Having worked in the law, journalism and numismatics, K.J. Parker now writes and makes things out of wood and metal.

Parker is married to a solicitor and lives in southern England.

Find out more about K.J. Parker and other Orbit authors by registering for the free monthly newsletter at www.orbitbooks.co.uk

PATTERN

The Scavenger Trilogy
Book Two

K. J. PARKER

orbit

www.orbitbooks.co.uk

An *Orbit* Book

First published in Great Britain by Orbit 2002
This edition published by Orbit 2003
Reprinted 2004

A CIP catalogue record for this book
is available from the British Library

ISBN 1 84149 182 9

Printed and bound in Great Britain
by Mackays of Chatham plc, Chatham Kent

Orbit
An imprint of
Time Warner Book Group UK
Brettenham House
Lancaster Place
London WC2E 7EN

Author's Note

As well as being an outstanding craftsman and one of the finest traditional blacksmiths in Europe, Ian Whitefield of Barrington Hill Forge, Somerset, is a man of infinite patience and the gladdest fool-sufferer in the business. He cheerfully spent many hours of his valuable time trying to teach me the basics of his craft, supported this project with advice and encouragement at every stage and even managed not to yell at me when I screwed up his best anvil. This book is therefore entirely his fault, since without him it could never have been written.

It should, of course, go without saying that nearly all the resemblances between Mr Whitefield and Asburn are entirely coincidental.

Poldarn's method of dealing with the mountain in Chapter Twenty may seem far-fetched: but a similar technique was used, successfully, during an eruption of Mount Etna in 1669.

Chapter One

He woke up out of a dream about faraway places, and saw smoke.

It was hanging in the air, like mist in a valley, and his first thought was that the chimney was blocked again. But there was rather too much of it for that, and he could hear burning, a soft cackle of inaudible conversation in the thatch above his head, the scampering of rats and squirrels in the hayloft.

Beside him, his wife grunted and turned over. He nudged her hard in the small of the back, and hopped out of bed.

'Get up,' he said. 'The house is on fire.'

'What?' She opened her eyes and stared at him.

'The house is on fire,' he told her, annoyed at having to repeat himself in the middle of a crisis. 'Come on, for God's sake.'

She scrambled out and started poking about with her feet, trying to find her shoes. 'No time for that now,' he snapped, and unlatched the partition door. It opened six inches or so and stuck; someone lying against it on the other side. That wasn't good.

It occurred to him to wonder where the light was coming from, a soft, rather beautiful orange glow, like an hour before sunset in autumn. The answer to that was through the gap where the partition didn't quite meet the roof – it was coming through from the main room. Not good at all.

He took a step back from the door and kicked it, stamping sideways with the flat of his bare foot. The door moved a few more inches, suggesting that he was shifting a dead weight. He repeated the manoeuvre five times, opening a gap he could just about squeeze through.

'Come *on*,' he urged his wife – comic, as if they were going to a dance and she was fussing about her hair. Hilarious.

The main room was full of orange light, but there wasn't any air, just smoke. As he stepped through, the heat washed over him; it was like standing right up close to the forge, as you have to when you're waiting for a piece of iron to come up to welding heat, and you feel the outer edge of the fire soaking into your skin. He looked down to see what the obstruction had been, and saw Henferth the swineherd, rolled over on his side, dead. No need to ask what had killed him; the smoke was a solid wall of fuzzy-edged orange. Just in time, he remembered not to breathe in; he lowered his head and drew in the clean air inside his shirt. Where had he learned to do that?

Only six paces, diagonally across the floor, to the upper door; he could make that, and once the door was open he'd be out in cold, fresh air. The bar was in place, of course, and the bolts were pushed home top and bottom – he grabbed the knob of the top bolt and immediately let go as the heat melted his skin. Little feathers of smoke were weaving in through the minute cracks between the boards; the outside of the door must be on fire.

So what? Catching the end of his sleeve into the palm of his hand, he pushed hard against the bolt. It was stiff – heat expands metal – but he was in no mood to mess about, and his lungs were already tight; also, the smoke was making his eyes prickle. He forced the top bolt back with an apparently disproportionate amount of effort, ramming splinters into the heel of his hand from a rough patch of sloppily planed wood, then stooped and shot back the bottom bolt, which moved quite easily. That just left the bar; and he was already gasping out his hoarded breath as he unhooked it. Then he put his shoulder to the door and shoved.

It didn't move. He barged against it again, but this wasn't just an annoying case of a sticky door, damp swelling the exposed end grain. He was out of breath now, and there was no air, only smoke. Most men would've panicked; fortunately, he remembered something else he must have picked up somewhere (where?) and dropped to the floor. Right down low, cheek pressed to the boards, there was clean air, just enough for a lungful.

As he breathed in he was thinking, The door's stuck, why? He hadn't stopped to think, Why is the house on fire? If his mind had addressed the problem at all, it had assumed some accident – a glowing cinder lodged in the thatch, carelessness with a lamp. But the door wouldn't open, the wood was burning on the inside. He knew exactly what that meant.

Behind him, someone was coughing horribly. He recognised the cough (she had a weak chest, always woke up coughing in winter). 'Get down,' he hissed, wasting precious breath. 'On the floor.' He didn't look round to see if she was doing as she was told, or even if she'd understood him. Right now, time was calibrated in units of air, and he had very little of it left. Certainly not enough to fritter away on fear or other self-indulgent luxuries; there'd be plenty of opportunities for that kind of stuff later, when he wasn't so busy.

The axe, he thought; the big axe. Of course the door was too solid to break down – he'd made it himself, he was just too damn painstaking for his own good – but with the big axe he could smash out the middle panel, at least enough to make a hole to breathe through. Where was the big axe, he wondered; there was something wrong with his memory, maybe the smoke had got in it and spoiled it, like oil curdling milk. Then he remembered. The big axe was in the woodshed, where the hell else would the big axe be? Inside there was only the little hand-axe, and he might as well peck at the door with his nose like a woodpecker.

Something flopped down next to him and he felt a sharp, unbearable pain in his left foot and ankle. Burning thatch, the roof was falling in. Oh, he really didn't need that. 'Bench,' he yelled, emptying his lungs (like spilling water in the desert; and when had he ever been in the desert?), 'smash the door down with a bench.' But she didn't answer, in fact he couldn't hear her at all, not even that goddamned horrible rasping cough. Oh well, he thought, can't help that now (plenty of time for that later, as well) and it screws up the bench idea. Come on, brain, suggestions. There's got to be another way out of here, because I've got to get out. The other door, or what about the window? And if they're blocked too, there's the hatch up into the hayloft, and out the hayloft door – ten-foot drop to the ground, but it'd be better than staying here.

But the other door was forty feet away; the window was closer, but still impossibly far, and the hatch might as well have been on the other side of the ocean. There simply wasn't time to try, and if he stood up he'd suffocate in the smoke. The only possible place to be was here, cheek flat on the floorboards, trapped for the brief remainder of his life in half an inch of air.

Another swathe of burning thatch landed on him, dropping heavily across his shoulders. He felt his hair frizzle up before he felt the pain, but when it came it was too much to bear – he couldn't just lie still and feel himself burn. He snuffed up as much air as he could get – there was a lot of smoke in it, and the coughing cost him a fortune in time –

and tried to get to his feet, only to find that they weren't working. Panic started to circle, like crows round a dead sheep, but he shooed it away as he lurched, overbalanced and fell heavily on his right elbow. The fire had reached his scalp and worked its way through his shirt to the skin on his back.

A man might be forgiven for calling it a day at this point, he thought; but he couldn't quite bring himself to do that, not yet. He'd be horribly burned, of course – he'd seen men who'd been in fires, their faces melted like wax – but you had to be philosophical about these things: what's done is done and what's gone is gone, salvage what you can while you can. Like his life, for instance. Yes, how about that?

It hadn't been so bad back in the inner room – why the hell had he ever left it, he wondered? Seemed like a good idea at the time. So he shrugged off the pain, like kicking away a yapping dog, and started to crawl back the way he'd just come. He made a good yard that way (the palm of his hand on his wife's upturned face; he knew the feel of the contours of her cheeks and mouth, from tracing them in the dark with his fingertips, tenderly, gently, like he meant it; but no air to waste on that stuff now) before the beam fell across his back and pinned him down, making him spill his last prudent savings of air. The pain – no, forget that for a moment, he couldn't feel his hands, even though he knew they were on fire, his back must be broken He tried to breathe in, but there was just smoke, no time left at all. Forget it, he thought, I can't be bothered with this any more.

(He expected death would come at that moment of abjur-ation; like a rough boys' game, you shout 'I give in' and it stops. But nothing seemed to change, as the time drew out – how was he paying for this time, now he was penniless for air? Had he discovered, in the very nick of time, the secret of breathing smoke? Nice trick, but pointless if his back was broken, and he was on fire too. Talk about irony.)

'What are you doing here?'

He looked up. He couldn't look up, because he was paralysed. He saw his grandfather looking down at him.

'What are you doing here?' the old bastard repeated. He sounded put out, as if his authority had been challenged. 'Get up,' he said, frowning, 'it's time to get up. You've overslept.'

You could put it that way, he thought; then he remembered. What am I doing here? How about what's *he* doing here, he's been dead for six months—

'What are *you* doing here?' the old man said—

'Sorry,' said the man facing him, 'am I boring you?'

Suddenly awake; he was sitting on a chair outside his grandfather's house at Haldersness, under the porch eaves, on a cold, bright day. The man opposite was Eyvind, his friend. His name was—

'No, of course not, go on,' he said. He hadn't fallen asleep, really, he'd just closed his eyes because the sun was so bright. His name was—

'All this talking,' Eyvind said apologetically, 'I'm not used to it. Truth is, among ourselves we don't talk much. Don't need to. Are you cold?'

'What? No, I'm fine, really.'

Eyvind smiled. 'You're huddled up in your jacket like a caterpillar,' he said. 'Perfectly understandable; where you've been all these years, it's much warmer. We sweat like pigs when we go there. Would you rather go inside?'

In front of him, over Eyvind's shoulder, was the great white-headed mountain. From its sides rose tall columns of milk-white steam, billowing out of the cracks and fissures where the natural hot springs bubbled up from the mountain's fiery heart. It was an amazing sight against a blue sky. 'No, thanks,' he replied. 'I like sitting here. Nice view.'

Eyvind laughed. 'I suppose it is,' he said, 'but I don't

notice it any more. Would you like me to get you a blanket or something?'

'No, really.' It was bitter cold; he could feel it in his feet, in spite of his thick leggings and felt-lined boots. Everybody said he'd get used to it.

'Wait there,' Eyvind said. 'I'll get a rug from the laundry.'

Well, it would give him an opportunity to wake up – not that he'd been asleep, of course. Once Eyvind had gone, he was able to wriggle a little deeper into the lining of his coat without appearing feeble in front of his friend. He didn't like the way everybody treated him like an invalid; after all, he was perfectly fit and healthy, he just felt the cold more than they did. And his name—

His name, he remembered, was Poldarn. At least, that wasn't his real name, it was the name of a Morevich god he'd impersonated while touring round the Bohec valley with a female confidence trickster who'd picked him up after he'd lost his memory a year ago. So far, only a part of that memory had come back; but these people, who lived an ocean away from where he'd woken up in the bed of a river surrounded by dead bodies, these people had told him his name was Ciartan, and he knew they were right. He'd grown up here, he could remember names (not his own, of course) and places, pictures in his mind that turned out to be real. Above all, now that he was here at least somebody knew who he was, and that was a great comfort after his experiences back in the empire.

Don't knock it, he thought, it's not everybody who gets a fresh start at the age of forty-one, especially a start like this. After all, his grandfather owned this enormous farm – 'owned' was the wrong word, of course, but it was easier to think of it that way – and everybody was going out of their way to be nice to him: they knew about his loss of memory, they understood how difficult it must be for him, they were only too pleased to help in any way they could, they even jumped up and fetched blankets for him without having to be asked. He couldn't have had a more luxurious, pampered life if he really had been a god.

On the far side of the yard, a peacock was clambering about on the thatched roof of the barn. When he'd first arrived he'd never seen a peacock before (as far as he could remember, though Grandfather insisted he'd killed one with his first bow and arrow, when he was seven) and even now he found it difficult to believe in the existence of such a gorgeous, unnecessary, stupid creature, because animals and birds were supposed to be above that kind of thing, they didn't have aristocracies and leisured classes. But the peacock was clearly some kind of duke or viscount, useless, troublesome and splendidly ornamental. Eyvind would have him believe they were just another breed of poultry, only there to get fat and then get eaten, but he didn't believe a word of it.

From the other side of the barn he could hear the shrill, musical clang of a blacksmith's hammer — Asburn the smith, getting down to some work at last. Properly speaking, that should have made him feel guilty, since by rights the job belonged to the head of the house, but Grandfather was too old now, his only son was dead, and his grandson, Ciartan, who'd only just come back from abroad, had left home before learning the trade and hadn't got a clue how to light the forge, let alone make anything in it. As a result Asburn, who was born to mend tools, sharpen hooks and scythes and generally make himself useful, had spent the last twenty years doing the wrong work; and the fact that he did it exceptionally well was neither here nor there. You could tell Asburn wasn't a smith just by looking at him: he was a little scrawny man with weedy arms and sloping shoulders. Poldarn, of course, looked every inch a blacksmith, and the sooner he knuckled down and learned the trade, the sooner everything could get back to normal.

But not today, Poldarn thought, even though it'd be nice and warm in the forge and out here it was freezing cold. Today he was far happier sitting and looking at the mountain, because he'd recognised it as soon as he saw it, and it reassured him more than anything else. As long as he could see it, he knew where he was. More than that, he knew *who* he was, just as long as he could see the mountain.

He'd nearly fallen over when they'd told him what it was called.

'Here you are,' Eyvind said, appearing suddenly behind him; and he felt the comforting weight of a thick woven rug descending round his shoulders. That was much better, of course, but even so he felt obliged to grumble.

'Wish you wouldn't do that,' he said quarter-heartedly. 'You're treating me like an old woman.'

Eyvind grinned and sat down. 'Hardly,' he said. 'My mother's seventy-one, and right now I expect she's out hoeing turnips. You wouldn't catch her lounging about on porches on a fine day like this.'

'Thank you so much,' Poldarn grunted, feeling even more useless than the peacock. 'Now, if only someone would tell me what I'm supposed to be doing, maybe I could muck in and start pulling my weight around here.'

'I wish you'd listen when I tell you things,' Eyvind replied, 'instead of falling asleep all the time. Makes it very boring for me, having to say the same thing over and over again.'

'Give it one more try,' Poldarn grumbled. 'You never know, this time it just might stick.'

'All right, but please try and stay conscious.' Eyvind leaned back in his chair, his hands folded in his lap, a wonderful study in applied comfort. 'The reason nobody's tried to tell you what to do,' he said, 'is that we just don't do things like that here. There's no need to. For example,' he went on, sitting up and looking round, 'there over by the barn, look, that's Carey. You know him?'

Poldarn nodded. 'Ever since I was a kid,' he replied. 'So they tell me.'

'Right. Now, Carey wakes up every morning knowing what he's going to do that day. If I'd been you, of course, I'd have said he knows what he's got to do; but that's not the way to look at it. He knows that today he's going to muck out the pigs, chop a stack of firewood, mend a broken railing in the middle sty and a bunch of other chores. He knows this because, first, he's got eyes in his head, he can see what needs doing, and he knows who does what around here; second, he knows because when he was a kid he watched his old man doing exactly the same sort of stuff, the same way his father watched his grandfather and so on. He doesn't need to be told, it'd be a waste of time telling him; more to the point, nobody could tell him because nobody knows Carey's work better than Carey does. Do you get what I'm driving at?'

Poldarn sighed. 'I think so,' he replied. 'Where I lose the thread is when it comes to why they all do it. If there's nobody in charge telling everybody else what to do, why do they bother doing all this work, when they could be – well, sitting around on the porch admiring the view?'

Eyvind laughed. 'If you need to ask that,' he said, 'you don't understand us at all. But you will, in time. It's really very simple. What you've got to do is simplify your mind, throw out all that junk that got lodged in there while you were abroad. God only knows how they manage to survive without starving to death over there, the way they do things.'

Poldarn didn't say anything. Every time Eyvind tried to explain things to him, they ended up at this point and never seemed to get any further. 'All right,' he said, 'so you tell me: how am I supposed to find out what I'm meant to be doing, if I don't know what my job is and neither does anybody else? You can see the problem, can't you?'

(Far away on the side of the mountain, at the point where

the snow began, a fat white cloud shot out of the rock and hung in the air.)

'Give it time.' Eyvind yawned. 'It'll come back to you, or you'll pick it up as you go along. Anyway, let's be realistic. In a month or so you'll have built a house of your own, you'll be starting from scratch with your own people – well, not from scratch, exactly, but once you're in your own house, running your own farm, you'll know what's got to be done without needing anybody to tell you. Believe me,' he added, 'I've done it.'

That really didn't help, of course. Poldarn knew, because he'd been told, that when Halder and his wife Rannwey were both dead, this house would be dismantled, pulled apart log by log and plank by plank and the materials piled up so that the farm people could help themselves to free building materials for their own houses and barns, and most of the household goods (apart from a few valuable heirlooms) would be divided up the same way. By then, Poldarn would be living in a brand new house a mile away down the valley, called Ciartansford or Ciartanswood or something like that – he'd still own all the land and the stock (not 'own', of course; wrong word entirely) and the grain and straw and hay and wood and apples and cheeses and hides and leeks and pears and cider and beer and everything else the land produced would be stored in his barn and eaten off his plates on his table; but for some reason he simply couldn't grasp – nobody had told him what it was, because either you knew or you didn't – he didn't have the option of living here in this house; it was like walking on water or flying in the air, it simply couldn't be done.

'So you say,' Poldarn replied. 'And we won't go into all that again, it made my head hurt the last time we talked about it. So let's put it this way: if you were me, what do you think you'd be likely to be doing, right now?'

Eyvind frowned, as if he'd been asked a difficult question

about a subject he'd never considered before. 'Well,' he said, as a particularly loud clang echoed across the yard from the direction of the forge, 'that, probably. Having a nasty accident, by the sound of it.'

'I see,' Poldarn muttered. 'That sounded like the anvil's just fallen on his foot. Would I absolutely have to?'

Eyvind shook his head. 'That wouldn't happen,' he explained. 'You see, you'd be the smith, you'd be more careful and the accident wouldn't happen. Asburn – well, he's a very nice man and he does some of the best work I've ever seen, but he's not a smith. Little wonder if he screws up from time to time.'

He could never tell whether Eyvind was joking or being serious when he started talking like this, probably both simultaneously. 'In other words,' he said, 'you're telling me I should be over there learning to bash hot iron, not sprawling around in a chair wasting your time.'

'*I*'m not telling you that,' Eyvind replied. 'But if you're asking me if I think it'd be a good thing for you to do, I can't see any reason why not.'

Poldarn nodded, and let his head rest against the back of the chair. It was a fine piece of work; old and beautifully carved out of dark, close-grained oak, with armrests in the shape of coiled dragons. Presumably it counted as an heirloom and he'd be allowed to keep it. 'Another thing you can help me with,' he said. 'That mountain. Is it meant to be doing that?'

Eyvind craned his neck round to look. 'Doing what?' he said.

'Breathing out all that steam,' Poldarn replied. 'Strikes me there's a lot more than usual.'

'Not really.' Eyvind shook his head. 'Some days there's more than others, that's all. Why, has somebody been trying to scare you?'

'No,' Poldarn said, 'unless you count what you just said. What's there to be scared of?'

'Nothing.' Eyvind smiled. 'It's just that some of the old jokers around here would have you believe that once every so often – about a hundred years, on average, which means it'd have happened exactly twice since we've been here – the mountain starts sneezing fire and blowing out great big rocks and dribbling rivers of red-hot cinders – like a bad cold in the head, except with burning snot. In case you're inclined to listen to them, these are the same people who tell stories about man-eating birds and islands in the middle of the sea that turn out to be sleeping whales. I thought maybe they'd been picking on you because suddenly there's someone on this island who might actually believe them.'

'Oh, I see. So that's all right, then.'

Eyvind nodded. 'There's a whole lot of things to be afraid of in this life,' he said, 'but an exploding mountain isn't one of them.'

That was reassuring enough, but there was still an itch at the back of his mind, a sore patch where a buried memory might be trying to work its way through before bursting out in a cloud of white steam. Perhaps it was just the name of the mountain that bothered him so much; and because, out of all the kind and helpful people and solid, reliable things he'd encountered since he'd been here, the mountain was still the only one he really trusted. 'One of these days,' he said, 'will you take me up there to see the hot springs? I've heard a whole lot about them but I can't really imagine it. Sounds too good to be true, all that boiling hot water just coming up out of a hole in the ground.'

'Sure,' Eyvind replied, 'though it's a hell of a climb, and most of the way you've got to walk. It's always struck me as a hell of a long way to go just to see some hot water you can't actually use for anything.' He shrugged. 'When I want hot water, I fill the copper and put it over the fire. Takes a while to come to the boil, but it beats hay out of all that walking.'

Poldarn nodded. 'Thanks,' he said, 'I'll hold you to that.'

'Please do; wouldn't have offered if I didn't mean it. Well,' Eyvind went on, glancing up at the sky, 'you may not have any work to do, but I've got a bucketful.' He jumped to his feet. 'Catch you later, probably.'

Poldarn got up as well. 'Can I come and help?' he asked.

'You don't know what the job is.'

'True. But I'm bored stiff with sitting around.'

Eyvind shrugged. 'Suit yourself,' he said. 'Your grandfather's given our house two dozen barrels of river gravel, for metalling the boggy patch at the bottom of our yard. All I've got to do is collect it and take it away.'

A slight twinge in Poldarn's left shoulder seemed to urge him to back out now, while he had the chance. 'I reckon I'm on for that,' he said. 'So, where is it now?'

Eyvind laughed. 'In the river, of course; that's where river gravel comes from.'

'Oh.'

'Thought you'd say that. First, we get a few long-handled shovels and dig it out, then we load it into barrels, which Halder's kindly lending us for the purpose, then we load the barrels onto a couple of carts, job done. It's bloody hard work and it'll take the rest of the day.' His face relaxed a little. 'Really,' he said, 'you don't have to if you don't want to. Turburn and Asley'll give me a hand.'

Poldarn knew who they were. Turburn was a huge man with a bald head and with shoulders as wide as a plough yoke; Asley looked like Turburn's big brother. Either of them could pick up a three-hundredweight barrel of gravel and walk right round the farm carrying it without realising it was there. 'Honestly,' he said, 'I don't mind, I need the exercise.'

Eyvind was looking at him as if he was a troll or a merman, some strange supernatural being who happened to look a bit like a human. 'That's something I'll never get used to,' he said. 'You say one thing, and you mean the exact opposite. I don't know how the hell you can do that. I couldn't, to save my life.'

Poldarn sighed. 'Well,' he said, 'obviously I'm not very good at it, if you can read me so easily.'

Judging by Eyvind's expression, he'd touched on some kind of important topic here, one that his friend didn't want to start discussing right then. 'Don't worry about it,' Eyvind said. 'All right, if you're dead set on volunteering, you come on. At the very least, it'll teach you never to do it again.'

It turned out to be an unspeakable job, back-breaking and shoulder-wrenching; and Poldarn made matters far worse by trying to keep up, at least to begin with, until he'd frittered away his strength and stamina, leaving fifteen barrels still empty. After that, all he could do was disconnect his mind and keep his arms and legs moving. He was painfully aware that he wasn't really contributing – his shovel pecked at the river bed, and he spilled most of what he dug up before it reached the barrel. Furthermore, his boots were letting in water, his knees had given out, and the strip of rag he'd bound round his hand wasn't really doing much to protect his blisters from the shovel handle. Anyone with any sense would've admitted defeat and crawled back to the house, but it appeared that he'd misplaced his brains along with his memory. It was lucky he didn't cause an accident when it came to hefting the barrels up onto the cart; he couldn't take the weight, and more than once the barrel nearly twisted out of his grip and fell on Turburn's leg. In the end, though, the job got done in spite of him, and he collapsed against the side of the cart, sitting down squarely in a pool of churned-up mud. Didn't matter, he was already filthy from head to toe. The other three weren't, of course.

'Thank you,' Eyvind said, and although all Poldarn's instincts insisted his friend was being facetious, chances were he really meant it. 'Don't know about you, but I'm ready for a beer. Coming?'

Poldarn nodded, and didn't move. It was nearly dark (they'd have finished long since without him, and the carts would've been on the road by now; as it was, they'd have to wait till morning, and the routine at Bollesknap would be out of joint for days), and the white clouds hanging over the mountain showed up as a dull, flat grey; on the opposite horizon, the sun was going down in fire. 'You go on,' he said. 'I'll catch you up. Think I'll just sit here for a bit.'

Some time later, when he'd got the use of his head back, it occurred to Poldarn that here he was again, sitting in the churned-up mud beside a river, still not really knowing who he was or what the hell he was supposed to be doing. He'd come a fair way since that first river – across a huge ocean, to an enormous island in the far west that the people back in the empire didn't even know about; couldn't come much further than that – and at least on this occasion he wasn't sharing the mud with any dead bodies. That said, he could close his eyes and it'd be the same river – that wasn't too hard to arrive at, if he supposed that the Bohec ran into the sea, the sun drew up water from the ocean and dumped it on this island as rain, it could easily be precisely the same water that he'd woken up beside – and the only change would be in his perceptions, because he hadn't *known* anything back then; for all he knew, he'd been digging gravel out of the Bohec when the unknown enemies attacked—

My perceptions, he thought. Well, for one thing, I perceive that I'm covered in mud, so I'd better have a wash before I go indoors. Taken one step at a time, any riddle you like can be broken down into little easy pieces; the trick is in putting them all back together again afterwards.

Getting his bum out of the mud was one of the hardest things Poldarn had ever had to do. All the engineers in Torcea couldn't have made it easy.

The place to wash was a little pool behind the house, where the stream collected in a natural stone basin before falling down the side of the combe on its way to join the river. It served the house as a combination bath house, laundry and mirror, performing all these functions rather better than any of the artificial facilities he'd seen in the crowded cities of the Bohec valley. The water was perishing cold, of course, but that was all right, it helped you wake up in the morning and gingered you up when you were tired at night. Like everything in this extraordinary place, even the disadvantages had their advantages.

Poldarn stood for a moment and looked at his reflection, backlit in sunset fire and blood, before smashing it to pieces with his hands; but, as usual, there was nothing to see except his face, no additional information. Maybe it was a true reflection, the only accurate mirror in the world, showing you what you really were: head, neck, shoulders and no past. He bent at the waist and dipped his hands through his face into the water. It was ice cold, and so clean it was hardly there at all.

When Poldarn reckoned he'd done about as much as could be achieved by way of damage limitation, he straightened his back, shuddered at the pain and hobbled back towards the house. Someone had said something, he seemed to remember, about beer.

Chapter Two

By the time Poldarn had finished washing and kicked off his mud-weighted boots in the back porch, they were ready to start dinner.

His instincts yelled at him to offer to help, but he knew better than that after the first time, when he'd tried his best but had managed to get under everyone's feet and had been banned on pain of certain death from ever helping again. Instead, he stood in the doorway, blissfully happy to have a door frame to lean against, and watched the curious, perfect ballet.

The first movement was the fetching-out of the tables. During the day, the tables and benches were pushed back against the panelled walls, leaving a broad empty space in the middle of the room large enough to accommodate a beached ship, provided its mast was unstepped first. Out of nowhere, four of the farmhands suddenly materialised, lifted the benches onto the tables and carried the tables into the middle of the room. Fifty years of instinctive precision had worn ruts in the baked-clay-and-cowdung floor to show where the table legs should be set down; as a result, every night they stood in exactly the same place, give or take the width of a sycamore leaf. There was no reason why the tables should be so exactly located, as far as Poldarn could judge. The ruts were just a visible display of the awesome power of force of habit, as silent and unregarded as an oak tree curled up in an acorn, or the fire sleeping under a volcano. When the tables were in place, they lifted down the benches and slid them into position in their own set of floor grooves.

(Bizarre, Poldarn thought. A man could go away for forty years and come home blind, and still be able to find his proper place at table by memory alone.)

At exactly the same moment as the benches slotted into place, Rannwey and five other women came through the doorway from the kitchen, carrying enormously long wooden trenchers, on each of which rested a colossal loaf. One loaf went to each table, perfectly centred – Poldarn knew without having to try the experiment that if he took a piece of string and measured, he'd find each crust-end of each loaf was definitely the same distance from the table's two top corners – while a gaggle of young boys followed on, each with an armful of wooden plates. Behind them came older boys and girls carrying wicker baskets clinking with cutlery – horn spoons, looted silver forks from the Empire, plain twisted iron forks from Asburn's forge, a jumble of misplaced heirlooms stolen out of other people's lives and practical home-made implements, all function and no history. By the time they'd finished setting the places, Rannwey and her party were back with earthenware beer-jugs, and as they returned to the kitchen they passed the boy-and-girl platoons on their way back with wooden and horn cups and beakers. Each item stood square on its mark like a runner at the start of a race, none of them so much as a finger's breadth out of line (as if standing a trifle to one side or another was likely to constitute an unfair advantage when the starting-flag fell). A place for everything, everything in its place. Perfection, even.

There was a heartbeat, two at most, dividing the setting down of the last mug and the entry of the first batch of farmhands, ready to take their seats. Poldarn recognised them as the long-barn crew: Eutho, Halph, Simmond and his twin brother Seyward – they worked furthest from the house, so presumably there was some kind of logic to their sitting down first. Next came Carriman and Osley from the stables, and after them Raffen, Olaph, Eyvind and his men (as long-term guests, apparently, they counted as honorary members of the trap-house crew); and so on, each outbuilding reproduced exactly as a grouping inside the house, until at the end Halder and Rannwey took their places in the centre of the middle table, and everybody pulled out their knives – alarming sight if you weren't used to it – and started carving up the long loaves.

At this point, Poldarn realised he should be sitting down, too. There was a place for him, of course, opposite Halder, an expanse of bench precisely the same width as his backside.

'There you are,' Halder said as he sat down. 'You're filthy.'

There didn't seem to be much Poldarn could say to that, apart from 'Yes'. Instead, he reached for the bread. There was one slice left, opposite his hand.

The young boys were back, this time with dishes of roast meat and round, flat bowls full of boiled leeks, baked apples, onions. A small mountain of food appeared on Poldarn's plate, filling up all the space not already taken up with bread. His cup had somehow filled itself with beer. Just as well – he was starving.

Halder had speared a small whole onion with the point of his knife, and was nibbling his way round it, like a squirrel. It occurred to Poldarn to wonder whether he'd done the same thing yesterday and the day before; there had to be some pattern to the actual eating of the food, or the whole business wouldn't make sense. He made a mental note to observe, over the next week or so. There were important questions to be asked: did everybody start with, say, the leeks, then the onions, then the apples, then the meat and finally the bread? How many mouthfuls of food did they take in between sips of beer? Did each individual have a degree of discretion as to which side of the plate he started from, or was there an orthodoxy about that, too? The night before last he'd caught someone on the table below staring at him in wonder as he ate a slice of beef; was this because he'd eaten it before he'd finished his onions, or because he'd gone six mouthfuls without a drink? If all else failed, of course, he could even grit his teeth and ask somebody; but it hadn't reached that point yet, as far as he could tell.

Six tables of hungry people eating together can't help but produce a certain volume of noise, but nobody was talking. This was another aspect of the ritual that Poldarn found somewhat oppressive, since it seemed fairly natural to him that mealtimes were a good opportunity for relaxed conversation, in the course of which he could ask useful questions without everybody suddenly going dead quiet and staring at him. But the man on his left, Raffen, and the woman on his right (whose name escaped him for the moment) were bent over their plates like clockmakers engraving a face, giving their full attention to the job in hand; if he tried to start a conversation, the shock might make them swallow something the wrong way and choke. At the very least, they'd probably lose their places and have to start the whole meal over again.

Never mind, Poldarn reflected; it was very good roast beef, and he hadn't had to kill anyone to get it. The beer was good too, although it disconcerted him slightly when he drained his cup only to find a serious-faced child standing over him, waiting to fill it up again.

After the main meal had been eaten (another point to check: did everybody finish eating at the same time?) the girls came round with slices of cheese, plums and fat red grapes, and a second refill of beer found its way into Poldarn's cup while his attention was distracted. Apparently cheese- and grape-eating wasn't such a serious business as putting away leeks and roast beef, because Poldarn could distinctly hear voices all around him – just one or two words, but speech nonetheless. He looked up from his plate to find Halder looking straight at him.

'Tomorrow,' Halder said, 'we'll go and take a look at your wood.'

That actually meant something to Poldarn: the memory burst out, like steam off the mountainside. He remembered quite clearly that on the day he'd been born, in accordance with the proper procedure, Halder and the middle-barn crew had planted out a stand of white ash down where the river curved round the side of the hill that marked the end of the combe. The idea was that when the time came for Poldarn to build his own house, those trees would be exactly ready. Although he hadn't been that far away from the farm buildings since he'd been back, he could picture the plantation perfectly clearly in his mind. He could see Halder, thirty years younger, strolling along beside him, pointing out which sapling would one day be his roof-tree, which were to be the joists, the door timbers, the great and lesser sills, the girts and the braces. At the time Poldarn remembered feeling a great surge of comfort and safety that came from knowing that everything was laid out ready for him, through every step of his life – there'd be no doubt or uncertainty, all he had to do was go forward, and everything he'd ever need would be waiting for him, ready in its appointed place, where he could reach out for it without even having to stretch.

'Good,' he replied. 'I'd like that.'

'You remember the time we went there when you were a kid.' It wasn't a question.

'I was thinking about it just now,' Poldarn replied. 'I don't suppose it looks anything like that now, though.'

'Pretty much the same,' Halder said, 'except the trees are bigger. Oh, and we lost one of the middle girts in a storm about fifteen years ago, but I know where there's a beech that'll drop in there just sweet.'

Poldarn nodded. 'That's good,' he said. 'Now I'm trying to remember where the house is going to go. I'm sure we went there that day.'

Halder actually smiled. 'That's right,' he said. 'Twenty paces south-east from the roof-tree, there's a rap of level ground with a good clay footing. First time I came here, it was touch and go whether I built my house there or here, but I chose here, because the other site – yours – is a bit more sheltered and closer to the water; and there's a fine little pool under some rocks for your washing-hole. Actual fact, I had Raffen and Sitrych clear the weeds out, winter before last.'

Sitrych, Poldarn thought, which one is Sitrych? Then he remembered; of course, the short, square man two down on Grandfather's left. At that moment, Sitrych was conscientiously chewing on a crisp, hard pear, his eyes fixed on a space about two feet over Poldarn's head.

'I can't picture it,' Poldarn admitted, 'but once we're there I expect it'll come back to me.'

His cup was empty, and there was that boy with the jug again. He put his hand over the cup. The boy stared at him, stood awkwardly for a moment, and then moved on down the line.

'You weren't at the forge today.' Not a question, or a reproach, or an accusation; just a statement of fact.

'No,' Poldarn said. 'I was helping Eyvind get in that gravel.'

Halder frowned, just slightly. 'I think you should make sure you put your time in there,' he said. 'There's still a lot you've got to learn.'

Poldarn looked up. 'Seems a bit pointless, really,' he replied. 'After all, we've already got a smith, best on the island by all accounts. I can't see where there's any need for me to get under his feet when he's busy.'

Halder's glare was like a slap round the face. 'I think mid-morning'd be a good time to go down to the wood,' he said. 'That way you can put in a good morning at the forge and be back when Asburn's ready to start again in the afternoon.'

Well, Poldarn thought, I tried; I failed, but nobody knifed me. So, no harm done, at any rate. 'That seems sensible,' he said. 'Very good cheese, this.'

'That's the last of the eight-weeks,' Halder said. 'The six-weeks'll be ready tomorrow.'

Well, yes, Poldarn said to himself, it would be, wouldn't it? 'Hope it's as good as this,' he said. Halder looked at him as if he'd said something that didn't make sense.

That night, when the tables had been put away and the fire was burning low, Poldarn made a conscious effort and called up the memory of that childhood walk among the trees. Mainly it was because he couldn't sleep – with the exception of Halder and Rannwey, who had the private room at the far end of the house, everybody slept on the floor of the hall, wrapped in blankets like a nest of silk-moths, and he found this hard to get used to – and recalling his childhood made a change from counting sheep. Partly it was conscientious reconnaissance in advance of tomorrow's expedition, in case there was something there he needed to be prepared for. To a certain extent, though, it was little more than self-referential tourism, a leisurely visit to the garden spot of his past, with a packed lunch and a parasol. In this respect, he was as limited as a citizen of Boc Bohec, whose choice of pleasant walks was limited to two rather crowded public parks; Poldarn had very few genuine memories to wander through, and several of them weren't places where he'd choose to spend time if he could help it.

Probably overtired, he told himself, which is why I can't get to sleep. He propped himself up on one elbow and looked round at the neat rows of sleepers, dim shapes in the flickering red glow of the fire, like a mass cremation. It stood to reason that these people (*his* people, must get used to thinking of them as that) should all roost together, all fall asleep together (because when the mind falls asleep, the parts of the body have no choice but to sleep too). Poldarn knew for a certainty that he was the only person awake in the whole house. In a way, it was a good feeling; for the first time in days, he could really be on his own, instead of being alone in the middle of a crowd.

But leaning on his elbow gave him cramp, so he lay down again and closed his eyes, summoning the memory like a nobleman calling for his jester. For some reason, though, the walk in the plantation wasn't available – someone else was dreaming it, or it was sulking and didn't want to come out. Instead, he remembered another walk with his grandfather, a month or so before or after the trip to the wood—

'Are we there yet?' he heard himself say.

He knew where he was; it was the reverse of the view from the porch, because they were standing on the lower slopes of the mountain, looking down at their valley. Behind them, the constant hiss and gurgle of the hot springs were almost loud enough to drown out Grandfather's voice. A dozen or so yards to his right, a solitary crow was tearing at the ribcage of a long-dead lamb.

It was his birthday.

'Not quite.'

'How much further?'

'Not far.'

'When will we get there?'

'Later.'

Grandfather was looking at the view; he seemed to like it a lot. Presumably he enjoyed looking at the farm from different angles, which was fair enough. Ciartan liked the view too, but now he'd seen it and he was getting cold and fidgety, and it wasn't as if anything about it was going to change. 'Can we go on now, please?'

Grandfather sighed. 'Yes, all right.' He dipped his head sideways, to say *this way*.

They were above the last scruffy patches of grass and heather now, in the belt of black rock and clinker that separated the marginal grazing of the lower slopes from the snowcap. It was foul stuff to walk on, particularly with short legs; every time you put your foot down it went over sideways on the chunks of black stuff, and you could feel the sharp edges right through the soles of your boots. Nothing at all lived up here, not even crows.

Ciartan was bored.

Grandfather sensed that; he was good at guessing people's moods. 'All right,' he said, 'let's see how much you know. Let's see: do you know the name of this mountain?'

That was a silly question. 'The mountain,' Ciartan replied. But Grandfather shook his head.

'All mountains are called The Mountain by somebody or other,' he said. 'No, this one's got a proper name, just as the farm's called Haldersness and the valley's called Raffenriverdale. Do you know what the mountain's proper name is?'

Ciartan shook his head.

'Thought not,' Grandfather replied.

'Tell me,' Ciartan said. 'Please,' he added, remembering his manners.

Grandfather stopped, either for effect or because the gradient was a bit too much for his bad knee. 'This mountain,' he announced, 'is called Polden's Forge.'

'Oh,' Ciartan said. 'Why's it called that?'

Grandfather shook his head. 'It's a long story,' he said. 'I don't suppose you want to hear it.'

'Yes, I do,' Ciartan replied eagerly. 'Please.'

'Well.' Grandfather dug the point of his short spear into a soft crack between two lumps of rock and leaned hard on the butt end. 'Many years ago, our people didn't live here. In fact, nobody even knew this country was here. We all lived far away across the sea, in what they used to call the Empire.'

'I know all about that,' Ciartan interrupted. 'That's where the men go raiding every year, to bring back the metal and stuff.'

Grandfather nodded. 'That's right,' he said. 'Now, the Empire's a very big place – bigger than our island, which is East Island, and almost as big as East Island and West Island put together. That's how big it is.'

Ciartan closed his eyes for a moment, visualising the enormous extent of the Empire. That was an impossible task, so instead he thought of the biggest thing he could think of, which at that moment happened to be the long barn. 'All right,' he said, 'go on.'

'Go on, what?'

'Please.'

'In the south of the Empire,' Grandfather said, wiping condensation out of his moustache with his left hand, 'is a country called Morevish, which is where our people used to live. That was over two hundred years ago, by the way; for what it's worth, Morevish isn't even part of the Empire now, it broke away a long time ago.'

Ciartan frowned. 'Broke away?'

'Rebelled. The people decided they didn't want to belong to the Empire any more, so they chased out the Empire's soldiers and became a free nation.'

'Oh, I see,' Ciartan replied, dismissing the image that had formed in his mind of a huge crack appearing in the ground, and the whole country slowly breaking away and drifting off into the sea.

'At the time our people still lived there, though,'

Grandfather went on, 'Morevish was still a province of the Empire, and the Imperial governors – that's the men who ran the country – were very harsh and cruel to our people. Every year they sent soldiers to steal a third of our corn, lambs and calves, and anybody who wouldn't give them what they wanted was dragged away and had his hands cut off, or even his head.'

Ciartan shuddered at the horror of such an idea. 'That's awful,' he said. 'So why didn't our people chase out the soldiers then, instead of later?'

Grandfather shrugged. 'Back then, the Empire was still strong,' he said. 'Later on, they got weak, because they were always quarrelling among themselves, and when that happened the people of Morevish were able to get rid of them. But we're getting ahead of the story.'

'Sorry,' Ciartan said. 'Please go on.'

A single solitary buzzard was wheeling in the air below them. It felt strange to be higher up than a bird.

'At the time I'm talking about,' Grandfather said carefully, 'two hundred years ago or more, our people still believed in gods. We don't do that any more, of course, just as you stopped believing in trolls and goblins when you were six. It's part of growing up.'

Ciartan nodded; though, to tell the truth, he still 'hadn't made up his mind about trolls. On the one hand, it didn't make sense to have people who turned to stone if they went out in the sun. On the other hand, he was almost sure he'd seen one once in the distance, on a bright moonlit night, when he and Grandfather had been out with the long-net.

'They used to believe in lots of gods,' Grandfather was saying, 'but their favourite god, the one they believed in the most, was a god called Polden. Now, the way with gods is that each of them's supposed to be in charge of something – like Grandma's in charge of the jam cupboard and the linen chest, or I'm in charge of the smithy. Polden was in charge of lots of things all at the same time, which was why our people believed in him so much. Polden was in charge of everything that had to do with fire; from keeping the house warm and cooking the dinner to making nails and horseshoes in the forge, right across to the fire that burns down houses when people fight each other. That made him different from the other gods; because, you see, all the other gods were either good or bad, depending on whether they were in charge of a good thing, like farming or making something, or a bad thing, like fighting. But Polden was both good and bad, all at the same time – because, you see, fire can be useful or it can be dangerous, and even when it's useful it's still dangerous, because if you're not careful when you're cooking the dinner you can set light to the chimney and set the thatch on fire, and the house'll burn down.'

Ciartan nodded sagely; he could understand that. In fact, this Polden sounded rather like himself, because he always tried to be good but somehow he kept managing to do bad things, or so the grown-ups told him.

'Anyway,' Grandfather went on, as the buzzard dwindled out of sight in the distance, 'lots of people from other parts of the Empire got to hear about Polden and started believing in him too; and this annoyed the men who ruled the Empire, because they believed in a whole different lot of gods; and that just made them treat our people even more cruelly than they'd done before. In the end,' Grandfather said, his eyes still fixed on the distant prospect of the farm, 'our people tried to fight the Empire's soldiers, but they lost; and the Emperor—'

'Who's the Emperor?'

'The man who ran the Empire. He told his soldiers to round up all our people who'd tried to fight the soldiers, and their families too, and put them on two hundred ships and launch them out into the sea.'

Ciartan gasped. It seemed a very harsh and unjust thing to do.

'It'd have been bad enough,' Grandfather went on, 'if they'd known these islands were here. But they didn't. For all they knew, there wasn't anything across the western sea but miles and miles of empty water, and our people would either have died of thirst or drowned. But they didn't. Just when they were at the very end of their food and drinking-water, they woke up one morning and saw the very top of a mountain – not this one, it was one of the Broken River mountains on West Island – and they knew they were saved.'

Ciartan had closed his eyes, as if to spare himself the horror of the exiles' plight. He opened them, and sighed with relief. 'What a terrible thing,' he said.

Grandfather smiled. 'Not so terrible, as it turned out,' he said. 'Because this country is far, far better than Morevish, which is very hot and dry, and very little grows there; and besides, back then it was part of the Empire, while out here our people could be free.'

'Ah.' That made sense, too; though Ciartan couldn't help feeling it had been pure luck, and the fact that it was so nice here didn't make what the Emperor had done any less wicked. 'So,' he said, 'why's this mountain called Polden's Forge?'

'I was coming to that,' Grandfather said. 'You see, when our people first came here and saw the clouds of steam and found that the water in the springs was boiling hot, they imagined that their god Polden must have his forge right underneath this mountain; and that's where the name comes from.'

'Oh,' Ciartan said, enlightened. 'I *see*.'

'Some people even said,' Grandfather went on, 'that when they first got here, they could see smoke and flames roaring up out of the top of the mountain, and the glowing coals of the forge fire. Mind you, nobody's ever seen that since, so they were probably making it up.'

A thought occurred to Ciartan, lodging in his mind like a fish-bone stuck in his throat. 'But Grandfather,' he said, 'if Polden was a god in Morvitch—'

'Morevish.'

'Morryvitch,' Ciartan amended. 'If he lived there, how could he have his forge here, if it's such a long way from there?'

He got the impression that Grandfather hadn't been expecting that. 'I don't know,' he said. 'Maybe they assumed Polden had come with them when they left.'

'What, on the ships, you mean?'

'I suppose so, yes.'

Ciartan shook his head. 'No, that can't be right,' he said. 'Because if he came with them, and reached this place the same time they did, he wouldn't have had time to build his forge, would he?'

Grandfather frowned. 'Oh, they believed gods could do anything,' he said. 'Well, it was all just superstition, anyway.'

'Maybe,' Ciartan said doubtfully. 'Actually, what I think is that Polden had his forge here all the time, and when our people were put in the ships with nowhere to go, he brought them here so they'd be safe and happy, where he could keep an eye on them.'

Grandfather looked like he didn't know what to make of that. 'I don't think so,' he said. 'Because, after all, Polden's only make-believe, he doesn't really exist. There's no such thing as gods, as we both know.'

Ciartan nodded, but he wasn't convinced. After all, Grandfather didn't believe in trolls, either, and he was almost certain he'd seen one that time. And if trolls could exist, maybe gods existed too. It'd be great, he couldn't help thinking, if there really was a big, powerful god living under their mountain, especially if he was a god who liked their people and had undertaken to look after them. The idea of it made him feel safe, somehow, as if the mountain he was standing on was really his home, not the farm way down below in the valley. It'd be fun living under a mountain, with a big fire to keep you warm and all the hot water you could ever want.

'Anyway,' Grandfather said firmly, 'that's quite enough of that. And now you know the name of this mountain, and a lot about where we all came from into the bargain. It's important that you remember it, all about the Empire and what they did to us. They were very wicked, and we haven't forgotten, or forgiven.'

Ciartan nodded dutifully. 'I'll remember,' he said. 'Now can we go to the hot springs, please?'

Grandfather smiled. 'Well, that's what we came for, isn't it?'

The hot springs were great fun; there was a great big pool, as big as the long barn, and the water was a strange light green colour. It was so hot Ciartan didn't dare get in it to start with, but once he'd got over the shock it was the most glorious feeling, and he wished he could find the god Polden and thank him for such a wonderful birthday treat. Then there was the waterspout, a hole in the ground out of which a great column of boiling water spurted just when you were least expecting it; and a dozen more hot pools, some of them green like the big one, some of them yellow (Grandfather said it was yellow because of something called sulphur; anyhow, they smelled horrible, and if you dipped your hand in, the smell got into your skin and wouldn't wash off when you went back in the green pool). Also, the noise was cheerful, the gurgling of the springs and the gruff whooshing sound the water made as it came huffing up out of the rock; if he closed his eyes he could imagine that he could hear words in those noises, as if someone jolly and cheerful was chattering away to himself, a long, long way under the ground. It was sad that they had to leave so early, but Grandfather wanted to be home by nightfall, and they had a long way to go. As they left the hot springs, walking carefully because of the hateful black rocks, Ciartan couldn't help turning his head and looking back one more time, just in case he caught a glimpse of old Polden, who he was almost certain did exist and did live there; but the mountain was deserted, just himself and Grandfather. Never mind, he thought, I know you're here, I can feel you; and you'll always be here when I need you, all I'll have to do is come back here and there you'll be. And then he happened to look down, and caught sight of a little pool of the nasty yellow water, and saw his reflection in it.

Chapter Three

Poldarn opened his eyes.

He was alone in the hall, and daylight was streaming in through the open door. Damn, he thought, I'm the last one to wake up again. It was embarrassing, though nobody had said anything yet; it made him feel sluggish and worthless, at a time in his life when his self-esteem didn't really need any further deflation.

The hall was empty because everyone else – those diligent, hard-working early risers – had gone off to the day's first chores. In a few hours they'd be back for the grand communal breakfast. Of course, there was nothing to stop Poldarn turning over and going back to sleep, or hauling his carcass out onto the porch, where he could wrap himself in three blankets and idle away the time till the next meal. He was tempted to do just that, as a protest against not being given a job to get on with.

But, quite apart from the self-worth and image problems involved, sitting on the porch would be very boring, so Poldarn got up, folded his blanket neatly, put it on the pile by the door, and went out into the yard. Properly speaking, of course, he ought to have headed over to the forge and watched Asburn getting ready for the day's work; it was what Grandfather would have expected him to do, though that was a long way removed from a direct order or even an explicit request. But he felt even more useless than usual hanging round the forge, because the house already had a smith, maybe the best on the island, and it seemed singularly pointless to learn the trade purely and simply with a view to supplanting him; the best *he*'d ever be, Poldarn knew perfectly well, was indifferent-competent, churning out mediocre hardware while Asburn went back to patching up kettles and mending fork handles. Crazy.

Still, it was either the forge, back to sleep or a rug and a chair on the stoop. It would be nice and warm in the forge. No point in being bored, useless *and* cold.

The smithy door stuck. It had dropped on its hinges shortly before Poldarn had been born, and when you pushed it, the bottom of the boards dragged along the ground like a prisoner being hauled off against his will; there were deep semicircular ruts in the yard clay to show how long it'd been since anybody had bothered about it. (Meanwhile, inside the smithy, Asburn was accustomed to make for other people the finest leaf-pattern door-hinges in the district, with forge-welded pintles and punched decoration.)

Inside, it was dark, as of course it should be in a smithy, and there was the usual smell of rust, filed steel and coal smoke. Asburn wasn't there, so Poldarn unhooked an apron from the wall and rummaged through the pile of tools and junk on the bench, looking for his gloves. Needless to say, the smith didn't wear gloves, since his hands had long since been cooked, pounded and rasped to the point where you could bend a nail on them; but Poldarn's skin hadn't reached that state yet, and he objected to pain. Visitors to the forge pretended not to notice.

First things first; he was earliest in, so he'd have to get the

fire lit. That wasn't good. Asburn hadn't insulted Poldarn by
showing him how to do such a simple, elementary job, and
Poldarn hadn't been able to bring himself to ask.
Accordingly the drill was that he'd make two, sometimes
three rather fatuous attempts, wasting good kindling (but
there was no shortage, so it didn't matter); and then he'd
make some remark about the coal being wet or the tue-iron
not drawing, and maybe Asburn'd have more luck with it;
and a few minutes later there'd be a fat red fire drinking the
air out of the bellows, and they'd be able to get on and do
some work.

There was coal in the barrel – good stuff, shop coal from
the mine on the other side of the island, clean enough to
weld in, unlike the garbage they scooped out of a wounded
hill two days to the west – and some split wood, dry twigs
and straw for kindling, even a tuft of parched moss and
some grain chaff for the tinderbox. No excuse, in other
words. Poldarn frowned and began raking the trash out of
the duck's nest, carefully piling up yesterday's half-burnt
coals around the edge. First a little pyre of straw spanned by
twig rafters, overarched by splints of split wood; a few turns
on the tinderbox crank produced smoke, and a few gentle
breaths coaxed a red glow. Getting somewhere; wouldn't
last, of course. He dumped the tinder onto his little wood-
and-straw house, then reached for the rake with his right
hand and the bellows handle with his left. The first few
draughts had to be smooth and gentle ('like you're blowing
in a girl's ear,' Asburn had put it once, rather incongruously) until the red glow woke up into standing flame. Then
there was no time to hang about: rake yesterday's leftovers
around the base of the splint frame and start pitching the
choicest nuggets on top, while at the same time gradually
increasing the force of air from the bellows (longer arms
would probably help). Once the splints were lightly covered with coals, both hands on the bellows and give it some

strength, watching the smoke getting squeezed out in plump fronds through the gaps between the coals. The result should have been a crocus-head of flame sprouting up in the middle. In theory.

As was only right and proper, the bellows was a big double-action, two goatskins closely stitched together and fitted with a valve; pumping it hard made Poldarn's shoulders and neck ache, probably because it had been fitted out for a shorter man. As he dragged the handle down, he watched the smoke. Predictably, depressingly, it was getting thinner with every blast of air, gradually sparser, like an old man's hair. Little yellow tendrils of fire were flaring out at the base of his coal-heap, but that was just the kindling burning up.

(Screw economy, he muttered to himself, I'm the smith here and I say from now on, we're using charcoal. Anything short of pissing on it lights charcoal; this stuff wouldn't burn if it got struck by lightning.)

Poldarn sighed, and raked out the mess he'd made, uncovering a little nest of grey ash and charred splinters where the kindling had been, buried under undamaged coals. Wonderful, he thought; everybody tells me I was born to make fire, and I can't do it for nuts. At least I'll never burn the house down.

He heard the door scrape, and looked round. 'Asburn?' he called out.

'Sorry I'm late. Got the fire in?'

At Haldersness, sarcasm was like charcoal; they knew about it, but they didn't seem to use it much. Accordingly, it was safe to assume that Asburn wasn't trying to be funny. 'Not having much luck with it, I'm afraid,' Poldarn replied. (He remembered standing on the black ash of the middle range of Polden's Forge; but it seemed he was doomed not to have much luck with fire.) 'Here, you know this layout better than me, you have a go. No point wasting good kindling.'

'Sure,' Asburn replied, and a minute or so later, the little cone of heaped-up black coals was shooting out jets of flame, just like a miniature volcano. 'It's the damp,' he said apologetically. 'Gets into everything. I keep meaning to do something about it, but you know how it is.'

Poldarn nodded; but of course there wasn't really any need for Asburn to waste his time curing the damp problem, since Asburn could make fire just by looking at a half-full scuttle. Imagine how embarrassing it'll be when I'm the smith here, Poldarn reflected; and every day of my life it'll take me half an hour and a barrelful of kindling just to get the bloody forge lit.

'Right,' he said briskly. 'Is there anything I can be doing to help?'

Asburn looked at him uncomfortably, as if he was talking a foreign language. 'Well,' he said, 'I was going to make a start on a scythe blade for Seyward – he's been on at me since the spring for one; and they want a new andiron for the kitchen, and the hay wagon needs a couple of tyres before the month's out.'

All that was undoubtedly true, but it didn't constitute an answer to a fairly simple question. 'How do you make andirons?' Poldarn asked.

'Oh, it's quite straightforward,' Asburn replied. 'You want something about two foot long, couple of fingers wide by a finger thick; I usually start with a scrap cart tyre. Make your ring at the top, split the bottom with the hot set, spread and shape the legs; then punch your hole, bend up your dog and swage down the end, take a welding heat, stuff the dog in the hole and weld it up. Simple as that.'

Poldarn nodded slowly. 'Supposing you showed me,' he said.

'Sure,' Asburn replied, and he disappeared into the scrap pile like a terrier diving down a rabbit hole. He emerged a few moments later with a long strip of rusty metal.

'Wonderful stuff, tyres,' he said. 'All your work's done for you, almost.'

Of course, Asburn didn't look anything like a smith; he was short and skinny, with little-girl's hands on the ends of thin, scrawny arms, and he had a plump, heart-shaped face nestling into a weak chin. Poldarn, by contrast, looked every inch the part. But when Asburn picked up the four-pound hammer and started swinging it, the hot iron moved; he seemed to be able to make it go where he wanted it to be by sheer force of personality, like an old sheepdog who can't be fussed with too much running about directing a flock of sheep into the pen. Poldarn watched in awe as the flat strip changed shape in front of him, curling like a snake or spreading like flood water, joining seamlessly as Asburn clouted the sparkling, incandescent joint, spraying white-hot cinders in every direction. Above all, what impressed him was Asburn's total lack of doubt or hesitation once the hot metal left the fire; here was someone who knew exactly what to do and how to do it in a very short, valuable space of time. Here was someone who knew who he was.

Having completed the weld, Asburn grabbed the finished piece and dunked it in the slack tub, vanishing for a few breathless seconds behind a white curtain of steam—

(Ah, Poldarn realised, that explains the hot springs)

—before fishing it out and attacking it vigorously with a two-handed wire brush, to scour off the firescale It was, of course, a superb piece of work; and after all that, Poldarn still didn't have a clue as to how to go about making one himself.

'And that's all there is to it,' Asburn said.

Poldarn took a deep breath. 'I see,' he said. 'Now, is there something I can be doing to help?'

The worried look again. 'Well, there's the scythe blade,' he said. 'Do you fancy having a go at that?'

'I'm not sure. What's involved?'

Asburn perched on the horn of the anvil. 'Depends. I

usually use a busted sword-blade or something like that. First job is drawing it down.'

Poldarn knew what drawing-down meant: you started with something short and fat and made it long and thin. It was usually a two-man job, the role of the second man being to wield the ten-pound sledge; hard work, but any bloody fool could do it. 'Fine,' he said. 'I'll strike, shall I?'

Asburn nodded. 'If you don't mind,' he said.

Poldarn didn't mind striking. All he had to do was hit a certain spot on the anvil very hard with a big hammer; and the noise was such as to make conversation impossible, no bad thing as far as he was concerned. Asburn was one of those people you have to make a special effort not to like, but Poldarn found him difficult to talk to.

Nevertheless, it was a great relief when Asburn, who appeared to have strange and occult powers where the detection of food was concerned, announced that it was getting on for breakfast time. While Asburn was banking up the fire and putting the tools away, Poldarn wandered down to the washing-hole and tried to get his hands clean. That was another aspect of the blacksmith's art that he hadn't mastered yet, which was unfortunate; his face cleaned up quite easily, but ever since he'd started in the forge, he'd never been able to shift the black marks from his palms, where the soot was ground into his skin by the hammer handle. No wonder everything he ate these days seemed to taste of coal.

They'd already set out the tables by the time he reached the house, and he went straight to his place. Oatmeal porridge, bread still soft and warm from the oven, and a slab of cheese large enough for a tombstone; you couldn't go hungry at Haldersness if you tried.

Curiously enough, Grandfather didn't show up for the meal. Having speculated as to the possible reason for this and failed to come up with any plausible explanation, Poldarn screwed up his courage and asked Rannwey where he was.

She looked at him patiently. 'Visitors,' she said.

Poldarn nodded. It didn't really answer his question, but since he found it almost impossible to talk to his grandmother, who terrified the life out of him, he was happy to let the matter drop. Unusually, though, she continued the conversation, actually volunteering information for the first time since he'd known her.

'Important visitors,' she said. 'From Colscegsford.'

Well, the name was vaguely familiar; it was one of the neighbouring farms, somewhere away down the valley, three or four days' ride in good weather. It was a fair bet that three-quarters of the household had never been there.

'Ah,' he said.

'Colsceg,' she went on, 'and Barn, that's his middle son, and Egil, his youngest. And Elja.' He could feel Rannwey's eyes skewering into his brain. 'That's his daughter.'

Oh, Poldarn thought. And then he thought, Well, why not? True, according to Prince Tazencius, who had no real reason to lie to me about the subject, back in the Empire I'm married to his daughter, with at least one child. But this isn't the Empire, and I won't be going back there again. So, yes, why not? No strong views on the subject, one way or another.

'So,' Rannwey went on – far and away the longest speech he'd ever heard her make – 'probably a good idea if you went over to the middle house after breakfast.'

'That's where they'll be, is it?'

Rannwey nodded, bringing the dialogue to a definite end. Well, well, Poldarn thought. If it means I can skip another session in the forge, why not indeed?

Accordingly, as soon as breakfast was over, he stood up to leave. Rannwey stopped him with a firm pressure of her fingers on his wrist. He was surprised at how cold her hands were.

'Better wait a bit longer,' she said. 'Probably still talking business.'

No point even wondering how she knew that; she was bound to be right. As to what the business was, Poldarn could probably guess if he wanted to, but he didn't. 'All right,' he said. 'Maybe I should get a clean shirt.'

'That would be a very good idea.'

At Haldersness, clothes were there for the taking; you went over to one of the big linen-presses at the far end of the hall, and poked about till you found something that looked like it'd fit. Clothes for the wash went in a big open-topped barrel in the opposite corner. Who washed them – and why – was just another of the mysteries of the place. Poldarn found a plain grey shirt, thick and comfortable, soft with age and washing but perfectly sound, clean and unfrayed. He put it on and carefully tied the neck-laces, taking his time; then he took a comb from the brush-and-rag box under the window and dragged it through his hair, using the blade of his knife as a mirror. Not that it mattered, of course – business was business – but he felt it showed willing.

The middle house was where things ended up when nobody had any immediate use for them. It had a high roof, half-boarded to form a gallery-come-loft, where the apples were spread out on racks and the onion-strings hung from hooks driven into the rafters. There wasn't a middle-house crew as such – people only went there to dump something or collect something – which made it one of the more peaceful places on the farm, somewhere to lurk when you didn't particularly want to be found. If only there was a bit more light in there, Poldarn thought, it'd be a good place to come and read a book, if only I had a book.

He couldn't hear any voices as he walked in through the door into contrast-induced darkness, but that didn't necessarily mean anything, given his people's tendency to long, solemn silences. Sure enough, when he located them, they were standing in front of a neat pile of scrap metal – mostly brass, with some copper and lead – staring at it without moving or speaking. If they noticed him come in, they didn't give any sign. He could only see their backs; Grandfather was easily identified, needless to say, and the older man would have to be Colsceg. Of the other two men, he took an arbitrary guess and assumed that the taller one was the middle son – name, name: Barn or Bran, something like that – which would make the shorter one Egil, the youngest. All Poldarn could see of the daughter was a hank of very long light brown hair, with a pair of heels poking out underneath. Still, he thought, at least she's not bald.

For what seemed like an insufferably long time, nobody moved or spoke. Then the man who was presumably Colsceg dipped his head, meaning Yes, and held out his hand. Grandfather took it and shook it, the inference being that a deal had been struck.

'Ciartan,' Grandfather said without looking round. 'Perhaps you'd like to come over here.'

Now they all turned to face Poldarn, though it wasn't until he was much closer that he could make out any degree of detail in the dim light. Understandably, he looked at the daughter first, and was pleasantly surprised. She was young – half his age, quite likely – and pleasant enough to look at; an oval, slightly flat face with a solemn mouth and round blue eyes, and she wasn't fat or bow-legged or anything. Colsceg was extremely broad, almost square, with a small nose and a stretched-looking white scar from his ear to his beardless chin, an affable-looking type. Barn or Bran was extremely tall, blank-faced, slightly gormless. Egil, if Poldarn had got them the right way round – Egil he recognised.

And Egil recognised him, because as soon as he came forward out of the shadows, Egil's face twisted with sharp, instinctive panic. It only lasted a moment, but so does a sudden loud noise; Poldarn knew that all of them had felt it, and were choosing to ignore it.

Here we go again, Poldarn thought.

Yes, he *recognised* the face (and it was a very nondescript sort of face, the kind you couldn't begin to describe, if you were asking someone if they'd seen him); but he couldn't *remember* him at all. There was just a picture in his mind – the same face, twenty years younger, little more than a boy, but staring at him in bleak horror. That was all. No backdrop, no words or movements or associations, nothing but a portrait, *Young Man Horrified*.

'Ciartan,' said Colsceg. 'Haven't seen you for a while.'

(If he tells me I've grown, Poldarn thought, so help me, I'll strangle him. And as he thought that, Colsceg's lips tweaked into a tiny smile.)

'I'm very sorry,' Poldarn replied, 'but—'

'You don't recognise me.' Colsceg nodded a couple of times. 'Halder's told me about all that. These are my sons, Barn and Egil; and my daughter, Elja.'

At least Poldarn had got the brothers the right way round. Egil's face was completely expressionless now, like plaster after you've smoothed away a blemish. They're all five of them as nervous as cats, Poldarn realised. Curiously enough, that made him feel a whole lot easier. Watching someone else getting twitchy made a pleasant change. 'Pleased to meet you,' he said, thinking sincere as he said it.

Elja smiled at him. She had a nice smile. That was good.

'Thirty years ago,' Halder said abruptly, 'Colsceg and I agreed that, as and when he had a daughter, it would make good sense for you to marry her.' He hesitated. It would be nice, Poldarn reckoned, if he'd paused because he wished he'd put that another way, but he felt sure that wasn't the real reason. 'But you left before Elja was born, and to be straight with you, nobody knew when or if you'd be coming back. Naturally, we both reckoned the deal had lapsed. As it turns out, though, Colsceg hasn't made any other arrangements, so there doesn't seem to be any reason why the original deal shouldn't go through.'

He's leaving something out, Poldarn thought. More than that, he's hiding something, and whatever it is, it's important enough that hiding it is almost the same thing as telling a lie; and Grandfather doesn't really know how to do that. They all know it's a lie.

'That's wonderful,' he heard himself say. 'And of course I'm deeply honoured. Assuming Elja will have me, of course.'

Now I'm talking gibberish, as far as they're concerned. Might as well ask the plough's permission before sticking its nose in the dirt. But they're going to be polite and pretend I didn't say anything. Elja's still smiling, though it's a reasonable bet her jaw's going to start aching if she has to keep it up much longer. Poor kid, he thought; in her shoes, I'd be dead with embarrassment by now.

Anyway, that seemed to conclude the meeting. Colsceg and Halder nodded to each other and walked out of the building, Barn and Elja following as if there was a string tied to their collars. Egil went with them as far as the door, then hesitated.

(I definitely know him from somewhere, Poldarn thought. Question is, do I really want to know the details? Probably not—)

'Ciartan,' Egil said; then he glanced nervously over his shoulder.

'Hello,' Poldarn replied.

The invisible string was pulling Egil hard; he staggered, slightly but perceptibly. 'You're back, then.'

'Yes,' Poldarn replied. 'Obviously we know each other, but I'm afraid I just don't remember you—'

Egil stared at him; curious expression, as if they were fighting and Poldarn had passed up an easy opportunity for a finishing cut, leaving himself wide open. 'Is that right?' Egil said.

Poldarn shrugged. 'Afraid so,' he said. 'Bits and pieces of

my memories about this place drift back from time to time, but that's all.'

There was a scar on the back of Egil's hand; Poldarn knew that, though he was sure he hadn't seen it. Only a little one, a patch of smooth white about a thumbnail's width long. No big deal.

'I see,' Egil said. 'And none of these bits and pieces have got me in them.'

'That's right. Not so far, anyway.'

'Good,' Egil said. 'You've changed since you've been away.'

Almost impossible to figure out what he meant by that. 'Have I?'

A short nod. 'You've changed a lot,' Egil said.

'For the better, by the sound of it.'

'Maybe. I'm in no position to judge.'

Poldarn couldn't help grinning. 'That makes two of us,' he said. 'You know, since I've been back, everybody's been trying to make me feel like I was only away for a week or so, not twenty years. But it stands to reason I'll have changed, people do.' He paused, trying to make a decision, then went on: 'Were we friends, then?'

Egil's face had gone dead. 'Oh yes,' he said. 'Very good friends.'

'We used to knock around together? Do things?'

'At one stage.'

A picture formed in Poldarn's mind. 'I think we went crow's-nesting once,' he said. 'I've got this image of us walking across a meadow towards a wood; you were about ten, eleven years old. We're carrying long, thin poles, for pushing the nests out of the trees with.'

'Fancy you remembering that.'

It's not what they say, these people, it's the way they say it. 'It happened, then?'

Egil nodded. 'It was Grather's wood,' he said. 'You know,

for his house. A big mob of crows had built in it, and they were flighting in on our spring wheat. Grather was supposed to come with us, but he couldn't make it. You remember Grather?'

Poldarn shook his head. 'Another friend of ours?' he said.

'My cousin.'

Well, that wasn't much help. 'And what happened?'

Egil didn't answer straight away. 'We did a good job,' he said. 'At least,' he went on, 'you did most of it. You and crows, it was like you couldn't bear to see the buggers. Every time one flew past you'd scowl at it, or throw a stone.'

'Grandfather's told me that, too,' Poldarn replied. 'Sounds like I had a real thing about them.'

'Meaning you don't, any more.'

Poldarn shrugged his shoulders. 'They don't seem to bother me particularly,' he said. 'I can see they're a major pest, after planting or when the corn's starting to sprout.'

'Well,' Egil said, 'I'd best be getting along – they'll want to know where I've been. Are you back for good now, then?'

For good, Poldarn thought; it's just an expression. 'Can't see why not,' he said. 'I've got no idea what sort of a life I had back over there, but it's no use to me if I can't remember it. Like buried treasure, if you've lost the map.'

'Buried treasure,' Egil repeated. 'Anyway, I'd better go. Expect I'll be seeing you around, now you're marrying Elja.' He laughed. 'Welcome to the family.'

'Thank you.'

'That's quite all right,' Egil said, and walked quickly away into the light.

Poldarn didn't follow. It was quiet and peaceful in the middle house, now that everybody had gone. He sat down on a broken sawhorse and rested his chin in his hands.

Whatever it was, he thought, it can't have been too bad; not if I'm going to marry his sister. If it was something dreadful, he'd tell his father and stop the wedding from happening.

Could be anything; something trivial from when he was a kid. If I'd done something dreadful here, everybody wouldn't be so annoyingly glad to see me all the time.

Poldarn pushed the thought out of his mind, like a host at daybreak shooing away the last overstaying guests. More important stuff to mull over: the future, rather than the past. Yes, on balance she seemed a perfectly nice girl—

And *perfectly nice* wasn't the sort of thing lovesick poets crooned under balconies. It wasn't so long ago that he'd arrived at the conclusion that he was in love with Copis, the lady con artist who'd saved his life, given him his name and briefly made him into a god. *She* hadn't been perfectly nice; she'd turned out to be a spy working for the monks of Deymeson, and hadn't she tried to kill him at one point? But that didn't necessarily change anything; and Poldarn had thought about her more than once since he'd been here, wondering if she was all right, what she was doing, whether their child had been born yet . . . Well, that was one relationship he did know about. There was also this wife of his, Tazencius's daughter, who'd married him for love, against her father's express wishes – probably not your 'perfectly nice' type either, by the sound of it. Bloody hell, he reflected, I'm old enough to be her father; what kind of life is that for a perfectly nice young girl? But she doesn't seem to mind the idea.

Doesn't seem to mind wasn't a standard phrase in love poetry, either. Maybe they didn't have love over here, or at least not that variety of the stuff. Thinking about it, Poldarn couldn't call to mind any examples of it that he'd observed (and you'd have thought you'd have come across at least one pair of starry-eyed young idiots while you'd been here; they weren't hard to spot when they were in that condition, after all). Maybe they made do with the sort of absent-minded affection he'd noticed between his grandfather and grandmother, for example, or Terwald and his wife, or whatever his name was who looked after the ewes, the one who was married to the fat woman. In a set-up as profoundly organised as this was, he could see where something as unruly and messy as genuine love wouldn't really fit in: it'd cause all sorts of problems with people missing shifts or even dodging off work altogether. Then there'd be quarrels and jealousies and fights, adulteries and girls kicking up a fuss about being married off to the wrong man, general disorder and disruption of agriculture. The likeliest explanation was that it was just one more of those charcoal things; they knew about it but had made a decision not to use it, probably for some good commonsense reason that everybody else on the island knew about but him.

Not that it mattered, since Poldarn couldn't remember ever having been really in love – Copis didn't count as that; for the short time they'd been together, their relationship had been more of a military and diplomatic alliance, offensive and defensive, against a mutual enemy consisting of the whole world. More than that, it was the next best thing to impossible to imagine being in love at Haldersness. In these parts, *perfectly nice* and *doesn't seem to mind* were probably about as ardent as it ever got.

Anyway; it could all be far worse. He could easily have been slated to marry someone twice his weight, with no teeth. He wasn't sure he'd have chosen those particular in-laws, but it was a safe bet that there was some kind of worthwhile property transaction in the background, and it was high time he started thinking like an heir apparent and giving such considerations their proper degree of weight. Mind you, that wasn't easy when nobody was prepared to tell him what was going on.

Which reminded him; at some stage this morning, Grandfather was supposed to be taking Poldarn to see the wood, the one they'd be building his house out of (like Grather, whoever he was). When the time came,

Grandfather would expect to find him in the forge, getting on with his lessons. He sighed; but he knew perfectly well that hiding in the middle house wasn't going to solve anything.

By the time he reached the forge, Asburn had finished drawing down the scythe blade on his own, and shaping it was very much a one-man job, for which Poldarn wasn't the right one man. So he found the nail sett, fished a strip of wire out of the scrap and set to making nails – couldn't have too many nails, after all, and it was so easy even he could do it. True, Asburn could turn out a bucketful in the time it took him to make one, and the nails Asburn made were straight. So what; it was the thought that counted.

But the fire was hotter than usual, for welding the iron to the steel, and Poldarn contrived to burn more wire than he shaped; his mind wasn't on his work, which wouldn't do at all in a forge. Egil, he thought, and killing crows. Why had he hated them so much, he wondered? It was hard to imagine himself feeling that strongly about anything, let alone slow-moving black birds. It seemed likely that, at some point, he and Egil had got up to some kind of mischief, and Egil was warily delighted to find that Poldarn had forgotten all about it. For the reasons he'd already considered, he was fairly sure that it hadn't been anything too bad, and whatever it was, they'd never been found out. So that was probably all right, too.

Poldarn pulled his strip of wire out of the forge and dropped it into the sett. Before he could start peening over the head, the door scraped open, and a face he recognised but couldn't put a name to appeared round it.

'You two,' said the newcomer, 'you want to come and take a look at this.'

Asburn was just about to take a weld on a complicated joint; the metal was glassy white and sparkling, it'd be a devil of a job to get it right again if he let it cool. But the newcomer's tone of voice was enough to make him lay the piece down on the anvil and hurry to the door. What the hell, Poldarn thought, and followed him.

Outside in the yard, most of the farm people were gathered in a tight group. They were staring up towards the mountain, and it didn't take Poldarn long to figure out why.

A column of crow-black smoke was rising out of a red gash in the mountainside, just to the right of the rather crooked summit.

Chapter Four

'What do you suppose that's in aid of?' someone asked.

Nobody seemed disposed to reply. The red gash was flickering in and out of sight, sporadically masked by plump white clouds – steam, presumably.

'How long has it been doing that?' Poldarn asked the man standing next to him, a long-barn hand called Rook.

'Well, since the noises,' Rook replied, as if stating the obvious.

'What noises?'

Rook shifted his gaze from the mountain and gave Poldarn a curious stare. 'The three loud bangs,' he said. 'You didn't hear them, then?'

Poldarn shook his head. 'I was in the forge.'

'Three loud bangs,' Rook said, 'and when we stopped for a look, there was all that black stuff coming out the top.' He frowned. This was clearly something outside his experience, and it occurred to Poldarn that these people – his people – probably didn't come across something new and unknown more than once or twice in a lifetime. 'You were abroad all those years,' Rook said. 'You got any idea what it is?'

Poldarn nodded. 'I think so,' he said. 'I think it's a—' He paused. No word in their language, his language, for *volcano*. 'I've never seen anything like it that I can remember,' he said carefully. 'But yes, I think I know what it is. Where's Halder?'

Rook indicated with a sideways nod of his head. 'So what is it, then?'

'It's a mountain with its head on fire,' Poldarn replied. 'What does it look like?'

He pushed his way through the crowd until he was standing next to Grandfather. 'So,' he said, 'what do you make of that?'

Grandfather shrugged. 'Beats me,' he said.

'I think there's a word for it in one of the languages I know. Basically, it's a mountain that gets stuffed up with fire, like a boil or an abscess under a tooth; and when it gets full, it bursts.'

'Oh.' Grandfather was frowning. 'Is it bad?'

'Usually,' Poldarn replied. 'Unfortunately, you now know as much about volcanoes – that's the foreign word for them – as I do.'

'Volcanoes.' Grandfather repeated the word a couple of times, as if trying out a new tool for balance and fit. 'How is it bad?'

Poldarn shrugged. 'I don't honestly know,' he admitted. 'But if that red stuff is fire and the white cloud is steam, chances are it's melting a lot of the pack snow, at the very least. Has the river ever flooded, do you know?'

Halder rubbed his chin. 'Once,' he said, 'when I was a boy. But that was just months of heavy rain, and everything got so waterlogged there was nowhere for it to go.'

'Fine,' Poldarn replied. 'All I'm thinking is, if there's a whole lot of melt water coming off the mountain all at once, it's got to go somewhere.'

'Not here,' Halder said, after a moment's thought. 'Come summer thaw, the melt always runs off down the other fork of the valley, out to Lyatsbridge and Colscegsford.' He pursed his lips. 'Colsceg's pretty high up, but I wouldn't want to be in Lyat's house if you're right about a spate coming down.'

Rook, who'd been listening in on the conversation, said, 'Maybe I'd better get over there, in case they haven't figured it for themselves.'

'The black mare's saddled,' Halder replied. 'I was going to ride back with Colsceg when he went on.'

Rook hurried off; and Poldarn noticed out of the corner of his eye that the stablehands had the horse outside and waiting for him some time before he reached the stable door. 'What happens next?' Halder asked.

'No idea,' Poldarn said. 'You sure it's never done anything like this before?'

'Could well have done, before we were here to see it. But not since we've been here.'

They stood and watched for a while, but nothing else seemed to be happening. Gradually, people started drifting away, back to work. They seemed uneasy, though, as if they'd suddenly woken up after an hour's unscheduled and unexplained sleep. 'Bloody thing,' Halder muttered resentfully. 'Always something.'

Indeed, Poldarn said to himself; how thoughtless of the mountain to catch on fire, just when everything was going so smoothly. 'Is Lyatsbridge a big place?' he asked, by way of making conversation.

'What? Oh, no, nothing much; not so big as here, or Colscegsford. Lyat was one of Colsceg's father's men, struck out on his own thirty years back. He took the ford because nobody wanted it, on account of the flooding.'

That seemed to cover that. 'Do you want to stay close to the house, in case something happens?' he asked.

Halder shook his head. 'Don't suppose there's anything to worry about,' he replied, in a voice that suggested he was making it so by saying it out loud. 'We might as well take that walk down as far as your wood, now you're here.'

And sure enough, Colsceg and his offspring were suddenly there, right behind him. Stands to reason they're invited too, Poldarn thought, since Elja's going to be living there one day. He looked up at the mountain again, just in case it had stopped performing while his back was turned; but it hadn't. 'Maybe Polden fell asleep,' he suggested, 'and his chimney caught alight.'

Halder didn't bother to reply to that.

Needless to say, nobody spoke, all the way from the house to the bottom meadow. When they reached the river, the whole party stopped; Poldarn wondered why, then realised that this was the last point from which they'd be able to see the mountain, without the reverse slope of the combe being in the way.

'Still at it, then,' Colsceg said.

He was right; the mountain was still pouring black smoke into the sky, like a leaking wineskin. They stood and scowled at it for a short while, then moved on.

More than once as they walked, Poldarn had looked sideways at Elja; but each time, she was looking straight ahead, absolutely no trace of an expression on her face. Egil, he noticed, stayed the other side of her, as far away from Poldarn as he could get, and he just looked bored and slightly constipated. Well, Poldarn thought, who wants chatty in-laws and a wife who talks all the time?

His first sight of the wood came as they rounded a slight bend in the river, where the western slope of the combe fell sharply down to the bank. Over its shoulder he could make out the tops of pine trees. The sight was extremely familiar – which didn't make any sense at all, he realised, since the last time he'd been here, the trees would have been too short to show above the hillside. He dismissed it as his imagination coining false memories for him.

The wood was smaller than he'd thought it would be; about six dozen tall, thin trees on a very gentle slope, next to a flat, bare platform standing on a pronounced mound; a highly suitable place to build a house, though the view wouldn't be up to much. As they approached, a mob of crows got up out of the treetops and flapped slowly, angrily away, like resentful tenants being evicted; not that far off the mark, Poldarn reckoned, since they'd lose their roost when the trees were taken down. Their problem, he told himself. As he watched them toiling laboriously into the air, he felt something on his face and the top of his head; a lighter touch than rain, more like snow. He ran his hand across his forehead and noticed a few specks of black ash. It reminded him of the awkward-to-walk-on black rocks on the mountain, between the snow and the grazing. If the others noticed it, they weren't curious enough to investigate, or else retrieving bits of debris off yourself in public was bad manners.

'Good lumber,' Barn said suddenly. It was the first thing Poldarn had heard him say.

'Scrawny,' Halder replied. 'Should've thinned them out fifteen years back. Didn't seem any point back then, though. Still,' he added, with a sigh, 'it'll have to do.'

It was just a clump of trees, a stand of timber – and then, quite suddenly and unexpectedly, Poldarn caught his breath, because it wasn't just that. As he stared at the trees, he began remembering them, only he wasn't seeing them as they had been or even as they were now, but how they would be, one day, one day *soon*. Just to the right of the middle of the stand grew the roof-tree, the backbone of the house; surrounding it were the girts, joists, floorboards and rafters; below them, slightly asplay on the gentle gradient, stood the braces, sills and plates, with the cross-beams standing out above them. He could see them as trees, still cluttered with branches and clothed in bark. He could also see them as sawn, planed timber, a skeleton of a house (like the skeletons of dead animals and men that litter the ground on a battlefield that nobody's dared go near for twenty years, on account of ghosts and ill fortune); he could see them in place, slotted together, tenon mated into mortice, joints lapped, dowels clouted home, waiting to be cladded in green-sawn planking, or else the outer skin had rotted or burnt away, leaving only the naked frame.

Poldarn passed his hand through his hair. It was thick with black ash.

'I remember this lot,' he said aloud. 'We came here when I was just a kid, and you pointed out all the trees, told me what they'd be used for. We even cut tallies on them, in case we forgot.' He lifted his head, then pointed. 'Look,' he said, 'there's one, you can still just about see it.'

Halder nodded. 'Thought it might ring a few bells,' he said. 'You used to come here all the time, about twenty-five years back.'

'Did I?' Poldarn frowned. 'That I don't remember.'

Halder laughed. 'You came up here flighting crows,' he said. 'You'd sit just inside the wood, just as it was starting to get dark; and when they dropped in and pitched to roost, you'd try and knock them down with a slingshot or a stone. Got quite good at it, too. Always struck me as a bit of a waste of time, but you always said it was too hard to get 'em out in the fields, you'd do better catching them where they lived. Some sense in that, I guess.' Halder shook his head. 'Always seemed to me you took it personal, them trespassing in your wood. Hated the buggers, you did.'

'Really.' Poldarn wasn't sure he wanted to hear about it. 'Well.' He took a few steps forward and rested the palm of his hand against the trunk of the tree that would one day be the middle cross-beam. He could feel it flexing ever so slightly, as the wind mussed up its branches. Then it occurred to him to wonder what they were doing there, at that particular moment. As he understood it, a man only built his house when his father (or grandfather) died, because then the old house would be pulled down and split up. It was as if, by bringing him here, Grandfather was serving a formal notice of his own impending death. Just the suggestion filled Poldarn with unanticipated panic; he looked round, just to make sure the old man was still there.

Halder was looking into the cupped palm of his right hand, which was grimy with ash. 'Bloody stuff,' he said.

'I think it's from the volcano,' Poldarn replied. Colsceg and his tribe seemed to recognise the word, although the only people he'd mentioned it to were Halder and the long-barn hand, Rook. 'I think it's what the big black cloud's made out of. The hot air from the fire shoots it way up in the air, and now it's starting to come down.'

'Figures,' Colsceg said, after a long pause. 'It's coming down everywhere, look. Like snow.'

Like black snow, at any rate. 'Let's hope it doesn't get any worse than that,' Poldarn said. 'A few cinders I can handle.' He dusted his hands off, but black smudges still clung to them. Like soot from Asburn's forge, he thought.

'Filthy mess,' Halder muttered, and Poldarn realised he was actually afraid of it – well, fair enough, fear of the unknown; he'd got over that quite some time ago, since he'd woken up beside a muddy river and found that nearly everything had suddenly become the unknown. In that respect at least, he was rather better off than all the rest of them.

'Maybe we should be getting back to the house,' he said.

Colsceg turned his head and looked at him suspiciously. 'What's the hurry?' he said. 'We only just got here.'

I don't know,' Poldarn admitted. 'It's just a feeling I've got; like, we shouldn't be too far from home, just in case something bad happens. How long will it take Rook to ride to the Lyat place?'

Halder scratched the back of his head. 'Couple of hours, maybe. It isn't far, good track all the way. Why?'

'I just wondered, that's all,' Poldarn said. 'Maybe it'll stop soon. After all, there can't be too much of the stuff in there, surely.'

'We might as well go back now,' Colsceg said.

As soon as they cleared the bend in the river, they all looked back at the mountain. It was still pumping out smoke, but far less than before, and the red glow had faded into a smudge. So that's all right, then, Poldarn thought. But he quickened his pace all the same. The cinders crunched as he walked on them, and he thought how uncomfortable it'd been, making his way over the black rocks on the way to the hot springs.

For some reason, Elja was walking fast too; in fact, she fell into step beside him, leaving her father and the rest of them behind. She didn't say anything, though.

'Well,' Poldarn said brightly, as he felt obliged to do, 'so what do you think of it?'

She looked at him as if he'd farted during a religious ceremony. 'Sorry?' she said. 'What do I think of what?'

'The site. Where the house is going to be.'

'Oh.' She shrugged. 'Very nice.'

Very nice. And said with such zest, too. 'It should be fairly well sheltered from the weather,' he said. 'And well above the river-line, in case of flooding. That's important, too.'

'I suppose so,' Elja replied. 'Did you really spend all your time killing crows when you were a boy?'

Poldarn cringed a little. 'So they tell me,' he replied. 'I can't remember anything about it myself.'

'Oh. I don't like crows. I think that horrid slow way they fly is creepy.'

'Well, yes,' Poldarn said awkwardly. 'To tell you the truth, I don't really notice them. I mean, everywhere you look, there one of them is.'

'Maybe. I think that just makes it worse.'

Well, at least they were talking about *something*. 'When I woke up,' Poldarn said, 'after I lost my memory, I mean, the only thing I could remember was a bit of a song. That was about crows.'

'Really.'

Poldarn nodded, passionately wishing he hadn't brought the subject up in the first place. 'It went, "Old crow sitting in a tall, thin tree—"'

'Oh, that one.' Elja nodded. 'That's an old one, everyone knows that. You know, you're a very strange person to talk to.'

I'm a very strange person to talk to. 'Really? In what way?'

'Well—' She made a vague gesture. 'I can't see what you're thinking. It makes things so difficult, I've got to say everything I mean. Don't you find it's a real nuisance?'

'No,' Poldarn admitted, 'not really. Look, maybe you can tell me about this, nobody else seems to want to. When you're talking to them – I mean, your family, other people – can you really see what they're thinking?'

'Sure,' she replied, faintly surprised. 'And they can see me back. And you can't, then.'

'No. In fact, I can't even imagine what it'd be like. Pretty strange, I should imagine.'

'Oh. I'd have said it was the other way round. Like being blind or something – you can't see what things are like, you can only hear. How can anybody manage to live like that?'

'People seem to cope, where I come from. I mean, where I've been. For a start, you listen to what people say, and then you know what they're thinking. If they want to tell you, that is. And if not, you've got to try and figure it out, from what they're doing, stuff like that.'

'Oh. But I always thought that over there –' she made a small gesture with her left hand '– they don't always tell things like they really are. I mean, they say things that aren't true.'

'That's right,' Poldarn said. 'Quite a lot of the time, in fact. You get used to it.'

'Really?'

'It's quite easy. Most people, when they're lying, they start acting funny. They won't look you in the eye, or their voices change slightly. It's because they're afraid of being found out.'

Elja thought about that for a moment. 'Yes, but that's only the ones you know about,' she said. 'What about the ones who're really good at it and don't know all that stuff? It could be that most people are saying untrue things most of the time, but you don't know how many of them are doing it because the only ones you find out are the ones who aren't good at it and give themselves away, like you said.'

It took Poldarn a moment to untangle that lot. 'It doesn't work like that,' he said. 'Actually, it's very hard to tell lies without getting caught out sooner or later. Besides, most of the time there wouldn't be any point. Like, suppose I'd fallen in a river and I couldn't swim, and someone shouted out, "Are you all right?" and I shouted back, "Yes, I'm fine". Then I'd drown.'

'Yes,' Elja replied thoughtfully, 'but that sort of thing doesn't happen very often, surely. Most of the time, you'd just be talking about ordinary stuff, where nobody can check up easily and really, you could say what you liked and nobody'd know, if you didn't make the silly mistakes.'

'True,' Poldarn replied, 'but why bother?'

Elja sighed. 'I don't know,' she said. 'But you see what I mean, about it being hard for me to talk to you. I can't even tell if you like me or not.'

'I—' Poldarn shrugged. 'If I told you I do, you might say I'm lying.'

'Exactly,' Elja said gloomily. 'It's so difficult, isn't it? Father says it's just because you've been away, and you'll get back to being normal sooner or later. Do you think you ever will?'

'No idea.'

'Oh.' Elja seemed to shrug the whole subject out of her mind. 'You know,' she said, 'it's funny you saying about that old song. What with the mountain and everything.'

Poldarn frowned. 'Is it?'

'Of course – or don't you know that bit of the song?'

'Which bit?'

She laughed. 'The bit you don't know, of course.'

'Oh. That bit.' He looked away. 'Tell me how it goes, it might come back if you jog my memory.'

'If you like.' She frowned. 'I won't sing it, because I'm not very good at singing. It goes something like –

> Old crow sitting on the chimney top,
> Old crow sitting on the chimney top,
> Old crow sitting on the chimney top;
> Dodger lit the fire and he made him hop.'

Poldarn thought for a moment. 'No,' he said, 'I don't remember that bit at all.'

'Oh. But you could've been telling an untruth when you said that.'

Poldarn smiled. 'And you could've just made it up, to worry me. I'd never know, would I?'

'I suppose not. That's a thought,' Elja said. 'It means I could tell you a whole lot of stuff that isn't true, and you'd never find out. That could be very good.'

Poldarn shook his head. 'I'd know,' he replied.

'Bet you wouldn't. Not if I was careful.'

'All right,' Poldarn said. 'Let's try it out, shall we? You say something, and I've got to guess if it' s true or not.'

She laughed again; she was good at laughter, unlike most of these people. 'All right,' she said. 'Oh, now I can't think of anything to say.'

'True.'

'Silly. I hadn't started yet.'

'Also true.'

'Stop it!' Elja's face was glowing with unexpected happiness, as if this was something she'd dreamed about once or twice but never believed could actually happen. 'You're teasing me. Now, let's start again and play the game properly.'

Poldarn twisted his face into a mask of terrible solemnity, making her burst out in giggles. He could feel four pairs of eyes boring holes in the back of his head, and was surprised at how very easy it was to ignore them. 'Ready?'

She spluttered. 'Yes.'

'Not true.'

'Not *fair*!' It was the joyful rage of a ten-year-old, everything forgotten except the game. 'If you're going to cheat, I'm not going to play any more.'

'It's not cheating.'

'It is too cheating. I can't see what you're going to say next.'

That brought Poldarn up short. For a while there, he could almost have believed he was talking to a regular human being, albeit a very young one. Now, though, she'd taken that one enormous difference and dropped it down between them. 'All right,' he said, 'we won't play any more. Besides, I think it's making your father nervous, all this laughing.'

Elja shook her head. 'Oh no,' she said. 'He's a bit taken aback and he's trying to figure out whether he approves or not, but he thinks he probably does. You know, on balance. Because, well, if I like you, he might as well like you too, since we're all going to be family.'

Poldarn nodded. 'I see,' he said. 'And you can read all that, can you, without even looking round?'

'Sure.'

He sighed. 'Well,' he said, 'at least it explains why you people don't go in much for jokes. No point, if the other person can see the punchline in your head before you've even started.'

She frowned a little. 'You think it's not as funny that way?'

'How do you mean?'

'I was wondering,' she replied, 'how you can ever make jokes, if you've got to do it a bit at a time. We see the whole thing all at once. You know,' she added, 'I've never actually thought about it before. It's really strange, talking to you. It makes me think about a lot of stuff I've always taken for granted.'

'Glad to be of service.'

'I'm not sure it's a good thing,' Elja said seriously. 'That's the whole point about being able to take things for granted, you can rely on them without having to check up on them all the time to see if they're still there. You know, like shoes, or the roof of your house. There's enough difficulties already without making new ones.'

Poldarn shrugged. 'Must be nice to be able to take things for granted,' he said. 'Not so easy when you're my age, and you can only remember back a few months. You can't really assume *anything*.'

Elja's eyes were wide as she looked up at him. 'It must've been terrible,' she said. 'I mean, not even knowing who you are, let alone other people. I bet you're glad you're home again, after all that.'

Poldarn thought before answering. 'I was,' he said, 'for a couple of days after we set sail. Actually, I'd had rather a rough time just before we left the Empire, I was really glad to see the back of it. Even here, though, it's not coming easily. There's so much about – well, us, I guess, that I don't know; and nobody's prepared to tell me, because it's usually so basic they can't begin to imagine I don't know it already.'

'Oh. Well, that's easily solved. You can ask me, and I'll tell you.'

'Truthfully?'

'On my word of honour.'

'That sounds impressive.'

'I mean it. I can explain stuff you don't know, and the other way around. Like,' Elja went on, 'this thing with the mountain. What did you call it?'

'A volcano,' Poldarn replied. 'At least, I'm pretty sure that's what it is. But really, I hardly know anything at all about them, except that they exist and that's what they're called.'

'That's more than any of us do. And you knew about the flash flood, which is why Rook went to Lyatsbridge.'

Poldarn shook his head. 'I just figured that out for myself,' he said. 'And it's far more likely that I was wrong and there's no problem at all, and the Lyatsbridge people will wonder what the hell we're making such a fuss about. At least, that's what I'm hoping.'

That thought soured the conversation somewhat, and neither of them said anything for a while. Elja's next words didn't improve matters, as far as he was concerned.

'You knew Egil when you were young,' she said.

Statement, not question; but clearly inviting comment. 'So he tells me,' Poldarn replied, 'and when I saw him I thought maybe I recognised him. But that's really as far as it goes.'

'That's strange,' she said. 'Because he's really afraid of you, for some reason. He's trying really hard not to think about it, and I don't think Dad or Barn have seen it in his mind yet. But I'm closer to him than they are, I can see things they can't.'

'So,' Poldarn said uncomfortably. 'Can you see what it is he's so frightened of?'

'No. That's buried so deep, you'd never be able to get it out without his help. It's odd, though. All the years I've known him, all my life, and I never thought he had anything in his mind I didn't know about.'

'The word "privacy" doesn't mean a lot around here, does it?'

'The word what?'

At first Poldarn thought Elja was making a joke; then he realised he'd used a word from another language. These people (his people) didn't have a word for it.

'Sorry,' he said. 'Don't worry about it – just me getting things muddled up.'

She shrugged, as if to say that he could keep his rotten old secrets for all she cared. 'You know,' she said, 'I don't think I've ever talked this much in my whole life.'

Poldarn grinned. 'You're a quick study,' he said. 'Do you like it?'

'What?'

'Talking.'

Elja considered for a moment. 'Actually, it's good fun,' she said. 'Like a game. I'm not sure I'd want to have to do it all the time, but it's interesting. Helps pass the time on a long walk.'

'Can't say I'd ever seen it in that light,' Poldarn confessed. 'But they all reckon I'll be back to normal before too long. Not sure how I feel about that. I mean, it must be very convenient to be able to see inside people's heads, but I can't say I'm happy about everyone being able to see inside mine. Especially,' he added, 'since I can't. How do you think it works? I mean, do you think you'll be able to see all the memories I've lost?'

'I don't know. Can't see why not.'

'Then I don't like the idea at all. You'd all know more about me than I do. And some of the stuff might not be very pleasant.'

'I can't believe that,' she said. 'And besides, it stands to reason that if you get back the trick of seeing inside heads, you'll be able to see into your own, and then you'll know all about yourself.'

'Yes,' Poldarn said. 'That's what I'm worried about.'

Elja looked at him as if he was talking in a foreign language again. 'Don't be silly,' she said.

'I'm not. Come on, think about it. What if it turns out that really I'm the most evil man that ever lived?'

'That's even sillier. Of course you're not. I can tell you that, and I've only known you for a couple of hours.'

'But you can't be sure. I might be lying.'

'I'm sure, really. I'd know if you were the most evil person ever. It'd be in your face.'

Poldarn shook his head. 'All you can see is what I'm thinking. Now, suppose I'd done all manner of dreadful things but I'd managed to make myself believe that I haven't done anything wrong.'

'Well, then,' she replied, 'in that case it wouldn't matter if we could all see inside your head, would it?'

'There's no point arguing with you, is there?'

'No, not really.'

By the time they got back to the house, Poldarn was distinctly worried. Since he'd woken up beside the river in his nest of blood-soaked mud, he'd had the problem of confronting a wide range of problems and perils, mostly unprepared, on the fly, and so far he'd managed to cope, in the sense that he was still alive and on his feet when a great many of the people he'd so far encountered weren't. Much more of this sort of thing and he'd start thinking of himself as resilient, resourceful or at least monstrously lucky. But the prospect of falling in love – for the first time, to all intents and purposes – was an emergency he simply wasn't prepared for; and the talents he'd so far excavated in himself, basically consisting of an ability to get a sword out of a scabbard and into an enemy faster than most people could do it, weren't going to be much use to him in this particular arena. So far, he reckoned, he'd managed to stay free and upright by virtue of that very isolation that his loss of memory had afflicted him with. Under all circumstances he'd been on his own, both imprisoned and protected by the wall of his enforced solitude. Without loyalties, attachments or encumbrances he'd been able to walk away from each threatening situation he'd found himself in – so long as he could get clear with his bones unbroken and the clothes he stood up in, he'd had all the options and choices in the world. Even here, where he had a real name and family and an inheritance, he'd been an outsider, an offcomer, unable to read or to be read; and if things went badly, he could always leave.

Falling in love would wreck all that. Love would arrest him, like a criminal nailed to the courthouse door by his ears, or a prisoner whose legs were smashed to make sure he couldn't escape. He'd have no choice but to participate, belong, get involved. He'd be stuck here, for ever.

Oh, there were worse places; the Bohec and Mahec valleys, for example. If Poldarn were still the boy called Ciartan who'd never left the farm or gone abroad, he couldn't have wished for anything more than love and stability. But he wasn't. He was someone out of a fairy story, the peasant's son who gets mistaken for the prince and just manages to pass himself off as royalty for a week or a month or a year until inevitably he gets found out (but then it turns out he really is the prince after all, and that's all right); and the point at which the reckless young fraud comes unstuck is always when he makes the mistake of falling for the princess, getting involved, the point where he sinks into the mud above the knee and finds he can't move any more.

Damn, Poldarn thought. But there's not a lot you can do about it when it happens, when you've already put your weight on a hidden patch of quicksand. No use looking where you're going after you've got yourself stuck.

The farmyard was black with ash.

Rook hadn't come back yet, and Colsceg decided it would

be sensible to get home, just in case something had happened or was happening. Of course, his horses were waiting for him, saddled and bridled and groomed, all his belongings stowed in the saddlebags, with an additional packhorse, heavily loaded with something or other in two coarse wool sacks. Elja didn't say goodbye as she crossed the yard to the mounting block and got on her horse, she didn't even look at Poldarn. Almost certainly there was no significance in the omission, but it didn't stop him thinking about it all afternoon, as he bashed a piece of inoffensive iron into a pair of very undistinguished pot-hooks.

Chapter Five

The vestry roof was burning.

When they told him, he was extremely annoyed. Damn it, he thought, as he yawned awake out of a delightfully pastoral dream (something about being a blacksmith on a farm, making pot-hooks), this is ridiculous. I'm a soldier, I'm supposed to be conducting an orderly defence of a fortified position, not fooling about with buckets of water. If they wanted a fireman, they should've hired a specialist.

But he left his post in the charge of a thoroughly terrified captain of archers, and hurried down the narrow spiral staircase. Twice he nearly lost his footing – the soles of his boots had been worn thin and smooth on the parade ground, and the stairs were polished – but luckily there was a guide-rope at the side he could catch hold of. Just as well; this wouldn't be a good time to fall and break his leg.

(*There was a crow in this dream; but it was floating on top of the hot air rising from the fire, a long way out of stone-throwing range. It called to him in crow language, but he couldn't understand what it was saying. Its presence implied that he was still dreaming, though he could distinctly remember having woken up.*

Were there really such things as crows when he was awake? Or were they some species of fabulous beast, the sort you can only believe in when you're dreaming?)

From the courtyard he had a good view of the problem. At some point during the night, the enemy had got tired of lobbing stones and arrows over the wall into an empty square with nothing left in it to break or hurt and had started sending over firepots instead. Most of them had smashed harmlessly on the flagstones and burnt themselves out – throughout the attack, he'd been convinced that his greatest asset and ally was the enemy's chief engineer, who clearly couldn't read a scale or set an accurate trajectory if his life depended on it – but one or two had overshot the yard completely and pitched on the vestry slates, where their burning oil could drip through the cracks made by their impact into the roof space below. It was a pity, all things considered, that the monks had decided to use the roof space to store a thousand years' worth of archives.

'I say let it burn,' said the ranking engineer, third from the top in the chain of command and clearly not happy at being woken up in the middle of the night. 'After all, it's free-standing – even if the wind changes it's not going to spread to the other buildings. And it's got no strategic importance, it's just a chapel.'

He couldn't agree more; but unfortunately he had his orders. 'Unacceptable,' he said. 'We've got to put it out. What I'm asking you is, how?'

The red and yellow light of the fire made the engineer's face shine grotesquely in the darkness. 'That's a very good question,' he said. 'Once a building like that makes up its mind to burn to the ground, there's not a lot you can do. What with the confined space and the lack of equipment, you're down to a lot of men with buckets. There's the well in the yard, but it's too deep and narrow to give you enough water for this job. You'd be better off with a longer chain, drawing off the carp ponds or the aqueduct. Both would probably be best.'

'Fine,' he replied. 'All right, you round up every bucket and basin you can find.' He turned to face the guard commander. 'You get anybody who can move, I want a chain from the ponds and another from the aqueduct, like he just said. See if you can get up the back stairs as well as the front; if we can tackle the fire from both ends at once, I reckon we'll have a better chance.'

Neither of them looked exactly hopeful as they scurried off on their respective errands, and he couldn't say he blamed them; from where he was standing the fire was already fairly well established, and even a slight breeze would turn the whole building into a furnace. He'd seen enough fires in his time to know that.

(*And yet, when you're camping out in the cold rain and what you need most in the whole world is a nice cheerful roaring fire, can you get one to light? Can you hell as like. Just like when you've got a busy day ahead of you in the forge, and the coal's damp and there's no kindling in the bucket. The fire god's sense of humour isn't his most attractive attribute.*)

They did the best they could in the circumstances, but that was never going to be enough. A hundred men dragged out of desperately needed sleep and told to put out a well-established fire in an entirely superfluous building with an inadequate supply of buckets and water were always going to be wasting their time. When the rafters and joists were starting to burn through and the situation got too dangerous to justify the risk, he called them off and told them to forget it. By that stage they were too exhausted to get back to sleep, and most of them stood aimlessly in the yard, watching the building gradually subsiding into the flames. They didn't seem to care particularly, one way or the other.

'It was a lost cause,' said a voice beside him. He looked

round, and saw the diminutive figure of the vice-chaplain, whose name he couldn't remember offhand.

'Even so, I'm sorry,' he said. 'I know how priceless those papers were. A thousand years of history—'

He stopped; not because the chaplain had interrupted him, but because he could sense that the little man was laughing at him. 'Please,' the chaplain said, 'don't worry about that, it really doesn't matter. True, we've just lost ten centuries of collected theological commentaries, speculation and debate. Good riddance. They were all wrong, you see.'

He frowned. 'Oh,' he said.

The chaplain laughed; not the sort of hysterical cackle you might expect from someone who's watching his entire world slowly drifting down in the form of thin slivers of white ash, but the genuine amusement of someone who's fully recognised his own absurdity. 'Well, of course,' he said. 'For a thousand years, we've been anticipating the return of the divine Poldarn. Every possible interpretation and analysis and hypothesis, every argument and refutation and counter-refutation – I don't know if you're familiar with the Sansory school of intaglio jewellery, but its main feature is that every last pinhead of space is covered with florid, intricate engraving and decoration, unspeakably vulgar and overdone. That's religious scholarship, only we don't just limit ourselves to the superficial level. We've left our tasteless little acanthus-leaf scrolls on *everything*. And now we have the satisfaction of knowing that everything we ever said and wrote about the subject was completely wrong.'

'You do?'

'Obviously we do,' the chaplain said. 'It's as plain as day. Poldarn has indeed returned, and he's nothing at all like what we'd thought he'd be. All in all, they've done us a favour, setting light to the archive, covering up the monumental waste of time, effort and money. Otherwise, we'd have had to do it ourselves, sooner or later.'

He scowled. 'No,' he said, 'you're wrong. Poldarn hasn't returned, and the man passing himself off as Poldarn is really nothing more than a vicious, unscrupulous two-quarter mercenary soldier. He's no more a god than I am, believe me.'

'Well.' The chaplain shrugged. 'I agree with you about the man's character and antecedents. But he's Poldarn, no doubt about it.'

The roof-tree of the vestry fell in, showering the courtyard with brilliant orange sparks that were burnt out by the time they reached the ground. 'Excuse me,' he said wearily, 'but that doesn't make sense. Either he's a god or a mercenary captain. He can't be both.'

'Why not?'

Dislodged by the fall of the roof-tree, the cross-beams gave way, one by one, pulling the rafters down with them. 'All due respect, Father,' he said, 'but it speaks for itself. Human beings are human beings, gods are gods. If they weren't gods, where's the point in having them?'

That amused the chaplain, for some reason. 'The truth is, Commander,' he said, 'you're far too clear-headed and straightforward to be a theologian.'

'You're too kind,' he grunted.

'Now I've offended you,' the chaplain sighed. 'I'm sorry. What I meant was, it takes a rather warped sort of mind to follow high doctrine. It's like doing arithmetic using only the odd numbers, and arbitrarily missing out any figures that begin or end with a seven. *You* live by logic and common sense, which is why you'll never understand theological theory.'

He coughed as the light breeze blew smoke into his face. 'Probably just as well,' he said.

'Oh, quite. You're far more use to everybody, myself and yourself included, doing what you were born to do, commanding a regiment—'

'Actually,' he interrupted, 'I don't. You've promoted me two ranks. I command a battalion, which isn't the same thing at all.'

'There,' the chaplain said cheerfully, 'that's exactly the sort of thing I have in mind. No, the point is, there's no reason at all why this bandit chieftain can't be the god Poldarn; and all the evidence suggests that that's precisely who he is. Of course,' he added, yawning, 'I'm not suggesting for one moment that he knows he's the god. In fact, it's almost certain he doesn't.'

'I see,' he said, inaccurately. 'Well, thank you for taking the time to explain. Can't say I believe any of it, but that's my loss, isn't it?'

'I suppose so. He's just as much a god if nobody believes in him; and since believing in him won't do you the slightest bit of good now that the world's coming to an end and we're all going to die, I can't see that it matters terribly much one way or another.' Almost absent-mindedly, the chaplain picked a glowing cinder off his sleeve. 'Which is why there's no earthly point in trying to save the archives; first, because they're all wrong, second, because even if they'd all been totally accurate and every prophecy and prediction had been correctly interpreted, we're all going to fry in a month or two, so, honestly, who cares? Still.' He shrugged his lean shoulders. 'My order has just lost its memory,' he said. 'From now on, for the very short time remaining to us, we don't know who we are, what we stand for, what we've said or done for the last thousand years. All that's left of us is us, and that simply isn't sufficient to justify our existence.'

He wished he hadn't got caught up in this conversation; the longer it went on, the more he could feel it oozing in over the tops of his boots. 'Well,' he said, 'if you're right about the end of the world and all that nonsense, pretty soon you won't have an existence to justify, and the problem won't arise.'

'True. And at times like this, it's a great comfort, believe me.'

The last of the girts and stays collapsed in a flurry of hot embers, filling the sky with spots of fire, like a volcano. It was obvious that the chaplain had come badly unstuck – hardly surprising, in the circumstances – and although he was talking in the most rational, lecture-to-first-years voice, all that was coming out of his mouth was half-digested drivel. On a basic infantry brigadier's pay of ninety quarters a month plus five quarters armour allowance, he wasn't paid enough to listen to elderly academics assuring him that the world was going to be burned to cold ashes before Harvest Festival.

'Anyway,' he said, 'I'll certainly bear that in mind. Still, just in case you're wrong, I suppose I'd better see about this fire.'

'Certainly,' the chaplain answered. 'You go right ahead. I think I'll stay here and enjoy the smoke.'

There was enough of it, no doubt about that. Something inside the vestry – whether it was the books or the tapestries or the wall hangings or the irreplaceable masterpieces of eighth-century religious painting – was spewing out rolling black clouds of the stuff, foul-smelling and probably very bad for your health if you breathed in too much of it. Not that there was anything he could do now, needless to say, but he very much wanted to get away from the chaplain; so he walked slowly towards the empty door frame where the bronze double gates had been.

Someone was yelling to him. He looked round and saw a young first lieutenant, whose name eluded him for the moment.

'Problem, sir,' the kid panted, wheezing like an old man. 'My platoon was on the bucket end in the south chapel when the roof came down. We were all accounted for except one. Now we've found him.'

'So?'

'It's where we found him,' the kid replied. 'He must've been in the Lady chapel when the roof fell in, and now he's got a rafter across his leg and can't shift.'

He thought for a moment: Lady chapel. Oh yes. No mouldy old books in there, but there'd been a pair of very nice gold candlesticks, a complete service of silver communion ware, and of course the offertory chest as well. All irreplaceable works of art, that went without saying, and it was very brave and heroic of the soldier to go back in there and try and save them for posterity, but now, thanks to his sheer bloody altruism, some poor suicidal fool was going to have to go in there and fish the bugger out.

Even from back here, the heat from the blaze was enough to blister someone's face. No way he could bring himself to send anyone in there; which left him with precisely one candidate for the mission. Fortunately, he'd just had it on the very best authority that the world was going to end any day now, so even if it was a suicide mission it was all as broad as it was long.

A few simple precautions, nonetheless; he confiscated a soldier's heavy overcoat and soaked it with water; did the same with two empty feed sacks and wrapped them round his face; no gloves to be found anywhere, of course, until someone suggested the bee-keeper's hut behind the guardhouse. The wet fabric felt clammy and revolting against his skin, but he couldn't think of anything better at such short notice.

He posted the young lieutenant in the doorway, with strict instructions to keep everybody else out; then a very deep breath, and inside—

Poldarn woke up to find that for some reason he'd tangled himself up comprehensively in the bedclothes, as if he'd deliberately twisted them round himself.

'Fire,' he shouted. 'Come on, the building's—'

He opened his eyes wide. Nothing to see. He was lying on the floor of the great hall. Everybody else had long since trooped off to work.

There'd been something utterly terrifying going on just a moment ago, but he couldn't remember what it was.

He stood up, rubbed his eyes until they could be trusted to stay open, and tottered out into the daylight. Nothing even remotely scary out there, either; all peaceful and industrious and as it should have been – apart from the carpet of black cinders lying over everything, of course.

One of the women came out of the house, carrying a basket. He stopped her.

'Rook back yet?' he asked.

She shook her head. 'Cettle's gone over there to see what's going on,' she told him. 'Mountain's playing up again.'

The way she said it made it sound like a job for the house handyman: mend the burnt skillet, the rat-house door's sticking, the yard broom needs a new handle, and when you've done that, the mountain's playing up again. 'Badly?' he asked.

'Terrible,' the woman replied. 'Been doing it half the night, puking up fire and god knows what else. That filthy ash everywhere.'

Now she was making it seem like the mountain was a naughty little boy given to vomiting on the rugs, just to get attention. 'Oh,' he said. 'Where's Halder?'

'In the cider house,' she answered, 'turning the apples.'

Poldarn nodded. 'Thank you,' he said, and crunched across the cinder-covered yard to find him. Why the hell bother turning the apples? In case they got bored, presumably.

On his way, he stopped to take a proper look at the mountain. There was that glow again, a red bruise on its cheek, and the black pillar standing out of the summit; it was ugly and unnatural, and he didn't like looking at it. And surely Rook had to be back by now?

Grandfather didn't look round when he clambered up the ladder into the cider-house loft. 'What was that word you used? About the mountain.'

'Volcano,' Poldarn replied.

Halder grunted. 'Well, it's at it again. Black shit all over the grass. God only knows where it'll end.' He made it sound like it was all Poldarn's fault, as if knowing a special word for the phenomenon made him guilty of causing it. 'You know any way of stopping the bloody thing?' he asked hopefully. 'I mean, if they've got them in the Empire, they must've figured out a way of dealing with them, or the whole place'd be knee-deep in ashes.'

'Sorry.' What was he apologising for, Poldarn wondered. 'Like I told you, I really don't know anything about them, except the word.' Halder didn't say anything and the silence was embarrassing, so Poldarn went on, 'But they can't be all that common over there, because I never saw one, or any black ash or anything like that.'

'Just our luck, then,' Halder said gloomily. 'Well, if there's nothing we can do, there's nothing we can do, so we might as well get on and get some work done.' That reminded him. 'You should be up at the forge,' he added. 'Isn't Asburn there, or something?'

'I don't know, I haven't been over there today. Is Rook back yet?'

Halder grunted. 'No,' he replied. 'I asked Asburn the other day how you're getting on, he says you're doing fine but maybe you'd care to try your hand at some of the less straightforward pieces.' He picked out an apple, rotated it in his fingers and threw it in a bucket. 'He's very polite, young Asburn; diplomatic, that's the word. What he means is, you aren't interested and you can't be bothered to learn. That's a pity. That's your work he's doing, you know that.'

He managed to make it sound like a reproach and a warning, that Asburn was encroaching on his prerogatives, of which he should be fiercely jealous. Poldarn picked a loose flake of dry timber off the wall with his fingernail.

'You know,' he said, 'I don't think I'm cut out for forge work. I think you need a feel for it, and I haven't got it. I'm sure I'd be much more use as a stockman or in the middle-house gang.'

Long silence, during which Halder rejected another apple. 'And then there's this wedding coming up,' he went on, 'and then you'll have your house to build. Bloody fool you'll feel, moving into your own house and all the hinges and nails and fire-irons and hardware's been made by someone else. You'll regret it the rest of your life if you let that happen, believe me. Really, you ought to knuckle down, learn your trade. I'm not going to live for ever, you know.'

'Yes, right,' Poldarn said. 'Will you let me know when Rook gets back?'

Halder stood up and looked round at him. 'Oh,' he said, 'I see what you mean. Yes, if you like. Now, why don't you get along to the forge and do some work?'

Indeed, Poldarn asked himself, *why don't I do just that?* 'You need any help with that?' he asked, more hopefully than realistically.

'No.'

'Fine. If Rook comes back, I'll be in the forge.'

'Good boy.'

The forge door stuck, of course; and when he dragged it back, it scooped up a little moraine of black ash. 'Asburn?' he called out.

'Morning,' the smith answered cheerfully. He was always cheerful, when he wasn't being worried. 'Is it still coming down out there?'

No need to ask what *it* was. 'Afraid so,' Poldarn said. 'Chucking it out all the time.'

'Filthy stuff,' Asburn replied. 'Come on in, you're just in time to see something.'

Oh, happy day. 'Just a moment,' Poldarn said, 'I'll get my apron on.'

As usual, it took him a little while to get used to the dim light. Eventually, however, he was able to make out a little stack of thin, narrow plates resting on top of the anvil. Each plate was about as wide as his thumb joint, as long as his hand from fingernails to wrist, and roughly the thickness of a bulrush. There were five plates in the stack, all the same size, and they were carefully wired together.

'You may not have seen this before,' Asburn went on – he was grinding something up in the mortar – 'and it's quite basic stuff, so it's just as well you're here.'

'Right,' Poldarn replied. 'So, what is it?'

Asburn took a pinch of whatever it was he'd been grinding between thumb and forefinger, testing its consistency. 'The regular term is pattern-welding,' he said, grinding doggedly with the pestle, 'though you'll hear people call it other things, like watered steel and the like. It's where you take, say, two bits of hard steel and three bits of ordinary soft iron, and you stack 'em up like this – iron, steel, iron, steel, iron, see? – and then you weld 'em together into a single billet, draw it out, fold it over, weld again, draw out, fold – you get the idea. What you finish up with is a piece of material that's as tough as iron and as hard as steel. Bloody useful for all sorts of things, and it's a wonderful use for all your odds and ends of scrap.'

'Ah,' Poldarn said. 'So what's that in the mortar?'

'Flux,' Asburn replied. 'When you're welding iron to steel, see, you've got to make sure you don't get any rubbish in the join. The flux draws out all the shit.'

'Ah,' Poldarn repeated. There didn't seem to be much else he could say about that.

'Nice thing about this stuff is,' Asburn went on, 'when

you've welded and folded a couple of times, you've actually got like – well, if you've ever seen where a river's cut a deep channel, and you can see all the different layers in the sides of the cut, one on top of the other, topsoil and clay and gravel and shale and rock and stuff. It's like that, only you've got maybe a hundred layers, iron and steel alternately; and when you make something out of it, if you etch it right with salt and vinegar, it brings out the most amazing patterns, like ferns or feathers or ripples in water, or the backbone of a fish. Which is why they call it pattern-welding.'

'I see,' Poldarn said, relieved to have that particular mystery cleared up before it had a chance to eat into his subconscious mind. 'Why not just use a piece of solid steel, though? We've got plenty in the scrap, haven't we?'

Asburn nodded. 'Loads,' he said. 'But some people reckon this stuff's better for holding an edge and not breaking, though I'm not so sure about that myself. Mostly because it looks good, and it's the way we've always done it, I guess.'

'Fine,' Poldarn replied. 'All right, so what happens now?'

Asburn reached up for the bellows handle and gave it an apparently effortless tug. 'First,' he said, 'we need a good heat.' His eyes took on that worried look. 'I don't suppose you'd just fetch over that sack, there by your foot?'

Poldarn nodded. As he lifted it, he realised what it was. 'This is charcoal,' he said. 'I thought we didn't use it.'

'Oh, got to use it for this job,' Asburn replied. 'Coal's too dirty and full of clinkers and shit. At least, there's a sort of coal they've got up north that welds really quite nicely, but—'

But Poldarn wasn't to be deflected so easily. 'So we can afford to use charcoal for this job, which by all accounts isn't really necessary; but when I want a couple of handfuls just to get the fire started—'

'I'll have a proper look at that tue-iron later on this week,' Asburn said quickly. 'I'm sure it's not drawing right, and that's why you're finding it hard to get a fire in. If you could see your way to just dumping a bit here, where it's handy to rake in when I need it.'

Poldarn grunted and poured a quarter of the sack out into the forge bed. Odd, he thought, the coal dust and debris in here looks just like the black ash from the volcano. 'Will that do you?'

'Oh, that's absolutely fine,' Asburn assured him, 'to be going on with.' He drew down on the bellows handle, smooth and slow, forcing a terrific blast of air through the heaped-up fire. A great spout of yellow flame burst out of the apex of the heap – again, just like the mountain outside. No wonder they'd called it Polden's Forge. 'Now we bung in the material,' Asburn continued, 'and heap up the fuel round it like so. There.' He pulled out the tongs and laid them on the anvil, ready for when he needed them next.

'Would you like me to do the bellows?' Poldarn asked.

'If you wouldn't mind.' Asburn made it sound like Poldarn had offered to take his place on the gallows. That sort of thing got annoying after a while. 'That's it,' he went on, as Poldarn's overstretched shoulder muscles registered the effort of pumping the bellows with little fissures of pain. After a long and uncomfortable interval, Asburn fished out the billet, which was now an even sunset orange all the way through, and sprinkled it with his magic dust, which sparkled as it burned on the hot surface. 'Now,' he said as he poked it back into the fire, 'we've got to listen out for when it gets hot enough.'

Poldarn frowned. 'Listen?'

Asburn nodded. 'It's a sort of hissy, scratchy sound, when the metal's just beginning to melt on the outside. You'll know it when you hear it.'

All Poldarn could hear was the creak of the bellows leather, the squeal of a dry bearing and the huffing of the blast as it aroused the fire. No hissy scratching, unless he'd gone deaf. But Asburn must've heard it, because he suddenly darted forward with the tongs and nipped the billet out of the fire, like a buzzard swooping on a rabbit. The metal was white-hot, very slightly glazed and translucent on the surface, and a few white sparkles were dancing in the air around it.

'All right,' Asburn said breathlessly, 'this is the—' He smacked the billet with his hammer; not particularly hard, but a cascade of incandescent sparks exploded from the point of impact, showering his arms and shoulders. Poldarn could hear them patter to the ground as they cooled and fell.

'– Good bit,' Asburn concluded, as he tapped and pecked at the billet, working so fast that Poldarn couldn't really follow his movements. Instead of ringing on the metal, the hammer made a sort of flat, squidging noise. When the billet had cooled to a bright yellow, Asburn stopped hammering and picked it up in the tongs. 'There,' he said, sounding thoroughly surprised, 'it's taken, see?' Poldarn leaned over close, until the heat radiating off the metal started to burn his face, and tried to see what all the fuss was about. Asburn was right: the weld had taken – he could see that by the way the heat was soaked evenly into the sides and edges.

'You could've warned me about the sparks,' he said. 'I nearly jumped out of my skin.'

'Sorry,' Asburn said, immediately looking the very image of horrified remorse. 'Are you all right? It didn't burn you, did it?'

'No, not at all,' Poldarn said, wishing he'd kept his mouth shut. 'I'm fine, really. Does it always do that?'

Asburn nodded. 'If it doesn't, you haven't got it hot enough,' he explained.

'I see. And then, if it hasn't taken, you've got to go back and do it again.'

'Well, you can try, certainly,' Asburn said. 'But usually, if you don't get it right first time, chances are it'll have got all full of clinker and rubbish and you'll never get it to go. Right,' he went on, 'back it goes in the fire, we take a normal working heat and draw it down till it's about twice the length it is now. Then we fold it and weld again.'

In spite of himself, not to mention the hard work of pumping the bellows and swinging the sledgehammer, Poldarn found he was almost enjoying this; particularly the rain of sparks, like a blizzard of burning snow, each time Asburn welded the folded billet. Quite why, he wasn't sure, since it was uncomfortably close to the view from the court-yard, and he'd come in here in the first place to get away from that.

'How many more times have we got to do this?' he asked, as Asburn put the billet back in the fire after the fourth weld.

'Depends,' Asburn replied. 'Mostly, on what you're figur-ing to make out of it. This time it's just a skinning knife for Raffen, so that'd probably do as it is. On the other hand, a couple more times won't hurt, and we'll get a better pattern. Not that I'm planning on anything fancy,' he added defen-sively, 'but if a job's worth doing, and all that.'

'Sure,' Poldarn said. 'I was just wondering, that's all. When you've done that, what next?'

Asburn shrugged. 'Just forge it like an ordinary lump of steel,' he said. 'You can do it if you like, Raffen doesn't want anything fussy or complicated.'

Then he's out of luck isn't he? Poldarn thought. 'All right,' he heard himself say, though why he wanted to volunteer for a job he didn't have to do he couldn't quite understand. After all, it'd be a crying shame for Asburn to do all this hard work and then have the result screwed up in the final, easy stage by an incompetent buffoon.

In the event, though, Poldarn made a reasonable job of it – the blade straight, the back very, very nearly level, no dirty lumps of clinker or scale carelessly hammered in, no ugly pits or stretch marks, and it didn't warp when he tempered it, either. True, compared with the knives he'd seen Asburn make it was ugly, graceless and pedestrian, but if the worst came to the worst and Raffen didn't have anything else handy to do the job with, it'd probably cut something up without snapping in two or wiping its edge off on a hazel twig. After Poldarn had filed it and burnt on a piece of staghorn for a handle, he let it lie on the bench and looked at it. I made that, he thought; well you can tell, can't you? Nevertheless.

While he'd been making the knife, Asburn had been up the other end of the building, fussing round a partly made lampstand with chalk and a piece of string. Asburn was capable of spending a whole day just measuring one piece, prodding and fiddling and fidgeting to get an exact fit on something that nobody but him would ever notice or care about. Poldarn had actually asked him once why he bothered; Asburn had replied that maybe right now nobody would be any the wiser if he sent out work that wasn't just right; but in a hundred years' time, or two hundred, a smith would come along and know in an instant what he'd done and where he'd gone wrong, and until then he wouldn't be able to lie still in his grave for fretting about it.

Poldarn reckoned that attitude was too silly for words, but decided not to say so.

All in all, he decided, as he gave the knife blade a few last touches with the stone, he'd had worse days. Which wasn't to say he was reconciled to this absurd system, whereby he was being politely frogmarched into a life and a line of work that he didn't like and wasn't good at; but when he compared this existence with what he'd been through on the other side of the ocean, there wasn't really any need to stop and think before choosing. Quite apart from the comforts and the security, he hadn't had to kill anybody since he'd arrived. That was the sort of thing he shouldn't get into the habit of taking for granted.

'I think I'm calling it a day,' Asburn said. 'How about you?'

'I think that'll—' Poldarn began, and got no further. Three bangs, absurdly loud, shook the floor and filled the air.

'What the hell—?' Asburn muttered; but Poldarn knew exactly what it was. Rook had mentioned them last time, he remembered distinctly because he'd been in the forge when they happened, and they'd been drowned out by the sound of his hammer. Well, he'd heard them all right this time, no question about that.

'The mountain,' Asburn said.

They ran outside and looked over the house roof. The first thing Poldarn noticed was how dark it had become. It took him rather longer to figure out why; the cloud of ash billowing out of the mountain was now so huge and thick that it was blocking out the sun.

'Not very good,' Asburn said.

Apparently he wasn't the only one who thought so; a mob of crows who'd been sitting on the middle-house roof flew up with a chorus of furious screaming and shrieking, and swirled in a barely controlled spiral over the house roofs. They're lost, Poldarn was shocked to realise, they don't know where they are or how to get to where they want to be. Somehow, that was almost more worrying than the sight of the volcano itself. He had no idea why they were having such problems, or even whether it was to do with the ash cloud or the mountain at all; but he'd been watching rooks and crows all his life (he could remember watching them) and he'd never seen anything like this before.

'Bloody stupid birds,' Asburn said, as a group of six or more sailed right over their heads, almost close enough to reach with a pitchfork or a long rake. 'It's like they can't hear their friends over in the long copse.'

The colony in the long copse was almost certainly where these birds were from; but the copse was an hour and a half away to the west. Then Poldarn realised what Asburn was talking about. Well, he thought; takes one to know one. 'You think so?' he said.

'It fits in with the way they're carrying on,' Asburn replied. 'At least, it's not the dark, because they fly home at night in darker than this; not the noise, because it's stopped; could be all the ash and shit in the air, I suppose, but if rain and snow don't bother 'em particularly, I wouldn't have thought flying through ash was so totally different as to spook 'em out completely.' He frowned, wiping black grime off his forehead – something of a waste of time, since he was already black and filthy from the forge's dust and scale. 'I think the noise pushed 'em out, and there's something about the ash that means they're suddenly out of touch with the others. It's like the body's still moving around, but the brain's dead or asleep or something.'

Poldarn wasn't paying attention. He was too busy watching the birds, as if he could somehow interpret the crazy patterns they were weaving in the air. He'd been wrong; he *had* seen them like this once before, years ago, the first time he'd managed to outwit them with his decoys. He'd been proud of the achievement, and rightly so; it was the day when he'd finally identified the scouts, the singletons who go in front of the main mob and check for signs of danger. Instead of opening up on them with his slingshot as soon as they pitched, he'd let them land and strut about on the ground, no more than fifteen feet from where he was lying, until the section leaders got up out of the roost trees and dropped in, putting their wings back, banking into the slight wind to slow themselves down. He'd spared them, too – it was torture, not moving for so long, hardly daring to breathe – and after they'd walked around for a while like they owned the place, in came the rank and file, tens and twenties at a time. And *then* he'd jumped up and started slinging, handfuls of stones to each release, so that he was killing and stunning them by threes and fours, so closely were they packed in their arrogance. They'd flown up at once, of course; but they couldn't understand, because there hadn't been an enemy in sight twenty minutes ago and they hadn't seen one come up, so there couldn't be any danger, could there? And while they debated and tried to figure it out, they swooped and circled and turned and banked and braked and fluttered, like drunks in the dark, while he crammed gravel into the pad of his sling and hurled till he felt the tendons in his forearm twang with pain, and each time he let fly it was a victory of unsurpassed sweetness; until quite suddenly the sky was empty, and the ground in front of him was littered with black objects, hopping and thrashing, twitching and fluttering broken wings, somersaulting bodies with brains already dead (it takes them a long time to stop moving after they die), cawing and screaming and struggling in their extreme pain; and black feathers floated in the air like volcanic ash, gradually drifting down to settle on the bare earth.

'You know,' Poldarn said, looking at the mountain, 'you may well be right. Screw this, let's go indoors.'

But a single crow swung over them, jinked away in terror as it saw what it was flying over, and sailed straight through the forge doorway. 'Bugger,' Asburn said. 'I hate it when that happens.'

'What?'

Asburn's shoulders drooped visibly. 'Bloody birds getting in the forge. They peck at the chimney hood and shit all over the tools and the scrap, and they're too stupid to leave when you try and shoo 'em out. Panic,' he explained. 'Would you mind—?'

Poldarn nodded, and followed Asburn back inside. It was even darker than usual, of course; the only light was red, bleeding out of the subsiding fire. At first there didn't seem to be any sign of the crow, and Poldarn wondered if it had flown under the hood and straight up the chimney. But no such luck; it had pitched on a cross-beam, and when they walked under it, the stupid creature erupted in a flurry of wingbeats and shot between them before either of them could react.

'Where the hell did it go?' Poldarn shouted.

Asburn shrugged. 'Too quick for me,' he replied.

And for me, Poldarn admitted, in shame. But it won't be the next time; he grabbed the poker from the hearth and held it down at his side, like a sheathed sword ready for the draw. Come on, he told himself, I thought this kind of thing was second nature to you.

'Right,' he said. 'You go up that end, I'll stay here. The thing about crows is, they're smart as anything, but they can't count.'

Asburn hesitated, as if he was having extreme difficulty with the idea of being told what to do. 'Yes,' he said eventually, 'I'll go this way.' He advanced down the workshop, clapping his hands over his head; and sure enough, the crow materialised as a burst of black movement out of a shadow and accelerated, flapping desperately, like a man learning to swim as he drowns. It passed Poldarn so fast that he didn't really see it; but the poker in his right hand lashed out, and he felt the shock of impact travelling down it and jarring his hand. He'd hit the crow like it was the ball in a game of stickball; it shot through the air, smashed into the tue-iron and rebounded onto the hearth, wings still pumping but not having any effect. With one long stride Poldarn was onto it. He slammed the poker down diagonally across the bird's outstretched wings, crushing it into the glowing embers, while his left hand fumbled for the bellows handle. The crow was strong, arching its body, thrusting with legs and neck and wings against the strength of his wrist and hand, but he held it there – as the bellows blasted air into the fire and made it flare up, he could feel the terrible heat frizzing the hair off his arm and scorching his skin, while the stench of

cooking meat and burning feathers made him feel sick. Three
more pumps on the bellows, as hard and fast as he could
work it, and the bird's feathers were crackling, all full of fire;
the force of its body against the poker was wrenching the
muscles of his arm, tearing his sinews, but he was past caring
about that, all that mattered now was the victory.

Poldarn was shocked at the suddenness of its death. It
died in the middle of a frantic shove, and the cessation of
resistance against his hand made him stumble forward,
almost lose his balance. At the same moment, the remaining
feathers ignited in a sudden flare that singed his face and
made his eyes smart. He hopped back two steps, dropping
the poker on the floor with a clang. Then he was aware of
Asburn, staring at him.

'What did you do that for?' Asburn asked.

It was as if the man who'd killed the crow had stepped out
of his body; he'd gone, and Poldarn couldn't remember a
thing about him, who he'd been or why he'd done what he'd
done. It didn't make sense. He'd never do a thing like that.

'Bloody thing,' he answered awkwardly, trying to sound
like his grandfather hating the mountain, and the blaze of
feathers died down, leaving a black cinder in the heart of the
fire. 'Serves it right for coming in here in the first place.'

Asburn looked at him, then looked away without saying a
word. Poldarn felt he owed him some kind of explanation,
even if it was only a lie, but he couldn't think of one.

The door opened, and one of the farm boys came in. 'God
almighty,' he said, 'what's that horrible smell?'

'Broiled crow,' Poldarn replied. 'What do you want?'

The boy shrugged. 'Halder sent me with a message. You
wanted to know when Rook got home. Well, he's back.'

Chapter Six

They found him in the hall of the main house, wrapped in six blankets and shivering helplessly, surrounded by silent, terrified-looking men and women, all keeping their distance as though he had some contagious disease. Two of the farmhands were banking up the fire, making the place uncomfortably hot. Halder was standing next to him, looking— the only word for it was frightened.

'What happened?' Poldarn asked. Everyone turned and stared at him, but he was getting used to that.

'Let him alone,' someone said. 'Can't you see he's near frozen to death?'

'All right,' Poldarn said, and as he walked down the hall he felt like a bridegroom on his wedding day, or the chief mourner at a funeral. 'Somebody else tell me what happened, I'm not fussy.'

Eyvind, who'd been sitting on the corner of the middle table, jumped up and came to meet him. 'You were right,' he said. 'In fact, the Lyatsbridge people are very grateful indeed, you probably saved all their lives.'

Well, Poldarn thought, that's nice, but I'd rather have some details. 'Was it a flood, then?' he ventured.

Halder nodded. 'Hell of a flood,' he said. 'And the devil of it was, it came down so quick, they would all have been at dinner, first they'd have known about it would've been the water smashing through the porch doors.'

'Bloody silly idea,' muttered Rook, through chattering teeth, 'building the house right in the bottom of the valley. Won't make that mistake next time.'

Eyvind put a hand on Poldarn's shoulder and gently eased him down onto a bench. 'It went straight through the middle of the main house,' he said. 'Lifted it up like you'd pick up a basket or something. Took out everything standing in the yard – barns, sheds, cider house, trap house, the lot. All the stock in the long pen, all the stores, everything; all they've got left is what they were wearing.'

Poldarn nodded slowly. 'So he got there in time, then.'

'Sort of,' Eyvind replied. 'Actually, he was on the other side of the valley when it came down – fast as a galloping horse, he said – and he just had to stand there and watch. But of course they'd known he was coming; they got out and went up the other side of the valley with only moments to spare.'

No need to ask how they'd known, of course; a useful thing, this mind-reading. 'How long did it last?' he asked.

'The rest of that day, and all night,' Halder said. 'Come first light, the water was going down, and by noon he managed to get across. Then it came down again, and he was stuck there.'

'But that was only the start.' Eyvind took up the narrative as if this was something they'd all rehearsed earlier, each of them knowing his cues. 'We thought we were getting a lot of ash down here – it's nothing compared with what they've been getting. A hand-span deep over everything, deeper in places; and sometimes it was coming down hot, like it'd just been raked off the fire.'

'Nowhere to shelter, see,' Halder said, 'they were all out in the open, so they had to lie down on their faces and hope they didn't get too badly burned. Nothing they could do about it, of course. There was one poor fool—'

'Iat,' Eyvind said, 'who worked in the dairy. He got hit with a lump of hot ash and his hair caught fire, so he ran down to the water and jumped in. Drowned, of course, the bloody fool. Too quick for anybody to stop him.'

Poldarn sighed, though he hadn't heard of this man Iat before. These things happen, he told himself; however bad things may be, human ingenuity and human determination will always find a way of making them worse.

'That was when it started raining,' Eyvind said.

Under his pile of blankets, Rook shuddered. Probably the cold.

'It happens like that,' Halder went on. 'It's because they're tight in to the foot of the mountain there; they get sudden flash rainstorms coming in off the hillside when the rest of us are having broad sunshine.'

'And all the steam,' Eyvind pointed out, 'from where the snow had melted; all that low cloud we could see from back here. Quite a downpour, even by their standards. Needless to say, it had to wait till the whole mountain was covered in ash.'

Maybe it's catching, Poldarn thought; because he knew what was coming next. 'Mud,' he said.

Halder nodded. 'That's right. Black mud, coming down off the slopes in a bloody torrent. At one point, it was actually moving faster than the flood water had done, if you can imagine that. God knows why, there's probably a simple reason. Anyhow, it filled up the valley right down as far as the lower bridge. In fact, valley's not the right word any more, it's a flat black plain.'

Eyvind shook his head. 'It's just like builder's mortar,' he continued. 'Same consistency, and it dries hard, not like ordinary mud. A few days of sun and that whole valley will be filled in with solid rock. Unbelievable,' he added, 'it's changed the country for ever. You should have seen the looks on their faces when they realised what it meant; they hadn't just lost their house and their animals and their stuff, their land's gone too – all the fields and meadows and orchards, buried under ten feet of black stone. You simply wouldn't credit it, outside of a fairy story.'

Quite so, Poldarn thought, the end of the world; and what we don't burn, we'll bury. His mind kept being drawn back, in spite of the atmosphere in the hall, the dead silence, the intense drama, to another issue, smaller but just as important to him personally; why on earth had he done that horrible, cruel thing to that crow, back in the forge? The more he thought about it, the more impossible to explain it became, and yet he could remember that at the time it had seemed logical, sensible, absolutely the right thing to do.

It went without saying that there couldn't possibly be a connection.

'Anyway,' Halder went on, 'soon as it stopped raining, Rook here sets off the long way round, over the hog's back, down to Callersfell and back up our river – on foot, mind, he couldn't get his horse across the flood, which is why it's taken him so long, and why he's frozen half to death, crossing the hog's back this time of year—'

'And his clothes all burned in tatters, don't forget,' Eyvind pointed out. 'It's bad enough up there if you've got a good fur coat and warm boots. But he knew we were worried about him and wanted to know what'd happened, so – well, here he is, just about. And bloody lucky too, if you ask me.'

Long silence; though, Poldarn knew perfectly well, it was only a silence as far as he was concerned. No doubt the rest of them were having a lively debate among themselves. Quite apart from everything else, it was such bad manners.

'So,' he said aloud, 'sounds like it's up to this house to do something for the Lyatsbridge people.'

Halder nodded. 'Us and Colscegsford,' he said. 'Assuming they were high enough up not to get a dose of the same.'

Poldarn frowned. 'And what about them?' he asked. 'Colsceg and Elja, I mean. If the river was right up and then the mudslides after that—'

'They're home,' Rook broke in, 'and safe. They heard what was going on, and took a detour through the Wicket Gate—'

'That's a sort of gap in the hog's back, on our side of the river,' Eyvind explained. 'They got home before the mudslides came on; and anyway, nothing came anywhere near them.'

Halder grunted. 'They've sent over blankets and sawn lumber,' he said, 'and food and beer, and a few changes of clothes. But it's more than they can spare; we'd better get something sorted out ourselves. I'm thinking it'd make more sense to bring the Lyatsbridge people here, rather than taking the stuff over to them. We've got room, and our fires get lit anyway, it'd make more sense, if this state of affairs is going to last any time. Being neighborly is all very well, but better not to waste fuel and food we might end up needing ourselves.'

Judging from the expressions on the faces around him, Halder was speaking in his capacity as spokesman for the whole farm. Not that Poldarn would've argued against the idea or the reasoning behind it, even if he'd had the option.

'There's another thing, though,' he said, thinking aloud as much as anything. 'If this mud stuff's blocked the river and filled in the valley, how's that going to affect us? What I mean is, next time there's a heavy burn and more snow gets melted, where's the flood water going to go, without that river to draw it off? You'll have to tell me, I don't know the country. Is there any danger it'll change course and come this way?'

They hadn't considered that, and in consequence nobody said anything, or had anything to say. Eventually Eyvind (interesting that it should have been him) broke the silence. 'It's difficult to say,' he said. 'I wouldn't have thought so, at least I wouldn't have thought this place was in any danger. But I'm thinking about our place; we're on the other side of the spur ridge, and lower than you are here. I'm not too bothered about floods, but what if there's a heavy rainstorm and one of these mudslides comes down? It'd only take a fall of rocks or something like that blocking the neck directly above our house, and anything that would've come down on Lyatsbridge could end up running off the other side of the spur and ending up in our yard. And if it moves that quickly—'

Halder nodded. 'Normally I'd say wait till morning, but if it carries on like this, it won't be any lighter then than it is now.'

'You're right.' Eyvind stood up. 'Sorry to abandon you like this,' he said to Poldarn, 'and I'll be back as soon as we've had a chance to figure things out at home. Till then – well, thanks for the warning. I wouldn't have thought of that if you hadn't mentioned it.'

Curious, Poldarn thought after he'd gone; is it possible that this wise and perceptive man whose foresight has saved so many lives is the same person who killed the crow? Oh. wouldn't it make everything so much easier if only I knew which of them was me.

The next morning, Poldarn woke up before everyone else and ran to the door, digging his feet into the ribs of several sleepers on the way (but they didn't wake up, of course). He was still full of undigested sleep, and it took him over a minute of cack-handed fumbling to cope with the bolts and the bar.

The mountain was on fire. All down the southern slope,

he could see black and red clouds, like some kind of exotic flowering lichen on the trunk of a dead tree. He assumed it was morning, simply because he was awake; the only light came from the dull glare of the fireclouds, but they lit up surprisingly well. He had no idea how long he stood in the porch staring – no sun meant no sense of time – but it was long enough for the cold wind to numb his hands and make his bare feet ache.

The first he knew of the next development was a gentle pattering sound, like rain. Bad, he said to himself, thinking of the mudslides; but it wasn't rain, it was cherry-stone-sized nuggets of black ash, and when one of them hit him on the forehead he found out that they were hot.

That woke Poldarn from his trance. The thatch, he thought; how hot did the ash nuggets have to be before they'd set the roof alight, and burn the house down with everybody in it? He made a solemn resolution that that wasn't going to happen, and ducked indoors.

'Grandfather,' he shouted, 'wake up, it's raining hot ash!'

Nobody even stirred, which was infuriating. But he knew what he had to do; he ran back the length of the hall – it didn't matter how many heads he kicked or hands he stood on, they weren't going to wake up until it was time – and through the double doors into the back room where Halder and Rannwey slept in magnificent privacy. If he could wake them up, he guessed, everybody else would come round too. Only logical.

Halder snapped awake and sat up as soon as Poldarn opened the doors. The older man stared at him as though he'd lost his mind.

'Hot ash,' Poldarn mumbled (Halder and Rannwey slept naked, he realised, and even with the world coming to an end all around him, he was still capable of acute embarrassment.) 'There's hot ash dropping out of the sky, and the thatch—'

'Bloody hell,' Halder growled, 'won't it ever stop? All

right, I'm coming. Just let me get some trousers on, will you?'

Poldarn backed out of the room and shut the doors firmly. He wasn't in the least surprised to find that the entire household was sitting up, reaching for their boots.

'Bloody mountain,' someone grumbled over to his left. 'Sneaking up on us while we're asleep. That's low, that is.'

He knew what the man meant. If it really was the divine Poldarn doing all this, he didn't think much of a god who attacked by night, trying to burn a sleeping house. A god should have more self-respect.

'All right.' Halder was standing in the doorway, mercifully betrousered, with his coat on but no shirt. 'You're the *volcano* expert – any suggestions?'

Poldarn was about to make it clear, yet again, that he didn't know any more about volcanoes than Halder did, when some voice inside his head told him exactly what to do. 'If I were you,' he said, 'I'd get every bucket and basin we can lay our hands on, and the long ladders from the hay barn. If we're quick, we should be able to save the house, at the very least.'

Halder scowled at him. 'Screw the house,' he said. 'We can't eat carpets or milk or furniture. What matters is the barns and the sheds.'

While he was speaking, the household was already snapping to it. In spite of the emergency, Poldarn couldn't help being amazed at the wonderful way they all managed to get out through the porch doors, just wide enough for two abreast, without any colliding, pushing or shoving. Instead, they timed their movements to perfection. How the hell do they do that? he wondered.

By the time he got outside, his original plan had been modified, rather intelligently; instead of just scrambling up ladders and sloshing buckets of water onto the thatch, they'd dragged out some heavy leather sheets – which were used to cover the hayricks – and the sails of Halder's ship. Normal people couldn't have done what came next, not unless they'd practised it as a drill for years under the command of exceptionally talented and cool-headed officers; but the Haldersness farmhands carried out the entire operation flawlessly, astonishingly quickly, and in total silence.

While the men unfolded the sheets and sails in the yard, the women were drawing buckets of water and passing them down a human chain that had apparently formed instantly while Poldarn's attention was elsewhere for a second or so. In consequence, it took no time at all to get each sheet thoroughly wet, ready for the next step.

The men spontaneously divided into two teams. One team brought up the ladders, while the others roped up the sheets. The ladders were laid up against the long barn, placed so that their topmost rungs were a foot or so clear of the top of the roof; this meant that the ropes could be drawn over the ladders without dragging on the thatch and ripping it out. Bracing the ladders while the sheets were being hauled turned out to be the hardest part of the job, but with the women and children helping as well, they managed to keep them in place until the sheets were lying astride the roof-tree, at which point the ladders were withdrawn and the ropes made fast. Later on, Eyvind told him that that was how they were used to covering hayricks, and the only difference was that the barn was somewhat taller and a whole lot longer; it was no big deal, Eyvind said, and Poldarn was prepared to believe that that was how he saw it.

After a few half-hearted and counterproductive attempts to make himself useful, Poldarn retired to the shelter of the turnip shed (which was one storey high and had a turf roof) and watched the show from there. He couldn't decide which was more impressive, the way they all worked together without having to stop and debate every step or be told what to do, or their apparent imperviousness to the hail of cinders that burnt holes in their coats, frizzled their hair and scorched their hands and faces as they hauled ropes and handled buckets. For the first time he understood what it was about them that made it impossible for the Empire's best generals to win or even survive a pitched battle against them. And yet, he remembered, when he'd woken them up and they'd realised what was happening, they'd stood gawping, faces blank, completely out of their depth when faced with something new and outside their experience; it was only when Poldarn had made his suggestion to Halder and Halder had, presumably, considered it and thought of something better that the entire household had suddenly burst into immediate, perfect action. That was a scary thought, possibly even more disturbing than the possibly impending end of the world; because when Halder was gone, the new head of the household would be the one man on the island who couldn't read minds or have his own mind read. Would they even be capable of waking up in the morning, Poldarn asked himself, let alone doing something like this?

Between completing the covering of the long barn and starting on the middle house there was no perceptible delay – the first team was already setting the ladders up while the second team were still pegging the guy ropes. In spite of the quite astonishing speed at which they worked, it was obviously going to be a long day, and there was still a depressingly large area of unprotected thatch for an unusually hot cinder to nest in. More than anything else, Poldarn wished there was something he could do to help, because he'd never been lonelier than he was now, crouched in a doorway on the edge of the yard. He'd saved the day again, of course; if he hadn't woken up when he had and realised the danger, the whole farm might be ablaze by now. But that didn't console him in the slightest. Of course, nobody was going to reproach him for lounging about gawping while everybody else was breaking their backs. They understood, they were happy to make allowances, until such time as he snapped out of this lost-memory business and started acting normal again. They couldn't be more tolerant or patient. That didn't make it any better; quite the reverse.

As if to make the point that the danger was real and immediate, the cider-house roof caught fire, just as the ladders were going up against the side wall. Instead of trying to put the fire out with buckets of water, they carried on hauling and laid a sopping wet sail on the blazing thatch. Of course the sail was ruined, but it put the fire out (and it'd be far easier to patch a sail than build a new cider house, not to mention the loss of a whole season's apples, the press and all the cider-making gear). That aside, they got the job done without any further damage, while the cinders continued to fall. They were getting larger, Poldarn noticed – some of them were now the size of pigeons' eggs – and the thick carpet of hot ash they made on the yard was now over a finger's length deep in places. Never mind about the thatch, the buildings themselves were timber-framed and timber-cladded. How much heat could they take before they started to burn?

One damn thing after another, he told himself; but he wrapped a couple of empty turnip sacks round his head and shoulders, twisted the corners over his hands, and went to find Halder.

'Good point,' Halder said, when Poldarn explained what was on his mind. 'I hadn't thought of that. When we've done putting on the covers, we'd better make a start on damping down the walls. Bloody thing isn't going to give us a moment's peace, I can see that.'

It occurred to Poldarn that his grandfather, who'd been shifting ladders and hauling ropes for over six hours, was well over eighty years old; his coat was more holes than cloth, and he'd taken three serious-looking burns to the top of his head, more still on the backs of his hands. 'Here,' he said, shrugging out of the turnip-sacks and draping them over Halder, 'better late than never.'

'Thanks,' Halder said. 'Any more where those came from?'

I should have thought of it for myself, Poldarn told himself, as he dashed from group to group handing out sacks, blankets, rugs, pillows, anything he could find that'd go between hot coals and bare skin. I've had long enough to think of it, God only knows. Still, maybe if I'm good they'll let me have a bucket to play with when they get on to the damping-down, if I promise to play nicely and not bother anybody.

They left covering the forge till last, since half the roof was slated rather than thatched; but in spite of all Poldarn's most earnest prayers and entreaties, the loathsome place stayed resolutely unignited. If I was to find a nice hot cinder and chuck it up there while nobody was looking, he said to himself as he filled his arms with leather aprons, would anybody know? Yes, of course they would. He abandoned the idea and hurried back outside, just in time to get hit right between the eyes by a scorching hot nugget as big as a child's fist. He turned back into the forge, rummaged around in the scrap and eventually found what he'd been looking for: an Imperial cavalry helmet, just the one round, jagged hole in the side of the left temple. Compromised, but a damn sight better than a severely burned scalp.

Back outside. The glow from the mountain was getting fainter, undoubtedly a good sign but inconvenient since it was still pitch dark. That didn't seem to bother the others, needless to say, and he guessed that they had some way of figuring out where they were in relation to each other, navigating by sounds inside their heads, like bats. There were times (and this was definitely one of them) when his fellow countrymen irritated the hell out of Poldarn.

But they couldn't read him, of course; which accounted for the fact that he walked straight into a ladder, being carried by

Eyn and Symond, and ended up on the ground, sitting on a carpet of very hot ash. He didn't stay there very long; he jumped up, bashed his head against the ladder, and passed out.

Well now, said the mountain, here we are.

He looked up. He was kneeling on the ground, but the ash wasn't hot any more, and the yard was deserted. He could see the mountain, though. It was glowing orange through a crown of burning cloud, and streams of liquid fire, like molten metal flowing from a crucible, cascaded down its flanks.

Go away, he replied. I can't hear you; and even if I can, it's just because I banged my head. Besides, you've got me in enough trouble already, I don't want to talk to you. Not now, not ever.

The mountain laughed; then, like an old man with a weak chest, it spat up three enormous spouts of fire. Don't be like that, it said. It's getting so we can't talk to each other unless something bashes your head in. I don't mind, but I'm sure it can't be good for you.

Go *away*, Poldarn thought. Damn it, I was certain I'd given you the slip when I left the Bohec valley. How dare you come sneaking after me like this?

Somehow, the mountain made the earth shake under his knees. Don't give me that, it said, you know perfectly well, where you go, I go, just like your shadow. Running away – you're like a cat with its tail on fire running through a corn- field. Believe me, it'd be far better if we talked it over like sensible people, got it all sorted out here and now. For their sake (a brilliant orange flare illuminated the whole farm), if not for yours and mine.

He shook his head. Get lost, he said. There's nothing to talk about, you know that perfectly well. I've finished with that life. I'm not going back and you can't make me. If you think torturing these people is going to make me have a change of heart—

Oh, come on, said the mountain impatiently (and one of the streams of liquid fire changed course and rushed down the eastern slope, towards a wooded valley). Where do you get that from, making out it's all my fault? It takes two, you know. It's all very well you coming over all pure as the driven snow, but I don't remember you being all squeamish and ladylike at the time. Quite the opposite. Such enthusiasm.

Shut *up*, Poldarn screamed. That wasn't me, that's what you tried to turn me into. I'm not responsible for what you did through me.

A gust of wind blew a handful of cinders straight into his face, but he didn't feel anything. Oh, for crying out loud, said the mountain, we've been over this again and again and again, can't you stop hiding behind this moral indignation thing and talk to me straight up, no more pretences? Come on, it's me you're talking to; you can't fool me, I know you too well.

He felt angry, more angry than he could remember having felt before. All right, he said, let's be straight about it, if that's what you want. Leave these people alone, they never did you any harm. And leave me alone, because I'm finished with you. It's over, can't you understand that?

The wind sighed all around him, hot and full of sparks. I don't know how you can say that, the mountain replied sadly, when you know, as well as I do, it'll never be over between you and me. As you proved just a few hours ago, right there, in the smithy.

Oh. He winced. You saw that, did you?

Saw that? The mountain laughed painfully. I didn't just see it, I felt it.

Served you right, then. You shouldn't have been hanging around here in the first place.

Do you honestly believe that?

He didn't reply.

Come on, the mountain said, and its voice was soft and charming, let's not have another fight, it really isn't going to solve anything. Like I keep telling you, if we could only talk it through, like rational creatures—

I don't want to be bloody rational, Poldarn shouted, not where you're concerned. It's gone way beyond rational. Look, I can understand why you're stalking me, but what the hell's the point of all this? You know it won't make me change my mind, it's just spite, viciousness. That's the whole point, it's why we're finished. You do things like this—

So do you, the mountain interrupted gently. That's how alike we really are. We can read each other's minds; I know exactly what you're thinking, under all that synthetic anger.

Oh, right. You can read my mind now. So what can you see there?

Easy, replied the mountain, you know I'm right, and deep down where it matters you want to come back to me, so it can be like the old days. You know, when we used to have fun—

You call that *fun*? Well, yes, I suppose you would; like you're probably enjoying this too. Yes, that's it, that's where I've been going wrong. You're not just doing this to get at me, you're doing this because you enjoy it. This is your idea of a thoroughly good time. God, you make me sick, you know that?

The mountain sighed. Here we go again, round and round in circles; it's like trying to catch one chicken in an empty barn. Do you truly believe that if you can wriggle your way out of talking to me long enough so that I'll lose my temper and go storming off, that'll actually *solve* anything? Well, no, of course you don't believe it, you know it's not true. All you're concerned with is getting me out of your hair for just a little while longer. But you can't make me go away, because I'm always there, right there inside you. Face it, can't you? I'll always be there, till death do us part – and I wouldn't go banking on that, if the thought had crossed your mind.

Kill myself? I wouldn't give you the satisfaction.

You think I want that? No, you don't, of course not; you're just saying that to get me angry. Can't you get it into your thick skull, I know what's going through your mind, it's like reading a public announcement nailed to the customs house door. Stop *lying*, can't you, just for a few minutes.

You're quite right, he said to the mountain, we do know each other too well. You know me, and I sure as hell know you. Why do you think I came here in the first place?

All right, the mountain said, here's the deal. Stop pushing me away, let me back in, and I'll leave these people in peace. No more clouds of fire, no more burning hot ash, no more darkness in the middle of the day. They can get on with their lives, we can get on with ours, and everybody's happy.

And if I tell you where you can stick your deal?

Then – the whole sky was red for a moment – then I'm going to have to do something to prove to you that it really isn't over, aren't I? I'm going to have to give you what you need, whether you want it or not. Not the way I'd have chosen, but I'm not the one being difficult here. If you won't come back to me, I'll show these people who you really are. And then I'll kill them. You see (the mountain went on), I tell it to you straight, like it is. Whatever else you say about me, I never lied to you and I never let you down. I was always there for you, always.

Screw you, he shouted—

Poldarn sat up. His backside was on fire.

'Are you all right?' Seymond was asking. 'That was one hell of a bang on the head you gave yourself there.'

'No,' Poldarn yelped, 'get me up, for pity's sake.'

They dumped the ladder, grabbed his arms and hauled him to his feet. He was a bit wobbly for a moment or so, but they held him up so he didn't fall or sit down again.

'Sorry,' Eyn said, 'didn't see you. Just as well you've got that helmet on your head, or you could've done yourself a real mischief.'

Blood was dripping into Poldarn's eyes. He remembered the gash in the helmet, its jagged lips curled inwards. Hence the bleeding, always so melodramatic from a little nick to the scalp. 'I'm fine,' he said. 'What's happening?'

'Looks like it's getting better,' Seymond told him. 'At least, the big puffy fireballs have stopped coming out of the mountain, and I do believe there's not so much ash falling as there was.'

'Not so hot, either,' Eyn put in. 'And it's getting lighter, too. You never know, maybe it's had enough, or it's run out or something.'

'Just as well,' Seymond muttered. 'We're keeping pace with it, going flat out, but we can't keep this game up for ever. How's the head now? Feeling dizzy? Sick? Spots in front of your eyes?'

Poldarn shook his head. 'It's fine,' he said. 'That's not the end of me that's hurting, if you must know.'

One of them laughed; too dark to see which. 'Well,' said Seymond, 'if you will go sitting on hot embers, what do you expect? Thought you'd have figured that out for yourself by now, you being a smith and all.'

Poldarn could have denied it, but they'd only have given him that funny look again. 'Guess it serves me right for not looking where I was going,' he said.

'It's fine. No harm done to the ladder.'

'That's all right, then.'

Poldarn found the aprons by feel – a simple process of elimination, they didn't scorch his fingertips – and carried on with his mission. Fortunately, there was one left over for him to huddle under on his way back to the forge. Inside, he found Asburn, calmly lighting the fire.

'What the hell do you think you're doing?' he asked.

Asburn looked at him. 'Getting on with some work,' he said. 'They don't need me out there, I'm just in the way.' He said that rather self-consciously, as if something was bothering him. 'Truth is, I sort of came over all clumsy – bumping into people, knocking buckets over, that sort of thing. Halder thought I might prefer to make a start on some hinges for the rat-house. The door's needed replacing for years – these bloody cinders can find their way in through the cracks.'

Poldarn frowned. He could see, intuitively, what the problem was; for some reason, Asburn was having trouble finding the minds of the rest of the household. He could think of several reasons why that might be, the likeliest being that since he'd been working in the forge, Asburn had had to get used to communicating in words, the old-fashioned way, and that was what had upset his inner eye or third ear, or whatever the proper term for it might be. My fault, like everything else around here, Poldarn told himself, though that was patently untrue.

The fire, he noticed, was drawing just fine on nothing more than dry coal and a handful of wood shavings. Why can't I get it to do that? he asked himself.

'Same here,' he said. 'All I've been doing all day is getting under people's feet, so I came in here to hide till it's all over. Need any help?'

Asburn thought for a moment. 'The hinges are more of a one-man job, really,' he said. 'If you felt like it, you could draw down a few dozen nails. They'll be needing them, God knows, when they come to fix up all this damage.'

He said *they*, Poldarn noticed; *they*, not *we*. He must really be out of touch. 'Sure,' he replied. 'Nails I can just about manage. Have you seen the header?'

'There, under the bench. And there should be some stock

the right size in the scrap if you don't mind rummaging about for it.'

Poldarn nodded, and knelt down beside the mountain of rusty iron and steel that filled one entire corner of the smithy. Mostly, looking through the scrap just made him feel depressed, because he knew perfectly well that he wouldn't even know where to start making most of the things that had ended up in there, and that anything he made would probably be inferior in quality and utility to the piece of broken junk he'd made it out of. How did one go about making a kettle, for example, or a door latch or a pair of tongs or a trivet or a candleholder or a pitchfork or an arrow-head or a spoon or a horseshoe or a sconce or a shovel or a ploughshare? He supposed he could figure it out if he absolutely had to, but he'd have burned a whole continent of coal and hammered the anvil bow-backed by the time he produced anything he'd be prepared to admit to being responsible for. And there, on the other hand, was the scrap; a thousand properly made articles, representing tens of thousands of hours of hard, skilled work by men who'd known and appreciated their craft, and they'd ended up here, defenceless prisoners awaiting execution at his hands. It was a tragedy.

(Except, he realised, that iron and steel are immortal. Men die and the damp gets into their bodies and spoils them, but iron and steel are too precious to waste. The broken tyre becomes a hinge, the broken sword becomes a cart-spring, the broken ploughshare becomes a spearhead, the broken pot becomes a ladle, the spindle that was once an axle that was once a beam becomes a handful of nails, and nothing ever dies. All that happens is that the metal is purged by the fire of the memory that had been pounded into it. The heat relaxes the constraints that hold it in one shape and the hammer eases it into some new form, a new life in a new setting – from field to house, yard to barn, war to peace, malignant to benign, lethal to helpful, like a man who wakes up one morning to find that his past has burned away, his identity scrubbed off like firescale. Fire and hammer impose the memory, fire and hammer grant pardon and amnesty; which may go some way to explain why superstitious people worship them as gods. It would, after all, be an easy mistake to make.)

A fat drop of water splashed on Poldarn's forehead, making the burnt skin sting.

Chapter Seven

The cinderfall stopped quite suddenly; and when the sun broke through they could see the mountain clearly, without any veils of smoke or steam. True, the landscape was an even dull black as far as the eye could see in every direction, but at least they could tell where it ended and the sky began. Things were looking up.

The first consideration, ahead of the house or even the barns and stores, was the livestock. The news wasn't good; a third of the sheep were dead, a quarter of the heifers, the horses had broken out of the stables in panic and bolted, and there hadn't been time to get the milch herd in, so God only knew what sort of a state they were in. The poultry and the pigs were all right, singed and distinctly offended at being cooped up for a day and two nights but still alive and productive. The bees had swarmed and cleared off, but that could happen at any time, end of the world or not.

Once the stock had been fed and secured, the next priority was patching up the buildings. When the drifts of cinders had been cleared away, the damage proved to be far less than anybody had any right to expect, in most cases little more than scorch marks and the filthy mess brought about by the hasty addition of water to piles of ash. Ugliness could wait for another day, however. Next on the list was clearing the yard, so people could get around the place without having to wade. Shovelling cinders into neat heaps wasn't exactly skilled work, and even Poldarn was allowed to join in (which, since it meant a holiday from the forge, he was delighted to do, until his grandfather spoiled it all by asking for more nails).

A day and a half of intense activity broke the back of that job; and, since the mountain was quiet and the farm now just looked scruffy instead of doomed, Halder convened a general meeting to decide what to do next.

Understandably, full household meetings were extremely rare events at Haldersness. This time, however, nobody knew what was going on or what would happen next or what they were supposed to be doing, so there really wasn't any option but to talk to each other.

'It's obvious what we've got to do,' Halder said. 'It's going to be one hell of a job, but I can't see as we've got any choice in the matter. Right now, all the grazing and the plough is a foot deep in this shit; the animals can't feed, nothing's going to grow, and the bloody stuff isn't going to shift itself. It'll take us months, maybe even years, but it's got to be done, and the sooner we make a start, the sooner we'll finish.'

Someone at the back stood up. Poldarn was sitting near the front and couldn't get his head round far enough to see who it was. 'That may not be the case,' this someone said. 'Remember what Rook here told us, about what happened at Lyatsbridge when it rained.'

'Bloody hell,' Raffen interrupted, 'don't wish that on us, it's bad enough as it is.'

'Let me finish, will you? All I'm saying is, what happened at Lyatsbridge proves one thing. When it rains, this stuff melts, like snow. Sure, it turns into filthy black mud and we really don't want to be around when that happens; but we can plan for that, we can figure out where these mudslides are going to go just by looking at the contours, and we can get the stock and our stuff well out of harm's way. What's the worst that can happen? The buildings could get washed away or buried in shit or whatever. So what? Big deal. We build new ones. So long as we're alive and safe and we've got our tools, we can do that, easy. Anyhow, it's not as if it's up to us, the mudslides'll happen whether we like it or not. All I'm saying is, rather than kill ourselves shovelling the stuff into big heaps and then seeing it turn into mud at the first drop of rain, we'd be better off spending our time getting ready, making sure we don't cop it like Lyatsbridge did; and when the rain's come and gone and it's all over, the grass and the plough'll still be there and we can get back to normal.'

A soft buzz of approval ran round the hall. Halder stood up again.

'Fine,' he said, 'assuming it's going to rain in the next few days. If it doesn't, what're the stock going to eat? And what are we going to eat in four months' time, when the crop's failed because we left it lying under a bloody great load of ashes?'

Someone else at the back – it might have been Seyward, or Torburn – called out, 'It'll rain, count on it. You looked at the mountain? All the snow's gone. I'm no weather expert, but it stands to reason that the snow turned to steam and it's up there somewhere right now, waiting to come down in a damn great flood. It'll rain all right, you'll see, and then we'll have rivers of mud, just like they did at Lyatsbridge. And I for one don't want to be here when that happens.'

It's not just me, Poldarn thought, it's all of them, they're shocked. Hardly surprising. All the time he'd been there, he'd never once heard anybody deliberately separating himself from Halder's viewpoint like that. He could see it in their eyes, a definite spark of panic as they realised what the mountain could do to them, over and above burning, burying and killing.

'All right,' Halder said, raising his voice even though the hall was deathly quiet, 'it isn't going to come to that, and yes, you've got a very good point there, something we've definitely got to bear in mind. But we've got to think about all the possibilities.'

'I agree.' This time it was one of the women – Aldeur, he was fairly certain, Scaptey's daughter; a tall, spare, gaunt-faced woman who washed clothes. 'And there's one we haven't even mentioned yet, though if you ask me it's the best idea of the lot. Look, this is a huge island, it's so big there's a lot of it nobody's even been to yet. Who says we've got to stay here? After all, what's here? It's just a house, and feeling comfortable because we know every stone and blade of grass in the valley. What've we got here that we wouldn't have if we upped sticks and went somewhere else? I'll tell you what, shall I? A horrible bloody great fire-breathing mountain, that's what, and you know, I think we'd be better off without it. After all – no offence, Halder, but it's got to be said – it won't be all that long before we're pulling this house down and building another one anyhow, so why the hell build it here, up to our necks in hot ashes, never knowing from one day to the next if we aren't going to wake up one morning cooked like a chicken in a crock? I'm telling you, I don't think I'll ever feel safe again so long as we're here, I'll spend all day long looking over my shoulder to see if the mountain's on the go again. It's a nice place, but it's just a place. I've got kids to consider, and I think their lives are more important than a few old traditions.' She paused, and frowned. 'There was more stuff I was going to say but I can't remember what it was now. Anyhow, that's what I think, and I'll bet you I'm not the only one.'

Poldarn felt sorry for Halder; he looked like he was having

a long, hard day. 'Well,' he said, 'there's definitely something to be said for that. Let's see who agrees with her. Right, anybody who thinks we should leave here and go somewhere else, stick your hand up.'

Aldeur's hand shot up straight away. Nobody else moved.

'That's that settled, then,' Halder said. 'It's a good idea, but let's try and come up with something else. Anybody?'

Nobody. Poldarn wriggled uncomfortably on his bench. He'd come very close to putting his hand up when Halder called the vote, but he'd been waiting for someone else (apart from Aldeur) to go first. By the looks of it, he hadn't been the only one to do that.

'Fine,' Halder said. 'So, basically we've got two options. One is to get stuck in and start clearing away this ash, the other is to wait and let the rain do it for us, assuming there's going to be any more rain – and yes, I grant you, it looks like it'll come tipping down any day now. The question is, do we all really want to bet our livelihood and our lives – same thing, really – on a weather forecast. Because you know what rain's like, it's an evil bugger; pisses down for weeks on end when you don't want it to, but when you need it desperately, it stays up there and will it hell as like come down. A week, we could probably manage. Three weeks, we're looking at losing the stock and next year's crop. It's a simple bet. Personally, if I was going to put everything I've got on a wager, I'd rather stick to the horse racing. It's easier to gauge form.'

Perhaps, Poldarn thought, I ought to form an opinion on this; after all, I'm part of this household, I should act like one and care. Of course, that would constitute getting involved—

'Halder's right.' Eyvind was on his feet, and everybody was looking at him, for a change. It occurred to Poldarn, for the first time, that Eyvind was an outsider too, he didn't belong to Haldersness, he had his own house on the other side of the mountain. In which case, he asked himself, what's he doing here? Shouldn't he be back home scraping ash off his own fields, or packing up his own pots and pans? What's keeping him here?

'Sure,' Eyvind was saying, 'we've got to think about mudslides. The worst thing anybody can say in a crisis is, I never thought of that. But sitting tight and doing nothing, or going and camping out while the sun shines, that doesn't make sense either. I say we've got to get the ash off the pasture and the ploughed ground first – keep an eye on the weather, I agree, but while we're waiting for it to rain, let's for God's sake do something useful.'

People were nodding their heads, muttering approval; even Aldeur, who'd wanted to leave the farm altogether just a moment ago. It was good to see the joint mind gradually coming back together, after the disconcerting spectacle of so many component parts starting to think for themselves. However— To his surprise, Poldarn found he was on his feet and about to say something.

'All due respect,' he heard himself say, 'but I'm not sure you've thought this thing through, either of you. You're saying, let's go and rake up the ash, like we raked up the yard. All right, now ask yourselves, how long did that take? All of you, working together, very hard? Now then. Any one of you knows a damn sight better than I do how large this farm is, how many head of cattle you're grazing, how many acres you've got ploughed and planted, so I'm not going to try and come up with any figures. You can do that for yourselves. How long's it going to take to clear the ash off enough ground to make doing the job worthwhile? A month? A year? Ten years? All right, you do the figuring. While you're doing that, ask yourselves this. If the whole household's out there dawn to dusk shovelling cinders, what about all the other work that needs to be done around the place? I've been watching ever since I got here, it takes all of you all of your time just to keep things running normally. That's fine; everybody's got work, everybody knows what to do, there's no waste of time or effort or materials. But everything's changed now – you can't just carry on doing what you've always done, you've got to deal with this new situation. And, to be honest with you, I don't see how any of the ideas that've been put forward is going to be enough, except maybe what she said just now: packing up and going somewhere else entirely. But you all agreed you didn't want to do that.'

They were all staring at him, of course; but this time there was something radically different in their faces, and he couldn't work out what it was. So he kept on talking instead.

'All right,' Poldarn went on, 'that's fine, we stay here. So let's see if we can't figure out how we can do that, without starving to death or drowning in mud. Anybody?' Nobody moved or made a sound; he really wished he could read what they were thinking. 'All right, then, how about this? We can't feed the stock here, so we drive them inland, as far as it takes to find empty country where there's enough grazing. Obviously, it's going to take a lot of manpower to do that, but the stock have got to be a priority: it'll take far longer to build up the herd from scratch than it would to get the arable side of things going again if we lose the crop. But I don't see why that's got to happen, either. If we're only talking about clearing the ash off the ground that's already been planted, I don't see why that shouldn't be possible, even with, say, a third of our people away with the livestock. After all, we don't have to get it all done in a week, it'll take a while for the crop to go bad under the ash, far longer than it'd take for the animals to starve to death. As for everything else that we do around here – well, we're going to have to look at that pretty carefully and see what we can cut out, if only for the time being. We don't need beer or cider, for one thing; we don't need the forge – sorry, Asburn, but that's two of us spending all day making stuff that's nice to have but not absolutely essential. Same goes for washing and mending clothes, all that sort of thing – I can't be specific about every single thing, because I haven't sat down and thought it all out, I'm just trying to put across the general principle; basically, if we don't need it for bare survival, it doesn't get done till the planted ground's clear. Now I'm sure there's a whole load of other things I haven't considered, because I don't know what they are yet. We can't think of everything right now, there's bound to be problems cropping up that we can't possibly foresee. But we'll just have to deal with them as we come to them, it's something you learn to do when you're living hand to mouth and on the fly, like I was doing back in the Empire before Eyvind here rescued me. As for the mudslides and whether it's going to rain or not; same thing goes for that, I think, as for the workload. We've got to be prepared to get out of the house and onto the higher ground literally at a moment's notice, so here's what I think we should do. Each of us wants to pack a bag – just a small cloth bag you can grab in a hurry, with just the things you absolutely need and no more – and we take that bag with us everywhere we go, sleep with it within arm's reach, so that as and when the mudslides start, we can grab it and run without even stopping to think. Anything too big to go in a bag, that we absolutely can't do without and can't readily make from scratch if we have to start all over again – I suggest that each of us is assigned one essential household item, and it'll be our job to rescue that one thing. It takes all the thought out of it, really; you don't have to stop and figure out what to take, you just get hold of your stuff and the thing you're responsible for, and hit the ground running.'

Poldarn paused for breath, then went on: 'I'm not saying I've got the answer to every damn thing we might have to face, because that'd be stupid. I'm not saying you can't think of better ways of dealing with specific problems, because I'm absolutely certain you all know far more about your particular job or function than I ever will, and so it makes much more sense for you to work out the details, rather than me. What I'm asking you to go along with is the general idea. First things first, get the stock safe, and then the planted crop. Be ready in case we get the mudslides, yes, but don't let them paralyse you with fear, like a mouse cornered by a weasel. Really, it's just common sense.'

That appeared to be all he had to say, so he sat down again. For what seemed like a very, very long time, nobody moved or spoke. Bloody hell, he said to himself, I've really done it this time. Then, just as he was wondering how he should set about apologising, Halder got up and looked round.

'Well,' he said, 'that's what we'll do, then. After all, you're the one who knows about these things.'

For a moment, Poldarn thought the old man was being funny. But if he was, nobody had got the joke. They didn't look particularly happy, but Poldarn could recognise resigned acceptance when he saw it. Amazing, he said to himself, I never knew I had such eloquence and leadership skills. Come to think of it, I'm not sure that's something I want to know about myself. Chances are if I've always had these qualities, I haven't done nice things with them.

Then he noticed the expression on Eyvind's face, and wondered what on earth was going on. He had no idea why, but Eyvind was scowling at him with genuine anger. What did I say? He wondered. He's glaring at me like I just set light to his beard.

'Right,' Halder went on, with an audible sigh, 'no use sitting here, we've got work to do. If anyone wants me, I'll be in the trap-house.'

A few moments later, the hall was empty, except for Poldarn and Eyvind; and Eyvind hadn't shifted or changed the expression on his face.

'Well,' Poldarn said, trying to keep the tension out of his voice, 'I didn't expect that.'

'Really?' Eyvind's voice was unusually quiet and flat; usually, he didn't just talk, he performed. 'Seems to me it all went off exactly the way you'd have wanted it to. I mean, they're all out there doing as they're told, aren't they?'

Poldarn shrugged. 'I suppose so,' he said. 'Though if they are, it beats me how. I mean, I was expecting we'd be here till midnight sorting out the details, like who's going with the herd, who's staying here, which jobs are essential and which ones we can put on hold for the time being. Instead—'

'Not what you wanted, then.' Eyvind sounded like a man who was barely in control of his temper, words leaking out of him involuntarily. 'I can see that.'

Poldarn knew it would have been better to let that go, but he was curious. 'What do you mean?' he asked.

'You know perfectly bloody well.'

'No.' Poldarn shook his head emphatically. 'I *don't* know, that's the point. Come on, you know as well as I do, I haven't got a clue how their minds work.'

'Our minds, you mean. And it doesn't look that way to me.'

Poldarn could feel an argument closing in, maybe even a fight. The question was whether he'd be able to get out of the way in time. 'Suit yourself,' he replied (and he knew at once that he'd used entirely the wrong tone). 'I'm just telling you, that's all. Really, I didn't mean to, well, take charge or anything. We were discussing what would be the best thing to do, and I gave my opinion. Honestly, I didn't mean anything by it.'

'Sure.' Eyvind jumped to his feet, every aspect of the movement suggesting that he couldn't stand being in a confined space with Poldarn for one moment more. 'That's all right, then. I believe you. Now I think I'll go and get my horse saddled. Time I was going home, I reckon.'

'Oh.' Poldarn hadn't been expecting that. 'I can understand you wanting to, 'he went on. 'It's just that – well, you've been here ever since I arrived, I guess I've got used to depending on you – to explain things, tell me what's going on, let me know when I've done something ignorant or offensive. It'll be hard having to cope on my own.'

'Really.' Eyvind had his back to him now. 'Well, I'm sure you'll manage. After all, you've got them eating out of your hand, which suggests you're more or less settled in, doesn't it?'

This is ridiculous, Poldarn thought. 'Look,' he said, 'I've obviously done something wrong. Would you mind telling me what it is?'

He heard Eyvind sigh, though he couldn't see the other's face. 'It's not about right and wrong, you should know that by now. There's no such thing as wrong, standing all by itself, not connected to anything. You did what you felt you had to do. That's not wrong.'

'But?'

'I wouldn't have done it. Nor would anybody else, in your shoes. It's not how we go about things here.'

Now Poldarn was starting to get angry. 'What isn't?' he insisted.

'Forget it, will you? I mean,' Eyvind added quietly, 'that's what you're good at, forgetting things. Must be a wonderful knack to have, that.'

More than anything, Poldarn wanted to hit him for that; he could feel how much satisfaction it would give him to drive his fist into the back of Eyvind's head. If anything ever seemed to be the right thing to do at a particular moment, that was it. Instead, he deliberately unclenched his hands. 'You may well be right,' he said. 'For some time, I've had this feeling that the reason why I can't remember anything is that deep down, I don't really want to; because whoever I used to be, I don't want to be him any more. I've got no idea if that's a sensible attitude or not. Really, all I can do is try and get along without hurting myself. Or anybody else, for that matter.'

(That last bit hadn't been there in his mind, he'd had to add it deliberately and it hadn't sounded at all right. Not so good.)

'Sure,' Eyvind said again, somehow contriving to bleach any hint of expression out of the word. 'Look.' He turned round, and Poldarn could see the strain in his face. 'Let me give you a bit of advice, just to show there's no ill feeling. Halder knows he's going to die soon; he was only hanging on because there wasn't anybody to take over from him, and then you turned up and he's been waiting to see if you'll shape up. But he won't last much longer, this bloody business with the mountain is going to kill him any day now; he knows it, everybody knows it – apart from you, apparently. When he dies, you'll be the farmer here, it'll be your house and your farm. Everybody knows that, too. So, if you start telling people what to do, naturally they're going to do it, because this is all new to us – I'm not just talking about the volcano, I mean this business of having to cope with things we don't know about or understand. But you – well, I don't think you really know any more about us than you did when you arrived. Oh, you've picked up a whole bunch of details, like a ball of wet dough picking up dust, but you've positively refused to join in or act like this is where you belong. Until now; and suddenly you're in charge, you're giving orders. Damn it, if I'd known you were going to do that, I'd have left you behind at Deymeson.'

Poldarn could feel anger building up inside him, a massive force of rage and fury pressing against his chest, making it hard for him to breathe. 'I'm really sorry you feel that way,' he said, 'and if I'd known, of course I wouldn't have said anything. I promise you, I won't do it again if it bothers you so much. Does that make it any better, or are you still mad at me?'

Eyvind shook his head. 'I don't know about you, really,' he said. 'First time we met, remember, I tried to kill you. And you killed Cetel, my best friend who I'd known since I was a kid – in self-defence, sure, and neither of us had a clue at the time who you were, so I'm not blaming you or anything. But at the time I had a feeling that we weren't going to turn out to be lucky for each other, one way or another. Oddly enough, it was you I felt sorry for. I got the impression you'd come out worse for us having met. But then again, I get these feelings every now and again, and nineteen times out of twenty they're just plain wrong.'

Poldarn wanted the anger to go away, but it wouldn't. 'One in twenty,' he said. 'That's a lousy average. In fact, it means that when you get one of these premonitions, there's a ninety-five per cent chance it isn't going to come true, so it looks like the best odds are that neither of us is going to come to a bad end. Excellent. You've cheered me up no end.'

Eyvind's face cracked into a smile. 'That's certainly one way of looking at it,' he said. 'But I really do think it's time I went home, just to have a look, see how they're getting on. Soon as I'm sure they're all right I'll come back. Will that do you?'

Poldarn nodded. 'That'll be fine,' he said. 'And I'm sorry I freaked you out like that. I just didn't know, that's all – which is why I need to have you around, to warn me about all this stuff. Otherwise, God only knows what damage I could do without realising.'

'You'll be fine, trust me,' Eyvind said, slapping Poldarn hard on the shoulder. It was, of course, the friendliest of gestures, but all Poldarn wanted to do was hit back, hard. He had just enough self-control to keep his hands by his sides. 'And anyway, I was wrong, probably. After all, that plan you came up with is pretty good – better than the alternatives, at any rate. That's the trouble with us all thinking basically the same way, we don't have the capacity to come up with original ideas. Not that we need them in the usual course of things; they only make life difficult.' He laughed. 'You know, I bet you think we're all weird.'

'Yes,' Poldarn said. 'Almost as weird as me. Mind you, I didn't find the Empire was all that rational, if you see what I mean.'

Eyvind stifled a yawn, and Poldarn realised that he hadn't had more than a few hours' sleep over the past few days. 'Maybe there's a place somewhere where everybody acts in a sensible, logical fashion and everything's just fine as a result. Let's just hope they never get it into their heads to invade, because we wouldn't stand a chance.'

The livestock was gone by next morning, along with a third of the men and most of the boys. Rook said they were headed north-west into the open country beyond the Tabletop mountains. 'Good grazing land out that way, I've heard,' he said. 'Better than these parts, by all accounts. Never been that way myself, but I once met a man who had. He liked it out there, reckoned that if he ever branched out on his own, that's where he'd probably go. Big plains, low hills, lots of woods, plenty of water. I've always had a fancy to see it, but the chance never came up.'

Poldarn nodded. 'So who lives there?' he asked.

'Nobody.'

'Oh.' That seemed strange. 'Why not?'

Rook shrugged. 'We haven't got there yet,' he replied. 'In a hundred years, maybe, when we've used up all the space between here and there.' He grinned. 'I heard an old boy say once, this island is so big you'd be an old man before you walked from one side to the other. He reckoned he'd talked to a man once who tried to sail all the way round it, just to see how big it is. He was gone for six months, and when he came back he said he'd just carried on going north until his crew reckoned they'd had enough, so he turned round and came back. Wonderful country up north, he said, bloody great big forests of cedar and maple, and grapevines growing wild with grapes on 'em the size of duck eggs. Makes you wonder why we stick around here, with that thing – ' he nodded at the mountain '– breathing fire and shitting ash on us. Still, I'm in no hurry to move on, not just yet. Around here suits me fine.'

Scraping up the ash proved to be harder than anyone had imagined. Asburn vanished into the forge and came out a day later with a massive iron rake-head, twice the size and weight of the regular farm version, which had proved to be far too flimsy and small for the job. His next effort was a third wider again, and was declared satisfactory by Halder and the raking crews. Poldarn, who'd never been so tired in his life after a day behind a farm rake on the lower home meadow, was actually glad to be back in the forge, swinging the big hammer for Asburn as he struggled to meet the demand for his new invention.

'Very simple, really,' Asburn said, when Poldarn asked him how the things were made. 'Take a good heavy bar, about three fingers wide; good steel if we've got it, something like a mill spindle or a waterwheel axle. First, make your socket; then take a good yellow heat about a forearm long, split the bar with the hot sett, bend the legs out at right angles and twist 'em half a turn, put the flatter on 'em and punch your holes for the tines; ordinary chain stock for the tines, a little finger long and thick, just draw 'em out, swage down a tenon to fit the hole, then rivet 'em in hard. Harden and temper, and that's all there is to it.'

Poldarn had come to dread that last phrase; but all that was asked of him was to hit the hot metal as hard as he could, so he didn't really care. For once, Asburn was working hard and fast, not stopping to measure up every five minutes or to agonise over a slightly asymmetrical taper or a tiny ding from a misplaced hammer strike. In this mood, he worked so fast that Poldarn's arms started to hurt and the side of his right little finger chafed into a long, fat blister; but it was better than standing around. What mattered was that he was working, helping, contributing, earning his keep—

'Are you sure you don't mind doing this?' Asburn said, as they waited for the steel to get hot. Asburn was working the bellows with his left hand, making it look as easy as swishing a fan on a pleasantly warm day. Poldarn had had to give up that duty on grounds of exhaustion. 'I mean, it's very kind of you, but don't they need you in the fields, or in the house?'

'Need me for what?' Poldarn replied, as he bound his blistered finger with a piece of rag.

'Well, to sort things out, make sure it's all being done right. After all, it's all your ideas, surely you should be there.'

Poldarn sighed. 'They seem to be getting on just fine without me,' he said. 'In fact, nobody's asked me about anything since the meeting. Which is good,' he added, 'because they know what needs to be done and I don't. I really wish I'd kept my face shut at that meeting – all I did was give people the wrong idea about me. I think Eyvind was ready to smash my face in at one point.'

Asburn frowned. 'I don't understand,' he said. 'What, do you mean he was angry or something?'

'You could say that, yes.'

'But why? What was there to be angry about?'

Poldarn laughed. 'Pretty much everything I said, I think. And, looking back, I can see his point. After all, it's not for me to come in here telling everybody what to do. God only knows what got into me.'

Asburn shook his head. 'That's not how it was,' he said. 'After all, you're Halder's next of kin, when he's gone you'll be the farmer. Of course it's your place to speak for us. I mean,' he went on, drawing the billet out an inch or so to check on its colour, 'it's not like you were ordering us about; and even if that's what you were trying to do – well, it'd never work, it'd be like trying to harden soft iron, it simply wouldn't take.'

Poldarn raised an eyebrow.

'I guess it's a bit like this,' Asburn said. 'And I'm really not sure if this makes any sense, because to tell you the truth I've never really had to think about this sort of thing before, like you don't have to think about how to breathe, you just do it. But anyway; suppose Haldersness is a man's body. We're all the different parts of it – hands, feet, joints, bones, muscles, lungs and so on. Halder's the head, and you'll be the head when he's gone. The head doesn't tell the feet what to do, it's just the part of the body where the command comes from. Otherwise it'd be like saying that if you punched someone, it was your hand's fault, not yours. Oh shit,' he added, jerking the billet out of the fire; there were tiny white sparkles dancing on the extreme end, where the steel was thinnest. 'Serves me right for chattering,' he added, swinging the billet through the air and laying it across the beak of the anvil at precisely the right angle. 'When you're ready.'

Poldarn lifted the hammer and struck; and by the time he'd beaten the bar from white through yellow and dull red into scale grey, the subject had gone cold as well, and he didn't try to raise it again. But that didn't stop him thinking about it; particularly the references to when Halder was gone, when Poldarn would take over and become the farmer. Very bad idea, he couldn't help feeling, because he'd be a head that couldn't communicate with the rest of the body, and Haldersness would become one of those people who end up paralysed because of some horrific accident, and all they can do is move their eyes. If that happened, it'd be a worse disaster than the volcano. Maybe the best thing would be if I just went away one night and didn't come back. So, what would happen if he did that? Either they'd have to choose someone else to be the farmer, or they'd all split up and go their separate ways; Rook would go north to the wonderful empty pastures he'd always wanted to see, Asburn could build his own forge and actually be the smith instead of a caretaker-impostor, things would get back to normal and Poldarn – I'd be free again, he heard himself think, just me to think about, and nothing but what I can carry. I don't suppose I can go back to the Empire; but why shouldn't I go north and build my own farm there, just me and an axe and a scythe and a bag of seedcorn—

Ridiculous. Sooner or later, of course, he'd be doing all that right here – building his house, sowing his first crop, shearing his own sheep and raising his own calves; and the house would be called Ciartanstead, and you can't own a farm more emphatically than by giving it your own name. Running away from Ciartanstead, from the wood his grandfather had planted for him on the day he had been born, was nothing more or less than running away from himself; and that, it went without saying, would be just plain impossible.

Chapter Eight

'We can probably get along without you for a day or so,' Halder said suddenly. 'Why don't you go over to Colscegsford? You should go and see how they're getting on.'

Poldarn was so taken aback by this unexpected reprieve that he almost forgot to take the hot iron out of the fire. 'All right,' he said.

'Splendid. You might like to take the dun gelding, it could do with the exercise.'

Disconcerting; but so was everything at Haldersness, and the thought of getting out of the forge and not having to bash steel bars into ash rakes for a couple of days was almost intoxicating. 'I'll go first thing in the morning, then,' he said.

Halder shrugged. 'You could go now if you like. I'm sure Asburn can cope.'

'Sure,' Asburn confirmed, and there was just a faint hint of relief in his voice. That wasn't very flattering, but Poldarn could sympathise. They'd been cooped up together in the dark heat of the forge for five days while the rest of the household had been out in the fresh air raking ash, and what little they'd had to say to each other had been said a long time ago. He liked Asburn, of course – what was there not to like? Nevertheless.

He found the horse saddled, groomed and ready at the mounting block, with saddlebags packed with bread and cheese, a heavy riding coat rolled up and strapped to the back of the saddle, and a light hand-axe with a long, slender handle hanging from the pommel by its wrist-loop. Nobody offered to tell him what the axe was supposed to be for, and he didn't feel up to asking.

Another thing nobody told him was how to get to Colscegsford but that was all right, since Eyvind had pointed out the head of Colsceg's combe – you could just about see it from the Haldersness porch, on a clear day – and once he'd found that it'd be easy enough to find the house. 'I'm not sure when I'll be back,' he told Halder as he shortened his reins and crammed his broad-brimmed felt riding hat onto his head. 'Figure on a couple of days, at least.'

'You take your time and don't rush,' Halder replied with ambiguous enthusiasm. 'If they need you for anything over there, you stay as long as you like.'

Poldarn decided to assume that that was well meant and ineptly phrased. 'Thanks,' he said. 'Any message?'

Halder shook his head. 'Can't think of anything,' he replied. 'Well, you could mention to Colsceg that we could use another half-dozen cartloads of hazel loppings, but there's no rush for them, we've got enough to be going on with. And I expect he'll have more pressing things to do than go out cutting twigs for us right now.'

It was undeniably pleasant to go for a ride in the weak sunshine, even though the crunch of ash under the horse's hooves grated on Poldarn's nerves every step of the way; undeniably pleasant to be out in the fresh air, each moment taking him further away from Haldersness; undeniably, supremely pleasant to be *alone*. He had no great opinion of his own company, having had a great deal of it during his time in the Bohec valley, but he'd been working and eating and sleeping surrounded by other people ever since he'd arrived at Haldersness, and he had the feeling that he wasn't as naturally gregarious as all that. There were times when he felt as if he was getting swallowed up in the household, almost as if he was being diluted, to the point where he no longer existed as an individual; and yet not a single day passed when he didn't feel the enormous gulf separating him from the others. Probably it'd be no bad thing if he could lose himself in the common mind of the farm. In a way, it was the best thing that could happen to him – since he had so very little of himself – to fill up the empty spaces in his mind with other people's lives and thoughts and memories. Unfortunately, for all the others' assurances that it'd all come flooding back any day now, there didn't seem to be any reason to believe that it really would. In consequence, he was stuck halfway, a perpetual guest in his own house, never quite certain what he should be saying or doing, or where he was meant to be, or where anything was.

From the top of the valley Poldarn had a fine, clear view of the farm. There was the main house, with the red and white sail incongruously draping the roof; beside it, the barns and sheds and stores, a grouping as large as a small village; behind them the animal pens and the kitchen garden, a splash of browns and greens in the ocean of black ash. Beyond that, flashes of green testified to the tireless efforts of the household and the efficacy of Asburn's excellent cinder-rakes, while the river sparkled cheerfully in the sunlight, long and silvery as a childhood scar. Under other circumstances, he thought, you'd be hard put to it to find a better spot, and you'd have to be a prince or an earl or a wealthy man to have such a fine spread back in the Empire—

(– And it's all mine, or it will be some day, but it doesn't feel like it's mine. More the other way around, like it owns me.)

Half an hour further on down the other side of the slope, the Haldersness valley was invisible – you'd never even know it was there unless you happened to know the country. That was a strange thought, that the whole of his new life could be so easily overlooked, when the farm and its people had become his whole, all-enveloping world. Remarkable; a stranger could ride on by, and never know any of it was there (except that there weren't any strangers in this country, of course, apart from himself).

The further he went, the less Poldarn enjoyed his day off. On every side there was nothing to be seen but black ash, masking the features of the landscape so that he found it hard to keep his bearings. It was as if someone had covered up the whole island with a dust sheet, like servants in a house to which the master isn't expected to return for a long time. True, he was heading towards the mountain rather than away from it, but seeing it like this brought home to him the full scope of the disaster. If the stuff dissolved in rain, the mudslides were likely to be terrifyingly destructive; and if it didn't, there'd be nothing for it but to pack up and go somewhere else, because it'd take a hundred years just to clean up the Haldersness grazing, assuming there wasn't more where that had come from. The sight of it made him feel uncomfortable. A fine inheritance this was turning out to be.

Three hours on, as Poldarn passed the hog's-back ridge that he'd been told to look out for – it marked the nominal boundary of the Haldersness pastures and the start of Colscegsford land, though from what he'd gathered, nobody really gave a damn – he decided he'd had enough. He dismounted, found the stone jug of strong beer he'd noticed in the saddlebag, and sat down under a scorched-looking thorn tree with the aim of drinking enough beer to restore his sense of perspective. That turned out to be harder to accomplish than he'd hoped; the beer was strong, but not that strong, and as soon as he sat down, a mob of crows formed in the air and circled over him, passing remarks he was delighted not to be able to understand.

It was undoubtedly the beer that put him to sleep. He was dreaming about something (but, as always, the dream left him, like someone else's wife at sunrise, before he was fully awake), and then he opened his eyes and realised he was looking straight at a large, unfriendly-looking black bear.

Not so good, Poldarn thought, though it did explain what the hand-axe was for. But the axe was hanging off the saddle of his horse, which was tugging on its reins hard enough to uproot the tree he was leaning against. Whether it was his horse or himself that the bear was taking such an unhealthy interest in he didn't know, but he guessed that this wasn't a guessing game in which it would do to win second prize.

Bears, he thought; according to Eyvind, they were so rare as not to pose a threat worth worrying about; they only came down out of the mountainside forests in atrociously bad winters, when there was nothing left for them to eat, and even then they confined their attention to sick sheep and elderly cows, being too cautious and timid to attack a man unless starvation had made them truly reckless. Of course, if you did happen to run into one in that condition, Polden help you; because when they were that desperate, you could rip their guts open and they'd still keep coming.

Indeed, Poldarn thought; I don't suppose there's much to eat in the forests right now, assuming the forests are still there. He watched the bear coming slowly towards him, weighing up the risks with each cautious stride, assessing the situation with all the scientific wisdom of a prosperous merchant figuring out the trends in malt futures. A dozen paces in, the bear must have reached the conclusion that it was on to a viable commercial proposition, because it started to run at him, unexpectedly fast, bounding in like a big friendly dog. When it was half a dozen paces away, it reared up onto its hind legs and roared, with an expression on its face so furious as to be almost comic.

Damn, Poldarn thought, and jumped to his feet. To his dismay, he realised that he had cramp in his left leg, from sleeping at a clumsy angle; even if a man is capable of out-running a hungry bear – if Eyvind had briefed him on this aspect of the matter, he couldn't remember the important part – he can't do it with pins and needles in his left foot. That really only left the axe, and he'd left it rather late to go with that option. Getting the axe would mean turning his back on the bear for the best part of a second. He simply didn't have that long. Oh well, he thought; it's probably better to die trying, though by what criteria these matters are judged, he couldn't remember offhand.

He knew he'd made the wrong decision as soon as he tried to move, and felt his left leg buckle under him. That left him kneeling on the ground, the bear out of sight over his shoulder, and he couldn't be bothered to exert himself any further. The bloody thing'll just have to eat me, then, he thought, as his eyes closed instinctively.

Nothing happened, for a whole heartbeat. That was a long time, in this context; long enough to live a whole life in and get to be old enough to grow doddery and forgetful. Then Poldarn heard a sound he couldn't identify: a thick, solid, wet, chunky noise, like the sound of moist dough being slammed on the kneading block. It was followed by a roar from the bear, but with a completely different intonation – anger, mostly, a protest to the heavens that this wasn't fair, that someone was cheating. Then the wet-dough sound again, but culminating in a dull, reverberating thump that Poldarn recognised as an axe driven into cross-grained wood (and instead of splitting the log neatly down the flaw-line, you shudder as the shock reverberates back up your arms and straight into your temples). Then a bewildering silence, for nearly a full half-heartbeat; and finally a dead-weight flump, like a bale of straw tossed down from the hayloft.

He opened his eyes. No bear.

Instead of the bear, he saw a man, standing with his legs apart, knees slightly bent. The man was catching his breath and grinning at Poldarn, as what had clearly been an extreme case of terror gradually thawed. If Poldarn hadn't heard the sounds and known better, he could easily have believed that the bear had changed its shape and turned into this man, because the fellow was unnaturally tall and broad, and his face was completely swamped in a curly black beard.

'Talk about fucking close,' the man said.

Poldarn found the bear; it was lying on its side, its neck outstretched and its head right back, like a dog asleep in front of the fire. There was a sticky red mess on its right shoulder, extending diagonally downwards about a hand's span. Poldarn looked up at the man, and saw an axe, very like the one whose lack had nearly cost Poldarn his life, lying on the ground at the big fellow's feet.

'Would've served me right,' the man went on; his voice was unexpectedly high and thin. 'Missed, didn't I? Aimed for the bugger's head, bounced off the side and nipped him in the shoulder. Lucky the axe didn't stick, or I'd be dead.'

'You got him, though,' Poldarn whispered.

'Oh, I got him,' the man replied. 'He'll keep. But I'm getting too old for this caper, I'm telling you.'

Poldarn frowned. 'You were hunting it?'

The man nodded. 'It's my living,' he said. 'And a bloody stupid way of making one it is, too. Lucky for you, though. Well, for both of us. You kept him occupied, it's half the battle. I don't know you, do I?'

'I wouldn't have thought so,' Poldarn replied. 'I haven't been here long.'

The man scowled. 'Where'd you come from, then?'

'It's a long story. I was born here but I went away for twenty years. My name's—' He had to think. 'Ciartan.'

The man shook his head. 'Doesn't ring any bells. But that doesn't mean anything, I'm not from these parts myself. I'm Boarci, by the way. You won't have heard of me.'

Poldarn laughed. 'That's true,' he said. 'But it doesn't mean much. While I was away I lost my memory, all of it, and it hasn't really come back yet.'

'You don't say.' Boarci shrugged. 'Heard of cases like that, never really believed them. Course, I don't believe in the marsh pixies either, and it's never seemed to bother them any.' He knelt down and wrestled the bear over onto its back; it took all his strength to do that. 'Fair-sized animal,' he said, 'now all I've got to do is dress the bugger out. I hate this job.' He paused, and then looked pointedly at Poldarn's horse. 'Mind you,' he added, 'dressing out's a piece of cake compared with lugging the meat to the nearest farm – a man can do himself a serious injury that way. Times like this, I really wish I had a horse.'

The hint was heavier than any bear that ever trod grass. 'Well,' Poldarn said, 'since you were kind enough to save my life, the least I can do is give you mine.'

'Oh.' Boarci looked slightly stunned. 'Actually, I wasn't meaning that. All I meant was, it'd be real handy if wherever you're going, you wouldn't mind walking and letting my bear ride.'

Poldarn smiled. 'I know that's what you meant,' he replied, 'but I think you've earned the horse. Besides,' he added, 'it isn't mine. Well, not really, it belongs to Haldersness, but everybody keeps telling me it amounts to the same thing, so you're welcome to it.'

'Haldersness,' Boarci repeated. 'Can't say as I know it. Close?'

Poldarn jerked his head back. 'Not far that way. But I was planning on going that way, to Colscegsford.'

Boarci shrugged. 'Broad as it's long to me, provided they can use some fresh meat at where you said. Doesn't bother me where I go.'

Poldarn nodded. 'Fine,' he said. 'Look, excuse me if this sounds ignorant, but am I right in thinking you're a professional hunter?'

'Yeah.' Boarci laughed; a deep, grumbling noise that seemed to happen somewhere around his navel. 'That's what I am, a professional hunter. More like, when I can find a bear or a wild ox or something worth eating that's dumb enough to hold still, I bang it on the head and take it on. Folks aren't quite so quick to show you the door if you bring dinner.'

'I see,' Poldarn exaggerated. 'So what else do you do apart from hunting, if you don't mind me asking?'

'I move around a lot,' Boarci replied, pulling a big knife out of the top of his boot and prodding the bear's stomach with a carrot-thick forefinger. 'If there's any work needs doing, I do it, until my face stops fitting and it's time to move on. I'll be straight with you, most folks don't seem to take to me, they worry when I'm around. Because I'm not settled, see, I don't belong anywhere. This thing with the mountain catching fire's been a godsend, actually; I got a week's work at some farm down the valley digging ditches to carry off flood water, and two days at another place shovelling this black shit out of their yard, and now a bear. I reckon it got pushed out of the forest, they don't hardly ever come up so far as this.'

Poldarn frowned. 'And when you get to the next farm, you sell the meat, right? Do people actually eat the stuff?'

Another laugh. 'Now I believe you about the memory thing,' Boarci said. 'Because if you'd ever had roast bear steaks, you wouldn't have forgotten it in a hurry. Best eating there is, barring spring beef and maybe wine-cooked venison.'

'Really.' Poldarn shrugged. 'Well, there's certainly plenty of it there.'

'You bet. And no, I don't *sell* it, that's not how it's done. I give the farmer the bear, he's more likely to let me stick around a while, find me some work to do. Not always, though. I've had 'em take a bear or a deer, thank you very much, and please close the door on the way out. Bastards,' he added dolefully.

'It does seem a bit ungrateful,' Poldarn said.

Apparently Boarci had found what he'd been looking for, because he slid the knife in and started sawing. 'Can't blame 'em, actually. Hell, if I was them, I'd probably set the dogs on me. How're they supposed to know I'm not a whole load of trouble – like, if I'm all right, what'm I doing straggling round all over instead of having a good place on a farm somewhere, like regular people?' He suddenly jerked the knife sideways, putting all his weight behind it. There was a terrific crack, like a branch snapping. 'Truth is, most of us you come across wandering around, it's because we did something bad or we can't get along with folks, so what do you expect? Course,' he added, wiping blood out of his eyes, 'I'm not like that. I'm out here on my own because of an unfortunate run of bad luck.'

'That's what I'd assumed,' said Poldarn mildly.

Boarci rolled up his sleeves and plunged his arms inside the bear's ribcage, right up to the elbows. 'It was all circumstances beyond my control,' he said sadly. 'That and a parcel of miserable neighbours who took against me for no reason, and saw fit to believe the worst of me on the strength of hardly any evidence at all. If it hadn't been for that, I'd be back in Ayrichsstead right now, with a nice house of my own and a herd of fat cows. Instead of which,' he added, hauling out a nauseating-smelling armful of bear guts, 'here I am, crawling up dead animals for a living and sleeping in shepherds' huts. Life can be a real arsehole sometimes.'

'So I believe,' Poldarn agreed. 'Well, if you want, you can come and stay with us at Haldersness for as long as you like. If you don't mind working, that is.'

Boarci looked at him over the mound of steaming guts. 'That's mighty generous of you,' he said, 'but I won't hold you to it, you not being used to people's ways and all. Thing is, farmers don't take kindly to the hands fetching in strangers off the hill. No offence, but I figure it wouldn't take long for this Halder to pitch me out in the straw, and then I'm back where I started. Thanks all the same,' he added, lifting his horrible burden and staggering a few yards with it before dumping it on the ash.

'I don't think that'll be a problem,' Poldarn said. 'You see, Halder's my grandfather, and my father's dead, so I'm sort of next in line. And when I tell him you saved me from a hungry bear, I don't think he'll be in any hurry to turn you away.'

'Well.' Boarci frowned. 'If you reckon there might be work going over your place—'

'Positive,' Poldarn interrupted. 'If you don't mind raking ash all day long. I think they'd be glad of the help.'

'You don't say,' Boarci muttered pensively. 'So, if there's all this needing doing at your place, can I ask what you think you're doing out here?'

'Visiting my future in-laws,' Poldarn answered. 'Which is just a polite way of saying they're so sick to the teeth of me having to have everything explained a dozen times, and getting under their feet when they're working, they bundled me off to be in the way somewhere else. Besides,' he added, 'they're much closer to the mountain, so I expect Grandfather was worried about how they're coping.'

'Right,' Boarci said, as he teased a bloody pink leg out of its skin. 'You're basically no bloody good round the farm, so when their best neighbour's in trouble, they send you. Guess I must've missed something basic along the way.'

Poldarn hadn't thought of it in those terms. 'I don't know,' he said. 'You'll just have to figure it out for yourself,' he went on. 'And besides, it doesn't matter what prompted them to send me. All that matters in the long run is what I actually do while I'm there.'

Boarci nodded. 'Can't argue with that,' he said. A moment later he stood up, bending his back and drawing away as he did so. The bear's pelt came off like a tight wet shirt. 'Not so bad,' he gasped, as he paused to let his lungs catch up with the rest of him. 'Look, about the horse.'

'Yours,' Poldarn said firmly. 'I said that and I meant it. There's plenty more where that came from. If you do come and stay with us, mind you, I can promise you you'll earn it twice over. Raking ash is a back-breaking job, so they tell me.'

Boarci was spreading out the bearskin. 'You don't know from first hand, then.'

'They wouldn't have me,' Poldarn told him. 'I'd just be in the way, slow everyone up. It's because – well, you don't need me to tell you.'

'Don't I?'

'Apparently you do. It's because they can't read my mind. Goes the other way about, too. But surely you can see this for yourself, can't you?'

Boarci shook his head slowly. 'Can't do that so well myself,' he said. 'Leastways, not with folks from these parts. Back where I came from, of course; but that's a long way from here, and also, most of 'em are dead now. Look,' he said, manhandling rather than changing the subject, 'I don't want to hurry you but it's not smart to hang around in bear country when you've just dressed out, the smell of blood and guts draws 'em in like crazy. If you could see your way to giving me a hand with this lot, we can get out of here. Where was it you said you were making for?'

Poldarn got up. His legs felt weak, but that was just the

aftermath of fear. 'Colscegsford,' he said. 'I'm engaged to Colsceg's daughter. Apparently,' he added.

'Fine.' Boarci had folded the bearskin, neat as a rug except that it had a bear's head and paws dangling off it, and laid it carefully over the saddle. 'You grab the front quarters, I'll get his arse. Now, on three—'

Even severely edited, it was a very heavy bear. 'You know,' Boarci said, while Poldarn was catching his breath, 'I'd have thought that just now, when you woke up and saw this old bear coming at you – Well, it should've solved this memory thing, right?'

Poldarn frowned. 'What, you mean I'd have been dead and it wouldn't have mattered any more?'

Boarci shook his head. 'No, you're missing the point. What I meant was, folks do say that when you're just about to die, your whole life flashes in front of your eyes. So, didn't it?'

Poldarn thought for a moment. 'No,' he said.

'Shit,' Boarci commiserated. 'And I always reckoned that old story. Still,' he went on, brightening up, 'maybe it only works when you're *really* about to die, not just when you think that's what's going to happen. And you're still alive, see.'

'Possibly.' Instinctively, Poldarn went to wipe his bloody hands on the grass, but there wasn't any, just black cinders. 'Except that if only people who actually die get to see it, how would anybody know that's what happens? Nobody would live to tell them.'

Boarci sighed. 'Damn shame,' he said. 'Though as far as I'm concerned it's no bad thing. Wouldn't want to see my life again, it'd just make me cranky. This way, you said?'

'That's right,' Poldarn confirmed. 'Just head for the middle spur. Over there, look, where those trees are.'

Walking on the cinders was slow, difficult and exhausting, like wading through coal. Boarci didn't seem to have much trouble, but Poldarn guessed he'd had more time to get used to it. Unfortunately, Boarci was the one leading both the horse and the way. 'Slow down, will you?' Poldarn panted eventually. 'What's the tearing hurry, anyway?'

'I wasn't hurrying,' Boarci replied. 'Sorry, it's been a while since I went any place in company. So, you been to this farm before? Guess you must have, if you're going to marry their girl.'

Poldarn shook his head. 'It was all sorted out by her father and my grandfather,' he replied. 'I've only seen her once, come to that.'

'Cute?'

'I guess you could say that, yes.'

'That's good. They're all as tricksy as snakes and bad-tempered, but if you've got to marry one, cute's better than ugly. Course, cute don't last, and then all you've got is the tricksiness and the bad temper. Still, better than nothing, I reckon.'

Poldarn grinned. 'You're not married, then.'

'Was married, once. She was cute, if you don't mind 'em small. But her folks turned her against me. They never liked me anyhow.'

For some reason, Poldarn wasn't surprised. But it was a pleasant change to have someone to talk to – talk in an almost normal way, as opposed to the strange bouts of communication he went through back at the farm, with people for whom speech wasn't the usual method. 'It was very impressive,' he said, 'the way you were able to get up close to the bear without being noticed. You must be good at stalking.'

Boarci laughed. 'And even if I was,' he said, 'it'd be a joke with all this black shit all over the ground, crunching under your feet like a thousand men eating celery. Truth is, if you hadn't gotten his attention, I wouldn't have had a prayer of getting that close, in daylight and in the open like that.'

'Glad I could help,' Poldarn muttered.

Boarci chuckled. 'You weren't planning on helping me,' he said, 'and I wasn't planning on saving you. Just kind of turned out that way, like a happy accident. Which is good. But don't go getting the idea I'm the sort of man who'd pick a fight with a fucking big bear just to stop some stranger from getting all chewed up. That's not my style, I'm afraid.'

'I've only got your word for that,' Poldarn said politely. 'For all I know, you could spend your whole life going round helping people, and just pretending to be a homeless drifter because you can't stand being made a fuss of.'

'Sure.' Boarci laughed again. 'That's me exactly, how did you guess?'

'Good judge of character, presumably.'

It was hard enough at the best of times to find the valley in which Colscegsford nestled. With nothing to see except black ash, the job proved to be too hard for Poldarn, distracted as he was by the unaccustomed luxury of talking to someone. It was only when they stopped to look down into the next valley along and found no house or buildings there that Poldarn paused to think and get his bearings.

'Of course,' said Boarci, 'the house not being there could be because it burned down or got buried, and the ruins are just under the cinders somewhere.'

They turned back and retraced their steps. Still no sign of Colsceg's farm. 'We could spend our lives doing this,' Poldarn grumbled. 'Damn it, the miserable place must be somewhere, whole farms don't just melt into the ash or vanish.'

'They do if it's the end of the world,' Boarci pointed out. 'Leastways, that's what my grandmother taught me. Didn't say anything about fire-breathing mountains, but the rest of it, the old lady wasn't so far off the mark.'

In the end, they found what they were looking for, after they'd walked past it three times. It was only a thin ribbon of light blue smoke briefly visible against the skyline that betrayed the farm's secret.

From the head of the combe, there was nothing much to see apart from a few chimney pots and the central ridge of one roof (and you had to be looking for them specifically). A river ran down the middle of the combe, fast and quite deep as it gathered momentum from the steepening gradient. They followed its course – Boarci pointing out that if the place was called Colscegsford, there was probably a ford there, so the river might be a good place to start their search – until they came to a sharp bend, almost a right angle, where the valley suddenly saw fit to drop away at an alarming angle. The river, though, switched over to the side of the combe, forced to follow the rather less precipitous western slope by a long knife-backed ridge that pulled it away like a deliberately built dam. The ridge petered out into a flat plain at the bottom of the combe, where the river slumped into a series of lazy S-bends, in the angle of one of which they found the farm. It wouldn't take much, Poldarn could see, to flood the plain completely; but the farm itself was built on a steeply banked platform between the river bank and the soaring bare rock of the western escarpment. If the river did slip out of its channel, the farm would be an island; but it would take a sea to fill up the valley enough to threaten its inhabitants.

'Good place to build,' Boarci said. 'Only it must get bloody tiresome having to carry all your water up that steep slope every day.'

Poldarn wasn't surprised to find a welcoming party waiting for them as they struggled up the hillside. He recognised Colsceg and Egil (who looked at him with a mixture of hatred and terror that must surely have rattled the brains of all the mind-readers in the district) and the gatepost-stolid Barn; Elja wasn't there, but what business was it of hers? She was only the girl he was engaged to, after all. Also included in the party were five or six chunky-looking men with expressionless faces poking out through impressive beards.

'Hello,' Colsceg said to him; then he turned slightly to face Boarci. 'We could certainly use the meat,' he said, 'but there's no work for you here. I'm sorry.'

Can mind-readers lie? Poldarn asked himself. Apparently they could – the yard was two-thirds buried in cinders, and one of the barns had only a few charred rafters for a roof – but not convincingly. It didn't take a mind-reader to see that Colsceg knew perfectly well that Boarci didn't believe him, and furthermore wasn't too bothered about it.

'This is Boarci,' Poldarn said. 'He saved my life by killing the bear, just as it was about to kill me. He's coming back with me to Haldersness as soon as I'm through here. I hope you don't mind if he stays here in the meanwhile.'

'That'll be fine,' Colsceg replied. 'Any friend of Haldersness is always welcome here.'

Definitely not convincingly, Poldarn thought. Still, that's their business. In any event, Boarci didn't seem unduly put out; he just grinned and kept his face shut.

'Thanks,' he said. 'Is Elja at home? I'd like to see her, if that's all right.'

The request seemed to puzzle Colsceg, but he nodded, and one of the bushy-faced men walked away, presumably to fetch her. The others started to unload the bear. 'That'll do nicely for tonight's dinner,' Colsceg said, and somehow Poldarn got the impression that dinner would've been considerably more sparse if they hadn't shown up when they did. The burned-out barn probably had something to do with that.

'You lost a building, then,' he said.

Colsceg nodded. 'The main storehouse,' he grunted. 'Flour, bacon, dried fish, apples, onions – couldn't save any of it. Won't be long before we're slaughtering the stock just to put food on the table. Not that we can pasture them anyhow; they're eating this winter's hay already, and God only knows what we'll do when that's gone. Terrible business, and we haven't got a clue what needs to be done. How about at your place?'

Poldarn shrugged. 'We're not much better off,' he said, 'except we've still got our stores, of course. But we decided to send our stock away up country; at least there's grazing for them there. Meanwhile, we're trying to scrape the ash off the ploughed land so the crop won't rot. There's a difference of opinion about whether that's a good idea or not; some of us reckon that as soon as there's any heavy rain, it'll wash all this stuff away for us, save us the bother.'

'We were wondering that,' Barn interrupted. 'They had rain over at Lyatsbridge.'

Poldarn nodded. 'From what I gather, getting rid of the ash was the least of their problems.'

'That's true,' Colsceg said. 'But we're all right on that score – we're high up, so mudslides won't be a problem.'

'Unless they come straight down off the mountainside at you,' Poldarn pointed out. 'But I expect you've considered that.'

Colsceg frowned. 'We're trying not to scare ourselves to death thinking of every bloody thing,' he replied. 'It's bad enough as it is without dreaming up new ways we could all get killed.'

That seemed to close that topic of discussion. 'I'm sure Halder will want to send you anything we can spare,' Poldarn said. 'I'll talk to him about it when I get home.'

Nobody seemed very impressed by what Poldarn reckoned was a very generous offer, not to mention a distinctly reckless one. He had a feeling that as far as the Haldersness people were concerned, charity began at home and stayed there. In fact, he wished he'd kept his mouth shut.

Chapter Nine

'I love organised religion,' said the old man with the long grey hair, wiping brains off the blade of his sword with the hem of his coat. 'I love its pomp and pageantry, its traditions, its stabilising influence on society.' He kicked a dead body just to make sure before pulling a ring off its finger. 'I just wish there was more of it. There don't seem to be nearly as many monasteries as there used to be when I was your age.'

The younger man (I know him; I'm sure I've seen him before, somewhere or in something) laughed. 'Too right,' he said. 'But you've burned down most of them. You can't have your cake and eat it, you know.'

(The crows were already beginning to circle. He couldn't see them, but he could hear their voices, as if they were calling out to him, trying to tell him something – a warning, maybe, or just vulgar abuse because he was in the way. He felt that he ought to be able to understand what they were saying, but either they were just too far away for him to make out the words, or else it was one of the arcane rules of the dream.)

The older man shrugged the point away. 'So what?' he said.

'If these people were really serious about religion, they'd rebuild them. Bigger and more splendid—' The ring didn't want to come off, so he knelt down, put the finger in his mouth and sucked. 'Useful trick, that,' he said, 'just the sort of thing you're here to learn.' He spat the ring out into his hand. 'Where was I?'

'Bigger and more splendid.'

'Absolutely.' The older man held out his arm, so that he could be helped up. 'Seems to me,' he went on, 'that if my country was being assailed by ruthless bands of wandering pirates—'

'It is.'

'—Then I'd do everything I possibly could to woo the favour of the gods,' the older man went on, grunting as he straightened his back, 'especially building monasteries and endowing them with fine silverware. Gods hate cheapskates, it's a well-known fact.' He frowned, drawing together his monstrous ruglike eyebrows. 'You aren't just going to leave that perfectly good pair of boots, are you?'

Of course, the older man was showing off (I know him, too; you couldn't forget someone like that) in front of his dazzled and devoted apprentice. He was usually like this after a massacre, clowning and cracking jokes to vent the stress and the anger and the self-loathing from his system. 'Sorry,' the younger man replied meekly, stooping and dragging off the dead man's left boot. 'I don't know what I could've been thinking of.'

Feron Amathy; the old man's name is Feron Amathy. I wonder if I'll remember that when I wake up. 'Hurry up, will you?' Amathy said, 'we've got a lot to get done. Oh, for pity's sake,' he added, as the younger man struggled with a tangled bootlace, 'just cut it and be done with it.'

The young man did as he was told. In fact, they weren't particularly good boots; the uppers were immaculately polished, but the soles were rough and thin. But Feron Amathy had to make his point.

Across the courtyard, a bunch of soldiers were making a long job of setting light to the thatched eaves of the stables; the thatch was still soaking wet after the morning's rain. 'Look at them, will you?' Feron Amathy sighed. 'No more idea than my old mother's parrot. What they want to do is get a pair of bellows – there's bound to be one in the kitchens or the smithy – and get some air behind it, otherwise we'll be here all day, till the sun comes out. If there's one thing I can't be doing with, it's sloppy workmanship.'

The younger man smiled dutifully. It pleases him, he thought, to play up this burlesque of what he actually is, as though it'll somehow diminish the offence. He's a fool to do that, the young man realised, it weakens him. Really, there's no need to be guilty or ashamed, this is just a perfectly natural transaction, in the order of things; if you leave valuable stuff lying about without proper security measures, you're asking for someone to come along and kill you for it. Good and evil have got nothing to do with it. 'So what's left to do?' he asked, in a businesslike tone of voice. 'We've done the chapel and the main building. How about the library?'

Feron Amathy pursed his lips. 'Now then,' he said, 'here's a test for you. In this library –' he pointed with his sword at the rather grand and over-ornate square building in the opposite corner of the quadrangle '– is a collection of very rare and precious books, many of them unique. What should we do?'

The young man thought for a moment. 'Books are heavy and bulky and a pain in the arse to handle,' he said, 'but if you can find the right market, they're worth a fortune. Rich people'll pay ridiculous amounts of money for rare old books.' He looked round. 'We could use those carts over there,' he said. 'It's a straight road over the hill, and we can store them in the big cave under the long escarpment.'

But Feron Amathy sighed. 'Sometimes I wonder if you ever listen to a word I say,' he said. 'Right; where do you propose getting rid of them?'

This time the younger man felt confident about his reply. 'Mael Bohec,' he replied. 'I happen to know there's a special book market there, behind the filler's yard in the old town. Our best bet'd be to sell them off to a trader, get a price for the whole lot, because—'

'Idiot,' said Feron Amathy. 'What did I say about the books?'

'Rare and precious, many of them unique,' the younger man said. 'Which surely means they must be worth—'

'A collection of rare and unique books,' Feron Amathy repeated. 'And since this is a monastery, what kind of books d'you think you'll find here? History? Poetry anthologies? Practical advice to farmers and craftsmen, profusely illustrated with several hundred line drawings?'

'Well, religious books, obviously. But they're the most valuable of all, someone told me, because—'

'Precisely.' Another piece of gold jewellery caught his eye, and he swooped like a jay. 'A magnificent, *world-famous* library of religious texts, many of them *unique*. For generations, monks have come here from all over the empire, because this library has the *only copy* of many crucial scriptural texts. Have you got any idea at all what I'm driving at?'

The young man nodded remorsefully. 'Of course,' he said. 'If there's only one copy and it suddenly shows up on a market stall, everyone'll know it came from here—'

'Which is impossible,' Feron Amathy went on, 'because everybody's been led to believe this town was razed to the ground by the pirates—'

'Who burn and kill everything and then disappear back across the sea to where they came from.'

'Which means?'

'Which means they don't sell the stuff they've stolen

through the usual fences. All right, I got that one wrong. I'm sorry.'

Feron Amathy sighed. 'That's all very well. But the day'll come when I'm not here to be apologised to, let alone save you from making incredibly dangerous mistakes. And then your head will end up on a spike over some gateway somewhere, and all this invaluable trade knowledge I'm passing on to you will have been wasted. So, all right then. What do we do with the books?'

'Burn them,' the young man said.

Feron Amathy sighed with exaggerated relief. 'Finally we're there. All right, you get the job as a reward for your performance in the test. Round up a dozen men and get on with it. We really haven't got all day.'

(*And that, he realised as he watched, was one of the crucial moments, the turning points, the places where it could so easily have gone either way.* I wish I knew how, precisely, he thought.)

The younger man nodded and trudged across the yard. It didn't take him long to assemble a working party – they weren't happy about being dragged away from looting the place and made to do hard, hot, unprofitable work, but they didn't hesitate or make excuses. Amathy house discipline was stronger and better than in any regular imperial unit.

Buoyed up by their confidence and high spirits, the younger man managed to kick in the library door, though he felt sure he'd broken a small bone in his foot after he missed the door itself and drove his boot hard against the metalwork. As a result, he was hobbling as he walked inside.

It was dark inside the library; the windows were shuttered, to prevent (he remembered) the light from fading the exquisitely illuminated capitals of the books set out on display on the great brass lecterns that stood in front of the rows of shelves. He drew his sword and held it out in front of him – no point in stubbing his toe on a lectern or a bench –

and edged his way across the floor until he came to the nearest bookshelf. He located a book by feel, grabbed a handful
of pages and tugged. But the book was best-quality parchment, far too tough to tear, so he dumped it on the ground,
knelt beside it and groped in his coat pocket for his tinderbox.

This would be the hard part.

Everybody else in the world, right down to tottering old
women and village idiots, could work a tinderbox. Little children who'd never been taught, who'd been expressly
forbidden to play with fire, could have a merry blaze crackling away in the dry moss within a few heartbeats. Any
bloody fool could do it, with one exception.

Painfully aware that his men were waiting for him, he
teased out the moss, making sure it was dry. He felt the edge
of the flint, which was good and crisp. All he had to do was
turn the little brass crank (he had a very fine, genuine
Torcean tinderbox, formerly the property of an Imperial
courier, state of the art and beautifully finished and
engraved) and by rights he'd have a little red glow in no time.
He cranked. He cranked slowly and fast, smoothly and
abruptly, with and without little wristy spurts. He blew into
the moss pan, soft as a summer breeze, hard as a tornado. He
stopped, slackened off the clamp and fitted a brand new
flint. He turned the moss over. Nothing.

'You all right in there?' one of the men called out from the
doorway.

'Fine,' he called back. 'Just lighting a fire.'

Needless to say, any one of them could have done it. The
requirements for joining the Amathy house weren't exactly
stringent – you had to be taller than a short dwarf and have
at least one arm – there certainly weren't any tests of practical everyday skills before you were allowed to sign on. But
any one of Feron Amathy's men could have lit a tinderbox,
not excluding the two or three old stagers who no longer

quite met the at-least-one-arm criterion. The only man in the whole house who couldn't was the man entrusted with starting a fire. Bloody comical, that was what it was.

He sighed. 'Bofor,' he shouted, 'get in here.'

Bofor, the sergeant, was a piss-poor excuse for a soldier, but he kept his mouth shut. 'Where are you?' he called out.

'Here. Watch where you're going,' he added, a little too late. He could hear the sergeant swearing softly and fluently in the darkness. 'Shut up and get a fire lit,' he hissed, handing over the tinderbox.

Two turns of the crank later, Bofor was nursing a tidy little blaze in the moss reservoir. 'Thanks,' the younger man sighed. 'All right, stay where you are. Soon as I've got this book going, you'll be able to see what you're about.'

He tipped the burning moss between the pages of the opened book, and fairly soon smoke was stinging his eyes. A vague circle of flickering red light seeped out into the shadows, thinning them. 'There we go,' he said. 'Now, give me back my box and go and fetch some books.'

Bofor grunted and went about his assigned duty. He found the shelf without difficulty; then, having apparently decided to do the thing methodically and start on the top shelf, he reached up and started pulling books down. The shelf fell on him, knocking him off his feet and burying him in literature.

Well, he wasn't to know, as the younger man was, that in monastery libraries the top shelves are reserved for restricted books, the ones that ordinary, unprivileged brothers aren't meant to read, and are locked and chained to the bookcase. Damn, the younger man said to himself, I should've remembered and warned him. Still, it seemed unlikely that Bofor would have survived upwards of thirty pitched battles only to be killed by an out-of-date copy of *Jorc On Building Disputes*.

He sighed. It's just not my day today, he thought, everything I touch turns to horse manure, I should've stayed in my tent and told them I had a headache. He looked down, and saw the cheerful glow of burning parchment. At least he'd been able to set light to one book, though at this rate torching the whole library would take him the rest of his life.

Think, he ordered himself, apply your mind, what's left of it. There was enough light from the burning book to guide him as far as the next bookshelf, which contained manuscripts and rolls rather than bound volumes. That was rather more like it; he gathered an armful and carefully stoked his little fire until it was burning vigorously – so well, in fact, that he felt the hair on his forehead frizzle, and jumped back. He carried on building the fire with supplies from the manuscript shelf, but even that was going to be too slow, if he had to carry every single book in the library over to his bonfire. What he needed to do was rig up torches that he could stuff into the gaps between shelves.

For someone of his ingenuity and resourcefulness, no problem; all it took was a big scroll, tightly wound so it'd burn steadily instead of flaring up and burning itself out before he could get it in place. Now that he had a viable plan of action, he could deploy his workforce; so he called in the rest of the men and told them what to do. It wasn't long before every case in the building was wreathed in sheets of billowing yellow fire – a rather attractive effect, he decided, reminding him of a set of very expensive silk wall hangings he'd seen in a government office somewhere. Not long after that, the soaring flames reached the rafters and cross-beams, burning off a couple of centuries of dust before catching on the timbers themselves. He stood for a moment or so with his hands on his hips, admiring the spectacle until the smoke got into his lungs and forced him outside.

'Right,' he said, once he'd stopped choking. 'Job done.'

A black pillar of smoke stood over the library roof, and little flakes of grey ash drifted down all around him, disintegrating as they touched the damp gravel. The heat made his face throb and glow, but it was a pleasant warmth, making him conscious of his achievement.

'Where's Fat Bofor?' someone said.

He felt his heart lurch in his chest. 'Anybody seen him?' he asked. 'He did come out, didn't he?'

Nobody said anything.

He stared at the burning library. Already, shoots of fire were sprouting out of holes in the roof tiles, where rafters and joists had burned through and collapsed. Smoke was pouring out of the windows between the charred stumps of the shutters, while a gaudy display of flames burgeoned out of the doorway like some exotic shrub growing in a ruin. Not a shadow of a doubt about it; if Sergeant Bofor was still in there, he was already dead and reduced to ash, and anybody who tried to go in after him wouldn't get very far before ending up the same way.

'Shit,' he said, because (now that he thought of it) it was his first command, and he'd lost ten per cent of his unit through sheer carelessness. 'Quick,' he barked, 'get me a bucket of water. You, give me your coat.'

The soldiers stared at him as he struggled into a second coat and upended the bucket over his head. 'Hang on,' one of them said, 'you aren't thinking of going in there, are you?'

'Shut up,' he replied, dowsing his hat in the dregs of the bucket. 'Whatever you do, don't come in after me, understood?'

'Don't be bloody stupid,' one of them said, but by then he was already on his way. He heard them yelling, 'Come back, what the hell do you think you're doing?' as he scrambled clumsily through a ground-floor window and landed awkwardly on one foot, standing in a pile of glowing ash.

He had one hoarded lungful of air, no more. Get your bearings, he ordered himself. Door's on my right, Bofor was by the first bookcase on the left. He dropped down onto his hands and knees – he could feel the skin on his palms

scorching, but physical pain was the least of his problems –
and scuttled like a hyperactive toddler across the floor in
what he hoped was the right direction. Of course he couldn't
see anything but smoke, so thick it was practically solid;
but he'd got this far, so it was inconceivable that he'd fail
now. Fat Bofor would still be alive, all he had to do was grab
his ankles and walk backwards, straight out through the
door. It would be simple, easy if he factored out the pain
and injury. He wouldn't be here and still alive if it wasn't
going to work out just fine in the end.

Something came down *thump* a foot or so to his left,
making him jump so sharply that he almost let go of his
breath. It could have been a bookcase collapsing, or a length
of rafter; or just a particularly thick and heavy book toppling off a burnt-through shelf; it didn't matter, there wasn't
enough time. He had to be crawling in the right direction,
Fat Bofor had to be here somewhere, already so close that he
could stretch out and grab him. He couldn't fail, because
otherwise—

He felt a stunning blow across his shoulders. It knocked all
the air out of him, and when he breathed in, all he got was
unbearable smoke. Oh, he thought; and—

'Hello,' he said. 'What are you doing here?'

His friend laughed at him. 'Don't be stupid,' he replied
cheerfully. 'I live here, remember?'

He frowned. 'Oh,' he said. 'I thought you'd got a transfer
to Deymeson.'

'I did,' his friend replied. 'I was there for years, on and off,
when I wasn't charging about running errands. But then
some bloody fool came along and set light to the place, so
here I am.'

This didn't make any sense. 'You've got to get out of here
quick,' he pointed out. 'Can't you see it's on fire?'

But his friend shook his head. 'They rebuilt it,' he said, as
if pointing out the painfully obvious. 'I ended up here as

Father Prior, would you believe? Me, of all people. Truth is, there were so few of us left, anybody with any seniority got made an abbot or a prior. Still, when you think of what old Horse's-Arse used to say about me when we were novices – *The day they make you an abbot, the world will come to an end.* Bloody odd to think he got that right.'

'Who are you?' the younger man asked.

'But here's me,' his friend went on, 'boasting about landing a rotten little priorship. Look at you, though, talk about the novice most likely to succeed. They may have made me a prior; they've gone and made you a fucking *god*.' His eyebrows pulled together into a comic scowl. 'Actually,' he said, 'I think that was taking it a bit too far. I mean, how can I be expected to fall down and worship someone who still owes me the two quarters I won off you for long spitting?'

'What's happening?' he demanded. 'Are you real, or is this a dream or something?'

His friend laughed. 'Is this a dream, he asks,' he crowed. 'Oh for pity's sake, Ciartan, of course it's a dream, otherwise you'd be dead. What you should be asking yourself is, which dream am I in, now or later? Bet you don't know.'

'You aren't real,' the younger man said accusingly. 'I'm hallucinating, and you don't exist.'

'There's no need to be offensive,' his friend replied. 'Anyway, you couldn't be more wrong if you tried. Of course I'm here. I'm at least twice as much here as you are. I'm just not letting it get to me, that's all.'

Suddenly he understood; about time, too. 'You're from years ahead in the future,' he said.

'Took you long enough to figure that one out, didn't it?' his friend mocked him. 'And you still aren't there yet. When did you get to be so stupid, then? Back when we were novices, everybody said how bright you were.'

'The future and the past,' he amended. 'You're from when we were both students, and you're from some time in the future where you've been made Father Prior. So, where am I, then?'

His oldest friend clicked his tongue impatiently. 'Oh, come on,' he said. 'Don't be so bloody feeble. You never used to be like this, you know. I think maybe it was the bash on the head, did more than just make you lose your memory. All right, then, let's see if we can't figure this out from first principles. I'm not really here, but you can see me and you can talk to me, back here in this place where we first met when we were novices together. Now, do you want to take a wild guess, or do I have to spell it out for you?'

'Spell it out for me,' he replied. 'I'm not proud.'

'Fine.' His friend shrugged, and became – naturally enough – a huge crow, pinned to the floor by a fallen rafter, as the fire caught in its feathers. 'Let me tell you a few things about yourself. I always wanted to tell you, but you know, you aren't the sort of person who takes criticism well. You've never wanted to hear unpleasant truths about yourself, and you've always been a bit too quick on the draw, so to speak. There was always a remote chance that pointing out your little weaknesses and faults of character might earn your helpful friend a swift chop to the neck. But here I am.' The crow tried to flap its broken wings, but couldn't. 'Nothing you can do to me, I'm as good as dead already. So here goes.'

The bird's feathers were full of fire and he couldn't bear its pain; but he couldn't move either, being trapped under the same rafter. 'No, please,' he said, but the crow didn't seem to hear him.

'Once upon a time,' said the crow, 'there was a young man who lived in a far country, a huge island in the middle of the sea. Everything was very pleasant there, if you like that sort of thing, and the people who lived there were a single-minded lot, rather like a mob of crows. You know what I mean by that; birds of a feather who flock together, and just the one fairly straightforward mind between them. But then the young man did something very bad; and although his grandfather forgave him and nobody else who mattered knew about it, it seemed sensible for the young man to clear out for a while, just a year or so, until things could be put right. So the young man got on a ship that was bound for the great and practically defenceless empire on the other side of the world. While he was away, he might as well make himself useful; so he was given the job of finding out as much as he could about the place he was going to – you see, his people had a very helpful sideline in robbing and plundering the great and practically defenceless empire, but they were hampered a bit by not knowing an awful lot about it, and a little reliable fieldwork would make life a whole lot easier. Besides, they had a friend in the empire, a very bad man who helped them out in exchange for a cut of the takings, but they didn't know very much about him, either, and it seemed like a good idea to get rid of him and maybe put in someone of their own, who could be trusted implicitly.' The crow's beak was starting to melt in the desperate heat, making it look faintly ridiculous. 'Are you with me so far, or do you want me to go back over all that?'

'It's all right,' he replied. 'It's coming back to me. Go on.'

'Ah well,' the crow said, 'in that case you don't need me to tell you about how you and I got to know each other. But just in case there's still a gap or two in your memory, there was a time when we were the very best of friends – really and truly, it wasn't just some part you were playing in the course of your research, or anything like that. Odd,' the crow continued, 'because after you left, I ended up making a career of sorts out of doing what you'd been sent over to do – spying, gathering information, always in and out of disguises, being a whole range of very plausible people, which I could always do because I never much enjoyed being myself. And now look at you.' Contempt and compassion in equal measure. 'You know, there were times when being one of my various personas was so much more bearable than being me that I nearly found the strength to run away, turn the deceit into truth, start again as someone else, crawling new-born out of a muddy river. But I didn't,' the crow added, with a palpable hint of superiority. 'People were depending on me, and I never forgot my flock, if you'll pardon the ecclesiastical metaphor.'

'I'm sorry,' the younger man said. 'About what I did to you in the forge. I don't know what came over me. You were flying around screaming and I guess I panicked.'

The crow laughed, a harsh, painful noise. 'Oh, that,' it said. 'Please, think nothing of it. You'd done it before and you'll do it again. You never could abide us when you were a kid, you'd sit out with your slingshot and your pile of stones and kill us by the dozen. And then you helped burn Deymeson, which was no better and no worse. You've been punished for that, of course. In fact, I'm not sure which tends to come first in your case, the punishment or the crime. If you will insist on being reborn every five minutes, it makes it bloody hard to keep track. Most people are content to live in a straight line, but you've always been a dog with a burning tail, running round in frantic circles trying to bite off your own arse. Of course, from here I can see it all so much more clearly – a bird's-eye view, if you like – and what really saddens me is the hopelessness of it all. Why bother? I ask myself; but that's hindsight for you. Did you know that we birds have all-round vision? Comes of having little round eyes on the sides of our heads, instead of oval ones in the front. You can't see what's beside you or behind you; we can. Very useful attribute, almost makes up for not having minds of our own. A bit like a religious order, with its centuries of tradition, its prophetic insights into the future, its access to additional dimensions of perception. And that, in case you're wondering, is why we wear the crow-black dressing gowns. I say "we", because of course you're one of us; just as much right to this livery as I have, if not better. Am I still making something vaguely approaching sense, or did I leave you behind some time ago?'

He shook his head. 'I think I can see what you're getting at,' he said. 'I just don't get the relevance, that's all.'

'Oh. Damn.' The crow's wings dissolved into black ash, which drifted up in a spiral as the hot air rose. 'And yet you were always top of the class in textual interpretation. Used to do my homework for me, or I'd never have got past fourth grade. All right, here it is in baby language. You killed me in the forge, and the mountain stopped puking up fire. You killed me in the fields, and you found true love – twice, actually, but that was a dirty trick, not my idea. You killed me here, and you shot to the top of the tree. You killed me at Deymeson, and that's how you came to be the heir apparent of Haldersness. Next time you kill me – or maybe the time after that, I'm a bit hazy about details – you'll usurp the imperial throne, get the girl, find out what you really wanted to know all along. Do you see a pattern emerging here, or what?'

'I see,' he said. 'You're my enemy.'

The fire turned to glowing cinders around the crow's skull. 'Absolutely not,' it said. 'I'm the best friend you ever had, even though you're going to burn me alive in your own house – and if you think this mess we're in now is rough, you just wait till then, it'll hurt you a whole lot more than it hurts me. But that's a given, because—'

The scorched and charred remains of the crow vanished and became Poldarn, holding the rake that was crushing him down into the forge fire. He screamed, flapped his wings desperately, but the weight of the rake pinned him down like a fallen rafter as the fire ran up his feathers into his flesh and bone. 'That's who you really are, you see,' the voice went on, 'just who you've always been. It's a cliché, your own worst enemy, but in your case it's absolutely appropriate.

When you're pinned down in Poldarn's forge and everything around you is burning – but you won't remember a word of this when you wake up, which is a real shame. Life can be so cruel.'

He sat up. He was in a cart, and Copis was beside him on the box, her face hidden by the cowl of her riding cloak. He lifted it away and saw her face, but the voice remained the same. It sounded like his own, but he was hardly qualified to be sure about that.

'It's what I was born for,' Copis said, 'to drive you around, round and round in circles, from this mountain to the next and back again, year after bloody year.' She sighed melodramatically. 'Always a priestess, never a god, just my rotten luck. I get the blame, you get all the burnt offerings. I really wish you could remember at least some of this when you wake up, it'd save me a great deal of physical pain, not to mention the emotional shit. But there we go. I think we're here,' she added, as the mountain, belching fire, appeared in the background. 'You're on. Break a leg.'

He opened his eyes.

'So there you are.' The older man's face: Feron Amathy, staring at him as if he'd seen a rather unsatisfactory ghost, not the one he'd been waiting for. 'You kept on dying and we were all set to bury you, and then you'd start breathing again, you bugger. God, you've cost me a lot of money.'

He tried to sit up, but that proved to be a very bad idea. Everything hurt, very badly.

'The good news is,' Feron Amathy went on (and behind his head was the peak of a tent, with other faces peering over his shoulder), 'apart from a broken leg and some scratches and singes, you're all right, you'll live.' He frowned. 'Did I say that was the good news? Matter of viewpoint, I guess. The bad news is, you fucked up and cost the lives of three good men, as well as buggering up my plans and ruining six months' work. If I didn't love you like my own son, I'd rip your stomach open and peg you out for the crows.'

He remembered what had happened. 'Sergeant Bofor—'

Feron Amathy shook his head. 'Make that three good men and one buffoon, though I'm not holding Fat Bofor against you. I'm assuming that it was his own stupidity that got him killed. Is that right?'

He tried to nod, but it hurt too much. 'He pulled a bookcase down on his head,' he croaked, 'I think it must have knocked him out.'

'Figures. But the other three are your fault, for rushing into a burning building to save a dead idiot. Different for them, of course; they rushed into a burning building too, but there was a slight chance their idiot was still alive. Since they were proved to be correct, I'm calling them heroes rather than irresponsible arseholes. Benefit of the doubt, and all that.'

He closed his eyes. 'I'm sorry,' he said. 'I was only trying to do the right thing.'

'I know,' Feron Amathy said tenderly. 'That's what makes you such a fucking menace. In case you're remotely interested, the men you killed – not too strong a word, in my opinion – were Has Gilla, Cuon Borilec and Fern Ilzen. Tully Galac got out alive – dragged you out with him – but he's burnt to hell and he's lost one eye, it's touch and go whether he'll make it or not. If this is what you achieve when you're trying to be good, Poldarn help us all if you ever decide to be bad.'

He could feel tears forming in his eyes. 'The library,' he said.

'Oh, that. You failed. I have no idea how you managed it, but only about half the books actually got burned; a wall fell in and cut the rest off from the fire – it's a bloody miracle, if you ask me. Anyway, who gives a shit about a load of old books? The point is, with you hovering on death's door like a hummingbird, we had to call off the attack on Josequin and hole up here; and now the bloody rain's set in, we haven't got a hope in hell of getting back down the mountain with the roads all turned to mud, so it looks like we're stuck here for a month at the very least. If the food holds out it'll be another bloody miracle. Can you do miracles? Apart from coming back from the dead, I mean. If so, now would be a really good time.'

A sharp pain shot up his leg and paralysed him for a very long moment. 'I don't think I can,' he said. 'I'm sorry.'

'Oh, great,' Feron Amathy sighed. 'A fat lot of use you turned out to be, then.'

He opened his eyes.

'Wake up, for crying out loud.' Colsceg was leaning over him, shaking him by the shoulder. 'We need you to tell us what to do.'

There was something in his mind, something incredibly important; but the light – and the sound of Colsceg's voice – washed it away, like a flood dissolving snow. 'What's the matter?' he asked sleepily.

(The main hall at Colscegsford; he could see the joists and cross-beams of the roof behind the old man's head. For some reason they seemed horribly threatening, as if they could fall in on him at any moment. Why? he wondered; I must have been dreaming.)

'What's the matter, he says.' Colsceg scowled at him. 'You bloody fool, can't you hear it?'

He could hear something; it was a gentle, familiar noise, one that he rather liked, because of pleasant associations he could no longer quite remember. 'Please,' he said, 'tell me. What's going on?'

(And then he recognised the sound—)

'I'll tell you what's going on,' Colsceg shouted, as if it was all his fault. 'It's raining.'

Chapter Ten

Poldarn pushed past Colsceg and burst through the door.

The rain was hard, each drop hitting his face like a slingstone, and so thick that he could only just make out the shapes of the encircling mountains. But he didn't need to see them. In his mind's eye, he had a clear vision of what was happening. The ash was dissolving into mud, slithering off the rocky slopes, following the channels and contours like sheep herded by a well-trained dog. Soon it would form its lines and columns, its ranks and files, ready to march; then it would move with terrifying speed (like the raiders, his people, swooping down on Josequin or Deymeson), gathering strength and pace as it went, before cascading in a black river into the valley, and filling it like molten metal poured into a mould. It would be here very soon, too soon to put together a coherent plan of action, organise the household, allocate duties and responsibilities, establish an effective chain of command – all the things that needed to be seen to if anything was ever to get done.

'Well,' Colsceg shouted at him, 'so what do we do?'

He thought about it for a whole second. 'Run,' he said.

'Fine. Where to?'

Ah, Poldarn thought, now there you have me. He looked round, more with his mind and memory than with his eyes. The valley plain was out of the question. He thought of Rook's account of the mudslides at Lyatsbridge; if they ran out onto the flat, there was every chance they'd be swamped and buried before they went more than a few hundred yards. Going up the slopes was no better, they ran the risk of being in the way of a mudslide coming down; it'd be quicker, though not by much, and that was the best to be said for it. Bloody hell, he thought, why's it got to be up to me, this isn't even my house. Why can't someone else tell *me* what to do, for a change?

'Up the hillside,' he said, and as he said it he knew perfectly well that he was only saying the first thing that came into his head, because there wasn't time to reach a considered decision. 'Keep to the high ground, away from the dips and trenches. You'll be just fine.'

Colsceg nodded and ran off; Poldarn could see people hurrying towards him. Of course, he and he alone was at liberty to please himself, he didn't have to go with the rest of them or allow his mind to be swamped by theirs. He could stay where he was, observe, collate more data, drown in mud, because he wasn't a part of this community. He only had himself to think about.

Not true. The hell with this, he thought; where's Boarci? Damn him to hell, Boarci was his responsibility now, and of course he was nowhere to be seen. Suppose it took him three minutes to find him, that'd use up his little allowance of grace and then it'd be too late to save either of them, even if he knew how to go about it. Waiting for him, looking for him would be an act of monumental stupidity, like running back into a burning house to try and save someone who was probably dead already. Only an imbecile would even consider doing something like that.

'Boarci,' he yelled, but he could only just hear himself over the hammering of the rain.

This would be a good time to be a mind-reader, Poldarn thought as he splashed and skidded across the yard. Already the rain had created pools in every bump and dip; it was flooding down off the eaves and gathering in miniature rivers, scuttling down the slight incline towards the edge of the plateau. The stables, he told himself; if I were Boarci, I'd try and get a horse, see if I could outrun the mud on the flat. Now that wasn't a bad idea, though needless to say it wasn't applicable to the Colscegsford household; there weren't enough horses to go round, and if they couldn't all go, none of them would even consider trying. But Boarci wasn't a part of this house, not even remotely, by betrothal; he could clear out and leave them all to die, and nobody would know he'd even been here. Now if only he could be trusted to think that way for himself, Poldarn would be relieved of the obligation of thinking for him, and that'd be one less thing to waste time on. But it wouldn't be safe to assume that Boarci would do that, and so Poldarn had no choice but to keep looking for him (and that'd be comical, if Poldarn died trying to save the one man in the place who managed to get away).

While he was standing in the yard trying to figure out this dilemma, the first mudslide made its spectacular entrance. It must have come down off the very steep escarpment at the far end of the plateau, because it landed on the roof of the grain store, smashed it into kindling and scooped up the mess before butting through the fence like an unusually ornery bull and slopping over the edge into the valley. Poldarn spun round to gawp, and by the time he'd seen enough the walls of the middle stable were being folded down flat as a torrent of black muck shouldered its way through, heading straight for the main house. That wasn't a problem, it was going away from where he was standing, and he'd noticed a nice sharp outcrop well above the channel it was following down the slope. If he looked sharp about it, he could see no reason why he couldn't get up there and be as safe as any man can be in this notoriously uncertain world. But before he could set off (time, of course, being very much of the essence) he realised that Elja was still inside the house. He didn't have a clue how he knew this, but he knew it.

Marvellous, he thought. But you'd have to be plumb crazy to try and outrun something moving that fast.

Poldarn ran; and, to his surprise, he found that he was making ground on the mudslide with every forced stride. By his calculations, the mud was shifting along at slightly more than a brisk walking pace, too slow for him to be able to abandon his responsibilities with a clear conscience. The door was wide open, as he'd left it, but he slipped in a pool of mud under the eaves and collided painfully hard with the door frame. He landed on his left knee, with a painful impression of having done it no good at all, but he couldn't spare the time for it to hurt or anything self-indulgent like that. Instead he pulled himself up on the edge of the door and charged into the house, howling Elja's name.

She came out of the inner room, looking sleepy.

'Mudslide,' he tried to say, but he was too out of breath to be able to shape words. Instead, he grabbed her arm and yanked her after him, reaching the doorway just as the mud caved it in.

Too late after all, Poldarn concluded sadly, as the mud swept his feet from under him and he flopped awkwardly onto his side, half falling and half collapsing, like an old shed in a high wind. He pulled Elja down with him, of course, and she screamed at him, bending back the fingers of his left hand where they were closed around her wrist. Now that really was painful, but he didn't have time or breath left to ask her to stop. The current carried him on a yard or so, twisting him round until he was lying on his back, watching the roof timbers getting pulled out of their mortices. He wondered whether he'd live long enough for the pain of having his head crushed by a falling beam to make him scream; he hoped not, since he didn't want to look pathetic in front of Elja.

But it didn't happen like that. Under the pressure of the mud, the walls were forced outwards, and the rafters and joists were pulled free of their sockets on the left-hand side before they cleared those on the right. In consequence, the roof beams folded rather than fell, crashing down diagonally into the mud and spraying it in all directions, but he was too far over to be in their line of collapse. Meanwhile, the wall nearest to him was floating on top of the mud, like a grotesquely oversized raft.

I could get on that, he thought. We could get on that, he corrected himself, and then at least we won't drown in the river of mountainshit. Death was one thing, but the thought of being sloughed over by a huge black slug of sodden ash was too revolting to bear thinking about. So he crawled, waded and flipped his way onto the flattened wall, like a salmon forcing its way upstream, and managed to haul himself over the precisely trimmed log-ends and flop, breathlessly, face down in a pool of his own mud.

A scream reminded Poldarn that he still had duties to attend to. Just in time, he reached out and grabbed Elja's wrist, before the current dragged her too far away. He pulled, and felt something go in her arm; she screamed again, this time from simple, everyday pain, and tried to shake him off. Instinct, he told himself, and pulled as hard as he could, ignoring whatever damage he was doing to her tendons and bones. A ludicrous picture of her hand coming off in his floated into his mind, somehow hopelessly mixed up with a memory of trying to wring a hen's neck, yanking straight when he should have twisted, and getting horribly scratched in the face by the claws of a decapitated chicken. But Elja's hand stayed on and she slopped down beside him on the wall-raft, flapping and wriggling like a landed fish.

'It's all right,' he shouted (but his mouth was full of mud), just as the roof subsided into the black mess, pushing up a wave that nearly submerged them both. He slid his own length down the raft on his belly, his feet ramming her in the neck and ear and almost shunting her off the timbers into the mud. Then – fortuitously – the raft came up against something solid and was jolted sideways, shooting them both back up the way they'd just come. Unfortunately, the impact was enough to wrench the wall-boards apart; the raft disintegrated into its component timbers (he saw Colsceg as a young man, marking each growing beam with his knife so he'd know which tree was to go where when the time came) and he needed both arms to grab on to a floating joist, just to keep his head above the surface. He couldn't look round to see what had become of Elja, but it didn't take much imagination to guess.

What a bloody mess, Poldarn said to himself, and he wondered how they were getting on at Haldersness, whether the rain was cleaning the ash off the fields, whether there were mudslides there, and was everybody dead. It didn't seem to matter; even if he contrived to keep his grip on the log he was hanging on to, sooner or later the current would sweep him off the plateau and he'd end up dead on the plain below, drowned in mud or crushed by house-lumber – if the fall itself didn't kill him. He'd failed, of course; Elja dead in spite of his heroic self-sacrifice, and Boarci clean forgotten about, though in the event he wouldn't have been able to do anything for him. It was almost annoying to be still alive, saved by the happy accident of the angle at which the roof fell, the conveniently handy wall that had served him as a raft – he'd had nothing to do with all that, he hadn't arranged it or done anything the least bit clever, and all that had come of it was that he'd lived a few rather unpleasant minutes longer, minutes he wouldn't have minded missing out on, at that. Pointless and faintly ridiculous, the whole thing.

I'll die, and I'll never know who I was. Maybe I should remember now; after all, what harm can it possibly do? But his memory remained obdurately locked, and he couldn't be bothered to argue with it. Something Boarci had said, about his life flashing before his eyes at the moment of death, flitted into his mind and made him smile. The rain was cold and brutal; he'd have preferred to die in the warm sun, but apparently that wasn't going to happen.

Ciartan, Ciartan. Maybe someone was calling his name, or maybe it was just a voice in his head, such as you sometimes hear in the middle of the night, mindlessly enunciating some word or other. On balance, Poldarn hoped it was the latter. It'd be dreadful if the last thing he saw was some poor fool trying to rescue him and getting himself killed in the process. To have that on his conscience at the final moment would be intolerable, particularly since his mind had gone to such elaborate pains to hide his past sins from him, in case they upset him. Above all, he wanted to die in peace; death and haircuts should both be free from idle and distracting chatter, he told himself, and regretted that he'd never have a chance to use the line in conversation, because he rather liked it.

'Ciartan, you bloody fool. Over here.'

Definitely not a voice in his head; but he couldn't look round to see who it was without loosening his grip on the timber. 'Go away,' he shouted. 'Leave me alone, for God's sake.'

'Fuck you,' replied the voice, and he recognised it: Boarci, his new best friend. Particularly galling, he thought; here he was in his last few moments of life, and his dependent, the man he felt most responsible for, was calling out to him to save him. Everything I do turns to horseshit on me, Poldarn thought sadly, as he realised that his grip was about to weaken. Why couldn't I have died back in the Bohec valley, where I wasn't any bother to anybody?

He tried to tighten his grip, but he had nothing left. The beam slipped out from under his fingers, and he felt the mud rushing into his nose and mouth, too quickly for him even to take a breath.

He was in some kind of dream, though for some reason there weren't any crows. The mud had turned to linen, and the soft pressure on his face was a sheet. He batted it away with the back of his hand and turned his head. Next to him on the pillow was a glorious tangle of golden hair. He caught his breath; and she yawned and rolled over to face him.

'Who are you?' he asked.

She giggled. 'Oh, just some girl you picked up at a dance,' she replied.

(The crazy part of it was, he could distinctly remember her saying that.)

He opened his eyes and immediately started choking.

'He's alive,' someone said. Good, he thought. Improbable, but I'll gladly take their word for it.

Someone was leaning over him. It was still raining, and drops of water dripped off the man's sodden fringe onto his face. 'It's all right,' the man said, 'you're going to be all right.'

'Boarci,' he said.

The man nodded. 'He got to you just in time. Damnedest thing I ever saw, the man must be crazy or something. But he pulled you both out, is the main thing, and no harm done.'

You both, us both – am I forgetting something here? 'Elja?' he said.

'She's going to be all right too,' Colsceg said. 'Absolutely amazing, how he managed to do it. Must be as strong as a team of plough-horses. Just as well for you, really.'

Poldarn started coughing again, which was infuriating because he badly needed to know what had happened. 'Tell me,' was as far as he managed to get between spasms.

Colsceg had grabbed Poldarn's arm. 'It'll be better if you can sit up,' he said, jerking him upright so hard he nearly dislocated his shoulder (and his muscles were all torn and bruised as it was; no wonder, after the games he'd put them through). 'There, you can breathe better now.'

Can I? Splendid, I'd never have known if you hadn't told me. 'What happened?' he croaked, through a mouthful of phlegm.

'Your friend,' Colsceg said, shaking his head as if he couldn't bring himself to approve of such goings-on. 'He was up among the rocks with us, and he saw what was happening, when the mud trashed the house. Of course, we all told him not to be a bloody fool, but he wouldn't listen, just hared off down the slope before we could grab hold of him. Slippery bugger, always dodging about.'

He stopped, turned his head slightly to the left, nodded. Behind his shoulder, Poldarn could see Colsceg's sons, Barn and Egil. He guessed they were passing on some new development or other.

'Like I was saying,' Colsceg went on, 'this friend of yours, he goes scrambling down the rocks, jumps a good fifteen feet onto a chunk of the old front door that's floating on top of the mud, then what does he do but he hops from one bit of timber to another, like a kid on stepping stones – you wouldn't credit it, I'd never have thought a big man like that could jump so far from a standstill – until he's close enough to reach over and grab you; Elja first, then you, one under each arm like a shepherd carrying lambs. Then of course the stupid fool realises he's stuck, standing there on a piece of sinking wood in the middle of the mudflow holding two people – dead weight both of you, we were sure you'd both drowned or choked to death. But then Egil here, and you could have knocked me over with a broom, I could have sworn he had more sense, Egil here sets off after him, catches up the rope we'd been using to get the kids up onto the rocks, and he goes out after him – not nearly so far, of course, but he gets close enough to throw the rope across, and your mad friend catches it; then Egil chucks the other end to me and Barn here, because of course we had to follow him, didn't we, and to cut a long story short we pulled you out, all four of you bloody maniacs. Amazing, the whole performance, but here you are.'

Poldarn screwed his eyes shut, then opened them again. 'Boarci rescued me,' he said.

'You and Elja,' Colsceg grunted. 'And then Egil rescued him, and we rescued Egil. Bloody miracle nobody was killed, of course. Never seen so many grown men acting so dumb.'

Oh, Poldarn thought. 'Thank you,' he tried to say, but his voice was too weak.

'Sort of rounded things off,' Colsceg was saying, 'us saving you after you saved us. Course, if there's a hero here today, it's got to be you. We'd never have thought of that, going *up* the hill like you said. Sounded like suicide when you said it, but we're bloody glad you did, else we'd all be dead and under the mud right now. Really was a stroke of luck, you showing up like that, and knowing all about volcanoes and mudslides and all.'

Poldarn breathed in slowly, trying to clear his mind. 'Is everybody all right?' he said. 'Did you all manage—?'

'All safe,' Colsceg told him. 'Right down to the old women and the kids, thanks to the rope. Couldn't say whose idea that was, who had the wit to bring it along. Wasn't me, that's for sure.' He chuckled. 'Closest call you ever did see but everybody's alive, nobody's busted up or anything like that, and that's got to be the main thing. Farm's gone, of course, completely fucking buried under all that shit, but so what, big deal. When I was twenty-six years old I started out with nothing but what I could carry on my back, and I can do it again, for sure, doesn't bother me one bit.'

His face told a different story, but Poldarn could hardly comment on that. 'Egil,' he said. 'I want to ask him.'

'What? Oh, right. Egil, he wants to ask you something. Don't tire him out, mind, he needs his rest.'

Egil shuffled forward, looking nervous and very, very wet. 'It wasn't you, it was her,' he said immediately. 'She's my sister, what else was I supposed to do?'

Poldarn nodded. 'I assumed it was something like that,' he said. 'Still, thank you.'

'Oh, that's fine. I owed you a good turn anyhow. So now we're quits, which is good.' He didn't look happy, however; in fact, he looked like a man who'd upset a keepnet full of carp trying to land a small eel. Poldarn got the feeling that if he'd stayed under the mud like he was supposed to have done, it'd have gone a long way towards reconciling Egil to the day's events.

'Suits me,' he said. 'Is Boarci anywhere near? I need to talk to him too.'

'Your friend.' Egil's tone of voice was pretty much the same as his father's. 'He was here a moment ago, then he went off to help with digging the shelter.' He scowled. 'You can tell things are bad, we're letting him help. A man like that.'

A man who saved your sister's life, Poldarn thought; then he added, And mine too, of course. That might well explain it. He wasn't convinced, though; the Colscegsford people just didn't like Boarci, and it seemed that nothing he could do was going to change that. 'Well, when you see him, tell him I'd like to thank him. That's twice he's saved my life. He must like me or something.'

Egil scowled. 'You want to watch him,' he said. 'He'll

make trouble for you if you let him stay around. And what you want is a quiet life.'

'That's true,' Poldarn replied. 'Who doesn't?'

Egil looked at him as if he was trying to be funny. 'Sure,' he replied, 'who doesn't? Of course, all this has been a stroke of luck for you. Oh, I don't mean you planned it or you wanted it to happen, but all the same. Bet you'll be resting easier in your bed from now on, with the farm under all that mud.'

Do I want to know what he means by that? Poldarn decided that, in spite of his better judgement, he probably did. 'Is that so?' he asked quietly. 'Why would that be?'

'Oh, right.' Egil gave him a look of pure hatred. 'I forgot, you lost your memory. Which is really convenient, now that you're back home and you're going to have Haldersness and be the big farmer. You know, I'm sure you're telling the truth and you really don't remember anything, which is just fine by me. And with the valley being buried in this ash and shit, there's really only what you and I remember, nothing else that could ever be a problem. So if you've forgotten, that just leaves me and I'm telling you, I can't remember anything either. In fact, my mind's a complete fucking blank, you know? And keeping it that way would be a very good idea indeed.'

'Egil.' Poldarn reached out quickly and grabbed a handful of Egil's coat. 'You're absolutely right, I have forgotten whatever it is you're talking about, and I keep telling myself that I don't want to know anything – well, anything bad about myself from the past, because I have a nasty feeling there's a lot of that kind of thing, one way or another. But that's not who I am; who I am now, I mean. I've been living with myself for a while, and I'm pretty sure that if I was some kind of evil monster, I'd have noticed. But really.' He let go of Egil's coat. 'Really, I haven't seen any signs of that, I think I'm just a straightforward man who doesn't mean any harm to anybody. At any rate,' he added, looking away, 'that's who I desperately want to be, and I'm pretty sure I can manage it, so long as I'm allowed to get on with it. Does that make any sense to you?'

Egil nodded, and smoothed his rumpled coat. 'It all sounds fair enough to me,' he said sullenly. 'Like, who wants trouble? Nobody. Not me, anyhow. Besides, we've got enough trouble as it is, with the mountain blowing up and losing the farm, that's a whole lifetime's worth all by itself. You think I'm going to stir up a load of old trouble, which'd screw things up for me just as bad as for you, you must be cracked in the head or something. And with you marrying my sister—' He broke off, as though he'd just swallowed something rotten.

'That's right,' Poldarn said gently. 'I'm going to be marrying your sister. We'll be brothers-in-law. I need to know there won't be anything bad to spoil that.'

'Not from me,' Egil said, staring past Poldarn's head. 'I mean, Polden knows I wouldn't have chosen you – I love my sister. But I'm not going to go saying anything and put my own neck on the block, you can bet your life. I may be a lot of things – leastways, I may have been a lot of bad things – but I'm not that dumb.' He was struggling, almost as if he was wrestling with some enemy. 'You take good care of her, you hear? You make sure you treat her right, God help us all, because it's not fair, what she's got stacked up against her, she never did no harm to anybody. So if you – you of all people – if you go treating her wrong, that'd be really bad. And like I said, I won't be telling anything to anybody, but even so I might just find myself killing you one of these days. I mean, I could do that and still nobody would ever know the truth, even if I got caught.'

There was something about his manner that made Poldarn feel very nervous indeed. 'That's interesting,' he said. 'But surely, if you did that, you'd just be swapping one problem for another. And the new one would be far worse, wouldn't it?'

'Sure.' Suddenly Egil grinned. 'Why do you think you're still alive, at that? If I killed you, next morning the whole household'd know what I'd done and I'd really be screwed. But only me, if you get my meaning; and my life's all shit anyhow, it doesn't bother me as much as some other stuff does. It makes no mind really what happens to me, I'd rather stay alive and keep going on, one day to the next, but I figure it's really only force of habit, or instinct or something.' He shook his head. 'Maybe the best thing for everyone'd be if you got your new friend to stick that axe of his in the back of my head some day. Quietly, when nobody's looking. Can't say it'd bother me a whole lot, and you'd really be clear then. Other than that—' He shrugged wearily. 'I've said what I wanted to say,' he continued. 'And you did real good, saving us all from the mudslide, so maybe you're not so bad, at that.' He stopped suddenly and looked up at the sky. 'You know what?' he said. 'It's stopped raining. About time.'

Egil was quite right. 'That's good,' Poldarn said. 'But don't try and change the subject. Can't you try and get it into your stupid thick head, nobody's going to get killed, there's no need for it. It seems to me, if something can be forgotten about so completely that only two people in the whole world know about it, and life goes on, it can't have been all that terrible to start with. God, that sounds all wrong, I know, but let's face facts. We're still alive, we came through the mudslide. I'd be dead if you hadn't risked your life for me, and Colsceg tells me you'd all be dead if I hadn't said go up the slope instead of down into the valley.' He stopped, trying to untangle the mess of unruly thoughts in his head. 'I see it like this,' he said. 'If I'd died that day beside the river, when I woke up and realised I'd lost my whole life up to that point, if whoever bashed my head in had hit me just a little bit harder, then you'd all be dead – half of Haldersness would be dead, too. If Boarci hadn't killed the bear before it got me, you'd be under the mud right now. If I hadn't gone away when I did – same thing, exactly. What I'm trying to say is, if I hadn't done this thing I'm supposed to have done, I'd never have left here, I'd still be one of you. But because I left, I became an outsider, and I came back just when an outsider was needed. Do you see what I'm getting at? If I hadn't done this thing, we'd all be dead because of the volcano or the mountain or the divine Polden, whatever you want to call it, we'd all be dead and there'd be nothing left, just mud and ash and a few burnt-out ruins. Whatever the hell it was that I did, was it so bad that it'd have been worth all our lives for it never to have happened? I don't know,' he said wretchedly, tense with frustration, 'maybe I did something you could never forgive, maybe I killed someone, I really don't want to know. But suppose that's what it was. If I'd never killed whoever it was, he'd be under the mud with the rest of us right now, and what the hell good would that be to anybody?'

Egil shook his head slowly. 'You don't understand,' he said. 'Like I said, you're lucky about the mudslide, and so am I. Let's say we leave it at that. Agreed?'

'Agreed.' Poldarn suddenly felt more tired than he could remember being before. 'Look, if it's all the same to you, would it be all right if I got some rest now? I've had a rather exhausting day and it's going to be a long way to Haldersness without any horses.'

'You do what the bloody hell you like,' Egil said, and walked away.

It would have been a long walk under any circumstances, up steep hills and down again, with the ground either bruising rock or infuriating bog after the torrential rain. Most of the ash and cinders were gone – no prizes for guessing where –

but there were dips and hollows waist-deep in thick black mud; after a near-disaster when they experimented briefly with wading through one of them, they resolved to go round them, even if it meant retracing their steps up a steep-sided combe. Poldarn did his best to walk on his own, but after the fifth or sixth unexpected detour his legs gave out completely and he sat down suddenly and hard in the grey shale of a particularly steep escarpment, after which Boarci grabbed him round the waist and wrenched an arm across his enormous shoulders. After an hour or so of trying to keep pace with Boarci's enormous strides Poldarn wasn't entirely sure that his new friend's help was making things any easier for him, but at least he kept moving, having no other option.

Covering the whole distance in one day proved to be out of the question, and they ended up spending the night huddled in the nominal shelter of a solitary thorn tree with an absurdly bowed and twisted trunk. It didn't take long for them to figure out how it had got that way; the wind was cold and brisk, and of course they had nothing in the way of blankets or even coats, while all their attempts to make a fire proved to be fatuous—

('You have a go,' Colsceg muttered at one point, dumping an inadequate bundle of scavenged twigs in Poldarn's lap. 'You're supposed to be a blacksmith, you should be good at starting a fire.')

In spite of the cold, and hunger that was steadily getting harder to ignore, and the general wretchedness of everything, Poldarn fell asleep – at least, he assumed he must have done, because he woke up with a horribly cramped back, pins and needles in both feet and a dreadful ache in his arms and shoulders to remind him of how he'd spent the previous day. The only way he could get up from the ground was by rolling onto his side and pulling himself slowly up the tree with his hands, which had clamped tight shut during the night and had to be prised open, like scallops. He took so long about it that they very nearly left without him.

The second day was much like the first, only worse; the hills seemed to get steeper, the ash-mud bogs more frequent, the wind harder and colder. When they passed the place where Boarci had killed the bear, it seemed to Poldarn like he was revisiting a scene from his childhood, a time long ago and wonderfully happy and carefree, when his whole life was still in front of him and he still had a horse.

'Fat lot of good it did you,' he said to Boarci, who was still hustling him along like a sheaf of cut corn.

'What are you talking about?'

'That horse I gave you, for saving me from the bear.'

Boarci shrugged. 'Serves you right for being too generous,' he replied. 'I could've told you at the time no good'd come of it.'

Faced with a choice between staggering painfully along on his own two feet and listening to much more of that sort of thing, Poldarn decided he preferred the pain. 'It's all right,' he said, wriggling out of Boarci's grip, 'I'm feeling much better now, I can walk on my own. Thanks all the same,' he added.

'Suit yourself,' Boarci grunted. 'I could do without you treading on my feet every third step, that's for sure.'

Poldarn slowed down, letting him get safely ahead, and this brought him up level with Elja, who was also walking on her own. He hadn't spoken to her since the mudslide, and she hadn't come near him; he wondered if there was anything wrong between them, or whether it was just a point of etiquette.

'So,' he said, 'how are you feeling?'

'Tired,' she replied.

He nodded. 'Me too,' he said. 'I feel like I've been walking my whole life. Still, it's not much further now.'

She frowned. 'Yes, it is,' she said. 'That's Riderfell over

there, and down in the dip is Fleot's Water, so at this rate we won't get there till just before dark, if we're lucky.'

'True,' Poldarn admitted. 'I was just trying to cheer you up.'

'Oh.' She looked at him. 'By telling me a lie?'

'Well, the truth's pretty depressing,' he said. 'Any bloody fool can tell you the truth and make you feel miserable.'

Elja stared at him for a moment, then laughed. 'I suppose so,' she said. 'You know, you're strange.'

'Thank you. That's probably the nicest thing anybody's ever said about me.'

'Really?'

'No,' he explained, 'that was a joke.'

'Another lie? To make me feel cheerful?'

'That's right. Oh, come on,' he added, 'you people have jokes, I've heard you making them.'

'I know. I was teasing you, but you seem to be a bit slow on the uptake today.'

It crossed Poldarn's mind that he might have been better off sticking with Boarci. 'You're probably right,' he said. 'It was getting soaked to the skin the day before yesterday – I think I'm brewing up a really high-class cold. The silly thing is, I can't remember having had one before. Weird at my time of life, having my first cold.'

'You'll get the hang of it pretty quickly, I'm sure. I expect it's like swimming, it'll all come back to you once you start.'

He shrugged. 'Maybe,' he said. 'Still, you could help me get into the right frame of mind. What comes first?'

Elja thought for a moment. 'Usually,' she said, 'you start off with a blocked nose, maybe a cough, some slight deafness even. A general feeling that your head's been stuffed full of unbleached wool.'

'That sounds familiar,' he said, stumbling over a rock but recovering his balance quite well. 'What about a slight headache? Is that orthodox?'

'It's not unknown, certainly,' she said. 'Though I'd tend to look for that in the next phase, along with the heavy sneezing, the runny nose, bleary eyes, that sort of thing.'

Poldarn pulled a face. 'So that's what I've got to look forward to,' he said. 'And do you get those things as well as the earlier stuff, the coughing and so on, or does one stop and the next one start?'

'Oh no, they all happen at the same time. Though sometimes you'll find that the runny nose clears up but the cough gets much worse. Followed,' she added, 'by a really horrible sore throat. That's a nasty combination, believe me.'

'I'm sure,' Poldarn said despondently. 'All right, so we've got as far as the sore throat. Then what?'

She sighed. 'Downhill all the way from there,' she said sadly. 'Next your arms and legs swell right up, you get these horrible blisters breaking out all over your skin, followed by massive internal bleeding, blackouts, madness and finally death. And that's assuming it doesn't go bad on you and turn into pneumonia.'

'Ah.' He bit his lip tragically. 'So how long do you think I've got? Give it to me straight, I can take it.'

She looked at him. 'A case like yours, I'd say three days, four at the very most. It's sad, really. I'd have enjoyed living at Haldersness.'

'Would you?' He heard something in his own voice, and quickly changed tack. 'You seem to know an awful lot about colds,' he said. 'Have you ever had one yourself?'

'Me? Loads of them.'

'And did you die?'

'Every time.'

He nodded. 'Well, in that case I guess you know what you're talking about.'

After that there was a slight awkwardness between them, as though one or the other of them had gone maybe a step too far, but neither was quite sure which of them it had been. Shortly after that, they came up against the worst quagmire

yet: between two escarpments was a small, steep-sided
defile that had completely filled up with mud. After standing and scowling at it for quite some time, they faced up to
the fact that there was no way round it except going back
down the road for half an hour and taking a long, gruelling
detour up the back face of the western slope.

'Marvellous,' Elja sighed as they trudged uphill. 'Now
we've got no chance of getting there before it gets dark.'

Poldarn would've said something extremely coarse if he
could've spared the breath. 'I don't like the idea of crashing
around in the dark,' he said. 'We could walk into one of
those bogs before we knew what'd hit us.'

'That's right,' Elja said. 'So I expect we'll end up sleeping
out again. I used to love doing that when I was a kid, but now
I'm not so keen.'

'I wouldn't mind if I had a blanket, or if there was anything we could make a fire with,' Poldarn groaned. 'It's bad
enough now with this wind. Once the sun goes down, it's
going to be *really* bloody cold.'

'I thought you were supposed to be telling me nice, cheerful things.'

'Yes, but they wouldn't be true.'

Elja furrowed her brows in studied thought. 'Truth is a
wonderful thing,' she said, 'and so is pea soup. You can get
tired of both of them if you never have anything else.'

They tried very hard to make up time, but it was pointless;
all they succeeded in doing was getting almost within sight of
Haldersness by the time it got too dark for any more trekking
to be safe. This time there wasn't even one lonely thorn tree
to sit under, so they had to make do with a small heap of
rocks, the remnants of a long derelict cairn. The shelter it
gave them from the wind was minimal verging on imaginary, but it felt better than sleeping out on the bare hillside,
even if they did get just as cold and (when it rained briefly,
around the middle of the night) wet.

As soon as they stopped, Elja went off without a word and joined the women on the other side of the cairn, leaving Poldarn on his own. He didn't mind that too much; he'd been in company of one sort or another all day, and one of the few things he was enjoying about this forced march was the occasional moment of solitude. It was undeniably pleasant to be able to crouch down on the ground a few paces away from the others and clear his mind at last, since he had a great deal to think about. He didn't manage it, though, since within a few heartbeats of getting moderately comfortable and closing his eyes, he was fast asleep.

When he woke up, his head was full of small pieces of a very unpleasant dream. He made a conscious effort to sweep them away, though he had a feeling that a few of them were still lurking in the inaccessible cracks and corners of his mind, like the last few tiny splinters of broken potsherd after you've dropped a plate or a cup, the ones you find with the soles of your bare feet three months later. It was broad daylight already, and there was a fine spray of moisture in the air, either a wet fog or low cloud. His knees and calves ached as he put his weight on them. Not far to go now, he told himself; but that was definitely another case of telling lies in order to cheer himself up – necessarily pointless when he was both the teller and the audience.

Long before Poldarn saw the farm, he located it by the mob of crows circling in the grey sky. He knew them pretty well by now; someone had walked them off their feed, and they were waiting for him to go away. He wasn't sure what they could have been feeding on; either a newly sown field or a dead animal, he guessed, but there was no way of telling which at this distance. He hoped it was the former, of course, since all the livestock should be a long way away by now, and sowing would imply that the rain had washed off the ash and life was getting back to normal. Typical crows, he told himself, to be so annoyingly ambiguous. He was relieved when he came close enough to distinguish the brown of newly turned earth directly underneath the cloud of slowly drifting black dots. It was going to be hard enough, with all these extra mouths to feed.

Needless to say, the Haldersness household was ready and waiting for them when they trudged down the last slope into the yard. He saw Eyvind and Rannwey and Rook and Scaptey, and Asburn at the back, looking anxious; no sign of Halder, which was odd.

'And another thing.' Boarci was at his side, almost protective, like a bodyguard. 'I lost all my kit back there, when the house got swamped. I'm not fussed about the rest of it, but it's a bloody shame about my axe. It was a good one, too, I'd had it for years.'

'No problem,' Poldarn replied, managing to keep the irritation out of his voice. 'I'll get our smith to make you a new one. He does good work, you'll be pleased.'

Boarci shrugged. 'Whatever,' he said. 'But it's a pity, all the same. Belonged to my father, about the only nice thing he ever had.'

Oh shut up, for crying out loud. 'I'll get Asburn on making you a new one straight away,' he said. 'And anything else you want, you just say the word, all right?'

'Like I said, I'm not bothered,' Boarci replied dolefully. 'I mean, when it comes right down to it, it's only stuff, right?'

Talking of stuff: behind the reception committee he could see a great stack of barrels and boxes and bundles, along with most of the major items of furniture – tables, benches, lamp stands, his grandfather's dining chair. There was no sign of any damage to the house, or indeed of any mud in the yard or the surrounding area, so it seemed odd that all the contents of the house should be packed up and outside.

Nobody on either side said anything until the two households were facing each other (like a mirror, Poldarn couldn't help thinking; they were practically identical in numbers and composition). At least he'd be spared the chore of explaining what had happened, thanks to the mind-reading business. He might have to fill in a few details, but he was certain they knew the broad outlines already.

Eyvind took a step forward and cleared his throat, rather self-consciously. 'Halder's dead,' he said.

Chapter Eleven

'Oh,' Poldarn said; and then, because that sounded crass and uncaring, he asked, 'How did it happen?', although he wasn't really in any hurry to hear the answer. Mostly, he discovered, he was extremely annoyed, as if his opponent in some game had unexpectedly outwitted him with a move that was within the letter of the rules but nevertheless was still extremely bad form. Who the opponent was – Halder himself, or Destiny, the divine Polden even – he wasn't really sure.

'Heart,' Eyvind replied. 'When the rain washed the mud down into the river, we'd left some tools and stuff; he went out with some of the men to see if they could salvage anything. Seyward got stuck in the mud up to his knees and Halder was trying to pull him out when he collapsed and fell down. By the time they got him back to the house, he was dead.'

Seyward was standing in the second row, looking absurdly solemn but otherwise none the worse for wear, so obviously they'd managed to get him out at some point. If he'd been in danger, then Halder's death was probably heroic, or at least meaningful. Otherwise it was a bloody stupid way to go, on account of some manky old tools.

Poldarn pulled himself together. As usual, he didn't know the correct procedures, but he guessed that the first step would be offering his commiserations to the widow. He turned to Rannwey. 'I'm so sorry,' he said.

But she only looked puzzled. 'Why?' she said. 'It wasn't your fault. You weren't even here. And who's that next to you? I don't know him.'

Poldarn had to think before he replied. 'This is Boarci,' he said. 'He's a friend of mine. Actually, he saved my life, twice.'

As far as he could tell from Rannwey's face, that wasn't enough to justify cluttering the place up with strangers. 'He staying, or moving on?' she asked.

Boarci started to say something, but Poldarn forestalled him. 'He'll be staying,' he said. 'With all these extra mouths to feed, one more won't make any odds.'

Rannwey made a small sighing noise in the back of her mouth, but didn't say anything. Poldarn hoped that that meant the subject was closed. 'So when did he die?' he asked.

'The day before yesterday,' Eyvind replied. 'About mid-morning.'

'I see.' He was about to ask about the funeral arrangements, but then he realised that he hadn't the faintest idea how these people (his people) disposed of their dead. For all he knew, they buried them in hollow trees, or ate them. Well; this was Eyvind he was talking to, albeit in front of several dozen witnesses. Eyvind knew how ignorant he was. 'You're going to have to tell me what happens about funerals,' he said. 'I'm afraid I don't know.'

Eyvind looked at him, and for a moment he was afraid he'd said something wrong, again. Then he realised that he'd used a foreign word. 'Funeral,' he repeated. 'It means any ceremonies or that sort of thing, when someone dies. Also, what happens to the body. You know,' he added, unrealistically hopeful.

Eyvind thought for a moment. 'Well,' he said, and Poldarn could feel him treading carefully, 'we put the body in the dungheap yesterday morning. Did you want to look at it – I mean, is there something you want to do?' Poldarn didn't need to be a mind-reader to sense the waves of embarrassment. 'I don't know how they do these things where you've been living,' he said. 'I'm sorry.'

'No, that's fine,' Poldarn said quickly, much to Eyvind's evident relief. So, that was that, then; the dead went in with the vegetable peelings and the horseshit, where they could perform one last function for the community. Reasonable enough, and absolutely consistent; certainly no worse than the pile of scrap metal in the corner of Asburn's smithy. It was all just a matter of shape-changing and memory, after all. 'So,' he went on, terribly brisk and businesslike, 'what happens now?'

Eyvind grinned bleakly. 'There's a question,' he said. 'Well, for a start, you've got to build your house. We've got all the furniture and stuff packed up and out already, so the next step is felling the lumber. Really we ought to get moving on that right away, before it starts raining again; we can store all the house contents in the middle barn, but it's going to be cramped in there, and now we've got to find somewhere for them to sleep—' He nodded very slightly towards the Colscegsford people, who didn't seem to have moved since they'd arrived. 'Of course, with them to lend a hand we'll be able to get the job done much quicker, which is a blessing. We'll be a bit short on tools, but that shouldn't be too much of a problem.'

Poldarn nodded, as if all this made perfect sense to him. 'And then what?' he said.

'Well, after your house is built, the next job'll be to tear down the old one. After that, once we've stacked the lumber—'

'Just a moment,' Poldarn interrupted. 'Surely it'd make better sense for Colsceg and his people to move into the old house. I mean, it seems a bit pointless to dismantle a perfectly good house and leave them camping out in the barns or wherever until they can put it back up again. Not to mention the lack of storage space for us,' he added quickly, hoping that this would constitute a suitably utilitarian line of argument. 'I quite understand that it's not the way it's usually done, but with things the way we are, it'd probably be sensible to stay flexible, if you see what I mean.'

Eyvind looked at him with undisguised dismay in his face. 'If that's what you want to do,' he said, 'that's up to you. After all, you're the farmer now.'

Yes, but what the hell does that actually mean? 'We don't have to decide that right now,' Poldarn said. 'I think it'd be a good idea if we all sat down and had something to eat. It's been a long, hard walk and I for one am absolutely famished.'

Rannwey nodded. 'There's fresh bread and cheese in the long barn,' she said. 'We baked the bread this morning for you. We're just drawing off a couple of pins of beer, and there's some stew warming up in the cider house.' She sounded tired – all that extra work, as if they didn't have enough to put up with – but that was all. For a woman who'd just lost her husband, it was simply bizarre. Even if she'd hated Halder solidly for fifty years, she ought to have been showing pleasure, or at least relief; but a normal person would've displayed more emotion over the demise of a favourite pair of shoes. Poldarn decided it was yet another aspect of the mind-reading thing – but that didn't really follow, because logically the entire household should have been as distraught as the widow herself, and nobody seemed particularly upset, just a little more pompously solemn than usual. He wondered how he could ever have lived among these people. When he'd been one of them, had he been like this? Come to that, was this what he really was – incapable of basic human feelings? That didn't seem likely, because even as he ran these speculations through his mind, he could feel a great wave of pain surging up inside him, like a volcano building up to an explosion, as he realised that he'd loved Halder, somehow and in a fashion he couldn't define; that without him he was completely lost, washed ashore on an unknown island populated by incomprehensible strangers.

'That's just fine,' he said, and that seemed to be the cue for the reception party to break up and get back to work, while Rannwey led the way to the long barn.

Poldarn felt ashamed as he ate, because the food tasted wonderful after two days of hungry trudging. As he stuffed bread and stewed beef into his face, he couldn't keep his mind off the obscure conundrum that these people represented; until he thought of the crows circling over the house, and it struck him that when one of their number died, they reacted in much the same way – no grief or heartbreak, just a slight readjustment of their order and patterns of flight, a closing-up of the gap that the dead individual had filled, so that within a few moments it was as if he'd never existed. That was the strength of the crows' organisation – it could lose a member or take back a straggler who'd been away for many years, without any noticeable disruption. Perhaps that was why killing them had been so fascinating; you could kill a hundred of them, and there'd still be just as many left, because really there was only one of them, as immortal as a god—

(And what else should a god be but undying, present everywhere that one part of Him happened to be, a single consciousness vested in the heart of a cloud of unimportant bodies? Killing crows was like trying to kill a river by drowning it. By that token, Halder wasn't dead; because Halder was the farmer at Haldersness, and there was still a farmer here, the only difference being in the small matter of his name, Ciartan. Ciartan, Poldarn thought: that's me. And a name is just an aid to memory, and memory washes out in fire the way dye washes out in water.)

'I'll say this for your outfit, the grub's not bad.' He hadn't noticed that Boarci was still next to him. 'The beer's a bit thin, mind, but you can't have everything in this life. Pass those boiled eggs.'

Boarci could swallow boiled eggs whole, provided he had enough beer to wash them down with. 'Why do you do that?' Poldarn asked, after he'd repeated the procedure for the fifth time.

'Don't like the taste,' Boarci replied. 'If you just gulp 'em down, you don't have to taste 'em. I was at a place once, they used to preserve eggs in vinegar. Didn't taste any better, but they tasted different, if you see what I mean.'

'I expect you've seen a lot of interesting things on your travels,' Poldarn said, spearing an egg before they all vanished.

'Not really,' Boarci replied. 'Once you've seen one farm, you've seen 'em all. Mind you, I did go raiding one year, when I was able to get a berth on a ship. We were away three months. But all you see when you're on that lark is a lot of open country and a few burnt-down towns. All places are pretty much the same, really.'

Or if they aren't to start with, they are when *you're* through with them. 'You may well be right,' Poldarn answered mildly. 'So, you'll be sticking around, then.'

'Not up to me,' Boarci replied with his mouth full. 'I hang around till they tell me to piss off. Some places it takes longer than others, that's all. But then, places don't really matter much. My old dad used to say, it's not where you are but who you are. Wouldn't go that far myself, but I suppose he had a point.'

'It sounds pretty convincing to me,' Poldarn said. 'What don't you agree with?'

'Ah.' Boarci swallowed, and gulped some more beer. 'I see it another way. I say, it's not where you are or who you are, it's *what* you are. Everything else can be fixed, so it doesn't actually matter a toss. Like, you can take a piece of iron, like an axle or a fireback, and you can make it into any bloody thing, but you can't turn it into brass. You get what I'm saying?'

Poldarn nodded. 'I don't really understand them,' he said, 'these people, I mean. You'd have thought it'd have meant something to them, my grandfather dying like that. But they don't seem to care.'

Boarci laughed. 'Of course not,' he said. 'They've got you now.'

'In which case, I'm truly sorry for them. I don't know spit about running a farm.'

'*They* do,' Boarci said. 'And unless you're as thick as mud, you'll let 'em get on with it and keep your nose out of what doesn't concern you. You've got other things to do, remember; you've got a house to build, and this business with the mountain – somebody said you know all about that, from being abroad.'

Poldarn sighed. 'Look,' he said, 'all I know is that in the empire, mountains that blow up are called volcanoes. That's it, really.'

Boarci shook his head. 'Don't think so,' he replied. 'Else how come you knew exactly what to do when the mud started coming down back at Colscegsford? You know a hell of a lot more about this shit than you're letting on, but if you don't want to share, that's no skin off my nose.'

For some reason, Poldarn found this infuriating. 'I said the first thing that came into my head,' he said. 'By some miracle, it turned out to be the right thing to do. It could just as easily have got us all killed.'

But Boarci only smiled. 'Maybe you don't know what you know,' he said, picking up a bone and gnawing it messily.

'People tell me I'm as weird as a bucketful of snails, but you're something else, believe me. It's like there's two of you, and they hate each other. I've seen married couples like that, been together forty years and spend their lives trying to jerk each other around, but they've grown so close you can hardly see where one ends and the other begins. God only knows what this lot make of you. But that's their problem, isn't it?'

'And mine,' Poldarn muttered. 'But I'm telling you the truth, I don't know any more than you do about volcanoes—'

'What?'

Poldarn closed his eyes. 'Volcano. It's the foreign word for exploding mountains.'

'Ah, right.' Boarci nodded. 'Of course, back where I grew up we had a different word.'

That made Poldarn sit bolt upright. 'You know about the bloody things?'

'Well.' Boarci frowned. 'Wouldn't say that, exactly. But my mother's cousin – we used to stay with them a few weeks each year in summer, to help out with the threshing and stuff – she used to tell a story about how a mountain blew up back in the old country.'

'Morevich.'

'What?'

'Morevich. It used to be part of the empire. Where we came from originally.'

Boarci shrugged. 'Is that so? Never heard it called that before, it was always the old country or back home. Anyhow, who gives a stuff, it's all ancient history anyhow. Point is, she had this story – mind, she was ninety and blind as a bat and a little bit daft in the head most of the time, and she dribbled her soup all down her front, but she loved to tell this yarn about how there was a big mountain right above the biggest city in the old country, and how one day a god came by in an old carrier's cart and told them the world was about to end. 'Course, they didn't believe him, because who ever heard of a real god rattling round the lanes in a dirty old cart, but the day after he'd passed through, the mountain burst open all down one side and burning shit came pouring down off it like molten metal out of a busted crucible, and the sky was so full of ash you couldn't see three feet in front of your nose, and the whole city was covered in the burning shit and that was the end of them.' He paused and wiped gravy out of his beard. 'There was a whole load more stuff to it than that,' he added. 'It had a regular story to it, with heroes and villains, and it was all somebody's fault for doing some bloody stupid thing, but I can't remember all that now, I reckon she made it up out of her head to make the yarn more interesting. Anyway, in her story the blowing-up mountain was always called Polden's Furnace, and that was the name of the god in the cart. There was some kind of woman involved in it, too – a witch or something – but you know what they're like, storytellers, they'll chuck in any old rubbish.'

Poldarn nodded. 'Like you said,' he replied. 'Though it's interesting, because when I was a kid, my grandfather told me this mountain used to be called Polden's Forge.'

'Well, there you go,' Boarci said, yawning. 'Practically the same thing, though you would know more about that side of things, you being a blacksmith. Though for what it's worth, furnace sounds more like it to me, because you melt stuff down in a furnace, like with the molten rock. Don't suppose there's more than a grain of truth in it, because most of these old tales are just a load of bullshit.'

After they'd eaten and the tables had been put away (they had to stack them diagonally in a corner, on top of a feed bin) the rest of the household dissolved like a morning fog, leaving Poldarn and the Colscegsford people to their own devices. As far as Poldarn was concerned, this meant sleep; if he was now the master of Haldersness, soon to be Ciartanswhatever, he could give himself permission to take the rest of the day off, which he did. Rather ostentatiously, he picked out a blanket, climbed up into the loft and made himself as comfortable as a human being can be while lying on bundles of unthreshed thatching reed. Typically, however, he couldn't get to sleep, even though he was dismally tired, so he lay on his side watching the others for a while, figuring that the sight of a parcel of these people (his people) sitting around with nothing specific to do would be enough to send any-body to sleep, overtired or not. It turned out to be a rather remarkable spectacle, because all they did was sit perfectly still, like birds roosting in a tree – conserving their energy, just as you'd expect with such perfectly efficient creatures. Most of them squatted on the floor, their hands folded in their laps, eyes open (in case of predators, presumably); one or two remained standing, by the door and the window, acting as the sentries for the rest of the flock. Nobody spoke, but Poldarn could tell they were engaged in a slow, quiet debate about something or other, anything from their future in their new environment to the proportion of rosemary to chives in the stew. He wondered about himself, roosting apart from the main body; was it useful to the community to have one far-flung sentry disconnected from the rest, a sep-arate mind constituting a back-up or fail-safe (knowing about volcanoes and what to do in the event of mudslides, because unexpected natural disasters and acts of the god in the cart are predators too, in their fashion), and if so, how had they ever managed to cope before he came home? But there was Boarci, just as separate as he was though in a less acceptable way. He was sitting astride a post vice-bolted to a beam set into the wall, and he was whittling something out of a bit of bone he'd saved from his dinner – something for himself, a purely selfish concern, contributing nothing to the well-being of the community. Confounded parasite, no wonder he's not welcome anywhere . . .

Poldarn drifted into sleep without realising, and had a dream in which he held a slow, quiet debate of his own

with someone he couldn't usually see. Whether or not anything useful was achieved he couldn't remember when he
woke up, which defeated the object of the exercise; it was
pitch dark, the door being bolted and the windows shuttered, and he could hear the busy sound of the two
households breathing in their sleep. It was annoying to be
awake and suddenly restless, out of time and step with
everyone else. Even if there was anything for him to do he
couldn't have done it: the floor was completely covered
with sleepers so he couldn't have got to the door without
treading on a dozen people; so he sat up and tried hard not
to fidget, searching for something to occupy his mind. But
the only thoughts he could come up with were uncomfortable ones, mostly to do with how different he was – asleep
when they were awake, awake when they were asleep,
perched up above them in the reed like a god or a nocturnal
carrion-feeder. He couldn't make out faces or identities in
the general sprawl of sleepers, but he reckoned that the
raw, vibrant snore coming from the far left corner could
only be coming from Boarci (like a cross-cut saw ripping
into green timber, with just a suggestion of an axe being
sharpened on a clogged grindstone). He closed his eyes and
tried to isolate different breathers – the head of a household
should be able to identify his people even in the dark – but
it was like trying to pick out the sound of one specific wave
breaking on a beach. He wondered; are they all dreaming
the same dream, are they all at the same point in the same
dream, do they dream at all or are they still in session, gradually debating their way down a long, comprehensive
agenda, like monks in chapter? He thought of how horses
and hawks slept with their eyes open, and wondered
whether these people (his people, now more than ever)
actually slept at all, or whether when their eyes were closed
their one shared mind was still awake, slowly chewing and
digesting facts into policies.

As Poldarn was turning this proposition over in his mind, he realised that someone was standing over him. That was strange – he hadn't heard anyone moving about and there was no other way up into the loft except by the ladder. Old instincts made his right hand twitch, but he made himself turn round slowly.

'You should be asleep,' Halder said. 'You've got a busy day tomorrow.'

You're dead, he thought. But not as dead as all that, apparently. 'I know,' he replied, though he couldn't hear himself speak. 'But you know how it is. I'm wide awake now.'

Halder nodded. 'I used to get that,' he said. 'Then I'd get to fidgetting, and that'd wake Rannwey up – she hated being woken up in the middle of the night. So we'd both be lying there, wide awake, sulking at each other, till it was morning and we could get up.' He sighed. 'I think it's something to do with the job,' he went on, 'being awake while the rest of 'em are asleep. Truth is, and don't ask me to explain it because I never was one of your deep thinkers, but there's times when you've got to be awake or else they wouldn't be able to sleep. Only when that happens, it's because there's something important on; and in your case, I don't see how it could apply, since you can't hear them.'

'I know,' Poldarn replied. 'I hate that.'

Halder nodded. 'It's going to be a real problem,' he said unhappily. 'Its a bloody shame you haven't been able to get it sorted out yet. Sooner or later you're going to have to, or else this place is going to grind to a halt. It'd be like when someone has a stroke, the body and the brain can't talk to each other. Can't have that, especially now, with the mountain – what was that word of yours again?'

'Volcano.'

'That's right,' Halder said. 'Fact is, I'm starting to forget things. You'd know all about that, of course. I can see now, it can't be easy for you.'

Poldarn frowned. 'What sort of things can't you remember?'

Halder laughed. 'I've forgotten. Which is a bugger, because it's like they never existed, and there's a lot of stuff I should've told you, but I could never make you hear. Won't be long now before it's all gone, and you'll really be on your own – no disrespect to your grandmother, she's a wonderful woman, salt of the earth, but it was never her business to know that sort of thing, so she'll be no help to you at all.'

'I see,' Poldarn said. 'How long do you think it'll be before you've forgotten it all?'

'Depends,' Halder replied. 'If the ground's wet, obviously much sooner than if it's dry. I'd give it a couple of months, this time of year, and then there'll be nothing left but a few bones, and they won't be much use to you, I'm afraid.' He shook his head. 'Everything loses its memory sooner or later, even if you don't melt it or bash it with a hammer it'll rust or rot or just fall apart and turn into dust; and then it's off and away, you'll never get it back again.' He smiled grimly. 'Sometimes it's just as well, other times it's a waste, but there's no getting away from it. You can't put anything back together again, all you can do is make something completely new using the bits of the old one. In your case, that's as close to hope as you're likely to get, though I have a feeling that you're like a really clever craftsman, you can make the same thing identical, over and over again. Which reminds me, you really have got to stick to the blacksmithing now that you're the head man around here. Asburn—' He made a vague gesture. 'He's a bloody good smith, don't get me wrong, but it's not his place, it's yours. You'll see exactly what I mean by that, sooner than you think, and then you'll understand why I've been banging on about it all this time. I wish I could have explained, but you couldn't hear me. You'll just have to take my word for it.'

Poldarn pulled a face. 'Yes, all right,' he said, 'I'll try and fit it in, when I'm not building houses or dodging mudslides. Was there something important, or did you come back from the dead just to nag me about my homework?'

'You shouldn't talk to me like that, it's not respectful. And yes, there was something. There's a whole lot of stuff, and if you'll just shut up for a moment I can tell you—'

Poldarn opened his eyes. He'd fallen asleep after all (and he'd done it in such a way as to crick his neck and his back and put his right arm to sleep; hardly a good start to a busy day) and now daylight was seeping through the bald patches in the thatch, thinning and curdling the darkness. What's the betting I'm the last to wake up, as usual? But not this time: down below in the main body of the barn, the household was just beginning to stir, all at the same time. It was an extraordinary sight, to see so many people waking up at precisely the same moment. Well, I was right about that, he told himself, though that doesn't make it any the less weird. I really don't want to know why they do that.

He stood up, and his legs were stiff and cramped; he had to steady himself, or he'd have fallen out of the loft and broken his neck. He closed his eyes to get rid of a brief moment of dizziness; and when he opened them again, he realised that he knew what he had to do today. All of it, the whole thing, as if he'd known it all along and only just remembered it (but he hadn't, he was sure of that; if this was a memory, it wasn't one of his).

Just as well, really, he said to himself, otherwise it'd have been really embarrassing. His legs felt much better now, and he scrambled down the ladder like a twelve-year-old. For the first time in a long while, he actually felt cheerful and confident about the day ahead, because he knew what he was supposed to be doing and knew how to do it. Of course, he reflected, this is what it's like for them every bloody day of their lives, no wonder they're always so damned smug. Feeling like this, there's absolutely nothing you couldn't do, it'd be like you're omnipotent. This is what it must be like if you're a god.

He knew who to look for first; Autcel, one of the Colscegsford men, and Horn, the Haldersness cooper and wheelwright, were the best tool-grinders in the two households, and he needed them to put an edge on the axes, hooks and adzes they'd be using today. He ran his gaze round the barn and saw them, yawning and stretching on their way to the door, which someone else had already unbolted and opened. They would go and start up the big treadle grindstone in the middle house, and by the time they'd finished, the rest of them would be kitted up and ready to make a start. What else would they need? Shovels and picks, which Raffen and Carey would fetch from the trap-house, and baskets – Rannwey and Jelda would see to them – and a line and a basin of water, of course, he'd get them himself, he knew where they were kept. For a moment, he fancied that he could see the whole job, every detail of it from beginning to end, all at the same time (like an illuminated manuscript chained to the desk in a sword-monks' monastery, where scenes from the beginning and the middle and the end are all played out in the same picture against the same background, with three identical heroes – one of them hearing the call of religion, one of them killing the dragon, one of them suffering martyrdom thirty years later in a different city five hundred miles away).

Easy, Poldarn said to himself, piece of cake, slice of duff, child's play. I could do this standing on my head. I can remember it like it was yesterday, from the last time—

(—the last time I did this? But it's a once-in-a-lifetime event, that's the whole point.)

Beer, he thought, we'll need plenty of that, and cold beef and cold smoked lamb and bread and cheese, can't expect men to work hard on an empty stomach (and he saw the Haldersness women packing up food in baskets, out in the cider house, filling a row of half-gallon barrels with beer from a newly tapped hogshead; he could see the beer was bright and clean, which meant it must have been racked and fined and left to settle at least a week ago, and how the hell had they known to do that, when Halder was still very much alive and showing no signs of being about to die?). Of course there'll be at least one thing we'll find we haven't remembered when we get there, and we'll have to send someone running back for it while we all stand around waiting; that's inevitable, it wouldn't be right unless that happened, it'd be bad luck on the house or something. But it'd be nice if we could keep it down to the one token forgotten thing.

At the back of Poldarn's mind there was a memory, a genuine one; he could feel it, like a bone stuck in his throat or a fibre of meat lodged between his teeth, but he couldn't prise it loose. It was infuriating, because he was sure it was something relevant (just as the one piece of steel you can't seem to find in the scrap pile would undoubtedly be just the right width and thickness for the job in hand, and the more you search for it, the more clearly you can picture it in your mind's eye; and nine times out of ten, when you come across it by chance a week later, after you've used something else, it turns out that it wouldn't have been suitable at all, it was just your imagination playing games with you). But as he worried away at it, he could feel it growing vague and flimsy, as if he was trying to pick up a page that had burned to ash.

Chapter Twelve

It must have rained heavily in the early hours of the morning, after Poldarn had fallen asleep for the second time, because the grass was very wet, soaking through their boots as they made their way down the combe to the wood. Nobody seemed unduly troubled by that; it was a pleasure to see it again, after what had seemed like a lifetime of staring at a carpet of black ash. As soon as the sun was up, of course, it'd all dry out in no time. Every indication suggested a fine, bright day, warm but not so hot as to make heavy work a burden. They walked quickly, gradually speeding up as they got closer to their objective. Two large crows shadowed them all the way from Haldersness to where the river bent just before they reached the wood, and then pulled off in a wide circle, as if they were expecting to be shot at.

The first job, needless to say, was a solid stone platform for a foundation. Poldarn didn't need to bother with troublesome mental arithmetic; they would need ten cartloads of double-hand-span wide flat stones, which they should be able to find in the bed of the river just before and after the bend; failing which, there was always the old fallen-down linhay two-thirds of the way up the slope, but it'd be savagely hard work to ship them down from there. Far easier to grovel around in the water for a few hours.

Picking the stones and building the foundation turned out to be a miserable job, which wasn't helped by the heavy rain that set in at mid-morning and carried on till just before sunset. There was also the small detail of how long and wide the foundation should be. Since all four sills were still growing up out of the ground with needles on their branches, they were left with three choices; guess, or fell the sill-trees early, or climb up the shortest trees with a piece of string and measure the wretched things.

'We fell them,' Poldarn decided. 'Like we should be doing with all the timbers, only we seem to have started in the middle instead of at the beginning. Stands to reason, you cut and shape before you build the foundation.'

So they chopped down the four sill-trees, trimmed them to length and pared off the branches; 'We'll leave roughhewing till tomorrow,' he said. 'I don't want to commit myself to dimensions more than I have to until I've got an idea of what shape this thing's going to be.'

The others could see his point; so they left the timbers in the bark and finished off the foundation, laying the last few stones just before dark. 'It'll do,' Poldarn announced, after he'd inspected it. The rest of the party were relieved. 'It'll do' in Poldarn's terms had turned out to mean that the work was irreproachably perfect; corners exactly square, levels checked with a stick floating in a bowl of water. If it had been a little out of true, not exactly right but good enough, Poldarn realised that he was perfectly capable of making them pull it all apart and do it again by torchlight. The things you find out about yourself when suddenly you're the one making the decisions, he thought. It left him feeling a little uncomfortable. Somehow, they'd been shifting away from the gloriously clear picture he'd had in his mind first thing that morning; a detail here, a measurement there slightly adjusted to save an hour's gruelling work with adze and drawknife, but every change knocked on, requiring two slight modifications to this piece or that, an extra wedge or a jowled post instead of a plain one. No big deal, nothing to worry about; but he could feel himself starting to drift, the perfect cutting edge of his earlier clarity gradually growing dull with every expedient compromise. It was annoying, not the way it ought to be. Illogical; but Poldarn couldn't help thinking that if someone else was doing the job, it wouldn't be getting out of hand like this.

An hour or thereabouts before it was time to pack up for the day, a thought struck him that was so utterly horrible in its implications that he had to say it out loud. Colsceg, Barn and Carey were working with him at the time.

'I suppose,' he said, 'it's all right to use green timber like this. Only, what if it shrinks or starts splitting as it dries out? The whole thing could pull out of shape.'

But Colsceg gave him a reassuringly contemptuous look. 'You hear a lot of bullshit about building with green timber these days,' he said. 'Bullshit,' he repeated. 'When my great-great grandfather first moved out here from the east, there wasn't time to season your timbers. It was either put 'em up green or spend six months camping out in the rain. So they put 'em up green, same as I did when I built my place, and you know what? It's still there. You build it right, as the timbers dry out they move together, you get stronger joints and tighter laps, not the other way around. Only time you need to worry about green timber's when you're putting it together with nails and straps, 'stead of regular joints and dowels; and only a damn fool of an easterner'd do such a thing to begin with.'

That seemed to settle that, and Poldarn was far too tactful to point out that Colsceg's house wasn't there any more. Irrelevant, anyway; even the most meticulously dried lumber wasn't supposed to be proof against freak cataracts of fast-moving black mud. All the same, it did occur to Poldarn to wonder where exactly, in Colsceg's view, the west ended and the feckless east began. Colsceg himself had never said anything definite on the subject, but Poldarn had an idea that the frontier lay somewhere just the other side of the eastern boundary of Colscegsford.

The Colscegsford household appeared to have worked up a substantial thirst during the day, because they were heavier than usual on the beer at dinner that night. That was unusual behaviour – Poldarn couldn't remember seeing anybody get drunk since he'd come home, and had come to the conclusion that it probably wasn't even possible: how could any one man drink enough beer to addle a brain he shared with several dozen other people? That night, however, the Colscegsford people seemed to be giving it their best shot, though they didn't succeed. The beer didn't seem to affect them in the slightest, as far as Poldarn could tell; no slurred words or loud behaviour, if anything they were quieter and more withdrawn than usual. If it had been the Bohec valley instead of the far islands, he'd have come to the conclusion that the loss of their home was finally beginning to get to them and they were trying to drown their sorrows, but that didn't seem very likely. Maybe they were just thirsty, at that.

Fortunately, the Haldersness contingent had the sense not to try and keep up with Colsceg's people on the beer, so there weren't any uncomfortably sore heads when Poldarn came round to wake them up an hour before dawn the next day. It was raining, needless to say, but no more than a light, cool drizzle, falling almost vertically out of a blue-patched sky.

They sharpened the axes on the big crank grindstone on the back porch, and set off for the combe, leaving trails in the long, wet grass. Poldarn led the way, with the slabbing rail over his shoulder – he was showing off, but the others must have figured that if he wanted to rick his back, this once he was entitled. Overladen or not, he kept up a smart pace all the way to the copse.

To begin with, they felled the thickest trees, the ones that would provide the rafters, joists, girts and braces. These had to be sawn into planks, and it made sense to bring those down first, so the fellers could move on while the sawyers were dealing with them. While he and Eyvind alternated cuts on either side of the main joist tree, Poldarn tried hard to put out of his mind the fact that he was cutting down one of *his* trees, harvesting it, killing it; but the thought was too stubborn and refused to go quietly. So far, the project had been all about growth; if the trees stopped growing, would he stop with them? At the back of his mind he could remember a story (whose story or where it was from he didn't have a clue) about the glorious hero who'd been cursed to live just as long as the oak sapling in the corner of his mother's kitchen garden – that had been a strange curse, he thought, because oaks live for hundreds of years if nobody fells them, and of course the hero's mother had built a wall round the little tree and set the household to guard and nurture it; and in time it grew mighty and strong, just as the hero did, and both of them shaded and sheltered their households for three hundred years, until the hero became cruel in his old age and tormented his people, until his own great-grandson lopped his head off with a felling axe, on the same night that lightning split the great tree, showing up the rot that was eating its heart out . . . He must have thought that was a pretty good story when he'd heard it, full of significance and inner meaning. But lumber is just lumber, and a man should be practical at all times; it was practical of grandfather to plant these trees, and now here was Poldarn, being practical, cutting them down.

After the first couple of hours, he was too weary and busy to bother with sentimental stuff. The tree that was supposed to provide the middle cross-beam turned out to be ring-shaken;

exposed to the wind on the edge of the copse, it had been twisted and flexed so much that the growth rings inside had pulled apart about a third of the way in, and great flakes of wood peeled off when they tried to rough-hew it. With luck, they'd be able to saw it cross-grain and get a couple of floor-joists out of it, but that was all. Accordingly, the third joist tree got a field promotion to middle cross-beam. Poldarn wasn't happy about that – he reckoned it'd be a bit too thin, because of the wane two-thirds up – but Colsceg and Carey and Eyvind looked it over and pronounced it suitable, provided they didn't hew it true square like the other cross-beams, but left more of the sapwood on. Poldarn agreed reluctantly but insisted that all the bark should come off, since woodworm and beetle love dry bark. Halfway through the morning, Rook's trick elbow gave out on him, and Poldarn had to take his place on the planking saw, which didn't exactly please him. He found the job absurdly difficult; his problem lay in maintaining a rhythm with the man on the other end of the saw (in this case, Colsceg's stolid elder son, Barn, who was known to be good at it). It worked out well enough, however. The hard part was always the first cut off the log, after it had been felled and dressed and heaved up onto the blocks. That was where the slabbing rail came in; you laid it over the curved back of the log and used its flat face to guide the saw, ensuring a flat, level finish on the bottom that would guide the next cut. As they went, they hammered wedges into the kerf to keep it from closing tight on the blade and jamming it. Even so, it was painfully hard work, tearing all the time at the tendons of the forearms.

Poldarn was happy to leave most of the hewing to the Colscegsford household. Whatever their faults, there was no doubt but that they were experts with the hewing axe and the lipped adze, chipping the timbers square as freely and easily as if they were hoeing a patch of earth. When Poldarn surreptitiously checked their work with a square, he found the angles were exact (how the hell could they do that, all by eye?) and there was hardly a toolmark to be seen; you'd think the work had been finished off with a plane. Essential, of course, to have all the surfaces flat and square if they didn't want to have to work twice as hard when the time came to cut the joints.

It took three days to fell, hew and plank out the timber, and suddenly there wasn't a copse there any more, just a huge pile of lumber, all carefully piled with wedges between each piece to allow the air to circulate in the stack and prevent warping. When they arrived on the fourth morning, the crows were sitting on the log pile, looking bewildered. How the hell do you expect us to roost on that? they seemed to cry as the work party walked them off. The fourth day was spent in cutting joints, and by now most of the enthusiasm had worn off. Poldarn got involved in a silent battle of wills with a Colscegsford hand called Bren over a sloppy mortice in the south end house-post; it'd have been all right if Bren had admitted at the start that he'd marked it out wrong, but he carried on working even though he knew the slot was skewed, which was just plain foolish (and typical of Bren, someone told Poldarn later, though on what authority he was left to guess). When he noticed and told him to stop, Bren tried to pretend that it was all perfectly good and that Poldarn couldn't judge an angle, so Poldarn had to fetch the gauge and show him. That made Bren even angrier, particularly when Colsceg started in on him as well. The issue gradually brought all work to a standstill, and it was only after Bren had suddenly got up and walked away that Poldarn and Eyvind were able to consider the problem calmly and decide what was to be done. Eyvind maintained that the post was useless and would have to be discarded; they'd have to hunt around for another piece of timber from somewhere, possibly rob a timber off the derelict barn. Poldarn wasn't having that. They were going to use this piece and no other, and if Eyvind was half the joiner he tacitly claimed to be, he'd be able to figure out a way of salvaging it.

Of course Eyvind didn't like that; luckily he took the implied slight as a challenge, and spent the next two hours cutting a block that exactly filled the defective mortice, dowelling it in tight and cutting a new mortice into the patch. The result, he claimed, would be even stronger than if it'd been cut from the whole wood, and if Poldarn wasn't entirely convinced by that, he could at least see that the job was good enough and would hold.

Things got better after that. Bren wandered back an hour or so after Eyvind had finished his patch; needless to say, the rest of the work he did that day was beyond reproach.

'Now all we've got to do,' Colsceg announced at the start of the fifth day, 'is put the bastard together.'

Poldarn had a feeling that Colsceg hadn't exactly dedicated his life to winning friends and getting people to like him, but that was a bit much, even coming from him. Still, nobody said anything – he'd have been amazed if they had – and they set to work with grim determination, boring the dowel-holes with augers and hammering in the pegs to assemble the sections of the frame. Much to Poldarn's surprise and relief, the plates, posts and sills slotted together perfectly – no yawning gaps, no frantic bashing to squash a fat tenon into a thin mortice – and once the sides were raised with the help of a gin-pole crane and a lot of bad language, the cross-beams and girts slotted in place without any fuss and the pegs went home without jamming or splitting.

'Don't panic,' Eyvind said, observing Poldarn's fraught expression. 'Something'll go wrong soon, and then you can relax.'

Poldarn shook his head. 'It's toying with me, I can tell,' he replied. 'Nothing fits together this easily, ever.'

'Bullshit,' Colsceg interrupted, his mouth full of pegs. 'You do the cutting-out right, it goes together first time. I never have any bother— Fuck,' he added, 'this goddamn tenon's too short. Who cut this tenon?'

Curiously, nobody could remember having worked on that particular timber; and, since it was out of the question that Colsceg could've made a mistake like that, they were left with the conclusion that at some point during the previous day, they'd been helped out by a bunch of careless elves.

'This is silly,' Poldarn said. 'We can't just pack in and start all over again because of one lousy inch.'

For once, Colsceg didn't seem to have an opinion on the matter in hand, and for a while, it was very quiet all round. Finally, Egil (who hadn't said a single word since the job began, as far as Poldarn could remember) cleared his throat and asked how it would be if they cut off the end and spliced in an extension?

Nobody said anything, and Egil shrugged as if to apologise for saying something crass. But then Poldarn said, 'Yes, we could do that', and Colsceg said, 'No, we couldn't, bloody thing'd pull itself apart soon as it took the weight,' and the two of them looked at each other for a while, and they decided to try it. Colsceg sketched out a joint with a scrap of charcoal – a murderously complicated affair that looked like two spiders fighting – while Poldarn solemnly picked up a saw and began to cut off the beam. The two of them worked in silence for over an hour while the others, who had nothing they could usefully do, looked on like a gaggle of expectant fathers.

'All right,' Poldarn said eventually. 'This ought to work.'

'And if it doesn't?' someone asked.

'Then we tear the whole bloody thing down and start again.'

The frightening thing was that he meant it. To everyone's relief, it didn't come to that. Colsceg's double-housed lapped dovetail, or whatever the hell it was, took the strain without so much as a creak, while Poldarn's joinery (When and where the hell did I learn that? he wondered) was so precise that they couldn't pull a single hair through the join.

'Not bad,' Colsceg admitted, frowning. 'Mind you, when I was your age—'

After that, things went well. The rafters dropped into their pockets in the plates, the pegs slid home and tightened in their tapers with a few light taps of the mallet and the collar ties lay sweetly in their blind mortices.

'Finished,' Poldarn said, taking a step back. 'Well, apart from the thatch and the doors, and planking up the sides. But the frame's up, anyway.'

Later, when the rest of them were well into their beer, he lit a torch, called Elja down from the loft and took her down the river path to see it. 'Of course,' he pointed out, 'it'll look different when it's got walls and a roof—'

'I imagine so, yes. A bit more waterproof, for a start.'

'– But you get the general idea.' He hesitated and looked away. 'What d'you think?' he asked.

'I think it's very nice,' Elja replied solemnly. 'Can we go back inside now, please? It's freezing, and my feet are all wet.'

'In a moment,' Poldarn replied. 'Wait there a moment, will you?' He disappeared out of the light, and came back a minute later with a wooden cup in his hand. 'I just remembered I left this out here,' he explained. 'Go on, have a sip. It's water from our river.'

Elja took the cup from him. 'It's not really our river,' she said.

'From here to the mouth of the combe it is,' Poldarn said. 'All right, from the spring head to here it belongs to Haldersness, and from the mouth of the combe as far as Swartmoor it belongs to your father, and after that I'm not sure; but for the minute or so it takes for the water to get from here to there, it's ours. Don't be so damned literal all the time.'

Elja sipped; then she pulled a face and spat it out. 'It's all muddy,' she said.

'Yes, well,' Poldarn admitted, 'probably I stirred it up a bit while I was washing the cup out. But I'll put in a gravel bed to filter it, and then we'll have the sweetest water this side of the mountains.'

'If you say so,' Elja said. 'And now, if it's all the same to you, I really would like to go back, because I'm getting married in a couple of days, and I don't want to say my vows with a streaming cold.'

'Don't fuss,' Poldarn said sternly, and kissed her; and although she knew she wasn't supposed to, she kissed him back. 'Anyway,' he said, 'I think it looks better that way.'

'What does?'

He nodded his head towards the house-frame. 'The copse,' he replied.

'Oh,' Elja said. 'That. I think it's a very nice house, even if it's still a bit bald in patches. But I really would like to go back now, if it's all the same to you.'

'Yes, it's all the same to me.' Poldarn sighed, feeling slightly ashamed of his petulance. 'Sorry, I shouldn't have snapped. I just thought you'd like to see it, that's all.'

'Thank you,' Elja replied gravely. 'But I'm going to be seeing it every day for the rest of my life, and it's late, and I'd like to get some sleep now. I'm sure it'll be a really nice house,' she added, 'when it's finished.'

Next day they started splitting the shakes for boarding in the walls. There was no easy way to go about it. Each felled log had to be carefully examined to see where the split-lines ran, and then it was a simple but tedious and exhausting matter of hammering in the froes, freeing them, driving them in a little further up the line, until the log cracked open lengthways to form two half-round planks. That was the theory, at any rate; but one log in three refused to split clean, leaving the chore of salvaging what material they could for filling and patching. As the day wore on, the hammers and axe-polls grew steadily heavier and more erratic, sometimes missing the froe altogether and landing a full-weight blow on the neck of the handle – whereupon the axe or hammer head would snap off and fly fast and wild through the air, adding a spice of danger to the monotony of the day's labours. By nightfall, the best that could be said was that half the job had been done and nobody had been killed yet; and when the Colscegsford people set to washing the dust out of their throats, Poldarn began to wonder how the beer could possibly hold out till the house was finished.

Another day to split the rest of the shakes and shingles, another two days to nail and peg them to the frames; then, quite suddenly early one afternoon, Colsceg stood back, looked at the house and said, 'Right, it's finished.'

Poldarn, who'd been fussing over a tight shutter, looked up in surprise. 'Are you sure?' he asked.

'Well.' Colsceg shrugged. 'It all needs sealing with pitch, of course, and that blacksmith of yours said the latches'd be ready two days ago and I haven't seen any sign of 'em so far, and there's a few bits and bobs that need sorting out, same as you get on any new building. But yes, it's finished.'

'Oh.' Poldarn took a few steps back. 'So it is,' he said. 'You know what, it isn't bad.'

'Seen worse,' Colsceg conceded. 'And so long as it keeps you dry and doesn't fall on your head in the night, who gives a damn?' He leaned on his axe and wiped his forehead with his sleeve. 'You're right, it's not so bad, though I say so myself. 'Course, if we had the job to do all over again, I'd use birds' mouths for the rafter seats instead of step laps and I'd probably stop the splayed scarfs with double wedges, but it's too late now to worry about that, not unless you want to tear the whole lot down and do it again.' He sighed. 'It'll get the job done, that's the main thing. Should see you out, anyway.'

'I like it,' Poldarn replied. 'You know what, I think I could get to know who I really am in a house like that.'

Colsceg frowned, as if to say that he didn't know what to make of a remark like that, and probably just as well. 'Let's just hope the mountain doesn't brew up again and flatten it,' he said. 'That'd be a choker, after all the work I've put in.'

Poldarn smiled. I dedicate this monument to my future father-in-law Colsceg, he said to himself, without whose dedication, hard work and helpful suggestions, this house would've been completed two days ago. 'I couldn't have done it without your help,' he said. 'Thank you.'

Colsceg seemed genuinely surprised by that; he frowned, and muttered that it was a job that needed doing, so he'd done it. 'Besides,' he went on, 'it's not just you that'll be living there, it's my daughter as well. Don't worry about it.'

Making Colsceg feel uncomfortable was almost as pleasant as building the house. 'No, honestly,' he said, 'I can't tell you how grateful I am. It was really kind of you to spare the time, especially when things have gone so badly for you. Most people in your position would've been far too preoccupied with their own business to have mucked in the way you did.'

'No, they wouldn't,' Colsceg protested, as if Poldarn had just said something outrageous. 'Look, it's no big deal, so let's not say any more about it, right?'

Poldarn shrugged. 'That's very generous of you,' he said, unable to resist a final twist of the knife before drawing it out of the wound. 'And the least I can do by way of thanks is to insist that you move into Haldersness, as soon as we're settled in here. After all,' he went on, barging through Colsceg's protests like an impatient carter running down chickens in the road, 'it's just standing there empty, and your people need a roof over their heads. Please, I want you to treat it as your own for as long as you like.'

'But—' Colsceg was now so bewildered that Poldarn

almost felt sorry for him. 'Well, for one thing, it's a good day's ride from our farm, we'd spend more time trekking back and forth than working. And there's a hell of a lot to do – well, you know that, you were there. If we moved into Haldersness, it'd be a nightmare.'

Reluctantly, Poldarn decided to let him off the hook. 'I suppose you're right,' he said. 'But at the very least, I want you to have all the timbers and the thatch, so all you'll have to do is take it down, cart it over to your place and put it back up again. I mean to say, where else are you going to find enough lumber to build with?'

There he had a point. Not long ago there had been a very fine wood at Colscegsford – Barn's wood, for building his house when Colsceg was dead – and another, rather smaller and less well looked after, for Egil; but both of them had been scooped up and smashed into kindling by the mud-slides, and the nearest stands of unclaimed timber were weeks away to the south-east. Cutting and carting so far from home would require the entire household to move out there for the best part of six months, during which time they'd have to fend for themselves as best they could by hunting and gathering. Or else they'd have to leave half the household camped out at Colscegsford to raise whatever crop they could grow in the mud, while the other half took twice as long to do the cutting and hauling. Poldarn fancied that he could see all these arguments tracking painfully across Colsceg's mind.

'Can't argue with that,' Colsceg said at last, a trifle resentfully. 'Guess we'll be taking you up on your offer. We're obliged to you.' He said the word *obliged* as if he'd just given his first-born as extra security on a mortgage of his entire property. 'We'll get started on tearing the old place down straight away.'

Poldarn shook his head. 'No hurry,' he said. 'You've all put in so much hard work here, you need a day or so to catch your breath before you start on that. Why don't you just hang around and take it easy for a while? You'll do much better work if you aren't exhausted.'

'All right,' Colsceg said reluctantly. 'And I guess there's the wedding to see to, that'll take a couple of days if we're going to do it properly. And if we don't get it done and out of the way now, while we're slack, it'll be awkward fitting it in later.'

He made it sound like a more than usually dreary chore, like forking out the poultry sheds. Charming, Poldarn thought, but then, I've never seen a wedding in these parts. Maybe it is a dreary chore, the way they do it. In fact, I wouldn't be at all surprised. 'What a splendid idea,' he said. 'And, like you say, no time like the present. How would the day after tomorrow suit you?'

Colsceg rubbed the bridge of his nose with thumb and forefinger. 'Sure, why not?' he said stoically. 'After all, every-thing's pretty well screwed up with the volcano and all, so the best thing would be to get it done as soon as possible – no point letting it drag on.'

Poldarn nodded. 'Assuming that's all right with Elja,' he put in.

'Huh? Oh, she won't mind. I mean, it's not like we're springing it on her out of the blue. Anyway,' he added, with a slight frown, 'she seems to like you all right, and a couple of days, you can get most of the furniture and stuff in. That'll be just fine.'

The two households were gathering up their tools, search-ing for lost froes and wedges, sorting the leftover timber into useful oddments and firewood. There was a general air of grim weariness, like the feel of a week-old battlefield when the scavengers are out gleaning the last pickings of useful property from the dead; all the good stuff having been taken already, and only torn clothes, worn-out boots and broken metalwork remaining. 'We could announce it straight away,' Poldarn pointed out. 'After all, everybody's here.'

Colsceg sighed. 'Good idea,' he said. 'Save having to call a meeting later on.'

Luckily, Poldarn hadn't been expecting wholesale rejoicing and mirth, so he wasn't disappointed; but even so, he wasn't too pleased by the dogged resignation that greeted the announcement. The best that could be said of it was that both households took it like men, with fortitude and without any undue display of protest or disgust. One damn thing after another, their attitude suggested, but it can't be helped, so what's the good of whining about it? Poldarn made a mental note that they were miserable bastards, every last one of them, and carried the slabbing rail back to Haldersness. It felt much heavier than it had done a week ago.

Chapter Thirteen

For once, the mind-reading thing turned out to be a blessing. If Poldarn'd had to break the news of the wedding to the combined Haldersness and Colscegsford households – calling a meeting, standing up in front of them, with their blank, bewildered faces glaring at him in the firelight – he wasn't sure he'd have been able to find the courage to do it. But they all knew without having to be told, and by the time the housebuilders arrived back at the middle house, Rannwey and the other women had already made a start on various nameless and inscrutable preparations, most of which seemed to involve tired, dank-looking vegetation in huge wicker baskets. Whether these would turn out to be things to eat or things to wear or things to hang on walls, Poldarn couldn't ascertain and didn't really want to know. Mostly, he got the feeling that it wasn't really anything to do with him, and his role in the forthcoming event would be both minimal and a considerable nuisance to everybody else.

He wanted to talk to Elja, if only to make sure that she didn't mind, but when he asked where she was, he was told by word, gesture and facial expression that even being in the same

building as her before the wedding would constitute an unmit-
igated abomination; she'd been moved to the trap-house, and
wouldn't be coming out until the actual day of the wedding, if
then. Meanwhile, it was suggested to him, if he was at a loose
end with nothing to do, wouldn't it be a good idea if he looked
in at the forge and did some work, for a change.

The last thing Poldarn wanted to do was stand in front of
a raging fire in a dark shed mangling a strip of hot iron; but,
since there wasn't really anywhere else for him to be, he
went. Asburn seemed genuinely pleased to see him.

'I hope you don't mind,' Asburn said, wiping a pink
furrow across his soot-blackened forehead with the back of
his hand, 'but I'm just finishing up these latches for the new
house. They should've been done by now, but if I can get
really stuck into them they'll be ready for when you move in.'

Poldarn frowned. 'Why should I mind?' he asked, but
Asburn didn't answer.

There still didn't seem to be anything for him to do;
making latch components was clearly a job for one skilled
man. He could always make a few nails, of course, but even
now that the house was finished there was still a full barrel of
nails in the corner, probably enough to last a decade, so there
didn't seem to be any point. Then he remembered the promise he'd made to Boarci, to make him an axe to replace the
one he'd lost.

'Asburn,' he said, 'how do you make axe heads?'

'Piece of cake,' Asburn replied promptly. 'All you do is,
you get a bit of square bar about a thumb-length broad and
about a foot long, you leave a square in the middle alone,
because that's going to be the poll, for hammering wedges
and stuff, but you draw down both ends to about the thickness of a tooth; then you fold these down at right angles
round a mandrel – that makes the eye for the handle to go
through – wedge a piece of hard steel between them, forge-
weld all three layers together, and then you just work it to

shape, take a good orange heat and quench in water. And that's all there is to it.'

'Ah,' Poldarn said. He'd followed that as far as the square in the middle, but the rest had soared over his head like a flock of startled teal. 'Thanks,' he said. 'I'll give it a try.'

Asburn went back to his work; he was measuring something with a pair of calipers, over and over again from a bewildering variety of angles. To Poldarn it looked like a little piece of bar, flat and straight and entirely uncomplicated, but obviously there was more to latchsmithing than met the eye. Piece of cake, he muttered sourly under his breath, as he rootled around in the scrap for inspiration.

What he'd been hoping to find, of course, was an axe head – a genuine one, made by a real smith, which he could grind and buff and pass off as his own work. There were halberds and glaives and bardisches and bills, both broken and intact, enough to fit out a regiment, but nothing as mundane and useful as a small hand-axe. But he did find half a heavy-duty cart tyre and the stub end of a broken rasp; and as he looked at them, it occurred to him (why, he had no idea) that he knew what to do.

First, he took a yellow heat and cut off a foot of the tyre with the hot sett, taking care not to let the glowing steel land on his foot or go flying across the forge when he severed it. While the cut-off section was still orange, he popped it back into the fire with the help of the offset-jaw tongs – undoubtedly not the right tongs for the job, but the only ones he'd figured out how to manage without trapping a blood-blister on the ball of his middle finger – got it as hot as he dared without burning it, and folded it into a U with a few smart taps over the anvil table. Back it went into the fire, while Poldarn rummaged in the heap of rusty tools under the bench until he found a tapered steel pin as thick as the axe handle needed to be. On this he hung the yellow-hot steel U, quickly clamped it in the vice, and tapped all round the pin with a light, well-crowned hammer to knock down the metal where the bend had flared it. That formed a nice, even, round eye, with two equal-length legs coming down on either side. Before the iron cooled, he hammered these together until they touched, then gripped the eye in the vice with the legs pointing upwards, and used the hot sett to open them up just enough to allow him to slide in the finger-length of broken rasp that would form the hard cutting edge. But he didn't do that yet; first he brought it up almost to a white heat, so the iron legs wouldn't burn before the heat soaked through into the middle. He was really proud of himself for thinking of that.

A few taps closed the legs around the insert; then a generous sprinkle of flux and back in the fire and some hard labour on the bellows handle, until the fire was so hot it frizzed his eyebrows. It took a frustratingly long time to get the work to a uniform welding heat, but Poldarn knew better than to be continually hauling it out and fiddling with it; he was listening for the sound of the iron starting to melt, even though he hadn't got a clue what that sound was supposed to be like. But, he figured, that was where his ignorance would come in useful; as soon as he heard a sound he couldn't identify, that'd be it.

It proved to be a soft, kittenish purr. He had the hammer in his hand all ready, a light dusting of flux on the anvil, loose firescale all carefully swept and blown away. As the work emerged from under the coals it was dripping fat white sparks like tame indoor stars, and as he started hammering the weld together the metal seemed to explode like a volcano, throwing out white-hot hailstones in every direction. Two of them settled on his bare skin and hurt like hell, but he knew he didn't have time to waste on pain; the iron and steel would only be half-molten together for a few precious heartbeats, and if he screwed up the weld this time, he'd probably have to start all over again with a new strip of tyre and another scrap of steel. He could see the brief opportunity in the hot metal, feel it squirming under the hammer, like a boot squelching in boggy ground (he imagined that it would feel like this to wade across the surface of the sun; something a god could probably get away with, though a man would be incinerated before his foot touched down).

The last few sparks went out, allowing Poldarn to feel the ferocious heat of the metal roasting his skin and flesh, though his hands were a hammer shaft and a pair of tongs removed from it. He stopped hammering and held the work up as close as he dared bring it to his face, trying to see if the weld had taken, but all he could make out was a glaring white hole burnt into his vision, which stayed there when he shut his eyes. He put the work back in the fire; after the trauma of taking the weld, pumping the bellows felt almost pleasant in comparison.

He concentrated this heat on drawing out the shape of the blade, tapering it on the flats and sides, first on the horn, to move it, then on the flat, to straighten it out. To Poldarn's joy and stark amazement, the weld seemed to have taken, right the way up to a point a fingernail's width under the eye. He was very impressed. He had no idea how he'd managed to do that.

The rest of the job – shaping, bevelling, smoothing, plenishing – he did in a sort of a daze, without really thinking about it, since his hands appeared to know what to do and his head didn't; they were *remembering*, just as they'd remembered how to draw a sword and slash through a neck vein. They'd remembered, because they were a blacksmith's hands, even if the blacksmith himself had seen fit to forget what he'd once been, who he was.

Damn, Poldarn thought, I was wrong and Grandfather was right, he said I was the Haldersness smith, it's who I've been all along and I wouldn't let myself admit it. I must have learned this trade – well, of course I learned it when I was a kid, that's what the heir apparent would do in a place like this. He looked round at the walls, at all the obscure and arcane tools roosting there on their hooks and brackets, and suddenly he knew them all by name, the way a leader knows his men, or the head of a household knows his family: the hardies and the swages and the flatters and the fullers, the stakes and setts and drifts and headers, straight-lip tongs and box tongs, wedge, hammer and side tongs, bicks, forks and scrolls. There you all are again, he said to himself, I've been away but I'm back again now, and here you all still are, just where I left you.

Asburn was coming over to him, smiling. 'How're you getting on?' he asked; then, 'Oh, that's really nice, you've got that just right.' For some reason, Poldarn felt patronised, insulted; and what was this stranger doing in his shop anyhow, using his tools, like he owned the place?

'Thanks,' he said sullenly. 'It isn't going to look much, but it's close enough for country music.' He leaned over the finished axe head, examining it with exaggerated interest, so he wouldn't have to look Asburn in the face. 'Bloody great scale pits there and there, look, they'll have to grind out, which is a pain.'

'That's a bloody good weld, though.' Asburn was genuinely pleased for him, but that was an unpardonable liberty, as though he needed anybody's praise or approval. 'I can never get the heat back up that far,' Asburn went on, 'I always end up peening over the tops just to cover up where it hasn't taken.'

Poldarn shrugged; the interloper's praise was almost physically irritating, like an itch or a cramp. 'I suppose it's not so bad, for a first effort,' he conceded unhappily. 'Not much of an axe, though, with no poll. Should've done it your way, but no, I had to know best. I reckon this ought to go back in the scrap, it isn't fit to give to anyone.'

'Oh no, really.' Asburn shook his head emphatically. 'A

touch on the wheel here and there and a bit of buffing soap, it'll be right as rain. Have you hardened it yet?'

Poldarn shook his head. 'It's all right,' he added, 'I can manage all right, thank you. Orange heat, then quench in water and draw it back to purple just going on blue. Right?'

Asburn nodded. 'That ought to do it,' he said cheerfully. 'Well, I'll let you get on with it, then, while I just finish up this latch tongue.'

No, you can just pick up your junk and get out of here. 'Thanks,' Poldarn said. 'Thanks, I appreciate it.'

'Oh, no bother,' Asburn replied, with the surprised awkwardness Poldarn had come to expect from these people when he said thank you for anything. 'Anyway, well done. Nice piece of work, really. Halder'd have been proud.'

When he'd done the hardening and tempering, Poldarn retired to the far corner of the smithy to do the grinding. Well, he thought, as the stone spat up yellow sparks, so that's what I used to do when I wasn't killing crows. No big deal, of course, it's just a skill, something you learn, something anybody can learn. It's not like finding out your name, or who your parents were. It can't matter very much, can it? Certainly can't do any harm; and it's kept me out from under their feet indoors. That's just as well, or I'm sure they'd have taken the meat-cleaver to me.

It's not like I've done anything clever or unusual. Bloody hell, if Asburn can do it, it can't be difficult.

After he'd ground up the blade and set a good edge, Poldarn went out to the woodpile and found a piece of seasoned straight ash branch as long as his arm, which he turned up on the rickety old pole lathe to make a reasonably functional handle (tapered, with a knob at the end so the head couldn't come off, and every blow would fix it on tighter). As a finishing touch, he served the grip with twine, right up as far as the head. Then he went to look for Boarci.

'Yeah, it's all right,' Boarci said, waggling it up and down in his hand. 'Ugly as hell, but who cares so long as it cuts and doesn't bust on me first time I use it. I liked the old one better, though. And this bloody string'll give me blisters.'

'Tough,' Poldarn said. 'It's like that so it won't get slippery with sweat and fly out of your hand.'

Boarci shook his head. 'My hands don't sweat,' he said. 'But it was a nice thought, I guess. Still, I'll strip that off when I've got a moment. A useful bit of string's worth having.'

Poldarn wasn't unduly impressed by that; so he retreated to the hayloft over the stables, where he could be sure of being out of the way for a while. It was dark there, but pleasantly warm, and he liked the smell of hay. He lay down with his hands behind his head, and tried to make sense of what had just happened in the forge.

Certainly, for a moment at least, he'd been somebody different, but he couldn't say for sure whether it had been someone else entirely or an extra part of himself that he hadn't known about (like a child growing up in a big house who finds his way into the attic for the first time). By way of experiment, he tried to think of a complicated piece of ironwork – the man-sized free-standing candleholder in the main hall was the first thing that came to mind – and settled down to figure out how he'd go about making it. He imagined a stack of iron bars, and tried to picture himself working them down, drawing out and swaging and jumping up and welding them until they became a finished piece of work. At first it was difficult, almost impossible to hold the shapes in his mind, but gradually Poldarn found that if he concentrated hard enough on the image, the pictures materialised behind his eyes, like the afterglow of the white-hot iron, and he knew that if he relied on instinct and let his hands and eyes do the work, he'd be able to make the wretched thing eventually. That set him speculating: was that how they read each others' minds, by staring with an extra eye until they could see what they were looking for?

'Something like that,' said a voice in the darkness. This time, Poldarn knew there wasn't anybody there, so he wasn't too worried. It was a girl's voice; he wasn't very good at identifying people's ages by their voices, but he was prepared to hazard a guess at somewhere between sixteen and twenty-four. 'Actually, it's easier than that, once you get used to it. Like walking; it takes you six months of desperate effort when you're a little child, and then you just stop thinking about it for years and years, until you're old and it gets to be a dreadful pain again.' The voice hesitated. 'That's not what I meant,' it continued, 'because I didn't mean that we have trouble hearing each other as we get older, I don't know why I said that last bit. I think it was the symmetry of it that took my fancy. But you can forget all that.'

'Thank you,' Poldarn said gravely. 'Forget what?'

'Well, all the—' The voice sighed. 'Don't tease,' it said. 'You never used to tease, it gets me flustered. That's a real boy thing, teasing.'

'I'm sorry,' Poldarn replied. 'I won't do it again. Would you mind telling me who you are, by the way? I'm sure I should know you, but I've forgotten.'

The voice tutted. 'More teasing. If you don't stop, I'm leaving.'

'No, really.' Poldarn sighed. 'It's too complicated to explain, but I promise you, I really don't remember—'

He stopped. The voice was giggling. 'My turn to tease you,' it explained. 'Yes, of course I know about you losing your memory, I was there at the time, I saw you. You didn't see me, of course. My name's Herda.'

Poldarn listened to the sound of the name, but it didn't mean anything at all to him. 'I'm sorry,' he said.

'Quite all right, I'm not offended or anything. Actually, I'm Elja's mother.'

'Oh. But I thought she was dead.'

'Well, of course I'm dead, silly.' The voice laughed. 'I've been dead for nineteen years – I died when Elja was born. You know that.'

'That's what I'd been told.'

'Ah, a cautious man, very sensible. But just this once, you're being told the truth. Make the most of it, it's not likely to happen to you very often.'

Something she'd said registered belatedly in Poldarn's mind. 'You said you were there,' he said, 'when I lost my memory. That's impossible, if you died when Elja was born.'

'Oh, you. You're always so damned literal. What I meant was, I was watching over you at the time. Like I always do. Your guardian angel, in fact. Do you want to know what happened, that day by the river?'

Poldarn found it hard to get out the word 'Yes,' but he managed it, somehow.

'Well.' The voice paused. 'You know, I don't really think I ought to tell you, it might upset you. You always were one for getting upset, the least little thing had you in tears when you were a little boy. Like the time you had that pet bird – oh come on, you must remember *that*, the old bald crow with the broken wing. You kept it for years, in a little hutch that Scaptey made for you.'

'Remind me,' Poldarn said, very quietly.

'All right. It was when you were – let me see, you can't have been more than five, possibly younger than that, and one day the poor thing was flapping around in the yard, I think one of my father's dogs had caught it and brought it down, but it managed to get away; and there it was, capering round the yard and flapping helplessly, and the dog was chasing after it in a frightful rage because every time he tried to grab it, the wretched creature did a flutter and a jump and just managed to get clear. The rest of us kids, well, you know how brutal children are, we were standing there watching and laughing our horrid little heads off, when you came thundering out of the trap-house waving a stick, and you whacked that dog across the back so hard I'm amazed you didn't kill it. And then you got a broken milk-pail, and you crept up on that funny old crow, really patiently, talking to it really gently and sweetly. It kept jinking about and it took you ages and ages, but you didn't lose your temper or give up, you carried on being nice and gentle until finally you got the pail over it; and then you picked it up so carefully, even though it panicked and scratched your face and pecked you till you were all covered in blood. You kept it in a feed bin, and Halder was furious, couldn't think why anybody could possibly want to make a pet of *vermin* as he called it; he couldn't read in your mind why you were doing it, you'd somehow managed to close your thoughts up so he couldn't see them. That was the first time you did it, and everybody was very shocked, of course, they said it was unnatural. But that's beside the point. Halder was livid, but old Scaptey – he was always so fond of you – he made you the hutch for your crow and you fed it and put in fresh straw every week and you'd sit there for hours chattering away to it – we used to creep up when you weren't looking and listen to you, and really, it was just like you were having a proper conversation with it, because you'd stop talking and crouch there like you were listening to what it was saying, and then you'd reply, and so on. We laughed at you like mad and teased you, but you didn't seem to mind, you said it was our loss not having a magic bird for a pet, because it told you all sorts of wonderful things, about the past and the future too; and then we got frightened, just in case it really was a magic bird, and we asked you, what sort of things was it saying to you, about the future? Well, then you started telling us things that were going to happen, really confidently, not as though you were making them up out of your head, and sure enough, they began to happen just as you'd told us – little things to start with, like when the old lame ewe was going to lamb, how many barrels of apples we'd get off the split tree, stuff like that; and after that, really big stuff – women getting pregnant and people dying. That went on for several years, I think, and all that time Halder was getting angrier and angrier, he said it wasn't right and no good would come of it, you were teaching the rest of us bad ways and all sorts of other dreadful things, and he was really worried because whenever he tried to tell you off, you'd close your mind up tight, like a box, and nobody could see what you were thinking at all. So he decided he'd have to get rid of the bird, but he couldn't bring himself to do it openly, because he knew you'd be so angry. Are you sure you don't remember this?'

'Positive,' Poldarn replied. 'Go on.'

'Well,' said the voice, 'one day when you were out with the sheep, he got a hammer and a sharp nail; and he had Scaptey hold the crow's head while he banged the nail into it and killed it. Then he broke up the slats on the roof of the hutch and put the dead crow back inside, and when you came home, he told you that while you'd been out, a big mob of crows had pitched on the hutch, smashed their way in and pecked your pet crow to death, because they were angry with him for leaving them and going to live with humans.'

'Halder said that?'

'Oh yes. What really bugged him, you see, was that you'd made friends with a scavenger, a pest who stole corn and pecked at the thatch and trampled down the laid patches in the barley, in preference to your own kind. For some reason he really hated that, he thought it was so perverse that it was positively *evil*. So he wanted you to think it was crows who'd killed your friend, so you'd stopped liking them.' She chuckled. 'It did that all right,' she said. 'That was when you took to sitting out in the headlands with a pocketful of stones and a slingshot. From one extreme to another, my father said – you carried on being just as crazy, except that instead of talking to crows, all you ever wanted to do was kill them, for revenge. Actually, that got Halder even more worried than when you had the pet, but he didn't say anything, just kept very quiet and gave you nice rewards for keeping the pests off the newly sown fields. Eventually you grew out of it, I suppose; but you kept that trick of being able to keep us out of your head, in fact you had your guard up more often than not, more and more as time went on. That was when Halder decided you'd got to go.'

'He decided that?'

'Oh yes, you were getting very unpopular, and people were saying things about you behind your back, how you weren't right in the head – you could see their point, you had a perfectly awful temper, you kept picking fights and beating people up, which had never happened before as far back as anyone could remember – well, how could it, when we can all see what everybody else is thinking? But we couldn't read *you*, of course, so you could walk up to someone and suddenly start being nasty, without any warning, and next thing there'd be a fight, and that someone'd be on the ground with you kicking and punching them. That started around the time you stopped killing crows, so naturally people drew their own conclusions.'

'Why the hell would I want to do that?' Poldarn asked.

'Exactly,' the voice replied, 'why would *anybody* want to do a thing like that? Nobody had a clue, except me, of course.'

'Except you.'

'Oh yes.' The voice sighed. 'You see, you only stopped killing crows when I told you it wasn't their fault your pet died, it was Halder and Scaptey who'd done it. I remember, I thought it was silly, someone declaring war on a species of bird, and it was time you got a grip on yourself and settled down. But as soon as you knew, you were really upset and you decided that you had to take revenge on people for all the crows they'd tricked you into killing. Really, I should have kept my mouth shut, but I was only trying to help. Well, it all came back on me in the end, didn't it?'

'Did it?'

'Yes. But you're making me get out of sequence. I was telling you how Halder decided you had to go away for a while. He wanted to send you up north, let you build a house up there and carry on where nobody knew you; but my father didn't like the thought of that. You see, he didn't like the way we'd become friends, ever since you were little and we played in the same gang, not with me being betrothed to Colsceg after his first wife died; he didn't think you'd stay up north, he was afraid you'd come creeping back. So he persuaded Halder that it'd be a good idea for you to go abroad, back to the old country, to be a spy for our raiding parties. If he wants to hurt people, he said, let him go and hurt people over there, where they deserve it. And Halder couldn't argue with that, because it was a good idea, of course. And you were definitely getting out of hand, no question about that. And then finally there was that other business.'

'What other business?' Poldarn asked.

But the voice only shushed him. 'You've made me lose track,' she said. 'Wasn't I supposed to be telling you about how you came to be lying there in the river, with all those dead people?'

Poldarn had clean forgotten about that. 'Yes,' he said. 'What about that? I really would like to know what happened.'

But the voice was silent for some time. 'I'm not sure,' she said. 'Like, think what happened that other time, when I told you something you didn't ought to know, because I thought it'd help. Look at all the trouble that made for everyone. No, I don't think I should tell you after all, not with the wedding coming up and all that. What if it made you go all crazy again? That'd be awful.'

Poldarn was so angry he could hardly keep still; but he

knew that if he moved, he'd wake up out of the dream, and then he'd never know. 'Please,' he said, 'stop teasing me. You said yourself, it's spiteful to tease. Tell me what happened.'

'All right,' she said, and she started to tell him. But her voice was getting softer and softer, so he couldn't make out what she was saying over the croaking and cackling of the huge mob of crows that had pitched on the roof – all the crows he'd ever killed, right down to the one he'd crushed into the coals of the forge fire, and they were talking about him, about various things he'd done, or else singing the song about the crows sitting in the tall, thin trees, and because he could hear every last voice, hundreds and thousands of them all at the same time inside his head, of course he heard nothing at all. Finally he got so angry that he grabbed an axe that happened to be lying beside him and jumped up to scare the crows away—

'Bloody hell,' said Boarci, 'calm down, for God's sake, and stop waving that thing in my face. It's only me, they told me to come and wake you up.'

Poldarn looked down at the axe in his hand. 'I was asleep,' he said.

'Too right you were, they could hear you snoring out in the yard. Having a bad dream, they reckoned, because you kept shouting stuff out loud.'

Of course, the dream had gone; it had opened its wings in a panic as he came rushing out of his sleep, and flown away into the air to roost in the darkness. 'What sort of stuff was I shouting?' Poldarn asked.

But Boarci only laughed. 'Search me,' he said, 'it was all in foreign, must've been the Empire language or something like that, we couldn't make out a word of it. Anyway, you were putting people off their food, so I came to wake you up.'

'Oh,' Poldarn said. 'Thank you, I suppose.'

'Don't mention it. Now, can I have my axe back, please? Or are you going to keep it for yourself after all? Feel free,'

Boarci added. 'After all, you made it. And I'm still not sure I like it. Bit front-heavy for my liking.'

Poldarn checked; it was the axe he'd made, sure enough, though he couldn't figure how on earth it had managed to get up there all by itself. 'I'll put a weighted pommel on the end if you like,' he said, 'that ought to sort out the balance for you.'

Boarci shrugged. 'Worth a try, I guess.' He laughed. 'Tell you what, though,' he said, 'it's just as well that girl of yours wasn't down there when you were snoring away like a grindstone. Not the sort of thing you'd want to hear just before you're about to get married to someone. If I was in her shoes, I'd probably run away while there's still time.'

Chapter Fourteen

'I've never been to a wedding before,' Poldarn said. 'At least, that's not strictly true. But I can't *remember* ever having been to one. What happens?'

Eyvind laughed. 'Oh, nothing much. Everyone troops into the hall, the head of the house says a few words, that's basically it. No big deal.'

Poldarn wasn't sure he believed him. The subdued frenzy of activity that had been going on behind his back for the last couple of days suggested otherwise. Of course, he hadn't the faintest idea what they'd been getting up to, because as soon as he turned up, everybody stopped what they were doing and stared at him in oppressive silence until he went away again; but it seemed to involve yards and yards of cloth, dozens of baskets of flora and vegetable matter, and pretty well every member of the two households except him. Even Asburn had been bashing away in the forge at all hours of the day and night, and had refused to let him in in case he saw something he shouldn't. Meanwhile, precious little work was being done around the farm, except by the prospective bridegroom (who, being at a loose end, had been pressed into deputising for all the busy people; he'd mended fences, laid hedges, weeded, spit and harrowed, mucked out cattle sheds and stables, fetched, carried, cooked, swept and polished, until he no longer needed to be told what to do. If he saw a job of work, he did it, knowing full well that if he didn't, nobody else was likely to. On reflection, it occurred to him that maybe that was the whole point).

'What sort of no big deal?' he asked. 'I mean, do I have to do anything, or do I just stand there like a small tree until it's all over?'

Eyvind shook his head. He was mending a broken staff-hook by binding the smashed shaft with wet rawhide, which gave him an excuse for not meeting Poldarn's eye. 'Actually,' he said, 'to be perfectly honest, I'm not sure. You see, as well as being the bridegroom you're also the head of the household – both households, really, since Colsceg and his mob are under your roof. So, properly speaking, you're the one who should be doing all the speeches and saying the magic words. It'll be interesting to see how it turns out, really.'

Poldarn sighed. Getting a straight answer out of Eyvind looked like it would take major surgery. On the other hand, nobody else was even prepared to talk to Poldarn, except Boarci, who probably knew the score but was pretending he didn't. 'That's just silly,' Poldarn said. 'I can't marry myself, it sounds all wrong. There must be some sort of established procedure in these cases.'

'You'd have thought so, wouldn't you?' Eyvind replied. 'But apparently not, it's never happened quite like this before. You see, usually the sons and grandsons of heads of households are married by the time they're nineteen, sometimes earlier. Old men like you and me roaming around free as birds is definitely the exception rather than the rule.'

'Oh,' Poldarn said. 'So why aren't you married, then? I've got an excuse, but you haven't.'

Eyvind shrugged. 'It just turned out that way,' he said. 'People like you and me, heads of houses or heirs apparent, can't just go marrying anybody – it's a serious thing, we've got to marry daughters of heads of other households, prefer- ably ones whose farms share a common boundary or two. Our place – well, it's tucked in rather awkwardly between several much bigger spreads and, as it turned out, after they'd all done deals with each other there wasn't anybody left over for me. So I'd have had to go marrying up-country, which would've involved a lot of messing around with graz- ing rights and water rights and overwintering agreements and stuff like that, and it's hard enough as it is screwing a living out of the collection of large rocks we call a farm with- out buggering up all our arrangements just so I don't have to sleep alone. Besides, there's no real need. When I die, the farm will go to my mother's brother's family, and every- body's quite happy with that. If I got spliced and had a son, it'd cause more problems than it'd solve.'

Oh, Poldarn thought. Isn't that missing the point rather? Obviously not. 'Do you mind?' he asked.

'Not terribly.' Eyvind grinned. 'I know what you're think- ing. But – no offence – you're forgetting the main difference between yourself and the rest of us. Take that into account, and maybe you can see how we've got a whole different set of motivations and priorities Or, at least, I'm guessing that, because I haven't got a clue how your mind works. Still, it seems to me that if you can go around thinking whatever the hell you like with nobody being able to look in on you, your approach to the whole subject has got to be completely dif- ferent. Much better in some ways, I guess, and far, far worse in others. We tend to keep that side of ourselves – well, in reserve, out of sight, even, until we go abroad. Doesn't matter a damn what we do while we're over there, after all.'

Well, not quite, Poldarn thought; that's how I came to be born, or didn't you hear about that? I'm sure you must have done, so that was a definite mistake, my otherwise tactful friend. Now maybe— It was the first time he'd thought of it. Maybe the reason he couldn't read and be read was because his mother was a foreigner, not part of the swarm, with a mind that couldn't be prised open and examined by everybody in the household. Not that it mattered; and the subject as a whole seemed to be embarrassing Eyvind, so he decided to change it. 'You were saying something about speeches and magic words,' he said. 'Can you be a bit more specific, perhaps?'

Eyvind pulled the last strip of rawhide tight and wiped his hands on his shirt. 'Let's see,' he said. 'It's been a while since I was at a wedding. I think what happens is that the head of household goes through a sort of list of do's and don'ts, asks questions about whether you really want to marry each other, are there any things you haven't told anybody about, like being brother and sister; that sort of thing generally. The sort of stuff that probably meant something once but now it's just a set of meaningless rote questions and responses that everybody reels off by heart without thinking.'

'Fine,' Poldarn said. 'So you're telling me I've got to ask all these dumb questions and then answer them myself. And with people watching, too. There's got to be a better way of going about it than that.'

'Such as?'

'Oh, I don't know. Can't I appoint someone as a stand-in head of household, just for the day of the wedding? Or what about Colsceg? He's a head of house, he'll do.'

'Yes, but it's not his house. I think there's specific rules about that.'

'All right, then,' Poldarn said with a touch of desperation. 'How about you? You're not a head of house but you're in line to be. I'm sure you could do it. The logical choice, really.'

Eyvind shook his head. 'You can forget that,' he said. 'I'd rather be trapped in a burning house, with the roof falling in on me.'

'Even to help out a friend in need?'

'I said forget it. Wouldn't be right, anyhow. Strictly speaking, I'm an offcomer, I shouldn't even be in the house when there's a wedding going on.'

'What does that mean?' Poldarn interrupted.

'Oh, superstition,' Eyvind replied. 'They say that if there's offcomers in the house on a wedding day, it's bad luck, to the bride and groom and the offcomers too. Just a load of old garbage, of course, but some people take that kind of thing pretty seriously – it wouldn't do to go upsetting them by having an offcomer actually taking the service.'

'Somebody's got to do it,' Poldarn snapped, 'and I'm bloody certain it isn't going to be me. Now come on, for pity's sake, I've got to go out there and get married in a few hours, there isn't any time for playing games. Think of someone.'

'I'm thinking,' Eyvind replied, somewhat nettled by Poldarn's outburst. 'But I can think till my brains boil out through my ears and it won't do any good if there's nobody to think *of*. Oh, I don't know, what about Colsceg's sons?'

Poldarn looked up sharply. 'What, you mean Barn? If he can do it, so could Colsceg, surely. And at least Colsceg's a bit more animated than a broken cartwheel.'

'I just said, he's disqualified. All right, if you've got something against Barn, what about Egil?'

Poldarn shook his head. 'He doesn't like me,' he said.

'How doesn't he like you?' Eyvind looked concerned. 'And what gave you that idea, anyhow?'

'Nothing. Forget I just said that.'

'Sorry,' Eyvind replied, 'but some of us can't forget things as easily as others. What's your problem with Egil?'

'Nothing, really. It's just an impression I got, so it's far more likely to be wrong than right, anyhow. I can't see inside his head, remember, so I have to go by other kinds of signal. And I wouldn't trust my judgement in such matters further than I could sneeze it out of my ear.'

That didn't seem to satisfy Eyvind at all. 'Fine,' he said. 'Be like that, don't tell me. But it strikes me that picking imaginary feuds with your prospective in-laws isn't the most intelligent thing in the world, especially if they're going to be living a few hundred yards from your front door.'

Poldarn smiled defensively. 'That's interesting,' he said. 'You make it sound like it's actually possible to have a quarrel with anybody in these parts. I wouldn't have thought it could be done, with everybody being so like-minded and knowing what everybody else is thinking.'

'Don't you believe it,' Eyvind replied. 'Oh, it's rare enough, but it happens. Not in the same household, of course, that would be impossible, but neighbours do fall out occasionally, and it can get rather unpleasant if you're not careful. Which is why getting it into your head that someone's got it in for you is a bad idea, believe me.'

'All right,' Poldarn said appeasingly, 'I promise to love all my fellow human beings to bits. And if you think Egil would do it, sure I'll ask him. I just doubt it, that's all.'

Eyvind stood up. 'I'll ask him for you, if you like,' he said abruptly. 'That way, you won't feel tempted to say something stupid or offensive.'

'Good idea,' Poldarn sighed. 'Why don't you do that?'

'All right.'

Poldarn had hoped that Eyvind wasn't serious, or that Egil would refuse; but apparently not. 'He says he'll be delighted,' Eyvind announced happily, a few minutes later. 'And he reckons he knows all the words and what to do, so that's all right. I think he liked the idea of playing at being a head of household for a while, since he won't ever get the chance otherwise. Pity, that,' Eyvind added, 'he'd be good at it, or at least better than his brother would be. Mind you, the same would hold true of a small piece of rock.'

Best not to go there, Poldarn decided. 'Fine,' he said. 'Thank you. Now, will you please tell me what I'm supposed to do at this wedding, because otherwise it's going to be extremely embarrassing.'

'Well,' Eyvind began; at which point an unfamiliar twelve-year-old girl came bounding up to tell them it was time to begin, and everybody was waiting. 'Actually,' Eyvind added, as the little girl led them away, 'it should all be pretty obvious, you'll know what to say when the time comes.'

Poldarn wasn't in the least convinced, but it was too late now to do anything about it. Quite apart from the details of the ceremony, there were a great many other connected issues he'd have liked to talk through, but clearly he wasn't going to get the chance. He had the feeling of being on the box of a runaway cart trundling slowly down a hill, just about to gather pace.

The wedding was going to take place in the hall of the house – the old house, Poldarn told himself; I don't live there any more, for some reason nobody's seen fit to explain to me. That bothered him for a moment; the house wasn't his now, and since the new house was built he'd been given to understand that he wasn't supposed to set foot in it. No doubt there was a very good reason why the wedding should be held on foreign soil, so to speak. If Halder had still been alive, where would they have held the wedding? In his house, presumably. Poldarn was sure there was a reason for every detail – that seemed to be the way of things here – but he couldn't help wishing that someone would explain it to him. After all, he was the head of the household, supreme ruler in a society where nobody ever told anyone else what to do, nobody ever *needed* to tell anyone else what to do (except when mountains exploded and flooded the world with black mud). Ludicrous, he thought; nominally, I'm the most important man in this valley, and I'm the only one who hasn't got a clue what's happening. It's like a religion where everybody worships a god who doesn't know he's divine.

The little girl led Poldarn to the door (the back door, he

noticed; any significance in that? Undoubtedly, though he could only guess at what it might be) and told him, rather abruptly, to wait there. So he waited. At first he stood up; then he began to feel fidgety, and leant against the door frame. Then he pulled over a log from the logpile and sat down. After a while, he wondered if they'd forgotten all about him, or whether the bride had changed her mind (assuming she had one to change), or if there was a furious debate raging inside about letting an offcomer marry into a respectable house; or maybe they'd all fallen asleep, or gone off to do something else, or died. Maybe they were all waiting impatiently for him, tapping their feet and picking at their sleeves, with Elja in floods of tears because she'd been left standing at the altar. He considered opening the door just a crack and looking in, but he couldn't quite bring himself to do that, for fear that he'd be noticed and everyone would swivel round and stare at him. Ridiculous, he thought; they can't leave me out here all day like a tethered donkey. Can they?

Apparently they could. After what seemed like a very long time – long enough for his left leg to go to sleep, at any rate – Poldarn came to the conclusion that if he was going to be stuck here indefinitely, he might as well find something useful to do, in accordance with the underlying philosophy of the place. He looked around, and saw a big splitting axe lodged in a big stump, with a stack of wood split into kindling, where someone had presumably downed tools in order to go to the wedding. There was still plenty of wood to be split, a whole pile of it, so he hauled himself painfully to his feet, levered the axe out of the chopping block, set a log on top and took a swing at it.

He'd taken aim at a shake-line in the log but he missed, and the axe bit deep into the log at a slant, sending a jarring shock up his arms into his shoulders. Poldarn winced, stood on the log and waggled the axe from side to side to get it free.

His next shot was in line and on target, and the log did indeed split in two; no doubt about that, because the two halves flew apart and sailed through the air at just under head height, fast enough to do a serious injury to anybody unlucky enough to be in the way. That suggested to him that maybe he was using a bit too much force; better, probably, just to lift the axe and let it fall in its own weight (which had no doubt been carefully calculated by a competent smith for this very reason). He retrieved the two halves of the log, put one up and studied it, taking care to fix all his attention on the place where he wanted the axe to bite. Then he swung it up, letting the momentum of the swing bring it through its course, and allowed it to fall, guiding it with his hands like a skilled helmsman.

He missed the log with the axe head but not with the shaft; with the result that the head snapped off and shot off at a ridiculous pace, thumping against the back door of the house with a noise that must've been audible at Colscegsford. As he stood there feeling incredibly stupid, the door opened and Eyvind came out.

'What the hell do you think you're doing?' he asked.

'Sorry,' Poldarn mumbled. 'I was just trying to make myself useful, that's all.'

'There's a time and a place, you know,' Eyvind said, shaking his head. 'Anyway, the hell with that. There's a problem.'

Poldarn nodded. 'I had a feeling there might be. What's up?'

Eyvind pulled a face. 'We haven't got a guarantor, is the problem.'

'Oh.' Poldarn looked grave. 'What's a guarantor?'

'What? Oh, of course, you wouldn't know. The guarantor is the man who guarantees the wedding vows.'

The way Eyvind said it made it sound like the most obvious thing in the world, until you stopped and thought about it. 'Ah,' Poldarn said. 'What does that mean? In practice,' he added quickly. 'What's he got to do in the ceremony, I mean.'

'Not a lot,' Eyvind admitted, 'but you can't have a wedding without one, because then it wouldn't be a wedding. All he's got to do is stand around looking solemn, and when you and the girl say your vows, he holds out a sword or a spear, and you rest your hand on it.'

'Oh,' Poldarn said. 'What's that in aid of?'

Eyvind fidgeted impatiently. 'The general idea is that if either side breaks one of the wedding vows, the guarantor's there to make sure they're punished for it. That's what the sword's for, it's symbolic. Like the seconds in a duel.'

'Really? At a *wedding*?' Poldarn shrugged. 'Still, what do I know about it? Anyway, why haven't we got one? Surely there's established procedures for figuring out who it's got to be.'

Eyvind laughed. 'Oh, it's easy. Younger brothers of the bride and groom, one on each side; failing which, male relatives in order. Unfortunately, there aren't any. You've got no living relatives, apart from your grandmother. On her side, Colsceg can't do it, because he's her father, and he's too old. Barn can't do it, because he'll be head of house when Colsceg's gone. Normally it'd be Egil, but he's conducting the ceremony. We're stuck.'

Poldarn thought about it for a moment. 'It's got to be family,' he said.

'Well, it should be. But in this case, obviously not.'

'Yes,' Poldarn said impatiently, 'but this can't be the first time something like this has happened. There's got to be a back-up procedure, surely.'

Eyvind nodded slowly. 'Well, yes, there is. Where there's no family, it should be two outsiders – neighbours, of course, but they shouldn't be under the jurisdiction of either side. Well, obviously,' he added, and Poldarn didn't ask for an explanation. 'Actually,' he went on, 'Colsceg suggested me for your side, and I suppose there's no reason why I shouldn't, it's just a ceremonial thing after all. But that still leaves us short for their side.'

Poldarn sighed. 'This is silly,' he said. 'Come on, there must be someone. Haven't they got cousins or nephews or something?'

'Oh sure. But not here, they all live a long way away, that's the problem. It'd be days before they could get here, and one thing you really can't do is stop a wedding once it's started. That's really bad.'

Poldarn nodded. 'And nobody considered all this before now?' he asked. 'All those people scurrying about with baskets of leaves and stuff, and no one thought about who was going to say the words or do this guarantor business?'

'No.' Eyvind grinned. 'If you knew us, you wouldn't be at all surprised. It's not usual, you see, it never happens like this, so nobody thought about it. Halder would've thought about it, of course, that'd have been his job, but he's not here. So you'd have thought about it, but you don't know.'

'Nobody told me.'

'It didn't occur to anybody you wouldn't know. Except me, I guess; but I'm not even supposed to be here. I can't suddenly stand up and start telling people what to do – I'm a guest in this household.'

He seemed to be getting upset, so Poldarn headed him off. 'That makes sense, I suppose. It's a bloody nuisance, though. What are we going to do?'

'No idea,' Eyvind confessed. 'Same for everybody. You're head of house, this sort of thing is up to you. It's what you're for.'

'Ah,' Poldarn said, 'well, that answers an important question that's been bothering me for a while. So I've got to choose someone, have I?'

Eyvind nodded.

'And if I make a choice, everybody's got to go along with it? No arguments or people stamping off in a huff?'

'Certainly not.' Eyvind looked mildly shocked at the thought. 'Of course, you've got to choose the right person.'

'Of course.' Poldarn leant the broken axe handle tidily against the woodpile. 'All right, we need an outsider. That narrows it down to two; and you're already in, and I'm the bridegroom . . .'

'You aren't an outsider.'

Poldarn pursed his lips, then went on: 'So that just leaves Boarci, doesn't it? Slice of good luck him showing up when he did, really.'

Eyvind made an exasperated noise. 'You can't choose him,' he said, 'he's an offcomer.'

'Isn't that the point?'

'Yes, but—' Eyvind stopped, then nodded slowly. 'All right,' he said, 'that's fine, I'll go and ask him if he'll do it. You wait there.'

'Well, but—' Poldarn said; but by then, Eyvind was back in the house and the door was closing behind him. Poldarn waited for a few minutes, then he picked up the axe handle, sat on his log and started whittling back the broken tongue with his knife.

He'd done one side and was scraping down the other when the door opened again. This time, though, it wasn't Eyvind; it was Barn, his future brother-in-law, looking uncharacter-istically anxious.

'There you are,' he said. 'We've been looking for you all over. Are you coming in, or not?'

Poldarn put down the axe handle and stowed his knife carefully away. 'Might as well,' he said. 'Have you sorted everything out yet?'

Barn frowned. 'Of course we have,' he replied. 'Everything's ready. Come on, will you, they'll be wondering what the hell's going on.'

They'll be wondering, Poldarn thought. 'Fine,' he said. 'Lead the way, then.'

Though it had been only a few days since he'd lived there, he'd forgotten quite how dark the inside of the house could be. The only light came through the small side windows (which on this occasion were firmly shuttered), the smoke-hole in the roof, and a battery of assorted pottery lamps lined up on a single table at the far end of the hall. Fortunately, people got out of his way before he blundered into them, and at least there wasn't any furniture left in the house for him to trip over. He followed Barn up to the top table. He felt horribly nervous, more so than if he'd been expecting to have to fight for his life (but that wasn't a fair comparison; he knew he was good at that sort of thing, but this was all new to him). He could feel a sneeze gathering momentum just above the bridge of his nose, and keeping it down was harder than carrying newly felled lumber.

Once Poldarn was inside the circle of pale yellow light, he was able to make out a few faces. There was Colsceg, right in the middle of the table, looking worried and depressed. There was Egil, white as a sheet and very tense, his left hand crushing his right fist. Next to Egil was Eyvind, doing a fine imitation of a dead body, and next to him was Elja, who gave him a very quick, conspiratorial smile before tightening her mouth into a thin line. It was that smile that made him think that, just possibly, this whole mess might somehow come out all right in the end. For some reason they'd draped her in bits of trailing greenery – for some reason, for some reason; he'd have given the farm and the clothes he stood up in for an insight into the coherent stream of logic that he was sure lay at the back of all this, but for the life of him he couldn't see why a young girl couldn't get married without having to be festooned with salad. That said, it suited her, in a bizarre sort of way. The dark, shining green of the leaves, reflecting the dull glare of the lamps, emphasised the thickness and body of her abundant, slightly coarse brown hair (and maybe that was the only reason; and a very good reason it would be, if only he could be sure). They'd put her in a plain light brown sack of a dress – somehow he knew without any doubt at all that she hadn't chosen it herself – but in spite of everything it looked just right, bringing out the creamy white of her skin and the very dark red of her lips. Pure luck that she should be so perfectly suited to the traditional outfit, which ought to have looked ridiculous; but at that moment, he was almost prepared to forgive and accept all the outlandish and inexplicable things about these people (his people; must remember that), simply because Elja proved that, once in a while, they worked pretty well.

I'm staring, Poldarn thought, that's got to be the wrong thing to do. Try to look properly solemn, or, failing that, stuffed. No sudden movements, and for pity's sake, let's see if we can get through this without killing anybody.

Egil stood up. He had some slight difficulty with the bench, it was too close to the table, and he had to slide and wriggle past it to get to his feet. Once he was there (he had to grab the table with his left hand to steady himself) he took a deep breath and looked Poldarn straight in the eyes.

'Ciartan,' he said – it took Poldarn just a fraction of a second to remember that Ciartan was him – 'do you accept this woman as your wife?'

Which woman? Oh, that woman, the one you're standing in front of so I can't actually see her. But there weren't any other females sitting at the table, apart from Rannwey, and he assumed that the chances of marrying her by accident were acceptably slim. 'Yes,' he replied, and hoped that would do.

Egil turned his head. 'Elja, do you accept this man as your husband?' There was a muted squeak from the shadows that might have been a yes, or a rodent narrowly avoiding a cat.

Egil seemed inclined to accept it as consent, or else he was too busy rehearsing his own lines in his head to listen; he grunted, and went on: 'Who is prepared to guarantee this marriage?', as if he were a general ordering brave men to their deaths. Eyvind stood up with the speed of a sword-monk's best draw; then nothing happened. Several heartbeats passed, and Poldarn finally sneezed.

'Here,' someone said in the darkness outside the yellow circle, and Boarci threaded his way through the crowd, some-how managing not to knock anybody over or cause any injuries with the axe in his right hand. Poldarn winced; if I'd only known, he thought, I'd have made more of an effort with the polishing. It made sense, of course; they'd never have allowed Boarci on the top table. For some reason, Poldarn had a picture of him being given his portion of the wedding breakfast in a bowl on the floor, with the other domestic animals.

'It's all right,' Boarci muttered in Poldarn's ear as he took his post directly behind him. 'Cheer up, nobody's going to eat you.' Eyvind scowled at him for that; nobody else appeared to have noticed.

'Guarantors,' Egil said crisply, whereupon Eyvind stooped and came up holding a backsabre, which he'd left on the floor where nobody could trip over it; he put it on the table as if he was waiting on a grand banquet and the sword was a tray of cinnamon cakes. Boarci leaned over, shoving Poldarn's head slightly to one side with his arm, and dumped his axe next to it; the two weapons clattered together noisily. 'All right,' Egil said. His sister stood up, reached across and laid the flat of her hand on the blade of the sword, nodding very slightly at Poldarn. He interpreted that as meaning that he was supposed to do the same thing, and rested his finger-tips on the axe head. It was cold and very smooth, like steel skin. Poldarn felt ashamed at the sight of the file marks around the eye.

'Bear witness,' Egil said, in a rather wobbly, high-pitched voice, 'these weapons, and if these vows are broken, avenge them.' He finished the speech with a stifled cough – he was standing over one of the lamps, and the smoke was tickling his throat. Poldarn managed not to laugh, though it was one of the funniest things he could remember having seen. 'Bear witness,' he repeated, coughing himself, and he picked up the sword and the axe and waggled them half-heartedly in the air.

At that point, he must have swallowed a mouthful of lamp smoke the wrong way, because instead of just coughing he choked, and the spasm must have messed up his coordination; in any event, he lost his grip on the axe, made a desperate attempt to recapture it, and dropped it right on top of the lamp, which shattered and flooded the table with oil, which immediately caught fire. At first, nobody seemed to realise what was happening. Then the burning oil set light to their cuffs and sleeves; they jumped up, swearing and flapping their arms like so many crippled birds, prancing round in circles, bumping into each other – under other circumstances it would have made a very pretty burlesque dance, appropriate for a country wedding, except for the presence of the uninvited guest and master of ceremonies, the spirit of fire. Poldarn immediately looked to see if Elja was all right; but she didn't have any sleeves, and she'd got her hand out of the way in time. Then he looked down at his own hands, and saw that although the cloth at his wrists was dark and shiny with oil, for some reason the fire hadn't taken to him. Egil was staggering backwards, pawing at his face; Eyvind was on fire from his wrists to his chin, contriving to set light to his whole body as he tried to slap out the flames. Apparently Colsceg had more imagination than the rest of them; he'd doused his sleeve with a jug of beer, but the oil refused to stop burning. Another lamp, a little further down, burst in the heat and showered the table with burning oil and sharp potsherds, like a miniature volcano.

Oh for pity's sake, Poldarn thought, because this was all so unnecessary; it was just a little fire to start with, and there was no earthly reason why it should be spreading so dramatically. He knew he ought to be doing something – head of the household, hero of the mudslides, a little domestic fire ought to be child's play to him – but for the moment all he could do was stand and stare. Nobody in the mob behind him seemed to be moving, so perhaps they all thought it was part of the ceremony.

'Hold still,' someone was shouting; it was Boarci, wrapping his coat round his left arm. 'For God's sake hold still, before you set the house on fire.' But nobody seemed prepared to listen to him, or else they simply couldn't understand a direct order; so he pushed past Poldarn, scrambled over the table, kneeling in the burning oil as he did so, and shoved Eyvind over onto the ground. Somebody was yelling at him, but he was too busy to notice; he was clubbing out the flames that Eyvind was wearing like a suit of clothes, as he did so choosing to disregard the fire that was clinging to his own legs and body. Egil had pulled off his coat by now, and was whacking at his father's arms and chest with it, while Colsceg stood perfectly still and stared at him as if he'd just gone mad. Another lamp exploded—

'Well,' said a voice by Poldarn's side, 'here we are again. Trouble really does seem to follow you around, doesn't it?'

He recognised the face, which hadn't been there a heartbeat ago; and the voice was even more familiar, though God alone knew where from. 'Who the hell are you?' he asked.

'Oh, don't mind me, I'm not really here.' The man laughed. 'I *was* here, many years ago, and of course I'll be here again. Right now, I'm somewhere else, but don't worry about it. You think I'd let a piddling little thing like geography keep me from my best friend's wedding?'

'Who are you?' Poldarn repeated.

'Good question,' the man replied. He was wearing the

robes of a sword-monk in full academic dress, with a broad crimson sash to hold his sword in, and a white fur trim to his hood. 'You know, I call myself so many names, it's a pain sometimes remembering who I'm meant to be. When in doubt, I just say Monach, which is the word for *monk* in some language or other that nobody knows any more. In case you're wondering,' he went on, 'this is actually some time later.'

Poldarn wanted to move, at least to get close enough to smash this idiot's face in, but found he couldn't. 'What've you done to me?' he shouted.

'Me? Nothing. How could I, when I'm not even here? Now pay attention, I'm trying to explain. You think you're still at the wedding, in the middle of the fire. Not so. Right now you're lying on a heap of straw in a deep sleep, with your devoted subjects and newly minted in-laws taking bets on whether you'll ever wake up out of it. Didn't I mention, you're one very sick man?'

'No,' Poldarn replied. In front of his eyes, Boarci and Egil were still flapping away with their coats; everything was moving, but nothing was changing. 'What happened?'

Monach laughed. 'Oh, it hasn't happened yet – in the time-frame you're looking at, I mean. In this time-frame, we're about twenty seconds away from the fire spreading to the thatch, which is where the trouble starts. In about five seconds, though, you'll fall over backwards and hit your head, so I'd better get a move on. You trip over your feet, bang your head and go to sleep – is this starting to sound familiar, by the way? – then the building catches light, everybody panics and squashes out through the door; it's only later, when the fire's taken hold and the roof's starting to fall in, that someone says, *Hey, where's Ciartan?* and they realise you must still be inside. You know,' Monach went on, reaching past a burning man and taking a honeycake off a plate, 'your life is woven from two dominant threads, tragedy and lack of originality. Not only do really shitty things happen to you, they happen over and over again.' He bit into the cake and chewed before continuing. 'There's a very good reason for that, by the way, like there's a very good reason for everything that goes on around here, and you're the only person in the whole wide world who isn't allowed to know what it is. That must really get up your nose sometimes, I guess.'

'I'm asleep,' Poldarn said. 'And dreaming all this.'

'Correct,' Monach said. 'Actually, it goes deeper than that; in fact, from a professional point of view, as far as I'm concerned, this is a real beauty, a genuine collector's item. You see, you aren't just dreaming this *now*, as you're lying on your pile of straw surrounded by your nearest and dearest. This is going to be one of your favourite recurring nightmares, you'll come back here time and again, sometimes weeks in a row; so I'm not just talking to you now, I'm talking to you all through your life, present, future *and* past. You know, I could work this up into a really good paper for the Founders' Day lecture, if you hadn't burned down Deymeson.' He grinned, and reached for another cake. 'Very good, these,' he said. 'Next time we meet up like this you must give me the recipe. Do you understand what I'm telling you? You bloody well ought to, you were top of the class in divinity theory in Third Year. I always had trouble getting my head around logical paradox, but it never bothered you any.'

'Please,' Poldarn said, 'I want to wake up now, I don't like this dream.'

'Not surprising. You aren't meant to like it. That's why they call them nightmares.' Monach sighed. 'What really amazes me is how few of them you have, considering the stuff you've got up to over the years. Compared to most of what you've done and been through, this is a picnic. Still, I guess it's all a matter of interpretation; and this is one of the main turning points in your life – well, we're just coming up to it, or else we've just passed it, depending on which direction we happen to be going in at the time.' He smiled. 'No, I'm not making it easy for you, I know. You'd hate that, you'd reckon it was patronising. Now, this girl you've just married—' He pointed; Elja was staring up at the roof and pointing. 'Lovely kid, she really likes you, I'd say you're on to a good thing there, even if she is young enough to be your daughter. God only knows what she sees in you, but that's her business, I suppose. Anyway, I trust you'll treat her a bit better next time you're here. She'll forgive you, I expect. That's the amazing thing about these people, this extraordinary knack they've got for forgiving and forgetting, or at least turning a blind eye.' Monach yawned – Poldarn could see bits of chewed cake on his tongue – then turned into a crow and, flapping the burning sleeves of his gown, lifted aloft, and flew slowly up into the smoke and flames of the roof.

Chapter Fifteen

'Wake up,' said a voice in his ear, 'for crying out loud.'

So he woke up. He was lying in the yard, next to the woodpile, and someone had just thrown a bucket of water in his face. No pile of straw, he noted, and no circle of anxious faces (so either Monach had got it wrong, or all that stuff was for next time; he repeated the thought in his mind, but this time none of it made any sense); just Boarci standing over him with an empty bucket.

'Bloody hell,' Poldarn croaked. 'What happened to you?'

'What? Oh, you mean my beard.' Boarci pulled a sad face. 'Got set on fire, didn't it? And when I looked at it just now, I figured, bloody fool I'd look with only half a beard. So I shaved the rest off. It'll grow back,' he sighed. 'Eventually.'

'How about the rest of you? You were all on fire,' Poldarn remembered.

'Just my clothes,' Boarci replied, 'though they're all ruined, of course, which is a pain. You know, I'm not having much luck here. When I arrived, I didn't have much but at least I had the clothes I stood up in. Not any more. This lot belongs to your middle-house stockman. Anyway,' he went on, 'it could've been worse. Nobody died, is the main thing, and they reckon they can patch up the house, given time. Not the most cheerful wedding I've ever been to, but livelier than some.'

Poldarn stood up. His legs were weak, but they seemed to be working. 'Where's Elja?' he said. 'Is she all right?'

Boarci nodded. 'A bit crispy round the edges, if you know what I mean, but yes, she's fine. Over there in the trap-house, cutting bandages and stuff. Only one who got anything like a nasty burn was your brother-in-law Egil, and it's only the backs of his hands, should heal up in time. I've seen worse.'

'That's a comfort,' Poldarn muttered. 'What happened to me?'

Boarci laughed. 'Bloody comical, that was. That lamp shattered, you jumped back, fell over your feet and nutted yourself on the deck. Out like a snuffed candle. Anyway, you were sleeping like a little lamb, so I got you out and here we are.'

Now that he mentioned it, Poldarn's head *was* hurting. 'What about the house?' he said.

'Oh, once they'd pulled themselves together it was business as usual. That's how come I've only just woken you up, there wasn't a bucket of water to spare till now. It's a bloody mess in there, but really it's just a few rafters and plates need replacing, the rest they can patch up. You know what they're like when they get started on a job.'

'That's good,' Poldarn said. 'So everything's under control, is it?'

Boarci laughed. 'As much as it ever is,' he replied. 'You ought to go and lie down – you look as sick as a pig. There's nothing for you to do, if that's what you're on about.'

'Good,' Poldarn said. 'I think I'll go and find Elja.'

'Yeah, why not? Of course, she'll probably tell you to get

lost, she's got work to do. But it shows the right spirit, I suppose.'

Poldarn nodded. The movement hurt. 'So,' he said, 'did Elja and me get married or not?'

'I think so,' Boarci said with a grin. 'Anyhow, close enough for government work. And it saved having to listen to all the speeches, so really it's a blessing. Though I was looking forward to yours.'

'Mine? I was supposed to make a speech?'

'Oh yes,' Boarci said solemnly. 'High spot of the event. There, see how lucky you are? If you fell in a shitheap you'd find a truffle.'

'Well,' Poldarn said nervously, 'there it is. Our house.'

Elja nodded. 'I've seen it before. It's very nice. Have they got the furniture in yet?'

'I think so,' Poldarn replied, guessing. 'I expect they have, it's the sort of detail they're good at. Anyhow, I'm sure there'll be something to sit down on and somewhere to sleep.'

'Mphm.' Elja nodded her head, neatly forestalling the implied topic. 'I don't suppose anybody's brought any food.'

'You're hungry?'

'Yes,' she replied firmly, 'very. I didn't have any breakfast, and we didn't get anything to eat after the wedding, what with the fire and everything. It's very important for you to know that I get extremely bad-tempered when I'm hungry.'

'Oh.' Poldarn froze, unable to think of anything intelligent to suggest. 'I suppose we'd better go back to the house – the old house, I mean – and see if we can dig up some bread and cheese.'

'Bread and cheese,' Elja repeated. 'Yes, all right. You go back, I'd better go inside and see what sort of a state the place is in.'

'Fine,' Poldarn snapped. 'I'll be as quick as I can.'

He didn't run, because his head was still hurting and every

step he took sent a shooting pain through his temples, but he walked briskly. It was just starting to get dark, and he missed his footing, stumbled and twisted his ankle. Bloody wonderful wedding day, he muttered to himself.

They were surprised to see him, back at the middle house. 'What are you doing here?' Rannwey asked, in a way that suggested that she wasn't at all happy at this latest display of eccentricity. 'Where's Elja?'

'Back at the house.'

'What, you left her there on her own, on your wedding night?'

'She wanted something to eat.'

Rannwey frowned at him. 'But there's plenty of food up there, I took it up myself this morning. Rye bread and cold smoked lamb and honeycakes and goat's cheese and some hard-boiled eggs in butter, and a quart of the new beer.'

'Oh,' Poldarn said. 'Oh, well, that's all right, then.'

So he trudged back, limping rather self-consciously on his pinked ankle, even though there was nobody to see him. When he reached the house, he could see a blade of yellow light showing under the door. He knocked before pushing it open.

'There you are,' Elja said with her mouth full, as she opened the door to him. 'You needn't have bothered, there's plenty of food.'

'I know,' Poldarn replied. 'They told me. Smoked lamb and eggs in butter.'

She nodded. 'Well, smoked lamb, anyway,' she said, 'I've eaten the eggs. Very good they were, too. And all the furniture's in, all nice and tidy, though I think I'll get you to move the linen chest out of the bedroom, you could bang your shin on it coming through the door. I've lit a fire, so it's nice and warm.'

Poldarn was already nice and warm, or at least warm, from toiling backwards and forwards up the river bank. 'Great,' he said. 'Thanks. I'll come in, then, shall I?'

'You do what you like.'

The house seemed very big with nobody in it but the two of them. It smelled rather disgusting – he hadn't been there when they laid the floor – two parts of potters' clay to one part of cowshit, the same mix as they used for lining furnaces; kept the heat in and the wet out – and the air was still full of sawdust and the clammy damp of newly cut green timber, drawn out by the large fire blazing in the hearth. Poldarn looked at it with disapproval; he'd seen enough fire for one day, and the sweat inside his shirt made him squirm. Mostly, he realised, he felt very tired, probably because of the headache and the day's melodrama.

'You sit down,' Elja said. 'I'll get you some food.'

Well, he thought, as he lowered his aching back into the big carved oak chair that Halder had always sat in, this is a bit more like it. Food on the table, his own fireside, his wife, domesticity. A man could get to feel his age in surroundings like this. That thought made him frown involuntarily, because ever since he'd woken up in the bloody mud beside the Bohec he hadn't felt any particular age; seventeen going on ninety, with an option on eternal youth and imminent certain death. According to Halder, he'd been born forty-two years ago, when the timbers that made up this fine house of his were little twiggy saplings, but he'd accepted that information as he'd accepted everything else Halder had told him about himself: a fact whose truth he had no reason to doubt, but clearly relating to somebody else. Now at least he had something to measure himself against; the timbers of the house, the house itself. By those criteria he was exactly the right age for the purpose in hand, and everything was working out the way it had been intended to.

'Elja,' he called out – she was at the other end of the hall – 'how old are you?'

'What?'

'I asked, how old are you?'

She didn't actually count on her fingers, but she paused before answering. 'Twenty-four,' she said. 'Why?'

'Just wondering, that's all. I didn't know.'

'Well, now you do. How about you?'

He didn't understand the question. 'Sorry, what do you mean?'

'How old are you, since it's so important.'

'Forty-two, according to my grandfather.'

'Well, he should know. You don't look it.'

He smiled inside. 'In a good way or a bad way?'

'Both,' she replied, slicing bread. 'From the chin down, you could pass for thirty.'

The inner smile faded. 'Fine,' he said. 'And from the chin up?'

'No idea,' she replied. 'Actually, you remind me of those stories where a young man visits the secret kingdom of the fairies; and next day he leaves, and he finds that it's a hundred years later and everybody he used to know's been dead for ages.'

'Thank you so much.'

'Oh, I didn't mean it in a nasty way,' she replied, hacking at the smoked lamb. 'Actually, it's rather—' She paused, wiping the knife. 'Interesting,' she said. 'Which is no bad thing, because when I'm all fat and wrinkly and old, you'll probably still look exactly the same.'

Poldarn nodded. 'Well, that'll be something to look forward to. Can I give you a hand with that?'

'No, you stay there, I don't want you under my feet. I saved you the last honeycake.'

She brought the plate and a mug of beer over to him, then went back to the other end of the hall and started clearing away. 'Start as you mean to go on,' she said, by way of explanation. 'If things aren't put away as soon as you've finished with them, next thing you know there's a big tangle of clutter, and it's much harder to get everything straight again.'

'That's very sensible,' Poldarn sighed. 'I don't know about you,' he added, 'but I'm tired out.'

'Really? You go on to bed, then. I'll be through as soon as I've finished in here.'

That sounded like a good idea; so he got up – his back was aching and his ankle hurt like hell – and tottered down the hall and through the partition door, which had learned to stick a little since he and Raffen had hung it, only a few days ago. He carried on into the bedroom.

There was a bed in it, presumably; it was hard to tell, because where the bed should have been there was a bed-shape, but completely buried under sheaves of green leaves, flowers and lengths of glossy creeper. All symbolic, he guessed, but a bloody nuisance; was he allowed to shovel the mess onto the floor, or was he supposed to lie on top of it, with the twigs and stems digging into the small of his back? Knowing his luck, there'd be beetles and earwigs as well; not really conducive to the occasion. He wanted to ask what he should do, but he didn't feel that he could, somehow. He compromised by shuffling enough of the foliage across onto the other side of the bed to allow him enough space to lie down on. There was a pillow; beautifully crisp linen, and stuffed with clover if the scent was anything to go by. It felt wonderful, soft enough to soothe his aching head with its support, and for the first time that day he felt his muscles unclench. I'll close my eyes, he thought, just for a second or two.

When he opened them again, there was sunlight in his eyes. He was lying uncomfortably on his right arm, which was numb from the elbow, on a mat of crushed fern and creeper; the rest of the bed was defoliated, and had been slept in. Bloody hell, he thought.

A head appeared round the door. 'If I were you, I'd get up now,' Elja said. 'Sun's up, they'll all be here any minute, and there's a lot of work to get through.'

Poldarn groaned. His head was still hurting, and when he tried to move his right arm, the pins and needles started with a vengeance. 'Yes, all right,' he said sadly. 'Is there any of that bread left?'

'No, sorry. It was getting stale, anyhow. With any luck there'll be time to do some baking later on; we'll have a whole household to feed this time tomorrow, remember.'

He swung his feet off the bed and rested them on the floor; he still had his boots on, and he felt uncomfortable all over, but there wasn't time to wash if the whole Haldersness outfit was due to show up at any moment.

'I was thinking,' Elja's voice drifted in through the open door, 'how about Ciartanstead?'

'What about it?'

'As a name for our farm, silly. Got to have a name, after all – we can't keep on calling it Haldersness.'

'Ah, right.' He stood up; his ankle now felt very bad indeed. 'Who's supposed to choose the name, then?'

'Well, you are, of course. After all, it's your farm. I like the sound of Ciartanstead, let's call it that.'

'All right,' Poldarn mumbled apathetically. 'Like you said, we've got to call it something.' Try as he might, he couldn't help feeling that this wasn't what they ought to be discussing, but he decided against pointing this out; if she didn't want to talk about it, then talking about it would most likely be counter-productive. Of course, if they could read each others' minds, there wouldn't be a problem—

'It's settled, then,' Elja announced cheerfully. 'Ciartanstead. I could get to like it.'

There was a knock at the door; two very hard thumps, suggesting to Poldarn that the art of knocking on doors wasn't widely practised here. (You wouldn't need to, when you could announce your imminent arrival just by thinking about it.) 'That'll be Dad and the rest of them,' Elja said, as if she hadn't already known.

The news, Colsceg announced, was good. They'd been up on the roof (what, already? It was only just daylight, for pity's sake) and they'd been right, the damage was far less severe than it looked; two days' work, three at the outside, and the place would be habitable. Egil would be out of action for a while, but everyone else was back on their feet; a few bandages here and there and some pretty odd-looking beards and eyebrows, but nothing to worry about. Certainly not enough to justify cancelling the games—

'Games?' Poldarn echoed.

Colsceg pulled one of those oh-for-crying-out-loud faces Poldarn had come to know so well. 'Games,' Colsceg repeated. 'Sports. Trials of strength and skill, to celebrate the wedding. It's a poor heart that never rejoices,' he added, as if reciting a particularly solemn passage from scripture.

'Oh, good,' Poldarn said, grateful that his thoughts on the subject were strictly private. 'When's that, then?'

After having known Poldarn for several weeks, it was surprising that Colsceg could still be so shocked at the man's ignorance. 'Well, *now*, of course. That's what we're here for. We've brought all the gear, and they're putting up the ring.' He paused, asking Providence under his breath to give him strength. 'So you're not ready, then.'

Poldarn shrugged. 'I suppose I'm as ready as I'll ever be. I don't know if I'm any good at sports. Maybe I should sit out and just watch and give the prizes or something.'

'No, that's completely wrong,' Colsceg snapped, then reined in his temper with an effort. 'It's you against all comers, that's the whole point. It's traditional,' he added, as if capping off an argument with a direct quote from the statute-book. 'When you say you're no good at sports—'

'Actually,' Poldarn interrupted, mostly out of devilment, 'I didn't say that. I said I don't know. Could be I'm brilliant at them. I guess we'll have to wait and see.'

One thing Colsceg was gaining from his alliance with the

Haldersness mob was a vastly increased ability to stay patient. 'Fine,' he said. 'Well, when you're ready.'

'No time like the present,' Poldarn said. 'Lead on.'

They'd already marked out the ring with ground chalk mixed with water; now they were sharpening stakes and hammering them in with a post-rammer. They'd cut the rails already and laid them by, handy to be nailed on to the stakes to complete the circle. 'We thought we'd start with javelin-throwing,' Colsceg said, 'it's fairly gentle, good one to warm up on. Then the weightlifting, axe-throwing, heavy running—'

'Heavy running? What's that?'

'You run five times round the ring carrying a half-hundredweight sack of coal. Light running's the same, but without the sack. We thought we'd do the light running after the log-chopping.'

I've got to do all this, Poldarn thought, me against all comers. Bloody hell. 'Good idea,' he said. 'Is that it, or is there more?'

'Well, yes,' Colsceg said. 'After the light running, we'll have the wrestling, quarterstaff, shying at marks and single-stick, and finally the home game to round off with. If that's all right with you,' Colsceg added.

'Oh, fine,' Poldarn replied; and as he said it he was thinking, If I say I've done my ankle after the third event, which probably won't be too far from the truth, they'll have to let me off the rest and I'll have shown willing, which is the main thing, surely. 'Actually, now you mention it, I guess I'm quite looking forward to this.'

Nothing to indicate which of his questions and statements had been the most offensive, but Colsceg sighed and walked away. Somehow, Boarci contrived to materialise out of thin air just behind his shoulder. 'How's you, then?' he muttered.

'What?' Poldarn turned round. 'Oh, I'm fine.'

Boarci was grinning like an elderly sheepdog. 'Sleep well?'

'Yes,' Poldarn replied accurately. 'I wish someone had told me about all this, I could've made up an excuse to get out of it.'

'Selfish bugger, aren't you?' Boarci replied. 'It's the best part of a wedding, this: making the bridegroom look really useless in front of his new bride. They're all looking forward to it.'

'You included, by the sound of it.'

'Too right. I'm really looking forward to the quarterstaff. They told you about that?'

Poldarn shook his head, which was hurting even more than before.

'It's a good laugh, the quarterstaff. They put up these two trestles with a thin plank between them, and you stand at one end, the other guy's at the other end, and you've both got big ash poles to hit each other with. Actually, there's a lot of skill involved, takes years to learn. Anyway, the object is to knock the other man off the plank, and there's a big pile of rocks underneath for him to land on. Hurts like shit. I'm bloody good with the staff, say so myself as shouldn't.'

'I see,' Poldarn said. 'So what happens if I lose? Presumably whoever wins stays up.'

Boarci laughed. 'Don't you wish. No, it's like he said, you against all comers. You get knocked down, you just pick yourself up and get back on, ready for the next challenger. If there's time, we get to go round again. Didn't it ever occur to you why I'm still a bachelor?'

There were seven entries besides Poldarn for the javelin-throwing. Six of them out-threw him by a rather offensive margin; he rather hoped that the seventh, Eyvind, had deliberately thrown short as a gesture of solidarity, but being realistic he reckoned it probably had more to do with the thick wads of bandages on both Eyvind's hands. Whatever the reason, he contrived to ace Eyvind's throw by a whole two inches. All nine other competitors beat him at weight-lifting, which turned out to be a very short event, concluding as soon as he gave up (on the third weight). The best that could be said for his performance in the axe-throwing was that he didn't kill anybody. Asburn won the heavy running; Poldarn did manage to complete the course, though only by turning round and dragging the sack backwards for the last fifty yards. By any standards it was a pretty hopeless showing; but the worse he did, the more good-natured, even affectionate grew the laughter and shouted commentary from the two households; for some reason (no doubt entirely logical, if you were in on the basic premises) the more hopeless and pathetic he made himself look, the more they seemed to like him. Actually, he could explain that: you tended to distrust, fear and dislike the stranger, the man you didn't know, couldn't properly assess. Once he demonstrated a complete lack of physical prowess, there was much less reason for fear and animosity. Accordingly, Poldarn postponed his feigned injury for a while and carried on.

The next event was wood-chopping; each of the ten competitors was presented with a log and given an axe, and the first to cut all the way through was the winner. Most likely Poldarn wouldn't even have tried to win, if the log put in front of him hadn't been quite obviously thicker than anybody else's. But that struck him as unnecessarily unfair; and when the referee (Colsceg) yelled 'Go!', he found that he was taking out his negative feelings on the log. Furthermore, after the first few cuts he realised that he was good at this; instead of trying to hit, he was putting all his effort into the swing, bringing the axe up as high as he could get it and then letting it drop, guiding it into the slot with a light but firm hand, making sure he cut at the most effective angle in the most effective place, never taking his eye off the mark – it felt right, the way forge-welding the axe head for Boarci had, and the upshot of it was that he won by a clear margin, much to the surprise and disgust of the other eight competitors. Everyone else cheered, in a slightly stunned way, and Poldarn found himself revelling in the pleasures of victory to an extent he wouldn't have thought possible. In fact, he realised, he couldn't have done better if he'd planned it out carefully beforehand. Losing the first five events had got rid of the mystery and the menace; winning the sixth against all the apparent odds was exactly the right thing to do. They still liked him, but now he wasn't quite the abject failure any more, there was at least one thing he was pretty good at. All in all, he decided that he approved of this wedding-games tradition. It definitely had its uses.

Poldarn lost the light running, of course; but he did come fourth out of a field of ten, which was also just right, from a tactical point of view. Next came the wrestling, and after the first two competitors had kicked his knees out from under him and dumped him unceremoniously on his back with gratuitous force, he might have lost his temper just a little; his next opponent, Seyward the middle-house hand, found himself flying through the air (Where did I learn to do that? Who gives a damn?), Barn got an elbow in his solar plexus and sat down with a pretty hilarious grunt of astonishment, and Eyvind didn't stand a chance. In the event, Poldarn came third out of seven, as well as getting a welcome chance to sublimate his growing frustrations with his life in general into quite natural and healthy acts of extreme violence.

While he was recovering from his exertions and flexing a painful left shoulder (though his ankle was hardly bothering him at all now, for some reason) the Colscegford party were setting up the trestles, planks and bed of rocks Boarci had threatened him with. That spoiled his otherwise fairly positive mood. Boarci had said, entirely plausibly, that staff-fighting was an art, and a difficult one at that. He'd seen a few staff-fights in the Bohec valley, and what he could remember of the moves seemed to bear that judgement out. Furthermore, the trestles were unnecessarily high, in his opinion, and the rocks looked positively dangerous. To make matters worse, Boarci was parading up and down on the other side of the ring performing a very impressive repertoire of twirls and juggles with a seven-foot ash pole, and his grin was plainly visible from twenty yards away.

Poldarn slumped against a ring-stake and made a cursory inventory of his aches and pains. As well as the shoulder injury and the dodgy ankle, he had a sinister twinge in his left forearm, a pulled muscle in his chest, another in the small of his back and a distinct ache in his left hamstring. On the other hand, his headache had cleared up altogether, which was nice. So, he told himself, cheer up. Be positive. Look on the bright side. Count your blessings.

As it turned out, he didn't have to face Boarci straight away – some other poor fool got up at the opposite end of the plank. Poldarn was so preoccupied with trying to figure out how to beat the shit out of the man who'd repeatedly saved his life that he didn't really take much notice of this first bout until it was over, and his opponent was crawling out from under the plank on his hands and knees.

Oh, Poldarn thought, I seem to have won. How did I do that? He thought about it, and remembered his moves, reviewing them as if he'd been watching someone else: the enemy's feint sparred up to the left, a pre-emptive parry with the butt of the pole joined with an aggressive step forward to force the opponent onto his back foot, followed by a jump back to make room and a deft flick of the wrist to jab the pole into the other man's teeth, swiftly doubled into a meaty jab to the right ankle and a finishing smack to the left ear. Did I do all that? he wondered. Apparently I did. He tried to remember who he'd been fighting, but he couldn't. He'd seen a target, not a face, and all targets look the same, after a while.

The next man to clamber up onto the plank wasn't Boarci, either; he lasted about five heartbeats before toppling off with a suspected broken collarbone. Next up was brother-in-law Barn, who presented a whole new set of problems. Barn was slow and physically inept, but so massive that hitting him didn't seem to achieve anything; and when he did swing his staff, parrying it was out of the question, given the necessity of staying on the plank. But either luck or repressed memory gave him the answer. A deft little prod to the back of the knee turned Barn's greatest asset into a liability, and he landed with a thump that shook the earth almost as much as the erupting volcano had. After him came Asburn, looking distinctly nervous. He seemed far more interested in defending himself than in attacking, whereas Poldarn had no wish whatsoever to hurt someone who was almost a friend. The upshot was a bout in which both parties pranced and feinted a lot, retreating to the far ends of the plank whenever their staffs happened to clack together. Whether Asburn really did fall over his feet, or whether he disguised a deliberate jump off the plank with a little cursory dumbshow, Poldarn wasn't sure; but he reckoned it was significant that Asburn landed cleanly on his feet well away from the carpet of rocks, and he made a resolution to thank him later, when nobody was looking.

Finally, Boarci stepped up, still fiendishly twirling his staff and pulling horrific faces. No doubt about it, he meant business, as his first onslaught amply proved – a lightning-fast lunge pulled at the last moment, followed up with a remarkably elegant quick-step shuffle up the plank, and converted into a hand-over-hand diagonal slash with the butt of the pole. By this stage, Poldarn had run out of plank to retreat onto; all he could do was duck, knowing as he did it that he was leaving his legs open to an extremely painful strike, which duly followed. Somehow, though, he kept his footing – not only that, but he improvised a side-swung riposte, fairly weak but sufficiently wristy to glance off the ball of Boarci's shoulder and clip his ear hard enough to draw blood.

Gratifyingly, Boarci jumped backwards out of the way, snapping into a perfect guard that was complete as soon as he landed. This gave Poldarn just enough time to catch his breath; then the next attack came in, and he realised that the first sally had been just a warm-up. He didn't have time to study or analyse the moves, it was all he could do to get his staff in the way of most of them, while the ones he didn't block landed on his knees and elbows, cramping him with pain. It was obvious that Boarci was taking his time, looking to wear Poldarn down with a series of carefully planned debilitating strikes that would inhibit his movements and lay him open for an artfully devised finishing strategy; the only way to counter it that he could see was one big, unexpected move to finish the fight in a heartbeat – and that was all very well, but he had no idea how to go about it. So he hung on, defending and trying to sneak back as much as he could of the ground he was continually forced to give, several times walking into punishing strikes simply in order to stay up the plank.

Then he saw his chance. Boarci swung a feint at Poldarn's face, intending to draw up his guard so as to open him for a crack across the left knee. Instead of parrying, however, Poldarn deliberately held still and took the blow – it was torture fighting down his instincts, waiting for what seemed like an eternity for the pole to smack into his cheekbone. Then, as the blow landed, he stepped forward into it and pushed rather than lunged, catching Boarci just below the navel. It was a weak contact, inflicting no pain, scoring no points; but Boarci was already on the move, stepping into a parry that hadn't happened but too late to adjust his strategy – he was thinking four moves ahead, and didn't have time to revise his plans on the fly. Just at that moment, his balance was a smidgeon too far forward, and Poldarn eased him off the plank with a gentle prod. Boarci disappeared, and a furious yell of pain suggested that he'd made an awkward landing on something hard, sharp or both. Poldarn smiled.

Nobody else seemed inclined to play, so Poldarn walked slowly to the end of the plank and jumped, like a little bird hopping off a twig. As he touched ground, his ankle gave way and he staggered, lost his feet and dropped down hard on his knees, just on the edge of the carpet of rocks. Something jagged bit into his left kneecap and he howled. For some reason the spectators seemed to find that unbearably amusing, as if he'd deliberately done something witty and clever.

He managed to get up again by planting the pole firmly in the ground and pulling himself up hand over hand, but that was about as far as he felt competent to go; so he clung to the top of the pole and remained there, swaying slightly, until Asburn and Eyvind trotted up and helped him over to a tree stump, where he could sit down and concentrate on feeling really sorry for himself without the distraction of having to maintain his balance.

'What the hell do you think you're playing at?' Eyvind whispered noisily in his ear. 'Are you out of your mind, or do you just enjoy hurting people?'

Poldarn looked up sharply. 'What?'

Eyvind stared at him; incomprehension staring at incomprehension, an optical effect like the well-known juxtaposition of two facing mirrors. Then he sighed. 'Right,' he said, 'I guess it's probably my fault, somebody's fault, anyhow. You weren't to know – you can't see things unless people tell you out loud. The point is, it's not meant to be serious. It's a game. The idea is, you let everybody beat you at sports, to show what a good sort you are, and in return they go easy on you in the fighting events; nobody gets beaten up, and we all have a nice drink afterwards. You're treating it like it's a battle to the death.'

'But that's not fair,' Poldarn objected, trying to keep his

cool but failing. 'They *weren't* going easy on me, far from it.
And I've got the bruises to prove it.'

'Yes, they were.'

And, now that Poldarn thought about it, yes, they had
been, until he'd lost his rag and made a fight of it in the
wrestling. His first few opponents in that event had bruised
his pride but not his bones; they'd taken extreme care to
throw him gently, which he'd taken for a patronising display
of superior skill rather than a logical reluctance to incapaci-
tate a member of the workforce. It was only when he'd taken
to throwing them in return – not to mention kicking and
elbow-slamming and various other over-effective techniques – that they'd hurt him at all, and that was purely
self-defence on their part, though as it turned out his skill
had been superior to theirs and their moves hadn't worked
terribly well. By the time they'd got to the quarterstaff,
they'd got wise to the change in rules and objectives, but all
the same they'd only fought seriously because he'd started it
and they didn't want to get hurt. Once again, it had so happened that he was better at bashing with a long pole than
they were; and now here he was feeling all smug because
he'd contrived to turn a cheerful burlesque into a ferocious
battle. Magnificent, he thought, and me all over. But none of
this would've happened if only they'd filled me in on the plot
beforehand . . .

'So what should I do now?' Poldarn asked plaintively.
'Should I back off and let them beat me?'

Eyvind shook his head. 'Not if you want to come out of
this alive,' he replied. 'For better or worse you've turned this
into a real contest – also, you've shown them you're unnaturally good at anything to do with weapons and fighting. You
can bet that they'll all be wanting to be the one to teach you
a lesson, so you'd better watch yourself. Bloody hell,' he
added, sighing deeply, 'you couldn't have made a worse mess
of it if you'd tried. If you want my opinion, the only thing

you can do is make absolutely sure you win; it'll be a sort of statement of intent that you mean to be – well, a different sort of head of house, leading from the front, the strong man, that sort of thing. It's not what they're used to, but at least they'll be able to understand what you're trying to do, instead of just standing there wondering why the hell you're beating shit out of your friends.'

'All right,' Poldarn replied. 'I'll give it a try – at least, that's assuming I can. What's left?'

'Single-stick and the home game,' Eyvind replied.

Poldarn shook his head. 'I don't know what that means,' he said.

Eyvind muttered something under his breath. 'Fine,' he said. 'Look, single-stick is like sword-fighting, but instead of a sword you've got a wooden rod, thick as your thumb, and the object is to land a blow that draws blood – just a little, mind, so for crying out loud don't go killing anybody. No hitting below the waist, no thrusting, and if the other man says "Hold", you *stop*. You got that?'

'I think so,' Poldarn replied. 'Put like that, it doesn't sound a bit like real swordfighting. I suppose you're all terribly good at it and practise all the time?'

Eyvind nodded. 'It's a very popular game,' he replied. 'Why do you think it's saved till the end of the show? Well, almost the end. And you're right, it's not in the least like real fighting with swords, it's all in the wrist and fingers. Oh God,' he added, glancing over his shoulder, 'they're ready for you. Just try and remember, this *isn't* a battle – don't go raving mad.'

'Right.'

'And make bloody sure you win,' Eyvind added, as Poldarn dragged himself unwillingly to his feet, 'or else they'll flay you alive. Got that?'

Poldarn's ankle was a little better, but he was painfully aware that he was limping, dragging his feet, and that anything like proper footwork was out of the question. A pity, that, because his instincts told him that mock swordfighting with bits of stick was probably more about footwork than anything else. As for Eyvind's parting advice, it seemed to boil down to *beat them to a pulp but don't hurt anybody*. And that, as Asburn would say, was all there was to it.

Piece of cake.

In the event, it came surprisingly easily to him, probably because his movements were so limited. As a result he was effectively limited to a solid but hostile defence; block three times, then counter just enough to drive his opponents back out of his space, his circle. (Now that was a familiar concept, something Poldarn knew he'd known a lot about once upon a time; he could remember having committed it to memory, but he couldn't remember it now.) Since there was no need for a proper attack, for moves that would give him scope to swing his arm hard and fast enough to slice meat and smash bone, there was nothing to be gained from taking the offensive; smart, stinging little backfoot ripostes, elegantly timed, were more likely to achieve the desired effect than big scything cuts and wraps, even if he'd been in any fit state to attempt them. Furthermore, his opponents were working on a new and to them unfamiliar agenda; they were more interested in hurting him than they were in winning, in a discipline where the techniques for causing real injury and those designed to produce formal victory were not only different but largely incompatible. The result was that they ended up fighting like they were expecting him to fight, while he quite effectively reinvented the gentle art of single-stick and performed it both elegantly and effectively. Accordingly he won all seven bouts quickly and without inflicting any damage beyond the required slight graze. Crazy, Poldarn thought; they're trying to be me and I'm succeeding at being them, making a rather better job of it than they are.

'How am I doing?' he muttered furtively to Eyvind, after the last challenger had retired in search of spider's web and a dock leaf. 'Look, I didn't kill anybody.'

'Not bad,' Eyvind replied, though he was clearly not happy about something. 'Where the hell did you learn single-stick like that?'

'I was just asking myself the same question,' Poldarn admitted. 'Maybe I was good at it when I was a kid, before I went away.'

But Eyvind shook his head. 'You didn't learn any of that stuff round here,' he replied. 'I've been fighting sticks since I was five, and I know every move in the game. Never saw anything like it in my life.'

'Oh,' Poldarn said. 'Then I guess I was just making it up as I went along.'

'Don't buy that, either,' Eyvind grumbled. 'You've obviously done this before, but Polden only knows where. Must've been over there, in the Empire. It's like a completely different game, only it works for how we do it, too. I figure you must've been pretty serious about it, though. Some of those moves looked like they took a lot of practice to get right.'

'I wouldn't know,' Poldarn replied. 'Look, when you feel like it, I can teach them to you if you like.'

'Thanks,' Eyvind replied, 'but I'd rather not. I don't think folks would take kindly to stuff like that.' He was frowning slightly, like a religious man who thinks he's just heard a blasphemy but can't quite work out what it was. 'I wouldn't go around pulling any more stunts like that if I were you, either. People can be very funny about things like that.'

Poldarn shrugged. 'Well, all right,' he said. 'Actually, I can't say the game appeals to me very much. Anything where you're likely to get hit isn't really my idea of a good time.'

That didn't seem to carry much weight with Eyvind, who looked away and changed the subject.

'The last event shouldn't be a problem,' he said. 'There isn't really much scope for hurting anybody in the home game, unless you happen to let go of the stick. Make sure you dry your hands before you start. In fact, rubbing a bit of sawdust on your palms might be an idea.'

'I meant to ask you about that,' Poldarn interrupted. 'This home game. What is it, exactly?'

Maybe Eyvind sighed a little, or maybe it was just Poldarn's imagination. 'Oh, it's quite simple. You and the other man stand facing each other, and you're both wearing a sash – any bit of old cloth, really – with a wooden sword stuck through it. It's supposed to be a proper carved job, but we generally just use a bit of old roofing lath, something like that. Anyhow, the game is to see who can draw the fastest; there's a referee watching in case it's not immediately obvious, but usually you can tell. It's called the home game because it used to be really popular back in the old country, apparently, before we left the Empire and came here. Sound familiar?'

Poldarn didn't reply straight away. 'No,' he said, 'but it sounds to me a bit like the swordmonks.'

'Same sort of thing,' Eyvind said. 'That's probably where it came from originally. Anyway, it ought to be perfectly harmless. Just don't go mad, you don't have to win this one. And make sure the stick doesn't slip, like I told you. All right?'

Poldarn nodded. 'I should be able to manage that.'

For the first time since the games began, Eyvind smiled at him. 'Be particularly careful,' he said, 'when it's you against me. I can't speak for the others, of course, but if you let go the stick and it smacks me in the face, I'll break both your arms.'

'Well, of course,' Poldarn said. 'Look, are you sure you're all right to take part, with your hands all burnt like that?'

Eyvind laughed. 'Listen,' he said, 'I may not be good at

much, but there's nobody in these parts who can touch me at the home game, even if I've got both hands tied behind my back. Not that I'm trying to put you off or anything,' he added innocently, 'just thought you ought to know that, is all.'

'We'll see about that,' Poldarn replied, grinning. 'You know, I won't be sorry when all this is over. I feel like I've just had a barn fall on me.'

'Really?' Eyvind said. 'Is that because of the fighting and stuff, or did you have a rough night?'

Poldarn sighed. 'If only,' he said. 'There, I think that means they're ready. Do I need to get something to use as a sash?'

He needn't have worried about that; Rannwey had one ready for him, a real sash rather than a strip of old sacking, with two silk tassels and a cord strap for a scabbard. Not made locally, that's for sure, he thought as he tied it on, I wonder how old it is? He was also given a proper wooden sword, remarkably similar in weight and feel to the steel version he'd been issued with during his time with Falx Roisin. It felt uncomfortably natural riding at his waist; he felt exposed by it, as if it was a dirty mark on a white shirt.

As Poldarn settled himself for the first bout, he thought about what Eyvind had said. No need to win this event in the interests of self-preservation; and it'd probably be smart to lose anyhow, so as not to leave the spectators with an impression of him as ferociously competitive. Anything like that, he felt sure, was probably frowned on in this community, and he'd done enough damage already on that score. Accordingly, he resolved to make a conscious effort to lose, assuming he wasn't hopelessly outclassed anyway.

Colsceg was the referee. Poldarn was expecting him to say something or give a signal for the start, but apparently that wasn't how the game worked, because his opponent drew quite unexpectedly, while Colsceg was busy talking to someone on the edge of the group. Even so, he'd have had trouble at all beating the draw, if he hadn't made a conscious effort not to. It felt quite extraordinary to miss the beat like that, and his hand shook so much he was sure that the spectators must have seen.

(Besides, he told himself, even if they hadn't been watching his hands, they'd surely noticed him shake all over, as his instincts tried their very best to override the conscious decision he'd made, like a dog pulling hard against its chain as a cat or a rabbit goes by. But, if they saw, nobody hissed or threw anything, so he could at least assure himself, without being rudely contradicted, that he'd managed to get away with it. Just as well they couldn't read his mind, though; otherwise he'd be wasting his time trying to deceive them.)

Poldarn managed to lose seven bouts. Once he'd got the hang of it, he found it relatively simple, mainly because his opponents were so slow and obvious about it that they didn't register in his mind as a threat. He was relieved to see that the eighth competitor was Eyvind, with his bandaged hands. Losing convincingly to someone who had to have his sash tied for him would be something of a challenge, but he reckoned he could handle it; after all, it looked as though he'd have plenty of time.

'Remember,' Eyvind hissed at him as they walked into the middle together, 'don't go raving mad. You're doing all right.'

'Thanks,' Poldarn replied. 'At least it's nearly over.'

Eyvind too had a proper sash, presumably his own – interesting, that he'd brought it with him from home, along with a finely carved oak dummy sword; presumably he practised every day, to keep his hand in, even when he was away from home. 'Leave it to me,' Eyvind added, as they reached the centre of the ring. 'You won't have to fake it, just follow me. All right?'

Poldarn nodded, and took a step back. Eyvind took a

moment to settle himself: three deep breaths while he adjusted the position of the sword in the sash, blade uppermost, handle diagonally across his body. No scabbard, of course, for a wooden foil, so he hooked his left thumb in the cloth and gently gripped the sword through it, simulating the scabbard's grip on the blade. Poldarn found it rather fascinating to watch; there was always something rather fine about a skilled practitioner of any art going about his business, and Eyvind's calm, solemn preparations were the antithesis of Poldarn's own experiences in sword-drawing – everything so deliberate, so carefully controlled. He made a mental note to ask Eyvind to run through his routine some time when his hands were better. As he watched, he almost believed he could see a circle in the air around his friend, fitting neatly into the circle of the fenced-off ring and the surrounding crowd of spectators, like ripples in a pool after a stone had been thrown in. Each circle, it seemed to him, bore on the circle next to it, so that disturbing one would disturb them all, as the ripples spread out. Where the circles ended, of course, he had no idea.

Then Eyvind drew. He was quick; extraordinarily so, there was almost nothing to see, only a palpable physical shock as his own circle was broken into—

(– And he was suddenly in a different place, though still inside the concentric rings; he was standing on the white sand of an arena ringed by raked stone benches, on which sat hundreds of men in the black robes of the sword-monks, all watching him and someone else, although which of them was which he couldn't quite make out. It was as if the rings spread out between them, as if he was looking through the ripples at his own reflection in the water just as it broke up, ruined by the sudden violence of the draw. He knew – he *remembered* – that the other man's name was Monach, that they were best friends, and that the swords in their hands were the finest grade watered steel, and sharp—)

The shock of contact brought Poldarn out of the memory. The first thing he saw was that real-but-imaginary circle, his circle, but once more whole; then the tip of his wooden sword, held out (arms straight, elbows locked) in the rest position, to which it must return after the draw and the cut have been completed. He looked past it and saw Eyvind stretched out on the ground, lying on his face with his arms under his body. At first Poldarn thought Eyvind was dead, but then he realised that he was remembering somebody else who'd lain exactly that way, at some unspecified point in the past. Eyvind wasn't dead, because he was twitching slightly and groaning softly. There was blood on the bevelled side of his foil.

Damn, Poldarn thought; and then, Serves him right for being so quick. It was all Eyvind's fault, he had no doubts on that score. His draw had been a hostile act, regardless of the intentions behind it, and an act is an act, speaking for itself. Poldarn realised that he was going through the closing moves of the drill – flicking the blood off his blade with a quick snap of the wrists, then sliding the sword back into the sash, resetting the sear for the next draw, whenever it came. Meanwhile, both households were staring at him in complete silence, and nobody was moving. What's the matter? Poldarn thought. Haven't you ever seen a swordfight before?

Chapter Sixteen

Two of the Colscegsford men – Poldarn couldn't remember their names – carried Eyvind into the house, while some of the women fussed round with basins of water and bandages. The rest of the crowd melted away, leaving Poldarn in sole possession of the field.

It was, of course, the worst possible thing he could have done in the circumstances; after ostentatiously losing seven bouts, to club down the one man who'd come up with a respectably quick draw, who also happened to be his benefactor and closest friend. (Yes, he told himself, but I couldn't help it, I wasn't even there, I was somewhere else back in the Empire, twenty years ago.) Besides, it was only foils. The last time – but the memory disintegrated as he touched it, like a dandelion clock or the ashes of a burnt page. Probably just as well.

At least the party seemed to be over. Men and women from both households were crossing backwards and forwards across the yard, busy with jobs Poldarn hadn't realised needed doing. Some of them were hefting timbers in a purposeful manner, some of them had tools for cutting and tools for digging – it was like watching ants, he decided, obviously they were all doing something necessary for the general good but no human being could ever understand what or why. He'd hoped that it'd all be different when it was his house, that he'd somehow be able to get a grip on it all, learn the mysteries from the very beginning, but apparently that wasn't going to happen; he'd missed some small but crucial element and now it was too late, the story had already become too complicated for him to follow. The hell with it, he thought, if they need me they can come and find me. He headed for the house without having any clear idea of what he could find to do when he got there.

He passed Elja in the doorway, but apparently she was too busy to stop and talk, though she smiled at him as they passed each other, in a perfunctory way. Inside, once he'd got used to the darkness, he saw Eyvind lying on a pile of blankets. He'd forgotten all about him for a while.

'How are you feeling?' Poldarn asked, kneeling beside him. Eyvind didn't move, but he said, 'Go away.'

'I'm sorry. Did I wake you up?'

'No. I just don't want to talk to you right now, that's all.'

'Oh.' Poldarn stayed where he was, mostly because he had nowhere else to go. 'Look,' he said, 'I'm really sorry about what happened. It was an accident—'

'No, it wasn't,' Eyvind said. There was a broad, messy cut running diagonally from his right eyebrow up to his hairline; someone had gummed it up with spider's web to stop the bleeding, but nuggets of caked blood glittered in the strands like jewels. 'God only knows what you thought you were doing, but it wasn't an accident.'

'No, you're right,' Poldarn said. 'What I meant was, I didn't do it on purpose, not consciously. One minute you were standing there fiddling with your sash, and then – I think I remembered something from when I was in the Bohec valley, something to do with fighting a duel in a ring with a load of sword-monks watching me. And then you were lying there, and I was so stunned I couldn't think what to do.'

Eyvind tried to prop himself up on one arm, but gave it up with a groan. 'What you're saying doesn't make sense,' he said. 'What happened was, I started my draw and you smashed me over the head. That's not how the game works, it's just a draw, not a draw and a cut.'

Poldarn shook his head. 'Not where I learned it, apparently. It was just reflex – I honestly didn't know what I was doing. It happened, but I can't actually remember pulling that wooden thing out of my sash, let alone hitting you. It's like I wasn't even there.'

'Sure,' Eyvind grunted. 'Look, didn't I tell you? Don't go raving mad, stay calm. And you managed it in all the other bouts, you did the moves just right, so don't go trying to tell me you don't know the rules. Then, when it's me you're facing, you suddenly go crazy and bash my head in. Everybody thinks you're a dangerous lunatic or something.'

Maybe they're right, Poldarn thought; how would I be supposed to know, anyhow? 'I promise you,' he said, 'I really didn't mean to hurt you, there wasn't any malice in it. It was like a cat batting at a bit of wool.'

Eyvind didn't reply immediately. 'Well, maybe,' he said grudgingly. 'And I guess it's just as well it was me you bashed, because I guess I can make allowances the way the others couldn't, me not being one of the household. But you've really screwed up this time; it's going to be years before they treat you like a normal person. They're going to think you did it to show off, or because you enjoy hurting people. The thing is, people here don't behave like that. I've been abroad, I know how different they are on the other side of the world. A lot of these people haven't ever been further than Roersbrook or Vitesness. How are we going to explain this to them?'

'I don't know,' Poldarn admitted. 'But that can wait – I don't actually care all that much. What bothers me is that I did this to you. And you've got to believe me, I didn't do it deliberately. I'd never do anything like that on purpose, to you or anybody else.'

Eyvind turned his head slightly so he wasn't looking at Poldarn any more. 'That I doubt,' he said. 'Seems to me you've had a lot of practice. You know, when I first met you I was sure I had you figured out, but now it strikes me I don't really understand you at all. We all thought that once you'd been here a while, it'd all come back to you and you'd slowly pick up where you left off. But maybe we were all wrong about you, and really you're nothing like us at all.' He sighed. 'And it's pointless asking you, because you know even less about who you are than we do. God, this is a mess. They'll just have to find a way of putting it out of their minds, I suppose. Don't ask me how, though.'

There didn't seem to be anything more to say, and Poldarn had aches and pains of his own to complain about, though he couldn't imagine anybody in either household wanting to hear about them. 'I'm sorry,' he said, and went into the inner room, where he was fairly sure of getting some privacy. He'd had enough of his people (these people) for one day.

He lay down on the bed, wincing as he did so. His clothes were filthy with dust and earth, but it was too much effort to take them off, and he was in no hurry to inspect the handsome crop of bruises that he suspected were coming into bloom all over his body. Not the sort of honeymoon he'd have chosen, given the choice. He closed his eyes.

When he opened them again, it was only because someone was prodding him on the point of his shoulder, where a couple of substantial hits had landed during the quarterstaff match.

'Are you going to lie there all day?' Elja said.

Poldarn turned his head. Light was flooding through the

crack between the shutter and the window frame. 'Bloody hell,' he groaned, 'what time is it?'

'Well after sun-up,' Elja replied. 'Come on, there's work to be done.'

'Is there really,' he grumbled. 'Can't see what that's got to do with me. Why can't they just get on with it, they all seem to know what they're supposed to be doing. Wish I did.'

'Get *up.*' She prodded him again, and he howled.

Elja wasn't very sympathetic. 'Now what are you fussing about?' she said. 'You're not the one who's laid up with a busted head.'

Poldarn groaned. 'No, but I wouldn't give more than scrap value for the rest of me. Can't I go back to sleep and wake up in a month or so, when I'm better?'

'No.'

'Oh, all right, then.' He swung his legs off the bed, but they were cramped and painful. His ankle protested as soon as he put his feet on the ground. 'I don't suppose you'll tell me, but I'd really like to know what I'm meant to do this morning. Just for once, it'd be nice to be in on the deadly secret. I thought it'd be different, after we all worked together building this house, but now it's like we're all back to where we were before.'

Elja laughed. 'You're strange,' she said. 'You really don't know, do you?'

'No.'

'All right,' she said, 'I'll tell you.'

'You will?'

'Of course, why shouldn't I?'

'Thank you,' Poldarn said gratefully, and tried to stand up, but his knees weren't up to the challenge. He sat down again and massaged them with the palms of his hands. *They* were painful, too.

'Well,' Elja said, pulling her shawl around her shoulders, 'mostly the men are working on the cattle pens, and laying the stone foundations for the main barn. We're going to be sewing, mainly: curtains for the doors and some shirts. That's the morning taken care of.'

Poldarn nodded gravely. 'That seems reasonable enough,' he said. 'What about this afternoon?'

'The pens should be finished by then, barring accidents, so the men'll probably head off down to the old house and start tearing down the outbuildings.'

'Oh. Why?'

'For the lumber, silly. Where else are you going to get materials from?'

Poldarn frowned. 'But your father and his lot,' he said. 'I thought it was settled, they're going to move in down there until they can rebuild Colscegsford.'

There was a disapproving tone in Elja's voice as she replied. 'They've agreed to stay in the house, for now,' she said. 'But you can't let them have the barns and buildings too, there just isn't enough timber to go round. Not unless you've got another plantation squirrelled away somewhere that you haven't told us about.'

Best not to argue, Poldarn told himself; after all, it wasn't as if he was talking to just one individual here. Everything Elja was thinking and saying had undoubtedly come direct from the Colscegsford household, popped into her mind like a pinch of sage sprinkled into a pot of stew. Somehow or other, what he'd assumed was the generous gesture of letting Colsceg and his brood have the use of Haldersness had turned into a mortal affront to their dignity, or something of the kind. He wished Elja'd explain how that worked too, but he didn't want to overtax her patience.

'Fair enough, then,' he said. 'If that's the way everybody wants to do it. But where's your dad supposed to get his timber from?'

'That's his business,' Elja replied promptly. 'I'm part of *this* household now, so there.'

She stood up and pushed her hair back over her shoulders, a gesture that Poldarn found strangely familiar. 'You really ought to get up,' she said. 'You know they can't start without you.'

Poldarn sighed. 'You mean,' he said wretchedly, 'that every day for the rest of my life I've got to be awake and up and about before everybody else, or nothing will ever get done. That's a really depressing thought.'

'You're just lazy,' she told him. 'Comes of spending all those years abroad, I guess. No wonder we can walk all over them, if they're all like you.'

It proved to be a very long day indeed. Against all expectations, theirs and his own, Poldarn found that he was able to do his share and more on the cattle pen, swinging the massive iron post-rammer and hauling rails; but the pain in his back and shoulders didn't go away, however hard he tried to ignore it, and by midday he'd had more than enough. But instead of crawling away and lying down somewhere out of the way he had to go and sit in the hall while the midday meal was eaten, because they couldn't have it without him, and as soon as it was over he had to get up and lead them all back to work. That made him feel ridiculous, like a duck leading a gaggle of ducklings down to the pond.

Prising apart the long barn turned out to be a nightmare of a job. The nails were mostly rusted in and wouldn't draw out, which meant their heads had to be chiselled or filed away. Even the dowels and pegs refused to come out clean; they broke off flush or cracked halfway through, leaving one or two inches of inaccessible taper to be drilled or bored out. Plank after plank proved to have splits or cracks in them – of course, they only found this out after they'd got them free, at which stage it was impossible to put them back, or use them for anything except firewood. The main timbers were in a rather better state by and large, but there were still a great many casualties (and each timber that failed would have to be replaced with a new one, which meant felling rather more of the scarce and precious trees than anybody would have chosen; nobody raised the problem of combining green and seasoned timber in the same structure, presumably because it was too depressing to contemplate). In the end, they were reduced to splicing patches into some of the broken timbers, which everybody knew was the wrong thing to do, but it wasn't as though they had any realistic alternative. The job was nowhere near finished by nightfall, but they left it and trooped back up to the new house, tired and silent. The evening meal was porridge, leeks and flat beer, because that was all that was left, thanks to the strain on the stores of feeding two households. When Poldarn expressed concern on that score, Rannwey told him there was nothing to get worried about, they had enough porridge and leeks and flat beer to last almost indefinitely; a prospect that depressed Poldarn rather more than the threat of starvation.

After the meal was over and the tables had been stacked away, the household immediately grabbed their blankets and got ready to go to sleep; Poldarn, who was tired but not at all sleepy, had no alternative but to retire to the inner room, since the pattern suggested that they couldn't close their eyes till he'd closed his. The mental image of a hall full of exhausted people wrapped in blankets and waiting impatiently for his first snore to filter through the partition was extremely disconcerting, and made him feel more awake than ever.

'It's all right,' Elja assured him. 'They can get their heads down now you're in here.'

He looked at her. 'How did you know what I was thinking?' he said.

She smiled at him. 'I saw it in your thoughts,' she said.

'But I didn't think you could do that.'

'Usually I can't,' she replied, slipping off her dress. 'But I guess you're so tired and fed up you let your guard down, and there it was, plain to see. It's all right,' she added with a grin, 'it's back up again now, I can't see a thing. Just goes to show, though, you really are one of us – you've just got this knack of shutting us all out.'

'Oh.' Poldarn sat down on the bed and tried to reach his boots, but his arms and legs were knotted with cramp. 'But I don't want to do that. I just want to be normal, like the rest of you.'

'Obviously you don't,' Elja replied. 'Not deep down. And I think I know why, too. You see, really you think you're normal and the rest of us are weird. That's why you keep us out. It must be very difficult.'

'You could be right,' Poldarn sighed. 'But I wouldn't know, I can't see. I guess I'm as closed off to myself as I am to the rest of you. Mostly though,' he added, 'I'm worn out.'

'Are you?'

He nodded. 'What with dragging around big lumps of wood all day, and all that stupid stuff yesterday; and the day before that getting bashed on the head when I fell over. I expect something horrible happened to me the day before that, too, but I can't remember that far back.'

'You poor thing.' She wriggled across the bed and draped her arms around his neck. 'One thing's for sure, it's been far more exciting around here since you showed up. Mostly horrible, of course, but exciting. Especially for me. If you hadn't turned up when you did, I'd probably have ended up marrying Turgren, from out over Vitesness.'

He gave up trying to reach his boot. The feel of her arm against his cheek was extraordinary. 'That wouldn't have been a good thing, then.'

She shook her head. 'He's bald and fat and about ten feet tall. I'd have needed to stand on a chair to kiss him, though why I'd want to do that God only knows. He's only got four teeth.'

He put his hands on her hips. 'Teeth aren't everything,' he said.

'True.' She traced round his lips with the tip of her tongue. 'So you think I should've married him instead?'

'Yes,' he replied. 'But you didn't, so I guess we've both got to make the best of a bad job.' Very carefully, he brushed his knuckles up and down her left nipple; she shivered, and her smile faded. 'Tell me something,' he said. 'Did they feel that next door?'

'I hope not. They need their sleep.'

Poldarn grinned. 'I expect they're asleep already.'

'Then they'll have interesting dreams.' Elja caught hold of his hand and steered it back to her breast. 'I've got a feeling you've done this sort of thing before.'

'Probably,' he replied, thinking about Prince Tazencius's daughter, who'd married him for love, apparently. 'I can't remember, though.'

'Pity.'

He repeated his earlier manoeuvre, finding that he knew exactly where to place his hand without having to look (it was like making the draw, in that sense). 'It's all right,' he said, 'I find that these things tend to come back to me, in emergencies.'

She called him an idiot and kissed him, suddenly and ferociously; and for some time after that he was too busy to think. But afterwards he listened for her in his mind, and still, in spite of everything that had happened between them, she wasn't there; so he lay on his back in the darkness, eyes open, feeling hopelessly alone and lost.

At some point he must have let his mind wander, because the voice had been speaking for some time before he started listening to what it was saying.

'That's the extraordinary thing,' she was saying, 'it's like suddenly I can feel you inside my mind, as well as the rest of me. I don't know, maybe everybody feels that way when it's someone they really love. It's a very nice feeling, though. Sort of complete.'

He had no idea who she was; but now she mentioned it, he could remember the moment she was talking about, when he'd taken advantage of her complete surrender to break into her mind. It had been much easier than he'd expected, he'd hardly needed to apply any material degree of force (and she, poor innocent thing, had probably assumed it was usual under such circumstances). Once he was in there, it had proved to be something of a disappointment, like battering into a castle and finding nothing but plain farmhouse furniture, wooden plates and bowls and one small box of brass jewellery. Somehow he'd assumed that such impressive defences must contain something worth stealing, but apparently not; just the ordinary thoughts of a commonplace young mind, and a great deal of rather nebulous infatuation.

'I know what you mean,' he mumbled sleepily.

She rolled over towards him and laid her hand on his chest; he found the intrusion annoying, but put up with it. 'Suddenly I felt like I really knew you,' she went on, 'all of you, like you'd taken the clothes off your soul and I could see it, all bare.'

'You liked what you saw.'

'Oh yes.' Somehow he doubted that. If she'd seen anything, it must have been what she wanted to see. He'd never really given his soul much thought, but he had a pretty shrewd idea that if she'd really seen it, she wouldn't be lying next to him purring like an overfed cat. She'd be halfway back to her father's house, and still running. 'Is it like this for everybody, do you know?' she asked. 'Or is it something special, just for you and me?'

'I don't know, I'd have to ask everybody. And that'd take a while.'

'Silly. My guess is that it's a bit like this, but for us it's something really special. I love you,' she added, sounding like a monk reciting a prayer; a formal phrase, constantly reiterated, encapsulating a great deal of scripture.

'I love you too,' he replied, wondering how long it'd take her to get to sleep. He made a rule of trying to be as accommodating as he could in such circumstances, but he never could see the point in this sort of aimless chatter at this stage of the proceedings. How nice it would have been, he thought wistfully, if he'd managed to get one who'd just shut up and go to sleep.

'I was thinking,' she went on. 'When Daddy gets back from the city, it'd be nice if we could go and visit, just for a day or so.' She paused, a little too self-consciously to carry conviction. 'You know, I'm sure that if you two really got to know each other—'

He smiled, safe in the darkness, and made a vaguely disapproving noise.

'I'm sorry,' she said, 'I'm being selfish; and of course I haven't forgiven him for what he said to you.'

'It's all right,' he replied, the perfect self-denying martyr, ready to overlook anything for his true love's sake. 'It doesn't bother me any more, really. I was just thinking, do we really need all those other people round us? There's sure to be a big crowd at your father's place.'

She sighed. 'Probably,' she said. 'There usually is.'

'Especially now,' he went on, gentle and careful as the crow glided down onto the pattern of decoys, 'with the big reconciliation thing, your father and General Cronan. I can't imagine he'd want us there, with all that going on.'

'Oh, he wouldn't mind,' she said, a little too quickly. 'And it'd mean he'd be busy a lot of the time, so we wouldn't be getting under each other's feet. It'd be showing willing more than anything else.'

He couldn't help grinning; she was headed right for the gap in the pattern, the killing zone. He'd learned this basic truth many years ago, in a ploughed field at Haldersness; you can't pull in a crow to the decoys unless it wants to come in. The trick lies in making it want to. 'If you really want to go,' he said, 'I suppose it'd be all right.'

She wriggled over and hugged him; he managed not to wince at the intrusion into his circle. 'That's so sweet of you,' she said – and for a moment he felt really bad about it, because she was young and beautiful and sweet, and he'd thoroughly enjoyed taking her, in spite of it all. But there was no reason for that, no reason why he shouldn't enjoy his work; mostly it was nasty and unpleasant, and the pleasure he usually got from it was definitely not something to be proud of; something relatively peaceful and normal, like making love to a lovely girl, was definitely an improvement on his usual daily round. Besides, he reassured himself, there's more ways of killing a crow than pulling its neck.

'That's all right,' he said, remembering to play up the part (attention to detail at all times). 'After all, I'm part of the family now, it's worth making the effort.' He yawned. Now he'd got what he wanted, he really would like to get some sleep. 'Come on,' he said, 'snuggle up.' He reached round and started stroking the small of her back, which never failed to put her to sleep. 'Busy day tomorrow,' he added, more to himself than to her. 'With any luck, we'll get the rest of the usable lumber off the old barn, and then we can make a start on the new one.

She grunted sleepily, while he thought, What was all that about? What old barn? And then he remembered – breaking up the old barn at Colscegsford after the heavy snow caved in the roof, all those years ago. What had put that into his head all of a sudden, he wondered; then he remembered that, too. Same moment, same half-lucid interval between waking and sleep, different girl. Very different girl, but somehow the moment was always the same. He was pleased with himself for thinking that.

'What?' Elja muttered drowsily.

'I was just saying,' Poldarn repeated, 'once we've finished salvaging the lumber, we can make a start on the new barn.'

'Oh,' Elja said, 'right. That's nice. I want to go to sleep now.'

'Sorry.'

'Mphm.' She wriggled away from him, pulling the bed-clothes with her. Typical, he thought, as the cold air hit his toes, they all do that (and then he stopped and wondered how he knew that, and who *they all* had been).

'Elja,' he said.

'Now what?'

'I love you.'

'Love you too,' she mumbled. 'See you in the morning.'

Yes, he thought. And that'll be something to look forward to.

Chapter Seventeen

E yvind was up and about early the next morning, still
obviously below par but determined to make himself
useful. He said good morning amiably enough but
didn't stop to talk, and Poldarn was left to guess whether
this signified forgiveness, diplomacy or just ingrained good
manners.

Of course, Poldarn didn't have a clue how to go about
building a barn; but although he'd lost his memory he still
had enough common sense to realise that he wouldn't go far
wrong if he used the old one as a pattern. So, when nobody
was looking, he carefully paced out the distances between the
corner posts, cut surreptitious witness marks on the main
timbers with his knife and even managed to scratch a ground
plan on the back of a bit of broken pot. It wasn't quite the
same as having a glorious revelation of how to go about the
job, as had been the case with the house itself; but he could
see that the shades of his ancestors, while obliged to enable
him to put a roof over his head, couldn't be expected to go
to the same degree of trouble over a grain store and junk
depository.

Dismantling the last few timbers and loading them onto carts took up the morning and most of the afternoon, and they finished unloading in the dark. Next day, it rained hard and if he'd had any say in the matter they'd have stayed indoors, but apparently he didn't; so they had to lay out and mark up with rain in their eyes and water trickling down the backs of their necks. Progress was slow, mistakes were made; Root, one of the Haldersness field hands, slipped in the mud while supporting a cross-beam, which fell and hit Eyrich, the Colscegsford wheelwright, on the point of the shoulder, breaking his collarbone. That held things up for a long time, and although nothing was said, even Poldarn could feel the tension it caused between the two households. Then, just when they'd got back into some sort of a rhythm, Barn contrived to miss a wedge with the big hammer and cracked himself on the ankle. Further delays, reduced manpower, loss of key personnel (not so much Barn himself; but Colsceg and Egil insisted on helping him back to the house, and Colsceg was the best mortice-cutter in either household); the further they fell behind schedule, the more jobs were rushed and therefore botched, resulting in more wasted time as skilled workers were called off what they were supposed to be doing to put right the mistakes, leaving the unskilled crews standing around with nothing to do. That was patently unacceptable, so Poldarn grabbed a chisel and a mallet and cut the mortices himself, only to find that it didn't come quite as naturally as he'd expected. That was embarrassing as well as counter-productive, and ended up with the whole job grinding to a halt until Colsceg came back and patched up the mess Poldarn had made of a particularly complicated step-lapped rafter seat.

'Cheer up,' Boarci said, appearing suddenly behind him. It was an order rather than a suggestion. 'Compared to most barn-raisings I've been on, this one's flowing like warm honey. It's when you've finished and you take a step back, and the whole lot slumps over to the left and flops down in a heap; *that*'s when you want to pack it all in and find a nice dry cave somewhere.'

'Fine,' Poldarn replied. 'I'll bear that in mind when the time comes. Are you any good at single shoulder tenons?'

Boarci laughed. 'Better than you, anyway,' he said. 'Mind you, so's my mother's cat. Here, give me that chisel before you fuck up any more dead trees.'

He turned out to be a very competent joiner, almost as good as Colsceg and considerably quicker. 'Outstanding,' Poldarn said, as the tenon snuggled into the mortice and the dowel slid home. 'Only, if you're so good at this, why've you been wasting your time lugging planks on and off carts? We could've used you here.'

'Not my place,' Boarci replied. 'If you weren't as blind as a bat, you'd have seen that for yourself. I'm not from around here, remember, I can't go pushing a man out of the way and doing his job just because I can do it a bit better than he can. All that'll get you is an open door and a boot up the bum, and serve you right. That's the sort of thing you need to know if you're going to run a house, basic stuff like that. Otherwise you'll only make trouble for yourself.'

Poldarn sighed. 'How about if I ask you to do my job for me?' he said. 'Does that make it all right?'

Boarci shook his head. 'Not really,' he said. 'But if it's that or risk the roof coming down on some poor bugger's head, I suppose you haven't got much choice.'

The closing stages, which should have been the easy part, turned out to be the most difficult of all. Half the boarding planks turned out to be shaken or rotten, but there wasn't enough new material to replace them. Accordingly, they had no alternative but to splice patches into the spoiled timbers, a hatefully fiddly job even for a fresh, dry crew, and nearly impossible for men who were tired, wet and thoroughly out of sorts. When the sun set behind the rain clouds that had been concealing it all day anyway and the light went, it looked like there was only a little bit left to do, so, rather than leave an annoying little tag end of a job unfinished over night, Poldarn sent up to the house for lamps and torches and they carried on, only to find that they'd underestimated the scope of the tiresome odds and ends, which they compounded in turn with a rash of small, stupid mistakes. Then the damp got into the lamp wicks, the rain got worse, and they were forced to drop their tools and run for shelter until it slackened off. By that time, nobody was prepared to carry on, and they trudged back to the house for their dinner of porridge and leeks. A day in the driving rain had made them all too wet to dry out, even if they hadn't been too tired to face the effort of undressing; so they banked up the fire with fuel they couldn't afford to waste and went to sleep in their wet clothes.

The next morning was hot and muggy. The bits and pieces they'd hoped to clear up by torchlight proved sufficiently awkward to keep them occupied until shortly after midday, and even then there were a few out-of-square window frames and uneven floorboards, things that could just about be ignored but which would have to be seen to sooner or later. Viewed from a distance of twenty-five yards or so, the end result could easily be mistaken for a barn, but if he closed his eyes, Poldarn could see every single glitch, snag and imperfection, from the clumsily nailed splices to the door that had to be lifted into its frame. That sort of thing could be overlooked in a building that'd been standing for fifty years, but in a newly built barn it was all rather shoddy and sad, and he knew perfectly well that until the faults were fixed, he'd notice them every time he walked through the doorway.

Even so, several minutes had passed and it was still standing, without even a couple of props wedged in against the walls – more than could be said for some barns on this side of the mountain. It wouldn't win any prizes, but Poldarn couldn't recall any being offered. When they began to move things in, he tagged along with one of the gangs and tried to look useful, in spite of his aching joints and pulled muscles.

'I can't see what you're making such a fuss about,' Elja told him as she rubbed his back with some singularly horrible-smelling embrocation. 'I mean to say, it's all going to get pulled down in forty years or so, and I dare say it'll manage to stay put till then. It's only a barn, not Polden's temple. You've still got two more barns to do, remember, and that's before you start on the small houses. If we're going to have all this agonising after each one, I think I'll leave you and go home to Daddy.'

'You do that,' Poldarn replied, 'and take that disgusting mess with you. What do they put in that stuff, anyway?'

'You're better off not knowing,' she told him cheerfully. 'And if you think it's nasty, what about me? I've got to put my hands in it, and sleep next to it.'

He pulled a face, though of course she couldn't see. 'I think that'll do,' he said. 'I feel a whole lot better now.'

'You do?'

'Yes. Or at least, I will as soon as you stop putting that stuff on me.'

More by luck than judgement, the other two barns weren't nearly so much trouble; they'd been rethatched more recently and so the damp hadn't swollen the joints, which meant that the wedges and pins came out cleanly and there were fewer breakages. That was just as well; they were almost out of new split and sawn lumber, and the last thing Poldarn wanted to do was send anyone to put an axe to the last few growing trees that had survived the volcano and the black ash. He'd already been putting out feelers about a logging expedition into the unsettled woods of the north and east, a project that would mean joining forces with three or four other households besides the two he was currently responsible for. The initial reactions weren't encouraging.

Lyatsbridge desperately needed timber, of course; they had a house to rebuild from the ground up, and no materials whatever. But unless Poldarn undertook to feed them through the winter, which he was in no position to do, they were going to be far too busy scraping together enough food to live on, and had already resigned themselves to camping out for the foreseeable future, or else packing up and moving away. Eyvind had sent home to Bollesknap to see if his father and brothers were interested in coming in on the project, but he didn't think they would be – they had more than enough timber for their own needs, but not quite enough that they could afford to spare any. Braynolphscombe was too far away to send a message to – it'd mean having a man away from the house for two weeks when they needed all hands for the rest of the buildings. It was a good idea, was the general consensus, but completely impractical.

So it was just as well that they seemed to have got the hang of taking apart the old houses without causing too much damage. The work was getting done, slowly but surely, and gradually Ciartanstead was starting to look like a farm, rather than a house that had got picked up by a freak gust of strong wind and planted down in the middle of nowhere. Needless to say, they'd taken far too long about it. Planting season would be on them before they knew it, with its entrancing prospect of a future that didn't involve porridge and leeks for every meal, but it seemed hopelessly inefficient to abandon the building works when they were nearly finished, and then go back to them several weeks later, when the pattern had faded from their minds. Unfortunately, 'nearly finished' proved to be an alarmingly imprecise and elastic measurement of time and quantity. Eventually, they had to face the humiliating reality of the situation and split the workforce into two; half to build and half to plant, which meant there were now two jobs that weren't getting done instead of just the one.

Poldarn had hoped that the coolness between Eyvind and himself following the wedding games debacle would gradually thaw as they worked together and made progress, but it didn't. There was no overt hostility; Eyvind was always polite, superficially friendly and unfailingly helpful and hard-working, but it didn't take a mind-reader to see the resentment behind his eyes, or hear the reserve in his voice. At first Poldarn pretended nothing was wrong, in the hope that it'd all sort itself out. Next he tried the direct approach and asked Eyvind if something was the matter or if he'd done something (something else) to upset him. In return he got a chilly assurance that everything was fine, whereupon Eyvind abruptly changed the subject and started talking about wall studs, wind braces and half-lap joints. In spite of himself, Poldarn couldn't help finding this annoying, and he told himself that if Eyvind wanted to sulk, that was his right as a free man and the heir to a fine house. His counter-sulk lasted two days, at the end of which Eyvind announced that he was going home.

'Just for a few weeks,' he added, looking away. Poldarn knew he was lying. 'I really ought to see how things are going at home, before they forget what I look like and all the dogs start barking at me.'

'Of course,' Poldarn said. 'I really appreciate all the time you've spent here and all your help, but naturally you've got to think about your own household.' He sounded like a diplomat, he realised, an experienced ambassador skilfully making an invasion sound like a routine patrol and fooling nobody, because both sides knew the truth. 'As and when you can see your way to dropping by again, we'll be delighted to see you, of course.'

Eyvind smiled weakly. 'I expect that by the time I get back, you'll have finished the outbuildings and made a start on the fencing; I won't know the place, probably.'

'We'll do our best,' Poldarn said. 'And remember, you're

always welcome here. I want you to treat this place like your own home.'

Poldarn wasn't there when Eyvind finally took his leave; he was up at the top pasture, where they were building a small linhay for storing winter fodder. He felt Eyvind's absence long before anybody mentioned his departure; apparently he'd said something about starting off early so as to make Nailsford by nightfall, which was why he hadn't wanted to wait till Poldarn got back. He'd taken the horse he'd had sent up from home and the clothes he'd brought with him, but he'd left behind everything Poldarn or the Haldersness household had ever given him, from the fine brass oil lamp Halder had brought back from the Empire to the new pair of working shoes that had been made for him when his old pair fell to pieces. To Poldarn's mind, that only made it worse; all Eyvind's things were there, in their usual place, and he couldn't get it out of his mind that his friend would walk in through the door at any moment. At the same time, he knew that it was highly unlikely that Eyvind would ever come back. This made him feel more isolated than ever before, his last link to his previous life severed. In a way, this should have been a good thing, but he found it hard to see it in that light.

Two days after Eyvind's departure, just as they were about to tackle the dismantling and relocation of the forge, a thin feather of black smoke appeared on the side of the mountain. The first Poldarn knew about it was when he came out of the old forge building at Haldersness and found virtually the entire combined household standing in the yard, their faces turned towards the mountain as if they were taking part in a religious ceremony. Nobody said a word – he was reminded of that night in Cric when he'd been the god in the cart, facing just such a wall of silent, staring faces from the other side of the curtain.

Once he'd found out what was going on, Poldarn's first

reaction was to load the carts with everything they could cram on board, and set off for the east. If he'd suggested it, the household would almost certainly have agreed; they were all quite obviously terrified, and it was probably only their strange unspoken communion that kept them from panicking. Somehow, though, he knew that it would be the wrong thing to do; it'd be like running because your shirt was on fire, pointless because wherever you ran to, the fire would go with you. Unfortunately, he couldn't think of a better alternative.

'Well,' somebody said at last, 'here we go again.'

'Maybe it won't be so bad this time,' someone else suggested hopefully. 'It's only a little bit of smoke, less than last time round.'

That would have been helpful and comforting if it had been true, but it wasn't, and everybody knew that. 'It'll be different down the valley,' someone else put in, 'we'll be further away, it won't be nearly so bad.'

'Just as well we haven't started on the thatching,' Raffen said, and Poldarn had to assume he was referring to the long barn and the middle house. They'd roofed all the other buildings with wooden shakes treated with pitch – nobody had actually suggested it out loud, but they'd gone ahead and done it as though they were following an architect's drawings, and Poldarn had assumed they'd had just such a contingency in mind. If so, it was an impressive example of foresight, and one less thing to worry about.

He pushed his way through the crowd to the front, then turned round to face them. 'It'll be all right,' he said. 'Even if the worst comes to the worst and we get another coating of that black shit, at least this time we know what to do, we can handle it. Look, we've got enough food laid in to last us a good long time – if needs be we can just settle down and sit it out. Or we can see if we can't figure out a way of beating the bloody thing.'

Nobody said a word, but Poldarn had no doubt that he had their complete attention, even if that was only because they thought he'd gone crazy. 'It's possible,' he said. 'I mean, how do we know there's nothing we can do about it — we haven't tried.'

The crowd stirred uneasily, as if they were afraid that the mountain would hear him and blame them for being associated with someone who could come out with such pernicious heresy.

'What did you have in mind?' Egil asked.

'I don't know, do I?' Poldarn replied impatiently. 'I don't know any more about these things than you do. But it seems to me that the sensible thing would be to try and find out a bit more, instead of just sharing out our ignorance among ourselves like a biscuit ration. I say that while it's just a little bit of smoke, what we ought to do is get up as close as we can to where it's coming from and get some solid information, instead of just guessing and going all to pieces.'

'Go up there?' someone said. 'You must be out of your mind. We all know what happened the last time. It could start puking up fire at any moment.'

Poldarn folded his arms. 'That's not entirely true,' he said. 'Last time, if you remember, it was several days before it started playing up. If we pull ourselves together, we can go up there, have a look round and maybe even come up with a few ideas before the trouble starts. It's got to be better than drooping round here like it was the end of the world or something.'

'All right,' Egil said. 'Who's going?'

That was more like it, Poldarn thought. 'Me for one,' he said. 'Anybody fancy coming with me?'

To his surprise, he got more volunteers than he knew what to do with, and he ended up turning people away. 'The rest of you,' he went on, once he'd made his selection, 'might want to make a start on a few basic precautions. Split up the food stores, for one thing, so we don't stand to lose the lot if the barn gets burned or buried. Get the roofs covered – it won't hurt even if nothing does happen, and it's got to be better than doing it all in a desperate rush with the cinders already falling. Luckily we don't have livestock to worry about this time round, which is something, but it might be an idea to make up a few extra buckets, things like that.' He knew he was being vague, but for the life of him he couldn't think of anything more specific. But surely they'd know what to do, they always seemed to.

'Right,' Colsceg said. 'When are you thinking of leaving?'

'Straight away,' Poldarn said, as much to his own surprise as anybody else's. 'No point in wasting precious time, and the sooner we leave, the sooner we'll get back.' As he said that, it occurred to him that Elja was down at Ciartanstead, and he'd just convincingly argued against sparing the time to go there and say goodbye. That seemed to strike him as a very bad and unlucky thing to do, but it was too late to go back on his decision.

He'd kept his reconnaissance party down to a round half-dozen, himself included: Egil and Raffen and Boarci (Poldarn was counting on him as a sort of lucky mascot), Rook and Barn. He had an uneasy feeling that he'd chosen most of them simply because he had no trouble telling them apart and remembering their names. But, he rationalised, Egil was smart, Boarci seemed to have a knack of not getting killed and of rescuing people when they'd got themselves into trouble; Rook had contrived to keep himself alive through the disaster at Lyatsbridge, so clearly he was nobody's fool, and the other two were stolid and fairly unflappable. He missed Eyvind very badly, of course, if only because Eyvind generally seemed able to understand what he was saying. They took with them as much food and water as they could carry, and the thickest leather boots, coats and hats they could find, in case it started raining big chunks of burning mountain on their heads before they could get out of the way. Apart from that, nothing obvious in the form of sensible precautions seemed to spring to mind. Boarci took his axe too, of course, but presumably from sheer force of habit, unless he was hoping they'd run into one or more slow-moving bears.

The first day they walked in silence, keeping up a pace that was just too fast for comfort, rarely taking their eyes off the mountain and the black smudge over it. They'd opted to head for the mountain in as close an approximation to a straight line as they could manage; this meant trudging up rather more hills than Poldarn would have chosen if the decision had been up to him rather than a wordless consensus. (It did occur to him that he'd wrongly presumed their intention, and they were just following him; but that was probably only because he was feeling depressed.) They carried on walking until it was too dark to see where they were going, then lay down where they stopped and went to sleep. The rising sun woke them all up, and they carried on along the line where they'd left off without stopping for anything to eat, an act of forbearance made somewhat easier by the knowledge that all they had in the way of supplies was the inevitable porridge and leeks.

As the mountain gradually grew larger in front of them, Poldarn found himself thinking back to his memory of visiting the hot springs with his grandfather and realised that something was very different about the silhouette he was walking towards. It didn't take him long to figure out what it was. Instead of a gently tapering, mostly symmetrical peak there was a swollen chimney, perched on the mountain top like a comical hat. They were treading on cinders by now, which made their progress slow and depressingly tiring, and the air stank of sulphur. Even at midday it was as dark as an hour after sunset; the black cloud was between them and the sun, and every fifth step or so they'd stumble over a larger than usual slab of brittle black rock.

Disconcertingly, the smoke wasn't coming out of the chimney; if anything, it appeared to be venting from somewhere on the other side of the mountain, hidden from view. Poldarn wasn't sure that he wanted to get close enough to see it, anyway, but he didn't really have any choice in the matter. It'd be too humiliating to turn back at this stage because of something so trivial as the fear of death. From time to time they heard ominous cracking and splitting noises, and the occasional deep rumble. More than once, the ground shook under their feet, an effect that Poldarn found horribly frightening.

'The way I see it,' Boarci said after a very long silence, 'it's a bit like a really big fat boil on your bum. It gets bigger and bigger and redder and redder, till finally it's so full of pus and crap that it bursts all over the place.'

The sun behind the cloud of black smoke went down just as they arrived at the hot springs. In spite of the darkness, Poldarn recognised the place at once. Not much had changed, except that the snow had gone and there was a narrow crack in the ground, no more than a foot wide but bewilderingly deep – Egil dropped in a pebble but nobody heard it land – running away up the hill as far as they could see.

'I don't like that at all,' Egil said. 'Seems to me that if it starts playing up while we're here, this is an obvious place for it to come up through.'

True enough, there were patches of grey mist and smoke hanging in the air above the crack, like little tangles of sheep's wool caught in a thorn bush. But they weren't confined to the crack, or even the area of the hot springs. The air was full of them; it was as if they were strolling through an orchard and the smoke was blossom on invisible trees.

'What are we supposed to be looking for, anyway?' Barn said nervously as he stepped over the crack.

'I don't know,' Poldarn answered promptly. 'Won't know till I see it, either.'

'Oh.' Barn nodded, as if that made perfect sense now that someone had taken the time to explain it to him clearly. 'So how much further have we got to go? My feet hurt.'

Poldarn looked round. 'We might as well stop here for the night,' he said. 'At least I've got some sort of idea where we are, in relation to everything.'

'Oh, sure,' put in Raffen. 'Let's camp out here, right on a crack. I mean, what's so special about waking up again?'

Poldarn ignored that and sank to his knees, struggling to get his arms free of the straps of his pack. 'The way I see it,' he went on, 'either we can keep going up till we get to the edge of the chimney, and then we can look down inside and see what's going on down there, or we can go round the side until we find out where all that smoke's coming from. Anybody got any preferences?'

Nobody seemed very taken with either option, but they seemed to prefer the former. 'I suppose it'll be all right,' Barn said, 'since the smoke's not actually coming out from there.' He wiped sweat off his face with his sleeve; it was decidedly hot, though they'd all felt chilly an hour or so ago.

'You all get your heads down,' Poldarn said cheerfully. 'I'm not particularly tired; I'll be quite happy just lying here, so if anything starts to happen I can give you all a shout in plenty of time.'

Immediately, Boarci twisted over onto his back, pulled his hat down over his face and appeared to go to sleep. The others took a bit longer – Egil even ventured to wash his face and hands by stepping into a shallow pool of hot water, but he yelped with pain and hopped out again straight away, announcing that the water was no longer pleasantly warm but boiling hot.

Although he was very tired, Poldarn had no difficulty at all staying awake; the thought of falling asleep in that place and dreaming was disturbing enough to keep his eyes wide open. In the dark he could make out a faint red glow behind the mountain that hadn't been visible in daylight, which worried him and made him feel grateful that they'd decided to go up instead of round the mountain top. A few hours before dawn, he became aware that a very fine shower of dust had started to fall; his eyes were gritty and he could feel it on his skin. He suddenly realised that he was hungry, dug a long-hoarded slab of hard cheese out of his pack and ate it slowly and deliberately.

The sunrise, when it came, was spectacular, a blaze of orange and red smeared across the sky in wild patterns and swirls. For a long time, all he could do was lie on his back and look up at it. Eventually, Boarci woke up.

'Bloody hell,' he yawned, 'is it morning already? How long have you been awake?'

'I didn't sleep,' Poldarn replied.

'More fool you, then. You'll be knackered this time tomorrow.'

They ate breakfast in a dull red glow, and set off immediately afterwards. As the day wore on the daylight started to fade, but the glare behind the mountain grew fiercer, so at least they could see where they were putting their feet. Rook was sure there was a lot more smoke coming out than there had been the day before – maybe twice as much, even. 'That's just because we're closer to it,' Poldarn replied, though he didn't believe what he was saying. Still, it seemed to cheer the others up, for some reason. The dust in the air grew steadily thicker, and they saw several more fissures like the one they'd noticed at the hot springs. Steam and yellow smoke rose up steeply from each one, making it hard to see where the cracks were, but they managed to cross them without anybody falling in.

As always seemed to be the way when struggling up a mountain, the peak proved to be much further away than they'd anticipated, and it was well past noon when they found themselves at the foot of the new chimney. Its walls were steep and black, in places hard and smooth as glass, extremely difficult and treacherous to climb, but now that they were this close, nobody seemed to want to hold back; it was as if the mere act of getting to the top was going to solve something, possibly even make the mountain stop misbehaving and go back to sleep. None of them said anything, or appeared to have anything to say. From time to time, Poldarn had the feeling that he was seeing something familiar, but he couldn't begin to think what it might be. More likely to be his imagination, he decided. One good thing: he wasn't feeling particularly tired, in spite of his lack of sleep. That too was something he couldn't readily explain.

So slow was their progress that when sunset came they were still dragging themselves uphill. But that was irrelevant; the benefit they got from the sun was minor enough anyway under the shadow of the cloud, whereas the red light from the other side of the mountain was getting stronger all the time, plenty good enough to see their way by. Besides, none of them liked the idea of trying to camp out on the steep ramparts of the chimney, for a number of quite obvious reasons. They kept going, somehow or other – it wasn't so much that they felt tired as that they'd been exhausted for so long that they seemed to have forgotten what it was like to feel any other way.

They hardly noticed the moment of arrival; one minute they were clambering up a particularly steep section of black rock, the next they were on a ledge, with no more mountain above them, only black cloud saturated with raw red light. The ledge was over a hundred yards across and perfectly level. They lay down, so thankful not to be climbing any more that they didn't have room for any other emotion, and stayed there without moving for a long time.

'Well,' Poldarn said eventually, 'we're here. We might as well go and have a look.'

Nobody seemed inclined to move, so Poldarn went on

alone. When he reached the edge, he lay down on his stomach and crawled the last yard or so; then he stuck his head out over the ledge and looked down.

The first thing that struck him, quite literally, was the heat. He knew the feeling very well; it was like standing over the forge while waiting for a piece of iron to come up to welding heat. The blast of rising hot air scrubbed his face and burned his cheeks, and instinctively he closed his eyes and pulled his head back out of the way. That wouldn't do at all, he decided, so he braced himself and tried again, making a conscious effort to keep his eyes open.

The inside walls of the chimney fell away sharply into a dazzling lake of pure white light. Once again, he thought *welding heat*, because it was the same colour and quality of light as iron glows with in that crucial moment of malleability before it melts and breaks up, the point at which it can be fused into another piece of iron with nothing more than a few light taps of the hammer. That explained the ferocious heat, even though it lay several hundred yards below him. At first he couldn't make out what it was; not iron or steel, he rationalised, in spite of the resemblance. Then, from somewhere in the back of his mind, came a recollection of watching glass-makers at work, and Poldarn realised that the huge pool of white liquid was molten rock.

The heat had become unbearable, and he pulled back, unable to see for the staring white blurs across his eyes, and the tears. All he could think about, for some reason, was the similarity between the chimney and the pool and a crucible of molten metal, the same shape and colour and glowing light. It must be an extraordinary thing, he thought, to melt rock in a furnace; who would do such a thing, and why? Given the sheer size of the undertaking, it would have to be a god of some sort, a huge and enormously thick-skinned god who could handle such a crucible and withstand such a heat. But even a god would need to have a reason for going to so much trouble, and that raised the question of what he was planning to make out of it. If there was a crucible and a pool of melt, somewhere there had to be a mould, pressed into the sand with a pattern. The only logical explanation was that this god was melting down the old world to make a new one, turning waste and scrap into useful material, loosening it from the bonds of memory, restoring to it its true and original nature by means of the intercession of fire, which forgives and redeems all past sins.

Poldarn opened his eyes again. Yes, he thought, that's all very well, but we didn't tramp all the way up here just to bask in the poetic symmetry of it all. Very reluctantly, he crawled back and examined the view a third time.

When he'd suggested the expedition, back at Haldersness, he'd had some idea of coming up with some scheme for dealing with the problem, stopping the volcano or making it harmless. Now that he'd had a chance to look at the thing, it was obvious that anything like that was out of the question, it was simply too big and too fierce; it'd be doomed to failure, like arm-wrestling with a god. They couldn't put the fire out with buckets of water, or fill in the chimney with earth and bury it, or even tap it like a beer barrel and draw the molten rock off through a spigot in some harmless direction. The problem was insoluble, he couldn't think of a way of dealing with it because there wasn't one.

'Well?' someone said behind him. Poldarn stayed where he was. 'Take a look for yourself,' he replied. They got down on their hands and knees next to him and crept forward. 'Watch it,' he added, 'it's a bit warm once you get your head out over the edge.'

They did as they were told, and after they'd gazed at it for as long as they could bear they dragged themselves back, just as he'd done, and sat still and quiet for a while.

'Might as well have stayed home,' Raffen said eventually. 'I can't see there's anything we can do about that.'

'No,' Poldarn replied, 'there isn't, unless we get on a ship and go back to the Empire. But that's assuming it's any better there. For all I know, every mountain north of Torcea's gone like this one has, and in a few weeks' time the whole Empire'll be gone, the world will have melted away and we'll all be dead. No way of knowing, really.'

They weren't particularly impressed with that statement – understandably, given the effort it had cost them to get there. 'We can't just go back and tell them they're all going to be killed but not to worry about it,' Rook grumbled. 'They'd think we've all gone crazy or something. Come on, you said all we have to do is figure out how it works and we can stop it.'

Poldarn pulled himself together, sighing. 'All right,' he said. 'Seems to me there's got to be an enormously hot fire right down there in the roots of the mountain, big and hot enough to melt rock, like a lime kiln. Once it's done that, I guess all the smoke and fumes get bottled up deep inside until eventually they burst out and punch a hole right through the top of the mountain. The cinders and ash that got all over everything must be molten rock that ended up being spat out high into the air, where it cooled off and came down everywhere like snow. Anyway,' he added, 'that's the way I see it. Anybody got a better explanation?'

'Sounds reasonable enough to me,' said Barn, wiping grit out of his eyes with his knuckles. 'So how does that help us?'

'It doesn't.' Poldarn shook his head. His cheeks and forehead were stinging horribly. 'I was wrong. There isn't a thing we can do about it. Let's go home, I'm sick to death of this place.'

Barn frowned. 'What about when it rains?' he asked. 'Surely if it rains hard enough, that ought to put it out.'

Poldarn couldn't be bothered to reply, so it was up to

Boarci to explain. 'It's too hot,' he said. 'The rain wouldn't get anywhere near the bottom of the chimney before it turned to steam. You remember all those fluffy white clouds the last time, once the rain started?'

Barn nodded. 'That's right,' he said. 'Not that it matters, we can't make it rain anyhow. But so what? As long as it stays down there it won't be doing us any harm.'

Poldarn looked up. 'Depends,' he said. 'What we don't know is how big the fire is or what's causing it. My guess is that it's the same fire as heats the water for the hot springs – in which case it's been going for thirty-odd years to my certain knowledge, and quite possibly a few thousand years before that.'

'Fine,' Barn replied. 'Like you said, it's been going on for centuries and never done anybody any harm till now.' He paused, then went on, 'I'm sure you're right about fumes getting trapped under the mountain and finally blowing out – I guess that must be what happened, and that's where all the ash and stuff came from. But now there's this huge great vent, like runners and risers when you're casting, so won't the fumes just rise up out of there and get blown away into the air, all nice and harmless?' He shrugged. 'All right, so it's very big and impressive, but I don't see what harm it's going to do us. I'm guessing that this new breakout is where another pocket of the fumes and steam and stuff must've built up, and it blasted a hole into the side of the mountain so it could get out. I don't know, maybe there's a whole load of them just getting ready to go pop, but doesn't it stand to reason that it must've used up most of its bottled-up fumes and shit by now? In which case, we may get a few more sprinklings of the cinders, but nothing too bad, just like this time around.' He shrugged. 'Come on, you're a blacksmith, you know what furnaces are like, and casting hot metal. If your sand's wet or you've got a blocked vent, it blows up and you get the whole lot in your face. If you've done your vents right and cooked your mould, there's nothing to it. Same here, I reckon.'

Poldarn thought about that for a while. 'I suppose so,' he said. 'I hadn't thought of it like that.'

'Makes sense to me,' Raffen put in. 'In which case, there's nothing to worry about and we can go home. I don't know about you, but this place gives me the creeps. I say we get back down the mountain and go do some work instead of roasting ourselves alive.'

'Fine,' Poldarn said. 'Let's do that, then.'

Getting back down the mountain was much quicker than getting up it, though not noticeably easier. Egil and Boarci led the way, both of them obviously keen to get away from there as soon as possible. Poldarn lagged behind. He found the place just as oppressive as the others did, but he felt sure there was something he'd overlooked, though he hadn't got the faintest idea what it might be. It wasn't just a vague feeling that he'd been there before – well, he knew that, he'd been there with Halder, and something about that visit had impressed him so much that the memory of it had forced its way to the surface of his mind (like the fire bottled up in the mountain). As he scrambled and skittered down the slopes of the chimney he found himself going over that memory in his mind, trying to winnow some degree of significance out of it; but the more he searched the more elusive the scene became, to the point where he was hard put to it to distinguish between actual recollections and appropriate-seeming details he'd made up to flesh it out and colour it. He could feel himself rewriting the scene, putting in words and inflections that would make some sort of sense of it all, justifying his belief that there was some secret or clue back up there on the rim of the crater – and wouldn't that be nice, he thought, if I could go back and mould the past into the shape I want it to be, if I could press a new pattern into the sand and then tap the molten rock and cast a whole new world; like a god, almost, bringing the old world to an end and creating a new one, he thought again. There was a fine notion, for sure; that the world which the god in the cart had come to destroy and replace wasn't the present but the past, a simple job of heating out the memory.

It started to rain as soon as they reached the foot of the mountain, and it didn't stop until they arrived back at Haldersness. By that stage they were all so wet that they couldn't think about anything else, not even how tired and hungry they were. But that was something that could be set right very easily, with a change of clothes, a bowl of porridge (and the inevitable leeks) and a brisk, tall fire, which quickly annealed the memory of the wretchedness of the last few days.

'So,' Colsceg demanded, as Poldarn soaked up the warmth, 'what did you find out up there?'

'Not a lot,' Poldarn answered. 'There's a big hole in the mountain where all the stuff got blown out, you can see right into it. There's a huge pool of molten rock, but it's a hell of a long way down.'

'Molten rock,' Colsceg repeated, as if Poldarn had just said something that didn't make sense, like *burning snow* or *wet fire*. 'Bloody hell, that sounds a bit grim. So what do you reckon we ought to do about it?'

Poldarn shrugged. 'Not a lot we can do – it's all too big. But I don't think there's anything to worry about, it's not like it's going anywhere. Now the mountain's got a way of letting off steam, it shouldn't bother us any more.'

Colsceg frowned. 'That's good,' he said. 'So, apart from that, did you see anything interesting?'

'No,' Poldarn replied. 'That's about it, really.'

'Long way to go just to see that.'

'Yes.'

Colsceg nodded. 'Well, I guess it's better knowing than guessing, at that.'

'True,' Poldarn said. 'Anything been happening here while we've been gone?'

'Not really. No more showers of ash falling out of the sky; a little bit of dust, is all, and not nearly as much of that as when you went away. At this rate, we'll be back to normal in a day or so.'

'Good,' Poldarn yawned, pulling his blanket tighter around his shoulders. 'The sooner that happens, the better for all of us. After all, we've got work to do.'

'We have that,' Colsceg agreed, as he rose to his feet. 'Looks like you'd better get some rest. If the rain holds off, we can finish digging up the turnip clump in the morning.'

'Great,' Poldarn said. 'I'll look forward to that.'

Chapter Eighteen

A day or so after Poldarn got back from the mountain, he was in his new smithy, now complete with a large and handsome brick forge and no less than three anvils. Curiously enough, he found himself drifting over to it more and more, whenever there was nothing obvious for him to do, or whenever he could manufacture a pretext. On this occasion all he had to do was straighten a handful of nails, salvaged from the Haldersness woodshed door – he could have done it easily enough on the mounting-block in the yard, with the back of an axe, but instead he'd gone to the trouble of lighting a fire and taking a heat on each one. Partly, he explained it to himself, it was the warmth he enjoyed; since he'd felt the heat of the volcano on his face as he hung over the ledge, he'd felt uncomfortably cold in the house or the fields, no matter how many layers of clothing he crammed himself into. A well-built fire in the forge, livened up by blasts of air from his magnificent new double-action bellows, was about the only thing that could stop him shivering.

Straightening the nails took him no time at all, so Poldarn

cast about for something else to do otherwise it'd be a waste of all the good coal he'd shovelled onto the fire, and as a good householder he couldn't countenance that. Already he was beginning to accumulate his own personal scrap-pile (he hadn't had the heart to confiscate Asburn's collection when he left Haldersness, where Asburn had remained to teach Barn the trade); mostly nails and brackets and hinges too badly damaged in the move to be used again, but also a fair quantity of junk retrieved from the various houses – worn-out scythe blades, files, ploughshares, axles, kettles, stirrup-irons, hoes, harrows, steelyards, leg-vices, the history of the settlement at Haldersness told through the medium of broken and discarded artefacts. At the bottom of the pile lurked the two halves of a snapped backsabre, partially rusted through, that had hung in the porch of the main house for as long as anybody could remember. Who'd put them there, or why, or who the sword had originally belonged to, had long since corroded away, but the two bits of steel had still been there, because there hadn't been any reason to get rid of them when the time came to leave the house. Someone had taken them down as an afterthought and thrown them in a basket of oddments; someone else had unpacked the basket and, on the basis that all bits of rusty old metal belonged in the forge, had slung them on the scrap-pile to await purification and rebirth.

A little scrabbling turned them up, and Poldarn laid them on the table of the middle anvil, fitted the pieces together along the fracture, and stared at them thoughtfully. There hadn't been any call for Asburn to make anything of the kind while Poldarn had been hanging about in the forge at Haldersness. There was no demand for weapons, generally speaking; they were something you inherited, or borrowed from the big chest with the four padlocks at the back of the hall as and when you needed one for a cruise to the Empire, and there were always more than enough of the things floating around without the smith having to waste time and effort making new ones. This one, the broken one from the Haldersness porch, looked like it was very old indeed, to judge by the depth of the rust-pits and the shrunken contours of the cutting edge, gradually thinned down and eroded by many years of sharpening with coarse stones. Out of curiosity Poldarn took a medium-grit stone and rubbed it up and down the flat of the blade to shift the rust. Once he'd got it back to white metal, he thought he could just about make out the faint pattern of ripples and ridges that marked out an old-fashioned pattern-welded piece, made back in the days when hard steel was rare and precious and a large object like a sword had to be built up out of scraps interleaved with layers of hard iron.

The thought of all the work that must have gone into it made Poldarn wince. Back at Haldersness he'd helped Asburn with some pattern-welding, swinging the big hammer while Asburn did all the clever stuff; it had taken hours of hard, slow work to produce one small billet, and Asburn had told him later that all they'd done was a very simple, utilitarian pattern, not to be mentioned in the same breath with the wonderful constructs the old-timers used – the four- or six-core aligned twists and countertwists, the maiden's-hair pattern, the butterfly, the hugs-and-kisses, the pool and eye and the Polden's ladder. Compared to what the old-timers used to get up to, according to Asburn, the little blank they'd rushed out was just a shoddy piece of rubbish, a parody, a travesty.

Whatever this one had been, he reflected, it hadn't done it much good. The blade had snapped right on the shoulder, the place where the concave bend of the cutting edge was most extreme. Judging by the corresponding chip and roll in the edge, it seemed likely that it had broken in the act of bashing on something hard and solid, quite possibly somebody's armoured head. So much, Poldarn decided, for pattern-welding.

Still; the shape itself was an interesting one, and he stood for quite some time figuring out how a man would go about making such a thing. First he'd have to draw down a steep taper, both thickness and width; then lay in the bevel, probably, keeping the blade straight as he went so as to give himself a chance of keeping everything even; then gradually introduce the curve, just an inch or so per heat, with gentle tapping and nudging over the anvil's beak; then more straightening and truing up, hot and cold – hours of that, in all probability, since flattening out one kink or distortion tended to set up two or three new ones further up or down the piece, as he knew only too well. Finally draw down a tang and either shape a point with the hammer or cheat by using the hot chisel and the rasp; it could be done, in fact now that he'd thought about it he could see every stage of the operation simultaneously, laid out side by side in his mind like a collection of memories. But it'd mean days of work, even using a solid piece of stock rather than pattern-welding, and since nobody wanted such a thing, where the hell was the point?

Poldarn shivered, and realised that while he'd been lost in thought he'd let the fire go out. Well; no excuse for lighting it again, so he might as well take his beautifully straightened nails back out to the yard and give them to someone to knock into a few bits of wood.

Before he could leave the forge, however, the door opened and Raffen came in, reflexively ducking his head to avoid the low beams that had been a feature of the Haldersness smithy, though the Ciartanstead forge didn't have that problem. 'Thought you might be in here,' he said. 'We've got a visitor.'

He made it sound like an infestation of rats. 'Oh,' Poldarn said. 'Who's that, then?'

'Leith,' Raffen replied with ill-concealed distaste, 'from Leithscroft, over the far side of Corby Wood. Haven't seen him round here for years.'

Poldarn shrugged. 'What does he want?'

'Don't ask me,' Raffen answered, 'he didn't tell me. You should be able to guess better than I can. After all, he's your friend.'

Poldarn had, of course, no memory of anybody called Leith. 'Is he?' he asked.

' 'Course. You two were always hanging round the yard when you were kids. Pair of bloody tearaways.'

'I'm sorry to hear that,' Poldarn answered gravely. 'Probably just as well I can't remember. Well, maybe he was passing and just wants to chat about old times. In which case,' he added, 'he probably won't be stopping long. Where did you leave him?'

'In the house, eating.' Raffen came a step or two closer. 'What's that you've got there, then?'

'Oh, that.' For some reason, Poldarn felt embarrassed. 'Just an old busted sword-blade. I was thinking of working it up into a pair of shears or something.'

Raffen squinted. 'Right, I remember it now. Used to hang in the porch – Halder's dad's old sword. I was wondering where that had got to, since the move.'

'Oh,' Poldarn said. 'Nobody told me what it was. In that case, I'll find something else to use.'

'Really? Why?'

Poldarn frowned. 'Well, it's an heirloom. Bit of family history.'

'Oh.' Raffen frowned, as if he'd just found a fish bone. 'Up to you, I suppose. But it's only two bits of old scrap. Better off as something useful than just lying around rusting.'

Leith turned out to be a big, tall man with startlingly broad shoulders and almost no remaining teeth. Poldarn couldn't remember his face at all, but Leith seemed to recognise Poldarn as soon as he walked in through the door, because he stood up and said, 'Hello, Ciartan,' in a rather worried-sounding voice.

'Hello,' Poldarn replied. 'Look, this is probably going to sound strange, but I don't know who you are. You see—'

Leith nodded abruptly. 'You lost your memory back in the old country, I know. I heard it from one of the Lyatsbridge people, they were out our way scrounging lumber and stuff. Soon as I heard, I came straight over. It's true, then.'

Poldarn nodded. He couldn't guess why his loss of memory had affected this stranger so much, but he guessed it wasn't just sympathy for an old friend. 'Apparently we knew each other years ago,' he said. 'Maybe you could tell me about it.'

'Yes.' Leith sucked in a long breath, as if he was bracing himself for something painful, like having a bone set. 'That's why I'm here – there's a few things you really ought to know.' But then he hesitated, as though he was having second thoughts, and a look passed over his face that Poldarn could only describe as sly. 'They also said you can't see anybody's thoughts now,' he said, rather too casually to be convincing. 'Is that right? Never heard anything like that before.'

'Perfectly true,' Poldarn said, trying not to be annoyed. 'And other people can't see mine, either. At least, that's what people have told me. I wouldn't know, of course.'

'Oh, that's true enough. It's like trying to see in through a shuttered window, you know there's something in there but the shutter's in the way. Damnedest thing I ever came across, actually.'

'Really.'

Leith scratched his chin and sat down again. There was a large empty bowl on the table next to him, with a few grains of drying porridge sticking to the side; also a jug and a horn cup, most likely empty now. 'Makes it a bit hard to talk to you, to be honest, but it doesn't bother me, really. So you don't remember anything at all?'

Poldarn shook his head. 'Bits and pieces, but nothing

connected. I can remember a few things I did as a boy – scaring birds in the fields, a trip I took with my grandfather, stuff like that. A few names and faces. No rhyme or reason to any of it, as far as I can make out.'

Leith nodded slowly. 'Didn't I hear somewhere that Halder had passed on?'

The euphemism sounded forced and awkward; Poldarn had got used to people saying things straight out. 'He died a few weeks back, yes,' he said. 'That's why we've moved house, of course.'

'Yes, of course, it stands to reason. I'm very sorry to hear that; he was a good man, for an old-timer.' That didn't sound right, either. 'So, did he tell you much about the old days?'

Poldarn shook his head. 'Not a great deal, he didn't seem very comfortable with the subject. Anyway, we didn't talk much.'

'Right.' Leith seemed rather uncomfortable, like a man sitting in a wet ditch. 'Well, that's a pity. And old Scaptey, the field hand; didn't somebody tell me he bought the farm last raiding season? Killed in a battle or something.'

'So I gather.'

'Really,' Leith said, 'Scaptey too. I've known him since I was a little kid. You remember my brother Brin?'

'No.'

'Ah. Well, he's dead too. We all used to go around together all the time, when we were young. Looks like there's just you and me left, out of the old gang. And you can't remember anything about it.'

'No.'

'There's a thought,' Leith muttered. 'So really it's just me, carrying round all those memories. I guess when I'm gone, it'll all be like it never happened. Not that it matters a damn,' he added. 'It's not as if we did anything much. Just a bunch of kids, really.'

Poldarn looked at him carefully. You came all this way

just to tell me that, he thought, you must have way too much time on your hands. 'How are things out your way?' he asked. 'With the mountain blowing up, and everything?'

'Oh, could have been worse,' Leith replied, his attention clearly elsewhere. 'Could have been a lot worse. Traphouse caught fire, but no great loss. We had that filthy black ash over everything for a while, but the rain washed it all off, down into the valley. Buggered up all the fishweirs, of course, but like I said, it could've been a whole lot worse. You seem to have got away with it all right out this way.'

'By and large,' Poldarn replied. 'Not like those poor devils at Lyatsbridge. They had it pretty rough, by all accounts.'

'Bloody tragedy,' Leith said blandly. 'Last I heard, they were packing up and moving on. We thought about it ourselves, to be honest with you, but we reckoned that on balance we might as well stay put, for now. No, it could have been a damn sight worse. A month later, and it'd have killed our crop stone dead in the ground.'

This was all very well, but hardly worth several days' gruelling ride. 'So,' Poldarn said, 'you mentioned there were some things I ought to know about.'

'That's right,' Leith said slowly. 'So, you're settling in here again, after being away so long. Making yourself at home, so to speak.'

'Well, yes,' Poldarn said. 'I suppose you could put it that way. At least, I've built this house, as you can see. I don't actually know why I needed to build a whole new house when the old one was perfectly good enough, but they told me I had to, so I did.'

'Nice place.'

'Thank you. I don't think it's so bad, for a first attempt. And what else? Oh yes, I got married.'

Leith looked up. 'You don't say.'

'That was another thing they told me I had to do. But it

could have been worse, as you'd say. I reckon I've been very lucky there, as it happens.'

Leith forced a smile. 'Well, there's something,' he said. 'You married. That's like the old story about the wolf who became a sheepdog. Still, at our age you've got to settle down, haven't you?'

'Apparently,' Poldarn replied.

'And you've found yourself a nice little girl,' Leith went on. 'Well, you would, wouldn't you?'

Poldarn nodded. 'Colsceg's daughter. You know her?'

'No.' Leith looked away. His hands were spread out flat on the table, palms down, fingers splayed out wide. 'Since my time. Anyhow, that's only one of the places we went. I never liked it much out that way, anyhow. Bleak old place in winter, Colscegsford.' He stood up. 'I think it's about time I was hitting the road,' he said. 'If I start straight away I can make Elletswater by dark.'

'What was it you came here to tell me?' Poldarn asked.

'Look.' There was a suggestion of panic in Leith's voice. 'If it's stuff only you and me would know about, and you've forgotten it anyway, who the hell cares any more? Besides, we're different people now. Married, with responsibilities, we can't go dwelling on the past. Take me, for instance, I'm nothing like I used to be. If I caught my eldest boy doing some of the stuff I used to get up to at his age, I'd skin him alive. People change, it's part of life; but if you're going to change, you've got to get rid of some bits of the past, break the old habits, get out of the patterns, that kind of thing. Like, if you and I were meeting now for the first time ever – well, I guess that's what we *are* doing, far as you're concerned – I mean to say, would we be best friends now? 'Course not, we've grown apart, nothing in common except the obvious stuff – the farm and the weather and running a house. Do you really want to hear a lot of things about someone who's nothing but a stranger to you now? That's me –

and you, of course, you as well.' Leith shook his head. 'I'll bet you anything you like, if it was the old you, like you were when we were kids, the old you stood here instead of me – do you think you'd recognise him, or have anything in common with him? I don't think so. You probably wouldn't like him, even. So why burden yourself with stuff that a perfect stranger did, twenty years ago? Makes no sense. I'm the only one who remembers now, and I won't tell anybody, for sure. So; it never happened. It's like a log of wood you put on the fire, it burns up and it's gone for ever.'

Or a book, Poldarn thought, the last copy of a book in a big old library; and I can remember burning the library down, but God only knows what was in the books. 'Looks like you've had a pretty pointless journey, then,' he said.

'Oh, that's all right,' Leith replied. 'Doesn't bother me. And it's done me a favour, when you think about it. Like, there's only so much room in a man's head for memories. Means I can clear out a lot of old stuff I won't ever need again. So that's that, then. And remember, if ever you're out our way, make sure to drop by. Always glad to see you, any time.'

'Thank you,' Poldarn said. 'And if ever you get one of those sudden urges to dash off somewhere a long way away for a bowl of porridge and a quick chat about the weather . . . you know where we are.'

'That's right,' Leith said. 'Though I don't get out much as a rule these days, I don't go raiding or stuff like that. I'm very quiet these days. It's better that way.'

'I think so too,' Poldarn said. 'There's always so much work that needs doing, for one thing. Some days, I hardly know what to do with myself.'

'Oh, same here,' Leith said emphatically. 'If it's not one thing it's another. Anyhow, take care, and my regards to your wife. I'd have brought her some flowers or a bottle of wine, only I left in such a hurry.'

'Of course. And besides, I only just told you I'm married.'

'Yes.' Leith took a step backwards. 'I really had better be going,' he said, 'it's a long way. We'll see each other again, I'm sure of it.'

'It's a small world,' Poldarn replied.

When Leith had gone, chivvying his horse into a canter as soon as he was out of the yard, Poldarn went and found Raffen, who was splitting kindling.

'Who was that?' he asked.

Raffen put down the hatchet and looked up. 'How do you mean?' he asked.

'That man who was here just now. You told me you knew him.'

'Of course I know him. Him and his brother, they lived here for years, when you and he were kids. You two went everywhere together.'

'So you said. But I don't remember, and he wouldn't tell me anything. In fact, he was acting like he was crazy or something. What else do you know about him?'

Raffen shrugged. 'Not a great deal,' he said. 'Really, you want to ask Colsceg, not me.'

'Colsceg.'

'That's right. They're related.'

'Oh.' Poldarn frowned. 'He didn't say anything about that.'

'Probably thought you already knew.' Raffen put a piece of wood on the chopping block and tapped it smartly with the hatchet, dividing it neatly into two. 'His uncle married Colsceg's sister, but she died young. And Colsceg married his other uncle's sister, that's his uncle on his father's side, of course. That was his first wife, Barn's mother. She died young, too, when she had Egil. Then Colsceg married Sterley's eldest daughter – Sterley was Leith's mother's brother, or at least properly speaking he was her half-brother, because their mother was married twice, once up north, which is where Sterley came from, and then again when she moved back here. There was some sort of trouble with a stranger, apparently, and she left her husband up there. Anyway, her second husband was Halder's uncle Crim; so when they both died, Leith and his brother – what was his name, now?'

'Brin,' Poldarn said.

'That's right, Brin. And there was an older sister, too – Essel, she married Suart, Lyat's dad, back when they lived at Suartsdale. I think she stayed there when Lyat moved on to Lyatsbridge. Leith and Brin, they came over here to live, till their dad died and it was time for them to go back and build their house. So you see, they're all family, one way or another.'

'I see,' Poldarn said. 'Well, I think I'll go and do some work. Is there any work I can be doing?'

Raffen frowned; then his face relaxed into a grin. 'So happens there is,' he said. 'Just the job for you, if you feel like it. You know the three-cornered field just below the old house, where we put in the peas, just before we left there?'

'Of course I do, I live here. What about it?'

'Bloody crows are tearing it all to pieces,' Raffen said, with a touch of anger he couldn't help. 'I was going to go up there later on and put up some bells, but that won't do any good. Waste of time, soon as my back's turned they'll be in there again. Where's the point of planting stuff if those bastards pull it all up, anyway?'

'I can see that,' Poldarn replied. 'And I used to be good at scaring birds, when I was a kid. Isn't that right?'

Raffen nodded eagerly. 'You really took to it,' he said. 'Made a good job, too. It isn't as easy as it looks, you know.'

'Then maybe it'll come back to me,' Poldarn replied. 'It'd be nice to find something I'm actually good at around here, even if it's just clapping my hands and shouting.'

Raffen pulled a face. 'There's a bit more to it than that,' he said. 'Just scaring the buggers off won't do any good. You've got to sort 'em out, once and for all.'

'Whatever,' Poldarn said.

The three-cornered field lay under a long, low, crescent-shaped hill topped with a knot of spindly fir trees. Along the western edge ran a ditch backed by an overgrown thorn hedge, with a thick mass of nettles and cow-parsley on the field side. The other two boundaries were open, marked only by a low drystone wall on the side facing the house, and a hump on the southern side where a bank had been grubbed out at some point, twenty or thirty years ago.

When Poldarn arrived, carrying a billhook, a leather bottle of weak cider and an old wooden bucket, the field was black with crows. They didn't get up as soon as he came into view, which annoyed him rather. About a third of them spread their wings and lifted off the ground in a spiral, the way dust blows up in a high wind; they swirled round in a tight circle and pitched a little further up the field, in good order. He stopped and studied them for a moment – careful reconnaissance is never wasted – taking note of the patterns they made on the ground, the way they aligned themselves to the wind, their spacing, the distances between groups, the gaps they left so that newcomers could pitch without overflying a contingent and spooking them into the air. Observing them, he couldn't help being impressed at the perfection of their society – their orderly conduct, unselfishness, consideration for others, flawless cooperation, unblemished unity of purpose. Against the grey of the turned soil they stood out like the shadow of a low cloud on a bright day, or the black ash that the volcano had dumped there, not so long ago.

Poldarn knew or remembered enough to keep perfectly still; but as the sun moved through the scattered clouds, the light changed, brightening up enough to flash a slight reflection off his pale face. At once, four or five crows got up from the edges and wheeled over him, slow, high and screaming; he froze, but they were aware of him now, and the whole flock lifted in a jarring explosion of harsh voices – you didn't need to know their language to get the gist of what they were saying. For a few heartbeats they hung in the air like smoke on a calm day; then they began to swirl and circle, winding broad, lazy hoops of concerted movement, boldly overstated brush strokes against the grey sky.

Poldarn had been expecting that, relying on it. On his way he'd picked up half a bucketful of flints from the headlands of the neighbouring fields, where generations of field hands had tossed them as they'd harrowed and mashed the clods. As the flock billowed over his head – they always made this mistake, just once, it was almost an arrogantly chivalrous gesture, allowing him one clear chance to take a few easy shots, satisfy his honour – he stooped down, grabbed a flint from the bucket, marked a point in the sky where the press of bodies was so thick he couldn't miss, and let fly. The first stone somehow managed to thread a way through the crowd without hitting anything, but the next five stones knocked down four birds – one dead in the air, two with broken wings landing indignant but in good order, and one pitching messily on its back, skipping and hopping in a dance of murderous rage until Poldarn got his foot behind its head and crushed it into the hard soil. The two broken-winged runners were harder to catch, they waddled with furious determination towards the hedge side, jinking and tacking out of the way every time he came within arm's length, so that in the end he had to resort to a desperate, flamboyant tackle to bring them down. Once he had his hand over their backs, it was a different matter – thumb pressed against the neck-bone, two forefingers to lever back the head until the neck snapped. Four crows had changed sides; not nearly as many as he'd have liked, but enough to make a start.

Next, Poldarn chose his place. That was a simple enough

decision; all he had to do was look at the pattern of the green haze of pea-sprouts just starting to show above the ground, and mark out the biggest bare patch, where the core of the flock had been feeding. The size of it made him very angry; almost a quarter of the crop was already ruined, an act of war against him and his household that he would have to make good against them, one way or another. Life was hard enough without this sort of thing, the sudden advent of a horde of merciless raiders who didn't care if the Ciartanstead house starved. Something had to be done, and it was already way past diplomacy or settlement.

Next, he built his hide. Again, he didn't need to think hard about that. The bare patch was tight in to the middle point of the hedge and ditch side; that was where they wanted to be, so that was where he'd have to go. Fortunately, it was the place he'd have chosen anyway; there was even a young oak standing up out of the hedge, to mask him from above. With that, the ditch to hunker down in, and the screen of weeds and nettles out front, he was practically invisible until he chose to show himself. Admittedly, it wasn't going to be comfortable crouching in the bottom of the ditch. The mud (silt from the recent rains, the last of the black ash filtered and ground small by the water) came oozing up round his ankles, and he had to sit on his heels with his back braced against the trunk of the oak, his head and neck craned forward so he could look out through a narrow gap in the weed-curtain. If he stayed here any length of time he'd be crippled the next day. As if that mattered.

Having marked his place in the ditch, Poldarn scrambled out and set up his decoys. From the thorn hedge he cut four straight sticks, each as long as his hand from fingertip to wrist. He sharpened these on the thin end and dug the points in under the dead crows' lower jaw, up through the brains until they stopped against the roofs of the skulls. That was enough to hold the dead birds' weights as he pegged them out, as realistically as he could manage, standing them upright with the heads raised and the beaks jutting out like spears at port arms, proud sentries at their posts. With only four of them to play with he couldn't suggest a convincing pattern, so they would have to be scouts, marking out the limits of the safe zone in advance of the main body. Accordingly he posted them at the extreme corners of his killing field, fifteen paces from his hide. The idea was that the crows would come in along the obvious flight-line from their castle, the knot of thin trees on the hilltop. Once they'd marked the position of the scouts and been made aware of the safe zone, they'd slow down by turning into the breeze, bank, and glide down to pitch in the centre of the approved space, gradually filling it from the middle outwards until there was no more room; whereupon another platoon of scouts would establish further safe zones in suitable adjoining areas, and so on until the field was carpeted with crows like black snow.

Before going back to his hide, he skirmished the headland for a few more handfuls of stones, just in case it turned into a good day (nothing worse than having to disrupt a fluent spell to go scrabbling out in the open for ammunition). Then he folded himself into the hide as best he could, wriggled his back into the closest approximation of comfort that he could find, and waited to see what would happen.

Poldarn knew, or remembered, that it was no good expecting birds to come in for at least half an hour after set-up – it was set down in the rules as a fundamental principle, unshakeable as the orientation of the rising and the setting sun. During that time, it was absolutely essential to keep perfectly still; you could just about get away with blinking so long as you had a first-rate hide, but anything more energetic than that and you might as well go home. After that, if you were really lucky, you'd hear the screams and squawks of the advance scouts, gliding slowly over at double-treetop height. You wouldn't see them, of course, because one thing you had not to do when the scouts were overhead was lift your head, or even raise your eyes; the flicker of the whites of your eyes would be enough to send the scouts into a scrambled, flustered turn, followed by a fast and noisy retreat, after which you might as well go to sleep for an hour for all the good you were likely to do—

He'd only just got himself into position when he felt a patch of darkness flicker across his forehead, the shadow of a crow hanging between himself and the sun. He caught sight of it a few heartbeats later as it crossed the bare patch in his line of sight; a T-shaped pattern of dark grey, unnaturally elongated, distorting as it dragged over humps and dips in the dirt. The first scout was over him already – impossible, unheard of, but there it was. A mere twenty years, and already they'd forgotten even the most elementary basics of their craft. He'd have to set them straight on a few points.

He held his breath until the shadow passed. First there'd be the singleton scouts, two or three of them flying high, cautious solo runs over the decoys. Next would come the corps of observers, describing two circuits at extreme range before closing in and pitching. They had to be spared, at all costs; they would be the unwitting traitors, his best friends and most valuable collaborators, because once they'd dropped in and walked up and down for a minute or so, the first detachment of foot soldiers would follow them up, and the battle could start. At that point, he knew or remembered, the crucial thing was *not to miss* . . . A crow rapped on the head with a stone as it drifted in to pitch would drop the last foot or so and land, quite dead, but looking to the rest of the army as though it was snuggling in to feed, and the sight of it would draw in another in its place, and so on. A crow missed, squirming round in the air and thrashing its wings in terror, would clear the air for a mile in every direction, leaving him with the whole miserable job to start again.

When the moment came and the first target presented itself, he found himself on his feet before he knew what he was doing. Is this right? he wondered helplessly as his throwing arm brushed his ear; then the crow's wings clamped against its sides as it died, and it bounced just a little as it hit the ground, and he knew it was going to be all right.

Don't be greedy, he told himself as he reached for the next stone; one at a time, let each one take its proper place, even if there's a dozen others in range to shy at, keep good order at all times. Sure enough, the fall of the first bird drew in another like a pawl lifting a gear in clockwork. He threw again – how very good he was at throwing stones, he realised, but he knew better than to stop and think about how he was doing it – and number two hit the ground, six yards to the left of number one. Number three was further out and for a heartbeat he thought he'd missed; the stone caught the back of the wing, shattering it, and the crow dropped on its feet and hopped about (excellent; live, moving decoys on the ground were the best sort) as number four spread its wings into the breeze and slid down into the path of a stone. By the time he missed, and the sky was suddenly empty and quiet again, he'd brought down nine birds; seven dead, one runner and one flapper.

Poldarn flopped against the tree-trunk, exhausted by the tension and the effort. His right shoulder was savagely painful and his knees were weak, but he hardly spared them a thought, so angry was he with himself for missing an easy mark. But when he looked up a moment or so later, he saw two more crows, one already on the ground, the other just pitching. With a heart full of love he thanked them for their kind forbearance, and picked a stone out of the bucket. Almost immediately a third crow began its glide, and he hit it beautifully on the side of the head, an exemplary throw at a full ten yards, but he knew before he let fly that he couldn't miss. The dead body plumped down and the machine started again, feeding crows into the slot as fast as he could pick up stones, until his tally reached fifteen. At that point there was a lull, for no cause that he could see (but he knew or remembered that such disruptions were in fact quite normal; there was probably a perfectly good reason, and maybe one day he'd figure out what it was). Without moving his body he craned his neck to see if there was anything in the air. Nothing coming in; so he stood up, being careful to keep his head down below the level of the weeds in front of him, and took stock of the field, with special reference to the pattern that was beginning to build. This would be a good time to consolidate – stake out the dead, tidy up the killing zone, do a little general housekeeping; but the pattern turned out to be good, the flapper had died of its injuries, the runner was still in play, there wasn't really anything that needed to be done. That was a slice of luck. If he left the hide now and walked about, it'd be half an hour at least before business could resume. He sat down again (his knees and thighs were hurting badly now) and chose a good smooth flint for his next throw, whenever it came.

He didn't have long to wait. Two scouts, then a dozen, a full echelon gliding straight at him from the trees, unheard-of confidence, ludicrous arrogance – If I was a crow you'd never catch me being so bloody stupid. The stone was digging uncomfortably into the palm of his hand, but he decided to let the dozen come all the way. If they were prepared to come in so boldly, it could only be because the pattern was just right, so that the crows were seeing exactly what they wanted to see. Very well, then; indulge them, let them make their appalling mistake. The dozen pitched and started waddling around, brushing past their dead brethren and pecking vainly at the already-plundered earth. Excellent, Poldarn thought; and he was right, because the flow that started after that lasted him another ten kills before he fumbled a shot and spoilt everything. The sky cleared, the trees in the distance flushed out the reserves and the general staff, and he was left alone with his dead.

Bloody ridiculous mistake. He was mortally ashamed; still, he had two dozen on the ground now, a big enough pattern to draw them back in spite of themselves. He didn't deserve another chance, but he was probably going to get one all the same. He wasn't wrong, at that; an hour later they were back, and only the barest going-through-the-motions flight of scouts before they started pouring in, pitching in twos and threes instead of singly. That should have been a problem; too many birds in play at any one time increases the risk of detection. But they didn't seem to care, and before long he was knocking down two, three, four in a row without breaking the rhythm. Somewhere around four dozen he lost count; they were drifting in like snow, and for all the notice they were taking of him, he might as well not have been there.

It was at this point that Poldarn became aware of someone sitting next to him in the hide. For a while he was too busy to do more than register the presence; whoever it was, he or she was sitting quite still, observing hide discipline, making no trouble. He guessed it was someone from the farm who'd come to see how he was getting on. It occurred to him to wonder how anybody could have got to the hide without showing himself and spooking the crows, but he only had enough spare attention to pose the question, not answer it. But then the tap turned off, as it had done two or three times already; the sun was too bright, or the wind had changed, or he'd killed all the birds in that particular detachment, and the reserves hadn't arrived yet. He turned his head to see who was crouching next to him.

'Hello,' he said (noise didn't bother the crows the way movement did, so it was all right to speak). 'Who are you? I'm sorry, but I don't know you.'

The boy smiled politely. 'My name's Ciartan,' he replied. 'I live at the farm up there on the hill. Do you mind if I just sit here and watch for a bit?'

Poldarn shrugged. 'Sure,' he said, 'so long as you don't move when there's birds in the air.'

'Oh, I know better than that,' the boy assured him gravely. 'I do a lot of crow-scaring myself, every chance I can get. But I've never had a day like this. You're really good at it.'

'Thank you,' Poldarn replied. 'It's just practice, that's all.'

The boy nodded. 'You've been doing it for a long time, then?'

'All my life,' Poldarn said, 'since I was your age. It's all about experience, really; that and keeping your eyes open, thinking about what you're looking at. That – and learning how to think like a crow, of course.'

'Exactly,' the boy said. 'You've got to be able to get inside their minds, really, otherwise you don't stand a chance. That's where I go wrong, of course. I can't seem to manage it.'

Before Poldarn could say anything, a big old crow with a ragged left wing appeared out of nowhere directly overhead. Poldarn froze, holding his breath, watching the bird's shadow on the ground as it flapped slowly away. 'He'll be back,' Poldarn whispered, 'you wait and see. He's just taking a look.'

'Scout?' the boy asked.

'Don't think so. Just occasionally you get a loner, out of touch with the rest of 'em. Look, he's on the turn. Keep still, he'll come back in straight at us.'

Sure enough, the crow executed a long, wide, sweeping turn, dropped low and came in with languorous, easy wing-beats, three feet or so above the ground. Poldarn let it come, knowing that if he could manage to drop it cleanly in the right place, its fall would bring in a new wave of scouts and the brief drought would be over. He could only just see the line it made in the air through his curtain of nettles, but he'd gauged its speed pretty well. When he reckoned it had reached the right spot, he straightened his protesting knees and threw at where the crow ought to be. Sure enough it was there, and the stone cracked it on the forehead. It dropped flat, wings tight in to its body.

'Shot,' the boy said, deeply impressed. 'I didn't even see it.'

Poldarn grinned. 'Nor me, I figured out where it was going to be. Now we should be in for some action.'

He wasn't wrong. Three scouts came over high, shrieking harshly, and slowly drew off; shortly afterwards, four more birds hobbled in on the line the singleton had taken. More or less at the point where Poldarn had killed the loner, they put their wings back and pitched.

'We leave them alone,' Poldarn said. 'Remember, for every one you can see, there's a couple of dozen that can see you.'

'I know,' the boy said. 'Right, here we go. Incoming on the left.'

Poldarn frowned; they hadn't come from that quarter before, or he hadn't seen them (he had a blind spot there). 'How many?'

'Two,' the boy replied immediately. 'One's on the glide, the other one's thinking about it.'

'Fine. We let the front one pitch and take the other one.'

He didn't see the second bird until it was a bare foot off the ground, but it was in the right place at the right time, so he killed it quickly and dropped back down as fast as he could. The first bird lifted, but spread its wings straight away and tacked into the wind to brake its airspeed. As it sailed over a gap he bobbed up and killed it. There was another bird in the air before he sat down.

'That's amazing,' the boy said. 'I can never get them to do that.'

'Watch and learn,' Poldarn replied smugly. 'The key to

this lark is patterns. Get the patterns right and all you've got to be able to do is throw a stone straight.'

No time for idle chatter for several minutes after that. They came in thick, almost too many of them, so that Poldarn had to keep throwing and killing just to keep the picture tight. 'You know,' the boy said during the next slight pause, 'it's starting to make sense to me now. It's like I can actually read the patterns and know what they're going to do. I can't explain it, though.'

'That's good, you're starting to think like them. They don't think in words, see; so you've got to be like them, think with your eyes.'

'That's right, think with your eyes. Like drawing a sword, really.' The boy stopped talking while Poldarn nailed a couple more crows. 'It all makes sense when you're doing it,' he went on, 'definitely what you said, patterns. You know exactly what's going to happen; it's almost like you've been here before and you're remembering it all, so you can remember exactly where each bird's come from and where it's going to be. Either that, or you're reading their minds. Or both.'

They came in again while the boy was still talking; but he must have seen Poldarn stiffen, because he abruptly fell silent and held still. Poldarn killed another three; then he reached into the bucket for a stone and found it was empty.

'Fuck,' he said, 'that's a bloody nuisance. Do me a favour, will you; nip out and get a few stones, the headland's covered with them.'

But the boy wasn't there any more; he must have slipped away while Poldarn was busy. Annoying; he was too stiff and cramped to want to get up. No choice in the matter, though; so he straightened his knees with an effort and clambered up the side of the ditch.

He hadn't seen the field, of course, not since he'd got down and worked himself in. It was an extraordinary sight.

There were dead crows everywhere, a black mat of wings and bodies; some on their backs with their claws curled in the air, some on their sides with a wing frozen in death, some flat on the ground with their wings spread. One or two were still twitching, straining their necks like athletes striving to lift weights. As he hauled himself out of the ditch, something thrashed frantically in the tall nettles. He stood and stared for a long time, remembering various things he had seen – the ground littered with dead monks at Deymeson, the aftermath of the battle in the river, when the old women in their black shawls had come out to rob the dead, and a host of other pictures from the back of his mind that were equally vivid, though he couldn't fit a story to them. But they all conformed to one pattern, in the alignment of the corpses, their spacing, the gaps between them. They lay just as they'd been when he'd arrived, when they were still alive and feeding (it was the picture he'd been trying to achieve, the pattern he'd held in his mind as he worked) and they covered the sprouting peas like the mountain's black ejecta, the only difference being that he'd put them there, and he'd been doing good.

Stones, he thought; but he didn't move. Instead, he looked towards the volcano, Polden's Forge, and saw a thick column of black smoke billowing out of the summit, exactly like a flock of crows put up out of a knot of tall, thin trees, their castle. He could almost believe that the smoke was crows, all the crows he'd killed that day and on other good days, when he'd blackened the fields with his mess. It reminded him of one day in particular, a turning point in his career as the death of crows – he'd forgotten all about it until now, but suddenly it appeared in his mind's sky, swooped and pitched in the killing zone of his memory, the day when a young boy called Ciartan had gone out to kill crows on a field of sprouting peas, only to find that a man he couldn't remember having seen before had got there first and built his hide in this very ditch, under this very oak tree. The offcomer (a strange and rather frightening man with a sad face) was having a very good day, the field was covered in dead bodies, and he'd sat with him in his hide for a while and watched him at work, learning ever so much about decoying and tracking the birds in night and building and maintaining patterns – the foundations on which he'd based all his subsequent triumphs, from that day to this. It was the sheer number of the dead that had impressed him then – after the man had gone he counted them, one hundred and seventy-two – and (he guessed) it was the similarity of that picture of slaughter to this that had jarred his mind back into the groove.

He let go of the bucket and went out to count the dead birds. There were a hundred and seventy-two of them. As he turned them over with his foot and reckoned up the total, he was singing:

> *Old crow lying on the cold brown clay,*
> *Old crow lying on the cold brown clay,*
> *Old crow lying on the cold brown clay –*
> *But there'll always be another for another day.*

He remembered that he'd left the billhook in the bottom of the ditch. For a moment he was tempted to leave it there – he was too tired and aching to go scrambling about in ditches, it'd be easier to go home, fire up the forge and make a new one – but he put that unworthy thought behind him and slithered back down the slope into the mud (much deeper now, where he'd churned it up.) The hook had managed to burrow its way into the bed of the ditch and he had to scrabble for it with his fingertips. The mud felt cold and rather disgusting, it was like paunching a rabbit you'd killed yesterday and forgotten to dress out; he found the hook eventually, but while he was groping for it he came across something else. At first it looked like just another stone (could've done with that a few minutes ago, when the crows were coming in) but something prompted him to scour away the surface mud with the ball of his thumb, and he realised that it was iron or steel, remarkably well preserved under the coating of mud, except that it had turned a stony grey colour. A knob of mud in the middle gave way under his finger and proved to be the eye of a small axe. Once he'd found the billhook he spent a few minutes scraping off the mud and rust coating, and was pleased to see that it was salvageable; all it'd need would be a touch or two on the grindstone and a new handle, and he'd have a perfectly usable tool. He tucked it into his belt, wondering how it had come to be there, sunk in the mud and deprived of its history. But there were no clues to be found just by looking at it; its memory had long since rotted away, along with its handle. Not to worry; whoever it had belonged to and whatever it had been, it was still a perfectly good axe, and so long as it could be made to remember how to cut, that, surely, was all that mattered.

By the time he'd hauled himself out of the ditch and trudged back across the field, the crows were already starting to drop in and pitch again, as if nothing had happened and he hadn't been there. That should have annoyed him, but this time he only shrugged and turned his back on them. There would, after all, be another day tomorrow.

Chapter Nineteen

The next day Poldarn could hardly move at all. From his hips to his knees, his legs ached unbearably, and he couldn't straighten them without yelping with pain. One trip from the bedroom round the back of the house to the privy was enough to persuade him that the crows could wait a day or so. He staggered back into the house and leaned against the door frame, feeling profoundly unhappy.

'What's the matter with you?' asked Carey the field hand, bustling past with a small cider barrel tucked under his arm.

'Done my legs in,' Poldarn answered dolefully. 'Six hours cramped up in a ditch'll do that to you.'

Carey grinned. 'Serves you right,' he said. 'Out enjoying yourself all day when the rest of us are working. Good day?'

Poldarn nodded. 'Hundred and seventy-two. Only quit because I ran out of stones.'

'Well, you must've saved a few for later. I was out there this morning and the whole field was black with the little buggers. Going out again later?'

'Certainly not,' Poldarn groaned. 'I'm wounded in action, that means I get a day off. Otherwise, where's the point?'

Carey grunted. 'Soft, that's what you are. Maybe you should try a day's biscay-spitting, that'll teach you a thing or two about really hurting.'

Poldarn made it back to his bed without falling over, though it was touch-and-go most of the way. Elja was in the bedroom, folding up the washing.

'You can't lie on the bed, I've just made it,' she said. 'You'll make the room look scruffy.'

'Go away,' Poldarn replied, collapsing onto the bed in a barely controlled fall. 'I want sympathy, not criticism.'

'You poor thing,' Elja said briskly. 'If you're going to lie there, take your boots off.'

'Have a heart,' Poldarn whimpered. 'It took me half an hour to get them on.'

She shook her head. 'It's your own silly fault for crouching in a muddy ditch,' she sighed. 'You can't expect sympathy if you crock yourself when you're out having fun.'

Poldarn pulled a face. 'It wasn't fun, it was serious work. You should see the damage they've done already, bloody things.'

'Sure,' Elja replied. 'I think you're cruel, picking on a load of defenceless birds.'

Poldarn straightened out his legs and closed his eyes. 'Please go away,' he said. 'As a special favour to me.'

'Just my luck,' Elja said with an exaggerated sniff. 'I end up married to an old man who can't sit in the sun all day without straining something. Fat lot of use you are to a growing girl.'

She left while he was still trying to think of an appropriate reply.

He closed his eyes and tried to go to sleep, but of course that didn't work. It was gloomy and dark in the bedroom now that the sun was up; it would have been too dark to read even if he'd had a book, which he didn't. He was too bored to stay still and his legs hurt too much to let him move. He longed for something to do — sewing shirts, or mending nets, or podding beans, anything useful that could be done with just the hands. Presumably if he summoned one of the women and *ordered* her to bring him a bucketful of apples to core and slice, she'd have to obey him, since he was the lord of Ciartanstead and his word was nominally law. Unfortunately he couldn't think of any way of attracting attention. Alternatively, he could lie back and think up brilliant, far-reaching schemes and reforms and ways of doing things much more efficiently and productively than ever before, or astoundingly original plans for dealing with droughts, floods and infestations of rats, or an amazingly simple way of protecting the farm from the volcano. Or he could write a poem (in his head; no paper) or compose a song. Or he could count sheep jumping over a low wall.

'Here you are.' There was someone in the doorway, but he couldn't see who it was from where he was lying. He tried to sit up but the angle was all wrong. 'No, don't get up,' the voice went on. 'Looks like you need your rest.'

He placed the voice; it was Egil, of all people. That in itself made him suspicious, in addition to the feeling of unease that his brother-in-law's tone of voice inspired in him. 'Sorry,' he said, keeping his voice carefully neutral. 'I've strained my legs, and I can't sit up.'

'I heard.' Egil appeared in front of him. 'Crouching in a ditch all day, hardly surprising. I did something like that once: I was sitting out waiting for the geese to come in on the long estuary at Brayskillness. Nine hours on the mud flats, and when the buggers finally showed up, I got one shot at extreme range, and I missed. But archery was never my strong point.'

'Nor mine,' Poldarn said. 'At least, I can't remember ever

trying it. Actually, I'm talking nonsense, for all I know I'm a crack shot. I should give it a try some time, it'd be a useful skill if I'm any good at it.'

Egil shrugged. 'Who knows?' he said. 'You were bloody pathetic at it when you were younger, but you seem to have learned a whole lot of skills while you were away, so maybe archery was one of them.' He shifted uncomfortably; he hadn't come here to talk about archery or swap hunting stories.

'Kind of you to drop by,' Poldarn said. 'You've no idea how boring it is lying here.'

'Actually, I have,' Egil said. 'I broke my leg, years ago. Nearly went off my head, staring at the roof timbers hour after hour. In the end I used to lie there with my eyes shut, imagining stuff.'

Poldarn raised an eyebrow. 'Stuff?'

Egil laughed, slightly off key. 'Swordfights,' he said, 'horse races, quarterstaff bouts. And, um, stuff with girls. All sorts of things. It passed the time.'

'I think I'll stick with staring at the roof, thank you,' Poldarn said. 'Though there's a botched lapjoint in the third rafter down that's bugging the hell out of me; what I want to do most in the world is get a ladder and a hammer and chisel and tidy it up. Soon as I'm back on my feet, I'm going to do that, I swear.'

'Well, that's good,' Egil said. 'It's nice to have a purpose in life. You must be wondering what the hell I'm doing here.'

Poldarn nodded. 'Ever since we met you've done your best to stay out of my way,' he said. 'And you keep hinting that it's because of some dreadful secret. I don't suppose you're here to let me in on it, are you?'

'No.' Egil shook his head. 'And I think you just answered the question I came here to ask. Thanks.'

'Hey.' Egil was about to leave the room. 'At least ask me the question.'

Egil frowned. 'All right,' he said. 'Someone told me Leith was here a day or so back. Is that right?'

'Yes. How did you – I guess someone told you. Or something like that.'

'Something like that. So he was here, then.'

'Came and went. Stayed just long enough to be annoyingly cryptic, then slung his hook. Why, do you know him?'

'I used to. But that was years ago. Look, I thought we had an understanding; you don't want to know about the old days, and I don't want to tell you.'

Poldarn dipped his head in acknowledgement. 'But Leith was something to do with it.'

'Very much so,' Egil said. 'So, he came over here because he knew you were back—'

'And he'd heard I'd lost my memory, but he wanted to make sure. Which he did. Then he went home. Simple as that.'

'Fine. So you must've set his mind at rest.'

'His mind, yes. Look, I've been thinking. This deadly secret, it must have been something I did. I'm starting to think I ought to know about it. In fact, I'm pretty sure I should. I've been second-guessing and third-guessing, I lie awake at nights trying to figure out what it could be, and it seems to me that it can't have been all that bad, or they'd never have brought me home. Halder knew, didn't he?'

'Oh, Halder knew.' Egil looked very thoughtful. 'You know, if anybody's to blame really, it's him. Other people – well, they made mistakes, I think it's fair enough to call it that – but Halder actually did a very bad thing, a *wicked* thing, and I'm positive he knew he was going to die soon afterwards and the truth would die with him. At least, that's what he thought, because he didn't know Leith and I were in on the secret too. But that doesn't make it any better.'

'Doesn't it?'

'Of course not. If you could commit a crime, something

really cruel and unspeakable, and you knew for a fact you'd never be found out, nobody'd even know the crime had been committed, it'd still be a crime. Wouldn't it?'

Poldarn thought for a moment. 'To be honest,' he said, 'I can't think of a really terrible crime that nobody would notice. I mean, there's got to be a victim or it isn't a crime: you can't blind someone or burn down his house without him realising what's been done to him. Well, I suppose you could kill a lonely stranger, someone with no family or friends who's just arrived in the district, so nobody apart from yourself knows he's there. That's not what happened, is it?'

Egil shook his head. 'Nothing like that,' he said. 'In fact, that wouldn't be such a bad crime, if you ask me, because someone like that – well, who cares? Apart from the stranger, of course; but if he's got no family, nobody depending on him, then it's not like it's a great loss, is it? There's nobody left to be affected by it.'

Poldarn's eyes opened wide. 'That's a pretty cold-blooded way of looking at things, isn't it?' he said.

'Maybe.' Egil sounded like he wasn't bothered. 'Truth is, it's so unlikely and far-fetched, it's hard to imagine what it'd be like. Everybody's got family and friends somewhere, even that new friend of yours, the bear-hunter who got you out of the mud over at our place. Like, if I killed him tomorrow, you'd notice he wasn't around any more, and if you found out I'd killed him, you'd be after me for revenge. And he's as close as you'll ever get to what you had in mind.'

'True,' Poldarn said. 'But supposing I'd killed him that first day I met him, out on the moors.'

Egil grinned. 'Before or after he saved you from the bear? No, think about it. If it was before, the bear would've got you. If it was afterwards, you'd have been too grateful to kill him. Like I said, that scenario of yours is just too improbable to be worth getting in a state over.'

'All right.' Poldarn straightened his right leg with a shudder of pain. 'And you're saying what I did was worse than that.'

Egil shook his head. 'Certainly not. Like I said just now, it was more of a mistake than a crime, anyway.'

'Fine. So what *Halder* did was worse than that.'

'No, not really. Oh, it was a despicable thing to do, but nothing like killing someone. It wasn't – well, *active*, if you see what I mean. There's a difference, isn't there? Between doing something bad and letting something bad happen?'

Poldarn decided to draw a bow at a venture. 'Like you did, you mean.'

'Like I did, yes. Except I just stood back and didn't interfere; what Halder did was worse than that. Except he thought nobody would ever know, so it'd all be all right. And in the end, it's been a blessing. Well, for a lot of people it has. Me, for one.'

'Really.' Poldarn scowled. 'You know, ever since I got here it's been like this. Everybody knows everything, except me. I'm getting bloody sick of it.'

But Egil shook his head. 'Don't be so damned selfish,' he said. 'It's just like your case, exactly.'

'How do you mean?'

'Think about it. Suppose there was a really bad man, a truly evil man who did terrible things; and one day he can't remember who he is or what he's done, and for ages he just wanders through his life, doing nobody any harm; and he comes to a place where there's no scope for his particular line of wrongdoing, and he just settles down and lives a fairly normal life, even does a bit of good when it's needed. And suppose where he's come to, nobody knows what he did, or nobody cares, or they wouldn't think what he did was wrong even if they knew about it. So: is he still a bad man? Was he ever a bad man, if nobody knows about it, nobody at all? Suppose the past is just something you can break or burn—'

'Like a book,' Poldarn interrupted.

'If you say so,' Egil replied. 'But suppose you can get rid of the past so it no longer exists. After all, the past is just memories. Suppose you can wipe them all out, wash them away like a stain in a shirt, so even you don't know any more. There's no past, just the present and the future. And the bad man's not bad any more, is he?'

Poldarn thought for a long time. 'I guess that depends,' he said. 'If he's really a bad man, won't he find a way to do evil again? Because it's his nature.'

Egil shook his head. 'But not necessarily,' he said. 'Suppose you were in a country where there's no such thing as property: if you want something you just take it and nobody gives a damn. You couldn't be a thief in that country, even if you tried. Or suppose there's a country where crows are sacred to the gods, and the worst crime is to kill one. There's a man who loves to kill crows; but he lives here, where crows are pests and we've got to kill them, or else they'll peck up the crops. He won't be doing evil, he'll be a useful member of society.'

'Maybe.' Poldarn looked away, up at the roof. 'But he kills crows because he likes killing, not because they damage the crops. That's evil.'

'That's his business,' Egil replied gently. 'And the more he tries to do evil, the more good he does. There's no harm done.'

'But he knows,' Poldarn insisted.

'So what?' Egil said. 'He knows he's trying to do evil, but no evil actually happens. What's inside his head doesn't matter, any more than a wiped-out past matters.' He looked around, and saw the axe head Poldarn had found in the muddy water of the ditch; it was lying on the table, beside the bed. 'All right, look,' he went on. 'You found this yesterday, right?'

'How did you know that?'

'You told someone, so I know. It's an axe, right? And you found it in the mud and brought it home. Put an edge on it, it'll do a useful job of work. Now let's say it got there because someone used it for a murder and dumped it there; but that was all a hundred years ago, nobody remembers the murdered man or anything like that. It's still a useful tool. Or should it go in a crucible and get melted down? And if you did that, would it be right to use the metal to make something else, or is it accursed for all time? Shouldn't we take it up to the top of the volcano and throw it in there, just to be sure?'

'Now you're being ridiculous,' Poldarn said. 'Sounds to me like you've got your own reasons for not wanting me to know what happened.'

'Of course I do,' Egil said angrily. 'You come back here, after all those years. You know what I thought when I heard what Halder had done? I was going to take my axe and smash your head in, because I'd rather be put to death for murder than let it happen. Then it turns out you've lost your memory, and suddenly it's all right again, I don't have to die after all. Can you imagine how wonderful that felt, being reprieved from having to kill someone, from having everybody think I was some kind of vicious wild animal, crazy in the head, couldn't be allowed to live? I'd have done it, you can be absolutely sure about that.'

'Really,' Poldarn said quietly. 'But when I was stranded in the mudslide at Colscegsford, you risked your life to help me. If I'd died, all your troubles would've been over.'

'Fuck you,' Egil shouted. 'What sort of bastard do you take me for? I couldn't stand by and watch someone die if I could help it.'

'Even so,' Poldarn said, icily rational, 'someone else could have gone. It wasn't your special assignment, keeping me alive.'

'I happened to be closest,' Egil said, clamping his hands to the side of his head. 'It was my job. Don't you understand us at all yet? There's a job to be done, whoever's closest does it. We don't have any choice in the matter.' He took a deep breath. 'Yes, I'd have been as happy as a lamb in springtime if you'd drowned in the mud. Or if it had been me, come to that. But it didn't turn out that way, that's all.' He walked over to the door, then looked back. 'You want to know my idea of a really evil man, someone so evil he could never be anything else? All right, I'll tell you. It's a man who's so selfish he'd follow up his curiosity without caring a damn who had to pay the price. Do you understand that?'

Poldarn nodded. 'I think so,' he said. 'Thank you for explaining it to me. Now I know.' In spite of everything, he couldn't help grinning. 'Like I keep saying, if people would just explain things, it'd make life so much easier.'

It took five days for Poldarn's legs to recover; five days during which the roof timbers of the bedroom at Ciartanstead grew steadily less and less interesting as the hours ground by. Every morning someone would drop by and assure him that it would be disastrous and irredeemable folly if he got up and walked about before his strained muscles were completely healed beyond any shadow of a doubt, and since they seemed to know ever so much more about the subject than he did, he had no choice but to go along with their advice. On the sixth day he got the same lecture, this time from Elja herself, but the thought of another minute, let alone another day, staring at that bodged lapjoint was more than he could bear. Far better to risk ending up crippled for life than certain death by tedium.

'You please yourself,' Elja sniffed, as he swung his feet off the bed and rested them tentatively on the floor. 'Just don't expect any sympathy from me if you end up rolling on the ground in agony.'

A quarter of an hour of hobbling round the yard, and

he'd more or less forgotten what strained muscles felt like; his legs were in full working order and fit to be taken entirely for granted once more. 'So,' he said briskly to Raffen, who happened to be passing, 'that's me sorted out, I can get back to work. I expect there's a whole heap of things piled up while I've been out of it.'

Raffen thought for a moment. 'Can't think of anything,' he said.

'Oh come on,' Poldarn pleaded. 'There must be something I should've been doing. Try and think of something, please, or I just might burst into tears.'

'Oh.' Raffen frowned. 'Well,' he said, 'the crows are back on the peas. Made such a mess up there, it'll hardly be worth getting 'em in.'

'Bugger the bloody crows. I can't face another five days staring at the roof, I'll go mad.' Raffen's expression suggested that this had already happened, but Poldarn couldn't be bothered to stop and explain; he'd remembered something. 'The roof,' he said, 'there's a lapjoint in the third timber, whoever did that made a really piss-poor job of it. Needs fixing, before the whole lot comes down on our heads.'

Raffen scratched his ear thoughtfully. 'I think *you* did all those joints,' he said. 'In fact, I'm sure it was you. Should've been Colsceg's job, but he was behind.'

'Oh.' Now he came to mention it, Poldarn had a feeling Raffen was right. Odd that he hadn't remembered that before. 'Well, anyway,' he said, 'it's got to be fixed. I'll get a ladder.'

Raffen shook his head. 'Don't talk soft,' he said. 'You're in no fit state to go fooling about up ladders. Carey can do it this afternoon, after he's finished the south paddock wall.'

Poldarn scowled. 'Carey's got his own work to do,' he said.

'No, he hasn't. He was going to help me out in the middle house, but I'll get Boarci to give me a hand. Carey's a damn good carpenter, you should see the work he's done on the linhay roof Besides, Boarci's got nothing to do, it'll keep him out of mischief'

What about keeping *me* out of mischief? I thought that was the whole point. 'Oh, all right, if you say so. I'll go over to the forge, make some nails or something.'

Raffen nodded approvingly. 'Always useful, nails. Can't have too many of 'em.'

So Poldarn wandered across the yard, coaxed up a fire after several false starts, and made a dozen nails out of a rusty old spit. Then he remembered the axe head he'd found in the ditch, the one Egil had preached him a sermon about. He fetched it from the house and spent the next few hours working it over mercilessly – files, coarse and smooth stones, polishing powder and the buffing wheel – until he could see his face in the flat and shave hairs off his arm with the edge. A rasp and a certain amount of effort turned a broken wheel-spoke into an acceptable handle, and he shaped an offcut from the nail stock into a wedge, complete with a series of deeply chiselled keys to bite in the wood and hold it in place. Finally he wrapped the last hand's span of the handle with thatching twine and dunked the head in the slack-tub to swell up overnight. There, he told himself, job done; the only thing left to do was find a home for it. A pity, really, that he'd already made an axe for Boarci; this one was much better in every respect, but he'd look stupid if he insisted on taking the other one back and exchanging it for this. Nobody else had mentioned wanting such a thing, so he had no real option but to keep it for himself – not that he wanted an axe particularly, but the thought of putting it into stock and letting it get rusty and mildewed offended him after all the work he'd put into it.

By this stage the fire had gone out, and it seemed pointless wasting good coal and kindling getting it going again, when there really wasn't anything that needed doing in the forge. By the same token, of course, there wasn't anything that needed doing outside it, at any rate by him, so Poldarn raked the clinker out of the ashes and perched on the anvil, turning over what Egil had said in his mind.

It wasn't as if he needed convincing; he'd acknowledged quite some time ago that he didn't really want to remember who he'd been or what he'd done. At the time he'd reached that conclusion, he'd had nobody to think of but himself; it was mere selfishness, made marginally acceptable by the very fact of his isolation. To a man on his own, wandering about in a strange landscape and trying to keep out of harm's way, it was an allowable indulgence, and he'd had the consolation of knowing that he was paying a high price for the privilege of not remembering, in the form of the substantial risks he'd taken precisely because he didn't know who he was, who was his friend and who was his enemy. Then all that had changed. Suddenly the universal enemy had reared up in front of him and claimed him for its own – but they'd turned out not to be demons and monsters, just a parcel of farmers and artisans seen out of context, and he'd been glad to go with them to claim his apparent inheritance, stepping off the road and into security, a place of his own in the world, a ready-made home and family and happy-ever-after. It hadn't quite worked out like that, but it couldn't be denied that they'd given him everything a rational man could expect out of life – food, clothes, a fine house, land and livestock, a lovely and compatible young wife; they'd even bestowed on him the highest rank a man could aspire to in that society, leadership of a household (and if he still hadn't any real idea of what that meant exactly, that was surely his fault rather than theirs). The argument from isolation, that it didn't matter because it was nobody's business but his own, was no longer valid, but it had been replaced by something far more compelling and, for what it was worth, morally defensible: the good of the community. Now, it appeared, there were extremely cogent reasons why he shouldn't find out the truth, why he should take all necessary steps to make sure the truth never came out. If that didn't let him off the hook, what the hell ever would?

They'd given him everything else; now they were giving him the priceless blessing of an excuse. They must love him very much, to go to such trouble. It'd be ungrateful and very, very selfish to jeopardise everything just to satisfy his own idle curiosity.

Poldarn stood up. He might be many things, but he wasn't so wickedly self-centred as to believe that setting his mind at rest was more important than another man's life, or the well-being of his household. It was a small enough sacrifice to make, and he was pleased to be able to give something back in return for everything they'd done for him. From now on, in fact, he was going to put a stop to all this shameful self-pity. It stood to reason that they valued him and needed him or else they wouldn't have given him so much, far more than his intrinsic merits could possibly deserve. It wasn't as though he had any rare or valuable skill, or an endless capacity for hard work. Left to himself, he'd be hard put to it to earn a living in a tough and pitiless world, let alone enjoy all the good things he had here; or, if there was something special about him that justified their indulgence, they knew about it and he didn't, so it'd be plain foolishness to imagine he knew better than they did. Either they loved him beyond his merits, in which case he should simply be grateful, or they could see in him qualities that he couldn't see in himself. In any event, it was high time he stopped moping about feeling lost and bewildered. When the time came, if there was work for him to do, he'd know it and be ready to get on with it. Until then, he owed it to them to be patient, to quit complaining, to be satisfied and to stop making a fuss. That wasn't so much to ask, was it? As for who he'd been . . . only a fool picks at a scab when it's nearly healed.

Fine, he thought. Now I really ought to get the fire going

again. There must be something I could be making, and
while I'm figuring out what it could be, I can fetch some
fresh coal from the coal shed.

So he went out into the yard, and the first thing he saw was
an astonishingly bright red glow in the sky, coming from the
direction of the mountain. By the look of it, he wasn't the
only one who'd decided to rake up a good, hot fire. And this
time Polden had beaten him to it.

Chapter Twenty

'Pretty soon,' Boarci grumbled, 'we'll be able to find our way blindfold.' He gave the lie to this assertion by catching his foot on a tussock of couch grass and stumbling, but he carried on: 'Probably just as well, if it starts shitting that black stuff again and blots out the sun like it did last time. Don't know about you, but I don't much like the thought of getting down off this mountain in the dark.'

It was three days since the side of the mountain had been ripped open and a glaring red strip had poked out of the fissure, as if the volcano was sticking its tongue out at them. It had taken Poldarn three hours of forceful argument, shouting and pleading to induce the two households to go along with his plan (whatever it was – he had a few vague ideas, but that was all; still, it wouldn't do to let them know that) but he'd won the day at last, or else they'd agreed to let him take a scouting party up the mountain simply in order to be rid of him and free of the sound of his voice. Nobody had had any other suggestions to make, but that didn't surprise him at all.

So, here they were again, struggling over the shale, ash and broken ground just below the place where the hot springs had been. Of the springs themselves there was no longer any trace. The fissure out of which the red tongue was sticking had opened right in the middle of where they had been before and within a few hours the whole area had filled up with red-hot molten rock, travelling (as far as they could judge from down below in the valley) a little faster than a galloping horse. At that point, the only option had appeared to be to leave everything behind and run as fast and as far as they could get, hoping that the fire-stream would chase someone else and pass them by. Then, quite abruptly, it slowed down to walking pace, then to a toddler's crawl. There seemed to be no reason to it, and no reason why it shouldn't pick up speed again at any minute, but Poldarn had a feeling that there was a logical explanation, and that finding out what it was would be a good idea. Hence the expedition, which had now arrived on the other side of the narrow hog's back that separated them from the fissure itself. We must be mad, Poldarn thought; and then, in fairness to his companions, he changed the *we* to *I*.

'Right,' he said, as the party ground to a halt. It was stiflingly hot, and everything they could see was washed in soft red light. 'Let's go and take a look, shall we?'

Nobody seemed very keen, for some reason, but he couldn't be bothered with leadership skills at that particular moment. He turned his back on them and started to climb the slope. 'Hold on,' someone said behind him – he recognised Boarci's voice, and felt a surge of thanks that he wouldn't be alone after all. 'Slow down, for crying out loud, I've got a blister on my heel the size of a cow's arse.'

The view from the top of the hog's back was spectacular, but somehow disappointing. It looked for all the world like a road; not one of your up-country cart trails, all ruts and grass growing up the middle, but a high-specification military road, the sort of thing that costs millions and takes a lifetime to build. It was so flat that it could have been trued up with a square and a level, one uniform slate-grey plane with arrowshaft-straight sides, a masterpiece of the road builder's art if ever there was one. It was only the stunning blast of heat rising off it that spoilt the illusion.

'It cools quick enough, then,' Boarci said. 'That's worth bearing in mind.'

Poldarn laughed. 'Depends what you mean by cool,' he replied. 'I'll bet you, if you pitched a bale of hay down there it'd catch fire as soon as it touched.'

'Wouldn't surprise me,' Boarci grunted. 'But that's not what I meant. Seems to me it only moves when it's red-hot. Like metal in the forge,' he explained. 'When it's blue-grey it'll still burn your hand, but you can't squidge it around like you can when it's red.'

Poldarn hadn't thought of it like that. 'It may have cooled down on the top,' he said, 'but my guess is that if you went down a foot or so you'd come to molten rock. I think that under this crust it's still flowing like a river, just not as fast as it did to begin with. Which would explain why it slowed down like it did. To start with, it was running at its top speed, but as the crust formed it acted like a sort of brake – it's squeezing in, closing up the channel the molten stuff runs through.' He frowned. 'That's good, isn't it?'

'Maybe.' Boarci was lying next to him, his chin cupped in his hands, as if he was on a picnic. 'All depends how much it'll slow it down. Maybe it won't have the legs to reach the valley, maybe it will. No way of knowing. But I don't think I'd take the chance if I were you.'

Boarci didn't need to enlarge on that. It didn't take a trained surveyor to figure out that if the molten rock carried on down its present course, it'd fill the valley and flatten both Ciartanstead and Haldersness; there'd be nothing left but this wonderful road, leading nowhere, because the road would obliterate the settlement it led to.

'I'm going to get a little bit closer,' Poldarn announced. 'You can stay up here if you like.'

Boarci groaned. 'I wish you'd stop doing this sort of stuff,' he complained. 'Have you noticed that every time you fling yourself into the jaws of death, I'm the poor bugger who's got to come and fish you out again?'

Poldarn shook his head. 'You stay there,' he said, 'please. I'd rather you did, there's no point us both taking stupid risks. I just have a feeling it isn't going to hurt me, that's all.'

'Bloody fool,' Boarci called out after him; but he stayed up on the ridge, as Poldarn had asked him to.

Poldarn scrambled about thirty yards down the slope, but it was soon fairly obvious that there was nothing to be gained by going any further, nothing to be seen that wasn't obvious from the top of the ridge. The heat, on the other hand, was unbearable, and when he tried to turn round and go back, he felt it like a crushing weight on his back. Damn, he thought, and held still, not from choice but because he no longer had the strength to move. If he stayed there, he told himself, he'd die, and how stupid that would be. So he gathered his remaining strength, like wringing water out of a dishcloth, and dragged himself upright. As he stood facing the steel-grey road, he saw a single crow, a scout, sailing overhead. As it passed over the road it hesitated – he could see it struggling, like an ant walking on water. He wanted it to break free, but it couldn't; its strength failed and broke, it spiralled slowly down with its wings beating furiously, and pitched in the exact centre of the road. It stood upright for a single heartbeat, then crumpled like a piece of brass subsiding into the melt, and burst into flames. The little fire flared up and went out, leaving a black smudge.

'You too, then,' Poldarn said to the mountain; but it'd have to do better than that to beat his score. He could feel exactly the same pressure (and he remembered applying it, back in the forge at Haldersness, with the back of the poker) but he refused to acknowledge it. His knees were still weak from crouching in the ditch, but he wasn't in the mood to give in to mere weakness. That's the difference between us, he told himself, and he walked upright back up the slope.

'Well?' Boarci said.

It took Poldarn some time to catch his breath. 'Nothing to see here,' he panted. 'We'd better follow it on down to where it's still hot. I've got an idea, but I'm not sure about it.'

'Fine,' Boarci muttered, 'but for God's sake don't tell them that. You tell them you had a divine revelation and the god of the volcano told you exactly what to do. Otherwise they'll be off down the mountain like a rat down a drain, and you can forget all about them getting closer to the hot end.'

That seemed sensible enough, though Poldarn decided against the divine-revelation story. Instead, he said, 'It's pretty much as I expected, but I need to take a look at it further down, where it hasn't formed the crust. It ought to be perfectly safe so long as we keep our distance.'

Surprisingly he got no arguments from the rest of the party, who managed to keep up the lively pace he was determined to set in spite of the pain in his legs and back. So long as they had the hog's-back ridge between them and the firestream it wasn't so bad; it was almost possible to pretend it wasn't there. But when the ridge petered out and glimpses of orange light became visible through the rocks and dips, that particular source of comfort was no longer available; so they changed tack and cut down the side of a steep combe to a plateau roughly level with where Poldarn guessed the stream had reached. Then there was nothing for it but to head back towards the source of the red glow; and at that point the rest of the party stopped and told him they were going home now. 'You don't need us,' one of them said. 'We'll see you back at the house.' Poldarn didn't object; he nodded and said that he'd be as quick as he could, but he'd probably need half a day to get to where he needed to go and back again. They divided up the food and water and went their separate ways, Boarci choosing to return to the house with the others. 'So I won't be tempted to get myself killed for nothing,' he explained graciously. Poldarn nodded his agreement, and said Boarci was probably very wise.

Poldarn came on it quite suddenly, tracing round the edge of a rocky outcrop. It stretched out in front of him like a sea of liquid glass; almost translucent, like a welding heat, but orange instead of white. Here and there on the meniscus were huge boulders, glowing a paler shade of orange, almost yellow round the edges. He found that so long as he kept back a stone's throw or so the heat wasn't too bad, no worse than the forge on a hot day. It was almost like a curtain, a discernible limit dividing bearable from unbearable. Once or twice he ventured through it, but the view wasn't any better on the unbearable side, so he stopped doing that and contented himself with a mid-range view. As he'd speculated earlier, the crust wasn't just the extreme edges of the stream cooling; a fair proportion of it was made up of the debris the stream collected as it went along, dirt and soil and shale that had burnt away and turned into ash. Where the stream had no channel to guide it, he realised, it was the crust that kept it together, preventing it from slopping out over the sides and dissipating its momentum. If he could find a way of breaking through the crust – it'd be like tapping a barrel, or caving in the wall of a dam – and if he could only manage to drain away enough of the stream, so that the material in front of his breach lost momentum and slowed down long enough to cool— It couldn't be stopped, no power on earth could do that, but it could be *diverted*, persuaded and tricked into pouring away down the other side of the mountain and missing his valley completely. From what he could remember, the contours fell away sharply on the eastern side. It'd have to flood the whole world with molten rock before it could threaten Ciartanstead.

Poldarn breathed in deeply and sighed. Well, he thought, I've got an idea now. Of course, there's no way anybody could actually make it work, but even so it's better than giving up and running away. Presumably.

(And then he thought: it may be a stupid idea, idiotic and far-fetched, but it's an idea nobody in this country could ever have come up with, because their minds don't work that way. They don't have ideas, because they always know what to do, instinctively, like animals. They can't *think*, they can only do things that have been done thousands of times before. And *that*'s why I'm here. Thank you. It all makes sense now.)

Boarci had waited for him after all. 'I thought you were going back to the house,' Poldarn said, as soon as he saw him.

'Yeah, well.' Boarci shrugged. 'I started off with those other idiots, but going all that way with only them to talk to, I couldn't face it. I'd rather stay up here and get burned to death. It's quicker than dying of boredom and not nearly as painful.'

Poldarn laughed. 'You may have a point,' he said. 'And I may have an idea.'

He explained what he had in mind as they hurried down the slope, bearing away from the fire-stream as fast as they could go. He was expecting Boarci to tell him he was off his head, but to his surprise Boarci thought about it for a while and then said: 'It could work, I guess. But there's a couple of things that need figuring out first. For a start, what're you going to smash through the crust with? You got any idea how thick it is, or how hard the skin is?'

'No,' Poldarn admitted. 'My guess is, it's not as thick as a brick wall, but not far short of that.'

Boarci nodded. 'Well, you're going to need special tools, then. Big hammers and cold chisels aren't going to hack it; you'll need to make up something specially for the job.'

'All right,' Poldarn replied. 'Shouldn't be impossible. Something like a quarryman's drill, basically just a long steel bar you bash in with a hammer and then twist.'

'Fair enough,' Boarci said. 'Next, you'll need to do something about the heat. You're talking about getting right up to the fire. At that distance it'll take all the skin off your face in a heartbeat.'

Poldarn frowned. 'I think I know what we can do about that. What else?'

'Oh, loads of things. For instance, suppose you do manage to break through the crust, what happens then? All the bloody hot stuff's going to come spurting out of the breach, and God help the poor bastard who's standing in the way.'

Poldarn thought about the crow, and the way it had burnt up in the time it took to sneeze. 'All right,' he said, 'but so long as we bear that in mind – We'll have to go in at an angle, I guess, and hope for the best. I didn't say it was going to be easy, I said it might be possible, that's all.'

'Sure,' Boarci said. 'But you'll need to have answers to all these points before you pitch the idea to that lot down there. They aren't going to like it one bit, I can tell you that right now.'

Boarci was right about that, too. The two households listened to Poldarn in stunned silence. On their faces he could see the sort of horrified embarrassment that he'd have expected to see if he'd got drunk and made an exhibition of himself – singing vulgar songs, dancing on the table, throwing up on the floor. Their reaction annoyed him so much that he forgot to be daunted by it.

'All right,' he said eventually, after the silence had gone on almost as long as his speech. 'Here's what I'll do. If anybody can come up with a better idea before dawn tomorrow, we'll forget all about my suggestion and go with his idea. What's more, he can have the farm; I'll give it to him or stand down or abdicate or whatever you want to call it, and he can be

head of household, and I'll spend the rest of my life muck-
ing out the pigs. Believe me, if someone takes me up on this,
I'll be the happiest man in the valley. You all got that? By
dawn tomorrow; otherwise we'll give my idea a go and see if
we can make it work. Good night.'

The silence followed him into the bedroom, where Elja
was placidly sewing, turning sheets sides to middle. 'Did
you hear that?' Poldarn asked as he closed the door.

'Your speech, you mean? Yes.'

Poldarn lay down on the bed, too tired and fed up to take
off his boots. 'I didn't mean that, I meant the reception it got
from that lot.'

'But they didn't say a word.'

'Exactly.'

'Oh.' Elja smiled. 'I see what you mean. Yes, I heard that.
Couldn't help hearing it. If they'd been any quieter, they'd
have been inaudible right down the other end of the valley.'

Poldarn laughed. 'They're bastards, the lot of 'em,' he
said. 'I wouldn't have minded if they'd shouted at me or
called me a bloody fool. But just sitting there like that, it's too
cruel for words.' He made an effort, sat up and groped for his
bootlaces. 'Last time I try and do anything for this household.'

'Don't be like that,' Elja said gently. 'They're just not used
to people like you, that's all. They don't know you the way I
do.'

'Oh really.' He tried to drag off a boot, but his foot was too
hot and swollen. 'Well, no, I suppose they don't. But that's
not the point.'

'Idiot.' She sat on the bed and tugged at the boot, without
making any perceptible difference. 'I don't think you realise
how scared of you they all are.'

That took Poldarn completely by surprise. 'Scared? Of
me? But that's ridiculous.'

Elja let go of the boot and stretched out beside him, hands

behind her head. 'What makes you say that?' she said. 'To all intents and purposes you're a stranger, an unknown quantity, and there aren't any of those here. Well,' she amended, 'there's tramps and layabouts like your friend Boarci, but we understand them, we know what to expect. You're completely different, and we can't even see what you're thinking. And if that's not bad enough, you do such weird things, nobody knows what you're going to get up to next. Not just that, but you go around telling people what they ought to be doing, when it's not what they know they should be doing; and sometimes, more often than not, you're right. Most of all, you know about the volcano, it's like you can see its thoughts. That's really scary.' She lifted her head and looked at him. 'Do you really mean to say you hadn't realised that?'

Poldarn nodded. 'Of course not. I mean, most of the time they treat me like I'm a kid or something. That's when they even acknowledge I exist.'

'They keep their distance, you mean. Actually, they talk to you far more than they talk to each other, or hadn't you noticed? That's another scary thing, you're always *at* them, asking questions, like you're interrogating a prisoner. If you were in their shoes, wouldn't you be scared?'

Poldarn thought about that. 'Not really,' he said. 'I might want to smash my face in from time to time, but I wouldn't be *scared*. Still, I guess I know me better than they do.'

Elja laughed. 'Are you sure? It strikes me that you know you less well than anybody. After all, you've only known you for a few months. Some of these people have known you forty-odd years, off and on.'

'True,' Poldarn replied. 'But I get the impression I've changed a bit since then.'

'Maybe. How would you know?'

'I don't,' Poldarn admitted. 'But anyway, that's not the point. I don't really give a damn whether they're scared of me, or they like me or hate me or whatever; not right now, anyway. What's important right now is doing something about the mountain. Just sitting there as though nothing was wrong – how can they do that?'

Elja smiled at him, quite tenderly. 'You poor thing,' she said, 'you really *don't* understand. They're scared of you, but they're absolutely terrified of the mountain. It's far more frightening than the thought of getting killed, or anything like that. They know about death, it happens every day, it's one of those things you live with your whole life. But the mountain is *new*. They've never even heard of anything like it before, not even in stories. And here you are, telling them they've got to go and *fight* this terrible thing. No wonder they just sat there. There aren't any words to say what they're all thinking right now.'

'Oh,' Poldarn said. 'And what about you, then? You seem pretty cool about it all.'

'Me?' Elja frowned. 'I don't really know, I hadn't thought about it. For some reason, I'm not frightened at all. I'm not frightened of you, or the mountain.'

'Good,' Poldarn said.

'Not really, no. I ought to be. I don't understand either of you. I just know that you aren't going to do me any harm. I know it's all going to be very bad for a while, and this plan of yours sounds absolutely horrible, but it's not going to hurt *me*. Something very bad is going to happen sooner or later, but not this.'

Poldarn leaned forward, not looking at her. 'You sound very sure about that.'

'Yes,' Elja said, 'I do. It's not a guess or even a conclusion I've reached – I just know it; like you know something you remember, because it's already happened. Does that make any sense to you?'

'Oddly enough, it does,' Poldarn said quietly. 'It's how I felt when we were building this house. I knew we'd be able to do it, because I felt I'd done it before – no, that's not it. I felt like I'd done it *already*, if you can see the distinction. I'd done it already, so it was already done and so it had to turn out right. The house couldn't not be built because I'd already built it.'

Elja nodded. 'You're weird,' she said. 'I hadn't realised quite how weird you really are.'

'Oh. So that's not how you see this, then.'

She shook her head. 'It's exactly how I see it,' she said. 'I never said I wasn't weird, did I?' She pushed her hair back behind her ears. 'Look at it from my point of view. I get this really strange, crazy feeling, it's so crazy it worries me. And then you say it's exactly how you felt when you were building the house. Now you *are* beginning to scare me. I mean, we mustn't both be crazy. Think of the children.'

Poldarn laughed. 'I think it's simpler than that. You love me so much you're absolutely sure I'll succeed and the firestream will go away. You have faith in me.'

'Oh, sure.' She rested her head on his shoulder. 'I worship you like a god, that goes without saying, I'm practically your high priestess. All you've got to do is snap your fingers and the fire'll crawl back into its kennel like a dog that knows it's been naughty.' A moth whirred past them and started to circle the pottery lamp beside the bed. 'Do you really think it could work, this idea of yours?'

'It could work,' Poldarn replied, 'but if you're asking whether I can make it work, that's another matter entirely. It could work, but only if we get a whole lot of difficult things right. Maybe we'd have a reasonable chance if we'd done it all before and we knew how to go about it. Getting it to work the first time, when we're making it up as we go along; that's a lot to ask, isn't it? We only get one try, after all.'

Elja yawned. 'It'll be all right,' she said. 'Trust me.'

'Why?'

'Because,' she told him, and snuggled down under the

blankets. 'Now shut up and go to sleep. You've got a big day tomorrow.'

He pinched out the flame of the lamp and lay still in the dark. Somewhere in the room the moth was fluttering round, trying to find out where the flame had gone. Stupid creature, Poldarn thought, I've probably saved its life and it doesn't even realise, let alone feel grateful to me for the exercise of my divine clemency. I'm glad I'm not a god; it must be soul-destroying, putting up with that sort of thing.

Next morning, early, he went to the forge. Asburn was already there, and a good fire was blazing in the duck's nest. 'These drills,' Asburn said. 'What did you have in mind?'

Poldarn couldn't remember having mentioned the drills to anybody except Boarci but he guessed that Boarci had told Asburn about them. 'Something like this,' he said, chalking a sketch on the face of the anvil. 'What do you think?'

Asburn nodded. 'Oughtn't to be a problem,' he said. 'Only, they've got to be drawn hard. Have we got anything long enough?'

Poldarn shook his head. 'I was thinking, make the shafts out of iron and weld a steel tip on.'

'That ought to do it,' Asburn said. 'In that case, we can draw down those old mill shafts.'

Poldarn stifled a groan, because that would mean several hours of swinging the big hammer, and he felt stiff and raw after his adventures on the mountain. 'Fine,' he said. 'Good idea.'

'I'll strike, then,' Asburn said, much to Poldarn's surprise. He'd assumed that he'd be striking, while Asburn did the skilled work. 'All right,' he said. 'If you don't mind.'

In spite of Poldarn's reservations, the drills more or less shaped themselves. First they drew down the shafts, reducing them in diameter by a third. Then they forged flats into the round bars, forming them into hexagons; Poldarn wasn't quite sure why this was necessary, but he knew it was the right thing to do – neither of them suggested it, they just did it as soon as they'd finished drawing down. In order to get the iron to work, they took a ferocious heat, almost white, and Poldarn's skin ached where the flare of the fire-stream had burned it. Next he cut lap scarfs into the tip of each drill with the hot sett, dressing them out clean with the hot and cold files, and smothered the scarfs with flux to keep the scale out while they were welding. As soon as the flux powder touched the hot metal it melted into a glowing yellow liquid, more or less the same in colour and texture as the bed of the fire-stream. They put the drill bodies in the edge of the fire so they'd hold their heat until they were needed, and jumped up some flogged-out old rasps to form the cutting tips. When these were ready they went into the fire until they were yellow, whereupon Poldarn fitted them into the scarfs in the shafts and peened them round to keep them in place as he brought the piece up to a full welding heat, turning them widdershins in the fire to keep the heat even. He raked the fire deep for this part of the process, which meant the metal was buried under burning coals and he had to rely on hearing the fizz as the surface started to burn in order to judge when it was ready to weld. He couldn't have been far out, because when he pulled the first drill out it was snowing fat white sparks. Asburn turned the shaft slowly, while Poldarn patted it smartly and evenly with a two-pound ball-peen. He could feel the iron and steel fuse together under the hammer, a curious scrunching sensation, like treading on a deep drift of virgin snow.

As soon as they'd finished one drill they started on the next, and by the time they'd hardened and tempered the blades and ground them to a cutting edge it was mid-afternoon. Poldarn left Asburn to finish up, and made a round of the other preparations. There weren't going to be nearly as many buckets as he'd have liked, but fortuitously there were plenty of skins, since nobody had got around to tanning the hides from last winter's slaughter. He found more than enough hammers, chisels, crowbars and axes in store, along with a reasonable quantity of rope, though not as much as he'd have liked. By the time everything had been stowed on the wagons, there was only just enough space left for the drills. Anything else – and he was bound to have forgotten something – they'd have to do without.

'That's the lot, then,' he announced, with rather more confidence than he actually felt. 'We'd better all get a good night's sleep,' he added, 'I want to get started first thing in the morning.'

Easier said than done. Poldarn lay awake most of the night, trying to visualise the job that lay before them, but the picture evaded him like an unreliable memory. When at last he slipped into a restless doze, the mountain was still there in his dreams – his mountain or another one very like it, only taller and steeper, coughing up fire like a dying man bringing up blood. The most vivid image in his dreams was the hot spring he'd seen so many years ago, with Halder beside him, except that now it was gushing fire instead of water. Somehow that seemed quite natural, as if his previous recollection of the scene had been at fault, and he'd only just corrected the mistake.

The fire-stream had put on a disconcerting turn of speed while Poldarn had been away. Its pronounced snout of rocks, shale and other debris now stood on a small plateau above a steep drop, with very little in the way of obstacles between it and the long, even slope that led directly to the mouth of the Haldersness valley. Once it made it over the edge, Poldarn couldn't see any force on earth stopping it. To make matters worse, the fissure in the side of the mountain was perceptibly wider, allowing a stronger flow. If this scheme didn't work there wouldn't be time to go home and think of something else. Whether he liked it or not, he was committed to

his chosen course of action. This struck him as an unfortunate state of affairs, since the more he thought about it, the
more fatuous it seemed.

'I'm sure I've forgotten something,' he complained, as they
came over the hog's back.

'So you keep telling us,' Elja muttered. She was carrying
two heavy buckets of water, covered with hides that had
been tied down to prevent wastage by spilling. 'And not just
something.'

'Forgotten to bring something we're going to need,'
Poldarn said. 'No chance of going back for it now.'

'Then let's hope it wasn't anything important.'

On the other hand, this was as good a place as any to try
out his idea – better, in fact, than most, because on the other
side of the plateau, where the rocks formed a low wall, there
was a plainly visible thin point, where it would be fairly
simple to break through. Channelled through that breach,
the tapped-off flow would run down an even steeper incline
that would guide it straight across the other side of the
mountain, following a deeply cut gorge to the level plain
below, and from there into a deep wooded valley, a natural
sump that would take a lot of filling before the fire-stream
could continue on its way. There was a farm down there –
Poldarn could just make out the tiny squares of the buildings
and the subtly differentiated colours of the home fields –
but it stood on high ground on the edge of the plain, a long
way above the valley. If everything went according to plan,
the fire-stream wouldn't come any nearer to the farm than a
mile and a half, missing the fields and the pasture completely.
An ideal arrangement, in other words. He couldn't have produced a more suitable landscape if he'd moulded it himself
out of potter's clay.

'Well,' Poldarn said, 'we'd better get started.'

He'd brought everyone with him, women and children
too, and nobody was empty-handed. He hadn't had to order

them to come, or plead, or even ask; they'd been ready and waiting for him when he emerged from the house, early on that first morning. Nobody said anything, but they'd managed to keep up a stiff pace all the way from Ciartanstead to the hog's back; so stiff that at times he'd been hard put to it to keep up.

The first step was obviously to breach the wall, and that was a simple enough job, though more than a little strenuous. For that they used pickaxes, hammers and stout cold chisels, cracking and chipping the rocks away from the other side (extremely awkward, since there were precious few places where a man could stand upright and still do any useful work; ten men could squeeze in at a time, and the rest of the workforce could only stand by and wait their turn to relieve them). They used the spoil to bank up the sides of the breach, in case weakening the crust wall in one place caused it to break out elsewhere. From start to finish the work took six hours, rather less than he'd anticipated, and there was still an hour of daylight left when they finished.

Waste not, want not, Poldarn thought; although daylight wasn't actually necessary, given the brightness of the fire-stream's orange glow. One last despairing attempt to remember whatever it was he'd forgotten; then he picked up one of the new special drills and led the way into the breach.

'I'll go first,' he announced, and nobody offered to take his place. 'Who's going to strike for me? Anybody?'

He'd been hoping Boarci would volunteer, but instead there was a long, awkward silence. Then Asburn shoved through to the front, picking up a heavy sledge on his way. 'I'll hold the drill and you strike, if you'd rather,' he said. It was a tempting offer, sure enough; it was the man holding the drill who had to stand closest to the fire-stream, and he'd be the first to die if the crust gave way and the molten rock came spurting out before there was time to get clear. But Poldarn shook his head. 'It's all right,' he said, 'you'll be more use behind the hammer. I don't think I could lift that thing, let alone swing it.'

Next came a rather ludicrous performance. Elja and a couple of the other women had soaked two large raw oxhides in water, and they proceeded to wrap them round him, tying them down at his wrists and ankles and swathing his face in loops of hide until only his eyes and the tip of his nose poked through. Then, for good measure, they splashed a few cups of water in his face and wrapped his hands with strips of sodden buckskin. Poldarn could feel water trickling down his cheeks inside the swathes, also down his chest and back into his trousers, gathering in reservoirs where the string was pulled tight around his ankles. Asburn had to put up with the same ritual humiliation, which gave some degree of comfort, but not much.

'Here goes, then,' Poldarn mumbled through the layers of wet leather. It wasn't the most inspiring speech of valediction, and it came out sounding sillier still. 'Get the next pair ready to take over as soon as we've had enough.'

He hadn't considered the problem of steam inside his clothes; it was hot enough to scald him wherever they touched his skin, and probably the hardest thing he had to do was keep his eyes open as drops of water dribbled off his forehead and turned into uncomfortably hot vapour before they could soak away. But the precautions proved to be more than amply justified; he managed to cling on to the drill long enough for Asburn to deliver five bone-jarring thumps on his end of the drill before the heat forced him back, his nose and fingertips red and tingling. On his way back he crossed with the next two, similarly cocooned in saturated hides. They only managed three hits before giving way to the next pair. It seemed like no time at all before it was his turn again, and with each thump and chink of the hammer he was torn between two horrible possibilities: that the crust was far too thick, and they'd never get through it at this rate, not if they played this game for a year; or that the crust would suddenly give way at the next hit, and he'd trip over his absurd skirts as he tried to run, and the fire-stream would surge over him like daylight flooding a room, and obliterate him completely. Each time he came off duty – he made it a point of honour to stand for at least five hits, a whole ten heartbeats in the face of the fire – his swaddle of hides was as dry as old shoes and moulded round him like armour, springy and tough, so that it took three pairs of hands to peel it off him.

The first casualty was one of the Colscegsford field hands, a man called Scerry; he was holding the drill and tried to get a step closer in, so as to direct the blow more accurately. But that one step was one too many; his wrappings dried out instantly and caught fire, and the shrinking and hardening effect on the oxhide made it impossible for him to run. He tried nevertheless, toppled over and landed on the edge of the crust, burning up in three heartbeats. He must have been dead before the fire burned through the hides, because he didn't make a sound. His replacement was in position before Scerry had finished burning, and the drill poked through his ashes to find the dent in the crust.

Hending, a Ciartanstead man, went out before the women had finished wrapping him properly. The bandages slipped off his face and it melted; his hammerman got him clear by grabbing the drill and hauling him in like a fish on a line. He died a few minutes later. Another Ciartanstead hand by the name of Brenny was hit on the side of the head by a splinter of rock – where it came from, nobody noticed; he was swinging the hammer for Carey, and someone else took his place in time for the next hit. A Colscegsford woman whose name Poldarn didn't know got in the way of a drill as it was being pulled clear at the end of a shift; the red-hot tip dragged down her arm from the shoulder to the elbow, burning her severely, but she carried on working for some time, carrying buckets in her other hand. Rook went out to hold a drill wearing heavy leather gloves instead of wrappings on his hands, but the leather turned out to be too greasy to take in water – they were a pair used in the wool store for hauling ropes, and the wool-grease had worked into the palms. The heat in the drill set them alight, taking all the skin off Rook's hands. Egil missed the end of the drill with the hammer head and hit it with the shaft instead. The head snapped off and went flying, hitting a Ciartanstead man between the shoulder blades; he was out of action for the rest of the day. Swessy, an old man who plaited ropes and weaved baskets for the Colscegsford house, took Rook's turn at the drill after Rook got burned. In spite of the wrappings, the heat was too much for him and stopped his heart. He was dead by the time they were able to pull him clear. They had no idea whether they were making any impression on the sidewall of the flow; there wasn't time to examine it, and the red glow dazzled their eyes. They still hadn't thought about what they could do as and when the wall finally did give way, but that possibility seemed too remote to worry about, compared to the other, more obvious dangers.

Finally, after two hours, they gave up and withdrew to the hog's back to rest. The general impression was that things weren't going too well. They'd already used up over half the water, and there wouldn't be time to go back and get any more. The heat had shrunk, curled, stiffened and cracked the hides to the point where they were starting to shrug off water, and it was taking more and more ingenuity to cover the bare patches. Nearly all of the men had minor burns to their hands and faces, not serious enough to count as an injury but sufficient to slow them down or reduce the time they could spend in front of the fire-stream. They were too exhausted to do any more, but everyone knew without having to be told that if they rested for too long, the stream would move on, taking the weakened patch they'd made (such as it was) with it. If that happened, the flow would miss the gap they'd made, and all their effort would go to waste. They kept still for an hour, but that was as long as they dared leave it. It was dark, of course, but there was enough firelight to work by. Nobody said anything. They trudged back to the breach and carried on.

(The crows do this, Poldarn realised. When there's danger they send out their scouts, and sometimes they come back, sometimes they don't, but the work, the joint effort of staying alive carries on. They don't stop to fuss over their dead and maimed, and they know what to do without having to be organised or told. Perhaps we're the crows this time, and I'm the mountain, an unknown quantity suddenly erupting into violence, changing everything. Maybe it's wrong of me to be on both sides at the same time; but there, I haven't known which side I'm meant to be on ever since I woke up in the mud beside the Bohec. The sensible thing would be to find a way not to take sides, but that's a luxury I don't appear to have. I'm lying on the anvil looking up at myself swinging the hammer.)

He was looking the other way when the crust finally gave way. It was only because some woman screamed that he looked around at all, just in time to see Barn, his stolid brother-in-law, drop his drill and spin round. But the breach in the sidewall opened up like a gate. releasing a flood of orange-hot liquid rock that moved faster than a galloping horse. Before Poldarn could catch his breath to shout the molten stone was round Barn's ankles, like the tide on a beach. Then Barn simply wasn't there any more, and his hammerman, a stranger, made a flamboyant standing leap for the built-up wall where the people from the two households were standing. Someone reached out a hand to pull him up, but they missed; he scrabbled at the rock with his fingers, apparently hanging off the sheer side of the wall like a fly, then he slid back down on his stomach, arms still flailing, and slipped into the fire-stream like a ship being launched. He made a very brief flare, but no sound.

But there were other things to look at besides the death of one stranger. For a very long heartbeat it looked as though the fire-stream had enough momentum to slop up the wall and push off the boulders they'd piled up to dam the flood. But it slid back, just as Barn's hammerman had done, found the breach they'd so carefully made, and ducked down into it, surging forward before vanishing over the edge. Poldarn closed his eyes into a dazzled white blur. It was doing what they wanted it to, at least for now. It was little short of a miracle, but it looked like they'd managed to pull it off. Remarkable, Poldarn said to himself; who'd have thought it?

He edged his way along the crowded ledge until he could look down into the valley. Already the fire-stream was slowing down, driving a furrow through the loose rock, dirt and shale, no longer shining bright (like a piece of hot steel shrouded in firescale as it cooled). But it was still moving – walking pace now, but much faster than its previous imperceptible creep. Poldarn stood watching it for a long time, as if afraid that if he looked away even for a moment it would stop dead in its tracks. Then in the back of his mind he realised that something had gone wrong.

He looked out over the fire-stream to the other side of the breach, where at least half of his company were now effectively stranded. They didn't seem to have realised it for themselves as yet; but there was clearly no way that they could cross the stream, either here, further up or down below. Unless they were planning on staying perched on the ledge for the rest of their lives, the only option open to them was to follow it round to the point where the slope behind them slackened off; from there, if they were very careful, they ought to be able to pick their way down onto the lower slopes and thence to the plain below, where Poldarn had noticed the farm. From there they'd have to go the long way round the base of the mountain to get back to Haldersness and Ciartanstead. If they managed to keep up a good pace, they ought to be home again in eight days or so.

It was a ludicrous position, and Poldarn found himself grinning, at least until he remembered that the last time he'd seen both Elja and Boarci they'd been on that side of the breach. That wiped the smile off his face, but it was hardly a disaster nonetheless. He looked round on his side, trying to spot familiar faces, but there weren't too many of them. When he looked back, he saw Colsceg trying to attract his attention, with Egil beside him looking worried. He knew immediately that neither of them was aware that Barn was dead.

'Ciartan,' Colsceg shouted, 'we're cut off here, we can't get across. We're stuck.'

Poldarn took a deep breath. 'I know,' he called back. 'You'll have to go the long way round, down into the valley and round.'

'Bugger,' Colsceg yelled. 'Should've thought of that before we broke through. Still, can't be helped.'

That was true enough. 'Will you be all right?' Poldarn shouted.

'Should be,' Colsceg replied. 'Got nothing to eat, but there's a farm down yonder – we can last out till we get there. See you in a few days, I reckon.'

'Longer than that, I'd say.' Poldarn hesitated. He felt that he ought to tell Colsceg about Barn, but it didn't seem right, howling the bad news at him across a river of fire; it would be a stupid, grotesque way of breaking the news, and he couldn't bring himself to do it. 'Still,' he went on, 'looks like we managed it, after all.'

'Looks that way,' Colsceg replied. 'Bloody good job, too. I never thought for a minute it was going to work, glad I was wrong. See you back home, then.'

'See you,' Poldarn replied. It was too far for him to see the expression on Colsceg's face, in the dark, with the air disturbed by the hot air rearing up from the fire-stream. He felt ashamed of himself, and his success didn't seem to count for anything, achieved this way. It was as if he'd bought it at the cost of Barn's life and didn't care. 'Sorry about this,' he shouted, but Colsceg was looking the other way, talking to the people on the far side. There didn't seem to be anything else he could do here, so he turned back to his own contingent and explained the situation as best he could. As far as he could tell, they'd already figured it out for themselves, which made the job a little easier.

'When it gets light, you go on ahead,' he told them, when he'd finished explaining. 'I'm going to hang on here for a while, just to make sure everything's going to be all right. I can't see any reason why it shouldn't be, but you never know.'

'Please yourself,' said Raffen. 'Me, I've had enough of this place to last me. I'm shattered, and I'm going to get some sleep.'

That sounded eminently reasonable, and the rest of the party quickly followed suit. Poldarn stretched himself out on the ledge with them, but for some reason he didn't want to close his eyes – maybe he knew he was too tired to sleep, or he was afraid of what he might see with his eyes shut. He lay for a long time staring up into the red sky, and when eventually he did drift into sleep, either he didn't dream or he forgot it as soon as he woke up, in the first light of dawn, with the orange glow of sunrise mirrored in the fire-stream.

Almost immediately, the two severed halves of the expedition team set about packing up and moving off. Poldarn tried to get a glimpse of Elja before she disappeared with the others; he caught sight of her briefly, but she didn't see him, and his view was obscured by other people getting in the way. Not long after that he was alone, perched on the edge of

the breach. Everything seemed to be all right; the diverted
stream had covered a surprising amount of ground during
the night, and was still moving fast enough for its progress to
be visible – not quite walking pace now, but at that rate it
wouldn't be long before it reached the valley below, and the
little wooded combe he'd aimed it at. Somehow it didn't seem
nearly as menacing, now that he'd imposed his will on it; as
it waddled down the slope it put him in mind of a flock of
sheep, bustled and bounced into going where it was supposed to go by a small but agile sheepdog. In a way he was
almost disappointed; the work had been painfully hard and
men had died, but *outsmarting* the enemy had been much
easier than he'd anticipated, and he no longer had the feeling
of being locked in battle with a worthy opponent. Not that
he felt proud of himself, particularly; in fact, he told himself,
since the solution had proved to be fairly simple and straightforward, chances were that they'd have thought of it for
themselves even if he hadn't been there. Quite possibly
they'd have done it better without him interfering, maybe
even without loss of life.

Poldarn shrugged. Looked at objectively, it was ridiculous
to feel a sense of anticlimax. If he hadn't taken charge, the
one practicable opportunity would've been missed, and the
fire-stream would be headed straight for Haldersness and
his new house. Sure, he thought, but would that really have
been so bad, compared with so many men dying? Barn and
his hammerman, Swessy and the others (he couldn't remember them all offhand, his mind was too ragged, but he
promised to remember them later, when he was himself
again). So; supposing the fire-stream had ploughed down
into Haldersness, forcing the river out of its bed and obliter-
ating his house – both his houses? So what? They were just
timber arranged in a pattern, nothing that couldn't be built
again, and even the farm, the river, the land weren't all that
important; it was a huge island that they lived on – all they'd

have had to do was pack up and move on, no big deal compared with what the first settlers here had faced, no big deal compared with the terrible malevolence of the fire-stream against human skin, the heat annealing all the memories out of their bodies, evaporating them, losing them for ever. It occurred to Poldarn that he'd made a very big, serious mistake, and that everything would have been better if only he'd left well alone.

Chapter Twenty-One

At first he assumed he was back in the peafield, and that the bodies lying out on the dry earth were the crows he'd killed. He could feel the pain in his knees – a pity I can't change the past, he thought, I'd get up and stretch my legs at this point, maybe save myself five days of misery – and the weary ache in his right shoulder. But then he realised that he wasn't alone in the ditch. It was full of men, in armour, clutching weapons and crouching low to keep their heads out of sight. Oh, he thought, I must be somewhere else.

He glanced sideways, doing his best not to be obvious about it. Whoever these people were, he had a feeling that they were under his command, and therefore had a right to feel confidence in their commander. It wouldn't do for him to start asking disconcerting questions, like *Where are we?* and *What the hell's going on here?* They might get the impression that he wasn't in complete control of the situation, and that would never do.

I must be dreaming again, he thought. In which case it's probably all right, nothing really bad can happen to me in the past, because if I'd died or lost an arm in this battle, I'd know it for sure back in the present. So that's all right, he added. This is just a holiday, a guided tour of some momentous event laid on for my benefit, as a reward for beating the volcano.

If he was dreaming, he rationalised, it seemed reasonable to suppose that he wasn't really here, and nothing he did could have a bad effect on the outcome; so he wriggled round to the point where he could put his weight on his feet and pushed up, just enough to let him see over the top of the ditch.

A column of soldiers was approaching. They looked remarkably like the soldiers next to him, as far as clothes, armour and equipment were concerned; the only difference he could see was that they were armed with straight-bladed swords, while in his own right hand he held a curved-bladed object that he recognised as an enemy backsabre—

(No, not enemy; at least, not as far as the present is concerned. The backsabre is our special design, unique to our people on the island. How he'd come by it, of course, he had no idea, but one of his men in the ditch seemed to have one, which suggested it was some kind of special trophy, an appropriate sidearm for a dashing and popular leader—)

There were, he realised an awful lot of soldiers drawing near, enough to make him very glad that he wasn't really there. Of course, he had no way of telling, crouched down there in the ditch, how many men he had on his side. For all he knew, there could be thousands of them, not just the couple of hundred in the ditch but other units hidden with equal skill and cunning, behind hedges, among the trees, maybe even hunkered down in cleverly disguised pits dug in the field. Since he had no idea just how wonderfully imaginative and inventive he was when it came to laying ambushes and conducting battles, all he could do was keep very still and hope for the best.

There didn't seem to be anything else he could glean from the approaching soldiers, so he turned his attention to the dead bodies. They weren't soldiers. Most of them weren't even men – there were a few old men, some boys, but the bodies were mostly those of women of various ages. All dead, of course, unless they were making a very good job of just shamming dead; but he didn't really think he was clever and imaginative enough to have staged that. Some of them at least were quite palpably dead: heads chopped off or necks slashed half through, ribcages opened, the sort of thing you couldn't really fake. The implication was that someone had massacred two or three hundred helpless civilians. He hoped very much that it hadn't been him, because the sight was pretty grim. The approaching soldiers didn't look too happy about it, for one thing, and they gave every indication of wanting to get their hands on whoever was responsible. That didn't bode well, particularly if he didn't have an extra thousand or so heavy infantry concealed about the place. He wasn't sure he cared much for this dream, after all.

The soldiers carried on advancing; they were no more than a couple of hundred yards away by now, rather too close for comfort. He wondered if he ought to be doing anything, or whether whatever was going to happen next could be left to take care of itself. Probably not. If he really was the leader of the men in the ditch, it'd be up to him; to give the order to attack – assuming that they were planning an ambush and not hiding, though if these few with him were all there were that could well be the case. Really, it was no better than being awake, the frustration of not knowing who he was or what he was meant to be doing. He could get as much of that as he wanted just by hanging round the farm, without having to travel back in time for it.

The man next to him budged him in the ribs. 'No offence,' he muttered, in a tone of voice that suggested the exact opposite, 'but you're cutting it bloody fine.'

'I know what I'm doing,' he replied, much to his own surprise (but that was the other man talking, the one who had a right to be here). 'Shut your face and wait for my mark.'

The man next to him froze, as if he'd just been hit across the face. He felt ashamed and embarrassed – the poor fellow had only been trying to help, and as far as he could see, the man had had a point, the enemy were getting closer all the time and it wasn't going to be easy getting out of this bloody ditch. By the time they'd scrambled up the bank and retrieved their weapons and kit, there wasn't going to be much in the way of an element of surprise. Still, he thought, there's no logical reason to believe that the momentous event I've come here to see is a victory. For all I know we're about to make a horrible mess of it and get slaughtered. He stole another look at the dead women and children scattered about the field like decoys, and added, Serve us right.

Then he realised what he'd been waiting for. The enemy, having come right down the field, within fifty yards of the ditch, were turning to the right, from column to file, with a view to marching off somewhere. You'd never try such an unwieldy manoeuvre on a battlefield in the face of the enemy; but they didn't know there was anybody in the ditch, so it was a perfectly reasonable thing to do. Obviously he'd foreseen that, his remarkably perceptive tactical brain allowing him to read the enemy commander's mind, right down to the minutiae of timing and procedure. He couldn't help admiring—

He was on his feet, clawing at the grass with his left hand to pull himself up the steep bank. On either side his men were doing the same thing, most of them rather more athletically than him. Already the first few dozen were up and on the move, hurling themselves against the enemy flank with a cold fury that argued a definite sense of purpose – probably they had a score to settle, some grievance that justified killing women and children, and prompted them to such a display of aggression. As for the other side, they didn't know what was happening. (By now he was out of the ditch, hands and knees filthy with mud, catching his breath and straightening his cramped back like an old man while all around him his soldiers were charging.) For one thing, it seemed, the other soldiers couldn't figure out why their own people were attacking them; they didn't seem to want to fight or use their weapons, not until they'd given away the advantage and lost all semblance of order and cohesion. Meanwhile, there was more movement going on in other parts of the field — he'd been right, there was a large contingent of his men tucked away behind the far hedge, another lot were rising up out of the ground like sprouting corn (another ditch, he assumed, or something of the sort) and it was soon pretty obvious that he had as many men as the other lot, if not more. That was a relief, at any rate. In fact, the result was already a foregone conclusion, if his instincts were anything to go by. He had the enemy in flank and rear, with another unit rushing up to block their front and complete the encirclement. His lot, the men from the ditch, were in the process of cutting the enemy column in two, which he was fairly sure was a very good thing in a battle. All things considered, the other lot didn't stand a chance, and all that remained was the tedious job of chopping them down where they stood. He was pleased to see that he, the leader of the winning side, was apparently content to leave the actual killing to his subordinates. It was turning into a very nasty business, and he didn't actually want to get involved, even if he wasn't really there and so couldn't come to any harm.

'Not bad.' Someone was talking to him; not the man he'd spoken to in the ditch, but presumably one of his officers, to judge by his manner and tone of voice. 'Not bad at all. I'll be honest with you, I thought it was a lousy idea and you were going to get us all killed. Glad I was wrong.'

He shrugged. 'Well,' he said. 'It's always worked for me before. No reason why you should know that, of course.'

The other man grinned. 'You're a ruthless bastard, though,' he said. 'I can't think of anybody else who'd knock off a whole village just to decoy a column into exactly the right spot. I thought it was just an excuse, because you like killing people.'

'What, me?' He was grinning, though he didn't know what was so funny. 'It's like I always say, you've got to set out the right pattern, let 'em see what they expect to see, otherwise they'll shy off and not drop in. We wanted them to think there were raiders in these parts, but they'd got no reason to believe that; so the obvious thing to do was make it look like the raiders had been through. Nothing does that like a couple of hundred dead bodies. Simple fieldcraft.'

'It's simple when you put it like that,' the other man said. 'Can't say I'd have thought of it myself, though. Still, you lot have always had a different way of going about things.'

'Sure,' he replied. 'We don't give a damn, it makes life much simpler.' He frowned. 'Your people take their time, don't they? We'd have been done and stripping their boots off by now.'

'Maybe it's because my men don't need dead men's boots,' the other man said mildly. 'Anyway, it's a certainty now, so that's all right. The general is going to be very pleased.'

He nodded. 'Where is he, by the way? Wasn't he supposed to be with the Seventh, coming in from the wood?'

'That's what I thought, too,' the other man said. 'Still, Cronan never did have a wonderful sense of direction. Maybe he wandered off and got himself lost.'

He laughed, for some reason. 'That'd be right,' he said. 'Of course, this is going to be the crowning glory of his brilliant career, so I guess it's appropriate, the bloody fool not even being here. Meanwhile, we do all the work and don't get a damn thing for it.'

The other man looked offended. 'I wouldn't say that, exactly,' he said.

'Yes, well. The main thing is, the job's done. I think I'll leave you to it, if you don't mind. I've got a long day ahead of me tomorrow.'

'That's no lie,' the other man said, with a certain degree of distaste. 'Have fun; and for God's sake, don't miss any of them. If Cronan finds out what we've been up to—'

'Oh, for crying out loud, Tazencius,' he said, 'what do you take me for, an idiot? It's not like I'm new at this.'

'No,' the other man said. 'You're not.' He smiled offensively. 'But mistakes happen – you should know that better than anybody. Otherwise you wouldn't be here, would you?'

He could feel that that, for some reason, was a deadly insult; he was conscious of forcing down the urge to lash out, of filing it away among his grievances, to be paid for later. 'Point taken,' he said. 'Right, I'm off. Are you heading back to town when this lot's done?'

The other man nodded. 'Soon as I can,' he said. 'Cronan can do without me for a week or so.'

'I'm sure. When you get back, be sure to give Lysalis my love.'

The other man abruptly stopped grinning, and gave him a look of pure hatred. 'Yes, all right,' he said. 'I'll tell her – well, I'll tell her you've been making yourself useful.'

'Thanks. Tell her I'll be bringing her back something nice for her birthday. I don't know what it is yet, mind, but there's bound to be something she'll like at Josequin.'

The other man was about to say something, but he wasn't there to hear it; he was sitting on a stone bench in the middle of a beautifully tended lawn, surrounded on three sides by an elegant sandstone cloister. Behind him he could hear running water, and he knew without looking round that the source of the sound was a small, rather ornate fountain in the shape of a grotesque dolphin. There was a woman next to him on the bench, cradling a baby girl in her arms. Between them lay a painted wooden box, about the size of a house brick. The hinged lid was open, and inside it was a necklace: woven gold with pearls and coral beads.

'It's lovely,' the woman said, with obvious pleasure. (He thought it looked flashy and vulgar, but he didn't say so.) 'Where on earth did you find it?'

'On a stall in the market at Boc,' he replied, knowing he was telling a little white lie. 'As soon as I saw it, I knew it was you all over.'

She beamed, as if the compliment mattered more than the gift. 'Thank you,' she said, and kissed him. Her lips were very soft and full. She was very pretty, and not more than nineteen, with masses of dark auburn hair piled up on top of her head in an over-elaborate coiffure. He noticed that the earrings she was wearing matched the necklace. Ah, he thought, that's probably why she likes it. How thoughtful of me.

'How long can you stay for this time?' she was saying, a little wistfully. She really was very attractive, and he awaited his reply with interest. 'Not long,' he heard himself say (he was disappointed), 'I've got to see some people and then get back. But I couldn't miss your birthday.'

She smiled. 'I think that's really sweet of you,' she said, 'coming all that way. We hardly seem to get any time together these days. Still, with all the wonderful help you've been giving Daddy I can't complain. I'm so glad you've decided to be friends at last.'

I remember you from somewhere, he thought, but of course he couldn't say anything like that. 'Well,' he said instead. 'The truth is, he's a bit out of his depth at the moment. It's this damned feud of his with General Cronan – it's going to cause a lot of trouble if something isn't done about it.'

'Oh.' The woman looked confused. 'But I thought that's what you'd been doing. Helping General Cronan, I mean.'

He laughed. 'That's exactly what we've been doing,' he said. 'That's the whole point. Only, our fool of an emperor assigned your father to Cronan's staff.' She looked even more confused, so he explained: 'That means he's working for Cronan, he's his subordinate. Well, you can imagine what he thinks about that. So nothing will do except he's got to steal all the glory; which is why he needed me, to pull off a really big coup, and beat General Allectus before Cronan could get to him. That was the idea, anyhow. Luckily for all of us it didn't turn out that way; your father rushed on ahead, trying to get to Allectus before Cronan could, and if he'd managed it, chances are Allectus would've had him for breakfast and there'd have been nothing I could do about it. But when your father did catch up with Allectus, he wasted two days dancing round him trying to get a good position, and by then Cronan was right behind him. So your father panics, tells me to think of something quickly—'

'Which you did, of course,' she interrupted, 'and it was brilliantly clever and you won the battle and everything worked out splendidly.'

'Well, sort of,' he replied, pulling a face. 'Actually, I hung around pretending to be clever until Cronan's men arrived, and then I managed to draw Allectus into an ambush. But for some reason Cronan wasn't there, he actually managed to lose his way in a forest on his way from the camp to the battlefield, of all the ridiculous things, and so he missed the whole thing. We had to go and look for him in the end. Of course, that pleased your father more than anything, far more than winning the battle. Silly, really. Still, it's over and done with now, and I don't suppose it'll make a blind bit of difference in the long run.'

She sighed. 'It does all sound rather childish,' she said. 'Still, I don't know anything at all about politics or war, so you mustn't pay any attention to me.' She reached out and gave his hand a quick, friendly squeeze. 'But if the war's over and horrid old General Allectus has been beaten, why've you got to go back again? And so soon, too.'

He shook his head. 'The rebellion wasn't really important,' he said. 'It'd have petered out of its own accord, probably. We only went after Allectus because the emperor wanted to make a point of crushing him immediately, Cronan wanted another victory for his collection, your father wanted to wipe Cronan's eye – all that sort of thing, you know what it's like. No, the real problem in the Bohec valley is the raiders, that's who we really have got to deal with, before they turn the whole province into a desert.'

She looked worried, frightened. 'Do they really need you to go?' she said. 'Oh, I know I'm being silly, but you hear such dreadful things about them. Couldn't they send somebody else instead?'

He put his arm around her shoulders. 'It's all right,' he said, 'nothing's going to happen to me, I promise. Trust me.' He grinned. 'I know for a fact that nothing's going to happen to me, because I can see into the future, remember?' That had to be some sort of private joke between them, he guessed. Anyway, it seemed to reassure her. 'Sorry,' she said, 'I'd forgotten about that. Silly of me.'

'You've got to stop saying you're silly,' he said, pretending to be stern and serious. 'No, I can see me coming home from the war without a scratch, raiders or no raiders.'

'No wonder you win all these battles,' she said, trying to sound bright and cheerful. 'Though really, I suppose it's cheating.'

'Well, of course. You wouldn't want me to play fair in a battle, would you? I might get hurt.'

'True.' She leant her head against his shoulder, winced, said 'Ow!' and lifted her head again. 'Sorry,' she said.

He smiled. 'Is your neck still hurting?'

'A bit. Silly old pulled muscle. It'll be better in a day or so.'

The baby opened its eyes and started to cry. 'It's getting chilly,' he said. 'Maybe we should go inside.'

They stood up; and they must have startled the old black crow that had been perched on the top of the fountain, because it screamed angrily at them and spread its wings noisily. The woman shrieked and shrank away, squeezing the baby against her chest as the crow flapped slowly upwards, exerting itself to gain lift in the still air. For some reason he felt extremely angry, as if the crow had no right to be there, let alone startle his wife; he stooped down and picked something up off the grass, a chess piece that someone had left there. The crow was rising steadily, just about to turn, but he anticipated the move (he knew exactly what it was planning to do) and threw the chess piece so hard that he felt a sharp pain in his shoulder. It was a good throw; the crow folded up in the air, wings tight to its body, and fell dead with a thump on the cloister roof.

He turned back and looked at her. She was upset, unhappy at the sight of killing, but she did her very best not to show it; still, he could see her thoughts quite clearly. 'Horrid thing,' she said. 'That was very clever of you,' she added.

He pulled a face. 'A friend of mine showed me how to do it,' he said, 'back when I was with the sword-monks. I'm sorry, I don't know what came over me. I guess I just don't like crows very much.'

'I hate them,' she replied quickly. 'Horrible gloomy creatures. And that one's been hanging around here for days, I keep shooing it away and it keeps coming back, like it was laughing at me or something. Well done,' she added firmly, convincing herself that he'd done a good deed.

He didn't reply; he was thinking of something his friend had told him, about the time he'd killed a crow in a blacksmith's forge, and never had a day's good luck since. He tried to remember the friend's name, but all he could recall was a nickname, Monach, which was just 'monk' in the Morevich dialect. Then he remembered that his friend was dead; killed by the raiders at Deymeson, possibly – most of the monks had died that day. But that was wrong, he wasn't even sure that had happened yet. He shrugged the thought away, and reminded himself that this was just a dream, and he wasn't really here.

The baby was howling, which made it impossible to think straight, anyway. 'You go on in,' he said, 'I'll join you in a minute or so.' She went, walking under an old carved arch he hadn't really taken any notice of before. He stood for a moment looking at it, until he saw what it was supposed to be: the divine Poldarn, standing up in his cart, bringing the end of the world to Torcea. Rather a gloomy subject for a carving, he thought; but of course, this house had once been a monastery, and the monks had a taste for the miserable and depressing in the decorative arts. He followed her, but as soon as he stepped under the arch he realised he wasn't in the cloister garden any more; he was home, in his own house at Ciartanstead, alone in the bed he shared with his wife.

He tried to close his hands on the dream, bring it down as it opened its wings and flapped screeching away; but this time his aim was bad, and the dream dwindled into a speck in the distance. He sat up.

Well, he thought, at least the house is still here. Of course, even if he'd failed, it would take the fire-stream a long time to get here; days, even weeks, depending on whether it gained or lost speed coming down the slopes. Someone would have woken him if the molten rock was lapping round the front porch, or if the roof was on fire. Even in the worst possible outcome, he wasn't likely to be burned alive in his bed. That was a comfort, he felt.

Nevertheless. The shutters were down and latched, but little blades of light were forcing their way through. It was time he was up and about, organising things, getting some work done. Assuming, of course, that there was anything for him to do.

By the time he'd dressed and got his boots on (a painful process; he'd escaped without anything he could properly describe as a burn, but his skin was horribly sensitive; like sunburn, only worse), the household was about its business, the tables were out and laid for breakfast, people were bustling in and out of the doors in pursuit of their appointed tasks. There didn't seem to be as many of them as there should have been, and Poldarn remembered the casualties before he remembered the mistake at the breach; the missing numbers weren't dead, just stranded somewhere in the valley on the other side of the mountain. He felt better after he'd realised that.

'You're up, then.' Rannwey was in charge of catering today. Usually it was Elja's job, but she wasn't there, of course, and wouldn't be back for days. 'We let you sleep in, you were dead beat when you got home last night.'

'Thanks,' Poldarn muttered, wondering how they'd managed to wake up before he did; that was supposed to be impossible, wasn't it? Well, maybe things had changed, either because half the household was away or for some other reason nobody had seen fit to tell him about. Better that way, needless to say. He was pretty sure he wasn't really a morning person at the best of times.

'You sit down,' Rannwey continued briskly, not looking at him. She never looked at him; always over his head or just past his shoulder, as if he wasn't there. 'Porridge and leeks again,' she added. 'Same as usual.'

He nodded. 'We're going to have to do something about that,' he said. 'We can't go on eating that muck for ever.'

Rannwey looked at him. 'Why not?' she said. 'It's good, wholesome food. Also, it's all we've got.'

'Yes, I know. But we must be able to get something different from somewhere. Trade for it with another house, something like that.'

'Really? Where? You don't suppose anybody else is going to be any better off, do you? Worse off, most of 'em, I shouldn't wonder. You want to count your blessings, before you go turning your nose up at good food.'

Well, that was him told; so he sat down and tried to look hungry. He wasn't. Thirsty, yes, but he had no appetite for food just then. But he got porridge and leeks anyway, and did his best to eat it. When breakfast was finally over, he jumped up and headed outside.

The red glow over the mountain was as bright as ever, and there had been a light sprinkling of black ash; nothing to worry about, though, just a slight film of dust, such as you'd find in a neglected house. The good news was that the fire-stream hadn't moved at all in their direction, and where it had been glowing red the last time he'd seen it from down in the valley, now it was just a black smudge on the mountain-side. Beyond the mountain, over its shoulder, so to speak, Poldarn could see a column of black smoke rising straight up into the air -- no wind to speak of, which was good, since it meant there wasn't anything to blow ash out their way. Nobody else was looking at the mountain, he noticed. That job was over and done with, evidently, as far as they were concerned.

Well, that was good too. Everybody was extremely busy, naturally enough -- with half the household absent, everyone had at least two jobs to do. Almost everyone. However busy and rushed off their feet they might be, they didn't appear to need Poldarn's help with anything. It was all right, they assured him, they could manage just fine, nothing needed doing that they weren't able to handle, or that couldn't wait. He must have far more important things to do than scrape down yards or chop firewood, and they wouldn't dream of keeping him from them.

After spending the whole morning unsuccessfully touting for work -- this must be what it was like for Boarci, he realised – Poldarn took a brush-hook and a small axe, and set off to cut back the greenery that was sprouting up all round the bridge over the river. It wasn't really a job that needed doing, the vegetation wasn't nearly tall or thick enough to clog the flow of the river or anything like that, but it was something that would have to be done sooner or later. He arrived only to find that Reed, Carey's eldest boy, had got there first and nearly finished one whole side. He sighed, and trudged back to the house.

'There you are.' Poldarn recognised the face of the man who'd spoken to him but couldn't put a name to it. 'They said you were around the place somewhere – I've been looking all over for you. Got a minute?'

Did he have a minute? Yes, he probably did. 'Excuse me,' he said, 'but who are you?'

The man looked confused, then laughed. 'Of course,' he said, 'they did tell me about your memory loss but I'd forgotten. My name's Hart. From Hartsriver, over the south ridge. Actually, I don't think I've seen you since you got back. You stayed over my place one summer, just before you went off.'

'Ah,' Poldarn said, 'I thought I recognised you. Anyway, what can I do for you?'

Hart was looking at him oddly, but he knew what that meant; it was that bemused look they gave him when they first realised they couldn't read his mind. He was used to that by now, of course. No need to say anything. They generally got the message soon enough.

'Really,' Hart said, 'it's more what I can do for you, though actually you'd be doing me a favour as well. Truth is, I was on my way to Eylphsness with twenty-six barrels of salt beef when the wheel came off my cart, just by your southern boundary there. I was wondering if you could run me up a new linchpin and weld my tyre.'

Poldarn frowned. 'Sure,' he said. 'At least, I think I should be able to. Or you can use our forge, if you prefer. I'm still rather new to blacksmith work, you see.'

Hart laughed. 'Well, you're better at it than me, that's for sure. My brother's the smith in our house. Anything you can do will be fine, I'm sure. Also,' he went on, 'how would you feel about a trade? You see, I owe Eylph fifteen barrels of beef, and I was going to trade him the some other stuff we need – hay and oats, mostly, and some apples if he'd got any. But like I said, what I mostly need is hay and oats. Since I'm here—'

'I'm sure we can work something out,' Poldarn said smoothly, trying not to show his emotions. 'All our stock's away at the moment,' he went on, 'till the mountain's stopped playing up, you understand. So we've got plenty of hay in hand, and oats—' He smiled. 'Oats won't be a problem. Can't help you with apples, I'm afraid, but if you could use a few leeks—'

Hart thought for a moment. 'So happens I could,' he said. 'Bloody ash wiped out half our crop. Yes, that sounds like a good deal as far as I'm concerned. And it'll save me trying to haul my stuff all the way to Eylphsness on a dodgy axle. I could take the fifteen barrels of beef up there, and then stop off for the hay and the rest of the stuff on my way back.'

Hart was a big man, very straight-backed and with broad shoulders, his hair thinning on top but compensated for by a dense bush of grey fur under the chin and swarming up both cheeks. He had the biggest hands Poldarn could remember having seen, and a pair of very watery pale blue eyes. 'Sounds ideal,' Poldarn said. 'In fact, if you like you can take one of our carts over to wherever it is you're going, and we can have yours spruced up and properly fixed by the time you get back.'

Hart seemed to think that was an excellent idea. 'All I need is a little two-wheeler trap,' he said. 'Tell you what; we can use it to run your barrels back here, along with my busted wheel; then once we've unloaded I'll run the trap over to Eylph's. How does that sound?'

It sounded just fine when compared with the alternative (mooching around the farm all day with nothing to do) so Poldarn smiled brightly and led the way to the trap-house. Disconcertingly, the ostlers had already backed the steady grey gelding into the shafts. He thought about that, and came to the conclusion that they must have seen it in Hart's mind, and taken his agreement for granted.

The trap badly needed new springs and a new axle; every bump and dip in the ground shot them out of their seats straight up in the air. 'It won't be so bad coming back,' Hart pointed out, 'the barrels'll weight it down a bit, damp most of this out. It wouldn't be so bad if it wasn't for the big chunks of ash still lying around.'

Two bone-rattling hours later, they reached Hart's derelict wagon. The wheel looked to be quite some way past repair. Five spokes were cracked, the tyre was nearly worn through in two places as well as being buckled, and the hub was three parts split. 'Don't worry about it,' Poldarn sighed. 'We can make you a whole new one. Horn down at the Colsceg house is a pretty fair wheelwright, and I can probably find a tyre to fit in the scrap – there's a whole bunch of 'em, hardly worn.'

It took a long time and a lot of effort to shift the barrels, but Poldarn didn't mind that. They were bigger than he'd expected, and a bigger barrel holds more. His bargain was looking more and more promising every minute. 'The trap ought to take it as far as the house,' he said, 'but you might as well borrow the hay cart for the rest of your trip I don't think this old heap's up to going that far.'

'If you're sure it's no bother,' Hart replied. 'That's very kind of you.'

'Don't worry about it,' Poldarn replied, imagining the look on his people's faces when they got meat with their dinners instead of porridge and leeks. 'If a man can't help out a neighbour, it's a pretty poor show.'

Laden down with barrels and the dead body of Hart's wheel, the trap was far more demure on the way home, though it creaked rather alarmingly. Poldarn took it more slowly on the way back, partly to save wear on the trap, partly because he wasn't in any great hurry to get home and resume doing nothing. 'It's interesting that you recognised me straight off after all those years,' he said. 'Sounds like I can't have changed much.'

Hart laughed. 'You've changed plenty,' he said. 'Truth is, I know all the Haldersness mob by sight. I didn't actually recognise you when I saw you, so it stood to reason you had to be Ciartan.'

'Oh.' Poldarn clicked his tongue. 'Oh, well,' he said. 'Changed in what sort of way?'

'Well.' Hart hesitated, and Poldarn could see he was getting ready to be tactful. 'You know how it is, twenty-odd years is a long time. I don't suppose *I* look much like I did twenty years ago.'

'As bad as that?'

'Oh, I don't know, in some respects you've improved. Not so skinny, for one thing.' Hart nodded gravely. 'All knees and neck and elbows,' he said, 'I've seen healthier-looking skeletons. My wife, rest her soul, she was convinced you were starving to death, she used to shovel food into you like stoking a furnace, but it never seemed to do a bit of good. Took a real shine to you, she did,' he added innocently. 'Mind, you always did have the knack of appealing to other men's wives.'

Poldarn looked up sharply. 'What's that supposed to mean?' he said.

'Just seeing how much you really do remember,' Hart replied, with a grin. 'No offence intended.'

'None taken,' Poldarn replied, drawing the trap to an

abrupt halt. 'But you're going to explain what you just said, or we aren't moving from this spot.'

Hart sighed. 'Another thing about you that's changed, you always used to be able to take a joke. I'm sorry, I really didn't mean anything by it.'

Poldarn grunted impatiently. 'I'm not upset,' he said, 'just curious. Really, I don't mind jokes so long as I'm let in on them. What's all this about other men's wives?'

'It was just the one time,' Hart said sullenly, 'or at least, just the one time I know about. That's how you came to be spending time over at my place, because you were having some kind of fling with a married woman. And before you ask,' he went on, 'no, I don't know who it was. I didn't want to know then, and I don't want to know now. That sort of thing doesn't happen very much in these parts – well, think about it, one thing you can't do is keep a secret. But you could. You had this knack you've got now, of closing off your mind so nobody can see what's going on inside it. They tell me you've pretty much stuck like it since you've been back, but in the old days you could turn it on and off whenever you wanted to, and I guess the woman, whoever she was, she could do the same. It's more common than we like to think, actually.'

Poldarn nodded. 'All right.' he said, 'but it seems a bit unlikely to me. I can't have been old enough to interest married women, back then.'

'Apparently you were,' Hart said, looking away. 'Your grandfather – he was the only one who knew about it, except for you and me – he said it was an old fool who'd married a young girl, which is usually a mistake, of course.'

'Quite,' Poldarn said coldly. 'And somebody local, presumably.'

'I guess so,' Hart said. 'Otherwise it'd have been a bit obvious, you'd have been spending too much time away from home.'

'Well,' Poldarn said thoughtfully, 'that must narrow it down a bit; one of the farms within a day or so's ride of Haldersness. Can you think of anybody who fits the bill?'

'No,' Hart said, a little too quickly. 'It was a long time ago, and my place is a long way from yours. I didn't get out this way often enough to know all the families round here. Look, all I know is this. I was over your place, on my way back from visiting my uncle's family on the coast. I stopped off at Haldersness just to be polite, say hello, and one evening Halder called me outside and asked if I'd do him a favour, put you up for a month or two until you'd got over this thing with some other man's wife. I didn't like the sound of it much, because – well, put yourself in my shoes, will you? I knew Halder, sure, always got on pretty well with him, but we weren't close friends or anything. Would you want some love-struck kid mooning about your place, with maybe a jealous husband turning up on the doorstep with an axe one morning? But Halder told me it was all right, it hadn't gotten very far and if you could be got out of the way for a while it'd all blow over sure enough. So I agreed, and you rode back with me – it was your idea, you knew this thing was trouble waiting to happen – and as it turned out you settled in, made yourself useful, no trouble to anyone. Most of the time you spent out on the barley, scaring off the birds. Then one day you came to me and said it wasn't working and you'd decided to go abroad for a while, completely out of harm's way, where you couldn't make trouble for anybody. Seemed a bit over the top to me – I mean, going to live abroad, it's practically unheard of – but you'd set your heart on it. Halder agreed, apparently he'd thought up something you could be doing while you were over there, and so when the raiding season came on, off you went, and that was the last I saw of you till today. And that's it,' he concluded, 'that's all I know. Sorry I can't tell you any more, but there you are.'

Poldarn was silent for a while. 'Well,' he said eventually, with an effort, 'thanks for telling me, anyway. You can see why I'm a bit concerned about this. For a start, what's going to happen if I run into this woman at some point? It could get very difficult.'

'No danger of that,' Hart replied. 'She's dead.'

'Oh. You didn't mention anything about that. I thought you'd told me everything.'

'I forgot,' Hart said lamely. 'So happens I ran into Halder a few years later. I asked after you, how were you getting on, when were you coming back, that sort of thing. He said he didn't know, he'd more or less lost touch; but it'd be all right for you to come back at that point, because the woman had died. Like I said, I really didn't want to know the details, so I left it at that and changed the subject quick. And that really is everything, I promise you.'

'Fine,' Poldarn said abruptly. 'And you're positive that you and Halder were the only other people who knew?'

'That's what he told me. Come to think of it, he reckoned he only found out because you'd told him – told him out loud, he didn't see it in your mind or anything like that. And if it'd been common knowledge at any point, I'm pretty sure I'd have heard about it. You can't keep stuff like that quiet for very long in these parts, once word gets out.'

Poldarn drew a long sigh. 'That's all right, then,' he said. 'It's just worrying, that's all. You can imagine, I'm sure – not knowing what you've done in the past, what secrets you might have been hiding, all that. At times, I feel like there's this other person who looks like me who's following me around, just waiting to cut my throat as soon as he figures I'm not looking. I'm getting a bit sick of him, to tell you the truth. I only came here to get away from him, but it seems like he's followed me. I wish to God he'd pack up and go away.'

Hart smiled. 'You should count yourself lucky,' he said.

'I've never been what you'd call a tearaway, but there's still nights when I wake up sweating, thinking about some of the really stupid things I've done over the years. I guess everybody does that. Except you, of course, because you've forgotten it all. That's a pretty good trick, if you ask me. I wouldn't complain about it if I were you.'

That seemed to be all that was fit to be said about the subject, and neither of them mentioned it again as they creaked back to Ciartanstead, unloaded the trap and stowed the rest of the freight in the hay cart. Once Hart was safely on his way, Poldarn took the damaged wheel down to the old house for Horn the wheelwright to look at. As he'd expected, the prognosis wasn't good; it'd be far easier and quicker to scrap it, salvage the unbroken spokes and make a new wheel. Fortuitously, both Horn and Asburn weren't too busy, and they reckoned they could get the job done before Hart came back; especially, they hinted, if they had prime salt beef to sustain them instead of the same old porridge and mouldy leeks, which didn't comprise the sort of diet a man needed if he was expected to exert himself over a rush job. Poldarn could see the sense in that; in fact, he'd anticipated it, because one of Hart's barrels had travelled down to the old house along with the wheel.

Back at Ciartanstead, the advent of the beef barrels was greeted with the closest thing to enthusiasm that Poldarn could remember having seen since he'd first landed on the island. People actually smiled at him, and even Rannwey made a point of saying that he'd made a good bargain. In fact, he got the impression that the beef coup had done more to raise him in the estimation of his household than taming the volcano. He could understand why they should see it that way; after all, they'd been making do with porridge and leeks for a very long time, and at least his latest exploit hadn't cost any lives. That was one trend he'd be delighted to see continued.

Needless to say, after the first gluttonous beef feast, the barrels were spirited away to a secret hiding place known only to Rannwey and her most trusted lieutenants, from which their contents emerged slowly and in very small quantities. But that was all to the good, Poldarn decided, because he wanted some to be left for when Elja got home; she was an enthusiastic carnivore, and the porridge-and-leek regime had affected her more than most. Indeed, that might have been at the back of his mind when he squirrelled away the extra barrel he'd extorted out of Hart as payment for the use of the hay cart.

Poldarn tried to figure out how long it would be before Elja could be expected back; but the days passed, refuting his calculations, and he had to make a conscious effort not to worry. Left to himself, he'd have taken a spare horse and gone out to meet her, but he got the impression that that wouldn't be proper. There weren't enough horses or places in carts for the whole party, and giving someone special treatment simply because she happened to be someone's wife was sure to be against the rules. To take his mind off her absence, he decided to throw himself heart and soul into his work; then, when he couldn't find any to do, he went back to aimless mooching and threw himself heart and soul into that, instead. Ten days dragged by; he did nothing all day and slept badly at night, chafing at his own company like an old married couple who discover, in the leisured evening of their lives, that they never really liked each other very much.

On the eleventh night, after lying on his back staring at the still unrectified mistake in the rafters (it was too dark to see it, but he knew it was there) he drifted into sleep and found himself in command of a wing of cavalry, drawing up outside a lonely farmhouse in the first dull glow of morning. He slid from the saddle, handed his reins to a trooper, and walked quickly up to the main door. There he paused, waiting for his men to take their pre-arranged positions: two to each shuttered window, two on the back door, six scrambling up onto the low roof, in case anybody tried to break out through the thatch and escape that way. He was impressed at his own thoroughness, though he had an uneasy feeling that it was born of a series of embarrassing failures resulting from carelessness and inattention to detail. When everyone was in position and ready – they'd been quick about it, knowing what they had to do without needing to be told – he stepped back from the door and gave it the hardest kick he could manage. The grey oak panels flexed but didn't give way. He was ready for that – the two men standing next to him stepped up and laid into the door with long-handled felling axes that smashed and splintered as much as they cut. He heard noises inside, shouting and scuffling, the sound of benches being dragged across a planked floor. His axemen quickened their strokes, striking alternately like well-trained hammermen in a smithy, concentrating on the middle panels where the bar ran across on the inside. A few heartbeats later they'd cleared away the panels and their axe blades were chewing on the bar itself; it was straight-grained seasoned oak, but they went about the job in the approved fashion, each cut slanting in diagonally opposite its predecessor and clearing out its chips. In no time at all the bar cracked downwards, clenting on the axes and then falling away. 'Right,' he said, and kicked the lower panels of the door again. This time it budged, only to come up against a blockage; benches, probably, or tables, thrust against it on the inside. He was ready for that, too. His reserve, half a dozen men plus the axemen and himself, slammed their shoulders against the side of the door and pushed, forcing the blockage back until the crack between door and frame was just wide enough for a man to wriggle through. He stepped back, and one of the axemen went ahead. He vanished into the house, but immediately they heard a grunt, and the sound of a dead weight slumping against the door. The rest of them shoved again,

until the door flew open and they stumbled into the house.
He saw a spearhead darting out at him like a snake's tongue;
he didn't have time to react, but fortunately as he fell forward
the spear passed over his bent neck. Now he could see the
man behind it, just enough of him to constitute a target for
a backhanded rising cut with the backsabre. His stroke connected with the spearman's wrist and sliced deep into the
bone; he gave the blade a sharp twist to free it, and followed
up with the point into the spearman's ribs. There too he
encountered bone, but the smooth curve of the sword-point
rode over it and into a gap. The dead man's own weight as he
slumped pulled him off the swords blade.

By now they were inside. The only light was the sullen red
glow of the embers in the long hearth, but it was enough to
show him the situation. Four sleepy-looking men were back-
ing away from him, hiding behind halberds and bardisches.
One look at them told him they weren't going to fight.
Behind them was a short, white-haired man in a long night-
shirt; it was patched at the knees, he noticed, and the collar
and cuffs were frayed. The man was holding a sword with an
etched blade and was standing in front of a piece of gilded
furniture, but almost immediately he dropped the weapon on
the floor, flinging it away as if it was still hot from the forge.

'Let them go,' the man said. It took him a moment to
realise the man was talking about the four halberdiers.
'They're just conscripts, they haven't done anything.'

He nodded, and the four guards knelt down, carefully
laying their weapons on the floor. He snapped his fingers,
and his men went forward and pushed them down flat on the
floor. When it was obvious they weren't capable of posing a
threat, he walked past them and grabbed the old man by the
hair on the back of his neck, jerking him off balance so that
he slipped and fell onto his hands and knees.

'Get up,' he said.

The man obeyed, moving stiffly and painfully – arthritis,

he guessed, bad enough to make him shake a little. Quite suddenly the man's name floated up from the bottom of his memory. He was called General Allectus.

Not that that signified; he wasn't going to start a conversation, he was there to arrest the traitor and bring him back to General Cronan's camp, near the village of Cric. He tightened his grip on the old man's hair and bundled him out roughly.

'Do you want us to set fire to the house?' one of his men asked.

He shook his head. 'We haven't got time to waste on that,' he said. 'Besides, there's no need. I don't know whose house this is, but I don't think he's ever done me any harm.'

The soldier shrugged. 'What about these?' he asked, meaning the four halberdiers.

'Them?' He frowned. 'They're rebels. Kill them.'

He didn't wait to see if his order was obeyed. A soldier helped him sling General Allectus over the back of the spare horse; he took the leading rein himself, looping it twice around his wrist to make sure. All in all, he thought, a pretty neat operation: the old bastard ought to be grateful, since I'm clearing up his mess. He won't be, but who gives a damn?

Apparently the soldiers had decided to burn the house down after all. He charitably assumed that they had a good reason for disobeying a direct order; there wasn't time to ask them what it was. With the red glow of dawn and burning thatch behind him, he spurred his horse into a canter.

He opened his eyes.

It was still dark, though there were traces of red seeping in past the shutters. Someone was standing over him; he shifted, intending to sit up, but something pricked his throat. He stayed exactly where he was, his weight uncomfortably on his wrists.

'He's in here,' the man called out. He could just make out a black line running up from under his chin into the man's hands. It was almost certainly a spear. It would make better sense, he thought, if he was still dreaming, but he was fairly sure he wasn't.

'What's going on?' he asked.

The man didn't answer; in fact, he didn't seem to have heard. So Poldarn stayed where he was. By this point he was certain he was awake, which made the situation he found himself in rather alarming.

The door opened, letting in a bit more light – enough, at any rate, to allow him to recognise the man who came in and stood next to the stranger with the spear. 'Eyvind?' Poldarn said. 'What's happening?'

It *was* Eyvind, no question about that. 'Hello, Ciartan,' he said. 'Don't move, or Elbran here'll kill you. I'd rather that didn't happen, but it wouldn't break my heart.'

'Please,' Poldarn said, 'for pity's sake, tell me what this is all about. I don't understand.'

Eyvind smiled, rather bleakly. 'It's quite simple,' he said. 'I'm taking your house.'

Chapter Twenty-Two

'I don't understand,' Poldarn repeated.

Eyvind looked down at him, the smile fading. 'No,' he said, 'I don't suppose you do. All right,' he told the man with the spear, 'that'll do. Give me that, I'll deal with him.'

The stranger – Eyvind had mentioned his name but Poldarn hadn't taken note of it – handed over the spear and left the room. Eyvind lifted the point away from Poldarn's face, just enough to let him stand up but no more. He looked as though he'd be delighted to have a pretext for using the weapon.

'Stand up,' Eyvind told him. 'I will kill you if I have to, so don't make trouble.'

As soon as Poldarn was on his feet, Eyvind stepped behind him, and Poldarn felt the spear-point digging into the small of his back. 'You go on through,' Eyvind said, 'I'll be right behind you.'

The main hall was even more crowded than usual. Poldarn saw his people, the household, lined up against the west wall; they looked confused and scared, which was very unusual.

He didn't recognise any of the other men, but they were all holding weapons of various sorts – spears, backsabres or axes. He guessed they must be Eyvind's people.

Eyvind made Poldarn sit down on a stool in the middle of the floor, which had apparently been put there for the purpose, to give the impression of a trial of some sort – or at least the conclusion of a trial, after the verdict had been brought in.

'Now, then,' Eyvind said, leaning on his spear, 'I don't suppose you know what I'm doing here. Do you?'

'No,' Poldarn said.

'All right, I'll tell you.' Eyvind took a deep breath, and it occurred to Poldarn that he was having trouble figuring out how to say whatever it was that he had in mind. He could sympathise with that; quite plainly, his friend was having a hard time, for whatever reason. Poldarn could feel his nervousness, he could discern traces of it in the way he spoke and moved, a slight and uncharacteristic degree of awkwardness and physical ineptness that suggested Eyvind was under rather more stress than he was used to. Not quite enough, Poldarn decided, to be useful tactically; enough to slow Eyvind down, so that it ought to be possible to get past him, get the spear away from him, but not enough to guarantee a certainty if Poldarn were to try and take him hostage, as a way of getting past the men with weapons and out of the house. Poldarn made a quick, rough estimate of the odds and decided against anything of the sort, at least until he had more to go on as far as the cause of all this was concerned. For all he knew it could be a ludicrous misunderstanding, something that could be set right with a few calm words. Escalating it into bloodshed was uncalled for at this stage.

'About a fortnight ago,' Eyvind said quietly, 'you took it upon yourself to go up the mountain and divert the stream – damn it, I don't know what to call it, all the burning shit that's coming out of the side. I've heard how you did it. I'm impressed, it was no end clever, and it worked just fine. You must be very proud.'

'Not really,' Poldarn said. 'Some people got killed. I don't think it was worth it, for that.'

Eyvind breathed in sharply through his nose, as if Poldarn's words had taken him by surprise. 'Interesting you should say that,' he said, 'because I'd assumed you were just showing off. You're always trying to do that.'

'I don't mean to,' Poldarn murmured.

'Maybe.' Eyvind scowled. He was having problems with something. 'I guess you do a lot of things you never meant to do. Is that right?'

Poldarn shrugged. 'I've got no idea,' he said. 'You know why.'

'Oh yes.' Eyvind nodded briskly. 'You lost your memory, you haven't got a clue who you are or what you've done, so we've all got to make allowances and forgive you. Well, that's fine, except that this time it isn't going to work, because you should have thought, you should have considered—' He paused, painfully aware that he wasn't expressing himself well. 'I'll tell you what you did, Ciartan. You diverted the stream. You turned it away from where it was going, and you sent it down the other side of the mountain. Is that right? I mean, I don't want to make any false accusations. You do agree with what I've said?'

'Of course. That's what happened.'

'Good, at least we haven't got to argue over the truth. So; did it occur to you to wonder where you were sending all that burning stuff? Did you even look to see where it was going to go?'

Poldarn frowned. 'Yes,' he said, 'I did. But it was just an empty valley. There was a farm, but a long way away, and the lie of the ground meant the fire-stream wouldn't go anywhere near it. There was a small, deep combe; I figured it'd flow into that, and no harm done. It wasn't even grazing land, just a bit of scrubby old woodland.'

Eyvind's face grew very tight, as if something was hurting him. 'Right,' he said. 'Just a bit of scrubby old woodland, so you decided – like a god or something, only gods are supposed to know things – you decided that the little combe didn't matter, you could just take it out, blot it out and there'd be no harm done. Is that what you thought?'

'Yes,' Poldarn said.

Eyvind took a moment before he replied. 'Fine,' he said. 'Do you happen to know who that little combe belongs to?'

Poldarn shook his head. 'No idea,' he replied.

'You're sure about that?'

'I'm sure.'

'I believe you. Well, you may be interested to know, it belongs to me. Not the farm; that belongs to my uncle. Just the wood. It was *my* wood. Do you understand what that means?'

Poldarn lifted his head and said nothing.

'I think you do,' Eyvind went on. 'I think you must understand; because this house we're in now, which I helped you build, this is *your* wood. Your grandfather planted it the day you were born, it was always here for you, for when it was time for you to build your house. It was your future. And that other one, that scrubby little bit of woodland, that was *my* wood. My future. And you destroyed it. Burned, flattened, filled in with rock so you can only tell where it used to be by seeing where the grass ends and the rock starts. Do you understand me?'

Poldarn didn't say anything.

'You took my *house*,' Eyvind shouted, suddenly ablaze with anger. 'You pointed your bloody fire at it and let it roll down the mountain right onto it, like it couldn't possibly matter, like nobody else could possibly matter. Because of you, I won't have a house of my own when my uncle dies, I'll never get to live in my own house. Killing me would've been so much kinder. You should've done it, that day when I tried to ambush your cart; then I wouldn't have brought you back here, and this would never have happened – my house, the mountain, everything. You know what? If you hadn't come back, I don't think the mountain would've burst, it never did anything like that until you came here, not in hundreds of years. You come here, ordering people about, closing your mind so we can't see, beating me up at your own wedding, and you take away my future. It's my fault for bringing you here, but it's your fault too. I ought to kill you right now.'

Poldarn relaxed a little, because the way Eyvind had said it made it clear that he wasn't prepared to do it. 'I'm sorry,' Poldarn said, 'it wasn't done on purpose. I was saving my house, it didn't occur to me that something like that would happen. I don't understand all your ways here, or I'd have known better.'

The anger in Eyvind's face swelled and halted, as the fire-stream had done when Poldarn had tapped it. 'I realise that,' he said, 'otherwise I'd have killed you and your people too. Obviously you didn't know, or you couldn't have done it. At least,' he added, 'a normal person couldn't have done it, not one of us. You I don't know about, maybe you'd be capable of something like that even if you did know, but I suppose I've got to give you the benefit of the doubt. We don't do things like that here, you see, we don't kill each other or beat each other up or order each other about. We couldn't, even if we wanted to. Maybe an outsider, someone who doesn't belong anywhere and just wanders about, like your friend Boarci, but not a normal person. We simply couldn't – our minds wouldn't let us.'

It occurred to Poldarn, in the abstract, that that was curious but probably true. Maybe it explained why they were so ruthless and brutal when they went raiding across the sea, because there was no outlet at home for all the violence and evil inside them, inside everybody. He could see where that made sense, if it was true.

'All right,' he said. 'So what are you going to do?'

Eyvind straightened up and looked away. 'Quite simple,' he said. 'You took away my house, so I'm going to take yours. I'll have this house, my uncle will have Haldersness, and you can have our place. That's fair, isn't it? I'm not stealing anything, it's a straightforward exchange. The only thing is, you don't have a choice, because you didn't give me one.'

It seemed like a ridiculous anticlimax, after the fear and the shock; a simple property transaction, an exchange of freeholds, no big deal at all somewhere else, where people chose where they lived and didn't automatically know every morning what they were going to do that day. 'I agree,' Poldarn said. 'It seems entirely fair. If only you'd come to me and suggested it—'

He'd said the wrong thing, of course; he knew it wasn't a sensible thing to say before the words were out of his mouth. For a moment, he thought Eyvind might be angry enough to attack him, but apparently not.

'Sure,' Eyvind said. 'We could've sat outside on the porch and talked it over, maybe haggled a little bit until we were both of the same mind, and then we'd have shaken hands on the trade and it'd all have been very pleasant and satisfactory, and you wouldn't have been *punished*. You'd have stood up in the hall that evening and told everybody what you'd agreed, and they'd never have known that you'd done anything wrong, burnt down my house, ruined my life. Well, that won't do, because everybody's got to know what you did, they've got to understand that you don't have any say in the matter, just for once you're the one who's being told what to do. I mean, you're quick enough to give orders, which is a shameful and disgusting way to behave towards your own people, so it's only fair you should be made to take orders. So this is what I decided to do, it was this or kill all your people, the ones I've got penned up back in my uncle's barn – your wife, people like that. Or had you forgotten about them? You and your memory.'

Eyvind was right; Poldarn had forgotten, or it hadn't occurred to him to wonder how Eyvind knew what he'd done. For the first time, he was genuinely frightened.

'You wouldn't have done that,' Poldarn said.

Eyvind scowled angrily. 'No, of course not,' he said. 'Not unless you refused to obey me, and you slipped past me and tried to make a fight of it. I'm insulted that you should think I could. This is the right way to do it, because now all your people can see me humiliating you, they can see you having to do as you're told, and how many of them do you think will stay with you after that? Well,' he added, spinning round to face the Ciartanstead household, 'what do you say about that? It goes without saying, any of you who want to stay here with me or go back to Haldersness, you're more than welcome. I know what I'd do.'

Nobody said anything; but it was one of those times when words weren't needed. Poldarn could see there and then who was going to stay and who'd be going with him, and there'd be precious few of the latter. In a way it was reassuring; because up till then, it had all struck him as too lenient, nothing that'd constitute the punishment Eyvind seemed set on inflicting on him, and so he'd been wondering what else Eyvind might have in mind that he hadn't seen fit to mention. But taking his people from him, he could see how that would be a fitting punishment as far as these people (his people) were concerned. Of course, Eyvind couldn't possibly hope to understand how Poldarn felt about the people of his household: that they bewildered him, made him feel uncomfortable, helpless and alone in a crowd of unfathomable strangers. It was almost funny.

Poldarn wondered if there was anything he could say to expedite such a mutually agreeable settlement; but anything he did say would most likely prove to be counter-productive.

As for the house; well, it was a nice enough house, but it would never be home, he'd never think of it as his, and the people who lived there would only ever be strangers who stared at him when he asked them perfectly reasonable questions, and wouldn't let him do anything. What he wanted most of all, he realised, was to be on his own again – well, to be with Elja, because she was different, she was *his*, and maybe his friend Boarci, who everybody else seemed to dislike so much for no apparent reason. Curious, that his idea of a happy life should be everybody else's notion of extreme punishment. It didn't seem right, somehow.

'Anyway,' Eyvind said, with an effort, 'that's how it's going to be. You can take a change of clothes but that's all, and if you ever come anywhere on this farm again, I'll kill you on sight, without saying a word. Do you understand?'

'Yes,' Poldarn said. 'I understand.'

'Good.' Eyvind breathed out; his whole body seemed to relax, shrink a little. Clearly he felt let down, frustrated, presumably because Poldarn didn't seem to be suffering at all, in spite of the fact that Eyvind had done everything he could do against him. That must be terrible, Poldarn thought, to do your very best to hurt your worst enemy, and see no sign of pain. It just goes to show, he told himself, I've got nothing at all in common with these people, after all. They can't even understand me enough to hurt me. That was disturbing too, in a way.

The departure from Ciartanstead was a comedy from start to finish. The spare cart had, of course, gone east with Hart the provider of salt beef, and the best cart turned out to have a bent rear axle, the result of a hidden pothole in the cart track down to Haldersness. Asburn (who was going with Poldarn) resolutely declined to straighten it, on the grounds that he didn't work for people who broke into other people's houses and threatened them with violence.

That was all very well, but the alternative was a long and miserable walk, so Poldarn volunteered to do the job. But Eyvind wouldn't let him, since blacksmithing was an honourable trade reserved for heads of households, and Poldarn no longer qualified. Someone suggested that in that case Eyvind had better do the work himself, since he was now the lord of Haldersness and Ciartanstead. Eyvind pointed out that he, being a younger son of the brother of the head of his house, who only stood to inherit because his cousin and elder brother had been killed in the last raid, had never learned the craft, and didn't know spit about hot metal. That left the trap, which would carry two people in comfort, three in discomfort and four in acute pain. Eyvind, who was rapidly losing patience with the whole business, declared that Poldarn and his party could take the trap, or they could walk, it was up to them. Someone else proposed a compromise: since there'd be no luggage to speak of, two (or three) of Poldarn's group could go in the trap, and the rest could ride. Eyvind objected most strongly to that, since his ideas of abject humiliation didn't include the loan of valuable riding horses. Someone else put forward the proposal that Poldarn's party (excluding the two, or three, who could fit in the trap) should be loaned something to ride on, but only something humiliating, such as donkeys or mules. That would be difficult, someone else said, because there weren't any at Ciartanstead; on the other hand, there were three elderly ploughhorses. After a mild tantrum, Eyvind agreed to that, but insisted that the horses would have to be returned. Poldarn replied that that would be fine by him, since he knew the three animals in question, they were no good for work any more and he'd be only too pleased not to be lumbered with them. That sent Eyvind into another rage, at the end of which he withdrew the offer of the trap; Poldarn and anybody misguided enough to go with him would have to walk, and that was his last word on the subject. At this point, the men assigned to escort duty objected that they were damned if they were going to walk all the way round the mountain just to satisfy Eyvind's lust for vengeance; and even if Eyvind issued them with horses, it'd still be a waste of time and a pain in the backside, since they'd have to ride at foot-walking pace, and the trip would take twice as long. They had other work they ought to be getting on with, they said, work that was rather more important than Eyvind's grand revenge.

By this point, Eyvind was close to tears from sheer frustration. He calmed himself down with an obvious effort, and called on Asburn to be reasonable; if only he'd agree to fix the bent axle, he and Poldarn and the rest of them could ride in comfort and reach their new home in half the time. Asburn relented and said he'd straighten the axle (under protest) provided he could take the best of his tools – his favourite hammers, tongs, swages, hardies and setts, and the smaller of his two anvils – with him. Eyvind refused outright. In that case, Asburn said, Eyvind could fix the damned axle himself. Once again, Poldarn offered his services, and was promptly told to shut up.

Then someone said that he'd just nipped out and taken a look at the axle, and in his opinion it didn't actually need straightening, at that. Eyvind said that, in that case, it might be a good idea to get the cart out and loaded straight away, before he did anything he'd regret later. They got the cart out of the shed, yoked up a couple of horses and brought it up towards the house. It hadn't gone ten yards when the rear axle snapped in half, like a carrot.

Asburn said that he thought there might be a spare axle down at the Haldersness forge. Almost certainly it'd be too long, but it wouldn't be too much of a job to cut it down; if it was too thick, however, it'd have to be heated up and swaged to the right diameter, assuming he had a swage the right size. If he didn't he could make one, but that'd be half a day's work. Alternatively, he added as an afterthought, there was always the Haldersness wagon.

Eyvind asked, what Haldersness wagon? Asburn replied, the Haldersness wagon, the old one that'd been there since he was a kid, probably longer than that; a high-sided back-sprung four-in-hand with a busted front rail, otherwise perfectly serviceable. Eyvind, totally confused, said that he thought that was the Ciartanstead spare cart; Asburn said no, the Ciartanstead spare cart was the old Haldersness hay wagon. He was talking about the Haldersness carrier's cart – they called it a cart, but it was bigger than a cart, being a four-in-hand. Eyvind said that he couldn't give a damn what it was so long as it was big enough to take Ciartan and his people round the mountain, or at any rate out of his sight, before he had them all cut into bits and thrown down the well. Two of his men got up without a word and left the hall.

They came back some time later and announced that there was indeed a backsprung four-in-hand at Haldersness, but someone had stripped off the back wheels, which were nowhere to be found. There was, however, a perfectly sound trap that would take two people in comfort, three or maybe four at a pinch. When Eyvind asked if they'd brought this trap back with them they answered no, they hadn't, because the only suitable horses down there were out of action on account of thrown shoes, but if he wanted they could take a couple of the Ciartanstead horses down and use those. Eyvind told them to do what the hell they liked.

By the time the two traps were ready to go – there was some problem about not being able to find the right harness – it was beginning to get dark, and the escort party said they didn't fancy the mountain track at night because of all the loose shale and big lumps of black cinder; so Poldarn was marched off to the rat-house along with the loyal remnants of his household – Asburn, Raffen and two men whose faces he recognised but whose names escaped him for the moment. When the door had been shut and barred behind them they sat in the dark and didn't speak to each other. Fairly soon, one of them started to snore, but Poldarn couldn't figure out who it was.

Just before first light they were hauled out. The traps were ready and waiting, with fine fresh horses in the shafts; one of them, a skewbald with a cropped mane, Poldarn recognised as Eyvind's own riding horse. He and Asburn got into the Ciartanstead trap, which was smaller and more rickety after its service as a salt-beef transporter. Raffen and the two unknowns squeezed into the other one. Eyvind's escort, six men armed with spears and axes, bracketed them – two in front, two behind and one on either side, in case anybody tried jumping out of the trap and making a run for it. They seemed to be in a bad mood and didn't say a word for the rest of the day.

They camped out on the lower slopes of the mountain, at the point where the largest and most boisterous of the western mountain streams cut the road. There had been a ford there when they came up that way the previous day, the escort leader said, but it didn't seem to be there any more. By the looks of it, there'd been a landslip or something of the sort, and the ford bed was now full of large rocks. Poldarn said that that didn't sound so good. Acknowledging his existence for the first time, the escort leader said no, it wasn't good; the nearest ford was half a day to the west, on Sceldsbrook land, and he wasn't minded to go there since the Sceldsbrook people could be very funny about other people going on their land without getting permission first. Getting permission would involve following the steam down into the valley to the farm, which was a good two days away, more like three. Raffen said that if the farm was that far away, it'd be highly unlikely for any of Sceld's people to be out in that direction, so maybe they should chance it. But the escort leader wasn't keen on that idea, pointing out that if they were caught out and it led to trouble between Sceld and Eyvind, he'd be the one who got all the blame. They argued about that until well into the night, until the escorts (who'd been up well before dawn the previous day, in order to launch their attack at first light) couldn't keep their eyes open any longer and fell asleep.

'Well,' Raffen announced in a loud whisper, 'now's our chance. We could make a run for it, and it'd be dawn before they could get after us.'

'True,' Poldarn replied with a yawn, 'but where in hell do you suggest we go?'

Nobody had an answer to that, so they went to sleep.

They were up again early the next day, still debating what best to do about the lost ford. Clearing it was out of the question – the rocks were far too big. In the end it came down to two possible choices: to press on to the next ford, or to turn round and head back to Ciartanstead. Neither option was in the least bit attractive. Taking liberties with the Sceldsbrook people was far too dangerous, the escort argued. True; but traipsing back to Ciartanstead and getting shouted at wasn't likely to solve anything. The ford would still be blocked when Eyvind sent them out again, and they'd have had a long and dreary ride for nothing.

'There's another way,' Poldarn said quietly. 'We could go up the mountain.'

The escort weren't at all keen about that. By now, however, they'd more or less forgotten that they were guards in charge of dangerous criminals, and when nobody else could come up with a better suggestion, they politely asked Poldarn what would be involved. He told them: they'd have to send back the cart and the horses and walk, but of course it would be a far shorter distance, as the crow flew, and there shouldn't be any danger from the volcano. They'd follow his original trail up the mountain, and when they reached the place where he'd diverted the fire-stream, all they'd have to do would be to follow it down into the valley, take a detour round the remains of Eyvind's wood and get to the farm that way. True, he admitted, if they were prepared to ditch the horses and the wagon they could probably get across the ford, using the fallen boulders as stepping stones, but then they'd have a very long walk round the edge of the mountain instead of a short one up and down it. It was up to them, Poldarn said; whereupon the escort said that they'd prefer to leave it up to him. since he seemed to be the man with the ideas.

So up the mountain they went. Poldarn set them a crisp pace, and they were able to reach the point where the fire-stream had been breached just before nightfall. The stream itself was grey now instead of cherry red, but it was still viciously hot, and the only water they had with them was in a couple of two-gallon leather bottles, carried by Asburn and Raffen. Only three of the escort were with them by this stage, the others having left to take back the horses and the wagon.

'And you actually smashed a hole in that?' one of the three asked in amazement, as the heat forced him to step back rapidly. 'Bloody hell.'

Poldarn grinned. 'It was a damn sight worse when we were working up here,' he said. 'Wasn't it, Asburn?'

'Much worse,' the blacksmith agreed. 'If we'd been standing as close as this, we'd be dead by now.'

The guard shook his head. 'Rather you than me, then,' he said. 'Even thinking about it gives me the horrors. Mind you, I've always been scared stiff of fire and stuff like that.'

'Oh, it's not so bad once you're used to it,' Poldarn said blandly. 'You've just got to treat it with a bit of respect, that's all. I learned that in the smithy.'

'Yes, well,' the guard mumbled. 'You wouldn't catch me doing that job, either.'

They were tired enough to be able to fall asleep immediately, in spite of their acutely uncomfortable surroundings, and they slept through till shortly after dawn, at which point they were woken up by a brisk shower of rain. At first, they couldn't figure out what was going on; it seemed as if they were being wrapped up in a small, predatory cloud that hissed at them like a small but fierce animal.

'It's the rain,' Poldarn realised. 'The rocks are so hot, it's turning to steam before it lands.'

As soon as they started walking through it, they discovered that the cloud was rather wetter than the rain would have been. They were soaked to the skin by the time they began the rather nerve-racking scramble down the steep incline that led straight towards Eyvind's ill-fated wood. The further down they went, the thicker the cloud became – presumably, Poldarn decided, because the surface of the fire-stream was hotter down below than up here, where its skin had thickened into a stout insulating wall – and finding their way without sliding or falling became a difficult and challenging pastime. Fortunately, the three escorts knew their own side of the mountain as well or better than the Haldersness people knew theirs; they were practically capable of navigating with their eyes shut. As was the way with terrifying experiences, the climb down to the relatively level plain seemed to take for ever, and then was suddenly over. Just when the ground started to level out under his feet, however, and the cloud seemed to be dispersing, Poldarn found that he was on his own. He couldn't see the rest of the party, not even as dim grey shapes at the edges of clarity, and he couldn't hear their footsteps or the sound of their voices. Also, he was looking at a very fine house, newly built and extremely smart, its pale yellow thatch not yet weathered to grey. That was very strange, since by his calculations he should be standing on the lip of the wooded combe, or the place where it used to be. He went a few yards further and realised that he could see the ground behind the house falling sharply away; that was the combe all right, no doubt about it, though there weren't any trees any more. He was wondering where he'd wandered off to when a cheerful shout made him jump.

He turned his head in the direction the voice had come from, and saw a shape taking form through the curtain of mist. He recognised it at once.

'Eyvind,' he said.

'There you are!' He sounded much happier than he had the last time they'd spoken to each other. 'I was starting to wonder where in hell you'd got to.'

'We got held up,' Poldarn said. 'The ford was blocked.'

'What, again?' Eyvind clicked his tongue and shook his head. 'I'm going to have to talk to Sceld about that. If he can't keep his damned cows from treading in the cutting, he'll have to find some other grazing for them. It's getting beyond a joke.'

For some reason, Poldarn felt prompted to look round at the mountain behind him. Its profile was entirely different, back the way it used to be before the volcano tore it apart, and it was capped with an elegant crown of pure white snow.

'Anyway,' Eyvind said, clapping an arm round his shoulders, 'you're here now, that's the main thing. Bersa'll be pleased. She's been hovering round the porch all day, looking to see if you were coming. She won't admit that, of course.'

Eyvind was frogmarching Poldarn along, giving him no choice but to walk with him towards the house. He had an idea that it wouldn't be advisable to go in there, but he didn't see how he could break away without giving offence. Then a crow lifted off the ground in front of them. Eyvind let him go and stooped to pick up a stone; he threw, and missed, and suddenly the cloud came down again. It lifted almost immediately, and Poldarn found he was looking at a very different landscape. There was no house, and no combe. Instead, the fire-stream marched straight as an army road towards a glowing red circle on the ground. On the edges, Poldarn could see the blackened stumps of trees. On either side, for about a hundred yards, the turf was burned down to ash and bare black soil. Boulders, dragged along by the stream and discarded at random, stuck out like a flock of feeding birds. The rain had stopped.

He looked round for the others and saw them, seven little dots in the distance, on the far edge of the red circle. The crow Eyvind had walked up swung in a wide circle overhead, screamed something offensive, and waddled across the sky towards the horizon.

The others were waiting for him.

'Where the hell did you get to?' demanded one of the escorts.

'I'm sorry,' he replied. 'I think I must've lost my way in the fog.'

They seemed to accept that, though they weren't happy. 'We thought you'd run out on us,' one of them said. 'We weren't looking forward to telling Eyvind when we got back home.'

'Sorry,' Poldarn repeated. 'Still, I'm here now. We might as well press on to the farm.'

Eyvind's uncle's house – Bollesknap, another member of the escort told him – was smaller than Haldersness or Ciartanstead, with fewer outbuildings. Its grey thatch was green with moss, and a broad, slow stream ran through the yard. 'That's new,' the man said. 'It must've changed course when you diverted the fire-stream. You'll want to watch that come the autumn, or you'll get flooded out.'

Poldarn shrugged. 'So long as it's only water, I'm not worried,' he replied.

The home fields were a reassuring sight: a promising crop of winter wheat just starting to stand up, a good show of cabbages and peas, some rather battered-looking leeks in a flat strip beside the house. Once that lot came in, there'd be plenty to eat, as well as seed for next year. No sign of any livestock, but he hadn't expected to see any; presumably they were on their way to Ciartanstead or Haldersness. He didn't imagine they'd like it there; the grazing wasn't nearly as good.

Waiting for them on the porch was a small group of people. Poldarn saw Elja there, and a great weight fell away from him; also Boarci, sitting in a chair with two men he didn't know standing over him, looking nervous, and four of the Haldersness hands, including Rook. The others were all strangers; Eyvind's people, presumably.

One of them stood up and came out to meet them. He ignored Poldarn and spoke to one of the escorts.

'So you got here at last, Tren,' he said sourly. 'What did you do, stop off to go fishing?'

The man he'd called Tren shook his head. 'Long story,' he said. 'Sceld's ford was blocked, so we had to go up the mountain and round; had to send the horses back, of course. Still, we're here now. Anything to eat inside?'

The stranger laughed. 'You'll be lucky,' he said, 'all the food's gone off in the carts to the new place, apart from a scrap or two for us for the journey. What do you mean, the ford's blocked? How are we supposed to get to the new place if we can't get across?'

Tren shrugged. 'Have to go back the way we've just come, I guess. Bloody hard slog it is, too, so you'd better have got your walking boots with you.'

The stranger frowned. 'What about the horses?' he said. 'We can't leave 'em here – Eyvind said we can't leave anything.'

'Well, you won't get 'em over the mountain, that's for sure. We'll just have to come back for them later, when the ford's clear.'

'Are you crazy?' The stranger jerked his head in the direction of the people on the porch. 'What the hell makes you think this lot'll give 'em back?'

Tren didn't seem to understand that at first; then he remembered that Poldarn and his people were their prisoners and enemies. The thought couldn't have bothered him much, because he said, 'I don't think you need worry too much on that score. Anyway, unless you've got another route I don't know about, it's not like we've got much choice.'

'Damn.' The stranger didn't know what to do. 'Oh well,' he said eventually, 'if we do have to come back for them, I don't see this lot giving us much trouble. As you can see, most of 'em decided to go to the new place.'

'So it would seem,' Tren said, and his tone of voice implied that he didn't think much of them for that. 'Well, that's their decision, none of our business.' The other man frowned, and Poldarn guessed there was more in Tren's mind than showed in what he'd said out loud. 'We'd better be on our way,' Tren continued. 'It's going to be a long walk, and the sooner we start the sooner we get there.' He turned to Poldarn. 'If we leave our horses here, you won't make trouble, will you?'

Poldarn shook his head. 'I don't pick fights,' he said. 'Particularly when I don't stand a chance. Besides, we aren't going anywhere, so we won't be needing horses. If Eyvind's taken all the feed we'll have to graze them outside, that's all.'

'I don't suppose they'll come to any harm like that,' Tren said, and his conciliatory tone suggested more than a touch of guilt. 'Soon as the ford's clear we'll take them off your hands, and then we'll leave you alone.'

'That'd be best,' Poldarn said.

He and his people watched them in silence till they were out of sight. Only when they'd vanished into a dip of dead ground did anybody speak.

'Father and Egil are going to move out west,' Elja said quietly. 'They said they'd feel uncomfortable at Ciartanstead, and they didn't want to stay here if the rest of the household went. I think that's probably the most sensible thing all round.'

Poldarn looked at her. 'You aren't going with them,' he said.

'No.' She looked away. 'I thought I'd stay here.'

'Good,' Poldarn said. He wanted to put his arms around her and hold on to her as hard as he could, but he felt she wouldn't like that. 'What about the rest of you?' he said. 'You don't have to stay if you don't want to. It's not going to be easy, just the twelve of us on a place this size.'

Nobody said anything for a while; then Rook said; 'It's not so bad. I had a look round; they've taken most of their stuff but they've left more than they meant to. The standing crops, for one thing.'

'They took all the tools,' said one of the men whose names Poldarn couldn't remember. 'I watched them loading up the carts.'

'The furniture, too,' Elja said sadly. 'No benches, no tables, no blankets even. We've got four walls and a roof, and that's it.'

Boarci laughed. 'No big deal,' he said. 'You've got a few trees still, and I think I saw what looked like a nice seam of potters' clay in the yard, where the stream's washed off the topsoil. We can make stuff; it's not exactly difficult.'

'Make stuff with what?' Raffen objected. 'They took all the tools.'

But Boarci shook his head. 'They *think* they took all the tools,' he replied. 'But in a place like this, you never take everything, there's always something left – a broken knife or a rusty old axe head in the corner of the barn.'

Asburn stood up and walked away; only Poldarn noticed him leave. 'That's all very well,' Raffen went on, 'but even if we can make a few things, that's not the most important thing. What really matters is, there isn't anything to eat.'

Boarci shook his head. 'Don't you believe it,' he said. 'It all depends on what you mean by food. When you've had to live rough as long as I have, you learn to get by on what you can find. There's five apple trees out back, for a start, just coming up nicely.'

One of the nameless men coughed. 'Actually,' he said, 'they're cider apples, not eaters.'

'Big deal.' Boarci grinned. 'They may taste like shit, but so what? And if it's meat you're after, they've left us half a dozen big, tall horses. After all those dinners of porridge and leeks, a nice red steak'll go down pretty sweet.'

But Poldarn shook his head. 'We won't do that,' he said. 'The last thing we need to do is give Eyvind a pretext. They're to be left alone till Eyvind's people come for them, understood?'

Boarci shrugged. 'Up to you,' he said. 'It's all right, though, we can do without. The mountain blowing its top means that all the deer and bears and wild goats and stuff have been pushed down into the valley, without even a wood to hide in. They'll tide us over for a month or so, easy, even if we don't find anything else. And there's plenty of other things you can eat, if you know what to look for. Anyone here ever tried earwigs? I have. They're not bad, if you just swallow and don't think about it.'

'It's not like we've got much choice,' Elja put in abruptly. 'At least, some of you can go to Ciartanstead, but I can't, I've got to stay here whether I like it or not. So yes, I'll eat anything that's edible, and be grateful. Anybody who doesn't think that way had better push off now, before Eyvind decides to shut the door on you.'

That killed the debate stone dead. Raffen sat down on the stoop, took off his left boot and examined the sole. Boarci got up and went into the house. The two unidentified men who'd come with Poldarn started talking to each other very quietly, apparently about a completely unrelated subject. For his part, Poldarn stared out in the direction of the fire-stream, thinking about what he'd seen when he came down off the mountain. They stayed like that until Asburn came bounding back, in apparently high spirits.

'I've just been to look at the smithy,' he said. 'They've taken all the tools but they've left a good anvil – it's bolted down to a big stump set in the floor, and I guess they couldn't get it out in time to take it on. And there's a decent enough vice mounted on the wall, and the forge and the bellows are all still there. And they've left most of the scrap, and,' he added with a big smile, 'I found this under the bench.' He held out a rusty lump of metal for them to see; it turned out to be a hammer head, a four-pound straight-peen with a nicely crowned face and the handle broken off flush in the eye. 'There's even coal in the bunker,' he went on. 'All I've got to do is put a new stem on this and we're in business. We can make all the tools we need.'

Everybody looked at him, as though he'd started telling jokes at a funeral. But Poldarn turned his back on the view and said, 'He's right. With a hammer and an anvil and a fire and some material, we can make any bloody thing we like. We can make axes and saws and chisels, we can make hoes and scythes and rakes and a plough.' He laughed suddenly. 'At least it'll be something to do,' he said. It looked like nobody else understood what he meant by that, but he didn't care. 'It won't be all that different from moving out to Ciartanstead; we'll have to make all the little things, but the house is here already, we don't have to build that. Oh, cheer up, for God's sake. At least we're still alive, not like Barn and those other poor bastards. I got up out of that river bed with nothing, not even any memories, and I've come this far. And just for once, I'll know what the hell I'm supposed to be doing.'

Asburn found a smashed-up wagon wheel in a ditch; he and Poldarn wrenched out one of the spokes, and Poldarn cracked a flint with the hammer head to make a sharp edge. While Asburn was fussing round his new forge, checking the bellows-leather for tears and sorting through the scrap pile, Poldarn patiently whittled down the spoke until it fitted into the eye of the hammer head; then he made a wedge out of a scrap of oak he found on the woodshed floor, split the top of the handle, slid in the wedge and slammed it down on the anvil a few times to drive it home. The weight and balance of his new hammer felt just about right, unlike the hammers he'd used back at the old place, which had never sat comfortably in his hand. By the time Poldarn had got that far, Asburn had lit the fire and found a couple of thick stakes that'd do for the makings of a pair of tongs. With tongs they could hold their work; they could make another hammer, another set of tongs, a set and a hardie and a punch, and with those they could make anything they chose, from an earring to a warship. Suddenly, there was nothing in the world they couldn't make or do.

'What do you think of the name?' Asburn asked, as they waited for the metal to get hot.

'What name?'

'Bollesknap,' Asburn replied. 'That's what they said this place is called.'

'I think it sucks,' Poldarn replied. 'I think we need a new name, don't you?'

Asburn nodded. 'How about Ciartansdale?' he suggested.

But Poldarn shook his head. 'Too confusing,' he said. 'Ciartanstead and Ciartansdale. Besides, I never liked that name much.'

'Fair enough.' Asburn drew the bar out of the nest of red coals; it was orange going on yellow, almost hot enough but not quite. He reached up for the bellows handle. 'You got anything in mind?'

'I have, as a matter of fact,' Poldarn said, lifting the hammer. 'I was thinking of Poldarn's Forge.'

Asburn looked at him. 'Funny choice,' he said. 'That's the old name for the mountain.' He drew the bar away from the fire, tapped it on the horn to shake off the scale, and laid it on the anvil. Poldarn fixed his gaze on the place where he wanted to strike.

'I know,' he said.

Chapter Twenty-Three

In spite of Boarci's enthusiastic recommendation, they didn't eat earwigs for dinner that night. By a pleasing coincidence, the first of the migrating geese appeared in the sky a few hours before sunset, and two plump but stupid specimens dropped in on the flood in the yard. They never knew what hit them.

By another pleasing coincidence, Asburn had already made spits to roast them on and a knife to carve them with. It was, everyone agreed, the best meal they'd had since before the volcano erupted, though Hand, one of the men who'd come from Ciartanstead with Poldarn, said they'd have been better for a bit of cabbage and a few leeks. Meanwhile, Elja had found five elderly but serviceable blankets in a mildewed trunk in the trap-house; she cut four of them down the middle and kept the fifth intact for Poldarn and herself. That left them short by two blankets, but Raffen and Boarci said they weren't particularly cold anyway, and if they were they weren't sleeping under anything that had come from the back of an outhouse. They smashed up the trunk and put the bits on the fire.

Poldarn woke up well before dawn and realised he had no chance of getting back to sleep. He felt as full of energy as a child on a holiday, so he crept out of the bedroom through the hall — it was dark, but he seemed to know the way, because he got through without treading on anybody — and across the yard to the forge. When he opened the door he found that Asburn was already there, nursing the beginnings of the day's fire with gentle nudges from the bellows.

'That's good,' Poldarn said. 'You know, I never dared admit this before, but I haven't got a clue how to start a fire. Not without plenty of hay and charcoal, anyhow.'

Asburn grinned. 'I'd gathered that,' he said. 'But it didn't seem right for me to say so, you being the smith by right of birth and all that. Here, I'll show you if you like.'

When the fire was full and hot, they started work. By alternating, they were able to share the anvil and the hammer, one man striking while the other took a heat. Asburn started by making a spearhead, 'so Boarci can go and kill things up the mountain.' Poldarn made three chisels, welding steel tips to iron bodies, since their stock of hardening steel was distinctly limited. The welds took first time without any trouble. Next Asburn made another hammer, a twelve-pound sledge, and once they'd fitted it on a stem carved down from a wheel-spoke with one of Poldarn's chisels, they used it to draw down and flatten out two broken sword-blades: one into a scythe, the other into a saw. The latter had to wait until Poldarn had made a file so that the teeth could be cut; he used a snapped-off halberd point, which already had the right degree of taper. Once he'd forged it triangular, he took a good heat, clamped it in the vice and used his new chisel to score in the cutting ridges. It was slow work; the heat in the metal kept drawing the temper of the chisel, which had to be rehardened over and over again before the job was done. Finally it was ready; he caked the file in mud before hardening it, so the fire wouldn't burn the ridges off as it came up to cherry red. The saw was filed and finished by nightfall, by which time Asburn had also made a sett, an axe head and a drill bit.

'It's getting late,' Asburn said, cutting a trail through the layer of black soot on his forehead with the back of his wrist. 'We ought to stop now, I suppose.'

'I guess,' Poldarn replied. The day had gone unbelievably quickly, and for once it had left behind tangible and valuable accomplishments. 'I was going to make a start on a shovel. That stream in the yard needs banking up straight away, before we get any more rain.'

'That's a long job,' Asburn replied. 'You'd be better off running up a couple more knives for the house.'

'We haven't eaten anything all day,' Poldarn remembered. 'We'd better do that, before we get weak and fall over.'

The treasures they brought with them ensured them a hero's welcome back in the house. Each piece of work was handed round and admired as if it had been dug up from a king's grave. In turn, they had to admire the achievements of the rest of the household. Raffen had been out gathering firewood, picking out bits and pieces from the charred mess of Eyvind's plantation. Boarci had spent the day waiting for the geese, and one of them had come home with him; they'd have to eat quickly and well to get through all the meat they had on hand before it spoiled. Hand and the other hitherto nameless loyalist, Reno, had filled half a blanket with apples, pears, quinces, chestnuts and various evil-looking varieties of fungus. Rook had scooped clay out of the seam in the yard and squidged it into cups, plates and bowls, which were drying in front of the fire. Elja had found a bed of osiers and was weaving them into something, though it wasn't big enough yet to tell what it was going to be.

'It's a shame Rannwey isn't here,' Poldarn said. 'She's very quick at basket-weaving.'

They turned their heads and looked at him. At last, Elja said, 'You don't know?'

'Don't know what?'

She took a deep breath. 'Rannwey's dead, I'm afraid. On the way down the mountain – we think it was her heart. I'm sorry.'

Poldarn froze, the basketwork still in his hands. 'Oh,' he said. 'Well, that's a shame. I'd assumed she'd gone to Ciartanstead with the others. I don't think she liked me very much.'

They were staring at him, that uncomprehending stare he'd seen so often. This time, it didn't bother him so much. The fact was that he felt nothing, except in an abstract, almost theoretical way. Rannwey had been his grandmother, his last living blood relative, and apparently she'd died. To him she'd been a pair of piercing eyes and a blank stare that he'd done his best to avoid; he'd always seemed to bewilder her more than he bewildered the others, and it had made him feel painfully embarrassed. The fact that he'd had no trouble in believing that she'd sided with his enemy was surely eloquent enough. He hadn't wanted her to die, but he was very glad she wasn't here, even if she could weave a good basket.

'Anyway,' Elja said with an effort, 'we're starting to get organised; that's good. Any chance of someone making a start on some furniture tomorrow? Two stools and the floor are all very well, but I could do with a little luxury, like a table.'

Then everyone began talking at once, urging the claims of their own favoured projects and laying claim to use of the tools. As for what Asburn and Poldarn should do the next day, there was no shortage of suggestions. Pot hooks and fire irons, rakes, pitchforks, hoes, mattocks, spades, more hammers, more files, more knives, more axes, more saws and chisels, an adze (Poldarn didn't happen to notice who asked for that, but he was impressed), pots and kettles, rasps, calipers, nails, a lamp-stand ('But we haven't got any lamps,' Asburn pointed out), new hinges for the barn door, bolts and hasps and brackets, and – if there was time – a lathe spindle, ploughshares and the metal parts for a spinning-wheel treadle. Poldarn kept nodding till he was dizzy; there didn't seem to be any reason why they couldn't make them all, if not tomorrow then the next day. It wasn't as if anything they were asking for was particularly difficult, it was just a matter of knowing what to do. And he did, he realised: somehow he'd known it all along but it was only just beginning to drift up from the depths of his memory. Suddenly he was having visions of himself beside an anvil, bending and twisting and drawing down and jumping up endless rods and bars and odd-shaped pieces from the scrap, while someone whose face he couldn't see was saying, *No, not like that*, and *Now you've got it, that's the ticket*. He found himself grinning because he'd known it all already, even when he'd been struggling to make a straight nail in the forge at Haldersness; he'd known the whole craft, even better than Asburn did – everything, of course, except how to get a fire going.

He woke up even earlier next day, and beat Asburn to the forge by several minutes. He still couldn't get the fire to catch, but this time at least he knew why. By the time he was so tired that the hammer was slipping through his fingers, he'd made a heap of priceless, indispensable tools and implements, each one a vital contribution to the life of the farm. Wire, Asburn was saying, if we could only make up some plates for drawing wire; but Poldarn knew exactly how to go about that, though he kept it to himself so he wouldn't look like he was boasting. He'd drawn wire before, any amount of it. It was like everything else, easy if you knew the trick. What a difference just a little scrap of memory made.

Poldarn thought about that as he dug a broken halberd-blade in under the coals. He considered the memory of steel, imparted by intense heat and sudden cold: take a piece of hardening steel, heat it until it glows red and quench it and heat it again until the colours crawl upwards, yellow and brown and purple and blue, and you can teach it to remember its own shape. Bend it back on itself and let it go, and it'll spring back into the shape you've taught it to keep. Heat it again and let it cool slowly in the air, and it forgets; bend it, and it stays bent, bend it back and forth often enough and it fatigues and breaks. Memory gives it not only identity, but strength.

Next he considered the memory of flesh, imparted by intense experience and sudden understanding: take a piece of flesh, fill it with knowledge, learning, wisdom, experience; quench it in pain, heat it again in friendship, love and understanding, and you can teach it to remember its own name. Bend it back on itself and let go, and it'll spring back into the identity it's learned to inhabit. Heat it again in horror, shame and understanding, let it cool slowly in confused sleep, and it forgets. Bend it, and it follows whatever force is applied to it, adapting itself without resistance to whatever shape will get it out of the way of the pressure, until in time it fatigues and breaks. Memory gives it not only identity, but strength.

Then he considered the broken steel and the broken flesh. One can be put back in the fire over and over again; each time it goes from intense heat to sudden cold to gradual, accumulating heat it accepts a new memory, gains new strength, becomes capable of taking and holding an edge. Put the other in the fire and it burns away, converted into smoke and ash, like the effluent of a volcano. The defining property of flesh is that it can only be worked once; unlike steel, which, if it warps in the quench and comes out distorted, crooked, bad, can be saved by fire and water and more fire, making it infinitely more versatile and enduring than muscle, skin and bone. Even supposing it were possible to take flesh with a bad set and heat out the offending memory, the result would inevitably be weak and ductile, unable to hold an edge, bending and stretching and buckling under pressure until finally the ignorant material fatigues, cracks, tears, snaps, fails. Memory is understanding. Memory is strength.

But supposing you were to take flesh that could withstand heat, even the heat of the fire-stream that had turned Barn and the old man who'd wanted to help into ash and smoke, but that had taken a bad set in the quench and become warped, distorted, untrue. Supposing you could find such a piece of flesh in a ditch or the corner of a barn or in the mud and blood of a river bank, annealed of its memory until it was as soft as a bloom of virgin iron, and supposing you heated and forged and heated and quenched and heated it, in the fire of burning houses and Polden's Forge and the river mud of the Bohec (as he'd coddled the file-blade in mud so the fine steel of the teeth wouldn't burn; yes, maybe that was how to save flesh from burning) – suppose you could do that, and keep on doing it over and over again until at last, eventually, it came out straight from the quench, filled with good memory and set in the desired shape. That would be the very best hardening flesh. That would be a god.

But he doubted that – because flesh burns, even when coated in mud or wrapped in oxhides saturated with water; a defining property of flesh is that it burns. That limits its usefulness and cramps its versatility, because nothing survives burning except smoke and the ash that covers fields and buries growth. The thought depressed him, because he'd had such high hopes for flesh as a material for the manufacture of useful and enduring things. But then he thought of how steel burns too, if too much heat gets into it, blanching the orange to white; he thought of the welding heat, the incandescent white that crackles and glitters with sparks, at which point it can be joined to another piece in marriage under the hammer, in the brief moment of love between taking a heat and burning. He considered the way Asburn had made the pattern-welded blade, binding together flat leaves of steel and bringing them to the very brink of burning, and how his hammer had joined the many into one (like the mind of the crows, or the people of Haldersness and Ciartanstead). It seemed to him that in order to make a join in steel or flesh, it was necessary to bring the material to the point of destruction, when the skin is molten and fluid and one piece can flow into another, as the Mahec and the Bohec merge into each other and then the sea, at Boc Bohec. Once joined, of course, they can take heat and sudden cold and incremental heat as well as a piece of the solid, and the only indication that they were ever separate is – of course – the pattern: the maiden's hair, the butterfly, the pools and eyes.

And that made him wonder whether the best hope for flesh wasn't the coddling in clay but the welding heat, the love of separate pieces achieving union at the point of burning. In the pattern weld, he remembered, Asburn had interleaved hardening steel and soft iron, so that the brittle strength of one should be saved by the soft ductility of the other while still being capable of taking and holding an edge, taking and keeping memory. He remembered what Asburn had told him; that when they first came to this country these people (his people) were dangerously short of good material and so learned the knack of burning and hammering separate pieces of scrap into useful and enduring things; at least until they'd grown strong enough to go across the sea and strip what they needed from the dead bodies of their enemies. Maybe, he thought, the answer to the problem of flesh is the pattern-weld, where muscle and skin and bone are fluxed out and burnt away, but the memory remains in the pattern, the ripples of the pools and eyes, the ascending rungs of Polden's Ladder.

'You look thoughtful,' Asburn said. 'Problem?'

Poldarn shook his head. 'Just trying to remember something,' he said. 'Did you ever come across a man called Hart? He lives over the other side of the moor somewhere.'

Asburn frowned. 'I think so,' he replied. 'Do you mean Egil Colscegson's friend, the one who breeds lurchers? I seem to remember seeing him once, over at Colscegsford, years ago. Tall man, big hands, not much good with horses.'

'That sounds like him,' Poldarn said, 'though I didn't know he was friends with Egil.'

'It was Egil or Barn,' Asburn replied. 'Most likely Egil, because Barn was always a bit timid around dogs. Why do you ask?'

'Oh, no reason. It was him I traded that salt beef with. I was wondering if he had any more going spare. We could do with it.'

'That's true. But what have we got that we could trade?'

'I don't know. It was just a thought.' Poldarn pulled his piece of steel out of the fire. It was still only dull red, so he put it back and hauled on the bellows handle.

Asburn shrugged. 'Come to think of it,' he said, 'if you want to know about Hart, you ought to ask Elja. I think she went to stay with him once or twice, when she was a kid. Her and Egil both. Or Barn. One of the two.'

Poldarn matched his breathing to the gusts of the bellows. 'It might be worth following up,' he said. 'If he's an old friend of the family, maybe he'd let us have the salt beef now and wait till later, when we've got something to trade for it.'

'Good idea. You should go over there and see him, when you've got the time.'

Poldarn stared into the fire. 'Yes,' he said, 'I could do that.'

That evening, when they gathered for dinner, Raffen happened to mention that a big mob of crows had settled on some flat patches in the barley and were making a mess of it.

So Poldarn got up early the next morning and took a bucketful of stones out to the long meadow. But his luck wasn't
in; the birds were there all right, but the hedge was too low
and thin to give him enough cover; they saw him in plenty of
time and flew wide rings round him, screaming and flinching
out of range whenever he drew his arm back, until he gave
up and went back to the house. According to Raffen, they
came back an hour after he'd gone and stayed there the rest
of the day.

During the two weeks that followed, Poldarn found himself
beginning to believe that life could, after all, be a pleasant
and rewarding affair, rather than the lamination of tedium
and horror he'd come to expect. He got up with the sun and
went straight to his day's work, knowing from the moment
he opened his eyes exactly what he was going to do that day,
and joyfully aware that by the time he closed them again,
he'd have achieved something that would make the next day
easier and more pleasant for himself and those around him.
He enjoyed the heat of the forge and the weight of the
hammer. He relished the challenge of imposing his will on
iron and steel, the satisfaction of teaching it shapes that it
would hold for a hundred years. He was delighted to find
that, as he went about each new project, he remembered in
precise detail how to do it. Some operations he knew he'd
done before at some time, others he was able to figure out
from basic principles that turned out to be ingrained in his
mind. Suddenly he could forge-weld better than Asburn,
knowing as soon as he drew the spitting white steel out of the
fire whether or not it would take. The four-pound hammer
became frustratingly light and slow, so he made himself a
six-pound straight-peen with a stem as long as his forearm
from fingertips to elbow. He found that he didn't have to
wrap a wet rag around a piece of heated bar before he could
bear to hold it. His arms and the backs of his hands became

pitted with scores of little burns from sparks and flying cinders, but instead of yelping and wincing when they landed on his bare skin, he ignored them and carried on working. Elja tanned the skin of a deer that Boarci had killed on the lower slopes of the mountain, and sewed it with its own sinew into an apron and a pair of long-cuffed gloves; he was delighted by the thought behind it, but rarely bothered to wear them.

On the rare occasions during the day when Poldarn wasn't working in the smithy, he either helped one of the others with some heavy job that needed two pairs of hands or walked over to the newly built pen to see to Eyvind's horses. They didn't need much looking after, but he felt an obligation to ensure that when they were called for they'd be in prime condition, groomed and combed, well fed but properly exercised; he felt he owed Eyvind that at least, for giving him this fine house and excellent farm. It was smaller than Ciartanstead but there was less waste — no hills too steep or too rocky for the plough, no bogs or outcrops. Several times, after the evening meal was over and the table (made by Raffen and Rook from chestnut planks sawn with the long two-handed saw he'd forged for them) had been put up against the wall, he wandered out of the house on the pretext of finishing up some job he'd been working on, and strolled round the home fields, taking note of new growth in the crops and the latest tactical manoeuvres of the enemy — the crows and pigeons and rabbits and rats. He couldn't think of anywhere he'd rather be, or anybody he'd rather be there with. Happiness, Poldarn decided, was a simple matter of being in the right place at the right time, with the right people, and the strange trail of circumstances that had brought him there, leading him step by step through the maze from the banks of the Bohec by way of burnt cities and battlefields and ambushes beside the road, murders and plots and betrayals, volcano and fire-stream and destruction of past and future, astounded him by its scope and complexity. Any wrong turning along the way, any apparent misfortune eluded, would have brought him to quite another place in entirely different company, and would have been a disaster. If he'd never left this country to begin with, he'd be a completely different person now – Ciartan of Haldersness, a dispossessed wanderer whose house lay buried under a huge fat worm of slowly cooling rock, conscious of nothing but his own unbearable loss. If he hadn't met with whatever the misadventure was that had stranded him in the mud beside the river, surrounded by dead men whose names he couldn't remember, he'd have lived out a totally different life on the wrong side of the sea, he'd never have ended up here in another man's house on another man's inheritance, which just happened to be the only place on earth where he could be who he was supposed to be. Time and again he tried to reconstruct the course of events in his mind, looking for the points in the story where things could have gone an entirely different way. Running into Copis and killing her partner, the god in the cart – but hadn't she turned out to be an agent of the sword-monks, trailing him before the incident beside the river, being on hand at that crucial moment to guide him along the right path? Stumbling on Tazencius when he'd fallen off his horse and hurt his leg – but hadn't he turned out to be part of some joint conspiracy, carrying him down the right path like the boulders dragged down the mountain by the fire-stream? Very well, then: being waylaid by Eyvind and his companion on the road to whatever that city was, the one ruled by clerks – *that* was pure chance, Eyvind having been cut off from the rest of his party and stranded in the middle of hostile territory. How easily he could have killed the wrong man that day, or even taken a different road or the same road at a different time or at a slightly slower or faster pace and missed him altogether. When he thought of how he'd got there, like a pilot navigating a ship blindfold through the shoals, he found it almost impossible to believe that it had all been mere chance, nothing but sheer good luck, like calling the spin of a coin correctly a hundred times in a row.

One day, just before noon, Poldarn was putting an edge on a bean-hook when Raffen burst into the forge, looking tired and extremely annoyed.

'Those bloody horses,' he said. 'Bust out of the pen and trampled right across the damned beans. Could be any bloody place by now.'

Poldarn frowned and put the hook down. 'Damn,' he said. 'You've got no idea where they could have gone?'

'That's what I just said.'

'That's bad,' Asburn put in as he hauled on the bellows handle. 'What's going to happen when Eyvind's people turn up here to collect them? They're going to think we've got them hidden away somewhere and don't want to give them back.'

Poldarn thought for a moment. 'We can't have that,' he said. 'It's their fault, the idle bastards, for leaving them here so long. All right,' he said wearily, 'we'll need to get the search properly organised, we've got a hell of a lot of ground to cover with just the twelve of us.'

They spent the rest of the day tramping up and down the slopes of the mountain. It was hard to figure out how anything as conspicuous as ten horses could escape being seen in such open country, but they couldn't even find any tracks, let alone the horses themselves.

'Which ought to tell us something,' Poldarn pointed out, when they met up again that night at the house. 'If they aren't leaving tracks, it's got to be because they're on stony ground, somewhere up the mountain.'

'Except you can see for miles up there,' Boarci pointed

out. 'You can take my word on that, I've spent the last couple of weeks stalking deer in the open without so much as a dandelion to take cover behind. If they were up there, I'd have seen them, you bet. I reckon they've got to be hiding out in one of the little dips on the other side of the fire-pit.'

Poldarn shook his head. 'But that's in completely the opposite direction to where they started from, coming from the pen across the bean field. To get down there they'd have had to double back, go right across the yard in plain sight of the lot of us.'

'Then that's what must have happened,' Boarci grumbled. 'Because it's the only place they could possibly be.'

'Fine.' Poldarn sighed. 'And did you bother to look down there?'

'Yes,' Boarci admitted. 'And no, of course I didn't find them. But I was on my own, they could've slipped past while I was in the dead ground, and I wouldn't have known a bloody thing about it. I've known deer do that before now.'

Poldarn slumped forward over the table, his face in his hands. 'Well,' he said, 'I suppose it's worth taking a proper look tomorrow, all of us strung out in a line so they can't slip by, if that's what they're doing. We've tried everywhere else, after all.'

'Bit late for that,' Boarci replied. 'If they kept on moving after sundown they could be any bloody place by now.'

'Sure,' Hand put in, 'but down there in the little combes they'd be bound to have left tracks, especially if there's been a heavy dew. We don't have to find them straight off, so long as we can pick up the trail.'

'That makes sense,' Poldarn said. 'All right, that's what we'll do, first thing in the morning. In the meantime, everybody just pray that Eyvind doesn't pick tomorrow to come collecting his property.'

Nobody slept well that night, and the household assembled some time before dawn, impatient to get on with the search so that the horses could be found and life could get back to normal. It was still dark when they set off – 'A mistake,' Boarci told them. 'We could be walking right past their tracks and never see the buggers. What I wouldn't give right now for a pair of good dogs.'

That made Poldarn think of Hart and Egil, but it didn't seem the right time to raise that subject. 'We'll just have to take the risk,' he said. 'I'm not turning back now. If we pick up the trail and it leads right back the way we've just come, you can say *I told you so*.'

The search wasn't exactly fruitless. They found a ring of big round yellow puffballs that Boarci swore blind were edible; and a solitary cock-pheasant jumped out of the grass at Raffen's feet, only to regret its bad timing when he brought it down with an instinctively aimed stone. They also stumbled across several unmistakable deer tracks, which Boarci took careful note of, and the ruin of a shepherd's hut, roofless and with a small oak tree growing inside it. No sign of any horses.

'Fine,' Poldarn said, as they dropped down to rest shortly after noon. 'So we can be fairly positive they aren't here. Where else could they be?'

No one replied. It was too hot for climbing up and down hills, and nobody had brought anything to drink. Poldarn could tell that they'd lost interest in the search some time ago and wanted to get home and carry on with the work they were supposed to be doing. He could sympathise with that; it did seem ridiculous to waste their valuable time combing the countryside for their enemy's property.

'I'll bet you they've headed straight back to Haldersness,' Rook yawned. 'Right now they're probably in the stable munching oats, and Eyvind is feeling pleased because he hasn't got to waste three days traipsing up here to fetch them.'

'Who cares?' Boarci muttered. 'If they're lost, let him go looking for them. We should ask him to send over some men and a cartload of lumber to fix up the pen; it was his damn horses that bust it up, after all.'

'All right,' Poldarn said. 'If nobody's got any suggestions, I say we should try a bit further down the ridge, where the rill comes out. In this weather, it's a fair bet they're thirsty. It's the closest water this side of the house.'

So they pressed on as far as the stream that came down off the side of the mountain and meandered over the flat before soaking away into a treacherous-looking marsh. No trace of any horses anywhere.

'Of course,' Hand said, 'it's possible they did come this way, wandered out into the boggy stuff and got sucked in. I saw a cow do that once, in the bog up behind the old house. One minute it was ambling along, next minute you'd never guess there'd been a cow there. Spookiest thing you ever did see.'

That didn't really help matters; so they agreed to forget about the search and headed for home. They were a long way out by that point, and the sun was starting to set by the time they reached the house. Outside, tied to the rail of the smashed-up pen, they saw four horses.

'Of course they could be ours,' Raffen muttered, 'and whoever found them could have saddled them up and ridden them back here. But I doubt it.'

Inside they found four men, sitting round the table looking bored. They didn't recognise them, but they had a fair idea who they were.

'Where the hell have you been?' one of the strangers asked.

Poldarn walked up the hall toward them. 'You're Eyvind's people,' he said.

'That's right,' another one of them replied. 'We've come to pick up those horses that were left here, but we can't find them, and there was nobody about. What's going on here?'

Poldarn took a deep breath. 'Your horses aren't here,' he said. 'When you were looking round, you may have noticed the pen out front. We had the horses in there but they broke through the rails and got out. We've just spent the last two days searching for them.'

The strangers looked at each other. 'Like hell,' one of them said. 'You don't really expect us to believe that, do you?'

'Maybe not,' Poldarn said, 'but you don't have to. You can do that mind-reading trick, can't you?'

'Not on you,' said another of the strangers. 'You're all barricaded up. Eyvind told us you're a freak.'

'Not on me,' Poldarn said patiently. 'One of the others. Look inside their heads, you'll see I'm telling the truth.'

But the stranger who'd spoken first shook his head. 'We don't trust you,' he said. 'There could be all sorts of reasons. Maybe it's just you who hid the horses, and you've had these people out looking for them, believing they're lost. Or maybe you can do things to their minds – there's no knowing what sort of tricks you're capable of. Aren't you the one who knew the mountain was going to blow up before it even happened?'

Poldarn sighed. 'The horses got out,' he said. 'We went looking for them, but we can't find any trace of them. That's all there is to it.'

'That's not very likely,' one of the strangers said. 'There'd be some tracks, no matter what. Ten horses don't just vanish. Not unless they get a lot of help.'

'Listen.' Poldarn sat down on the bench, gently pushing a stranger aside and making him move down. 'We're tired and hungry, we've just wasted two days chasing after horses that don't even belong to us, which you left here without even asking permission. You can believe us or not, that's up to you, but in any event, go away. We aren't in the mood.'

'It's dark,' one of them said. 'We can't go back round the mountain in the dark, it'd be asking for trouble.'

'Fine, then you can stay here. Just shut up and let us go to bed.'

The stranger who'd spoken first stood up. 'He's lying,' he said. 'Otherwise he wouldn't shut off his mind like that, obviously he's got something to hide. He knows perfectly well where the horses are.'

'Sit down, for God's sake,' Poldarn said. 'You're getting on my nerves.'

The stranger hesitated for a moment, then sat down. 'Look,' he said, 'we haven't got any quarrel with you, but if we go back without those bloody horses, Eyvind'll skin us alive. You don't want him for an enemy. Trust me, I've known him a long time.'

'Funny,' Boarci said to nobody in particular, 'I wouldn't have called throwing us out of our own house all that friendly. Still, you folks in these parts have some pretty strange ways.'

'Boarci, shut up,' Poldarn said. 'Listen to me,' he went on, looking the stranger in the eye. 'If I knew where the horses are, I'd tell you. I don't want to pick a fight with Eyvind or anybody else. If you think we've got them hidden somewhere, please go ahead and look. Take all the time you need, make a really thorough search. Tell me what you want us to do to prove to you that we haven't got them, and we'll do it. Now, is that fair, or what?'

The stranger pulled a tragic face. 'I can't go back and tell him that,' he said. 'The bloody things have got to be somewhere. For God's sake, quit fooling around. This sort of thing just doesn't happen here.'

'I know why we couldn't find them,' put in one of the other strangers. 'It's damned obvious, when you think about it. Like, when we left them here they didn't have any food. They've killed them and eaten them, for sure.'

Poldarn would have laughed out loud, except that he remembered what Boarci had said on the first evening. 'Don't be ridiculous,' he said. 'We wouldn't do that.'

'Oh really?' The stranger leant forward across the table. 'So what *have* you been eating, then? Tell me that.'

'Roast venison, mostly,' Boarci said with a yawn. 'Also goose, duck, pheasant, stuff like that. Better than what you've been eating, I'll bet. What's for dinner at Haldersness these days, boys? Porridge and onions?'

The expression on the strangers' faces suggested that Boarci was probably right. 'Bullshit,' one of them said. 'There's no game in this valley; I lived here all my life, never seen a deer closer than a mile away.'

Boarci grinned. 'That I can believe, he said. 'You're too fat and dumb to get closer than a mile to any deer, unless it's dead already.'

Poldarn scowled at him, then said, 'It's since the mountain blew up, it's driven the deer down from the high ground. There's quite a lot of them about, thank God. Otherwise yes, we'd have had a hard time of it. If you like, I'll take you out back and you can see the bones in the midden.'

'Sure,' the stranger muttered. 'Horse bones. Maybe we can take a few back to Eyvind. He'd be interested in seeing them, I'll bet.'

'If he's so dumb he can't tell horse bones from deer bones—' Boarci started to say, but Poldarn interrupted him with a furious glare. 'Once and for all,' he said, 'we haven't eaten your goddamned horses. We haven't hidden them away, we don't know where they are, otherwise we'd give them to you and get you out of our lives. That's the truth, and you can tell Eyvind what the hell you like.' He stood up, and the rest of his household stood up with him. 'Now,' he went on, 'you're welcome to stay the night here, in the barn, or you can be on your way tonight, whichever you like. Meanwhile, we're very tired and we want to have our dinner and go to bed.'

The strangers looked at each other. 'You're making a big mistake,' one of them said.

'Maybe,' Poldarn replied. 'Don't suppose it'd be the first time, or the last. But my offer still stands: you tell us what we've got to do to convince you and we'll do it. But if you aren't going to take me up on it, you can go to the barn, or you can set off home. Is that clear?'

After a long pause the strangers stood up, all but one of them. He folded his arms across his chest and said, 'I'm not budging from here till you tell us what you've done with the horses.'

His companions shifted uneasily, and one of them gestured to him to get up. He ignored the signals and pulled a face that was presumably intended to express irresistible resolve, though Poldarn reckoned it just looked silly.

'Come on, Terfin,' one of the other strangers said. 'Let Eyvind deal with these clowns – it's not worth it.'

'Screw you,' Terfin said angrily.

Poldarn was trying not to laugh; but suddenly Boarci darted forwards, grabbed Terfin's arm, twisted it savagely behind his back until he screamed, and hauled him to his feet. 'Ciartan told you to leave,' he said quietly. 'Are you deaf as well as stupid?'

'Boarci, let him go, for God's sake,' Poldarn shouted; but Boarci was grinning. 'It's all right,' he said, 'he's just leaving, him and his pals. And if I ever see them round here again, they'll be going home on their backs. You got that?' One of the other strangers started to move, but Boarci twisted Terfin's arm a little further, making him howl like a cat.

Poldarn closed his eyes. 'Boarci,' he said, 'you let that man go or you'll need somewhere else to live. Whatever it is you think you're doing, it isn't helping.'

Boarci laughed, and pushed Terfin across the room. He hit the wall and fell down. 'I'm not afraid of any little turd like that,' he said.

'No,' Poldarn said, 'but I am, and I don't give a shit who knows it. You,' he said to the strangers, 'get out now, before this gets any worse. And you,' he went on, turning to Boarci, 'I'll forgive you this once, because of how you saved me from the bear. But if you ever do anything like that again, I'll throw you out of here so fast your head'll spin.'

Boarci grinned; the strangers left without a word, and a moment or so later Poldarn could hear them mounting up in the yard. He sighed, and rested his head on his elbows. Nobody spoke for a long time.

'Well,' Elja said, 'that could have gone better.'

'You think so?' Boarci yawned. 'I'd say we handled it pretty well, considering.'

For a moment Poldarn wanted to hit him, but he was too tired. 'I meant what I said,' he told him. 'One more stunt like that and you're out. Do you understand me?' But Boarci only grinned, and asked what was for dinner.

'Well, there's the pheasant,' Elja said, 'and those revolting looking fungus things. Or there's the last pickings off that hare from the day before yesterday. Or I suppose I could fix up some soup.'

Raffen looked up. 'What kind of soup?' he said.

'No particular kind,' Elja replied. 'Just soup.'

'In that case,' Raffen replied, 'I suggest you make it the pheasant. What're you groaning at?' he added, as Asburn let out a long sigh. 'Got the guts-ache or something?'

Asburn shook his head. 'Nothing,' he replied. 'I was just thinking of all that salt beef we got off that up-country type. What I wouldn't give for a plate of that right now.'

Boarci made a show of being offended. 'What, better than fresh roast venison?' he growled. 'Some people are just plain ignorant.'

'I like salt beef,' Asburn replied plaintively. 'All this wildlife stuff's all very well, I guess, but it's not what you'd call proper food. Salt beef, some good strong cheese and a big fat chunk of new bread; now *that*'s what I call food.'

Boarci shook his head sadly. 'You'll just have to dream,' he said. 'Now,' he went on, 'I know where I can get you a nice neck fillet of horse—'

'That's very funny, Boarci,' Poldarn said. 'You could die laughing at a joke like that. All right,' he went on, 'let's have the pheasant and the poison mushrooms, and then for God's sake let's go to bed and get some sleep.'

Later, when they were lying alone together in the dark, Elja asked him: 'What do you suppose Eyvind'll do now?'

Poldarn stared up at the roof. 'I don't know,' he replied. 'From what I know of him, he'd be prepared to leave the business with the horses. Whether he believes us or not, he's got more sense than to pick a fight over something trivial. And he's got all *my* horses, those and his own are more than he needs. It's not in his nature to quarrel with his own kind, even with a freak like me.'

'Ah,' Elja said drowsily. 'So that's all right, then.'

But Poldarn shook his head. 'It's not the horses I'm worried about,' he said. 'It's Boarci starting a fight with that man. You can be sure they'll tell Eyvind all about that; they'll want to make a big deal about it so he won't think too much about them coming home empty-handed. If they make it sound like we slung them out, Eyvind won't take that well, it'll offend his sense of what's right. It's us freaks beating up on regular folks, it'll get him worried and angry. The point is, he's afraid of me. He thinks I made the mountain blow up.'

'He's an idiot,' Elja mumbled.

'Maybe.' Poldarn sighed. 'But he feels responsible, because he brought me here, and ever since then, nothing's been the way it ought to be. First the mountain blew up, then I was telling people what to do, and now I'm stealing horses and beating up his men when he asks for them back.

If I was going out of my way to make him afraid of me, I couldn't have done a better job.'

'Then it's your own silly fault,' Elja said. 'Next time, think carefully before you go setting off any volcanoes.'

Poldarn shifted, but he couldn't get comfortable. The blanket felt hot and heavy. 'I wish I understood him better,' he said. 'It's like I can see one half of him but not the other. This is all going wrong, just when I thought I was making some sense of it.'

Elja yawned, and pulled the blanket over to her side of the bed. 'Shut up and go to sleep,' she said.

Chapter Twenty-Four

A week went by, and every day Poldarn did his arithmetic – a day and a half for them to get back to
Ciartanstead, two at the most; a day for Eyvind to get
his people organised; a day and a half to ride over here, two
at the most – and every morning he adjusted the variables
like a good actuary, allowing half a day here for a house
meeting, a day there for making weapons or other such
preparations, a day lost because of a stream in spate or a
blocked ford. By the end of the week he was convinced that
Eyvind was either coming with a fully equipped army, or he
wasn't coming at all.

Eight days, and no sign of him. Nine days, and Poldarn
allowed himself to tip the balance ever so slightly in favour of
the second hypothesis. Ten days, and he found that he
needed to exercise considerable ingenuity to stay worried. A
fortnight, and he'd have been able to dismiss the whole incident from his mind – if Boarci hadn't gone missing.

He'd set off one morning, early, before anybody else had
been awake, and they'd assumed that he was out killing
things, as usual. At dinner time, Raffen said that Boarci had

probably decided to sleep out on a trail so as to catch a particularly large and juicy buck on its way to its morning feed. At noon the next day, Asburn wondered if Boarci had fallen down somewhere on the mountain and damaged his leg. That night, nobody mentioned him at all, and conversation was generally subdued.

'It's just the sort of solution Eyvind would go for,' Poldarn told Elja, as they got ready for bed. 'Rather than pick a quarrel with all of us because of what Boarci did to that man, he's decided to make it a personal thing, himself and Boarci. It's quite clever thinking, actually, because after all, Boarci's the outsider, we wouldn't be under any real obligation to take the matter further. Eyvind knows he's got to do something, but he's giving us a way out of having to hit back.'

Elja nodded. 'Or maybe Boarci's slipped on loose shale and twisted his ankle,' she said. 'Or he's got bored with being in the one place for so long and gone off somewhere else. He's a drifter, it's what they do.'

'He wouldn't just go, without saying a word.'

'You reckon?' Elja shook her head. 'I think it's exactly what he'd do. And even if I'm wrong, there's another way of looking at it. Suppose he got to worrying about what he'd started, and he figured that the best thing he could do is clear out. That way, Eyvind can't touch him, because he can't find him; and Eyvind won't bother us, because we can say it was all Boarci's fault, nothing to do with us. Solves the problem neatly, don't you think?'

Poldarn hadn't thought of that. 'That's not like him at all,' he said. 'His idea of sorting out the mess would be going over there and planting an axe between Eyvind's eyebrows.' He paused. 'God,' he said, 'let's just pray he hasn't, or we really *are* in trouble.'

He slept badly that night, and was woken up out of a mystifying dream by the sound of horses in the yard outside. He jumped up and groped in the dark for the axe he'd put beside the bed the previous evening. Instead, he caught hold of Elja's toe, and got sworn at.

'Shut up,' he hissed, 'they're here. Horses, in the yard. Can't you hear?'

That woke her up. 'Maybe it's the missing horses,' she whispered. 'Maybe they found their own way home.'

Poldarn didn't answer. He felt his way along the wall with his hands, looking for the door. It took him far too long to find it; by then, the rest of the household was awake. He could hear someone unbolting the door, calling out, 'Who's there?' Not a sound tactical move, he thought.

'It's all right,' replied a familiar voice. 'It's only me.'

'Bloody hell,' Poldarn whispered under his breath. Then he found the door and pushed through it.

'Boarci,' he shouted, 'for crying out loud. Where have you been?'

Someone had managed to get a lamp lit. It was only a little one, squidged out of stream-bed clay and fitted with a rush wick, but it gave just enough light to show Boarci's face, grinning. 'Ciartanstead,' he said. 'And I've brought you all a present. Anybody going to help me get it in from the cart, or have I got to do every damn thing myself?'

'What cart?' Poldarn asked, but nobody was listening to him. A moment or so later, they were all helping him to haul a big, fat, strangely familiar barrel in through the doorway.

'Is that . . .?' Asburn said, in a voice quiet with wonder.

'Yes,' Boarci replied. 'And don't say I never do anything for you.'

It was one of Hart's salt-beef barrels. There was a rope tied round the top and another round the base. It hadn't been opened, though one of the staves was cracked, and the pickle was seeping through.

'Well, don't all thank me at once,' Boarci said.

Poldarn found that extreme anger made him talk softly. 'Where did you get that from?' he asked.

'From Ciartanstead,' Boarci replied. 'Where else?'

'I see.' Poldarn nodded. 'I thought for a moment you might have run into Hart and traded it for something. So you went over there and stole it.'

Raffen laughed. 'Wasn't stealing,' he said. 'It's our salt beef' Then he caught Poldarn's eye and shut up rapidly.

'Yes,' Boarci said. 'After they had the nerve to come over here, saying we were telling lies about their fucking horses. Also, Asburn said he fancied some salt beef.'

'Fine,' Poldarn said. 'Now, what's this about a cart? Where did it come from?'

'Same place,' Boarci said. 'Actually, it's not a cart, just the old trap.'

'So as well as stealing the beef,' Poldarn purred, 'you stole the trap and the horses.'

Boarci grinned. 'I found the trap out on the mountain road,' he said. 'Wheel'd come off, they'd ditched it. In open ground. I call that salvage, not stealing.'

'Actually, he's right,' Rook put in; then he shut up, as well.

'I found it,' Boarci went on, 'and I put the wheel back on – bloody fools don't know how to fix a busted cotter-pin out of an old nail, don't deserve to have a decent trap. The rule is, if you find something that's been ditched and you fix it up, it's yours to hang on to and use till the owner squares up with you for your time and trouble. Always been that way, hasn't it?'

The rest of the household seemed to agree, but they did so in dead silence. The only person who didn't seem to feel the tension was Boarci himself.

'So you fixed the cart,' Poldarn said. 'Then you went down to the farm and stole the horses, and then you used them to steal the barrel.'

Boarci shook his head. 'Catch me being so obvious,' he replied. 'Can't go stealing horses, they'd miss 'em and get upset. Different, of course, if you just happen to find a string of horses wandering about on the hill. Same rules as the trap, you see.'

'You found the horses—' Poldarn stopped abruptly and stood with his mouth open for a heartbeat or so, until his composure returned. 'All that time those men were here, and you knew where the bloody things were.'

'Don't talk soft,' Boarci replied cheerfully. 'It was after they'd pissed off home I found the horses. I was right, you see, they *had* been down in the combes there. That's why I went back, to see if I could pick up the trail. One of you lot must've walked right past it, I could see a man's trail clear as anything. So I followed it up, right onto the mountain, and there the buggers were, in a little fold beside the small rill.'

Poldarn nodded. 'But you didn't bring them back,' he said. 'You decided you'd steal them instead.'

'No, actually.' Boarci perched on the corner of the table. 'I thought, I'll take them back to Ciartanstead and that'll clear everything up. So I set off, and next thing I found was the trap, like I told you. Well, that was too good to miss, so I fixed it and carried on; and when I got there – it was just before dawn, nobody about, the idle bastards – I suddenly thought, I wonder if that barrel of beef's still there; you know,' he added, looking at Poldarn, 'the one you stashed away from the rest of us, in the back shed.'

This time, everyone looked at Poldarn. He was tempted to explain, because they were giving him those kind of looks and he'd hoped he'd seen the last of them; but he decided against it.

'So I thought,' Boarci went on, 'it's a dead certainty they don't know it's there; after all, nobody knew about it except you and Hart, and me because I just happened to see you sneaking it in there, all furtive. Well, it was still there, so I got some rope and some timbers and made up a sort of rough block-and-tackle; and here we are. And the joy of it is, they don't even know they've been robbed. Now we can take the horses back, and the trap too, and say, excuse me but we think these belong to you, all innocent and virtuous, and that'll put *that* right; and meanwhile, we're up a barrel of beef, just when it'll do us the most good. Now, is that neat, or what?'

Poldarn didn't know what to say. Inside, he knew what he had to do. He had to tell Boarci to leave the house and never come back. But why? Boarci had done a stupid thing, put all their lives at risk, but he'd done his stupid thing in such a clever way that it seemed pretty well certain that he'd got away with it, and all for their sakes; there was the barrel, crammed with Hart's exceedingly fine salt beef, at a time when they desperately needed it. It wasn't as though Boarci had acted selfishly; he'd been putting food on the table for them ever since they'd got there, and now he'd done it again, in style, as well as finding the wretched, elusive horses and given Poldarn a wonderful opportunity to snatch back the moral upper hand. It was a daring exploit, not a bloody stupid thing to do; at least, that was how everybody else in the house was taking it. Everybody except himself.

But Poldarn knew what he ought to do; not because of the risk, but because he'd told Boarci not to pull any more stunts after his fight with Terfen, and Boarci had disobeyed him. That was unforgivable, an abomination; things like that didn't happen here, because the hands didn't disobey orders, because heads of households didn't give orders for them to break. God, Poldarn thought, I'm starting to think like Eyvind. As if that's a bad thing, in this country.

'Well,' Elja said, 'what're you going to do? We can't give it back, if that's what you're thinking. If we give it back, we've got to tell them we stole it. And anyhow,' she said, 'what were you doing hiding it away in the first place?'

'It was for you,' Poldarn said at once. 'I could see you were sick to death of porridge and leeks. And the salt beef was getting eaten so fast, I wanted to make sure there'd be some left for you by the time you got back.'

'Oh.' Elja looked at him, and shrugged. 'Well, next time I'll thank you not to make me your accomplice without asking me first. Anyway, all's well that ends well: we're a barrel of beef to the good, thanks to Boarci. Now, I suggest we let the matter drop and go back to bed.'

No, Poldarn thought, we can't do that, it's far too serious. If we just forget about it, there'll be big trouble in the end. 'All right,' he said, 'let's do that. Only, please,' he added, grabbing Boarci by the arm as he passed, 'I want you to give me your word that you won't do any more stuff like that. We got away with it this time, but we won't be so lucky again.'

'Sure,' Boarci replied with a grin. 'Whatever you say.'

A few hours later, they were up and about again, and they had to choose who was going to take the horses and the trap back to Ciartanstead. Much to Poldarn's annoyance, Boarci claimed the right, since he'd found them. 'I want to see the look on their faces,' he explained, and apparently everyone apart from Poldarn reckoned that was fair enough.

'All right,' Poldarn said. 'But in that case I'm going with you, just to make sure you don't get tempted to play any more games while you're there. Is that all right with you?'

Boarci shrugged. 'Whatever,' he replied. 'Just us two? Or do you want anybody else along?'

'Two men out for four days is bad enough,' Poldarn said. 'We can't spare any more than that, not with all the work we've got on. Do you want to drive the trap, or would you rather ride and lead the horses?'

Boarci thought for a moment. 'I'll ride,' he said. 'The springs on that trap are shot. I'd rather stay behind than get shaken to death.'

'Suit yourself,' Poldarn said. 'All right, we'll be as quick as we can. But remember, we're going to have to walk back, so expect us when you see us.'

Packing didn't take long and, once assembled, their luggage proved to be light, the food bag in particular. They left quickly, without fuss, as if they were just going as far as the top of the yard.

'Don't know about you,' Boarci said, as they laboured up the mountain, 'but I'm getting sick to the teeth of this trip. Maybe they've got the ford open again.'

'Or maybe not,' Poldarn replied. 'And in any case, this way's quicker than skirting the edge. I want to get there and get back as soon as possible, if it's all the same to you.'

Boarci laughed. 'You didn't have to come at all,' he said. 'I'm perfectly capable of delivering a few horses. Or you could've sent Raffen with me, or one of the others.'

'You know perfectly well why I'm here. For your sake as much as mine. You ask for trouble so much, one of these days somebody's going to oblige you.'

Boarci laughed.

They made good time, as it happened, reaching Ciartanstead an hour before noon the next day. It felt strange to see the place again; now it looked remarkably foreign, so that Poldarn had trouble remembering that he'd built the house with his own hands. Eyvind had made changes; not great ones, but enough to set his mark there. The cider house was gone, and where it had stood there was a handsome new long barn, built mostly of stone and roofed with turf. 'Someone's been thinking sensibly about the next time the mountain blows its top,' Boarci said. 'That Eyvind's brighter than you'd give him credit for. We could do something like that back home; there's plenty of good building stone in the lower combes.'

Poldarn agreed; the same thought had occurred to him more than once, but he hadn't dared suggest it, because it would be too different, and probably an abomination – coming from him, at least. 'That's new,' he said, pointing to a long cultivated strip that started just below the north wall of the house. 'Something else we should have thought of. I can't remember – what was there before?'

'The smithy,' Boarci replied. 'Fancy you forgetting that.'

'Of course.' Poldarn looked round, but there was no sign of anybody. 'Where have they all got to?' he said aloud. 'This time of day, there ought to be loads of people about the place.'

Boarci nodded. 'My guess is,' he said, 'they're out the other side of the house. Eyvind's building a smoke-house, or he was a few days ago when I was last here. I guess they're raising the frames or something.'

Boarci was right. The whole household – the old Bollesknap outfit, and most of the former Haldersness and Ciartanstead houses – were there, pulling on ropes and lifting timbers, with nobody giving orders or directing the work. For an outsider, it was an amazing sight to see. As soon as they'd finished the stage they were working on, they stopped and turned to stare at Poldarn and Boarci. That was unnerving, to say the least.

After what felt like a very long time, Eyvind emerged from the crowd and walked slowly towards them. He looked different too; more solid, somehow, slower and more assertive in his movements, as if every step had to be taken seriously. Poldarn noticed a new, fresh scar on his right arm, and wondered how he'd come by it.

'You,' he said, and Poldarn realised he was talking to Boarci. 'You must be out of your mind coming here.'

'Maybe,' Boarci replied, grinning. 'We've found your horses, look. And your trap, the one your men broke and left for dead. We've even put the wheel back on for you.'

But Eyvind just stood looking at him, clearly trying to choose between various courses of action. The decision must have been a difficult one, to judge by the unease in his face.

'Boarci found the trap on the mountain,' Poldarn said, with the uncomfortable feeling that nobody was listening to him. 'We brought it straight back. You can have it, we don't want anything for finding it or doing the wheel.'

Eyvind wrestled with his decision silently for a while longer, then made a small gesture with his head. At once, a dozen or so men surged forward. One of them grabbed the reins of the trap; two more stood either side of Boarci's horse, while a third took hold of its bridle. A fourth pulled Boarci's spear out of its bucket on the saddle and levelled it in a vaguely menacing manner.

'Take him to the barn and bar the door,' Eyvind said. 'We'll have to decide what to do with him later.'

'Hold on,' Poldarn said urgently. 'What the hell is all this about?'

Eyvind scowled at him. 'All right,' he said, 'maybe you don't know, at that. Anyhow, I'll give you the benefit of the doubt. Your man, this one, came sneaking over here a few days back and stole a barrel of salt beef. One of my men saw him at it, but he was long gone by the time he could raise the alarm. He's going to have to pay for that.'

Poldarn felt cold. His own stupid fault, he told himself, for assuming that they'd got away with it just because Eyvind hadn't come storming over the hill with weapons. 'I did know about it,' he said, 'after the event. Boarci told me.'

'Doesn't matter,' Eyvind replied sharply. 'I'm choosing to see it as your man acting off his own hook, so I won't have to take action against the rest of you. Count yourself very lucky,' he added. 'And I won't be so forbearing again.'

Poldarn could feel the blood pounding in his arms and hands. Any moment now, he knew, something could happen that would set off the instincts he knew lay buried deep inside him; someone would try to grab hold of him or pull him down off the cart, and he'd strike out before he had time to stop himself. He didn't know much about the man who'd lived in his body before Poldarn had inherited it, that day he'd woken up in the mud beside the Bohec; but he'd come to know a little about how he reacted to perceived danger. He was afraid of himself, far more than he was afraid of Eyvind or his people.

Distracted as Poldarn was, he didn't actually see what happened, only the aftermath. Afterwards, in his mind's eye and in recurring dreams, he figured out that it must have started when someone tried to pull Boarci down off his horse. Boarci must have pulled his axe out from inside his coat – he generally carried it concealed, even among friends – and struck out, catching the man in the forehead, just above the bridge of the nose. Immediately, the man who'd confiscated Boarci's spear tried to stab him with it, but apparently Boarci had anticipated that and dodged sideways, trying to slip off the horse and run. Unfortunately he couldn't have seen the man who stepped up on his blind side, intending to force him to surrender by prodding him with a four-tine hay-fork. The outcome was that Boarci slid onto the fork; two of the tines passed through his neck on either side of the spine, killing him instantly. By the time Poldarn realised that something was happening it was nearly all over; the man with the fork was staggering backwards, carrying Boarci's substantial weight on the fork handle, like a youngster showing off by trying to pitch a stook that was far too heavy for him. After a moment of agonised stillness he let go of the handle and Boarci flopped out of the saddle onto the ground, knocking another man off his feet and landing on top of him.

Everybody held perfectly still; it was as though they were unable to accept what they'd just seen – two men killed in a matter of seconds by their own kind. It was the same sort of bewildered horror Poldarn had noticed when the mountain had first erupted, the sort of reaction you'd expect if some malignant and terrifying supernatural creature had suddenly appeared in the middle of the farmyard, without warning.

Quite calm inside, Poldarn weighed up the options available to him. The men who were supposed to be marking him were looking the other way; it'd be easy for him, with his proven abilities in this field, to get past them, take a weapon away from one of them, and kill three or four men before anybody could be ready to oppose him; there was a good chance, better than evens, that he'd be able to get to Eyvind, and he knew he was Eyvind's match with weapons any day of the week. He could kill him, or use him as a hostage, to be sure of getting clear. Or he could go the other way, make for the man with the hay-fork and kill him – that'd be easier, there were fewer people in the way and they were all in a state of profound shock, no real opposition at all. After he'd killed the man with the fork he could take a hostage – really, any of them would do just as well as Eyvind, nobody would be expendable – and get out just as easily, if not more so. Either way, he'd need a horse (but he could demand that, with a hostage, and be sure of getting what he asked for) and a good head start if he wanted to reach Poldarn's Forge in time to organise some vestige of a defence. That would be difficult but – given how well he'd come to know the road across the mountain – by no means impossible. As to whether he should try and fight his pursuers at the Forge or tell his people to get up the mountain and hide there (no chance of them outrunning Eyvind's people, with only one horse), Poldarn wasn't able to reach a quick decision. It was all reasonable enough up to that point, but thereafter it could turn out very badly.

On the other hand, he didn't have to kill anybody at all. It was good to have that option to fall back on, it made a pleasant change. He realised that he didn't really want to kill anyone, or at least not now, under such adverse conditions. If he didn't (leaving aside issues of retribution for the time being) he couldn't guarantee his own temporary safety with a hostage, but he wouldn't be setting up a far more dangerous situation further down the line. He asked himself: Is it likely that if I sit still and do nothing, they'll kill me or do me any harm? On balance he concluded no, the crowd wasn't in that sort of mood; if anything, they were less likely to harm him now than they had been before Boarci was killed. On the other hand, he couldn't just slip away – the men marking him were too close and too well placed for him to be able to get by them without violence; and his own condition was such that if he had to fight to get past them, he couldn't be sure of being able to use only limited, non-lethal force.

So, what should he be looking to do? All things considered, the best odds lay with staying exactly where he was and waiting to see what they'd do next. His first priority, after all, was getting out of there and home in one piece. Killing the pitchfork man would be pointless, since the fellow was just some unfortunate clown who'd happened to get in the way. Killing Eyvind was definitely something Poldarn would like to do at some stage, but not enough to warrant taking unnecessary risks with his own life or the lives of the eleven people at Poldarn's Forge. Finally, on basic and fundamental principles, he wasn't willing to commit himself to a course of action without being at least fairly sure that he could predict what Eyvind was likely to do next; quite simply, he didn't have the faintest idea what the accepted protocol was in a case like this, assuming that there was one. To embark on any course, especially a drastic and irrevocable one, in the absence of such elementary data would be thoroughly irresponsible. Furthermore, there was a chance, albeit a remote one, that Eyvind might misjudge his response and commit a tactical error that could be exploited at some point in the future. With everything except instinctive anger pointing towards a policy of cautious observation, Poldarn resolved to stay where he was and do nothing.

No sooner had he arrived at this conclusion than Eyvind turned round and faced him. 'I'm sorry,' he said. 'I didn't mean for that to happen.'

Poldarn took a deep breath before answering. 'No,' he said, 'I don't suppose you did.'

They'd pulled Boarci's body clear of the man he'd knocked down. Poldarn stood up on the box of the trap, and they made way for him. He went over and looked down at Boarci's face, with its wide-open eyes and slightly parted lips. One more stunt like this, he thought, but it was only fair to say that he didn't think Boarci had intended it to turn out like this. He felt like a small boy whose friend has thrown a stone and broken a slat in the fence, and then run off and left him to face the anger of the grown-ups.

'The other man,' he said. 'I suppose he's dead, too.'

Someone nodded, and Poldarn threaded his way through the crowd to look at him. He recognised the face, with its incongruous bloody mark gouged out of the forehead: it was Scild, one of the Haldersness field hands who'd chosen to stay home; formerly one of his own, until he'd chosen to forfeit the obligation.

When he'd seen enough he turned round to face Eyvind. 'Right,' he said. 'What happens now? I'm afraid I don't know the right procedure.'

Eyvind looked like he wasn't too sure of it himself, but he wasn't going to admit anything of the kind in front of his household. 'There's got to be some sort of settlement, obviously,' he said. 'Normally, I think the thing to do would be to set off your man against mine – we can forget about the theft, obviously, since that was Boarci's business, not something between our houses.' He paused there, clearly hoping Poldarn would agree; but Poldarn kept quiet and said nothing. 'On the other hand,' Eyvind went on, 'it's arguable that my man provoked the whole thing by trying to lay hands on your man; your man overreacted, I think we can agree on that, but I'm prepared to accept the extra blame, in the circumstances.'

Poldarn stayed quiet, and dipped his head slightly to mark

his agreement. Eyvind swallowed, and went on: 'In which case, I'd be agreeable to waiving any claim for Scild and offering a full settlement on Boarci – which is generous, I'd say, since he was an offcomer, not a regular household man – with all other issues stayed. Does that sound reasonable to you?'

'I think so,' Poldarn said. 'As I told you, I'm not familiar with the way these things are handled, so I'm having to rely on you to do what's right. But I think I can take your word for it.'

'Good.' Eyvind didn't seem overjoyed at the rather grudging praise; chances were that he felt he'd been more than generous in the circumstances, and was annoyed that Poldarn hadn't acknowledged the fact. 'In that case, how would you like to fix the amount of the settlement? We can do it here and now, or if you prefer we can find someone to arbitrate. I don't mind.'

'Let's get it over and done with,' Poldarn replied. 'What did you have in mind?'

Eyvind frowned, thinking on his feet. 'What about this?' he said. 'First, you can have the trap and the horses. On top of that, I'd suggest five barrels of salt beef and five barrels of oats, say a dozen blankets, and twenty yards of the ordinary wool cloth. And for good measure I'll throw in the dead man's personal things, all the stuff that was confiscated when we moved in here. Will that do, do you think?'

Poldarn made a show of giving it careful thought, as though he was doing long division in his head. 'I won't argue with that,' he said. 'I don't know what the going rate is, obviously, but I'm sure you aren't going to try and cheat me or anything like that. Mostly I'd like to get things settled as quickly and quietly as possible, so we can put all this behind us. I'd just like to remind you that I didn't start this quarrel, not intentionally at any rate, and I really don't want to see it continue, let alone get worse. Losing a man means a great deal more to our house than to yours, obviously; we're so much smaller than you are, and Boarci was our hunter – he was pretty much feeding us single-handedly, until the first crops came in. On that basis, the beef and the oats should tide us over, if we're careful, so yes, it's a fair deal. I'll be glad to accept it, on the understanding that it puts everything square between us.'

'That's exactly what I want too,' Eyvind said, obviously relieved. 'It's very bad that something like this had to happen, but it's good that we're able to deal with it in a reasonable manner, like sensible people.'

It took a fair amount of ingenuity and patience to get the beef barrels loaded onto the trap, and even more to rig up frames so that the horses could carry the oats and the rest of the stuff. But they managed it somehow, and found a way to fasten the horses' leading rein to the bed of the trap. 'Take it slowly and you should be all right,' the man who'd done the fixing told him. 'And they're good steady horses, shouldn't give you any trouble on the way back.'

The last horse in the string carried Boarci's body, slung over the saddle like a carpet or other saleable merchandise. As for his few possessions, Poldarn stowed them in between the barrels in the trap; all except Boarci's axe, the rather scruffy one Poldarn had made for him before they left Ciartanstead; Poldarn tucked it through his belt and drew his coat round it to conceal it.

His journey home was quick and uneventful, and he arrived at Poldarn's Forge in mid-afternoon. They were surprised to see him back so soon. They were even more surprised to see the horses and the trap. They asked where Boarci was.

'He's dead,' Poldarn replied, easing himself off the trap box. He was painfully stiff after several days driving a trap with defective suspension, and the last thing he wanted to do was talk to anybody or explain anything. Clearly, though, he had no choice. 'He was killed by one of Eyvind's people.' (He didn't say who, or that the killer had been a Haldersness man. Best to keep it simple, for now.)

The household received the news in stunned silence, pretty much as Poldarn had expected. By now it was pretty apparent that killings – homicide, murder, whatever you chose to call it – simply didn't happen here. It was as if he'd told them that the sky had opened and Boarci had been lifted up into the courts of heaven on the back of a snow-white eagle. 'It was partly his fault,' he went on. 'Apparently, someone saw him taking that barrel; they started to grab hold of him, he lashed out with his axe and stoved somebody's head in; then he tried to get away and fell on a hay-fork somebody happened to be holding. It was more of an accident, really.'

Now at least they believed him, but they still couldn't understand. 'Then what happened?' Elja asked.

Poldarn sighed, and sat down on the porch. 'Oh, Eyvind offered compensation for him, and they gave us some barrels of beef and oats, plus the horses and the trap. Then I came home.'

Raffen had noticed the corpse-sized lump under a blanket, slung over the back of one of the horses. He didn't say anything, but pretty soon they were all staring at it.

'Anyway,' Poldarn went on, 'that's about the size of it. There's some cloth, too, and some blankets – useful stuff. Oh, and his things, everything they took from him when they moved in. Would someone else mind doing the unloading? I'm dead on my feet.'

Automatically, Raffen and Asburn slipped away and set to work. The rest of the household stayed exactly where they were, silent and motionless, like tools on a rack. Poldarn decided he couldn't be doing with any more of that, so he went inside and lay down on the bed. Very soon he was fast asleep.

As he slept, he found himself once again on the box of the

trap; except that it was now a cart, and the back was full of dead crows. He couldn't imagine what he could be doing (that in itself had a familiar feel to it) carting a load of carrion down what appeared to be a long, straight, dusty road across a dry moor; but he knew that, just beyond the ridge to his left, the moor fell away steeply into the Bohec valley, and that his job was to deliver his cargo to the Falx house in Mael Bohec. That made sense; after all, he was just a courier, it wasn't his business to know what he was carrying or why.

The crows were talking behind his back, which was annoying, but he couldn't be bothered to make anything of it.

'What about you?' one of them said. 'You're new, aren't you?'

'Just got in,' another one replied. The voice was, of course, familiar.

'What happened to you, then?' asked a third voice.

'My own silly fault,' said the voice he recognised. 'Tried to start a fight where I was surrounded. Got jabbed in the neck with a fork, would you believe. Bloody ridiculous way to die, but there it is.'

Several of the crows cackled, but the first voice said gravely: 'I never heard where there was a good way. Doesn't matter, anyhow. Here we all are, and there's an end to it.'

'True enough,' the familiar voice said. 'So, how about you?'

'Oh, I just keeled over and turned up my toes,' the first voice said; and it too was familiar, now that he thought about it. 'Died of a broken heart, you could say, though really it was just overdoing it. That and the worry, with the mountain blowing up and all. Tried to do more than was good for me at my age.'

'Accident, then?' asked the second voice.

'Misadventure,' the first voice replied, 'same as you. Same as the rest of us, if the truth be told. Like, he didn't kill any of us because he hated us, or anything like that. No, we just happened to get in the way, or we were soldiers in a battle trying to do our job, and met him trying to do his, or we were living in a city that had to be burned down and all the people killed so there'd be no witnesses. He never kills anybody for a bad reason, such as because he hates them. Mostly he doesn't even want to hurt them, particularly. We all just happened to be in the wrong place at the wrong time.'

'It's usually to do with what side you're on,' put in another voice. 'It's like we're on one side, wanting to eat the corn or the peas or whatever, and he's on the other side, wanting to keep 'em safe. Or else we're defending our homes or our friends or our leaders, whatever, and he's on the attacking side. Nothing personal in it, it's just the way things are.'

'Sounds fair enough to me,' commented the second voice. 'Sure are a lot of us, though.'

'I think he leads an unhappy life,' said a fourth voice. 'At least, he's always getting into trouble and danger and having to cut his way out again. I kind of feel sorry for him, actually.'

Poldarn felt something brush against his shoulder, and saw that there was someone with him on the box. It was the man he'd killed shortly after he first woke up beside the river, the original god in the cart. 'Don't mind them,' he said. 'They just chatter on. Don't mean anything by it.'

Poldarn frowned. 'But they're making it sound like I killed them all,' he said. 'And that's not right. Boarci got killed by one of Eyvind's people. And Halder's heart stopped when I wasn't even there.'

The god laughed. 'Oh, you killed them all right,' he said. 'But it doesn't matter. You didn't mean anything by it, same as they don't. I mean, if we held a grudge, would I be sitting here talking to you like this?'

'I suppose not,' Poldarn conceded. 'In your case it was simple self-defence.'

'Sure.' The god grinned sheepishly. 'I was smashed out of my head, and I went for you with a halberd or something. Served me right, I never did well by drinking. Truth is, it's never your fault. Either it's just bad luck, happening to get in the way when there's something you need to do, or else it's our own damn stupid fault, like pitching in and wrecking the peas, or it's self-defence, or something like that. You don't want to go worrying about it, or you'd never sleep at night.' He laughed. 'It's all a game, isn't it? Chances are you don't even remember most of us. Some of us you never even knew about, where we died a long way away because of something you did someplace else. Isn't that right?' he called out over his shoulder.

The dead crows in the back mumbled their agreement. 'Like he said,' one of them replied, 'there's nothing for you to feel guilty about. You were only ever doing what you had to do.'

That sounded eminently reasonable, but deep down he knew it wasn't true. 'I'm sorry,' he said, 'but these things tend to happen to me a lot, and there's very little time, always.'

'It's fine, really,' the god replied. 'I know for a fact that I'd have done the same in your shoes. Anyhow, who's to say it won't be completely different next time around?' He leaned across the box, confidentially. 'Don't tell anybody I told you this, but I was you once. Poldarn, I mean; I was the god who brought the world to an end, driving round in my little cart, like some travelling hawker selling buttons. Hell of a long time ago, of course, the cities that burned down then are just grassy mounds now; you'd have to get a spade and dig real deep to find 'em. Take that island you were raised on, for instance. A thousand years ago, maybe two or five thousand, a squirrel could've run across the rooftops from one coast to the other; but now it's just grass and woodland, and all the houses are buried under the ash – you'd never find *them* again. And in another thousand, five thousand years, there'll be houses and workshops and temples and God only knows what where your grandfather grew his onions, all sitting round the foot of the mountain ready for when Poldarn blows his top and smears a whole new country over the top of 'em. Makes no mind. And that's why nothing matters, of course, because all they can ever do is just kill the scouts. You could fill a whole valley with stones and kill a crow with every stone, and still all you'd be doing is killing scouts.'

Poldarn frowned. 'I'm not sure I understand,' he said. 'How could you have been me?'

This time the god laughed out loud. 'I forgot,' he said. 'How dumb can you get, huh? Of course, you don't know. All right, go figure. Poldarn can read Poldarn's thoughts, because Poldarn is the flock, not just a scout. Poldarn sends out scouts, and the scouts get dead as often as not, but Poldarn never dies. That's what being a god's all about, see. Every time the world ends, Poldarn buries it in burning melted rock, and it all starts over again, each time the old man dies and the youngster builds his house. Houses, shops, temples, palaces, doesn't signify; they'll all die and get buried under the ash. But that's how it's meant to be – hell, you know that as well as I do. The single dots aren't worth shit, only the pattern. Which is why we have memory, in the gaps between the fires.'

Poldarn thought for a moment. 'Often when I go to sleep,' he said, 'I have these dreams, where I'm somebody else. And while I'm dreaming I'm this other person and me at the same time. Can you tell me anything about that?'

'Simple,' the god replied. 'You're an islander, you can see inside other people's minds – which is putting it the wrong way round, of course, but let's get your question answered first, and then we can put this shit straight. You can see inside these people's heads, so you know what they were thinking; it's all bits of memory in the scrap, and you pull out what you need whenever you make something. But that's starting at the end, like I said. The reason you know what the others are thinking, it's because you're remembering, way back, from the time round when you were them. Like, this time round you're Ciartan, right? Well, the time before the time before last, let's say you were Colsceg, or Tazencius, or Feron Amathy; and this time you're Ciartan, but you remember. That's how it's done; no magic, no big deal. Round and round and round again; none of it exists, the people and the buildings and the places, the same way a hummingbird's got no wings.'

'You've lost me,' Poldarn confessed.

The god grinned. 'You ever seen a hummingbird hover? 'Course you have. Now, have you ever seen its wings? No way, they move too fast for your eye to follow; all you see is the pattern, little wings pumping up and down, making a blur where you know the wings should be. You don't see any damn thing, just the pattern everything moves in as it spins round and round; like you've never seen the spokes of a cart-wheel spinning, just the blur. And that's all you ever see, the blur, not the thing or the person.'

Poldarn nodded slowly. 'I think I understand,' he said. 'Like looking at a big flock of birds a long way off; you don't see the individuals, just the flock.'

The god stamped his foot cheerfully. 'Now you're getting it,' he said. 'A god lives for ever, right, so time goes real slow past him; your life and mine, we're moving too fast, so all he sees is the blur. But of course, he's not watching with his eyes, he's remembering with his mind – thousands of Ciartans and Cronans, millions of Raffens and Eyvinds, a blur where they go round. The pattern is memory. Everything's memory, locked right down into the grain of the steel; so, when you bend it, it jumps right back to exactly where it was before. Otherwise, it'd be a fucking shambles; every time a kid was born he'd be like a damn animal, having to figure every single thing out for himself, instead of just learning it. You do see that, don't you?'

Poldarn rubbed his chin thoughtfully. 'I guess so,' he said. 'But *I* woke up in the mud with no memory at all.'

The god smiled and shook his head. 'You remembered it all,' he replied. 'You just didn't know what it meant. But you remembered. It was all in the song.'

What song? Poldarn wondered; and then it came back to him—

Old crow sitting in a tall, thin tree—

('That's right,' said the god. 'That's what I've been trying to tell you, all this time.')

Old crow sitting in a tall, thin tree,
Old crow sitting in a tall, thin tree—

('Which is the same words,' the god pointed out, 'over and over.')

—And along comes the Dodger, and he says—

'That's me,' said the god. 'And you, of course, and every other damn fool in the flock. Couldn't have made it much plainer if I'd drawn diagrams.'

Poldarn sighed. 'Then why can't I see into their minds, or they see into mine? That really bothers me, sometimes.'

'Because they're too fast, and you're too slow. You can't interpret the blur, and they don't recognise just the one spoke, not moving. Of course, it'll all be different at the end, you'll see. Well,' the god added, 'here we are. You jump out, and you can give me a hand unloading this lot.'

They'd stopped in a place Poldarn recognised, except that he remembered it as a battlefield. It was only after they'd dragged out all the dead bodies and put them where they had to go that he was able to get the two pictures to fit, one superimposed exactly on the other—

He woke up with a start, and as he opened his eyes he heard himself say, 'So that's fine, all I've got to do is not forget —' And then the dream was gone, not leaving so much as the shape of a single black feather behind.

Chapter Twenty-Five

After that, nobody mentioned Boarci again. There was no need to; the salt beef took the place of the venison and duck and hare, and since he'd done precious little around the farm other than bringing home dead meat, there was no need to rearrange patterns of work to cover for his absence. Nobody mentioned Eyvind either, or where the blankets had come from. Apart from a few barrels stacked in the stores of memory, Boarci had never existed and nothing out of the ordinary had happened.

Perhaps because the mountain had screwed up the weather in some way they couldn't fathom, the crops came in late and all at once. This was something between a nuisance and a disaster. There weren't enough hands to get them in before they started to spoil, there wasn't enough storage space, not enough barrels and sacks and jars. In the end, well over a quarter of the crop went to waste, though that wasn't as bad as it might have been; Eyvind had planted to feed a full household, whereas now there were only eleven of them.

*

Typically, everything except the main wheat and barley crops were in and stored when the strangers showed up. There were ten of them; six men and four women, dirty and ragged and lame from walking too far on too little shoe leather. Nobody had any idea who they were, or where they'd come from, and of course their minds were closed tight shut as far as Poldarn's people were concerned.

'Still,' Poldarn pointed out, as they watched them trailing down the yard towards the house, 'the fact remains, we're badly short of hands here, we've just proved that. And I'm not going to turn anybody away just because they're offcomers.'

He hadn't expected enthusiasm, so he wasn't disappointed. When the strangers were close enough to be talked to without shouting, he stepped forward and waited for one of them to speak.

'I'm sorry,' one of them said, 'I don't know you. Isn't this Bollesknap?'

He was a big man, tall and broad, though hunger and hard walking was starting to hollow him out. He had a small, squat nose and a round face, and his hair was grey with a few untidy smears of dark brown.

'It used to be,' Poldarn replied. 'But now it's called Poldarn's Forge. If you're looking for Eyvind, you've missed him by about four months.'

The man looked confused. 'He's gone, then.'

'Round the other side of the mountain,' Poldarn replied. 'Do you know Haldersness?'

'Heard of it,' the man answered doubtfully, as if to say that he'd also heard of two-headed goats and sea serpents, but he didn't necessarily believe in them. 'Never been there, though.'

'Well, that's where he's gone,' Poldarn said. 'Will we do instead? My name's Ciartan.'

'I'm Geir.' The man hesitated for a moment, as if he was about to say something rude. 'Truth is,' he went on, 'we're in a bit of trouble. Have you heard of our place, Geirsdale, about six days west?'

Poldarn shook his head. 'Can't say I have,' he replied. 'What sort of trouble?.'

'That.' Geir nodded resentfully towards the mountain. 'Cut a long story short, our house is somewhere under a bloody great big pile of ash. There used to be seventy-two of us, but the rest are still in the house.' He grinned painfully. 'That's about it,' he said. 'Except that we're off-relations of Bolle – that's Eyvind's uncle, if you didn't know already.'

'Off-relations,' Poldarn repeated. 'How off, exactly?'

'Oh, a long way, something like fifth cousins on his mother's side. Is that good or bad?'

'Could be worse,' Poldarn said. 'You'd better come in and have something to eat.'

They ate like crows on sprouting corn, finishing everything, taking whatever was offered, gazing warily at their hosts while they ate, just in case it turned out to be a trap. Eventually, Poldarn figured out that the only way to stop them eating was not to provide any more food.

'So,' he said, when he reckoned he had their attention. 'What are your plans?'

Geir shrugged. 'Plans are for people who know where their next meal's coming from. I suppose what we're aiming to do is head out into the new territories, stake out some land, start over. But obviously we won't be in a position to do that any time soon, with no stock or gear. Till then, we'll go where we can, stay as long as we're allowed, and do whatever we have to do to earn our feed.'

'Well, that's putting it straight enough,' Poldarn said. 'Sounds like you haven't got your hearts set on getting your own place; at least, not at the moment. Am I right?'

Geir smiled wanly. 'Going hungry is a pretty good cure for ambition,' he said. 'You look a bit short-handed here, if you don't mind me saying so.'

'That's no lie,' Poldarn replied. 'What you see is all of us. I think we can quit treading carefully and say it out loud. If you want to stop here, you're welcome, for as long as you like. But you'll have to work, and you're not much use to us if you're planning on moving on in a week or so.'

'Not much chance of that,' Geir said.

'That's all right, then. But there's one thing we need to get absolutely straight. If you want to stick around here, that'd suit both of us. But I'd better warn you, we had a bad falling-out with Eyvind and his people, and it's just got a whole lot worse. If you're relations of his, you'd probably be better off carrying on to where he's living now; it's only a day or so further on, and you'll be more comfortable there for sure – they've got far more of everything than we have and there's a whole lot more of them than there is of us. If things get any worse it could easily come to fighting. You don't want to find yourselves up against your own family, or on the losing side.'

For a moment, Geir had that bewildered look on his face; but it came and went quickly, and he shook his head. 'I'll be honest with you,' he said, 'I don't know cousin Bolle from a pile of dirt, let alone cousin Eyvind, and we only came here because the relationship gave us a tiny scrap of a claim on his hospitality. You've said you'll take us in, and we're kin to your enemy, so I get the feeling we'll be better suited here. Besides, it looks like you could use us.. If Eyvind's house is as big and prosperous as you say it is, there's no place for us there and sooner or later we'd have to go. We're outsiders now, offcomers, and we're coming to terms with that: it's the worst thing anybody could ever be, though I don't suppose you can begin to imagine.'

Poldarn smiled. 'Well,' he said, 'I might; but that's a long story, and there's plenty of time for it later. Just remember, that's all. This is more likely to be the start of all your troubles than the end.'

*

The new arrivals couldn't have shown up at a better time. Eyvind had planted fine and extensive crops of wheat and barley, which stood up well and ripened quickly, untroubled by blight or crows, in a flurry of late sunshine. If Poldarn and the others had had to try getting it in with just ten men, they'd have been forced to leave at least a third of it to wilt and rot. As it was, they stood a reasonable chance of making a decent harvest of it; which would mean a substantial surplus over and above what they'd need for themselves, something they could trade with other farms for things they needed but didn't have the time or the materials to make. From what they gathered from such contact as they'd had with other farms in the area, the volcano had done serious damage in many places, so that quite a few houses would be only too glad to buy in food, if they could find anyone to buy it from. This was, of course, an unfamiliar, unheard-of concept, the idea of not being able to provide for all one's needs from one's own resources, and it was taking people a long time to get used to it. Ironically, there was a strong possibility that Eyvind would be a customer. Halder had planted his usual quantities of wheat and barley at Haldersness and it had done reasonably well, though not as well as usual; the Ciartanstead crop had more or less failed, after the overlay of ash had poisoned the ground. Since Eyvind had more mouths to feed than either Halder or the Ciartanstead people had contemplated when they planted, he was facing a serious problem in the not too distant future. Poldarn's heart bled for him.

Grandiose plans for a far-flung commercial empire all depended, of course, on being able to get the crop cut and threshed, and that was no foregone conclusion, even with six more scythes and four more binders and gleaners.

The first day of the cut dawned bright and clear, with a mild breeze to keep the workers cool. They started early, leaving the house before sunrise, so as to get as much as possible done before the sun came up and the heat slowed them down and wore them out. Poldarn couldn't see any reason why they shouldn't start with the nearest parcel and work their way out, so they didn't have far to walk that first morning, with their scythes balanced on their shoulders, the blades pointed carefully down so as not to maim anyone walking behind. It occurred to Poldarn as they reached the field that he might not know how to cut corn; fortunately, this turned out not to be the case.

They started with the headlands, clearing a swathe round all four sides. Then they lined out and moved forward, like well-drilled heavy infantry following up the skirmishers in an attack that was actually going according to plan. At first Poldarn made the mistake of trying to make the scythe cut, instead of lifting it and letting its own weight do the work. Once his shoulders and back started to ache, however, he stopped putting effort into it and found he was making much better progress, letting the scythe hang off his right hand and lightly guiding it with his left, with a slight flick up and back at the end of the stroke to make good use of the full length of the blade. The shearing click of the corn against the steel reminded him of many things, some of which he decided he could do without remembering, but once he'd got the hang of the job he found it came easily, as easily as killing crows. As the day wore on and the sun started to chafe his skin he found himself stopping to whet his blade rather more often than it needed. But he wasn't the only one by any means; he reckoned it'd be safe to bet that by the time the scythes were put away for the night, they'd be considerably sharper than they'd been when they started work.

After the midday break, Poldarn handed his scythe over to Raffen and took his turn at stacking and binding; it was harder work, but simpler, and he decided that on balance he preferred it. Not only that; but it gave him a chance to watch a true artist at work, and that was something he enjoyed.

Raffen was good at cutting. He knew how to read the lie of each swathe he cut, so that where the stems were bent or drooping he moved his feet and altered his angle of attack, always taking full advantage of the angle and the curve of the cutting edge. As he studied Raffen's technique, it seemed to him as though Raffen wasn't cutting the corn; the corn was crowding up against the scythe and cutting itself. There seemed to be no effort in the procedure, only the bare minimum of movement in the forward and back strokes. It was like religion as practised by the sword-monks – the draw, the cut, the follow-through, the return to rest that set up the next cut perfectly. Definitely there was religion in the way Raffen sliced and moved on, and every stem he cut through was a sacrifice, exactly the way it was with the monks of Deymeson. Poldarn wondered about that. Was that the secret of religion, a measured and controlled process of severing, separating the good from the evil, the stem from the root, the wheat from the chaff? He'd always assumed that the monks cut and sliced because their enemies had to be dealt with, that the objects of their swords were the weeds, not the wheat. But suppose that was wrong, and that the very act of drawing steel through matter was the essence of religion, that the sacrifice was what counted, not the victim. It was an intriguing hypothesis, particularly when transferred to the killing of crows, or other living things traditionally slaughtered in the open field, in the name of some cause.

Maybe, he thought as he bent and gathered and knotted, maybe the difference lay in the picking-up afterwards; and he couldn't help thinking of the old women in black who'd flocked round the carrion after that battle in the river, when he'd saved the life of a wounded soldier. Perhaps the purpose of the battle was the carrion, an equitable means of distributing wealth among the rural poor; in which case it was not religion to drive off the old women or kill the crows, since he had no use for the bodies and the crows themselves were the appointed beneficiaries of slaughter. That, or the crow-killer was doubly blessed, since he preyed on the predators who fed upon the dead. Perhaps that latter function was the proper office of a god, in his capacity as the ultimate remainder-man of all mortality.

Of course, a god would know that kind of thing without having to stop and figure it out from first principles; much as he'd turned out to know how to handle a scythe, or a sword, or a small stone, or a four-pound straight-peen hammer. That brought him back to the old question, like a man wandering round in circles in a thick fog: what did he know by light of nature and what was simply seeping through from his bottled and caulked store of memories, and were the gods omniscient only because they were remembering it all from the last time they'd swooped round in their endless circling over the world? Once he reached that point, Poldarn decided to give it up and think about something else.

For some reason, however, the sword-monks stayed in the back of his mind all the rest of that day, and he found himself following up that line of thought to Copis, who had been their loyal servant and spy, and who was carrying his child; in fact (he tried to figure out the dates), wasn't she due any time now? And what would become of his son or daughter, whose mother he hadn't seen since she'd tried to kill him in the ruins of Deymeson? He shook his head at that. How many wives and children had he got, for God's sake? Who and where were they, and how had he happened to come by them? Some girl had been the reason why he'd left home in the first place; then there was Tazencius's daughter, and apparently he'd been genuinely fond of her, according to her father; and Copis, of course, and now Elja. The thought of so much activity in that field of endeavour appalled him rather, and what they'd all seen in him he couldn't begin to imagine. Still, it made him grin as he stooped over the fallen corn; maybe he'd taken rather too many people out of the world in his time, but by all accounts he'd done his best to make up for it by replacing them with his own offspring. Very appropriate, he decided; very godlike. Give him twenty more years at this rate, and he could populate the entire world with innumerable first cousins.

Each day of the harvest grew a little longer and a little easier, as the work became more familiar and less interesting. Poldarn's back started to hurt after two days, and was fine again after six. When they were through with cutting they started on threshing, and for several days the area around the long barn was covered in a thin layer of white chaff, lighter than the ash from the volcano and less destructive but just as pervasive. Halfway through the job they realised that they were facing a desperate shortage of jars, sacks and barrels; they couldn't spare the hands or the time to make any more, and they couldn't do without them, either. The best they could come up with was a stake-and-plank silo built into the corner of the barn, all done in one night by a tired and bad-tempered workforce. They looked at it when it was finished and could see perfectly well that it wasn't really good enough; but it wasn't as though they had any alternative, and there'd be time to do a proper job later, after the rush was over. Finally, when the threshing was done and the straw had been stooked up and stored away, Elja told Poldarn she was going to have a baby. He wanted to tell her what a curious coincidence that was, since he'd been thinking about that only a week or so before, but he realised it probably wouldn't come out sounding right if he tried to share it with her, so he told her it was wonderful news and left it at that.

'I think we ought to call him Halder,' she said, 'after his great-grandfather. What do you think?'

'Good idea,' Poldarn replied. 'Unless he turns out to be a girl, just to spite us.'

Elja frowned. 'Well, in that case we'll call her Cremeld, after my grandmother. But he'll be a boy, I'm sure of it.'

'Good,' Poldarn said, 'though a girl would be nice too, of course. Can women be heads of houses, by the way, if there's no son to succeed?'

'I'm not sure,' Elja confessed. 'It's not something that ever happens, because they get married and their husbands take over. But I suppose that if a girl was the only child and her father died before she got married, she'd have to be, wouldn't she? That's an odd thing to ask about, isn't it?'

'It just crossed my mind, that's all. I like the name Cremeld, by the way. I suppose I ought to think about planting some trees.'

Elja nodded. 'Just not too close to the house, if you don't mind. The last thing we want is a rookery, right next to the barn.'

First, of course, Poldarn had to find some trees to plant. It hadn't occurred to him to wonder where they were supposed to come from; should he have thought about it long before this, planted out a nursery with pine seeds and trained up a hundred or so saplings, so as to be ready? He'd have to ask someone about that, Raffen or Rook or one of the other old hands. As to where it ought to go, that was another awkward question. Normally he'd have been looking at the far end of the farm, where Eyvind's wood had been; but now that he'd diverted the flow of molten rock from the volcano, any future eruption could well send a fire-stream rushing down in that direction, and his unborn grandson wouldn't thank him for a stream of red-hot liquid stone running through the kitchen garden. That really only left the spur at the other end of the farm, and that'd be an awkward place to build a house, with Poldarn's Forge standing in the way between the new house and the fields. It was strange to think that a choice he made now could have such a profound effect in twenty years' time on someone who wasn't born yet. With that in mind he compromised, and surveyed a patch halfway between the house and the filled-in combe. It wasn't what he'd have chosen, but it would have to do. It wasn't as if he was spoiled for choice.

Colsceg had to be told, of course. Since they weren't entirely sure where he was, they resigned themselves to sending out a messenger who might not be back for some weeks. Raffen volunteered to go, but Poldarn didn't like the thought of being without his best worker for so long and in the end they chose one of the newcomers instead – a young man called Stolley.

('But I don't know the way,' Stolley protested, when they told him he'd just volunteered. 'I've never been west of Locksdale in my life.'

'You'll be all right,' Rook assured him. 'Just follow the trail over the mountain till you get to Ciartanstead and ask there. They'll tell you where Colsceg's gone. Be reasonable; if it wasn't something any bloody fool could do, do you think we'd be sending you?')

One morning, when Poldarn was busy in the forge making a pot-hook, one of the offcomer women – her name was Birta, and she was Geir's kid sister – came by with the water jug.

'That's good timing,' Poldarn said, and he took a long drink straight from the jug. 'Thanks.'

'That's all right,' Birta replied; as usual, she was slightly taken aback at being thanked. One of these days, Poldarn promised himself, I'll get out of the habit, and then maybe I won't get stare at quite so much. 'Oh, and there's a message for you,' she went on, 'from my brother. He said to tell you the Ciartanstead men came by and picked up the horse.'

Poldarn rested the jug on the anvil. 'Sorry?'

'The Ciartanstead men. They came by and picked up the horse.'

He frowned. He could ask again, and she could repeat her

message, and maybe they could carry on having the same conversation all day. 'Where's Geir now?' he asked.

'In the trap-house, fixing the roof,' she replied. 'At least, he was a minute ago.'

Geir was still there. 'Yes,' he said, 'two men, I didn't catch their names. That's all right, isn't it?'

Poldarn looked up at the roof. There was a hole in the thatch. 'I'm not sure,' he said. 'What did they have to say for themselves?'

Geir shrugged. 'That they'd come to collect the horse, and you knew all about it, you'd fixed it up with Eyvind. Why, is something wrong?'

'It's probably nothing,' Poldarn replied. 'Chances are there's a perfectly good explanation, only nobody's bothered to tell me about it. That sort of thing happens a lot round here, you'll find that out for yourself.'

But nobody else knew anything about any horse, so Poldarn went back to Geir and asked him for more details.

'Well,' Geir told him, 'one of them was a big, thin man, something between forty and sixty, with a nose like the beak on an anvil. The other one was short and quite broad, with a little thin beard. Does that help at all?'

The thin man sounded like Carey, the Haldersness stockman. 'Nothing to worry about,' Poldarn said. 'But I just might run over there sometime and sort it all out.'

He thought about it some more, and went and saddled up a horse. He told the stable hands to tell Elja he'd be away for a day or so, but it was no big deal, just something that needed clearing up.

He needn't have bothered them with the message, because he met Elja coming out of the rat-house. 'Where are you off to?' she asked.

'Ciartanstead,' he replied, tightening the girth. 'There's some kind of silly mix-up about a horse, I thought I'd better go over there and put it straight before it gets out of hand.'

She nodded. 'Got any food for the journey?'

'Salt beef and a bottle of water,' he replied. 'I don't plan on being very long.'

'Good,' she said. 'It's not a good time to go swanning off on sociables.' Elja pushed aside the saddle-blanket. 'You're taking Boarci's axe with you,' she observed.

'I thought I might,' Poldarn said. 'Just in case there's still any bears left that he didn't bash on the head.'

'Well, have a safe trip,' she told him. 'See you in a day or so.'

On his way up and down the mountain, Poldarn put the missing horse out of his mind and thought about the future. Planting some trees; that was definitely something he was going to have to do. There was also the question of the Haldersness herd, which was presumably still somewhere out west, along with a dozen or so of the Haldersness men. The mountain hadn't played up at all since they'd moved into Poldarn's Forge, and fresh milk, meat, cheese and wool would come in very handy indeed; so would the herdsmen, if they could be induced to come and settle at the Forge. He could remember the names of two of them – Odey and Lothbrook – but nothing else about them at all. In their shoes, of course, he'd throw in his lot with Eyvind and use the herd to pay his membership dues; but of course he wasn't a bit like these people (his people) and what he'd do in any given situation wasn't a reliable guide. He couldn't see that Eyvind had any justifiable claim on the herd, simply because he'd stolen the house and the farm; if they saw it differently, however, he recognised that there was precious little he could do about it. The most sensible thing would be to agree a compromise with Eyvind and divide the herd between them – after all, he didn't have the manpower to look after the whole herd, even if he could get his hands on it. That would be the most practical, logical course of action. No question about it.

Poldarn slept badly out in the open, and woke up with a stiff neck. Halfway through the next morning it came on to rain, and he realised he'd come out without a proper coat. The horse blanket, draped round his shoulders and tucked in under his chin, made him feel happier for a while, until it soaked up so much water that its presence became a nuisance rather than a help. Half an hour before he reached Ciartanstead it stopped raining and the sun came out, filling his nose with the stench of drying blanket.

He remembered a small patch of dead ground not far from the house, with a tree he could tie the horse to. From there he walked slowly and carefully, making sure he kept just below the skyline. At some point in his career – at Deymeson, presumably – he'd learned how to make himself inconspicuous in a rural landscape. If anyone saw him as he approached the farm, he wasn't aware of it.

The closest cover was the cider house. Leaning against the wall was a stack of long poles; he crept in behind it and looked up the sky. Not far off noon; in which case, Carey would be fetching water from the spring. That meant crossing the yard, and there were bound to be people about. Fortunately, he appeared to have covered that part of the syllabus, too. He found a bucket, picked it up, and crossed the yard briskly and openly. Nobody ever takes any notice of a man with a bucket who looks like he's working.

Just for once, he'd got it pretty much right. Carey was at the spring, stooping down to fill his own bucket. Another part of the course must have dealt with sneaking up behind people without being heard, because the first Carey knew about Poldarn was the edge of Boarci's axe, pressed against the side of his neck.

'Hello,' Poldarn said; quiet, ordinary speech, in a pleasant tone of voice, because few things are as conspicuous as whispering. 'Why did you steal my horse?'

Carey had the sense to stay very still. 'I'm sorry,' he said.

'It was Eyvind's decision. Just happened to be my turn to go, is all.'

'I understand,' Poldarn replied. 'I don't blame you, it's not your fault. Where's the horse now?'

'In the stable,' Carey replied. 'Fifth stall on your right from the door.'

'Thanks,' Poldarn said. 'Out of interest, why did Eyvind decide to steal my horse?'

Carey sighed. 'He didn't want to,' he said. 'But Melsha — you know, Orin's daughter; Orin, the man Boarci killed — Melsha was making trouble, said it was wrong how he'd put aside Orin's death without a settlement, when he hadn't been doing anything wrong. She kept nagging Eyvind to do something, Eyvind said no, she said there had to be a settlement, even if it was just a gesture, and they decided on taking a horse. Nobody's happy about it. Eyvind reckoned it'd cause trouble, and he doesn't want that.'

Poldarn frowned. 'He should have thought of that when he turned me out of my house,' he replied, and drew the edge of the axe firmly across Carey's jugular vein.

Chapter Twenty-Six

The spurt of blood splashed him before he could duck out of the way. It was humiliating, like being laughed at by the rest of the class for getting the exercise wrong. He felt a fool as he wiped the warm, thick stuff out of his eyes.

Now then, he thought, looking down at the dead body (lying on its face half in and half out of the water, which was brown with disturbed silt and red with blood; here we are again, back at the beginning): what did I go and do that for? It was a good thing that the face was mostly submerged, because he'd known Carey, though only for a short while, and now he was gone, his life had broken out of its pen and escaped, and there was no chance of catching up with it and bringing it back. There were things he'd have liked to have asked him, and he couldn't now.

Then he remembered; of course, Eyvind and the stolen horse and the stolen house, the broken settlement, the act of war that he was obliged to take notice of. He hadn't really had any choice in the matter, once he'd been told about it and the sharp facts had embedded themselves in his memory, in over the barbs and up to the socket. You can't ignore stuff like that when you're the head of a house, or what would the world come to?

Pity, though; he'd neither liked nor disliked the man, but now Carey was firmly planted in his memory, a fixture in his mind for ever, or until his own life flew the coop. He wondered which bloody fool it was who'd put such a vulnerable thing as the jugular vein in such an exposed position on the neck, where any vicious bastard with a sharp edge could just reach out and snip through it, easy as picking apples. If it was the work of some god, he wasn't impressed. To him it suggested carelessness or outright malice, and either of those was good grounds for contempt.

Well; it wasn't very smart to stand out here in the open, at midday, a known enemy of the house, with a dead man at his feet and blood all over his face. If he'd done that back at Deymeson, they'd have made him stand in the corner for the rest of the lesson.

First, it'd be a good idea to get rid of the blood. He dropped to his knees and plunged his hands in the water, tearing apart his own reflection (which was fine by him, it wasn't something he wanted to see at that precise moment). It didn't take him long to scrub the blood out of his eye sockets with his balled fists, and that would have to do to be going on with. A quick scout round in case anybody was watching, then a brisk but relaxed walk across the open ground between the pool and the trap-house; brief pause for another look round, then across the yard to the rat-house and the sanctuary of his nest of leaning poles.

Time to think sensibly about the next step. If he was going to do this thing properly, he ought really to go over to the stable and retrieve his stolen horse. That would be the right thing to do, and if he didn't, killing poor old Carey would begin to seem less like a tactical necessity and more like cold-blooded irrational murder. By the same token, stealing the horse was the most effective way he could think of to sign his name to the killing; and then there'd be retribution, and the cycle would gather speed, the pattern repeating, until one side or the other was wiped out. If he were to sneak quietly away without being seen, that might not happen; sure, Eyvind would suspect him and his house, he couldn't help but do so, but he'd have no proof and so wouldn't be obliged, or able, to take the matter further. That was all very well; but he'd come here to deliver a message. He'd done that, but did a message really count as having been delivered if you whispered it in the other man's ear while he was asleep?

Furthermore, he thought, if I show up at Poldarn's Forge with the missing horse, and a day or so later Eyvind's men arrive, my people will know for sure that it was me who killed Carey – and I'm not entirely sure I want them to. They're the ones who stand to suffer most if this turns into a regular killing feud, simply because there's so many more of Eyvind's lot than there are of us.

At times like this, duty to those one leads and to those who are under one's protection must be the overriding consideration. Otherwise, what would become of us all?

He frowned; and then he knew what to do. It came into his mind by intuition, or he remembered having been at this point before; it was like suddenly remembering how to do the forge-weld, or how to use a scythe properly.

But that was some way in the future. Right now, there wasn't really all that much he could usefully do here – and besides, it was his unshirkable duty to keep from getting caught and killed, because who else was there who could run things at the Forge? Better that he should go home, keep his face shut and quietly figure out a defence strategy that'd give his side even a remote chance of surviving if Eyvind saw past his anonymous act and took the next step. After that, of course, he knew exactly what had to be done, so there was no need for detailed planning.

Forget the horse, then, and concentrate on getting out of there in one unobserved piece. That was a tough enough assignment to pose a worthwhile challenge for anybody.

Just strolling along with a bucket had been enough to get him in, but he had an uncomfortable feeling that it couldn't be relied on to get him out again. On the way in, he hadn't done anything wrong yet, and so the worst he could have suffered was embarrassment. If he was stopped and detained now, they'd find the body and that'd be that: worst possible outcome.

A diversion, then, so they'd all be looking the other way. That was the classic approach; unlikely that he'd be able to better it by figuring out something from scratch. Quickest, easiest and best value in terms of effect would be to set fire to one of the buildings – but he knew for a stone-cold certainty that if he tried that, he'd be a quarter of an hour trying to get a spark to catch in the tinder, and even then it'd smoke feebly for a few seconds and then go out. Even with charcoal and a big set of bellows it was still always a pleasant surprise when he managed to get a fire going in the forge. Out here, in these circumstances, with the materials available to him – forget it.

Not a fire, then. He could go over to the stables and turn out all the horses; but that'd leave him exposed, in the middle of all the confusion, and someone would be bound to see him. He could chop through the rafters of the barn roof and collapse it, but that'd take too long, and the roof would probably fall on him. He could yell 'Fire!' and hope someone believed him. He could kill someone else, to divert attention from the first killing . . .

None of the above. He slumped against the wall, furious at his own lack of ingenuity. It was a bad time to have his mind go blank. If only—

He looked up sharply. A thump, so loud that it made the ground shiver under his feet, filled the air, and instinctively he looked up towards the mountain. He knew what he was going to see: a red glow under a black cloud near the summit. *He* might not be much good at causing diversions, but the *divine* Poldarn had a flair for it.

At once the yard was full of people, running out to stare. As on every previous occasion they stood still, eyes fixed on the skyline, no words. Well, he thought, no point in hanging about; certainly no point in standing there gawping like the rest of them. As he walked quickly away from the yard, he couldn't help reflecting on that. Here was the sight everyone in the district dreaded most, and here was one man, not like the rest of them, who was looking the other way.

Once he was a safe distance from the yard, screened from it by the lie of the land, he stopped and did some gawping of his own. Compared to the previous outbursts it was fairly small-scale, a little cut instead of a gaping wound; but red-hot molten rock was gushing out of the mountainside like blood from a severed vein, spurting and dribbling down the neck of the mountain, and he'd have had to be deaf and blind as well as stupid not to get the gist of what the divine Poldarn was trying to tell him. When the god under the mountain chose to deliver a message, *he* didn't whisper.

Bloody hell, he thought; I've got to go home past that.

It was, of course, far too soon to hazard a guess as to where the fire-stream was headed. It looked as if it had burst out just above the place where the hot springs had once been but he didn't know the upper reaches of the mountain well enough to be able to visualise the area in detail and extrapolate the stream's likely route. He wondered if Eyvind would feel obliged to try and do something about it, so as to eclipse the memory of his predecessor in title. It would be hilarious, screamingly funny, if Eyvind led a party up there with drills and goatskins and buckets to divert the course of the stream, and inadvertently sent it tumbling down onto Poldarn's Forge, smashing and burning the house, burying the fields. Seeing Eyvind's face under those circumstances would be better than a day at the bear-baiting.

He retrieved his horse, turned his back on Ciartanstead and rode towards the mountain. By now the road was as familiar as an old coat, and he made good time. As far as he could tell at this stage (and it really was too early to judge) the fire-stream was headed down the Ciartanstead side of the mountain, but slightly further west than it had been before, when its threat had prompted him to divert it. He tried to plan out the route in his head. At the moment, the red smudge was working its way down towards a trough and ridge; once it hit that, it would have to follow the line of least resistance, which would lead it further west to a steep drop. That would make it gain pace and momentum, so that when it reached the bottom of the escarpment it could very well have enough impetus behind it to jump over the little lip just below and carry on in a straight line until it hit the long, flat decline directly underneath; and that would carry it, smooth and quick as a paved street in Boc Bohec, directly onto the roof of Haldersness.

He frowned, startled by the coincidence; then he shrugged. They'd have several days' notice, so there was no real danger to the household there. They'd evacuate to Ciartanstead in good time, taking with them a judicious selection of their goods and chattels, only those things that would be less trouble to find space for than to make again. It'd be a tight squeeze in Eyvind's new house – his people, the Ciartanstead household and the Haldersness refugees as well – but it was wonderful how many people you could fit into a confined space if you really had to. All of them, together under one roof. From one point of view that would be a definite advantage, the divine Poldarn helping him to cover an angle he'd overlooked in his original concept. From another point of view it was rather a pity, but it certainly wasn't his fault, not this time.

(Well, maybe it was. Maybe it was because he'd diverted the previous outburst that this one had broken out in exactly that spot. Or maybe it was the fault of the god under the mountain. Or both.)

In any event, if the fire-stream followed the route he'd figured out for it, it oughtn't to cause him any problems in getting home; a slight detour, over marginally rougher ground, perhaps adding an extra hour or two but no more. As far as that side of it was concerned, the divine Poldarn had been delightfully considerate. As was only right and proper, of course.

As it turned out, the detour shortened the journey home by at least three hours, though he had more than one awkward moment as he picked his way across sloping beds of deep shale. That was good. Almost certainly, Eyvind had found the body by now. If he'd found it fairly soon after Poldarn had left, and had immediately come to the conclusion that Poldarn had been responsible, there was a chance that retribution was already on its way. Once again, the divine Poldarn was on his side, since by the time the putative expeditionary force reached the mountain road, the fire-stream would be an hour or so further on its way, cutting off the route he'd taken himself and forcing them onto a longer, slower track. Even so, the extra three hours he'd shaved off the trip would come in handy, just in case.

They came out to meet him, clearly aware that something was wrong. At first he assumed it was the mountain that was bothering them – he was feeling quite blasé about it himself, and as he drew close he started to figure out what he'd say to put their minds at rest. But it wasn't the mountain, as it turned out; because Elja's first words to him were, 'Where have you been?'

'Ciartanstead,' he replied casually. 'I told you, I had some business over there.'

Elja looked at him steadily, as if she already knew what she was looking for. 'There's dried blood all over your shirt collar,' she said. 'But I can't see any cut or anything, so I'm guessing it's not yours.'

'No,' he confessed. 'It's not.'

'Has it got something to do with the business you had at the old house?'

He nodded. 'Quite a bit to do with it, yes.'

'I see.' Elja didn't look surprised, or angry, or disappointed, or even pleased. 'Did it go the way you wanted?'

He nodded. 'The mountain breaking out again was an unexpected help,' he said. 'It got me out of there without any bother at all.'

'Glad it's turned out useful for something,' Elja said, looking straight at him. There had been a time when a look like that would have bothered the hell out of him, but he couldn't spare attention for it right now. Maybe later, but probably not.

'I think we'd better make ourselves scarce for a while,' he said, sliding off his horse and stumbling as his cramped legs buckled under him. He straightened up and waited for the strength to come back. 'Just a precaution,' he added. 'I think they'll have other things on their minds right now. But I may be overestimating their intelligence, so we'd better play it safe.'

Asburn said: 'You'll be wanting a lookout, then.'

'Yes,' he replied. 'That'd be a sensible idea. You volunteering?'

'I'll go up the side of the mountain, to where there's that fallen-down old hut,' Asburn said. 'If anybody can spare the time to bring me up some dinner later on, I'd appreciate it.'

'Actually,' Geir put in, 'we could all do worse than head up there, if there's a chance trouble could be on the way. We'd see them long before they could see us, we'd be able to get out of there and scatter up the mountain before they could get up to us, and at least there's the best part of a roof on there if it comes on to rain while we're waiting.'

Poldarn agreed. 'All right,' he said, 'you get together whatever we're likely to need and head on up there; take the horses, just in case. I'll join you in a short while, there's a few things I need to see to first.'

'Such as?' Elja asked him, but he didn't answer. Instead, he hurried away to the barn, where he reckoned he'd be able to find pretty much everything he'd need. The errand took longer than he'd expected – there was never a ball of strong thatcher's twine around when you really needed one – but eventually he had everything neatly piled, bagged and stashed where he'd be able to find it in a hurry. Then he trudged up to the ruined hut; slowly, because by now he was very tired. He hadn't really been able to sleep the previous night, perched on a ledge on the side of the burning mountain, and what little sleep he'd managed to get had been spoilt by a bad dream.

When Poldarn rejoined the others, he was immediately aware that they knew what he had in mind. That was disconcerting, to say the least, and he wondered what it signified; but it cut out the need for long, difficult explanations and justifications, neither of which he was really in the mood for.

'You found everything you wanted?' Asburn asked. His voice was low and strained – part of it was fear, part of it something uncommonly like embarrassment, as if he felt awkward talking to someone who was in disgrace with the rest of the group.

'Ready and packed,' Poldarn replied. 'Now it's just a matter of waiting for the mountain to do its part.'

'And how long do you figure that'll be?' someone asked; he

couldn't be sure who it was, in the growing dark. One of the offcomers.

'Difficult to say,' he answered. Though in his own mind he was quite sure: the fire-stream would reach Haldersness on the morning of the fourth day from tomorrow, but the evacuation would be fully complete by nightfall on the third day. Since the schedule was in his mind and so, presumably, visible to them all, he didn't bother to say anything else out loud, and nobody asked.

'You think that's the best way to go.' Elja wasn't asking him to reconsider or anything; it was a statement, not a question. He confirmed it with a slight nod of his head. 'All right,' she said. 'I think we should be able to go back to the house in the morning, so long as we leave someone up here to keep an eye out, just in case Eyvind does come. But I don't believe he will.'

'I agree,' Poldarn said. 'Still, the very worst famous last words a man can utter are *I was sure he wasn't going to do that.*'

In the morning they went down to the house, feeling stiff, bad-tempered and rather foolish for having spent the night on a damp earth floor when they hadn't had to. Nobody seemed to have any work to do; they sat around on the porch or pottered about, not talking, not even looking at each other. Sullen was the best word to describe it; they were like children ordered to go on a treat they didn't fancy. Poldarn spent most of the day watching the mountain. He couldn't see the progress of the fire-stream, of course; he tried to deduce what he could from the direction of the smoke and ash, but mostly he knew he was fooling himself. It was frustrating to have to rely on an ally he couldn't watch, or talk to, one he'd never even met, whose existence he didn't really believe in, but whose contribution was vital and on whose timing everything depended.

He tried to prise his way into Eyvind's mind, but that turned out to be impossible; so instead Poldarn had to rely on his imagination. He tried to think the way his old friend would be thinking, the way he'd always been able to do when killing crows. Uppermost in Eyvind's concerns would be the pressure of responsibility, the priorities forced on him by events, the need to think clearly and pay attention to detail. That would be hard, with his entire world cracking up and burning all around him – Carey murdered, and he'd be sure he knew who'd done it, but what standard of proof would he need to show before he could take the decision to act on it? And the mountain, choosing this moment to flare up and reach out towards Haldersness; what the hell was he supposed to make of that, for pity's sake? Then he'd be constantly itching in his mind about what he'd already done, the extent to which he'd been right and wrong, how much of it was someone else's fault and how much was his own. There would be a voice in the back of his mind urging him to change tack, to find some way to deflect the course of events from the terrible conclusion that was being forced on him. Wouldn't it be possible, that voice would be urging him, to chip a hole in the side of that unbearable chain of consequences, tap it and draw off the heat and the violence, sending it rushing away in some other direction where it couldn't do any harm? Failing that, couldn't he just get out of the way, leave, go somewhere else where the stream of consequences couldn't follow him? But he'd know that was out of the question; because every stream diverted flows into someone else's valley, and such a horrible force of heat and destruction can never soak harmlessly away, all he'd be doing would be changing the place where the end would come, possibly disrupting the schedule a little, almost certainly making things worse for himself, reducing his chances of being the one left alive when it was all over.

Poldarn thought about that. There had been a time when

he'd pulled himself out of the mud and had realised his memories had all been washed out, like bloodstains from a shirt; a time when he'd had infinite choices, with no inevitable course he was bound to follow, no channels and slopes and lips and troughs forcing him to flow in any certain direction. He'd felt alone then, terrified, one defenceless little man in a vast open space, where everybody had to be presumed hostile until proven otherwise. Then his course had been aimless, he'd been sure of that. He'd chosen his turnings on a whim, allowing the most trivial factors to sway his decisions. But, as he'd flowed on and gathered speed down the side of his mountain (moving down and out from the peak of Polden's Forge, the sharp apex at the beginning from which he could see everything and recognise nothing), so as he went he'd gathered up dust and stones and ash that stuck to him and formed a skin, an armoured crust that constricted him more and more as his descent gathered pace, forcing him to follow the contours and the features of the terrain, directing him . . . here, to the point where he was rushing down on the roof of his own house, the house he'd built for himself from the timber that had been ordained for that purpose since the day of his father's birth. That conceit pleased him – the trees growing up to meet the fire-stream coming down, the perfectly timed confluence of fire and fuel, destroyer and victim, Poldarn and Ciartan; the threads drawn together to complete the obscure and complex but ultimately satisfying pattern.

Well now, he thought, how about that for a neatly planned conclusion?

He stayed watching the mountain until it was quite dark. The evening was unusually warm, and somehow he didn't want to go into the house (any house, at this particular time) so he sat in a chair on the porch and closed his eyes. The chair was newly made and really rather fine – Raffen's work, the man had a definite flair for making furniture – and he thought how pleasant life could have been here, if only he'd arrived in this place by a more auspicious route.

The chair was so comfortable that he slipped away into a dream, where he was sitting in a chair on a porch, watching a glowing red sunset over a mountain. But in the dream he was wide awake, because he was waiting, nervously, for a very important appointment. Beside him was a door, a rather magnificent thing made of bronze, with eight panels and slightly over-ornate hinges. Just as the sun set – such timing – the door opened and a grave-looking man in an ecclesiastical robe beckoned to him to come in.

The room he found himself in was big and rather dim; there were scores of candles, but all down at the other end. There wasn't any furniture apart from the table the candles stood on, but there was a mat – a wholly inadequate word to describe such a glorious piece of work. It was dark red, patterned with black and gold lines intertwined in a way that made him dizzy, so that he looked up, and saw the ceiling. That was even more spectacular. It was covered in a fresco, executed in a style he recognised as very old indeed, and it seemed to be telling a story, though he hadn't a clue what it was about. In one corner, a man and a woman were riding in a cart across a field covered with dead crows, while in the background a volcano was erupting, spewing red lava out of one side of the summit. In another corner, the same man who appeared in the cart was getting married, apparently to four women at the same time. Opposite to that, the same man was engaged in the sack of a city, amid scenes of graphic and very artistic carnage. In the fourth corner, he was standing in the bed of a river, surrounded by dead bodies. There was no indication as to the order of events, and the four panels converged on each other in such a way that they formed a continuous circle. In the centre, two sword-monks faced each other in a crowded room, transfixed in the moment of the draw; somehow the painter had contrived to give the impression that the events surrounding that central scene were all taking place in that same frozen moment. Although he reckoned he knew pretty much everything there was to know about the draw by now, he couldn't make out from the position of the figures which one was going to win; in fact, it looked almost certain to be a dead heat.

Someone walked between him and the bank of candles. Actually, there were two men: one of them a young man, the same age as himself, the other older by some twenty years or so. They both wore the standard robes of the order, perfectly plain and ideally suited for the exercise of religion, and both had swords in their sashes, just like his own.

'Has it stopped raining?' the older man asked.

'Quite some time ago,' he replied. 'In fact, it's a lovely evening.'

The older man nodded. 'It's about time we had some better weather. Now, Monach, Poldarn, when you're both ready.' He stepped back a pace or two and stood with his arms folded, while the younger man loosened his sash and tied it again, twisting two turns of cloth around the scabbard of his sword before tightening the knot.

'Can we begin?' he asked.

'Whenever you like,' the older man replied.

The young man took a deep breath and knelt down on the floor, slowly drawing his sword and laying it on the mat in front of him. He did the same; then, at the same moment, they bowed to each other, sat up on their heels and sheathed their swords. The older man clapped his hands once, and they both stood up. 'Poldarn,' the older man said; and the younger man bowed again. 'Monach.' He returned the bow. It was all very polite and graceful, but it wasn't making him feel any less nervous. Quite the reverse, in fact.

'You may begin,' said the older man; but neither of them moved. The younger man, Poldarn, took two deep breaths, drawing the air slowly down into the pit of his stomach, holding it there and slowly letting it out again. Suddenly he realised, as if remembering something obvious but temporarily forgotten, that when Poldarn had finished taking in his third breath, he'd draw; that would be the moment. He also knew that it was far too late to prepare himself to meet that draw, that inevitably he'd lose. He took two steps back and held up his hand.

'I'm sorry,' he said.

Poldarn relaxed, slumping forward slightly as the tension drained from him. 'That's perfectly all right,' the older man said. 'Take a moment and start again.'

This time, he knew exactly what he had to do. Instead of watching Poldarn he ignored him completely, concentrating instead on his own breathing, making sure he knew where his own hands and feet and head were, building his circle so that he'd be able to tell when something broke into it even if his eyes were shut. He drew in his third breath until his lungs and stomach were full; only then did he look for his opponent – found and marked him, though really it wasn't necessary, his hand would know where his enemy's neck would be. As soon as there was no more room left for air inside him, he felt his right hand relax—

In the event, he did the draw perfectly, flawlessly, to perfection, in accordance with all the precepts and observances of religion. The back of his hand found the hilt and flipped over so that the fingers could close around the sharkskin-wrapped handle. His left thumb flicked the swordguard forward to free it from the jaws of the scabbard and the draw launched: the sword slipped effortlessly free and began its precisely directed journey, sweeping forward like a lava flow, unstoppable and deadly. It was a perfect draw.

But apparently Poldarn's was better. As he fell backwards, in the last moment of consciousness, he wondered how on earth anybody could draw so fast; and he realised that the difference between them was one of time, because somehow his draw had been in the present, whereas Poldarn's had already happened, Poldarn had already drawn and struck and beaten him before they'd even faced each other on the mat.

Then he opened his eyes. Poldarn was kneeling over him, looking worried. The older man was standing behind Poldarn's shoulder, with a faintly disappointed look on his face.

'Never mind,' the older man said. 'My mistake. I believed you were ready, and you aren't. It's just as well we had this practice, before we tried it with sharps.'

'I'm sorry,' he heard himself say. 'It was the wrong time. I hadn't realised.'

'That's all right,' the older man said. 'It's all part of learning, after all. Help him up, Poldarn, and get him a drink of water.'

Poldarn pulled him to his feet and steadied him with an arm around his shoulders. 'I hope I didn't hurt you,' he said.

'No, I'm fine,' he lied. 'My own silly fault – seems like I've been missing the point all along.'

'Quite,' the older man said. 'In fact, it's quite remarkable that you were able to fool me into thinking you were ready. If you can draw that fast with just your hand and arm, you ought to do well once you've learned the proper way.'

That sounded like a compliment, but he was feeling too groggy to parse it thoroughly. 'It's because—' he started to say, but he couldn't find the words.

The older man nodded approvingly. 'It's because once Poldarn set his hand to his hilt, the draw was already done and over,' he said, 'whereas in your case it was just beginning. You still exist in the moment.' And he pointed up at the ceiling, to the two painted swordsmen frozen in the instant of the draw. 'You have everything, all the technical accomplishments, but you have no religion. It's very perplexing,' he added, 'because usually, at your stage of training, it's the other way round: still not perfect technically, but perfect in religion, which is all that matters in practice. You're still nothing but a human being with superb reflexes. Poldarn, on the other hand, is a relatively slow and cack-handed god. Now,' he went on, 'if I were you I'd go and sit down outside for a while, since it's such a pleasant evening, and take a moment to catch your breath and pull yourself together.'

That seemed like an excellent suggestion, so he followed it; and after a while he began to feel drowsy and closed his eyes. When he opened them, he knew at once that he was actually asleep and dreaming, because the first thing he saw was a huge black crow.

It was sitting on a fire-blackened timber that stuck out from a pile of rubble and ashes, and as soon as it saw him it spread its wings with a resentful squawk and lifted laboriously into the air. He felt an urge to grab a stone and kill the horrible creature, but he couldn't be bothered; instead, he watched it flap away until it was out of sight. Crows, at that precise moment, were the very least of his worries.

'Well,' someone standing next to him said, 'that's that, then. A pity it had to end this way, but it wasn't your fault. Wasn't anybody's fault, really.'

Far away in the distance, the mountain was leaking glowing red blood. 'How can you say that?' he replied, finding enough passion to be angry, much to his surprise. 'It was their fault for starting it. It was my fault for finishing it. Of course,' he added bitterly, 'you can't be expected to understand, since you're just an offcomer.'

'Fair point,' the other man said – he hadn't turned to look at him yet, couldn't be bothered to do so now. 'But it was all just trivial stuff, a quarrel about a cart. Odd how it always seems to begin with a cart – there's some sort of pattern there. I think I'll go and see if there's anything worth having in the barn.'

Some of the embers were still smoking, but mostly there

was just black ash. He ground some of it under his foot and listened to the crunch. It had been a fine house, but now it was just so much charcoal. That thought made him grin in spite of himself; maybe he should come back here with a cart and some sacks and bag it up, then there'd always be plenty of charcoal to get the forge lit. He considered that for a moment, but dismissed it as profoundly lacking in taste and respect for the dead.

There was nothing more to do here, so he turned his back and walked away. Nearby, next to the trap-house wall, he saw a nice sturdy log and sat down on it, his back to the wall. Once he'd taken the weight off his feet, he suddenly became very much aware that he hadn't slept for several days. This was hardly the time or the place for a nap; but resting his eyes for a moment or so couldn't do any harm.

As soon as his eyelids closed, he knew he was somewhere else, in a dream; he was sure of that, because he was sitting at a table, in the middle of which stood a wonderfully lifelike ebony statue of a crow with a ring in its beak. It was extraordinarily realistic; in fact, it looked more like a crow than any crow he'd ever seen, especially the live ones. The urge to throw a doughnut at it was almost impossible to resist.

But that would have been a waste of an exceptionally fine doughnut – there was a plate piled high with the things right next to his hand, and beside that another plate of honey-cakes, and a silver basket of cinnamon biscuits. In the distance – it was a very long table – he could just make out a parcel-gilt fruit bowl overflowing with oranges, apricots and peaches. Closer to hand was a huge chunky wine goblet, silver with gold inlays – vulgar, but impressive nevertheless. This was clearly a better class of dream altogether.

'And just then,' someone was saying, 'the stable door opened and in walked the sergeant; and he looked at the young officer, and he said, "Actually, what we do is, we use the mule to ride down the mountain to the village."'

Everyone – everyone but him, of course – burst out laughing, and someone suggested that that called for a drink. A pair of hands appeared over his shoulder; they were holding a gigantic silver wine-jug, which gurgled a stream of red wine into his cup. Then someone out of sight at the far end of the table called for a toast, and everyone started to get up. Naturally, he followed suit.

'His majesty,' said the distant voice, and everyone repeated, 'His majesty,' and had a drink. Then they sat down again. As he settled back in his chair he noticed that everyone was staring at him, though they stopped doing so almost immediately and started talking to the person next door. It was only then that he realised that he was sitting at the head of the table, and the toast had apparently been aimed at him; hence their surprise when he joined in. Bad form, to drink your own health.

They were all substantial-looking types, wearing some pretty fancy clothes – lots of velvets and heavy silks, the men as well as the women – but they didn't look like the sort of people you'd expect to see gathered around a royal dining table. In fact, they looked more like bandits or pirates or the men who hold horses for money outside theatres and brothels. Or soldiers, of course. But their appearance didn't seem to be bothering him unduly, which suggested that he'd had a drop or so to drink already (and a vicious twinge of heartburn went a long way towards corroborating that theory).

'Now then,' someone said, 'we've all had a nice dinner and a nice drink. How about the entertainment?'

That was a popular suggestion; all the villainous-looking men were shouting and banging their cups on the table; the women were trying to be a little bit more refined, so they just clapped and cheered. If anything, they looked marginally rougher than the menfolk.

'Well?' someone said, looking at him. 'How about it?'

Well indeed, he thought, why not? Naturally he had no

idea what the entertainment would turn out to be, though if he had to hazard a guess he assumed it'd be either fire-swallowers or young ladies with very few clothes on. But he had no deep-rooted objections to either category; and since the decision seemed to rest with him, he nodded. That made everyone very happy indeed, and a lot of perfectly good wine ended up soaking away into the tablecloth.

After a few bumps and thuds off stage, eight men in over-stated livery brought in two large wooden frames (like window frames without glass or parchment). Inside each frame a human being was stretched like a curing hide, hands and feet pulled tight into the corners. One of them was a woman, and she looked familiar; he thought for a moment, and the name Copis came into his mind, though he couldn't fit a context to the name. The other was a man, and he was familiar too – in fact, he'd seen him a few moments before, in his first dream: he was one of the two monks (Monach, he remembered, and Poldarn) but offhand he couldn't recall which one. Both of them were naked and dirty and thin, with rather disgusting ulcers and sores on their ribs and shins. Their heads had been recently shaved, which was a blessing – there were few things more likely to put a man off his food than the sight of matted, greasy hair – and their eyes and mouths were red and swollen. If this is what passes for entertainment in aristocratic circles, he decided, I don't think much of it.

The men in livery lugged the frames up onto a raised dais on the right-hand side of the room – they tripped, dropping the woman, which caused a great deal of mirth around the table – and someone passed ropes over hooks in the ceiling beam. From these they hung the frames, securing them at the bottom with more ropes passed through rings set in the floor. The presence of these rather specialised fixtures suggested to him that this performance, whatever it might turn out to be, was a regular event. Personally, he'd have preferred a string quartet or the ladies with very few clothes, but obviously the customs of the royal court overrode his personal tastes.

Once they'd finished fastening the ropes, the servants got out of the way in a great hurry; which turned out to be a sensible move on their part, because the company around the table were busily arming themselves with missiles of every sort, from soft fruit to the chunkily vulgar wine goblets. The barrage they let fly was more vigorous than accurate. Most of their projectiles banged and splatted against the wall rather than against the poor devils in the frames; but such was the volume of missiles that inevitably a proportion found their mark. He saw the man's head knocked sideways by a goblet, splattering the wall behind with wine or blood or both. Two of the men in the middle of the table were having a contest, to see who could be the first to land a napkin ring on one of the woman's breasts. Other diners were throwing spoons and knives. He wasn't sure whether he ought to join in; he didn't really want to, so he kept his hands folded in his lap and just watched instead.

It wasn't long before the table was stripped bare. The ebony crow had been the last missile to fly; it had been claimed by a tall thin man with a very long beard, who took a long time over his aim and managed to catch the woman square in the ribs with considerable force. The thin man got a good round of applause for that, and it was hard, in all conscience, to begrudge it to him.

Well, he thought, that was rather childish, but I guess it does them good to let off steam after dinner; and presumably these two are wicked, antisocial types who've done something to deserve it. It was impossible to tell just by looking at them what their particular malfeasances might have been. Anybody who's been locked up in prison and starved for a month or so will inevitably come out looking guiltily wretched, whether they were locked up for infanticide or stealing clothes from the public baths. He wasn't sure he approved of the proceedings, at that; but he was a stranger here and didn't know the score, so who was he to pass judgement?

After the last missile had been thrown there was a general round of cheering, mixed with shouts for more wine (and more cups). When these basic needs had been provided for by the impressively efficient table-servants, one of the men down at the far end of the table called out, 'Get on with it!' Everybody laughed and cheered, and two men appeared from the direction they'd brought the frames in from. They were clearly very serious men indeed; they were dressed in military uniforms, with gleaming black boots and white pipeclay belts, immaculate red tunics and breastplates whose metallic gleam hurt the eyes, especially after a drink or two. One of them was carrying a long stick like a broom handle, and the other a long knife with a curved thin blade.

The man with the knife stopped, right-wheeled, saluted him and said, 'By your leave, sir.' That caught him offguard, but he heard himself say, 'Carry on, sergeant,' so that was all right.

The sergeant turned to the man stretched in the frame and wiped a section of his midriff clean of fruit pulp and wine dregs. Then he pinched a fold of skin near the solar plexus and carefully inserted the point of the knife, working it in with the skill and concentration of a high-class surgeon. Once he'd made his incision he pushed the knife in an inch or so – he was taking care not to puncture any of the internal organs – and drew it down in a straight line, slitting the skin like a hunter paunching a hare. He tucked the knife into his belt without looking down, then pushed his two forefingers into the incision and gently drew the skin apart to reveal the intestines. His skill and delicacy of touch earned him a round of applause from the diners that actually drowned out the noises the man was making; it was hard to see how the sergeant could keep his mind on his work with such a terrible racket going on, but apparently he was used to it, because he didn't seem to be taking any notice. Retrieving his knife from his belt he hooked a strand of the man's stretched gut round his finger and sliced through it. Then he nodded his head and the other soldier handed him the stick, around which he started to wind the severed gut.

I'm not sure I care for this, he thought, though nobody else seems to mind; in fact, they're lapping it up, and this substantial gathering of important people can't all be wrong. But he wished, he felt an urgent need to remember, which of the two this one was, Monach or Poldarn; he wasn't sure why, but he had an idea it was extremely important, if not now then at some point in the future. But, for some reason, he couldn't see clearly what was going on. It was as though he was being carried further and further away, or his sight was fading, or perhaps this was what happened to your senses when you died; he was a long way from the scene by now, so that the noise was an indistinct blur, screaming and cheering scrambled together, and the people were just shapes melting into a mass of colour, and then nothing.

Chapter Twenty-Seven

He sat up and opened his eyes. The sudden movement disturbed a pair of crows that had settled on the porch rail while he'd been dozing; they spread their wings and lifted up, cawing furiously while they found their balance in the air. Poldarn's hand reached out for a stone or a cup or something to throw, but he was out of luck. They took their time leaving, as if they knew they were safe. They sailed away towards the mountain, the tips of their long wings flicking gracefully down at the end of each stroke.

It's time, he thought. Sitting around here won't do anybody any good. It's time we were on our way.

The red glow over the mountain was dawn, and something else as well. He went into the house and woke up Raffen and Asburn with the toe of his boot.

'We're leaving,' he said.

Raffen turned over and scowled at him. 'Already?' he grumbled.

Poldarn nodded. 'The fire-stream's gained a lot of speed going down the lower slope; it'll reach Haldersness by noon tomorrow. We're going to have to take a pretty wide detour because of it, and we can't take the horses, let alone the trap, so we need to allow an extra half-day to get there; the sooner we start, the better.'

He left them to get ready and went across the yard to the barn. Everything they needed was there, ready where he'd left it; not very much of anything, since they'd have to carry it a long way over difficult ground. He checked it all over one last time, and as an afterthought he added Boarci's axe to his pile. If everything went right he wouldn't be needing a weapon — there was no reason why it should come to that — but there was always the risk of a bear, evicted from its territory by the latest eruptions on the mountain, or something of the sort. He hadn't cleaned the axe properly since the last time he'd used it, and it had acquired a coating of gritty, sticky red rust; but it hadn't exactly been a thing of beauty to begin with, so who gave a damn?

They got themselves up and ready as quickly as anyone could reasonably expect, but Poldarn's nervousness had made him irritable, and he wasn't very polite to any of them. By the time they moved out, nobody was talking to anybody else; the silence was grim and awkward and miserable, but they started at a good pace and kept it up all morning.

At noon they stopped for a brief rest, while Poldarn went on ahead to look at the fire-stream. Nobody had asked him how he'd known all that stuff he'd told them, about how it had picked up speed and had made a longer detour necessary. He had no idea himself — maybe he'd had a vision or the divine Poldarn had appeared to him in a dream — but when he got to the top of the ridge and looked down, he found it all exactly as he'd expected it to be. The fire-stream itself was much wider and longer than it had been, and it was moving at nearly twice its previous speed. A tributary stream had broken out from the main body as it rode over the little crest he'd noticed from Ciartanstead. It was comparatively minor and wouldn't have the legs to make it over the next crest, but

crossing it was nevertheless out of the question; they'd have
to skirt round it, and that meant going right down to the
terraces at the foot of the mountain. They'd be able to go a
little way on the flat, but then they'd come up against a rill in
spate that was too fast and wide to ford. The only way round
that was to go back up the mountain and get across it while
it was still just a frothy white splash falling almost vertically
off the rocks. That was going to be a long, tiresome climb;
they'd have to rest for at least an hour afterwards; and from
there to the old road it wouldn't exactly be a gentle stroll. All
things considered, even with the early start they were going
to have to keep up a stiff pace if they wanted to get to where
they had to be before nightfall tomorrow.

'Come on,' he called out, as soon as he'd rejoined the main
party, 'that's plenty long enough. We're going to have to get
a move on.'

Elja, who'd taken off her shoes, gave him a scowl. 'We
can't go any faster,' she said. 'I've got blisters on both heels as
it is.'

'Then you should've worn your boots,' Poldarn snapped.
'The fire-stream's thrown us out more than I'd expected –
we've got to go right down into the valley, then right up
again. There's no time for dawdling.'

Elja didn't say anything as she pulled her shoes back on.
They were just rawhide moccasins with thin wooden soles,
quite unsuitable for scrambling over rocks. He should have
checked she was wearing her boots before they'd left, but
he'd assumed she'd have had more sense.

The next eight hours were uncomfortable and unpleasant.
They were all doing their best to keep up, but little things
kept going wrong: knapsack straps broke, Raffen slipped on
some shale and turned his ankle over, they tried a short cut
that ended up costing them an hour. When it was too dark to
see, they stopped beside a little pool under a waterfall and
refused to go any further. Poldarn gave in, with a very bad

grace. They had something to eat – dry bread and an onion each and went to sleep without exchanging a word.

Poldarn closed his eyes but stayed wide awake. He was afraid of going to sleep, for various reasons – cramp and stiffness, dreams, things like that. The sensible thing would have been to use the time productively, to go over his plans, work out alternative courses of action to meet predictable contingencies, but he couldn't concentrate. Instead, that wretched song kept jingling through his mind, and he couldn't keep himself from straining after the words he couldn't remember—

> Old crow sitting on the cinder heap,
> Old crow sitting on the cinder heap,
> Old crow sitting on the cinder heap—

But the last line wouldn't come, it was just out of reach in the back of his mind, where he could feel it but not get hold of it. He thought of waking someone up and asking, but even he could see that that wouldn't be a good idea in the circumstances. So he had to put up with the itch, like a pain in a tooth that had fallen out years ago. The night was dark and starless; he had no way of gauging the passage of time, so that what felt like an hour might only have been a minute. He wondered if death was anything like this, a matter of lying in the timeless dark, straining to remember things that would never come back again.

But although the last line of the verse kept eluding him, he found that as he trawled his memory, other things came up in the net. Mostly they were trivial and he had no idea what they meant – little broken glimpses of himself, random as dug-up potsherds, each bearing a tiny fragment of the pattern but never enough to make any sense. In one he was climbing out of a stream, all wet, while people on the bank were laughing at him. In another, he'd just been stung by a bee, in a field of nearly ripe oats. In another, he was sitting on the deck of a ship, looking straight up at the mast above his head. In another, he was throwing a stick for a dog. In another, he was stuck in a deep patch of muddy bog, which had just sucked the boot off his left foot. In another, he was up a ladder, picking cherries off a tree. In another, he was waking up out of a recurring bad dream, in which he'd seen a man tortured to death, and either he was the victim, or else he was the evil monster who'd given the order to the executioners—

He tried to catch hold of that memory, but it was too far back; the version of himself who'd had that dream was only a boy, maybe nine or ten years old. He could see himself waking up out of that dream – he was on the porch at Haldersness, curled up in a nest of blankets and pillows, and he was howling and sobbing with terror, as people came running to see what the matter was. Was it that dream again? they were asking, and he was nodding tearfully, the salt stinging his eyes (and a tear dribbled down onto his lips, and a calm part of his mind savoured the interesting taste).

When it finally deigned to show up, the dawn took him almost by surprise. It came out of the dull red glow of the volcano like a party of soldiers sneaking out from an ambush; it was only when the sun showed its rim over the red clouds that he recognised it for what it was.

It was a spectacularly beautiful dawn, an extraordinary fusion of shapes and colours, in which the familiar landscape suddenly appeared strange, different and new. He sat for a while and stared at it, trying to remember the last time he'd paid a sunrise the attention it deserved; and he found himself thinking, what if there was a day so perfect in every respect that a man could be entirely content, simply living that day over and over again? What if a man could pull up the ends of the straight line from birth to death and forge-weld them together, making his life a circle, a closed loop into which nothing bad could intrude and nothing good escape? Even if the day wasn't perfect, what would it be like to circle endlessly over life, observing rather than participating, like the crow scouts? Nothing would matter, and so there could be no pain or sorrow, nothing behind or ahead to be afraid of; there would be no death overshadowing the future, no hidden guilt casting its shadow over the past, no causes or consequences, nothing ever irrevocable, nothing that couldn't be put right next time around, nothing that needed putting right to begin with. Wouldn't it be fine to divert the fire-stream and make it turn a wheel driving a shaft powering a mill or a lathe or a pump or a trip-hammer, something capable of doing useful work, tirelessly and for ever?

Then he remembered who he was and where he was going; and as the memory came back, he considered the thing he had to do that day. Before the sun rose again, he would have taken an utterly irrevocable step, channelling the fire-stream down onto the roof of his own house. In theory, here in the dawn's apparent infinity of choice, he could simply get up and walk away, keep walking until he reached the sea; in practice he couldn't turn back because he was already there, he couldn't abandon the job in hand because it had already been done. Understanding that, he realised that he was already committed to the circle, not the straight line, but his endlessly recurring day was the opposite of perfect. This was the day where he would have to live for ever, and he was locked into it just as he was locked into every previous day of his life, and that every past day controlled every day yet to come. The hammer-weld that kept the world out kept him in, and there could be no escape. The circle was nothing more than the steel band of memory, circumscribing his life as a tyre surrounds a wheel, supporting and confining the spokes.

Then the others started waking up, and he turned his attention to details.

'On your feet,' he told them all. 'We've got a long way to go today, and we're behind as it is.'

As they marched he went over the minutiae of the plan until he'd annoyed all of them to the point of mutiny. After he'd finished doing that, none of them said a word, to him or to each other. That made for a very long day.

Fortunately, he'd figured out the necessary diversions pretty well, and had estimated accurately the time their journey would take; as he'd anticipated, they came within sight of the roof of Ciartanstead just as the light was beginning to fade. When they'd reached the patch of dead ground where he'd paused after killing Carey, he ordered a halt.

'We'll hang on here for a while,' he said.

Raffen, who'd sat down and was rubbing his neck where the straps of his rucksack had bitten into it, grunted. 'How long's a while?' he asked.

'As long as it needs to be,' Poldarn replied. 'If you like you can get some sleep, all of you. I'll wake you up when it's time.'

They didn't need to hear the suggestion twice. How they could sleep, so close to the house, was beyond him entirely. While they slept, he kept watch from the lip of the rise. As he'd hoped, there was nothing to see. The Ciartanstead household were all inside, eating dinner, resting after what must have been a tense, fraught day. By now, he knew the routines so well that he could picture them all with total clarity – pulling out the benches and tables, sitting down, waiting for the food to be brought, passing round the dishes, porridge and onions again, why can't we have a bit of meat for a change? Of course he couldn't hear their voices or read their minds, but he could make himself think he could hear the silence as they concentrated wholeheartedly on the job in hand, eating and drinking with the same diligent efficiency that these people, his people, brought to everything they did. It would be a bit cosy in there tonight, needless to say, with all the Haldersness people as well as the Ciartanstead hands; they'd be squashed up tight on the benches, no room to spread elbows, they'd all be sitting up straight, shoulder to shoulder. Now they were done eating, and tables and benches were put away and the blankets were fetched out and laid on the floor; not to worry, room for everyone provided that nobody was selfish about personal space. Nobody was going to have any trouble getting to sleep tonight, not after such a tiring and eventful day; nobody was going to want to sit up late nattering, there was serious sleeping to be done. He wondered: when they sleep (when we sleep), do they dream, or is dreaming too frivolous and unproductive for them to countenance? And if they dream, do they all share the same words and images, do they all go to the same place and relive the same moments? Do they share the dreams of the head of house, taking their lead from him in that as in everything else? Where Eyvind was concerned, he could believe they did – he was a good householder, one you could confidently take as a model of a perfect community leader, a paradigm of his people. So; what did Eyvind dream about, he wondered, and did he remember his dreams when he woke up, or did they fade with the darkness? And even if he didn't remember, how about the rest of them? Did they retain the dreams he forgot? Did they all share the same recurring nightmares?

(He hoped that the Poldarn's Forge hands didn't share his dreams, or at least not the one he'd been having lately, where he watched the executioners cut open the man who was either his best friend or himself, while either he or his best friend watched approvingly. That dream, for some reason, he had no trouble remembering, though on balance he'd have preferred it otherwise.)

By now they should all have been fast asleep; but he kept still and quiet, resolved to wait a little longer, just to be sure. Behind him as well as in front, his people were fast asleep (and whose dreams were Raffen and Rook and Asburn and

Geir and Elja sharing, he wondered) and it seemed only fair to let them be peaceful for a little longer. After they were through here, they might not find it quite so easy to get to sleep, or if they did they might have bad dreams to contend with. He lay on his stomach and gazed at the red glow from the mountain and the fire-stream seeping over the horizon like a rival dawn, or like blood soaking through a bandage.

(In theory I could still abandon the whole idea; in theory, none of this has to happen – not this time round, anyway, it'll keep till the next evolution of the wheel. But the little voice that kept whispering that in the back of his mind had missed the point completely. What was about to happen was even more inevitable than tomorrow's dawn; it was the point of contact between the wheel and the ground as Poldarn's cart rolled slowly towards the next condemned city.)

Suddenly he sat up. He'd arrived; this was the right time.

Gently, he nudged Asburn's shoulder. 'Wake up,' he said, 'we're here.'

The blacksmith opened his eyes, and maybe there was a very brief moment when he wasn't aware of where he was or what he was about to do. But it was over very quickly, and Poldarn could feel the weight of memory settling on him. 'All right,' Asburn said. 'I'm ready.'

The rest of them woke up without having to be prodded. One or two of them yawned, but nobody said anything as they gathered their tools and equipment and slowly got to their feet. They didn't wish each other luck – that would have been wildly inappropriate, and unnecessary as well. Whatever other problems they might be about to face, the risk of failure wasn't one of them. After all, it wasn't as if what they were about to do was difficult.

They walked slowly down the slope to the yard. It was very dark, but Poldarn didn't need light to find his way around the farm he'd built himself. They stopped outside the barn, opposite the main door of the house. They all knew what to do; there was no need for Poldarn to give orders or instructions. Each of them took a couple of deep breaths to steady their nerves, and went to work.

As was only fitting, Poldarn and Raffen saw to the most important task, that of barring the main door. It was perfectly straightforward, simply a matter of dragging the heavy timbers that leant up against the side of the barn across the yard, butting one end into the ground and wedging the other end against the door. That would be enough to keep the people inside from crashing their way out long enough for Poldarn and Raffen to do a proper job, passing stout battens across the door and nailing them securely into the frame on either side. Once they'd jammed the door with the timbers they waited for the others to do their part – Asburn and Lax to do the same for the side door, Rook and the rest of Geir's people to board up the shutters, the rest to stand by with the long poles from the woodstack, ready to push back anybody who tried to break out through the thatch.

Once he was satisfied that everyone was in place, Poldarn reached in his bag and found the hammer and the cloth bag that held the nails he'd forged for this purpose. Raffen held the battens up while Poldarn drove the nails home. He worked quickly but carefully, knowing that the first blows of the hammer would wake up everybody inside, and it wouldn't take them long to figure out what was going on. That shouldn't matter, with the long beams holding the door shut, but Poldarn wasn't minded to take any risks. If the people inside did get out, he and his crew would be hopelessly outnumbered and the whole project would founder. From the back of the house he could hear Asburn's hammer counterpointing his own, while further pounding of steel on iron at either side of him reassured him that the others were keeping up, as they drove in the staples through which they'd pass the iron bars that would keep the shutters cramped down.

He'd got one side finished before he heard any voices from

inside; then he felt the door quiver, as someone tried to open it. The vibrations in the wood intensified – whoever it was, he was trying to kick the door open or burst it out with his shoulder. But the timbers did their job admirably, just as he'd hoped they would, and he knocked in the remaining nails without any problems.

He knew without needing to be told when Asburn finished with the back door; the shutters were already secure. He put the hammer carefully back in his bag – it was a good hammer, he didn't want to drop it in the dark – and took a step back. Inside they were shouting, but it was all right, all the angles were covered, everything was still perfect. Hand and Rook brought up the big sack full of kindling, and emptied it on the ground. Poldarn took out his tinderbox and tried to get it to light.

No luck. It was the moment he'd been dreading most. It's not me who should be doing this, he thought ruefully, it should be Asburn or one of the others, I never could get a fire started to save my life. But, just as he was about to give up and call for help, a little spiral of smoke stood up out of the dry moss in the pan of the box; he gave it a couple of puffs, and a tiny orange ember started glowing brightly. Quickly he piled the moss up round it while Hand made a little nest of dry leaves and straw; then Poldarn dumped the box's contents into it, dropped to his knees and let go a series of long, slow breaths until the tinder caught and the first flame broke through, like the first corn-shoot of spring.

The others were standing by, waiting to light the torches they'd made, hay and straw wrapped tight around a stick and drenched in lamp oil. Once the torches were ablaze there was light to see by, not that they needed it; and once they'd tossed the torches up onto the roof and the thatch had started to burn, it was soon as light as day.

So far, he thought, so good; the roof was burning cheerfully, and they could turn their attention to the rest of the house. Raffen, Geir and Reno were carrying armfuls of kindling out from the woodshed; Asburn was on his way back from the forge with the first sack of charcoal. Surprisingly quickly, they built up a series of small pyres all round the house, primed with oil from the quench and lard and beeswax from the storehouse. Some of these they lit with their torches and portfires; others were set alight by handfuls of burning thatch sliding down from the roof.

Someone inside was attacking the main door with an axe; but that wouldn't do him any good – the battens themselves would take a quarter of an hour to chop through, let alone the main timbers of the door itself. They were screaming in there now, as well as shouting, but so far nobody had thought to try getting out through the roof; that was surprising, he'd given them credit for more ingenuity than that.

The smoke was stinging his eyes; he closed them, taking a step back, and in that moment he realised that what he could hear, muffled and indistinct in the background, wasn't the shouting or the screaming, all that was quite different in tone and pitch; what he could hear were the thoughts passing through their minds, a confused jumble of voices all talking at the same time. He couldn't make any sense at all of it, so he concentrated until he found the one voice he was looking for—

I'm waking up out of a dream about faraway places. I can see smoke.

It's hanging in the air, like mist in a valley; the chimney's blocked again. But there's rather too much of it for that, and I can hear burning, a soft cackle of inaudible conversation in the thatch above my head, the scampering of rats and squirrels in the hayloft.

Beside me, my wife grunts and turns over. I nudge her hard in the small of the back, and hop out of bed.

'Get up,' I tell her. 'The house is on fire.'

'What?' She opens her eyes and stares at me.

'The house is on fire,' I tell her, annoyed at having to repeat myself in the middle of a crisis. 'Come on, for God's sake.'

She scrambles out and starts poking about with her feet, trying to find her shoes. 'No time for that now,' I snap, and unlatch the partition door. It opens six inches or so and sticks; someone's lying against it on the other side. That isn't good.

It occurs to me to wonder where the light's coming from, a soft, rather beautiful orange glow, like a distant view of the fire-stream slipping gently down the side of the mountain. The answer to that is through the gap where the partition doesn't quite meet the roof – it's coming through from the main room. Not good at all.

I take a step back from the door and kick it, stamping sideways with the flat of my foot. The door moves a few more inches, suggesting that I'm shifting a dead weight. I repeat the manoeuvre five times, opening a gap I can just about squeeze through.

'Come on,' I urge my wife – comic, as if we're going to a dance and she's fussing about her hair. Hilarious.

The main room's full of orange light, but there isn't any air, just smoke. As I step through, the heat washes over me; I look down to see what the obstruction had been, and see Henferth the swineherd, rolled over on his side, dead. No need to ask what had killed him, the smoke's a solid wall of fuzzy-edged orange. Just in time, I remember not to breathe in; I lower my head and draw in the clean air inside my shirt.

Only six paces, diagonally across the floor, to the upper door; I can make that, and once the door's open I'll be out in cold, fresh air. The bar's in place, of course, and the bolts are pushed home top and bottom – I grab the knob of the top bolt and immediately let go as the heat sears my skin. Little feathers of smoke are weaving in through the minute cracks between the boards; the outside of the door must be on fire.

So what? Catching the end of my sleeve into the palm of my hand, I push hard against the bolt. It's stiff – heat expands metal – but I'm in no mood to mess about, and my lungs are already tight; also, the smoke's making my eyes prickle. I force the top bolt back, ramming splinters into the heel of my hand from a rough patch of sloppily planed wood, then stoop and shoot back the bottom bolt, which moves quite easily. That just leaves the bar; and I'm already gasping out my hoarded breath as I unhook it. Then I put my shoulder to the door and shove.

It doesn't move. I'm out of breath now, and there's no air, only smoke. I drop to the floor. Right down low, cheek pressed to the boards, there's clean air, just enough for a lungful.

As I breathe in, I'm thinking, The door's stuck, why? The door won't open, it's burning on the outside. No prizes for guessing what that means

The axe; the big axe. Of course the door's too solid to break down but with the big axe I can smash out the middle panel, at least enough to make a hole to breathe through. Where's the big axe? Then I remember. The big axe is in the woodshed, where the hell else would the big axe be? Inside there's only the little hand-axe, and I might as well peck at the door with my nose like a woodpecker.

Something flops down next to me and I feel a sharp, unbearable pain in my left foot and ankle. Burning thatch, the roof's falling in. 'Bench,' I yell, 'smash the door down with a bench.' But nobody answers. Come on, brain, suggestions. There's got to be another way out of here, because I've got to get out. The other door, or what about the window? And if they're blocked too, there's the hatch up into the hayloft, and out the hayloft door – ten-foot drop to the ground, but it'd be better than staying here.

But the other door's forty feet away; the window's closer, but still impossibly far, and the hatch might as well be on the other side of the ocean. There simply isn't time to try, and if I stand up I'll suffocate in the smoke. The only possible place to be is here, cheek flat on the floorboards, trapped for the rest of my life in half an inch of air.

Another swathe of burning thatch lands on me, dropping heavily across my shoulders. I feel my hair frizzle up before I feel the pain, but when it comes it's too much to bear. I snuff up as much air as I can get – there's a lot of smoke in it, and the coughing costs me a fortune in time – and try to get to my feet, only to find that they aren't working. I panic, lurch, overbalance and fall heavily on my right elbow. The fire's reached my scalp, it's working its way through my shirt to the skin on my back.

A man might be forgiven for calling it a day at this point, but I can't quite bring myself to do that, not yet. I'd be horribly burned, of course – I've seen men who've been in fires, their faces melted like wax – but you've got to be philosophical about these things, what's done is done and what's gone is gone, salvage what you can while you can.

It hadn't been so bad back in the inner room – why the hell did I ever leave it? Seemed like a good idea at the time. So I start to crawl back the way I've just come. A good yard (the palm of my hand on her upturned face; I know the feel of the contours of her cheeks and mouth, from tracing them in the dark with my fingertips, tenderly, gently; but no air to waste on that stuff now) before the beam falls across my back and pins me down, making me spill my last prudent savings of air. The pain – no, forget that for a moment, I can't feel my hands, even though I know they're on fire, my back must be broken. Try to breathe in, but there's just smoke, no time left at all. Forget it, I can't be bothered with this any more—

Poldarn opened his eyes. 'He's dead,' he announced.

They looked at him. 'Who's dead?' one of them asked.

'Eyvind.' Poldarn let out the breath he'd been holding (as if he'd been the one trapped in the smoke, hoarding air like a prudent farmer stockpiling grain against a hard winter). 'All of them. It's finished.'

Someone – Raffen or Rook, in the darkness they all looked the same – coughed a couple of times and said, 'Well, we did it, then.'

'Yes,' Poldarn replied. 'We did it, and it's over. I wish we hadn't.'

'Bloody fine time to say that.' He wasn't sure who'd spoken. 'Bloody fine time. Next you'll be telling us it was all a mistake.'

Poldarn shrugged. 'I don't know,' he said. 'It seemed like a good idea at the time.'

'Is that supposed to be funny?' That sounded like Hand, but he couldn't be sure. 'Because if it was, I don't think much of it.'

'Sorry.' Poldarn wanted to look away – the brightness of the flames was hurting his eyes – but he couldn't. 'But it's true, at the time it seemed like the right course of action. Now, I'm not so sure. It was a terrible thing to do.'

'That's no lie.' This time, he was almost certain it was Raffen. 'But the bastards asked for it. They had it coming, turning us out of our own house.'

Someone else said, 'That's right,' but it sounded like he was trying to convince himself. And failing.

'And the way they went about it.' Asburn's voice, slightly hesitant. 'Sure, we've just done something pretty bad, but they started it. They got what they deserved. We showed them. And anyway, it's too late now.'

'What the hell are you all moaning about?' That was Elja, and she sounded hard, firm, resolute. 'It was all Eyvind's fault; he was supposed to be your friend, and he started this stupid feud. If it hadn't been for him, we'd all be getting on with our lives in the places where we ought to be. Come on, we all knew that before we started this. Otherwise we wouldn't have done it.'

The roof-tree fell in, lifting up a cascade of sparks, like a mob of crows put up off a newly sown field. It was a beautiful sight, regardless of context. 'If anything's to blame,' someone said, 'it's the mountain. If that hadn't started playing up, we'd none of us be in this mess.'

'Yes,' Poldarn said, 'but it was my decision. It all went wrong when Boarci died. I could overlook the rest, there was a sort of cack-handed justice about it, but he saved my life, and there wasn't anybody else to stand up for him. But getting killed like that was his own fault. He should never have stolen that barrel.'

'True,' Elja said. 'But if you hadn't hidden it, he couldn't have stolen it. You shouldn't have done that.'

'I did it for you,' Poldarn mumbled. 'So you'd have something to eat besides porridge and onions. It was only a little thing.'

'So's the peak of a mountain,' Elja replied, 'but everything else stems from it. I don't suppose it matters now, but if you want to know where it all started to screw up, that was it.'

'You should have killed Eyvind back in the old country,' Asburn said. 'Didn't he try to kill you the first time you met him?'

'He saved my life,' Poldarn replied. 'And anyway, it's not as simple as that. Nobody's to blame here except me. I killed a man, for no reason. I hid the barrel. I turned the fire-stream away. I brought Boarci home, and if I hadn't he'd still be alive.' He tried to look away, but the burning house held him, as though he was the one lying pinned by a fallen rafter. 'I did it all, everything. At the time, each time round, I thought I was doing the right thing – no, I *was* doing the right thing. At every turn, all I wanted was to be a good man, honourable, putting others ahead of myself. And this is where I've brought you all to, by doing the right thing. I

guess that's the way it's got to be, with me. Everything I do
turns bad on me, and I've never knowingly done anything
wrong, in the small part of my life that I can remember. I
don't know; Raffen, you're a sensible sort of man, what
would you have done, if it'd been up to you? If you'd been
the head of house and the fire-stream was headed straight at
you down the mountain, what would you have done?'

Raffen laughed. 'Not what you did, that's for sure. But
only because I wouldn't have had the wit to think of it.
Maybe you're too smart for your own good.'

'You can't say you're sorry for doing that,' Asburn put in.
'It was amazing, how you thought of it. Anybody else
would've run away, but you didn't. You figured out a way to
save the house, and you made it happen. Nobody else
could've done it but you.'

Poldarn closed his eyes. 'And look what happened. I saved
the house from being burnt down by the fire-stream, then
came back and did the job myself.'

Someone was pulling at his arm. 'Stop it.' Elja's voice.
'Listen to yourself, will you? You're trying to make out you're
some kind of evil monster. Well, if you were, wouldn't I be
the first person to know it? After all, I'm married to you. But
I know for a fact you aren't evil, you're just a man who's
done what he had to do, and in the end it's meant you've
done some pretty unpleasant things. So, that's how it is
sometimes. But I don't blame you, because it's not your fault,
really it isn't. I don't think it was anybody's fault, it was just
the way things turned out. Worse things than this happen
every day, and the world doesn't come to an end. Don't stand
there staring at me,' she went on. 'You've all done worse
things than this, and for less good reasons – or haven't any of
you gone raiding over the winter, and burned down whole
cities, not just one house, all so there won't be witnesses,
anybody who can say what we look like or where we come
from? Is that a good reason for killing people, women and

children? Oh, you can say it's because of what was done to us in the old country, hundreds and hundreds of years ago, but that's not why you do it, and you know it. It's just the most efficient way of going about the job, and you don't care about the people who get killed any more than you care about smoking out a wasps' nest. And that's all right,' she continued, 'because everybody does it and nobody even thinks about whether it's right or wrong. But you –' she tugged at his arm again, like an impatient child – 'you've been fretting and worrying yourself about whether you're doing the right thing or not, but it's not like you ever had any choice – well, except for hiding the barrel, but you didn't mean for any harm to come of it, you were just trying to be nice. And when Boarci got himself killed, you did the right thing, you sorted out a settlement; and then they had to go and break it, sneaking over here and stealing that horse because Eyvind changed his mind. That was that, there was no way we could trust them after that. One morning we'd have woken up and there we'd be again, them pointing spears at our throats and moving us on because they wanted their farm back, or killing us even, because Eyvind had changed his mind again. You thought, the only way we'll ever be safe is if Eyvind and all his people are dead and can't hurt us any more. There really wasn't anything else you could have done, honestly.'

Poldarn pulled his arm free. 'I know that,' he said. 'That's what I've been trying to tell you. Even when I do the right thing, it comes out bad. In which case, what sort of a man am I? I don't know, I can't remember. But even if a fire can forget it's a fire, if you stick your hand in it, it'll still burn you. The only thing that matters is what people do. Everything else is beside the point.'

'And you're forgetting something really important,' Raffen added. 'We won, remember? They're all dead and we're all alive. Isn't it obvious what that means? We must've been right and they must've been wrong. Otherwise, nothing makes any sense.'

Nobody replied to that. Instead, there was an uncomfortable silence, until Asburn said: 'Well, so what're we going to do now?'

Poldarn opened his eyes and turned round to face them all. 'We're going to go home and get on with our work,' he said. 'There's nothing more to be done here, and plenty to be getting on with at home.' He looked up at the sky, but the red glow in the east was the fire-stream rolling over Haldersness. 'We'll have to stay here for the rest of the night,' he said. 'It's still four or five hours before sun-up. I don't think this is a good place to hang about, but we can get our heads down in the barn. Even if anybody does turn up looking for us, they won't expect to find us there. Then, as soon as it's light, we'll be on our way.'

'Fair enough,' said Reno. 'I suppose someone'd better stay awake and keep an eye out, just in case.'

'I'll do that,' Poldarn replied. 'I don't suppose I'd be able to sleep tonight.'

He was wrong about that. About an hour after the rest of them had settled down in the hayloft, he opened his eyes and found himself in a garden. It was a stunningly beautiful place (I must be remembering, he thought, I'd never be capable of imagining something like this). A closely mown raised camomile path led arrow-straight from the steps of the house behind him, which he couldn't see, to an ornate wrought-iron gateway. On either side of the path were neatly trimmed enclosures surrounded with knee-high hedges of box and lavender; inside each enclosure, intricate flowing patterns were picked out in flowers, their colours matching and contrasting to emphasise the clarity and grace of the design. In the centre of each enclosure there stood a small arbour, iron trelliswork covered in climbing roses. Another path bisected the first at right tangles, dividing the garden into four perfect squares; and at the point where the paths met, there was a circular fountain. Without being aware of having moved, he found himself sitting on a marble bench looking down into the water. He couldn't see his reflection because the streams from the fountain jets disturbed the surface, but that didn't matter, because he knew perfectly well who he was: this was his garden, and he was at home. Everything here was in its right place, because he'd put it there; he'd directed the placement of each flower, each bush, each slab of stone; it was his creation, a place he'd made where everything was right and all the choices had been good.

There was someone sitting beside him, though he couldn't see his face. 'You did well today,' the other man said. 'It was difficult and dangerous, it took some planning and seeing through, but you managed it. Nobody else could've done it but you.'

He looked up, because that was more or less what Asburn had said to him earlier, and he'd known it was true. 'Oh, that,' he heard himself say. 'That wasn't anything clever. Still, I don't suppose we'll be having any more trouble from that quarter for a while.'

The other man laughed. 'You're being modest,' he said. 'You planned the whole business out from the start, and none of them ever suspected a thing, right up to the last minute. And then, of course, it was too late. Really, I don't know how you did it. It's as if you could read their minds or something.'

He nodded gravely. 'Something like that,' he said. 'It's just a knack I've got. Everybody can do it, where I come from.'

The other man whistled in admiration. 'That must be a very strange place to live,' he said. 'Really, are you serious? They can all see what everybody else is thinking?'

'Pretty much. There's a few exceptions, but they're very rare.'

The other man was clearly impressed. 'And they can do this all the time?'

'All the time, without even trying. It's a way of life with them, like being able to see or hear. They don't think anything of it.'

'No wonder they wipe the floor with our lot, then,' the other man said. 'Just think of it, an army of soldiers who know exactly what they're supposed to be doing without having to be told. Is that how it is?'

'Exactly.' He yawned; it was warm, and he was feeling drowsy. 'No disagreements, either; there's no one man giving orders, the whole lot of 'em decide what to do, and then they do it. There's nothing else special about them, though. They're just a bunch of farmers the rest of the year.'

'Remarkable,' the other man said. 'You know, that must be a wonderful thing, to be linked so intimately to so many people. I'd love to be able to do that. If I'd have been you, I don't think I'd have left there.'

He laughed. 'Oh, I had my reasons,' he said. 'Truth is, I made myself a bit unpopular, and it seemed like it was time to be on my way.'

'Ah.' The other man didn't press for further details. 'So, do you think you'll ever go back there? On the one hand, I don't suppose you're in a hurry to get back to the farm and dig turnips. On the other hand, being so close to the rest of them, I don't see how you could give that up, once you'd got used to it.'

'Oh, I'll go back again some day,' he replied, 'once things have calmed down a bit. I left there once before, when I was still just a kid – things hadn't worked out very well, one way and another. Then I went back, a year or so ago, and everything was fine for a while until someone let me down badly and I had to do something about it. Well, that was a pity, because it meant I had to clear out again; but it'll all blow over sooner or later. They're a very forgiving people.'

'I suppose it's hard to bear a grudge when you can see what's in the other man's mind,' his companion said. 'I really would like to go there one day, it sounds absolutely fascinating.'

At the far end of the path, the gates were opening, though he couldn't see who was coming through. 'It's all right, I suppose,' he said, 'if you like the quiet life. Nothing much ever happens, but that's the whole point of the place, really.' He laughed abruptly. 'You know, if all the generals and elder statesmen in Torcea could go there and actually see these people they're so terrified of, they'd never believe it. This whole empire, scared stiff of a bunch of farmers. There isn't enough gold in the whole country to make up a year's wages for a palace clerk.'

Behind him the sun was setting, and the fiery red light glowed in the streams gushing down from the fountain. It put him in mind of a mountain far away; and that made him think of another pool, circled round with ferns and tall grass, where he'd first seen his face, on the day he stood up out of the river. He wondered about that; but the logical conclusion was disturbing, so he thought about something else instead. 'Well,' he said, 'tomorrow's the big day. Are you feeling nervous?'

'Me?' The other man laughed. 'Well, yes and no. After all, it's not as though it actually means anything, we both know that. But standing up in front of all those thousands of people, and trying not to make a bog of the ceremony, that sort of thing – I don't think I'd be human if I wasn't a bit nervous. So, yes.'

'I'm not,' he replied. 'It's just a theatrical performance, after all, and I've had a bit of experience in that line myself. Of course, I wasn't playing at being a king or an emperor, and the audience was rather smaller, too. But I should imagine the principle's the same.'

The sunset was closing in, and it was starting to get cold.

He stood up. 'Come on,' he said, 'we might as well go inside. Neither of us is going to do any good if we're sneezing and snuffling all through the ceremony.'

'True,' said the other man. 'Look, do you mind if I ask you a question?'

'Fire away.'

'If you had your time over again,' the other man said, 'would you do things differently?'

He smiled. The fountain was a bubbling cauldron of red-hot lava, and it was all his doing. 'First, yes, I will. And second, no, I won't. All right?'

'Fine,' said the other man. 'I was just asking, that was all. No offence, by the way.'

'None taken,' he replied. 'After all, when I haven't done anything wrong, what's there to be offended by?'

Chapter Twenty-Eight

They walked back over the mountain to Poldarn's Forge. Two crows followed them all the way. By the time they got their first view of the house, Poldarn knew he'd lost the ability to see the others' thoughts. He'd hardly noticed it coming or going, and he was left with the conclusion that it was no big deal. Most of what he'd seen on the night of the burning was the sort of thing he'd have been able to guess quite easily anyway – I'm cold, I'm scared, I don't like what we're doing, maybe this wasn't such a good idea – and none of it was important. In a way, he felt cheated because gaining and losing the knack had both been such an anticlimax; it had come and gone and he'd hardly noticed, being preoccupied with other concerns.

They reached home in the middle of the afternoon, and the rest of them went straight back to work, pausing only to dump their knapsacks and change their boots. Poldarn sat down on the porch and sat for a while, staring at the sky over the mountain, but that wasn't really achieving anything; so he hauled himself up out of the chair and crossed the yard to the forge.

Asburn had already laid in the fire; he had a long double-edged spearhead in the coals, which Poldarn couldn't remember having seen in the scrap, so he asked where it had come from.

'Oh, I picked it up at Ciartanstead,' Asburn replied, his gaze fixed on his work. 'I saw it there when I went over to their forge for charcoal, and I knew we needed something to make a long-handled bean-hook out of. So I brought it on.'

Poldarn shrugged. 'Good idea,' he said. 'What else needs doing? I'm at a loose end.'

Asburn pulled out the steel, but it was only just starting to blush, so he put it back. 'Well,' he said, 'we're pretty much up to date, really. Saying that, it wouldn't hurt to draw down some more wire. Or there's always nails.'

'Fine,' Poldarn replied. 'I'll make some nails, then.'

He made a show of prowling round the workshop floor looking for splinters and offcuts that couldn't be used for anything else, but he wasn't in the mood for nail-making. Instead, he leaned up against the west wall and watched Asburn as he pulled out the orange-hot spearhead with the inside tongs, laid it over the anvil beak and started bending it round with a succession of quick, hard blows from the four-pound sledge. Once he'd got the curve he wanted, he slapped it down on the face and straightened out the crinkles and twists with six mighty smacks, then nudged it back under the coals and hauled on the bellows handle until the fire began to flare. He took another good heat, waiting till the metal was bright orange, almost ready to burn; then he thickened the convex edge into a spine by slamming it against the anvil face, stopping every now and then to straighten and square it with deft nips from the hammer. The whole job only took him five heats; then one more to get the whole thing up to cherry red (patience and diligence, passing the curved blade to and fro through the fire, turning it over to spread the heat evenly) before dumping it into the slack tub. The thin oil caught fire, but he put out the flames by dunking the hook an inch deeper; then he held it still until the oil had stopped bubbling, pulled it out and laid it on the anvil to cool. Under the broken skin of burnt oil the blade was a dull slate-grey, a sure sign that it had hardened properly. Asburn took a few moments to rake up the fire and damp down the backplate with a splash of water from the ladle; then, gripping the socket of the hook with the tongs and supporting the spine on the head of the hammer, he held it up to the light to see if it had warped. The expression on his face suggested that it hadn't. He nodded to himself, put the hook down again, and took down a coarse grey stone from a rack on the wall.

(So that was that, Poldarn said to himself; from an abandoned weapon to a useful farm tool in six heats – seven, to include the tempering. Once he'd done that, drawn out the brittle hardness and left it springy and tough, it'd be a hook. Anybody looking at it would assume it had always been a hook, there was nothing to show that it had once been a spear. It had been purged of its old memory and supplied with a new one. There was no risk that it would ever remember its old life and suddenly uncurl back into a spear, like a shoot standing up out of the earth in spring, and there was no reason to suppose it would be likely to suffer from unpleasant dreams.)

'Sorry,' Asburn said, noticing him, 'did you want to get to the fire?'

'Thanks.' Poldarn gripped his silly little shaving of iron in the small tongs and snuggled it into the coals, while Asburn ground off the scale and burnt oil from his hook. 'Just the job, that spear,' he said, 'as it turned out.'

Asburn nodded. 'Nice bit of hardening steel,' he said. 'It'd have been a pity to waste it.'

How true, Poldarn thought. His scrap took no time at all to heat up, and he transferred it to the other anvil and started to draw it into a taper. Almost at once the wedge flew out of his hammer. He swore and looked round for it, but it could have been anywhere. 'Might as well make a new one,' he grumbled. 'Quicker in the long run.'

He found a piece of thick iron strap in the trash and drew it down in two heats into a fan; then he closed in the sides and cut it off with the hot sett. It wasn't much to look at, but it was what he needed, and it went in smoothly enough. He rapped the bottom of the handle sharply on the anvil to settle the head, and dunked the hammer in the water tank to swell. It'd have to stay there overnight before it was fit to use, so at least he wouldn't have to make any nails that day.

He managed to get an hour or two of sleep that night, which left him wide awake in the early hours of the morning, at the time of day when even small worries cast long shadows. He lay in the dark, staring at the shadow where the roof ought to be, and wondered what it would feel like to be a bean-hook that suddenly woke up remembering what it had been like to be a spear. It was a ridiculous notion, not the sort of thing you could contemplate without grinning at any other time of day, but it clamoured for his attention like an obstreperous child, and wouldn't go away until he played with it. What would it be like to be a farmer who suddenly realised that he'd once been a soldier, a leader of armies, a deviser of strategies, figuring out the best way to achieve an objective through the use of violent force? An academic question if ever there was one, but interesting, as a case study in human temperament.

As he lay there, he felt the stuffed-straw mattress under his back soften into the churned mud beside the Bohec; and somewhere nearby, two people were talking.

You again, said one voice. How many times have I got to tell you, we don't want you here.

We, the other voice repeated, that's a new one. Since when have you been we? Oh, I forgot, you're married. You're in love. Two hearts, one mind, one flesh. Excuse me while I do the figures; is this the third time, or the fourth?

It's the last time, the first voice said firmly. This is the time that matters. She's having my baby, and we're going to stay here and grow old together. And three's a crowd. Go away.

Sure, replied the other voice, that's what you always say, there's a definite pattern to it. Every time, before you snap out of it and come back to me, you find some girl, father a kid, it's some kind of gesture you feel the need to make so I'll know you don't need me. Then you realise that you do need me after all, and off we go together. Actually, I'm glad. I'm patient, but not that patient. It's about time.

You just don't listen, the first voice said angrily. You're out of the picture, you don't exist any more, you're buried and cremated and gone. The sooner you come to terms with that, the better for both of us.

The other voice laughed; a cold, patronising laugh that made Poldarn shiver. That's what you always say, it said, around about this stage in the proceedings. I love it when you're predictable.

The first voice tried to object, but the second voice overrode it. Imagine what it'd be like, the second voice said, if you were a farmer who woke up and remembered he'd once been a soldier, a master of a free company. Think how you'd feel, bending down to prod cabbage plants into the dirt, knowing that once upon a time, all you had to do was say the word and cities would burn. Think of the shame—

Exactly, the first voice put in. Shame, guilt—

I didn't mean it like that, said the other voice calmly. You know perfectly well what I meant. I'm talking about the shame you'd feel at how low you'd fallen, how little and pathetic and grubby you'd become – it could break your heart, knowing that. But we don't have to do it that way. All you've got to do is come with me, and it can be smooth and easy and *enjoyable*—

Never, the first voice said. That's where you completely fail to understand me, because deep down, we're totally opposite, no common ground between us whatsoever. Which is why I pushed you out of my life, and why I won't ever let you back. What's so difficult to understand about that?

It's a lie, the other voice said simply. It's not true. So there's nothing to understand. It's just you playing hard to get, as usual. Or are you trying to pretend you don't remember us having exactly this conversation about ten years ago, in Mael? Or five years before that, in Deymeson?

Of course I don't remember, the first voice said. Obviously. That wasn't me back then, it was you. Really, what kind of an idiot do you take me for?

It's the other way round, the second voice replied, as if explaining something simple to a backwards child. You're trying to make me believe something that's patently untrue. I could take offence at that, if I didn't love you so much.

You don't love me. You never loved anybody.

That's a lie. The second voice flared into anger, then slipped easily back into its quiet, superior tone. Don't be ridiculous, of course I love you. For pity's sake, just look at the things I've done for you. I've burned cities to the ground, churned up a whole empire, killed thousands of people. You can try and bury my love, but that just makes things worse; you can pile a whole mountain on top of it, and it'll still burst through and come streaming down the mountainside in fire. I've moved heaven and earth for you, literally, so don't you ever say I don't love you. And I'll tell you another thing, the voice went on, quieter and more urgent; if you care a damn about that woman of yours, or about any of these people, you won't let them come between us. You know what happens to people who come between us. If you're capable of any kind of affection – well, I won't spell it out, you're not that dense. But you need to think about stuff like that before you go plunging into things. You've got obligations, you ought to remember that.

I hate you, the first voice said.

Really? The second voice sounded insufferably amused. That's something else you always say, just before we get back together again. Come on, don't be a pain. Give in easily for a change, it'll be better for everybody, you'll see. All you've got to do is close your eyes.

I don't care what you do, the first voice said, you do what the hell you like, because it'll be your fault, not mine. This time I really mean it. We're finished. I'm going to stay here, even if you turn the whole place into a desert.

I can do that, the second voice said pleasantly. You've seen how I can do that: all I've got to do is push a little harder, and the next time you won't be able to deflect me so easily. Oh, for crying out loud, you don't think *you* did that? You don't honestly believe you pushed me aside, do you? You didn't push me, I got out of the way, to please you – and because I could see where it'd lead, of course, where you'd have me believe you couldn't. You know me, I'm the dog you throw sticks for. You tell me to go right instead of left, I can do that, for sure. You tell me to make a loud noise so the bad guys will look the other way, I'll do that too. And when you ask me to come and huff and puff and burn a little house down, that's not a problem, I come running – and exactly on time, I hope you noticed, I was in position to the minute. I hope you noticed that.

I was busy, the other voice whispered. I didn't see.

No? Pity. Never mind, I held up my side of the bargain. Now you're obligated. And don't pretend you didn't know – you knew perfectly well, the moment you started it all.

I *didn't* start it, the first voice said, almost pleading.

The hell you didn't. Let's see, where exactly did it all start? Was it when you cut that man's throat, out by the washing pool? Or when you diverted the fire-stream, or when you hid the beef barrel, or when you took in your killer waif off the mountainside? Or was it earlier than that, even – you know, I lose track sometimes, you're so busy when you're on your own, always getting up to mischief. That's why you need me, to keep you on the straight and narrow, not dissipating your energy on silly little jobs. Anyway, it was definitely you, each and every step of the way. It could only have been you, because of course I wasn't there. I've got the perfect alibi, you see. I wasn't there, because you turned me away, told me to get lost. You do understand that, don't you? Because it's absolutely crucial. You can't blame me for anything, because it was all you.

All right! the first voice shouted. It was me, it was me. But it's all your fault, because you made me like this. Even without you, I still do these horrible things. That's why I can never go back to you. Because if I do, it'll be worse—

No. There was a smile in the second voice, an audible grin of triumph. The only difference between what you do on your own and what you did when we were together is that your solo efforts are meaningless, they don't achieve anything, they're just random chaos and destruction. All right, when we're together we do the same sort of stuff, but just think for a moment about what we've *achieved*. That's the difference. You know, the voice went on, you seem to believe that I'm the bad side and you're the good side; but that's horseshit, it's the other way around. You and I together, we were getting somewhere. On your own, you're just a fox running through a cornfield with a burning switch tied to its tail. Besides, by any standards, what you do on your own is worse. It doesn't mean anything. It's just blind malevolence, like the volcano.

There was a long silence. Then the first voice said, No. All right, so maybe some of what you're saying is true. But that doesn't change anything, it really doesn't matter. I don't care if I'm as evil as you are, or worse, even. I don't care if I'm the devil incarnate and you're an angel. I hate you, and I'm never going back. Not ever—

Poldarn sat up. His face and chest were dripping wet with sweat. Beside him, Elja grunted irritably and clawed at the blanket. 'Go to sleep,' she mumbled. 'It's the middle of the night.'

'I heard something,' he replied. 'Stay there, I'm going to look.'

He slid out of bed and crept across the floor in his bare feet, out through the partition door into the hall and onto the porch. At once he looked up towards the mountain, expecting to see a river of orange fire; but there was nothing, just a smear of dawn. He sat down on the chair Raffen had made and started to shake, though he hadn't a clue why.

After a while, the shakes wore off; he relaxed, told himself it was just a bad dream, nothing unusual about that. He watched the red seep into the clouds on the skyline and tried to remember the rhyme: red sky in the morning – it was either good or bad, but he couldn't recall which.

'Shepherd's warning,' said a voice to his left. He recognised it.

'That's it,' he said, 'it means rain later or something like that. What are you doing here? I thought I heard somewhere that you died.'

'I did. And it was a nasty way to go, too. Blood poisoning, after I gave birth to our daughter. To be honest with you, I can't really say it was worth it. I mean, she's a nice enough kid, quite pretty in a washed-out, everyday sort of way, but not a patch on me.'

'True,' Poldarn replied. 'But that's a pretty high standard you're setting her. There's not many that could measure up to it. And she's kind and understanding and loyal, and she's got a great sense of humour.'

'And I bet she's mustard at embroidery and brewing, too, but who gives a shit about all that sort of thing?' Whoever she was, she laughed. 'Listen to me, I'm jealous of my own daughter now. No, I'm not, because I know for a fact that she can't compare to me. If it came down to a straight choice, right now, you'd dump her and come away with me without even having to think about it.'

'Yes,' Poldarn said, 'I would. But you're dead, so the question doesn't arise. It never did. You were married, to that moron Colsceg, and you wouldn't leave him.'

She laughed again. 'Oh, I'd have left him like a stone from a sling, if the right man had come along. But he didn't. Instead, I got you. And it killed me. I suppose you could say it served me right, but I'm not convinced. I deserved better, a whole lot better than either of you. Instead—' She sighed. 'Instead, by the time I was her age, I'd been dead six years. Not much of a fair go, was it? Eighteen years, that's all I had, and in that time I was *wonderful*. Oh, he didn't appreciate me, my useless turd of a husband. I think you did, a bit, but you were just a kid, you'd only just learned how to tie your bootlaces. No, you always were inclined to think with your dick, especially back in those days.'

'That's not fair,' Poldarn said equably. 'If things had been different, if we could've got married and settled down, things would have been so much better for everyone—'

'Oh, please.' She was laughing at him. 'What on earth makes you think I'd ever have married *you*?'

'Well, you married Colsceg. This suggests that you weren't inclined to be picky.'

'Shows what you know. I married him to get out of my father's house, simple as that. He was exactly what I needed at that time: he had his own house, he wasn't living under the shadow of his father or his grandfather or anybody else, so I'd be in charge at home, no raddled old cow telling me what to do or how things should be run. He had two sons already, so he didn't have any call to use me as a brood mare. And since we're being honest, which I don't remember ever happening back when I was alive, he might have been stodgy and middle-aged but he was twice the man you were. There was never anything much to you. In fact, God only knows what all your other women ever saw in you.'

'Thank you so much,' Poldarn said. 'It's so kind of you to tell me that.'

'Well, for pity's sake,' the voice said contemptuously. 'Just look at them, will you? There's been so many of them, and every single one of them about as interesting as last night's porridge. I mean, take that mimsy little blonde bitch, the prince's daughter—'

'I loved her,' Poldarn objected.

'Did you hell. You only married her so you'd have her father by the balls.'

'Oh sure, to begin with,' Poldarn admitted readily. 'That was the original idea; but then I fell in love with her. She was so giving, so—'

'Weak and pathetic,' the voice cut in. 'A doormat, a little plaster doll. How you managed to stay awake when you were seeing to *that* beats me, really it does. And what about the last one – sorry, the one before last, it gets so confusing. You know, the one who never washed, with the hairy armpits. You're not seriously asking me to believe you were ever even fond of *her*.'

'Yes, as a matter of fact,' Poldarn replied. 'Actually, she reminds me a lot of you.'

For a moment, the other voice was too angry to speak. 'That's sick,' it said. 'I know you only said that to annoy me, but you shouldn't say things like that, even in spite. And so, all right, maybe you were *fond* of her. You were absolutely besotted with me.'

'Very true,' Poldarn said, 'I was. But as you yourself said just now, I was only a kid at the time. Shallow, immature, only interested in one thing. You can't have it both ways, you know.'

She giggled. 'Very true,' she said. 'You know, you've some-how managed to get a bit of an edge since the last time I saw you.'

'Really. Next you'll be saying, haven't I grown?'

She ignored that. 'About time, too,' she said. 'God, you were so damn soppy back then, it turns my stomach just thinking about it. Giving me flowers all the time. I don't want to sound hard or anything, but what earthly use is a bunch of dead vegetation? If I'd wanted flowers, I'd have picked my own. As it was, soon as you were gone, I buried them in the compost heap. Oh, now I've hurt your feelings; but be reasonable, I couldn't very well have gone back home with them. First thing he'd have said, where did you get those?'

'Sorry,' Poldarn said. 'I thought you liked them. You always said you liked them.'

'Dear Ciartan,' she said, 'I was just trying to be nice. You know, pretending. I always did a lot of pretending when I was with you. After all, you were so terribly brittle, one word out of place and you were no good for anything. Of course I pretended, it's what we all do. Or did you really think I was melting at your every touch?'

'Fine,' Poldarn replied. 'You know, if I was so useless, I don't know why you bothered.'

She thought for a moment. 'It was something to do, I suppose.'

'Something to do,' Poldarn repeated. 'Have you got any idea how much trouble you've caused?'

This time, she sounded genuinely shocked. 'Me? For heaven's sake, if anybody's the victim, it's me. You're not the one who died in childbirth, remember.'

'You,' Poldarn said firmly. 'If it hadn't been for you, I'd never have left here, I'd have stayed here and been a good little farmer, I'd never have gone abroad; and hundreds of thousands of dead people would be alive today.'

A moment of silence. 'I hadn't actually thought of it in those terms,' she said. 'But no, I think you're wrong there. Yes, I'm sure of it. After all, if it hadn't been me there'd have been some other reason, you'd have got yourself into trouble one way or the other. You were born to it, for pity's sake. You were born because your father raped your mother, and then she killed him. You're nothing but trouble, you know that perfectly well. Someone whose idea of fun is killing crows isn't exactly normal, you must admit. For all we know, if it hadn't been for me, and getting thrown off the Island when you did, you might've ended up doing something even worse.'

Poldarn was extremely angry. 'Worse? What could I possibly have done that could've been worse? I've had cities burned down and innocent people massacred. Everybody I've known has come to a bad end. Everybody I've loved, either they're dead or they're so screwed up that they'd be better off dead. And now, as if that wasn't enough, I've come home, started a blood-feud and got my own daughter pregnant. And it's your fault.'

Her reply was as cold as ice. 'Don't be ridiculous,' she said. 'At every turn you had a choice. You were the one who did all those things. Oh, at the time it was always the right thing to do – for your people, for the cause, to save your skin, whatever. And don't try pretending that this losing your memory thing excuses anything. When you came back here, you had a perfect fresh start, a whole new life, everything anybody could possibly want – and now look at what you've done. You've got us fighting among ourselves, killing each other. Nobody else could've done that, only you. So leave me out of it, thank you very much. I'm just another one of your victims, and don't you ever try and pretend otherwise.'

'I did it because I loved you,' he said quietly. 'And I thought you loved me.'

'Like you hid the barrel of salt beef? Well, quite. You thought that what you were doing was right. But don't you see, that's exactly the sort of person you are. You know what, Ciartan? You're like a mother polecat in a chicken run. You believe that the right thing to do is feed your babies, so you kill all the chickens. And yes, in a way it is the right thing to do, but you can bet your life nobody else is going to see it that way. You're like a weapon, Ciartan, an axe or a spear. The right thing for a weapon to do is to kill people and hurt people, and at the right time in the right place, that's very good. But the rest of the time— What I'm trying to tell you is, it's in your nature to wreck everything you touch. Maybe you can't help it, I don't know. Now, if you were in the right place at the right time, you could be very useful, you could do a lot of good, even. But when you're out of context you're a menace, and you ought to be knocked on the head and buried in quicklime.' She sighed. 'Nobody would think it to look at you,' she went on. 'You come across as dumb and sweet, a bit vulnerable, maybe not the sharpest chisel in the rack but quite endearing, in a passive sort of way. And people see that, and they overlook this simple talent you've got for breaking things, and the fact that when you lash out there's usually something sharp in your hand and people tend to fall down dead. Oh yes, and you have a sneaking suspicion that you're a god, and it's your destiny to bring about the end of the world. That really helps things, of course. You know, if you really wanted to help other people and make the world a better place, you'd find a nice strong tree, a milking stool and ten feet of good quality rope.'

He didn't answer for a very long time. 'I'm sorry you feel that way,' he said at last. 'But that's definitely not going to happen.'

'Please yourself. But you wanted my advice and now you've got it. If you're just going to ignore it, don't ask me again. And now, if it's all the same to you, I think I'd like to carry on being dead, please. It doesn't have a lot to recommend it, but at least it means I don't have to associate with the likes of you.'

He opened his eyes; and his first thought was, it's all right, I never remember my dreams. In a second or so it'll have gone, and I'll never know. But for once he was wrong. It was still there in his mind, the whole thing; and he knew it was true. He could remember it all.

Herda, Colsceg's second wife: young and very beautiful, but wild and dangerous. That was how he'd thought of her when he'd been eighteen and had seen her for the first time. She was everything he'd dreamed of, and he fell in love like a dead crow tumbling out of the air. Whether she'd loved him or whether she was just amusing herself and pretending, he never knew and didn't care. The adventure was the main thing, and the tiny brief escape from the unrelenting certainty of Haldersness, where everybody knew what everybody else was thinking, all the time. It hadn't been Herda's sweeping red hair or glowing green eyes or the breathtaking softness of her slim body; what he'd fallen in love with had been the opaqueness of her mind, which she could hide from him whenever she wanted (and she wanted, all the time). It was from her that he had somehow picked up the trick of shutting the door on everyone else, keeping them out of the part of his mind where he was really himself. It had been a useful knack, because even he couldn't prise open that door; whenever he chose he could stop being himself and be somebody quite different, separated and protected from who he really was. But it hadn't gone well. Suddenly she'd told him she was going to have a baby, and he was the father, and she wasn't going to see him any more. For a while he'd moped about the place, and nobody had known the reason, though a few people seemed to have had their suspicions – her brother Egil, for one. He found out quite early, somehow or other, but he'd had his own reasons to keep his mouth shut. There had been a morning, he remembered, shortly before the affair ended, when he'd got up just before dawn to go out and decoy crows and he'd met Egil in the yard, with blood all over his face and clothes. Nobody else was up and about and he'd wondered where the boy had been, how he'd managed to get himself in such a dreadful state, so he'd stopped and asked him. Egil didn't want to say, which made him all the more curious; finally the boy broke down and told him what had happened. He'd been up on the mountainside, exercising his dogs, and two strangers, offcomers from the other side of the island, had come on him unexpectedly. One of the dogs bit one of the men; both men seemed to get very angry and said that they were taking the dogs as their settlement for the bite. Egil was furious and when the men tried to take the dogs he hit one of the would-be thieves on the side of the head with his stick. That was the wrong thing to do. They were big, strong men, and one of them held his arms while the other one slapped and punched him – not hard enough to do any damage, he was most careful about that, but just enough to make him burst into tears and beg the man to stop. Then they'd laughed at him and taken the dogs anyway and Egil had come home; and all he wanted in the whole world was to see them punished. He told him that, and then a strange expression came over his face, and he said, 'You ought to help me. After all, you're a friend of the family.'

'I suppose so,' he'd replied. 'But it's none of my business, really.'

'I think you ought to do something about it,' Egil had said. 'Like I ought to tell Dad a thing or two, only I haven't. Not yet, at any rate.'

That had been enough; so he'd gone into the barn and found a small axe. Then he told Egil to take him to the place where he'd last seen the two men. They were easy enough to track down, and when he confronted them, they didn't seem the least bit worried – not until he pulled the axe out from under his coat and pecked it into the sides of their heads, one after the other, as neat and quick as a bird with a worm.

Egil was scared stiff, but he'd told him, 'It'll be all right, they're only offcomers. Nobody's going to miss them, and if they do, they won't care.' So they dragged the bodies up the mountain – it took a long time and wore them out – and pitched them into the big crack where the hot springs burst out. Then they went home, and he'd told everyone a story about having a bad feeling about something and going up the mountain and finding Egil lying there all bloody, after being chased and batted about by a bear. Everyone thanked him and told him how well he'd done; and later on, he took the little axe and tossed it into a ditch, in that same field where he'd killed all those crows a short while before he diverted the fire-stream.

And that was how Egil had known, and why he couldn't tell anybody; it was lucky that he'd got a touch of the same knack of hiding his thoughts, because nobody ever seemed to have found out the truth from him. (Though, looking back, there had been that off-relation who'd come to visit, and who'd been so pleased when he'd heard he'd lost his memory; and Hart too. Maybe they'd seen a little of it in Egil's mind, enough to let them know there was something wrong.)

Shortly after he'd killed the two men, Herda had told him about the baby; he'd gone to stay with one of Halder's friends, hoping he'd get over it, but there wasn't much chance of that. Then some men had called at the farm, talking about going raiding come the autumn, and he'd asked to go with them. They'd said yes, and nobody'd seemed to mind; and on the way there, they'd started talking about how useful it would be to have a spy inside the Empire, someone who'd stay there and find out about the place, stuff that'd be useful to the raiding parties. That seemed like the best possible idea: a new start in a new country where nobody at all knew him, where he'd have a second chance at his life, all the mistakes wiped away.

He remembered all that; and now he'd come home and married Colsceg and Herda's daughter, to please his grandfather by beginning a clean new life, his second fresh start. In a way, it was ludicrous, as if the only reason he'd been allowed to forget what had happened for a while was so that he'd stroll blithely into his own trap, do something so unbearably wrong that even he would never have done it if only he'd known. Tactically, it was inspired. Whoever it was who'd thought of it deserved to be congratulated for their imagination, economy of force and painstaking attention to detail.

Well, he thought; time I wasn't here.

It was still early. If he took a horse and rode quickly, he could be on the other side of the mountain before they'd even noticed he was gone. A few days at a good pace, assuming he didn't get lost and start going the wrong way, would get him to the coast, and it wasn't long till the start of the raiding season, a few weeks at most before the first ships left for the Empire. Till then, he'd have to find work, doing the sort of thing offcomers and outsiders were allowed to do, but something told him he'd manage somehow or other. One thing he couldn't do was stay here another day; even if he could still mask his thoughts from the others (from Elja? Little chance of that), it couldn't be long before Geir's son got back from telling Colsceg about Elja being pregnant – and what if Egil came back with him? But if he went away immediately, there was a chance that nobody else would ever know; and what nobody knew didn't exist, for all practical purposes. And one had to be practical, or else how the hell could anybody expect to survive?

That wasn't the only reason why he ought to leave; but it would do as well as any other. He stood up, wincing at the cramp in his legs, and went over to the stable.

When he opened the door, he realised he wasn't alone. Someone else was in there, he could hear movement. Whoever it was, he was acting as though he had a right to be there; Poldarn heard the sound of a bridle jingling as it was lifted onto a hook. That told him that the stranger had stabled his horse and was putting the harness away neatly, in the proper methodical fashion. Look after your horse before you look after yourself (someone had told him that, years ago, and he knew it was the right thing to do). Taking pains to walk silently, he headed for the sound, and presently he discovered the source. It was Egil.

Either Egil knew he was there, or it was pure coincidence that he turned round at exactly that moment, leaving Poldarn no time to get out of sight. They stared at each other for a moment; then Egil said, 'I heard the news.' He had his saddle in one hand, and a rusty, pitted old axe in the other. Poldarn recognised it as the one he'd found in the ditch.

'What news?' Poldarn said.

'About Elja, of course,' Egil replied. Without breaking eye contact, he let the saddle fall off his forearm onto the ground. 'Judging by the way you're looking at me, I think you know why I hurried over here as soon as I heard.'

Poldarn nodded.

'Fine,' Egil said, 'because I didn't want to have to explain it to you, and I reckoned you had a right to know, before we settled things.'

'You think there's something to settle, then,' Poldarn said.

'Yes. Don't you?'

'I suppose so. And you look like you've made your mind up already, so there's no point arguing. What sort of settlement had you in mind?'

Egil shook his head. 'Seems to me there isn't much choice,' he replied. 'You know what I mean.'

The axe head was still black, crusted with flakes of rust, but the cutting edge had been worked up recently with a stone. 'It doesn't take a mind-reader to know that,' Poldarn replied. 'Have you told anybody else?'

'Are you out of your mind? No, of course not. And I'm not planning to, either. The way I see it, there's only two of us that know, and that's one too many.'

Out of the corner of his eye, Poldarn could see a hay-fork, just out of arm's reach to his left. 'I'll go along with that,' he said. 'So, what are you going to do?'

Egil twitched, as if he'd been about to move but had decided not to, or had found that he couldn't. 'I'm not sure,' he said. 'I hadn't thought that far ahead. I suppose that if I'd got here and you'd been still asleep, I was going to cut your throat as you lay there. But you're here now, which is much better. At least we can be straightforward about it.'

Poldarn took a deep breath, then let it go. 'You're going to kill me, then.'

'I don't really see any other way, do you?'

'Go on, then,' Poldarn told him.

Egil stood perfectly still for a moment or so; then he took a long stride forward and swung the axe over his head. As soon as his arm started to move, Poldarn knew that it wasn't going to be difficult or dangerous, or anything like that. Even as he sidestepped the cut and reached for the hay-fork, it seemed to him as though he was remembering something from long ago, a scene he'd witnessed, maybe something from a recurring dream. The fork handle snuggled comfortably into his right hand; he took a short step diagonally, passing behind Egil's right shoulder, and as his foot touched the floor the top half of the handle dropped into his left hand. The thrust itself must have happened, because the results were plainly obvious a fraction of a second later, but afterwards Poldarn never could remember what he did. All he remembered was the instant when the tips of the fork's four slim tines showed through the back of Egil's coat, like the growing season's first green shoots.

Egil slumped off the fork and dropped to the ground in a messy heap. Well then, Poldarn said to himself, there was nothing to that. He stooped down, retrieved the axe and stood up again. It was a pity, of course, a great shame that something like this had to happen, but it was over and done with, so there was no point fretting about it. As luck would have it, Egil had fallen face down, so Poldarn didn't have to look him in the eye afterwards. By anybody's standards it was self-defence, though of course Egil had been right in trying to do what he did, just as what Poldarn himself had done was entirely proper and justifiable. After all, they'd agreed beforehand among themselves what the outcome had to be, and that was precisely what had happened. The secret had been contained, and now it only existed in one mind. From now on, Poldarn was the only person who knew; and his word, uncorroborated, was opinion, not fact. Henceforth it would exist only in his memory, and as the years passed he'd begin to doubt it, wondering if perhaps he could have been wrong, and what he thought was a memory of reality was only a fragment of an undigested dream, taken out of context, vivid enough, perhaps, but entirely false. And what if the circle went round again, and he woke up a second time beside a river, unable to remember his name or anything else? If that were to happen, then none of it would ever have happened, and everything would have been put right.

He shook his head sadly. It was a great pity that Egil had had to die in order to correct his bad memory, but at least it wasn't his fault now. The outcome was the main thing. It could have been far worse. It could have taken the mountain blowing wide open and drowning the whole island in molten rock to cover up that false version of history, but luckily it hadn't come to that. Thank the divine Poldarn for small mercies.

He chose the small grey mare, as being the least useful and valuable horse to steal; for the moment at least he was still head of this household, so he had a duty to minimise its losses where he could. His hands didn't shake or anything like that as he saddled and bridled the horse, which gave him a certain degree of satisfaction. It made him feel that he could at least control his own body, and that was always a good feeling to have.

At the top of the ridge he stopped and wondered if he should look back, take a last sight of Poldarn's Forge. But the sun was rising, and the whole valley was blotted out in a flare of bright red light, so there wouldn't really be anything to see.